THE BORROWERS OMNIBUS

THE BORROWERS OMNIBUS

MARY NORTON

With illustrations by
DIANA STANLEY

Plates coloured by
TIM PARKER

containing
THE BORROWERS
THE BORROWERS AFIELD
THE BORROWERS AFLOAT
THE BORROWERS ALOFT

GUILD PUBLISHING
LONDON · NEW YORK · SYDNEY · TORONTO

To Mary and Boz

Introduction

To John Cromwell, Esq.

Dear John,

It is early morning in this small whitewashed room, and I am sitting up in bed trying to answer this question of yours about what kind of events or circumstances led me first to think about the Borrowers.

Looking back, the idea seems to be part of an early fantasy in the life of a very short-sighted child, before it was known that she needed glasses. Detailed panorama of lake and mountain, the just-glimpsed boat on a vague horizon, the scattered constellations of a winter sky, the daylight owl – carven and motionless against the matching tree trunk – the sight of romping hares in a distant field, the swift recognition of a rare bird on the wing, were not for her (although the pointing fingers and shouted 'look-looks' in no way passed her by: on tiptoed feet and with screwed-up searching eyes she would join in an excitement which for her held the added element of mystery).

On the other hand, for her brothers country walks with her must have been something of a trial: she was an inveterate lingerer, a gazer into banks and hedgerows, a rapt investigator of shallow pools, a lier-down by stream-like teeming ditches. Such walks were punctuated by loud, long-suffering cries: 'Oh, come *on* ... for goodness' sake . . . we'll never get there . . . What on earth are you staring at *now*?'

It might only be a small toad, with striped eyes, trying to hoist himself up – on his bulging washerwoman's arms – from the dank depths of the ditch on to a piece of floating bark; or wood violets quivering on their massed roots from the passage of some sly, desperate creature pushing its way to safety. What would it be like, this child would wonder, lying prone upon the moss, to live among such creatures – human oneself to all intents and purposes, but as small and vulnerable as they? What would one live on? Where make one's home? Which would be one's enemies and which one's friends?

She would think of these things, as she scuffed her shoes along the sandy lane on her way to join her brothers. All three would climb the gate, jumping clear of the pocked mud and the cow pats, and stroll along the path between the coarse grass and the thistles. On this particular walk they would carry bathing suits in rolled towels because, beyond the wood ahead, lay a rocky cove with a deserted patch of beach.

'Look, there's a buzzard! There! On that post!' But it wasn't a buzzard to her: there was a post (or something like a post) slightly thickened at the top. 'There she goes! What a beauty!' The thickened end of the post had broken off and she saw for a second a swift, dim shadow of flight, and the post seemed a great deal shorter.

Buzzards, yes, they would be the enemies of her little people. Hawks too – and owls. She thought back to the gate which so easily the three human children had climbed. How would her small people manipulate it? They would go underneath of course – there was plenty of room – but, suddenly, she saw through their eyes the great lava-like (sometimes almost steaming) lakes of cattle dung, the pock-like craters in the mud – chasms to them, whether wet or dry. It would take them, she thought, almost half an hour of teetering on ridges, helping one another, calling out warnings, holding one another's hands before, exhausted, they reached the dry grass beyond. And then, she thought, how wickedly sharp, how dizzily high and rustling those thistle plants would seem! And suppose one of these creatures (Were they a little family? She thought perhaps they might be) called out as her brother had just done, 'Look, there's a buzzard!' What a different intonation in the voice and a different implication in the fact. How still they would lie – under perhaps a dock leaf! How deathly still, except for their beating hearts!

Then for this child, as for all children, there were the ill days – mumps, chicken-pox, measles, flu, tonsillitis. Bored with jigsaw puzzles, coloured chalks, familiar story-books, (and with hours to go before the welcome rattle of a supper tray), she would bring her small people indoors – and set them mountain climbing among the bedroom furniture. She would invent for them commando-like assault courses: from window seat to bedside table without touching the floor; from curtain-rod to picture rail; from corner cupboard, via the chimney-piece to coal-scuttle. To help them achieve such feats she would allow them any material assistance they could lay their hands on: work baskets were for rifling – threads and wools for climbing ropes, needles and pins for alpenstocks. She would allow them the run of any half-opened drawer or gaping toy cupboard; then, having exhausted all the horizontal climbs, she would decide to start them from the floor and send them upwards towards the ceiling. This, she found, was the hardest task of all: chair and table legs were polished and slippery and the walls (except for a large picture called 'Bubbles' and one called 'Cherry Ripe') terrifyingly stark. At this point she would encourage them to build teetering pagodas of strong-smelling throat lozenges on down-turned medicine glasses which would serve them as stairways to greater heights. Long curtains helped with this too, of course, and trailing bedclothes where they touched the carpet. Wicker-work waste-paper baskets also had their uses. After a while she began to realize that there was no place in the room they could not reach at last – given time, privacy and patience.

What did they live on? she began to wonder. The answer was easy: they lived on human left-overs as mice do, and birds in winter. They would be as shy as mice or birds, and as fearful of the dangers surrounding them, but more discerning in their tastes and more adventurously ambitious.

In the dull, safe routine of those nursery years, it was exciting to imagine there were others in the house, unguessed at by the adult human beings, who were living so close but so dangerously.

It was the maturing demands of boarding-school which swept them away at last. The Powers That Were discovered that she could not see the blackboard. There were eye tests; and eventually the much stamped, oblong box arrived by morning post, fiercely bound by sticky tape; and (after some nail-breaking and sharp work with a penknife) there at last, in cotton wool, lay a round-rimmed pair of spectacles.

Magic. The girls on the far side of the long classroom had faces suddenly; the trees outside the window had separate leaves; there was a crack in the ceiling like the coast of Brittany; the heel of Miss Hollingworth's stocking, as she turned towards the blackboard, had been darned in a lighter wool; and, not only that, she was losing a hairpin.

They were off and on sort of spectacles, easily mislaid, because while more distant objects stood out with eye-smiting clarity, close things became more blurred. It had to be 'glasses off' to read a book, write a letter, examine an ant nest, search for wild strawberries or four-leaved clovers – or even to pick up a pin; 'glasses on' to follow the hockey ball, see the unrolled map on the wall, watch the weekly lantern lecture or the fourth-form Latin play ('Where did you last have them? Try to think! Very tiresome! Take an order mark!').

In the midst of such diversions there was little time for the Borrowers who, denied even humble attention, slid quietly back to the past.

Anyway, ghosts had become the craze by then – ghosts and ghost stories (as small girls, wide-eyed, huddled in groups around the bubbling radiators of the 'gym'); heavy objects heard after dark, dragging across the boot-room floor; skeletal shadows in the ill-lit corridors joining up the houses; a silent figure who, in moonlit white, would be seen to cross a dormitory. We knew in our hearts that the heavy objects dragged across the cloakroom floor were the sacks of muddy hockey boots collected by the boot-boy; that the skeletal shadows were a trick of the corridor lights where preceding and receding outlines momentarily met and blended; we knew too that our cubicled dormitories were *peopled* by white-robed figures – most of whom were snoring gently and safely tucked in bed; and that one or two of these, in the silent hours, would make slippered expeditions to the bathroom.

But we loved to frighten ourselves. Life perhaps in those days seemed a little too secure – in spite of the

1914-18 war and the mud and blood across the Channel which engaged our elder brothers, but which to us, at our convent school, seemed wearily familiar yet somehow not quite real. As we told our stories, grouped around the radiators, we knitted balaclava helmets and long, long khaki scarves.

It was only just before the 1940 war, when a change was creeping over the world as we had known it, that one thought again about the Borrowers. There were human men and women who were being forced to live (by stark and tragic necessity) the kind of lives a child had once envisaged for a race of mythical creatures. One could not help but realize (without any thought of conscious symbolism) that the world at any time could produce its Mrs Drivers who in their turn would summon their Rich Williams. And there we would be. Apart from this thought, these are meant to be very practical books. Pod's balloon does work. I wonder if anyone has tried it?

With love, dear John. I hope this answers your question.

Yours,
Mary
Positano. June, 1966

THE BORROWERS

For Sharon Rhodes

Chapter One

It was Mrs May who first told me about them. No, not me. How could it have been me — a wild, untidy, self-willed little girl who stared with angry eyes and was said to crunch her teeth? Kate, she should have been called. Yes, that was it — Kate. Not that the name matters much either way: she barely comes into the story.

Mrs May lived in two rooms in Kate's parents' house in London; she was, I think, some kind of relation. Her bedroom was on the first floor, and her sitting-room was a room which, as part of the house, was called 'the breakfast-room.' Now breakfast-rooms are all right in the morning when the sun streams in on the toast and marmalade, but by afternoon they seem to vanish a little and to fill with a strange silvery light, their own twilight; there is a kind of sadness in them then, but as a child it was a sadness Kate liked. She would creep in to Mrs May just before teatime and Mrs May would teach her to crochet.

Mrs May was old, her joints were stiff, and she was — not strict exactly, but she had that inner certainty which does instead. Kate was never 'wild' with Mrs May, nor untidy, nor self-willed; and Mrs May taught her many things besides crochet: how to wind wool into an egg-shaped ball; how to run-and-fell and plan a darn; how to tidy a drawer and to lay, like a blessing, above the contents, a sheet of rustling tissue against the dust.

'Why so quiet, child?' asked Mrs May one day, when Kate was sitting hunched and idle upon the hassock. 'What's the matter with you? Have you lost your tongue?'

'No,' said Kate, pulling at her shoe button, 'I've lost the crochet hook . . .' (they were making a bed-quilt – in woollen squares: there were thirty still to do), 'I know where I put it,' she went on hastily; 'I put it on the bottom shelf of the book-case just beside my bed.'

'On the bottom shelf?' repeated Mrs May, her own needle flicking steadily in the firelight. 'Near the floor?'

'Yes,' said Kate, 'but I looked on the floor. Under the rug. Everywhere. The wool was still there though. Just where I'd left it.'

'Oh dear,' exclaimed Mrs May lightly, 'don't say they're in this house too!'

'That what are?' asked Kate.

'The Borrowers,' said Mrs May, and in the half light she seemed to smile.

Kate stared a little fearfully. 'Are there such things?' she asked after a moment.

'As what?'

Kate blinked her eyelids. 'As people, other people, living in a house who . . . borrow things?'

Mrs May laid down her work. 'What do you think?' she asked.

'I don't know,' said Kate, looking away and pulling hard at her shoe button. 'There can't be. And yet' – she raised her head – 'and yet sometimes I think there must be.'

'Why do you think there must be?' asked Mrs May.

'Because of all the things that disappear. Safety-pins,

for instance. Factories go on making safety-pins, and every day people go on buying safety-pins and yet, somehow, there never is a safety-pin just when you want one. Where are they all? Now, at this minute? Where do they go to? Take needles,' she went on. 'All the needles my mother ever bought – there must be hundreds – can't just be lying about this house.'

'Not lying about the house, no,' agreed Mrs May.

'And all the other things we keep on buying. Again and again and again. Like pencils and match-boxes and sealing-wax and hair-slides and drawing-pins and thimbles—'

'And hat-pins,' put in Mrs May, 'and blotting-paper.'

'Yes, blotting-paper,' agreed Kate, 'but not hat-pins.'

'That's where you're wrong,' said Mrs May, and she picked up her work again. 'There was a reason for hat-pins.'

Kate stared. 'A reason?' she repeated. 'I mean – what kind of a reason?'

'Well, there were two reasons really. A hat-pin is a very useful weapon and' – Mrs May laughed suddenly – 'but it all sounds such nonsense and' – she hesitated – 'it was so very long ago!'

'But tell me,' said Kate, 'tell me how you *know* about the hat-pin. Did you ever see one?'

Mrs May threw her a startled glance. 'Well, yes—' she began.

'Not a hat-pin,' exclaimed Kate impatiently, 'a – what-ever-you-called-them – a Borrower?'

Mrs May drew a sharp breath. 'No,' she said quickly, 'I never saw one.'

'But someone else saw one,' cried Kate, 'and you know about it. I can see you do!'

'Hush,' said Mrs May, 'no need to shout!' She gazed downwards at the upturned face and then she smiled and her eyes slid away into distance. 'I had a brother—' she began uncertainly.

Kate knelt upon the hassock. 'And he saw them!'

'I don't know,' said Mrs May, shaking her head, 'I just don't know!' She smoothed out her work upon her knee. 'He was such a tease. He told us so many things – my sister and me – impossible things. He was killed,' she added gently, 'many years ago now, on the North-West Frontier. He became colonel of his regiment. He died what they call "a hero's death" . . .'

'Was he your only brother?'

'Yes, and he was our little brother. I think that was why' – she thought for a moment, still smiling to herself –

'yes, why he told us such impossible stories, such strange imaginings. He was jealous, I think, because we were older – and because we could read better. He wanted to impress us; he wanted, perhaps, to shock us. And yet' – she looked into the fire – 'there was something about him – perhaps because we were brought up in India among mystery and magic and legend – something that made us think that he saw things that other people could not see; sometimes we'd know he was teasing, but at other times – well, we were not so sure . . .' She leaned forward and, in her tidy way, brushed a fan of loose ashes under the grate, then, brush in hand, she stared again at the fire. 'He wasn't a very strong little boy: the first time he came home from India he got rheumatic fever. He missed a whole term at school and was sent away to the country to get over it. To the house of a great-aunt. Later I went there myself. It was a strange old house . . .' She hung up the brush on its brass hook and, dusting her hands on her handkerchief, she picked up her work. 'Better light the lamp,' she said.

'Not yet,' begged Kate, leaning forward. 'Please go on. Please tell me—'

'But I've told you.'

'No you haven't. This old house – wasn't that where he saw – he saw . . .?'

Mrs May laughed. 'Where he saw the Borrowers? Yes, that's what he told us . . . what he'd have us believe. And, what's more, it seems that he didn't just see them but that he got to know them very well; that he became part of their lives, as it were; in fact, you might almost say that he became a borrower himself . . .'

'Oh, *do* tell me. Please. Try to remember. Right from the very beginning!'

'But I do remember,' said Mrs May. 'Oddly enough I remember it better than many real things which have happened. Perhaps it was a real thing. I just don't know. You see, on the way back to India my brother and I had to share a cabin – my sister used to sleep with our governess – and, on those very hot nights, often we couldn't sleep; and my brother would talk for hours and hours, going over old ground, repeating conversations, telling me details again and again – wondering how they were and what they were doing and—'

'They? Who were they – exactly?'

'Homily, Pod, and little Arrietty.'

'Pod?'

'Yes, even their names were never quite right. They imagined they had their own names – quite different from human names – but with half an ear you could tell they were borrowed. Even Uncle Hendreary's and Egg-letina's. Everything they had was borrowed; they had nothing of their own at all. Nothing. In spite of this, my brother said, they were touchy and conceited, and thought they owned the world.'

'How do you mean?'

'They thought human beings were just invented to do the dirty work – great slaves put there for them to use. At least, that's what they told each other. But my brother said that, underneath, he thought they were frightened. It was because they were frightened, he thought, that they had grown so small. Each generation had become smaller and smaller, and more and more hidden. In the olden days, it seems, and in some parts of England, our ancestors talked quite openly about the "little people."'

'Yes,' said Kate, 'I know.'

'Nowadays, I suppose,' Mrs May went on slowly, 'if

they exist at all, you would only find them in houses which are old and quiet and deep in the country – and where the human beings live to a routine. Routine is their safeguard: it is important for them to know which rooms are to be used and when. They do not stay long where there are careless people, unruly children, or certain household pets.

'This particular old house, of course, was ideal – although as far as some of them were concerned, a trifle cold and empty. Great Aunt Sophy was bedridden, through a hunting accident some twenty years before, and as for other human beings there was only Mrs Driver the cook, Crampfurl the gardener, and, at rare intervals, an odd housemaid or such. My brother, too, when he went there after rheumatic fever, had to spend long hours in bed, and for those first weeks it seems the Borrowers did not know of his existence.

'He slept in the old night-nursery, beyond the school-room. The schoolroom, at that time, was sheeted and shrouded and filled with junk – odd trunks, a broken sewing-machine, a desk, a dressmaker's dummy, a table, some chairs, and a disused pianola – as the children who had used it, Great Aunt Sophy's children, had long since grown up, married, died, or gone away. The night-nursery opened out of the schoolroom and, from his bed, my brother could see the oil-painting of the battle of Waterloo which hung above the schoolroom fire-place and, on the wall, a corner cupboard with glass doors in which was set out, on hooks and shelves, a doll's tea-service – very delicate and old. At night, if the school-room door was open, he had a view down the lighted passage which led to the staircase, and it would comfort him to see, each evening at dusk, Mrs Driver appear at the head of the stairs and cross the passage carrying a tray for

Aunt Sophy with Bath Oliver biscuits and the tall, cut-glass decanter of Fine Old Pale Madeira. On her way out Mrs Driver would pause and lower the gas jet in the passage to a dim, blue flame, and then he would watch her as she stumped away downstairs, sinking slowly out of sight between the banisters.

'Under this passage, in the hall below, there was a clock, and through the night he would hear it strike the hours. It was a grandfather clock and very old. Mr Frith of Leighton Buzzard came each month to wind it, as his father had come before him and his great-uncle before that. For eighty years, they said (and to Mr Frith's certain knowledge), it had not stopped and, as far as any one could tell, for as many years before that. The great thing was – that it must never be moved. It stood against the wainscot, and the stone flags around it had been washed so often that a little platform, my brother said, rose up inside.

'And, under this clock, below the wainscot, there was a hole . . .'

Chapter Two

It was Pod's hole – the keep of his fortress; the entrance to his home. Not that his home was anywhere near the clock: far from it – as you might say. There were yards of dark and dusty passage-way, with wooden doors between the joists and metal gates against the mice. Pod used all kinds of things for these gates – a flat leaf of a folding cheese-grater, the hinged lid of a small cash-box, squares of pierced zinc from an old meat-safe, a wire fly-swotter . . . 'Not that I'm afraid of mice,' Homily would say, 'but I can't abide the smell.' In vain Arrietty had begged for a little mouse of her own, a little blind mouse to bring up by hand – 'like Eggletina had had.' But Homily would bang with the pan lids and exclaim: 'And look what happened to Eggletina!' 'What,' Arrietty would ask, 'what did happen to Eggletina?' But no one would ever say.

It was only Pod who knew the way through the intersecting passages to the hole under the clock. And only Pod could open the gates. There were complicated clasps made of hair-slides and safety-pins of which Pod alone knew the secret. His wife and child led more sheltered lives in homelike apartments under the kitchen, far removed from the risks and dangers of the dreaded house above. But there was a grating in the brick wall of the house, just below the floor level of the kitchen above, through which Arrietty could see the garden – a piece of gravelled path and a bank where crocus bloomed in spring; where blossom drifted from an unseen tree; and where later an azalea bush would flower; and where birds came – and pecked and flirted and sometimes fought. 'The hours you waste on them birds,' Homily would say, 'and when there's a little job to be done you can never find the time. I was brought up in a house,' Homily went on, 'where there wasn't no grating, and we were all the happier for it. Now go off and get me the potato.'

That was the day when Arrietty, rolling the potato before her from the storehouse down the dusty lane under the floor-boards, kicked it ill-temperedly so that it

rolled rather fast into their kitchen, where Homily was stooping over the stove.

'There you go again,' exclaimed Homily, turning angrily; 'nearly pushed me into the soup. And when I say "potato" I don't mean the whole potato. Take the scissor, can't you, and cut off a slice.'

'Didn't know how much you wanted,' Arrietty had mumbled, as Homily, snorting and sniffing, unhooked the blade and handle of half a pair of manicure scissors from a nail on the wall, and began to cut through the peel.

'You've ruined this potato,' she grumbled. 'You can't roll it back now in all that dust, not once it's been cut open.'

'Oh, what does it matter?' said Arrietty. 'There are plenty more.'

'That's a nice way to talk. Plenty more. Do you realize,' Homily went on gravely, laying down the half nail scissor, 'that your poor father risks his life every time he borrows a potato?'

'I meant,' said Arrietty, 'that there are plenty more in the store-room.'

'Well, out of my way now,' said Homily, bustling around again, 'whatever you meant – and let me get the supper.'

Arrietty had wandered through the open door into the sitting-room – the fire had been lighted and the room looked bright and cosy. Homily was proud of her sitting-room: the walls had been papered with scraps of old letters out of waste-paper baskets, and Homily had arranged the hand-writing sideways in vertical stripes which ran from floor to ceiling. On the walls, repeated in various colours, hung several portraits of Queen Victoria as a girl; these were postage stamps, borrowed by Pod some years ago from the stamp-box on the desk in the morning-room. There was a lacquer trinket-box, padded inside and with the lid open, which they used as a settle; and that useful stand-by – a chest of drawers made of match-boxes. There was a round table with a red velvet cloth, which Pod had made from the wooden bottom of a pill-box supported on the carved pedestal of a knight from the chess-set. (This had caused a great deal of trouble upstairs when Aunt Sophy's eldest son, on a flying mid-week visit, had invited the vicar for 'a game after dinner.' Rosa Pickhatchet, who was housemaid at the time, gave in her notice. Not long after she had left other things were found to be missing and, from that time onwards, Mrs Driver ruled supreme.) The knight itself – its bust, so to speak – was standing on a column in the corner, where it looked very fine, and lent that air to the room which only statuary can give.

Beside the fire, in a tilted wooden book-case, stood

Arrietty's library. This was a set of those miniature volumes which the Victorians loved to print, but which to Arrietty seemed the size of very large church Bibles. There was Bryce's *Tom Thumb Gazetteer of the World*, including the last census; Bryce's *Tom Thumb Diction-ary*, with short explanations of scientific, philosophical, literary, and technical terms; Bryce's *Tom Thumb Edi-tion of the Comedies of William Shakespeare*, including a foreword on the author; another book, whose pages were all blank, called *Memoranda*; and, last but not least, Arrietty's favourite Bryce's *Tom Thumb Diary and Proverb Book*, with a saying for each day of the year and, as a preface, the life story of a little man called General Tom Thumb, who married a girl called Mercy Lavinia Bump. There was an engraving of their carriage and pair, with little horses – the size of mice. Arrietty was not a stupid girl. She knew that horses could not be as small as mice, but she did not realize that Tom Thumb, nearly two feet high, would seem a giant to a Borrower.

Arrietty had learned to read from these books, and to write by leaning sideways and copying out the writings on the walls. In spite of this, she did not always keep her diary, although on most days she would take the book out for the sake of the saying which sometimes would comfort her. To-day it said: 'You may go farther and fare worse,' and, underneath: 'Order of the Garter, instituted 1348.' She carried the book to the fire and sat down with her feet on the hob.

'What are you doing, Arrietty?' called Homily from the kitchen.

'Writing my diary.'

'Oh,' exclaimed Homily shortly.

'What did you want?' asked Arrietty. She felt quite safe; Homily liked her to write; Homily encouraged any form of culture. Homily herself, poor ignorant creature, could not even say the alphabet. 'Nothing. Nothing,' said Homily crossly, banging away with the pan lids; 'it'll do later.'

Arrietty took out her pencil. It was a small white pencil, with a piece of silk cord attached, which had come off a dance programme, but, even so, in Arrietty's hand, it looked like a rolling-pin.

'Arrietty!' called Homily again from the kitchen.

'Yes?'

'Put a little something on the fire, will you?'

Arrietty braced her muscles and heaved the book off her knees, and stood it upright on the floor. They kept the fuel, assorted slack and crumbled candle-grease in a pewter mustard-pot, and shovelled it out with the spoon. Arrietty trickled only a few grains, tilting the mustard spoon, not to spoil the blaze. Then she stood there basking in the warmth. It was a charming fire-place, made by Arrietty's grandfather, with a cog-wheel from the stables, part of an old cider-press. The spokes of the cog-wheel stood out in starry rays, and the fire itself nestled in the centre. Above there was a chimney-piece made from a small brass funnel, inverted. This, at one time, belonged to an oil-lamp which matched it, and which stood, in the old days, on the hall table upstairs. An arrangement of pipes, from the spout of the funnel, carried the fumes into the kitchen flues above. The fire was laid with match-sticks and fed with assorted slack and, as it burned up, the iron would become hot, and Homily would simmer soup on the spokes, in a silver thimble, and Arrietty would broil nuts. How cosy those winter evenings could be. Arrietty, her great book on her knees, sometimes reading aloud; Pod at his last (he was a shoemaker, and made button-boots out of kid gloves —

now, alas, only for his family); and Homily, quiet at last, with her knitting.

Homily knitted their jerseys and stockings on black-headed pins, and, sometimes, on darning needles. A great reel of silk or cotton would stand, table high, beside her chair, and sometimes, if she pulled too sharply, the reel would tip up and roll away out of the open door into the dusty passage beyond, and Arrietty would be sent after it, to re-wind it carefully as she rolled it back.

The floor of the sitting-room was carpeted with deep red blotting-paper, which was warm and cosy, and soaked up the spills. Homily would renew it at intervals when it became available upstairs, but since Aunt Sophy had taken to her bed Mrs Driver seldom thought of blotting-paper unless, suddenly, there were guests. Homily liked things which saved washing because drying was difficult under the floor; water they had in plenty, hot and cold, thanks to Pod's father who had tapped the pipes from the kitchen boiler. They bathed in a small tureen, which once had held *pâté de foie gras*. When you had wiped out your bath you were supposed to put the lid back, to stop people putting things in it. The soap, too, a great cake of it, hung on a nail in the scullery, and they scraped pieces off. Homily liked coal tar, but Pod and Arrietty preferred sandalwood.

'What are you doing now, Arrietty?' called Homily from the kitchen.

'Still writing my diary.'

Once again Arrietty took hold of the book and heaved it back on to her knees. She licked the lead of her great pencil, and stared a moment, deep in thought. She allowed herself (when she did remember to write) one little line on each page because she would never – of this

she was sure – have another diary, and if she could get twenty lines on each page the diary would last her twenty years. She had kept it for nearly two years already, and to-day, 22nd March, she read last year's entry: 'Mother cross.' She thought a while longer then, at last, she put ditto marks under 'mother,' and 'worried' under 'cross.'

'What did you say you were doing, Arrietty?' called Homily from the kitchen.

Arrietty closed the book. 'Nothing,' she said.

'Then chop me up this onion, there's a good girl. Your father's late to-night . . .'

Chapter Three

Sighing, Arrietty put away her diary and went into the kitchen. She took the onion ring from Homily, and slung it lightly round her shoulders, while she foraged for a piece of razor blade. 'Really, Arrietty,' exclaimed Homily, 'not on your clean jersey! Do you want to smell like a bit-bucket? Here, take the scissor—'

Arrietty stepped through the onion ring as though it were a child's hoop, and began to chop it into segments.

'Your father's late,' muttered Homily again, 'and it's my fault, as you might say. Oh dear, oh dear, I wish I hadn't—'

'Hadn't what?' asked Arrietty, her eyes watering. She sniffed loudly and longed to rub her nose on her sleeve.

Homily pushed back a thin lock of hair with a worried hand. She stared at Arrietty absently. 'It's that tea-cup you broke,' she said.

'But that was days ago—' began Arrietty, blinking her eyelids, and she sniffed again.

'I know. I know. It's not you. It's me. It's not the breaking that matters, it's what I said to your father.'

'What did you say to him?'

'Well, I just said – there's the rest of the service, I said – up there, where it always was, in the corner cupboard in the schoolroom.'

'I don't see anything bad in that,' said Arrietty as, one by one, she dropped the pieces of onion into the soup.

'But it's a high cupboard,' exclaimed Homily. 'You have to get up by the curtain. And your father at his age—' She sat down suddenly on a metal-topped champagne cork. 'Oh, Arrietty, I wish I'd never mentioned it!'

'Don't worry,' said Arrietty, 'papa knows what he can do.' She pulled a rubber scent-bottle cork out of the hole in the hot-water pipe and let a trickle of scalding drops fall into the tin lid of an aspirin bottle. She added cold and began to wash her hands.

'Maybe,' said Homily. 'But I went on about it so. What's a tea-cup! Your Uncle Hendreary never drank a thing that wasn't out of a common acorn cup, and he's lived to a ripe old age and had the strength to emigrate. My mother's family never had nothing but a little bone thimble which they shared around. But it's once you've *had* a tea-cup, if you see what I mean . . .'

'Yes,' said Arrietty, drying her hands on a roller towel made out of surgical bandage.

'It's that curtain,' cried Homily. 'He can't climb a curtain at his age – not by the bobbles!'

'With his pin he could,' said Arrietty.

'His pin! I led him into that one too! Take a hat-pin, I told him, and tie a bit of name-tape to the head, and pull yourself upstairs. It was to borrow the emerald watch from Her bedroom for me to time the cooking.' Homily's voice began to tremble. 'Your mother's a wicked woman, Arrietty. Wicked and selfish, that's what she is!'

'You know what?' exclaimed Arrietty suddenly.

Homily brushed away a tear. 'No,' she said wanly, 'what?'

'I could climb a curtain.'

Homily rose up. 'Arrietty, you dare stand there in cold blood and say a thing like that!'

'But I could! I could! I could borrow! I know I could!'

'Oh!' gasped Homily. 'Oh, you wicked heathen girl! How could you speak so!' and she crumpled up again on the cork stool. 'So it's come to this!' she said.

'Now, mother, please,' begged Arrietty, 'now, don't take on!'

'But don't you see, Arrietty . . .' gasped Homily; she stared down at the table at loss for words and then, at last, she raised a haggard face. 'My poor child,' she said, 'don't speak like that of borrowing. You don't know – and, thank goodness, you never will know' – she dropped her voice to a fearful whisper – 'what it's like upstairs . . .'

Arrietty was silent. 'What is it like?' she asked after a moment.

Homily wiped her face on her apron and smoothed back her hair. 'Your Uncle Hendreary,' she began, 'Eggletina's father—' and then she paused. 'Listen!' she said. 'What's that?'

Echoing on the wood was a faint vibration – the sound of a distant click. 'Your father!' exclaimed Homily. 'Oh, look at me! Where's the comb?'

They had a comb: a little, silver, eighteenth-century eyebrow comb from the cabinet in the drawing-room upstairs. Homily ran it through her hair and rinsed her poor red eyes and, when Pod came in, she was smiling and smoothing down her apron.

Chapter Four

Pod came in slowly, his sack on his back; he leaned his
hat-pin, with its dangling name-tape, against the wall
and, on the middle of the kitchen table, he placed a doll's
tea-cup; it seemed the size of a mixing-bowl.

'Why, Pod—' began Homily.

'Got the saucer too,' he said. He swung down the sack
and untied the neck. 'Here you are,' he said, drawing out
the saucer. 'Matches it.'

He had a round, currant-bunny sort of face; to-night it
looked flabby.

'Oh, Pod,' said Homily, 'you do look queer. Are you all
right?'

Pod sat down. 'I'm fair enough,' he said.

'You went up the curtain,' said Homily. 'Oh, Pod, you
shouldn't have. It's shaken you—'

Pod made a strange face, his eyes swivelled round
towards Arrietty. Homily stared at him, her mouth open,
and then she turned. 'Come along, Arrietty,' she said
briskly, 'you pop off to bed now, like a good girl, and I'll
bring you some supper.'

'Oh,' said Arrietty, 'can't I see the rest of the borrowings?'

'Your father's got nothing now. Only food. Off you
pop to bed. You've seen the cup and saucer.'

Arrietty went into the sitting-room to put away her
diary, and took some time fixing her candle on the
upturned drawing-pin which served as a holder.

'Whatever are you doing?' grumbled Homily. 'Give it
here. There, that's the way. Now off to bed and fold your
clothes, mind.'

'Good night, papa,' said Arrietty, kissing his flat white cheek.

'Careful of the light,' he said mechanically, and watched her with his round eyes until she had closed the door.

'Now, Pod,' said Homily, when they were alone, 'tell me. What's the matter?'

Pod looked at her blankly. 'I been "seen,"' he said.

Homily put out a groping hand for the edge of the table; she grasped it and lowered herself slowly on to the stool. 'Oh, Pod,' she said.

There was silence between them. Pod stared at Homily and Homily stared at the table. After a while she raised her white face. 'Badly?' she asked.

Pod moved restlessly. 'I don't know about badly. I been "seen." Ain't that bad enough?'

'No one,' said Homily slowly, 'hasn't never been "seen" since Uncle Hendreary and he was the first they say for forty-five years.' A thought struck her and she gripped the table. 'It's no good, Pod, I won't emigrate!'

'No one's asked you to,' said Pod.

'To go and live like Hendreary and Lupy in a badger's set! The other side of the world, that's where they say it is – all among the earthworms.'

'It's two fields away, above the spinney,' said Pod.

'Nuts, that's what they eat. And berries. I wouldn't wonder if they don't eat mice—'

'You've eaten mice yourself,' Pod reminded her.

'All draughts and fresh air and the children growing up wild. Think of Arrietty!' said Homily. 'Think of the way she's been brought up. An only child. She'd catch her death. It's different for Hendreary.'

'Why?' asked Pod. 'He's got five.'

'That's why,' explained Homily. 'When you've got

five, they're brought up rough. But never mind that now . . . Who saw you?'

'A boy,' said Pod.

'A what?' exclaimed Homily, staring.

'A boy.' Pod sketched out a rough shape in the air with his hands. 'You know, a boy.'

'But there isn't – I mean, what sort of a boy?'

'I don't know what you mean "what sort of a boy." A boy in a night-shirt. A boy. You know what a boy is, don't you?'

'Yes,' said Homily. 'I know what a boy is. But there hasn't been a boy, not in this house, these twenty years.'

'Well,' said Pod, 'there's one here now.'

Homily stared at him in silence, and Pod met her eyes. 'Where did he see you?' asked Homily at last.

'In the schoolroom.'

'Oh,' said Homily, 'when you was getting the cup?'

'Yes,' said Pod.

'Haven't you got eyes?' asked Homily. 'Couldn't you have looked first?'

'There's never nobody in the schoolroom. And what's more,' he went on, 'there wasn't to-day.'

'Then where was he?'

'In bed. In the night-nursery or whatever it's called. That's where he was. Sitting up in bed. With the doors open.'

'Well, you could have looked in the nursery.'

'How could I – half-way up the curtain!'

'Is that where you was?'

'Yes.'

'With the cup?'

'Yes. I couldn't get up or down.'

'Oh, Pod,' wailed Homily, 'I should never have let you go. Not at your age!'

'Now, look here,' said Pod, 'don't mistake me. I got up all right. Got up like a bird, as you might say, bobbles or no bobbles. But' – he leaned towards her – 'afterwards – with the cup in me hand, if you see what I mean . . .' He picked it up off the table. 'You see, it's heavy like. You can hold it by the handle, like this . . . but it drops or droops, as you might say. You should take a cup like this in your two hands. A bit of cheese off a shelf, or an apple – well, I drop that . . . give it a push and it falls and I climbs down in me own time and picks it up. But with a cup – you see what I mean? And coming down, you got to watch your feet. And, as I say, some of the bobbles was

34

missing. You didn't know what you could hold on to, not safely . . .'

'Oh, Pod,' said Homily, her eyes full of tears, 'what did you do?'

'Well,' said Pod, sitting back again, 'he took the cup.'

'What do you mean?' exclaimed Homily aghast.

Pod avoided her eyes. 'Well, he'd been sitting up in bed there watching me. I'd been on the curtain a good ten minutes, because the hall clock had just struck the quarter—'

'But how do you mean – "he took the cup"?'

'Well, he'd got out of bed and there he was standing, looking up. "I'll take the cup," he said.'

'Oh!' gasped Homily, her eyes staring, 'and you give it him?'

'He took it,' said Pod, 'ever so gentle. And then, when I was down, he give it me.' Homily put her face in her hands. 'Now don't take on,' said Pod uneasily.

'He might have caught you,' shuddered Homily in a stifled voice.

'Yes,' said Pod, 'but he just give me the cup. "Here you are," he said.'

Homily raised her face. 'What are we going to do?' she asked.

Pod sighed. 'Well, there isn't nothing we can do. Except—'

'Oh, no,' exclaimed Homily, 'not that. Not emigrate. Not that, Pod, now I've got the house so nice and a clock and all.'

'We could take the clock,' said Pod.

'And Arrietty? What about her? She's not like those cousins. She can *read*, Pod, and sew a treat—'

'He don't know where we live,' said Pod.

'But they look,' exclaimed Homily. 'Remember Hen-dreary! They got the cat and—'

'Now, now,' said Pod, 'don't bring up the past.'

'But you've got to think of it! They got the cat and—'

'Yes,' said Pod, 'but Eggletina was different.'

'How different? She was Arrietty's age.'

'Well, they hadn't told her, you see. That's where they went wrong. They tried to make her believe that there wasn't nothing but was under the floor. They never told her about Mrs Driver or Crampfurl. Least of all about cats.'

'There wasn't any cat,' Homily pointed out, 'not till Hendreary was "seen."'

'Well, there was, then,' said Pod. 'You got to tell them, that's what I say, or they try to find out for themselves.'

'Pod,' said Homily solemnly, 'we haven't told Arrietty.'

'Oh, she knows,' said Pod; he moved uncomfortably. 'She's got her grating.'

'She doesn't know about Eggletina. She doesn't know about being "seen."'

'Well, said Pod, 'we'll tell her. We always said we would. There's no hurry.'

Homily stood up. 'Pod,' she said, 'we're going to tell her to-night.'

Chapter Five

Arrietty had not been asleep. She had been lying under her knitted coverlet staring up at the ceiling. It was an interesting ceiling. Pod had built Arrietty's bedroom out of two cigar-boxes, and on the ceiling lovely painted ladies dressed in swirls of chiffon blew long trumpets against a background of blue sky; below there were feathery palm-trees and small white houses set about a square. It was a glamorous scene, above all by candle-light, but to-night Arrietty had stared without seeing. The wood of a cigar-box is thin and Arrietty, lying straight and still under the quilt, had heard the rise and fall of worried voices. She had heard her own name; she had heard Homily exclaim: 'Nuts and berries, that's what they eat!' and she had heard, after a while, the heart-felt cry of 'What shall we do?'

So when Homily appeared beside her bed, she wrapped herself obediently in her quilt and, padding in her bare feet along the dusty passage, she joined her parents in the

warmth of the kitchen. Crouched on her little stool she
sat clasping her knees, shivering a little, and looking from
one face to another.

Homily came beside her and, kneeling on the floor, she
placed an arm round Arrietty's skinny shoulders. 'Arrietty,' she said gravely, 'you know about upstairs?'

'What about it?' asked Arrietty.

'You know about the two giants?'

'Yes,' said Arrietty, 'Great Aunt Sophy and Mrs
Driver.'

'That's right,' said Homily, 'and Crampfurl in the
garden.' She laid a roughened hand on Arrietty's clasped
ones. 'You know about Uncle Hendreary?'

Arrietty thought awhile. 'He went abroad?' she said.

'Emigrated,' corrected Homily, 'to the other side of the
world. With Aunt Lupy and all the children. To a
badger's set – a hole in a bank under a hawthorn hedge.
Now why do you think he did this?'

'Oh,' said Arrietty, her face alight, 'to be out of doors . . . to lie in the sun . . . to run in the grass . . . to swing on twigs like the birds do . . . to suck honey . . .'

'Nonsense, Arrietty,' exclaimed Homily sharply, 'that's a nasty habit! And your Uncle Hendreary's a rheumatic sort of man. He emigrated,' she went on, stressing the word, 'because he was "seen."'

'Oh,' said Arrietty.

'He was "seen" on the 23rd of April 1892, by Rosa Pickhatchet, on the drawing-room mantelpiece. Of all places . . .' she added suddenly in a wondering aside.

'Oh,' said Arrietty.

'I have never heard nor no one has never seen fit to tell why he went on the drawing-room mantelpiece in the first place. There's nothing on it, your father assures me, which cannot be seen from the floor or by standing sideways on the handle of the bureau and steadying yourself on the key. That's what your father does if he ever goes into the drawing-room—'

'They said it was a liver pill,' put in Pod.

'How do you mean?' asked Homily, startled.

'A liver pill for Lupy.' Pod spoke wearily. 'Someone started a rumour,' he went on, 'that there were liver pills on the drawing-room mantelpiece . . .'

'Oh,' said Homily and looked thoughtful. 'I never heard that. All the same,' she exclaimed, 'it was stupid and foolhardy. There's no way down except by the bell-pull. She dusted him, they say, with a feather duster, and he stood so still, alongside a cupid, that she might never have noticed him if he hadn't sneezed. She was new, you see, and didn't know the ornaments. We heard her screeching right here under the kitchen. And they could never get her to clean anything much after that that wasn't chairs or tables – least of all the tiger-skin rug.'

'I don't hardly never bother with the drawing-room,' said Pod. 'Everything's got its place like and they see what goes. There might be a little something left on a table or down the side of a chair, but not without there's been company, and there never is no company – not for the last ten or twelve year. Sitting here in this chair, I can tell you by heart every blessed thing that's in that drawing-room, working round from the cabinet by the window to the—'

'There's a mint of things in that cabinet,' interrupted Homily, 'solid silver some of them. A solid silver violin, they got there, strings and all – just right for our Arrietty.'

'What's the good,' asked Pod, 'of things behind glass?'

'Couldn't you break it?' suggested Arrietty. 'Just a corner, just a little tap, just a . . .' Her voice faltered as she saw the shocked amazement on her father's face.

'Listen here, Arrietty,' began Homily angrily, and then she controlled herself and patted Arrietty's clasped hands. 'She don't know much about borrowing,' she explained to Pod. 'You can't blame her.' She turned again to Arrietty. 'Borrowing's a skilled job, an art like. Of all the families who've been in this house, there's only us left, and do you know for why? Because your father, Arrietty, is the best borrower that's been known in these parts since – well, before your grandad's time. Even your Aunt Lupy admitted that much. When he was younger I've seen your father walk the length of a laid dinner-table, after the gong was rung, taking a nut or sweet from every dish, and down by a fold in the table-cloth as the first people came in at the door. He'd do it just for fun, wouldn't you, Pod?'

Pod smiled wanly. 'There weren't no sense in it,' he said.

'Maybe,' said Homily, 'but you did it! Who else would dare?'

'I were younger then,' said Pod. He sighed and turned to Arrietty. 'You don't break things, lass. That's not the way to do it. That's not borrowing . . .'

'We were rich then,' said Homily. 'Oh, we did have some lovely things! You were only a tot, Arrietty, and wouldn't remember. We had a whole suite of walnut furniture out of the doll's house and a set of wineglasses in green glass, and a musical snuff-box, and the cousins would come and we'd have parties. Do you remember, Pod? Not only the cousins. The Harpsichords came. Everybody came – except those Overmantels from the morning-room. And we'd dance and dance and the

young people would sit out by the grating. Three tunes that snuff-box played – *Clementine*, *God Save the Queen*, and the *Post-Chaise Gallop*. We were the envy of everybody – even the Overmantels . . .'

'Who were the Overmantels?' asked Arrietty.

'Oh, you must've heard me talk of the Overmantels,' exclaimed Homily, 'that stuck-up lot who lived in the wall high up – among the lath and plaster behind the mantelpiece in the morning-room. And a queer lot they were. The men smoked all the time because the tobacco jars were kept there; and they'd climb about and in and out the carvings of the overmantel, sliding down pillars and showing off. The women were a conceited lot too, always admiring themselves in all those bits of overmantel looking-glass. They never asked any one up there and I, for one, never wanted to go. I've no head for heights, and your father never liked the men. He's always lived steady, your father has, and not only the tobacco jars, but the whisky decanters too, were kept in the morning-room and they say those Overmantel men would suck up the dregs in the glasses through those quill pipe-cleaners they keep there on the mantelpiece. I don't know whether it's true but they do say that those Overmantel men used to have a party every Tuesday after the bailiff had been to talk business in the morning-room. Laid out, they'd be, dead drunk – or so the story goes – on the green plush table-cloth, all among the tin boxes and the account books—'

'Now, Homily,' protested Pod, who did not like gossip, 'I never see'd 'em.'

'But you wouldn't put it past them, Pod. You said yourself when I married you not to call on the Overmantels.'

'They lived so high,' said Pod, 'that's all.'

'Well, they were a lazy lot – that much you can't deny. They never had no kind of home life. Kept themselves warm in winter by the heat of the morning-room fire and ate nothing but breakfast food; breakfast, of course, was the only meal served in the morning-room.'

'What happened to them?' asked Arrietty.

'Well, when the Master died and She took to her bed, there was no more use for the morning-room. So the Overmantels had to go. What else could they do? No food, no fire. It's a bitter cold room in winter.'

'And the Harpsichords?' asked Arrietty.

Homily looked thoughtful. 'Well, they were different. I'm not saying they weren't stuck up too, because they were. Your Aunt Lupy, who married your Uncle Hendreary, was a Harpsichord by marriage and we all know the airs she gave herself.'

'Now, Homily—' began Pod.

'Well, she'd no right to. She was only a Rain-Pipe from the stables before she married Harpsichord.

'Didn't she marry Uncle Hendreary?' asked Arrietty.

'Yes, later. She was a widow with two children and he was a widower with three. It's no good looking at me like that, Pod. You can't deny she took it out of poor Hendreary: she thought it was a come-down to marry a Clock.'

'Why?' asked Arrietty.

'Because we Clocks live under the kitchen, that's why. Because we don't talk fancy grammar and eat anchovy toast. But to live under the kitchen doesn't say we aren't educated. The Clocks are just as old a family as the Harpsichords. You remember that, Arrietty, and don't let any one tell you different. Your grandfather could count and write down the numbers up to – what was it, Pod?'

'Fifty-seven,' said Pod.

'There,' said Homily, 'fifty-seven! And your father can count, as you know, Arrietty; he can count and write down the numbers, on and on, as far as it goes. How far does it go, Pod?'

'Close on a thousand,' said Pod.

'There!' exclaimed Homily, 'and he knows the alphabet because he taught you, Arrietty, didn't he? And he would have been able to read – wouldn't you, Pod? – if he hadn't had to start borrowing so young. Your Uncle Hendreary and your father had to go out borrowing at thirteen – your age, Arrietty, think of it!'

'But I should like—' began Arrietty.

'So he didn't have your advantages,' went on Homily breathlessly, 'and just because the Harpsichords lived in the drawing-room – they moved in there, in 1837, to a hole in the wainscot just behind where the harpsichord used to stand, if ever there was one, which I doubt – and were really a family called Linen-Press or some such name and changed it to Harpsichord—'

'What did they live on,' asked Arrietty, 'in the drawing-room?'

'Afternoon tea,' said Homily, 'nothing but afternoon tea. No wonder the children grew up peaky. Of course, in the old days it was better – muffins and crumpets and such, and good rich cake and jams and jellies. And there was one old Harpsichord who could remember sillabub of an evening. But they had to do their borrowing in such a rush, poor things. On wet days, when the human beings sat all afternoon in the drawing-room, the tea would be brought in and taken away again without a chance of the Harpsichords getting near it – and on fine days it might be taken out into the garden. Lupy has told me that, sometimes, there were days and days when they lived on crumbs and on water out of the flower-vases. So you can't be too hard on them; their only comfort, poor things, was to show off a bit and talk like ladies and gentlemen. Did you ever hear your Aunt Lupy talk?'

'Yes. No. I can't remember.'

'Oh, you should have heard her say, "Parquet" – that's the stuff the drawing-room floor's made of – "Parkay . . . Parr-r-kay," she'd say. Oh, it was lovely. Come to think of it, your Aunt Lupy was the most stuck up of them all . . .'

'Arrietty's shivering,' said Pod. 'We didn't get the little maid up to talk about Aunt Lupy.'

'Nor we did,' cried Homily, suddenly contrite, 'you should've stopped me, Pod. There, my lamb, tuck this quilt right round you and I'll get you a nice drop of piping hot soup!'

'And yet,' said Pod as Homily, fussing at the stove, ladled soup into the tea-cup, 'we did in a way.'

'Did what?' asked Homily.

'Get her here to talk about Aunt Lupy. Aunt Lupy, Uncle Hendreary, and' – he paused – 'Eggletina.'

'Let her drink up her soup first,' said Homily.

'There's no call for her to stop drinking,' said Pod.

46

Chapter Six

'Your mother and I got you up,' said Pod, 'to tell you about upstairs.'

Arrietty, holding the great cup in both hands, looked at him over the edge.

Pod coughed. 'You said a while back that the sky was dark brown with cracks in it. Well, it isn't.' He looked at her almost accusingly. 'It's blue.'

'I know,' said Arrietty.

'You know!' exclaimed Pod.

'Yes, of course I know. I've got the grating.'

'Can you see the sky through the grating?'

'Go on,' interrupted Homily, 'tell her about the gates.'

'Well,' said Pod ponderously, 'if you go outside this room, what do you see?'

'A dark passage,' said Arrietty.

'And what else?'

'Other rooms.'

'And if you go farther?'

'More passages.'

'And, if you go walking on and on, in all the passages under the floor, however they twist and turn, what do you find?'

'Gates,' said Arrietty.

'Strong gates,' said Pod, 'gates you can't open. What are they there for?'

'Against the mice?' said Arrietty.

'Yes,' agreed Pod uncertainly, as though he gave her half a mark, 'but mice never hurt no one. What else?'

'Rats?' suggested Arrietty.

'We don't have rats,' said Pod. 'What about cats?'

'Cats?' echoed Arrietty, surprised.

'Or to keep you in?' suggested Pod.

'To keep me in?' repeated Arrietty, dismayed.

'Upstairs is a dangerous place,' said Pod. 'And you, Arrietty, you're all we've got, see? It isn't like Hendreary – he still has two of his own and three of hers. Once,' said Pod, 'Hendreary had three – three of his own.'

'Your father's thinking of Eggletina,' said Homily.

'Yes,' said Pod, 'Eggletina. They never told her about upstairs. And they hadn't got no grating. They told her the sky was nailed up, like, with cracks in it—'

'A foolish way to bring up a child,' murmured Homily. She sniffed slightly and touched Arrietty's hair.

'But Eggletina was no fool,' said Pod; 'she didn't believe them. So one day,' he went on, 'she went upstairs to see for herself.'

'How did she get out?' asked Arrietty, interested.

'Well, we didn't have so many gates then. Just the one under the clock. Hendreary must have left it unlocked or something. Anyway, Eggletina went out . . .'

'In a blue dress,' said Homily, 'and a pair of button-boots your father made her, yellow kid with jet beads for buttons. Lovely they were.'

'Well,' said Pod, 'any other time it might have been all right. She'd have gone out, had a look around, had a bit of a fright, maybe, and come back – none the worse and no one the wiser . . .'

'But things had been happening,' said Homily.

'Yes,' said Pod, 'she didn't know, as they never told her, that her father had been "seen" and that upstairs they had got in the cat and—'

'They waited a week,' said Homily, 'and they waited a month and they hoped for a year but no one ever saw Eggletina no more.'

'And that,' said Pod after a pause and eyeing Arrietty, 'is what happened to Eggletina.'

There was silence except for Pod's breathing and the faint bubble of the soup.

'It just broke up your Uncle Hendreary,' said Homily at last. 'He never went upstairs again – in case, he said, he found the button-boots. Their only future was to emigrate.'

Arrietty was silent a moment, then she raised her head. 'Why did you tell me?' she asked. 'Now? To-night?'

Homily got up. She moved restlessly towards the stove. 'We don't never talk of it,' she said, 'at least, not much, but, to-night, we felt—' She turned suddenly. 'Well, we'll just say it straight out: your father's been "seen," Arrietty!'

'Oh,' said Arrietty, 'who by?'

'Well, by a – something you've never heard of. But that's not the point: the point is—'

'You think they'll get a cat?'

'They may,' said Homily.

Arrietty set down the soup for a moment; she stared into the cup as it stood beside her almost knee high on the floor; there was a dreamy, secret something about her lowered face. 'Couldn't we emigrate?' she ventured at last, very softly.

Homily gasped and clasped her hands and swung away towards the wall. 'You don't know what you're talking about,' she cried, addressing a frying-pan which hung there. 'Worms and weazels and cold and damp and—'

'But supposing,' said Arrietty, 'that *I* went out, like Eggletina did, and the cat ate *me*. Then you and papa would emigrate. Wouldn't you?' she asked, and her voice faltered. 'Wouldn't you?'

Homily swung round again, this time towards Arrietty; her face looked very angry. 'I shall smack you, Arrietty Clock, if you don't behave yourself this minute!'

Arrietty's eyes filled with tears. 'I was only thinking,' she said, 'that I'd like to be there – to emigrate too. Uneaten,' she added softly and the tears fell.

'Now,' said Pod, 'this is enough! You get off to bed, Arrietty, uneaten and unbeaten both – and we'll talk about it in the morning.'

'It's not that I'm afraid,' cried Arrietty angrily; 'I like cats. I bet the cat didn't eat Eggletina. I bet she just ran away because she hated being cooped up . . . day after day . . . week after week . . . year after year . . . Like I do!' she added on a sob.

'Cooped up!' repeated Homily, astounded.

Arrietty put her face into her hands. 'Gates . . .' she gasped, 'gates, gates, gates . . .'

Pod and Homily stared at each other across Arrietty's bowed shoulders. 'You didn't ought to have brought it up,' he said unhappily, 'not so late at night . . .'

Arrietty raised her tear-streaked face. 'Late or early, what's the difference?' she cried. 'Oh, I know papa is a wonderful borrower. I know we've managed to stay when all the others have gone. But what has it done for us, in the end? I don't think it's so clever to live on alone, for ever and ever, in a great, big, half-empty house; under the floor, with no one to talk to, no one to play with, nothing to see but dust and passages, no light but candlelight and firelight and what comes through the cracks. Eggletina had brothers and Eggletina had half-brothers; Eggletina had a tame mouse; Eggletina had yellow boots with jet buttons, and Eggletina did get out – just once!'

'Shush,' said Pod gently, 'not so loud.' Above their heads the floor creaked and heavy footfalls heaved deliberately to and fro. They heard Mrs Driver's grumbling voice and the clatter of the fire-irons. 'Drat this stove,' they heard her say, 'wind's in the east again.' Then they heard her raise her voice and call, 'Crampfurl!'

Pod sat staring glumly at the floor; Arrietty shivered a little and hugged herself more tightly into the knitted quilt and Homily drew a long, slow breath. Suddenly she raised her head.

'The child is right,' she announced firmly.

Arrietty's eyes grew big. 'Oh, no—' she began. It shocked her to be right. Parents were right, not children. Children could say anything, Arrietty knew, and enjoy saying it – knowing always they were safe and wrong.

'You see, Pod,' went on Homily, 'it was different for you and me. There was other families, other children . . . the Sinks in the scullery, you remember? And those people who lived behind the knife machine – I forget their names now. And the Broom-Cupboard boys. And there was that underground passage from the stables – you know, that the Rain-Pipes used. We had more, as you might say, freedom.'

'Ah, yes,' said Pod, 'in a way. But where does freedom take you?' He looked up uncertainly. 'Where are they all now?'

'Some of them may have bettered themselves, I shouldn't wonder,' said Homily sharply. 'Times have changed in the whole house. Pickings aren't what they were. There were those that went, you remember, when they dug a trench for the gas-pipe. Over the fields, and through the wood, and all. A kind of tunnel it gave them, all the way to Leighton Buzzard.'

'And what did they find there?' said Pod unkindly. 'A mountain of coke!'

Homily turned away. 'Arrietty,' she said, in the same firm voice, 'supposing one day – we'd pick a special day when there was no one about, and providing they don't get a cat which I have my reasons for thinking they won't – supposing, one day, your father took you out borrowing, you'd be a good girl, wouldn't you? You'd do just what he said, quickly and quietly and no arguing?'

Arrietty turned quite pink; she clasped her hands together. 'Oh—' she began in an ecstatic voice, but Pod cut in quickly:

'Now, Homily, we got to think. You can't just say things like that without thinking it out proper. I been "seen" remember. This is no kind of time for taking a child upstairs.'

'There won't be no cat,' said Homily; 'there wasn't no screeching. It's not like that time with Rosa Pickhatchet.'

'All the same,' said Pod uncertainly, 'the risk's there. I never heard of no *girl* going borrowing before.'

'The way I look at it,' said Homily, 'and it's only now it's come to me: if you had a son, you'd take him borrowing, now wouldn't you? Well, you haven't got no son – only Arrietty. Suppose anything happened to you or me, where would Arrietty be – if she hadn't learned to borrow?'

Pod stared down at his knees. 'Yes,' he said after a moment, 'I see what you mean.'

'And it'll give her a bit of interest like and stop her hankering.'

'Hankering for what?'

'For blue sky and grass and suchlike.' Arrietty caught her breath and Homily turned on her swiftly: 'It's no good, Arrietty, I'm not going to emigrate – not for you nor any one else!'

'Ah,' said Pod and began to laugh, 'so that's it!'

'Shush!' said Homily, annoyed, and glanced quickly at the ceiling. 'Not so loud! Now kiss your father, Arrietty,' she went on briskly, 'and pop off back to bed.'

As Arrietty snuggled down under the bed-clothes she felt, creeping up from her toes, a glow of happiness like a glow of warmth. She heard their voices rising and falling in the next room: Homily's went on and on, measured and confident – there was, Arrietty felt, a kind of conviction behind it; it was the winning voice. Once she heard Pod get up and the scrape of a chair. 'I don't like it!' she heard him say. And she heard Homily whisper 'Hush!' and there were tremulous footfalls on the floor above and the sudden clash of pans.

Arrietty, half dozing, gazed up at her painted ceiling. 'FLOR DE HAVANA,' proclaimed the banners proudly. 'Garantizados . . . Superiores . . . Non Plus Ultra . . . Esquisitos . . .' and the lovely gauzy ladies blew their trumpets, silently, triumphantly, on soundless notes of glee . . .

Chapter Seven

For the next three weeks Arrietty was especially 'good': she helped her mother tidy the store-rooms; she swept and watered the passages and trod them down: she sorted and graded the beads (which they used as buttons) into the screw tops of aspirin bottles; she cut old kid gloves into squares for Pod's shoemaking; she filed fish-bone needles to a bee-sting sharpness; she hung up the washing to dry by the grating so that it blew in the soft air; and at last the day came – that dreadful, wonderful, never-to-be-forgotten day – when Homily, scrubbing the kitchen table, straightened her back and called 'Pod!'

He came in from his workroom, last in hand.

'Look at this brush!' cried Homily. It was a fibre brush with a plaited, fibre back.

'Aye,' said Pod, 'worn down.'

'Gets me knuckles now,' said Homily, 'everytime I scrub.'

Pod looked worried. Since he had been 'seen,' they had stuck to kitchen borrowing, the bare essentials of fuel and food. There was an old mouse-hole under the kitchen stove upstairs which, at night when the fire was out or very low, Pod could use as a chute to save carrying. Since the window-curtain incident they had pushed a match-box chest of drawers below the mouse-hole, and had stood a wooden chest on the chest of drawers; and Pod, with much help and shoving from Homily, had learned to squeeze up the chute instead of down. In this way he need not venture into the great hall and passages, he could just nip out, from under the vast black stove in the kitchen, for a clove or a carrot or a tasty piece of ham. But it was not a satisfactory arrangement: even when the fire was out, often there was hot ash and cinders under the stove and once, as he emerged, a great brush came at him wielded by Mrs Driver; and he slithered back, on top of Homily, singed, shaken, and coughing dust. Another time, for some reason, the fire had been in full blaze and Pod had arrived suddenly beneath a glowing inferno, dropping white-hot coals. But usually, at night, the fire was out, and Pod could pick his way through the cinders into the kitchen proper.

'Mrs Driver's out,' Homily went on. 'It's her day off. And She' – they always spoke of Aunt Sophy as 'She' – 'is safe enough in bed.'

'It's not them that worries me,' said Pod.

'Why,' exclaimed Homily sharply, 'the boy's not still here?'

'I don't know,' said Pod; 'there's always a risk,' he added.

'And there always will be,' retorted Homily, 'like when you was in the coal-cellar and the coal-cart came.'

'But the other two,' said Pod, 'Mrs Driver and Her, I always know where they are, like.'

'As for that,' exclaimed Homily, 'a boy's even better.

You can hear a boy a mile off. Well,' she went on after a moment, 'please yourself. 'But it's not like you to talk of risks . . .'

Pod sighed. 'All right,' he said and turned away to fetch his borrowing-bag.

'Take the child,' called Homily after him.

Pod turned. 'Now, Homily,' he began in an alarmed voice.

'Why not?' asked Homily sharply, 'it's just the day. You aren't going no farther than the front door. If you're nervous you can leave her by the clock, ready to nip underneath and down the hole. Let her just *see* at any rate. Arrietty!'

As Arrietty came running in Pod tried again. 'Now listen, Homily—' he protested.

Homily ignored him. 'Arrietty,' she said brightly, 'would you like to go along with your father and borrow me some brush fibre from the door-mat in the hall?'

Arrietty gave a little skip. 'Oh,' she cried, 'could I?'

'Well, take your apron off,' said Homily, 'and change your boots. You want light shoes for borrowing – better wear the red kid.' And then as Arrietty spun away Homily turned to Pod: 'She'll be all right,' she said, 'you'll see.'

As she followed her father down the passage Arrietty's heart began to beat faster. Now the moment had come at last she found it almost too much to bear. She felt light and trembly, and hollow with excitement.

They had three borrowing-bags between the two of them ('In case,' Pod had explained, 'we pick up something. A bad borrower loses many a chance for lack of an extra bag'), and Pod laid these down to open the first gate, which was latched by a safety-pin. It was a big pin, too strongly sprung for little hands to open, and Arrietty watched her father swing his whole weight on the bar and his feet kick loose off the ground. Hanging from his hands, he shifted his weight along the pin towards the curved sheath and, as he moved, the pin sprang open and he, in the same instant, jumped free. 'You couldn't do that,' he remarked, dusting his hands, 'too light. Nor could your mother. Come along now. Quietly . . .'

There were other gates; all of which Pod left open ('Never shut a gate on the way out,' he explained in a whisper, 'you might need to get back quick') and, after a while, Arrietty saw a faint light at the end of the passage. She pulled her father's sleeve. 'Is that it?' she whispered.

Pod stood still. 'Quietly, now,' he warned her. 'Yes, that's it: the hole under the clock!' As he said these words, Arrietty felt breathless but, outwardly, she made no sign. 'There are three steps up to it,' Pod went on, 'steep like, so mind how you go. When you're under the clock you just stay there; don't let your mind wander and keep your eyes on me: if all's clear, I'll give you the sign.'

The steps were high and a little uneven but Arrietty took them more lightly than Pod. As she scrambled past the jagged edges of the hole she had a sudden blinding glimpse of molten gold: it was spring sunshine on the pale stones of the hall floor. Standing upright, she could no longer see this; she could only see the cave-like shadows in the great case above her and the dim outline of the hanging weights. The hollow darkness around her vibrated with sound; it was a safe sound – solid and regular; and, far above her head, she saw the movement of the pendulum; it gleamed a little in the half light, remote and cautious in its rhythmic swing. Arrietty felt warm tears behind her eyelids and a sudden swelling pride: so this, at last, was The Clock! Their clock . . .

after which her family was named! For two hundred years it had stood here, deep-voiced and patient, guarding their threshold, and measuring their time.

But Pod, she saw, stood crouched beneath the carved archway against the light: 'Keep your eyes on me,' he had said, so Arrietty crouched too. She saw the gleaming golden stone floor of the hall stretching away into

distance: she saw the edges of rugs, like richly coloured
islands in a molten sea, and she saw, in a glory of sunlight
– like a dreamed-of gateway to fairyland – the open front
door. Beyond she saw grass and, against the clear, bright
sky, a waving frond of green.

Pod's eyes slewed round. 'Wait,' he breathed, 'and
watch.' And then in a flash he was gone.

Arrietty saw him scurry across the sunlit floor. Swiftly
he ran – as a mouse runs or a blown dry leaf – and
suddenly she saw him as 'small.' 'But', she told herself,
'he isn't small. He's half a head taller than mother . . .'
She watched him run round a chestnut-coloured island of
door-mat into the shadows beside the door. There, it
seemed, he became invisible.

Arrietty watched and waited. All was still except for a
sudden whirr within the clock. A grinding whirr it was,
up high in the hollow darkness above her head, then the
sliding grate of slipped metal before the clock sang out its
chime. Three notes were struck, deliberate and mellow:
'Take it or leave it,' they seemed to say, 'but that's the
time—'

A sudden movement near the shadowed lintel of the
front door and there was Pod again, bag in hand, beside
the mat; it rose knee deep before him like a field of
chestnut corn. Arrietty saw him glance towards the clock
and then she saw him raise his hand.

Oh, the warmth of the stone flags as she ran across
them . . . the gladdening sunlight on her face and hands
. . . the awful space above and around her! Pod caught
her and held her at last, and patted her shoulder. 'There,
there . . .' he said, 'get your breath – good girl!'

Panting a little, Arrietty gazed about her. She saw great
chair legs rearing up into sunlight; she saw the shadowed
undersides of their seats spread above her like canopies;

she saw the nails and the strapping and odd tags of silk
and string; she saw the terraced cliffs of the stairs,
mounting up into the distance, up and up . . . she saw
carved table legs and a cavern under the chest. And all the
time, in the stillness, the clock spoke – measuring out the
seconds, spreading its layers of calm.

And then, turning, Arrietty looked at the garden. She
saw a gravelled path, full of coloured stones – the size of
walnuts they were with, here and there, a blade of grass
between them, transparent green against the light of the
sun. Beyond the path she saw a grassy bank rising steeply
to a tangled hedge; and beyond the hedge she saw fruit
trees, bright with blossom.

'Here's a bag,' said Pod in a hoarse whisper; 'better get
down to work.'

Obediently Arrietty started pulling fibre; stiff it was
and full of dust. Pod worked swiftly and methodically,
making small bundles, each of which he put immediately
in the bag. 'If you have to run suddenly,' he explained,
'you don't want to leave nothing behind.'

'It hurts your hands,' said Arrietty, 'doesn't it?' and suddenly she sneezed.

'Not my hands it doesn't,' said Pod; 'they're hardened like,' and Arrietty sneezed again.

'Dusty, isn't it?' she said.

Pod straightened his back. 'No good pulling where it's knotted right in,' he said, watching her. 'No wonder it hurts your hands. See here,' he exclaimed after a moment, 'you leave it! It's your first time up like. You sit on the step there and take a peek out of doors.'

'Oh, no—' Arrietty began ('If I don't help,' she thought, 'he won't want me again'), but Pod insisted.

'I'm better on me own,' he said. 'I can choose me bits, if you see what I mean, seeing as it's me who's got to make the brush.'

Chapter Eight

The step was warm but very steep. 'If I got down on to the path,' Arrietty thought, 'I might not get up again,' so for some moments she sat quietly. After a while she noticed the shoe-scraper.

'Arrietty,' called Pod softly, 'where have you got to?'

'I just climbed down the shoe-scraper,' she called back.

He came along and looked down at her from the top of the step. 'That's all right,' he said after a moment's stare, 'but never climb down anything that isn't fixed like. Supposing one of them came along and moved the

shoe-scraper – where would you be then? How would
you get up again?'

'It's heavy to move,' said Arrietty.

'Maybe,' said Pod, 'but it's movable. See what I mean?
There's rules, my lass, and you got to learn.'

'This path,' Arrietty said, 'goes round the house. And
the bank does too.'

'Well,' said Pod, 'what of it?'

Arrietty rubbed one red kid shoe on a rounded stone.

'It's my grating,' she explained. 'I was thinking that my
grating must be just round the corner. My grating looks
out on to this bank.'

'Your grating!' exclaimed Pod. 'Since when has it been
your grating?'

'I was thinking,' Arrietty went on. 'Suppose I just went
round the corner and called through the grating to
mother?'

'No,' said Pod, 'we're not going to have none of that.
Not going round corners.'

'Then,' went on Arrietty, 'she'd see I was all right like.'

'Well,' said Pod, and then he half smiled, 'go quickly

then and call. I'll watch for you here. Not loud mind!'

Arrietty ran. The stones in the path were firmly bedded and her light, soft shoes hardly seemed to touch them. How glorious it was to run – you could never run under the floor: you walked, you stooped, you crawled – but you never ran. Arrietty nearly ran past the grating. She saw it just in time after she turned the corner. Yes, there it was quite close to the ground, embedded deeply in the old wall of the house; there was moss below it in a spreading, greenish stain.

Arrietty ran up to it. 'Mother!' she called, her nose against the iron grille. 'Mother!' She waited quietly and, after a moment, she called again.

At the third call Homily came. Her hair was coming down and she carried, as though it were heavy, the screw lid of a pickle jar, filled with soapy water. 'Oh,' she said in an annoyed voice, 'you didn't half give me a turn! What do you think you're up to? Where's your father?'

Arrietty jerked her head sideways. 'Just there – by the front door!' She was so full of happiness that, out of Homily's sight, her toes danced on the green moss. Here she was on the other side of the grating – here she was at last, on the outside – looking in!

'Yes,' said Homily, 'they open that door like that – the first day of spring. Well,' she went on briskly, 'you run back to your father. And tell him, if the morning-room door happens to be open that I wouldn't say no to a bit of red blotting-paper. Mind out of my way now – while I throw the water!'

'That's what grows the moss,' thought Arrietty as she sped back to her father, 'all the water we empty through the grating . . .'

Pod looked relieved when he saw her but frowned at the message. 'How's she expect me to climb that desk without me pin ? Blotting-paper's a curtain-and-chair job and she should know it. Come on now! Up with you!'

'Let me stay down,' pleaded Arrietty, 'just a bit longer. Just till you finish. They're all out. Except Her. Mother said so.'

'She'd say anything,' grumbled Pod, 'when she wants something quick. How does she know She won't take it into her head to get out of that bed of Hers and come downstairs with a stick ? How does she know Mrs Driver ain't stayed at home to-day – with a headache ? How does she know that boy ain't still here ?'

'What boy?' asked Arrietty.

Pod looked embarrassed. 'What boy?' he repeated vaguely and then went on: 'Or may be Crampfurl—'

'Crampfurl isn't a boy,' said Arrietty.

'No he isn't,' said Pod, 'not in a manner of speaking No,' he went on as though thinking this out, 'no, you wouldn't call Crampfurl a boy. Not, as you might say, a boy – exactly. Well,' he said, beginning to move away, 'stay down a bit if you like. But stay close!'

Arrietty watched him move away from the step and then she looked about her. Oh, glory! Oh, joy! Oh, freedom! The sunlight, the grasses, the soft, moving air and half-way up the bank, where it curved round the corner, a flowering cherry-tree! Below it on the path lay a stain of pinkish petals and, at the tree's foot, pale as butter, a nest of primroses.

Arrietty threw a cautious glance towards the front doorstep and then, light and dancey, in her soft red shoes, she ran towards the petals. They were curved like shells and rocked as she touched them. She gathered several up and laid them one inside the other . . . up and up . . . like a card castle. And then she spilled them. Pod came again to the top of the step and looked along the path. 'Don't you go far,' he said after a moment. Seeing his lips move, she smiled back at him: she was too far already to hear the words.

A greenish beetle, shining in the sunlight, came towards her across the stones. She laid her fingers lightly on its shell and it stood still, waiting and watchful, and when she moved her hand the beetle went swiftly on. An ant came hurrying in a busy zigzag. She danced in front of it to tease it and put out her foot. It stared at her, nonplussed, waving its antennae; then pettishly, as though put out, it swerved away. Two birds came down, quarrelling shrilly, into the grass below the tree. One flew away but Arrietty could see the other among the moving grass stems above her on the slope. Cautiously she moved towards the bank and climbed a little nervously in amongst the green blades. As she parted them gently with her bare hands, drops of water plopped on her skirt and she felt the red shoes become damp. But on she went, pulling herself up now and again by rooty stems into this jungle of moss and wood-violet and creeping leaves of clover. The sharp-seeming grass blades, waist high, were tender to the touch and sprang back lightly behind her as she passed. When at last she reached the foot of the tree, the bird took fright and flew away and she sat down suddenly on a gnarled leaf of primrose. The air was filled with scent. 'But nothing will play with you,' she thought and saw the cracks and furrows of the primrose leaves held crystal beads of dew. If she pressed the leaf these rolled like marbles. The bank was warm, almost too warm here within the shelter of the tall grass, and the sandy earth smelled dry. Standing up, she picked a primrose. The pink stalk felt tender and living in her hands and was covered with silvery hairs, and when she held the flower, like a parasol, between her eyes and the

sky, she saw the sun's pale light through the veined petals.
On a piece of bark she found a wood-louse and she struck
it lightly with her swaying flower. It curled immediately
and became a ball, bumping softly away downhill in
amongst the grass roots. But she knew about wood-lice.
There were plenty of them at home under the floor.
Homily always scolded her if she played with them
because, she said, they smelled of old knives. She lay back
among the stalks of the primroses and they made a
coolness between her and the sun, and then, sighing, she
turned her head and looked sideways up the bank among
the grass stems. Startled, she caught her breath. Something had moved above her on the bank. Something had
glittered. Arrietty stared.

Chapter Nine

It was an eye. Or it looked like an eye. Clear and bright
like the colour of the sky. An eye like her own but
enormous. A glaring eye. Breathless with fear, she sat up.
And the eye blinked. A great fringe of lashes came curving
down and flew up again out of sight. Cautiously, Arrietty
moved her legs: she would slide noiselessly in among the
grass stems and slither away down the bank.

'Don't move!' said a voice, and the voice, like the eye,
was enormous but, somehow, hushed – and hoarse like a
surge of wind through the grating on a stormy night in
March.

Arrietty froze. 'So this is it,' she thought, 'the worst and most terrible thing of all : I have been "seen" ! Whatever happened to Eggletina will now, almost certainly, happen to me !'

There was a pause and Arrietty, her heart pounding in her ears, heard the breath again drawn swiftly into the vast lungs. 'Or,' said the voice, whispering still, 'I shall hit you with my ash stick.'

Suddenly Arrietty became calm. 'Why ?' she asked. How strange her own voice sounded ! Crystal thin and harebell clear, it tinkled on the air.

'In case,' came the surprised whisper at last, 'you ran towards me, quickly, through the grass . . . in case,' it went on, trembling a little, 'you scrabbled at me with your nasty little hands.'

Arrietty stared at the eye; she held herself quite still. 'Why ?' she asked again, and again the word tinkled – icy cold it sounded this time, and needle sharp.

'Things do,' said the voice. 'I've seen them. In India.'

Arrietty thought of her *Gazetteer of the World*. 'You're not in India now,' she pointed out.

'Did you come out of the house ?'

'Yes,' said Arrietty.

'From whereabouts in the house ?'

Arrietty stared at the eye. 'I'm not going to tell you,' she said at last bravely.

'Then I'll hit you with my ash stick !'

'All right,' said Arrietty, 'hit me !'

'I'll pick you up and break you in half !'

Arrietty stood up. 'All right,' she said and took two paces forward.

There was a sharp gasp and an earthquake in the grass : he spun away from her and sat up, a great mountain in a

67

green jersey. He had fair, straight hair and golden eyelashes. 'Stay where you are!' he cried.

Arrietty stared up at him. So this was 'the boy'! Breathless, she felt, and light with fear. 'I guessed you were about nine,' she gasped after a moment.

He flushed. 'Well, you're wrong, I'm ten.' He looked down at her, breathing deeply. 'How old are you?'

'Fourteen,' said Arrietty. 'Next June,' she added, watching him.

There was silence while Arrietty waited, trembling a little. 'Can you read?' the boy said at last.

'Of course,' said Arrietty. 'Can't you?'

'No,' he stammered. 'I mean – yes. I mean I've just come from India.'

'What's that got to do with it?' asked Arrietty.

'Well, if you're born in India, you're bilingual. And if you're bilingual, you can't read. Not so well.'

Arrietty stared up at him: what a monster, she thought, dark against the sky.

'Do you grow out of it?' she asked.

He moved a little and she felt the cold flick of his shadow.

'Oh yes,' he said, 'it wears off. My sisters were bilingual; now they aren't a bit. They could read any of those books upstairs in the schoolroom.'

'So could I,' said Arrietty quickly, 'if someone could hold them, and turn the pages. I'm not a bit bilingual. I can read anything.'

'Could you read out loud?'

'Of course,' said Arrietty.

'Would you wait here while I run upstairs and get a book now?'

'Well,' said Arrietty; she was longing to show off; then a startled look came into her eyes. 'Oh—' she faltered.

'What's the matter?' The boy was standing up now. He towered above her.

'How many doors are there to this house?' She squinted up at him against the bright sunlight. He dropped on one knee.

'Doors?' he said. 'Outside doors?'

'Yes.'

'Well, there's the front door, the back door, the gun-room door, the kitchen door, the scullery door . . . and the french windows in the drawing-room.'

'Well, you see,' said Arrietty, 'my father's in the hall, by the front door, working. He . . . he wouldn't want to be disturbed.'

'Working?' said the boy. 'What at?'

'Getting material,' said Arrietty, 'for a scrubbing-brush.'

'Then I'll go in the side door'; he began to move away but turned suddenly and came back to her. He stood a moment, as though embarrassed, and then he said: 'Can you fly?'

'No,' said Arrietty, surprised; 'can you?'

His face became even redder. 'Of course not,' he said angrily; 'I'm not a fairy!'

'Well, nor am I,' said Arrietty, 'nor is anybody. I don't believe in them.'

He looked at her strangely. 'You don't believe in them?'

'No,' said Arrietty; 'do you?'

'Of course not!'

Really, she thought, he is a very angry kind of boy. 'My mother believes in them,' she said, trying to appease him. 'She thinks she saw one once. It was when she was a girl and lived with her parents behind the sand pile in the potting-shed.'

He squatted down on his heels and she felt his breath on her face: 'What was it like?' he asked.

'About the size of a glow-worm with wings like a butterfly. And it had a tiny little face, she said, all alight and moving like sparks and tiny moving hands. Its face was changing all the time, she said, smiling and sort of shimmering. It seemed to be talking, she said, very quickly – but you couldn't hear a word . . .'

'Oh,' said the boy, interested. After a moment he asked: 'Where did it go?'

'It just went,' said Arrietty. 'When my mother saw it, it seemed to be caught in a cobweb. It was dark at the time. About five o'clock on a winter's evening. After tea.'

'Oh,' he said again and picked up two petals of cherry-blossom which he folded together like a sandwich and ate slowly. 'Supposing,' he said, staring past her at the wall of the house, 'you saw a little man, about as tall as a pencil, with a blue patch in his trousers, half-way up a window curtain, carrying a doll's tea-cup – would you say it was a fairy?'

'No,' said Arrietty, 'I'd say it was my father.'

'Oh,' said the boy, thinking this out, 'does your father have a blue patch on his trousers?'

'Not on his best trousers. He does on his borrowing ones.'

'Oh,' said the boy again. He seemed to find it a safe sound, as lawyers do. 'Are there many people like you?'

'No,' said Arrietty. 'None. We're all different.'

'I mean as small as you?'

Arrietty laughed. 'Oh, don't be silly!' she said. 'Surely you don't think there are many people in the world your size?'

'There are more my size than yours,' he retorted.

'Honestly—' began Arrietty helplessly and laughed

again. 'Do you really think – I mean, whatever sort of a world would it be? Those great chairs . . . I've seen them. Fancy if you had to make chairs that size for every one? And the stuff for their clothes . . . miles and miles of it . . . tents of it . . . and the sewing! And their great houses, reaching up so you can hardly see the ceilings . . . their great beds . . . the *food* they eat . . . great, smoking mountains of it, huge bogs of stew and soup and stuff.'

'Don't you eat soup?' asked the boy.

'Of course we do,' laughed Arrietty. 'My father had an uncle who had a little boat which he rowed round in the stock-pot picking up flotsam and jetsam. He did bottom-fishing too for bits of marrow until the cook got suspicious through finding bent pins in the soup. Once he was nearly shipwrecked on a chunk of submerged shinbone. He lost his oars and the boat sprang a leak but he flung a line over the pot handle and pulled himself alongside the rim. But all that stock – fathoms of it! And the size of the stockpot! I mean, there wouldn't be enough stuff in the world to go round after a bit! That's why my father says it's a good thing they're dying out . . . just a few, my father says, that's all we need – to keep us. Otherwise, he says, the whole thing gets'— Arrietty hesitated, trying to remember the word – 'exaggerated, he says—'

'What do you mean,' asked the boy, '"to keep us"?'

Chapter Ten

So Arrietty told him about borrowing – how difficult it was and how dangerous. She told him about the store-rooms under the floor; about Pod's early exploits, the skill he had shown and the courage, she described those far-off days, before her birth, when Pod and Homily had been rich; she described the musical snuff-box, of gold filigree, and the little bird which flew out of it made of kingfisher feathers, how it flapped its wings and sang its song; she described the doll's wardrobe and the tiny green glasses; the little silver tea-pot out of the drawing-room case; the satin bedcovers and embroidered sheets . . . 'those we have still,' she told him, 'they're Her handkerchiefs . . .' 'She,' the boy realized gradually, was his Great Aunt Sophy upstairs; he heard how Pod would borrow from her bedroom, picking his way – in the firelight – among the trinkets on her dressing-table, even climbing her bed-curtains and walking on her quilt. And of how she would watch him and sometimes talk to him because, Arrietty explained, every day at six o'clock they brought her a decanter of Fine Old Pale Madeira, and how before midnight she would drink the lot. Nobody blamed her, not even Homily, because, as Homily would say, 'She' had so few pleasures, poor soul, but, Arrietty explained, after the first three glasses Great Aunt Sophy never believed in anything she saw. 'She thinks my father comes out of the decanter,' said Arrietty, 'and one day when I'm older he's going to take me there and she'll think I come out of the decanter too. It'll please her, my father thinks, as she's used to him now. Once he took my mother, and Aunt Sophy perked up like

anything and kept asking why my mother didn't come any more and saying they'd watered the Madeira because once, she says, she saw a little man *and* a little woman and now she only sees a little man . . .'

'I wish she thought I came out of the decanter,' said the boy. 'She gives me dictation and teaches me to write. I only see her in the mornings when she's cross. She sends for me and looks behind my ears and asks Mrs D. if I've learned my words.'

'What does Mrs D. look like?' asked Arrietty. (How delicious it was to say 'Mrs D.' like that . . . how careless and daring!)

'She's fat and has a moustache and gives me my bath and hurts my bruise and my sore elbow and says she'll take a slipper to me one of these days . . .' The boy pulled

73

up a tuft of grass and stared at it angrily and Arrietty saw his lip tremble. 'My mother's very nice,' he said. 'She lives in India. Why did you lose all your worldly riches?'

'Well,' said Arrietty, 'the kitchen boiler burst and hot water came pouring through the floor into our house and everything was washed away and piled up in front of the grating. My father worked night and day. First hot, then cold. Trying to salvage things. And there's a dreadful draught in March through that grating. He got ill, you see, and couldn't go borrowing. So my Uncle Hendreary had to do it and one or two others and my mother gave them things, bit by bit, for all their trouble. But the kingfisher bird was spoilt by the water; all its feathers fell off and a great twirly spring came jumping out of its side. My father used the spring to keep the door shut against draughts from the grating and my mother put the feathers in a little moleskin hat. After a while I got born and my father went borrowing again. But he gets tired now and doesn't like curtains, not when any of the bobbles are off . . .'

'I helped him a bit,' said the boy, 'with the tea-cup. He was shivering all over. I suppose he was frightened.'

'My father frightened!' exclaimed Arrietty angrily. 'Frightened of you!' she added.

'Perhaps he doesn't like heights,' said the boy.

'He loves heights,' said Arrietty. 'The thing he doesn't like is curtains. I've told you. Curtains make him tired.'

The boy sat thoughtfully on his haunches, chewing a blade of grass. 'Borrowing,' he said after a while. 'Is that what you call it?'

'What else could you call it?' asked Arrietty.

'I'd call it stealing.'

Arrietty laughed. She really laughed. 'But we *are* Borrowers,' she explained, 'like you're a – a Human Bean or whatever it's called. We're part of the house. You might as well say that the fire-grate steals the coal from the coal-scuttle.'

'Then what is stealing?'

Arrietty looked grave. 'Supposing my Uncle Hendreary borrowed an emerald watch from Her dressing-table and my father took it and hung it up on our wall. That's stealing.'

'An emerald watch!' exclaimed the boy.

'Well, I just said that because we have one on the wall at home, but my father borrowed it himself. It needn't be a watch. It could be anything. A lump of sugar even. But Borrowers don't steal.'

'Except from human beans,' said the boy.

Arrietty burst out laughing; she laughed so much that she had to hide her face in the primrose. 'Oh dear,' she gasped with tears in her eyes, 'you are funny!' She stared upwards at his puzzled face. 'Human beans are *for* Borrowers – like bread's for butter!'

The boy was silent awhile. A sigh of wind rustled the cherry-tree and shivered among the blossom.

'Well, I don't believe it,' he said at last, watching the falling petals. 'I don't believe that's what we're for at all and I don't believe we're dying out!'

'Oh, goodness!' exclaimed Arrietty impatiently, staring up at his chin. 'Just use your common sense: you're the only real human bean I ever saw (although I do just know of three more – Crampfurl, Her, and Mrs Driver). But I know lots and lots of Borrowers: the Overmantels and the Harpsichords and the Rain-Barrels and the Linen-Presses and the Boot-Racks and the Hon. John Studdingtons and—'

He looked down. 'John Studdington? But he was our grand-uncle—'

'Well, this family lived behind a picture,' went on Arrietty, hardly listening, 'and there were the Stove-Pipes and the Bell-Pulls and the—'

'Yes,' he interrupted, 'but did you see them?'

'I saw the Harpsichords. And my mother was a Bell-Pull. The others were before I was born . . .'

He leaned closer. 'Then where are they now? Tell me that.'

'My Uncle Hendreary has a house in the country,' said Arrietty coldly, edging away from his great lowering face; it was misted over, she noticed, with hairs of palest gold. 'And five children, Harpsichords and Clocks.'

'But where are the others?'

'Oh,' said Arrietty, 'they're somewhere.' But where? she wondered. And she shivered slightly in the boy's cold shadow which lay about her, slant-wise, on the grass.

He drew back again, his fair head blocking out a great piece of sky. 'Well,' he said deliberately after a moment, and his eyes were cold, 'I've only seen two Borrowers but

I've seen hundreds and hundreds and hundreds and hundreds and hundreds—'

'Oh no—' whispered Arrietty.

'Of human beans.' And he sat back.

Arrietty stood very still. She did not look at him. After a while she said: 'I don't believe you.'

'All right,' he said, 'then I'll tell you—'

'I still won't believe you,' murmured Arrietty.

'Listen!' he said. And he told her about railway stations and football matches and racecourses and royal processions and Albert Hall concerts. He told her about India and China and North America and the British Commonwealth. He told her about the July sales. 'Not hundreds,' he said, 'but thousands and millions and billions and trillions of great, big, enormous people. Now do you believe me?'

Arrietty stared up at him with frightened eyes: it gave her a crick in the neck. 'I don't know,' she whispered.

'As for you,' he went on, leaning closer again, 'I don't believe that there are any more Borrowers anywhere in the world. I believe you're the last three,' he said.

Arrietty dropped her face into the primrose. 'We're not. There's Aunt Lupy and Uncle Hendreary and all the cousins.'

'I bet they're dead,' said the boy. 'And what's more,' he went on, 'no one will ever believe I've seen *you*. And you'll be the very last because you're the youngest. One day,' he told her, smiling triumphantly, 'you'll be the only Borrower left in the world!'

He sat still, waiting, but she did not look up. 'Now you're crying,' he remarked after a moment.

'They're not dead,' said Arrietty in a muffled voice; she was feeling in her little pocket for a handkerchief. 'They live in a badger's set two fields away, beyond the spinney.

We don't see them because it's too far. There are weasels and things and cows and foxes . . . and crows . . .'

'Which spinney?' he asked.

'I don't KNOW!' Arrietty almost shouted. 'It's along by the gas-pipe – a field called Parkin's Beck.' She blew her nose. 'I'm going home,' she said.

'Don't go,' he said, 'not yet.'

'Yes, I'm going,' said Arrietty.

His face turned pink. 'Let me just get the book,' he pleaded.

'I'm not going to read to you now,' said Arrietty.

'Why not?'

She looked at him with angry eyes. 'Because—'

'Listen,' he said, 'I'll go to that field. I'll go and find Uncle Hendreary. And the cousins. And Aunt What-ever-she-is. And, if they're alive, I'll tell you. What about that? You could write them a letter and I'd put it down the hole—'

Arrietty gazed up at him: 'Would you?' she breathed.

'Yes, I would. Really I would. Now can I go and get the book? I'll go in by the side door.'

'All right,' said Arrietty absently. Her eyes were shining. 'When can I give you the letter?'

'Any time,' he said, standing above her. 'Where in the house do you live?'

'Well—' began Arrietty and stopped. Why once again did she feel this chill? Could it only be his shadow . . . towering above her, blotting out the sun? 'I'll put it somewhere,' she said hurriedly, 'I'll put it under the hall mat.'

'Which one? The one by the front door?'

'Yes, that one.'

He was gone. And she stood there alone in the sunshine, shoulder deep in grass. What had happened seemed too big for thought; she felt unable to believe it really had happened: not only had she been 'seen' but she had been talked to; not only had she been talked to but she had—

'Arrietty!' said a voice.

She stood up startled and spun round: there was Pod, moon-faced, on the path looking up at her. 'Come on down!' he whispered.

She stared at him for a moment as though she did not recognize him; how round his face was, how kind, how familiar!

'Come on!' he said again, more urgently; and obediently because he sounded worried, she slithered quickly towards him off the bank, balancing her primrose. 'Put that thing down,' he said sharply, when she stood at last beside him on the path. 'You can't lug great flowers about – you got to carry a bag. What you want to go up there for?' he grumbled as they moved off across the stones. 'I might never have seen you. Hurry up now. Your mother'll have tea waiting!'

Chapter Eleven

Homily was there, at the last gate, to meet them. She had tidied her hair and smelled of coal-tar soap. She looked younger and somehow excited. 'Well—!' she kept saying. 'Well!' taking the bag from Arrietty and helping Pod to

fasten the gate. 'Well, was it nice? Were you a good girl? Was the cherry-tree out? Did the clock strike?' She seemed, in the dim light, to be trying to read the expression on Arrietty's face. 'Come along now. Tea's all ready. Give me your hand . . .'

Tea was indeed ready, laid on the round table in the sitting-room with a bright fire burning in the cog-wheel. How familiar the room seemed, and homely, but, suddenly, somehow strange: the firelight flickering on the wallpaper – the line which read: '. . . it would be so charming if—' If what? Arrietty always wondered. If our house were less dark, she thought, that would be charming. She looked at the home-made dips set in upturned drawing-pins which Homily had placed as candle-holders among the tea things; the old teapot, a hollow oak-apple, with its quill spout and wired-on handle – burnished it was now and hard with age; there were two roast sliced chestnuts which they would eat like toast with butter and a cold boiled chestnut which Pod would cut like bread; there was a plate of hot dried currants, well plumped before the fire; there were cinnamon breadcrumbs, crispy golden, and lightly dredged with sugar, and in front of each place, oh, delight of delights, a single potted shrimp. Homily had put out the silver plates – the florin ones for herself and Arrietty and the half-crown one for Pod.

'Come along, Arrietty, if you've washed your hands,' exclaimed Homily, taking up the teapot, 'don't dream!'

Arrietty drew up a cotton-reel and sat down slowly. She watched her mother pulling on the spout of the teapot; this was always an interesting moment. The thicker end of the quill being inside the teapot, a slight pull just before pouring would draw it tightly into the hole and thus prevent a leak. If, as sometimes happened, a trace of dampness appeared about the join, it only meant a rather harder pull and a sudden gentle twist.

'Well?' said Homily, gingerly pouring. 'Tell us what you saw!'

'She didn't see so much,' said Pod, cutting himself a slice of boiled chestnut to eat with his shrimp.

'Didn't she see the overmantel?'

'No,' said Pod, 'we never went in the morning-room.'

'What about my blotting-paper?'

'I never got it,' said Pod.

'Now that's a nice thing—' began Homily.

'Maybe,' said Pod, munching steadily, 'but I had me feeling. I had it bad.'

'What's that?' asked Arrietty. 'His feeling?'

'Up the back of his head and in his fingers,' said Homily. 'It's a feeling your father gets when' – she dropped her voice – 'there's someone about.'

'Oh,' said Arrietty and seemed to shrink.

'That's why I brought her along home,' said Pod.

'And was there any one?' asked Homily anxiously.

Pod took a mouthful of shrimp. 'Must have been,' he said, 'but I didn't see nothing.'

Homily leaned across the table. 'Did you have any feeling, Arrietty?'

Arrietty started. 'Oh,' she said, 'do we all have it?'

'Well, not in the same place,' said Homily. 'Mine starts at the back of me ankles and then me knees go. My mother – hers used to start just under her chin and run right round her neck—'

'And tied in a bow at the back,' said Pod, munching.

'No, Pod,' protested Homily, 'it's a fact. No need to be sarcastic. All the Bell-Pulls were like that. Like a collar, she said it was—'

'Pity it didn't choke her,' said Pod.

'Now, Pod, be fair; she had her points.'

'Points!' said Pod. 'She was all points!'

Arrietty moistened her lips; she glanced nervously from Pod to Homily. 'I didn't feel anything,' she said.

'Well,' said Homily, 'perhaps it was a false alarm.'

'Oh no,' began Arrietty, 'it wasn't—' and, as Homily glanced at her sharply, she faltered: 'I mean if papa felt something – I mean— Perhaps,' she went on, 'I don't have it.'

'Well,' said Homily, 'you're young. It'll come, all in good time. You go and stand in our kitchen, just under the chute, when Mrs Driver's raking out the stove upstairs. Stand right up on a stool or something – so's you're fairly near the ceiling. It'll come – with practice.'

After tea, when Pod had gone to his last and Homily was washing up, Arrietty rushed to her diary: 'I'll just open it,' she thought, trembling with haste, 'anywhere.' It fell open at the 9th and 10th of July: 'Talk of Camps but Stay at Home. Old Cameronian Colours in Glasgow Cathedral, 1885' – that's what it said for the 9th. And on the 10th the page was headed: 'Make Hay while the Sun Shines. Snowdon Peak sold for £5,750, 1889.' Arrietty tore out this last page. Turning it over she read on the reverse side: 'July 11th: Make Not a Toil of your Pleasure. Niagara passed by C. D. Graham in a cask, 1886.' No, she thought, I'll choose the 10th, 'Make Hay while the Sun Shines,' and, crossing out her last entry ('Mother out of sorts'), she wrote below it:

'What are you doing, Arrietty?' called Homily from the kitchen.

'Writing in my diary.'

'Oh,' said Homily shortly.

'Anything you want?' asked Arrietty.

'It'll do later,' said Homily.

Arrietty folded the letter and placed it carefully between the pages of Bryce's *Tom Thumb Gazetteer of the World* and, in the diary, she wrote: 'Went borrowing. Wrote to H. Talked to B.' After that Arrietty sat for a long time staring into the fire, and thinking and thinking and thinking . . .

Chapter Twelve

But it was one thing to write a letter and quite another to find some means of getting it under the mat. Pod, for several days, could not be persuaded to go borrowing: he was well away on his yearly turn-out of the store-rooms, mending partitions, and putting up new shelves. Arrietty usually enjoyed this spring sorting, when half-forgotten treasures came to light and new uses were discovered for old borrowings. She used to love turning over the scraps of silk or lace; the odd kid gloves; the pencil stubs; the rusty razor blades; the hairpins and the needles; the dried figs, the hazel-nuts, the powdery bits of chocolate, and the scarlet stubs of sealing-wax. Pod, one year, had made her a hairbrush from a toothbrush and Homily had made her a small pair of Turkish bloomers from two glove fingers for 'knocking about in the mornings.' There were reels and reels of coloured silks and cottons and small variegated balls of odd wool, pen nibs which Homily used as flour scoops, and bottle-tops galore.

But this year Arrietty banged about impatiently and stole away whenever she dared, to stare through the grating, hoping to see the boy. She now kept the letter always with her, stuffed inside her jersey, and the edges became rubbed. Once he did run past the grating and she saw his woollen stockings; he was making a chugging noise in his throat like some kind of engine, and as he turned the corner he let out a piercing 'Ooooo—oo' (it was a train whistle, he told her afterwards) so he did not hear her call. One evening, after dark, she crept away and tried to open the first gate, but swing and tug as she might she could not budge the pin.

Homily, every time she swept the sitting-room, would grumble about the carpet. 'It may be a curtain-and-chair job,' she would say to Pod, 'but it wouldn't take you not a quarter of an hour, with your pin and name-tape, to fetch me a bit of blotting-paper from the desk in the morning-room . . . any one would think, looking at this floor, that we lived in a toad-hole. No one could call me house-proud,' said Homily. 'You couldn't be, not with my kind of family, but I do like,' she said, 'to keep "nice things nice."' And at last, on the fourth day, Pod gave in. He laid down his hammer (a small electric-bell clapper) and said to Arrietty: 'Come along . . .'

Arrietty was glad to see the morning-room; the door luckily had been left ajar and it was fascinating to stand at last in the thick pile of the carpet gazing upwards at the shelves and pillars and towering gables of the famous overmantel. So that's where they had lived, she thought, those pleasure-loving creatures, remote and gay and self-sufficient. She imagined the Overmantel women – a little 'tweedy', Homily had described them, with wasp waists and piled Edwardian hair – swinging carelessly outwards on the pilasters, lissom and laughing; gazing at themselves in the inset looking-glass which reflected back the tobacco jars, the cut-glass decanters, the bookshelves, and the plush covered table. She imagined the Overmantel men – fair, they were said to be, with long moustaches and nervous, slender hands – smoking and drinking and telling their witty tales. So they had never asked Homily up there! Poor Homily with her bony nose and never tidy hair . . . They would have looked at her strangely, Arrietty thought, with their long, half-laughing eyes, and smile a little and, humming, turn away. And they had lived only on breakfast food – on toast and egg and tiny snips of mushroom; sausage they'd have had and crispy bacon and little sips of tea and coffee. Where were they now? Arrietty wondered. Where could such creatures go?

Pod had flung his pin so it stuck into the seat of the chair and was up the leg in a trice, leaning outwards on his tape; then, pulling out the pin, he flung it like a javelin, above his head, into a fold of curtain. This is the moment, Arrietty thought, and felt for her precious letter. She slipped into the hall. It was darker, this time, with the front door closed, and she ran across it with a beating heart. The mat was heavy, but she lifted up the corner and slid the letter under by pushing with her foot. 'There !' she said, and looked about her . . . shadows, shadows, and the ticking clock. She looked across the great plain of floor to where, in the distance, the stairs mounted. 'Another world above,' she thought, 'world on world . . .' and shivered slightly.

'Arrietty,' called Pod softly from the morning-room, and she ran back in time to see him swing clear of the chair seat and pull himself upwards on the name-tape, level with the desk. Lightly he came down feet apart and she saw him, for safety's sake, twist the name-tape lightly round his wrist. 'I wanted you to see that,' he said, a little breathless. The blotting-paper, when he pushed it, floated down quite softly, riding lightly on the air, and lay

at last some feet beyond the desk, pink and fresh, on the carpet's dingy pile.

'You start rolling,' whispered Pod. 'I'll be down,' and Arrietty went on her knees and began to roll the blotting-paper until it grew too stiff for her to hold. Pod soon finished it off and lashed it with his name-tape, through which he ran his hat-pin, and together they carried the long cylinder, as two house-painters would carry a ladder, under the clock and down the hole.

Homily hardly thanked them when, panting a little, they dropped the bundle in the passage outside the sitting-room door. She looked alarmed. 'Oh, there you are,' she said. 'Thank goodness! That boy's about again. I've just heard Mrs Driver talking to Crampfurl.'

'Oh!' cried Arrietty. 'What did she say?' and Homily glanced sharply at her and saw that she looked pale.

Arrietty realized she should have said: 'What boy?' It was too late now.

'Nothing real bad,' Homily went on, as though to reassure her. 'It's just a boy they have upstairs. It's nothing at all, but I heard Mrs Driver say that she'd take a slipper to him, see if she wouldn't, if he had the mats up once again in the hall.'

'The mats up in the hall!' echoed Arrietty.

'Yes. Three days running, she said to Crampfurl, he'd had the mats up in the hall. She could tell, she said, by the dust and the way he'd put them back. It was the hall part that worried me, seeing as you and your father – What's the matter, Arrietty? There's no call for that sort of face! Come on now, help me move the furniture and we'll get down the carpet.'

'Oh dear, oh dear,' thought Arrietty miserably, as she helped her mother empty the match-box chest of drawers. 'Three days running he's looked and nothing there. He'll give up hope now . . . he'll never look again.'

That evening she stood for hours on a stool under the chute in their kitchen, pretending she was practising to get 'a feeling' when really she was listening to Mrs Driver's conversations with Crampfurl. All she learned was that Mrs Driver's feet were killing her, and that it was a pity that she hadn't given in her notice last May, and would Crampfurl have another drop, considering there was more in the cellar than any one would drink in Her lifetime, and if they thought she was going to clean the first-floor windows single-handed they had better think again. But on the third night, just as Arrietty had climbed down off the stool before she overbalanced with weariness, she heard Crampfurl say: 'If you ask me, I'd say he had a ferret.' And quickly Arrietty climbed back again, holding her breath.

'A ferret!' she heard Mrs Driver exclaim shrilly. 'Whatever next? Where would he keep it?'

'That I wouldn't like to say,' said Crampfurl in his rumbling earthy voice; 'all I know is he was up beyond Parkin's Beck, going round all the banks and calling-like down all the rabbit-holes.'

'Well, I never,' said Mrs Driver. 'Where's your glass?'

'Just a drop,' said Crampfurl. 'That's enough. Goes to your liver, this sweet stuff – not like beer, it isn't. Yes,' he went on, 'when he saw me coming with a gun he pretended to be cutting a stick like from the hedge. But I'd see'd him all right and heard him. Calling away, his nose down a rabbit-hole. It's my belief he's got a ferret.' There was a gulp, as though Crampfurl was drinking. 'Yes,' he said at last, and Arrietty heard him set down the glass, 'a ferret called Uncle something.'

Arrietty made a sharp movement, balanced for one moment with arms waving, and fell off the stool. There was a clatter as the stool slid sideways, banged against a chest of drawers and rolled over.

'What was that?' asked Crampfurl.

There was silence upstairs and Arrietty held her breath. 'I didn't hear nothing,' said Mrs Driver.

'Yes,' said Crampfurl, 'it was under the floor like, there by the stove.'

'That's nothing,' said Mrs Driver. 'It's the coals falling. Often sounds like that. Scares you sometimes when you're sitting here alone . . . Here, pass your glass, there's only a drop left – might as well finish the bottle . . .'

They're drinking Fine Old Madeira, thought Arrietty, and very carefully she set the stool upright and stood quietly beside it, looking up. She could see light through the crack, occasionally flicked with shadow as one person or another moved a hand or arm.

'Yes,' went on Crampfurl, returning to his story, 'and when I come up with m'gun he says, all innocent like – to put me off, I shouldn't wonder: "Any old badgers' sets round here?"'

'Artful,' said Mrs Driver; 'the things they think of . . . badgers' sets . . .' and she gave her creaking laugh.

'As a matter of fact,' said Crampfurl, 'there did used to be one, but when I showed him where it was like he didn't take no notice of it. Just stood there, waiting for me to go.' Crampfurl laughed. 'Two can play at that game, I thought, so I just sits m'self down. And there we were the two of us.'

'And what happened?'

'Well, he had to go off in the end. Leaving his ferret. I waited a bit, but it never came out. I poked around a bit and whistled. Pity I never heard properly what he called it. Uncle something it sounded like—' Arrietty heard the sudden scrape of a chair. 'Well,' said Crampfurl, 'I'd better get on now and shut up the chickens—'

The scullery door banged and there was a sudden clatter overhead as Mrs Driver began to rake the stove. Arrietty replaced the stool and stole swiftly into the sitting-room, where she found her mother alone.

Chapter Thirteen

Homily was ironing, bending and banging and pushing the hair back out of her eyes. All round the room underclothes hung airing on safety-pins which Homily used like coat-hangers.

'What happened?' asked Homily. 'Did you fall over?'

'Yes,' said Arrietty, moving quietly into her place beside the fire.

'How's the feeling coming?'

'Oh, I don't know,' said Arrietty. She clasped her knees and laid her chin on them.

'Where's your knitting?' asked Homily. 'I don't know what's come over you lately. Always idle. You don't feel seedy, do you?'

'Oh,' exclaimed Arrietty, 'let me be!' And Homily for once was silent. 'It's the spring,' she told herself. 'Used to take me like that sometimes at her age.'

'I must see that boy,' Arrietty was thinking – staring blindly into the fire. 'I must hear what happened. I must hear if they're all right. I don't want us to die out. I don't want to be the last Borrower. I don't want' – and here Arrietty dropped her face on to her knees – 'to live for ever and ever like this . . . in the dark . . . under the floor . . .'

'No good getting supper,' said Homily, breaking the silence; 'your father's gone borrowing. To Her room. And you know what that means!'

Arrietty raised her head. 'No,' she said, hardly listening; 'what does it mean?'

'That he won't be back,' said Homily sharply, 'for a good hour and a half. He likes it up there, gossiping with

Her and poking about on the dressing-table. And it's safe enough once that boy's in bed. Not that there's anything we want special,' she went on. 'It's just these new shelves he's made. They look kind of bare, he says, and he might, he says, just pick up a little something . . .'

Arrietty suddenly was sitting bolt upright: a thought had struck her, leaving her breathless and a little shaky at the knees. 'A good hour and a half,' her mother had said and the gates would be open!

'Where are you going?' asked Homily as Arrietty moved towards the door.

'Just along to the store-rooms,' said Arrietty, shading with one hand her candle-dip from the draught. 'I won't be long.'

'Now don't you untidy anything!' Homily called out after her. 'And be careful of that light!'

As Arrietty went down the passage she thought: 'It is true. I am going to the store-rooms – to find another hat-pin. And if I do find a hat-pin (and a piece of string – there won't be any name-tape) I still "won't be long" because I'll have to get back before papa. And I'm doing it for their sakes,' she told herself doggedly, 'and one day they'll thank me.' All the same she felt a little guilty. 'Artful' – that's what Mrs Driver would say she was.

There was a hat-pin – one with a bar for a top – and she tied on a piece of string, very firmly, twisting it back and forth like a figure of eight and, as a crowning inspiration, she sealed it with sealing-wax.

The gates were open and she left the candle in the middle of the passage where it could come to no harm, just below the hole by the clock.

The great hall when she had climbed out into it was dim with shadows. A single gas jet, turned low, made a pool of light beside the locked front door and another faintly flickered on the landing half-way up the stairs. The ceiling sprang away into height and darkness and all around was space. The night-nursery, she knew, was at the end of the upstairs passage and the boy would be in bed – her mother had just said so.

Arrietty had watched her father use his pin on the chair and single stairs, in comparison, were easier. There was a kind of rhythm to it after a while: a throw, a pull, a scramble, and an upward swing. The stair rods glinted coldly, but the pile of the carpet seemed soft and warm and delicious to fall back on. On the half-landing she paused to get her breath. She did not mind the semi-darkness; she lived in darkness; she was at home in it and, at a time like this, it made her feel safe.

On the upper landing she saw an open door and a great square of golden light which like a barrier lay across the passage. 'I've got to pass through that,' Arrietty told herself, trying to be brave. Inside the lighted room a voice was talking, droning on. '. . . And this mare,' the voice said, 'was a five-year-old which really belonged to my brother in Ireland, not my elder brother but my younger brother, the one who owned Stale Mate and Oh My Darling. He had entered her for several point-to-points . . . but when I say "several" I mean three or at least two . . . Have you ever seen an Irish point-to-point?'

'No,' said another voice, rather absent-mindedly. 'That's my father,' Arrietty realized with a start, 'my father talking to Great Aunt Sophy or rather Great Aunt Sophy talking to my father.' She gripped her pin with its loops of string, and ran into the light and through it to the passage beyond. As she passed the open door she had a glimpse of firelight and lamplight and gleaming furniture and dark-red silk brocade.

Beyond the square of light the passage was dark again and she could see, at the far end, a half-open door. 'That's the day-nursery,' she thought, 'and beyond that is the night-nursery.'

'There are certain differences,' Aunt Sophy's voice went on, 'which would strike you at once. For instance . . .' Arrietty liked the voice. It was comforting and steady, like the sound of the clock in the hall, and as she moved off the carpet on to the strip of polished floor beside the skirting-board, she was interested to hear there were walls in Ireland instead of hedges. Here by the skirting she could run and she loved running. Carpets were heavy going – thick and clinging, they held you up. The boards were smooth and smelled of beeswax. She liked the smell.

The schoolroom, when she reached it, was shrouded in dust sheets and full of junk. Here too a gas jet burned, turned low to a bluish flame. The floor was oilcloth, rather worn, and the rugs were shabby. Under the table was a great cavern of darkness. She moved into it, feeling about, and bumped into a dusty hassock higher than her head. Coming out again, into the half light, she looked up and saw the corner cupboard with the doll's tea-service, the painting above the fire-place, and the plush curtain where her father had been 'seen.' Chair legs were everywhere and chair seats obscured her view. She found her way among them to the door of the night-nursery and there she saw, suddenly, on a shadowed plateau in the far corner, the boy in bed. She saw his great face, turned towards her on the edge of the pillow; she saw the gaslight reflected in his open eyes; she saw his hand gripping the bed-clothes, holding them tightly pressed against his mouth.

She stopped moving and stood still. After a while, when she saw his fingers relax, she said softly: 'Don't be frightened . . . It's me, Arrietty.'

He let the bed-clothes slide away from his mouth and said: 'Arri-*what*-y?' He seemed annoyed.

'Etty,' she repeated gently. 'Did you take the letter?'

He stared at her for a moment without speaking, then he said: 'Why did you come creeping, creeping, into my room?'

'I didn't come creeping, creeping,' said Arrietty. 'I even ran. Didn't you see?'

He was silent, staring at her with his great, wide-open eyes.

'When I brought the book,' he said at last, 'you'd gone.'

'I had to go. Tea was ready. My father fetched me.'

He understood this. 'Oh,' he said matter of factly, and did not reproach her.

'Did you take the letter?' she asked again.

'Yes,' he said, 'I had to go back twice. I shoved it down the badger's hole . . .' Suddenly he threw back the bed-clothes and stood up in bed, enormous in his pale flannel nightshirt. It was Arrietty's turn to be afraid. She half turned, her eyes on his face, and began backing slowly towards the door. But he did not look at her; he was feeling behind a picture on the wall. 'Here it is,' he said, sitting down again, and the bed creaked loudly.

'But I don't want it back!' exclaimed Arrietty, coming forward again. 'You should have left it there! Why did you bring it back?'

He turned it over in his fingers. 'He's written on it,' he said.

'Oh, please,' cried Arrietty excitedly, 'show me!' She ran right up to the bed and tugged at the trailing sheet. 'Then they are alive! Did you see him?'

'No,' he said, 'the letter was there, just down the hole where I'd put it.' He leaned towards her. 'But he's written on it. Look!'

She made a quick dart and almost snatched the letter

out of his great fingers, but was careful to keep out of range of his grasp. She ran with it to the door of the schoolroom where the light, though dim, was a little brighter. 'It's very faint,' she said, holding it close to her eyes. 'What's he written it with? I wonder. It's all in capitals—' She turned suddenly. 'Are you sure you didn't write it?' she asked.

'Of course not,' he began. 'I write small—' But she had seen by his face that he spoke the truth and began to spell out the letters. 'T–e–double l,' she said. 'Tell y–o–r–e.' She looked up. 'Yore?' she said.

TELL YORE ANT LUPPY TO COM HOME

11th July.
Make not a toil of your pleasure.
Niagara passed by C. D. Graham
in a cask 1886.

'Yes,' said the boy, 'your.'

'Tell your a–n–t, ant?' said Arrietty. 'Ant? My ant?' The boy was silent, waiting. 'Ant L–u– Oh, Aunt Lupy!' she exclaimed. 'He says – listen, this is what he says: "Tell your Aunt Lupy to come home"!'

There was silence. 'Then tell her,' said the boy after a moment.

'But she isn't here!' exclaimed Arrietty. 'She's never been here! I don't even remember what she looked like!'

'Look,' said the boy, staring through the door, 'some-one's coming !'

Arrietty whipped round. There was no time to hide : it was Pod, borrowing-bag in one hand and pin in the other. He stood in the doorway of the schoolroom. Quite still he stood, outlined against the light in the passage, his little shadow falling dimly in front of him. He had seen her.

'I heard your voice,' he said, and there was a dreadful quietness about the way he spoke, 'just as I was coming out of Her room.' Arrietty stared back at him, stuffing the letter up her jersey. Could he see beyond her into the shadowed room. Could he see the tousled shape in bed ?

'Come on home,' said Pod, and turned away.

Chapter Fourteen

Pod did not speak until they reached the sitting-room. Nor did he look at her. She had had to scramble after him as best she might. He had ignored her efforts to help him shut the gates, but once, when she tripped, he had waited until she had got up again, watching her, it seemed, almost without interest while she brushed the dust off her knees.

Supper was laid and the ironing put away and Homily came running in from the kitchen, surprised to see them together.

Pod threw down his borrowing-bag. He stared at his wife.

'What's the matter?' faltered Homily, looking from one to the other.

'She was in the night-nursery,' said Pod quietly, 'talking to that boy!'

Homily moved forward, her hands clasped tremblingly against her apron, her startled eyes flicking swiftly to and fro. 'Oh, no—' she breathed.

Pod sat down. He ran a tired hand over his eyes and forehead; his face looked heavy like a piece of dough. 'Now what?' he said.

Homily stood quite still; bowed she stood over her clasped hands and stared at Arrietty. 'Oh, you never—' she whispered.

'They are frightened,' Arrietty realized; 'they are not angry at all – they are very, very frightened.' She moved forward. 'It's all right—' she began.

Homily sat down suddenly on the cotton-reel; she had

begun to tremble. 'Oh,' she said, 'whatever shall we do?'
She began to rock herself, very slightly, to and fro.

'Oh, mother, don't!' pleaded Arrietty. 'It isn't so bad
as that. It really isn't.' She felt up the front of her jersey; at
first she could not find the letter – it had slid round her
side to the back – but at last she drew it out, very
crumpled. 'Look,' she said, 'here's a letter from Uncle
Hendreary. I wrote to him and the boy took the letter—'

'You wrote to him!' cried Homily on a kind of
suppressed shriek. 'Oh,' she moaned, and closed her eyes,
'whatever next! Whatever shall we do?' and she fanned
herself limply with her bony hand.

'Get your mother a drink of water, Arrietty,' said Pod
sharply. Arrietty brought it in a sawn-off hazel shell – it
had been sawn off at the pointed end and was shaped like
a brandy glass.

'But whatever made you do such a thing, Arrietty?'
said Homily more calmly, setting the empty cup down on
the table. 'Whatever came over you?'

So Arrietty told them about being 'seen' – that morning
under the cherry-tree. And how she had kept it from them
not to worry them. And what the boy said about 'dying
out.' And how – more than important – how imperative
it had seemed to make sure the Hendrearys were alive.
'Do understand,' pleaded Arrietty, 'please understand!
I'm trying to save the race!'

'The expressions she uses!' said Homily to Pod under
her breath, not without pride.

But Pod was not listening. 'Save the race!' he repeated
grimly. 'It's people like you, my girl, who do things
sudden like with no respect for tradition, who'll finish us
Borrowers once for all. Don't you see what you've done?'

Arrietty met his accusing eyes. 'Yes,' she said falter-
ingly, 'I've – I've got in touch with the only other ones still

alive. So that,' she went on bravely, 'from now on we can all stick together . . .'

'All stick together!' Pod repeated angrily. 'Do you think Hendreary's lot would ever come to live back here? Can you see your mother emigrating to a badger's set, two fields away, out in the open and no hot water laid on?'

'Never!' cried Homily in a full, rich voice which made them both turn and look at her.

'Or do you see your mother walking across two fields and a garden,' went on Pod, 'two fields full of crows and cows and horses and what-not, to take a cup of tea with your Aunt Lupy whom she never liked much anyway? But wait,' he said as Arrietty tried to speak, 'that's not the point – as far as all that goes we're just where we was – the point,' he went on, leaning forward and speaking with great solemnity, 'is this: that boy knows now where we live!'

'Oh no,' said Arrietty, 'I never told him that. I—'

'You told him,' interrupted Pod, 'about the kitchen pipe bursting; you told him how all our stuff got washed away to the grating.' He sat back again glaring at her. 'He's only got to think,' he pointed out. Arrietty was silent and Pod went on: 'That's a thing that has never happened before, never, in the whole long history of the Borrowers. Borrowers have been "seen" – yes; Borrowers have been caught – maybe: but no human bean has ever known where any Borrower lived. We're in very grave danger, Arrietty, and you've put us there. And that's a fact.'

'Oh, Pod,' whimpered Homily, 'don't frighten the child.'

'Nay, Homily,' said Pod more gently, 'my poor old girl! I don't want to frighten no one, but this is serious.

Suppose I said to you pack up to-night, all our bits and pieces, where would you go?'

'Not to Hendreary's,' cried Homily, 'not there, Pod! I couldn't never share a kitchen with Lupy—'

'No,' agreed Pod, 'not to Hendreary's. And don't you see for why? The boy knows about that too!'

'Oh!' cried Homily in real dismay.

'Yes,' said Pod, 'a couple of smart terriers, or a well-trained ferret and that'd be the end of that lot.'

'Oh, Pod . . .' said Homily and began again to tremble. The thought of living in a badger's set had been bad enough, but the thought of not having even that to go to seemed almost worse. 'And I dare say I could have got it nice in the end,' she said, 'providing we lived quite separate—'

'Well, it's no good thinking of it now,' said Pod. He turned to Arrietty: 'What does your Uncle Hendreary say in his letter?'

'Yes,' exclaimed Homily, 'where's this letter?'

'It doesn't say much,' said Arrietty, passing over the paper; 'it just says "Tell your Aunt Lupy to come home."'

'What?' exclaimed Homily sharply, looking at the letter upside-down. 'Come home? What can he mean?'

'He means,' said Pod, 'that Lupy must have set off to come here and that she never arrived.'

'Set off to come here?' repeated Homily. 'But when?'

'How should I know?' said Pod.

'It doesn't say when,' said Arrietty.

'But,' exclaimed Homily, 'it might have been weeks ago!'

'It might,' said Pod. 'Long enough anyway for him to want her back.'

'Oh,' cried Homily, 'all those poor little children!'

'They're growing up now,' said Pod.

'But something must have happened to her!' exclaimed Homily.

'Yes,' said Pod. He turned to Arrietty. 'See what I mean, Arrietty, about those fields?'

'Oh, Pod,' said Homily, her eyes full of tears, 'I don't suppose none of us'll ever see poor Lupy again!'

'Well, we wouldn't have anyway,' said Pod.

'Pod,' said Homily soberly, 'I'm frightened. Everything seems to be happening at once. What are we going to do?'

'Well,' said Pod, 'there's nothing we can do to-night. That's certain. But have a bit of supper and a good night's rest.' He rose to his feet.

'Oh, Arrietty,' wailed Homily suddenly, 'you naughty wicked girl! How could you go and start all this? How could you go and talk to a human bean? If only—'

'I was "seen,"' cried Arrietty. 'I couldn't help being "seen." Papa was "seen." I don't think it's all as awful as you're trying to make out. I don't think human beans are all that bad—'

'They're bad and they're good,' said Pod; 'they're honest and they're artful – it's just as it takes them at the moment. And animals, if they could talk, would say the same. Steer clear of them – that's what I've always been told. No matter what they promise you. No good never really came to no one from any human bean.'

Chapter Fifteen

That night, while Arrietty lay straight and still under her cigar-box ceiling, Homily and Pod talked for hours. They talked in the sitting-room, they talked in the kitchen, and later, much later, she heard them talk in their bedroom. She heard drawers shutting and opening, doors creaking, and boxes being pulled out from under beds. 'What are they doing?' she wondered. 'What will happen next?' Very still she lay in her soft little bed with her familiar belongings about her: her postage stamp view of Rio harbour; her silver pig off a charm bracelet; her turquoise ring which sometimes, for fun, she would wear as a crown, and, dearest of all, her floating ladies with the golden trumpets, tooting above their peaceful town. She did not want to lose these, she realized suddenly, lying there straight and still in bed, but to have all the other things as well, adventure and safety mixed – that's what she wanted. And that (the restless bangings and whisperings told her) is just what you couldn't do.

As it happened, Homily was only fidgeting: opening drawers and shutting them, unable to be still. And she ended up, when Pod was already in bed, by deciding to curl her hair. 'Now, Homily,' Pod protested wearily, lying there in his night-shirt, 'there's really no call for that. Who's going to see you?'

'That's just it,' exclaimed Homily, searching in a drawer for her curl-rags; 'in times like these one never knows. I'm not going to be caught out,' she said irritably, turning the drawer upside-down and picking over the spilled contents, 'with me hair like this!'

She came to bed at last, looking spiky, like a washed-out golliwog, and Pod with a sigh turned over at last and closed his eyes.

Homily lay for a long time staring at the oil-lamp; it was the silver cap of a scent-bottle with a tiny, floating wick. She felt unwilling, for some reason, to blow it out. There were movements upstairs in the kitchen above and it was late for movements – the household should be asleep – and the lumpy curlers pressed uncomfortably against her neck. She gazed – just as Arrietty had done – about the familiar room (too full, she realized, with little bags and boxes and make-shift cupboards) and thought: 'What now? Perhaps nothing will happen after all; the child perhaps is right, and we are making a good deal of fuss about nothing very much; this boy, when all's said and done, is only a guest; perhaps,' thought Homily, 'he'll go away again quite soon, and that,' she told herself drowsily, 'will be that.'

Later (as she realized afterwards) she must have dozed off because it seemed she was crossing Parkin's Beck; it was night and the wind was blowing and the field seemed very steep; she was scrambling up it, along the ridge by the gas-pipe, sliding and falling in the wet grass. The trees, it seemed to Homily, were threshing and clashing, their branches waving and sawing against the sky. Then (as she told them many weeks later) there was a sound of splintering wood . . .

And Homily woke up. She saw the room again and the oil-lamp flickering, but something, she knew at once, was different: there was a strange draught and her mouth felt dry and full of grit. Then she looked up at the ceiling: 'Pod!' she shrieked, clutching his shoulder.

Pod rolled over and sat up. They both stared at the ceiling: the whole surface was on a steep slant and one side of it had come right away from the wall – this was what had caused the draught – and down into the room, to within an inch of the foot of the bed, protruded a curious object: a huge bar of grey steel with a flattened, shining edge.

'It's a screwdriver,' said Pod.

They stared at it, fascinated, unable to move, and for a moment all was still. Then slowly the huge object swayed upwards until the sharp edge lay against their ceiling and Homily heard a scrape on the floor above and a sudden human gasp. 'Oh, my knees,' cried Homily, 'oh, my feeling—' as, with a splintering wrench, their whole roof flew off and fell down with a clatter, somewhere out of sight.

Homily screamed then. But this time it was a real scream, loud and shrill and hearty; she seemed almost to settle down in her scream, while her eyes stared up, half interested, into empty lighted space. There was another ceiling, she realized, away up above them – higher, it seemed, than the sky; a ham hung from it and two strings of onions. Arrietty appeared in the doorway, scared and trembling, clutching her night-gown. And Pod slapped Homily's back. 'Have done,' he said, 'that's enough,' and Homily, suddenly, was quiet.

A great face appeared then between them and that distant height. It wavered above them, smiling and terrible: there was silence and Homily sat bolt upright, her mouth open. 'Is that your mother?' asked a surprised voice after a moment, and Arrietty from the doorway whispered: 'Yes.'

It was the boy.

Pod got out of bed and stood beside it, shivering in his night-shirt. 'Come on,' he said to Homily, 'you can't stay there!'

But Homily could. She had her old night-dress on with

the patch in the back and nothing was going to move her. A slow anger was rising up in Homily: she had been caught in her hair-curlers; Pod had raised his hand to her; and she remembered that, in the general turmoil and for once in her life, she had left the supper washing-up for morning, and there it would be, on the kitchen table, for all the world to see!

She glared at the boy – he was only a child after all. 'Put it back!' she said, 'put it back at once!' Her eyes flashed and her curlers seemed to quiver.

He knelt down then, but Homily did not flinch as the great face came slowly closer. She saw his under lip, pink and full – like an enormous exaggeration of Arrietty's – and she saw it wobble slightly. 'But I've got something for you,' he said.

Homily's expression did not change and Arrietty called out from her place in the doorway: 'What have you got?'

The boy reached behind him and very gingerly, careful to keep it upright, he held a wooden object above their heads. 'It's this,' he said, and carefully, his tongue out and breathing heavily, he lowered the object slowly into their hole: it was a doll's dresser, complete with plates. It had two drawers in it and a cupboard below; he adjusted its position at the foot of Homily's bed. Arrietty ran round to see better.

'Oh,' she cried ecstatically. 'Mother, look!'

Homily threw the dresser a glance – it was dark oak and the plates were hand-painted – and then she looked quickly away again. 'Yes,' she said coldly, 'it's very nice.'

There was a short silence which no one knew how to break.

'The cupboard really opens,' said the boy at last, and the great hand came down all amongst them, smelling of

bath soap. Arrietty flattened herself against the wall and
Pod exclaimed, nervous: 'Now then!'

'Yes,' agreed Homily after a moment, 'I see it does.'

Pod drew a long breath – a sigh of relief as the hand
went back.

'There, Homily,' he said placatingly, 'you've always
wanted something like that!'

'Yes,' said Homily – she still sat bolt upright, her hands
clasped in her lap. 'Thank you very much. And now,' she
went on coldly, 'will you please put back the roof?'

'Wait a minute,' pleaded the boy. Again he reached
behind him; again the hand came down; and there,
beside the dresser, where there was barely room for it,
was a very small doll's chair; it was a Victorian chair,
upholstered in red velvet. 'Oh!' Arrietty exclaimed again
and Pod said shyly: 'Just about fit me, that would.'

'Try it,' begged the boy, and Pod threw him a nervous
glance. 'Go on!' said Arrietty, and Pod sat down – in his

night-shirt, his bare feet showing. 'That's nice,' he said after a moment.

'It would go by the fire in the sitting-room,' cried Arrietty; 'it would look lovely on red blotting-paper!'

'Let's try it,' said the boy, and the hand came down again. Pod sprang up just in time to steady the dresser as the red velvet chair was whisked away above his head and placed presumably in the next room but one. Arrietty ran out of the door and along the passage to see. 'Oh,' she called out to her parents, 'come and see. It's lovely!'

But Pod and Homily did not move. The boy was leaning over them, breathing hard, and they could see the middle buttons of his night-shirt. He seemed to be examining the farther room.

'What do you keep in that mustard-pot?' he asked.

'Coal,' said Arrietty's voice. 'And I helped to borrow this new carpet. Here's the watch I told you about, and the pictures . . .'

'I could get you some better stamps than those,' the boy said. 'I've got some jubilee ones with the Taj Mahal.'

'Look,' cried Arrietty's voice again, and Pod took Homily's hand, 'these are my books—'

Homily clutched Pod as the great hand came down once more in the direction of Arrietty. 'Quiet,' he whispered; 'sit still . . .' The boy, it seemed, was touching the books.

'What are they called?' he asked, and Arrietty reeled off the names.

'Pod,' whispered Homily, 'I'm going to scream—'

'No,' whispered Pod. 'You mustn't. Not again.'

'I feel it coming on,' said Homily.

Pod looked worried. 'Hold your breath,' he said, 'and count ten.'

The boy was saying to Arrietty: 'Why couldn't you read me those?'

'Well, I could,' said Arrietty, 'but I'd rather read something new.'

'But you never come,' complained the boy.

'I know,' said Arrietty, 'but I will.'

'Pod,' whispered Homily, 'did you hear that? Did you hear what she said?'

'Yes, yes,' Pod whispered; 'keep quiet—'

'Do you want to see the store-rooms?' Arrietty suggested next and Homily clapped a hand to her mouth as though to stifle a cry.

Pod looked up at the boy. 'Hey,' he called, trying to attract his attention. The boy looked down. 'Put the roof back now,' Pod begged him, trying to sound matter of fact and reasonable; 'we're getting cold.'

'All right,' agreed the boy, but he seemed to hesitate: he reached across them for the piece of board which formed their roof. 'Shall I nail you down?' he asked, and they saw him pick up the hammer; it swayed above them, very dangerous looking.

'Of course nail us down,' said Pod irritably.

'I mean,' said the boy, 'I've got some more things upstairs—'

Pod looked uncertain and Homily nudged him. 'Ask him,' she whispered, 'what kind of things?'

'What kind of things?' asked Pod.

'Things from an old doll's house there is on the top shelf of the cupboard by the fire-place in the school-room.'

'I've never seen no doll's house,' said Pod.

'Well, it's in the cupboard,' said the boy, 'right up by the ceiling; you can't see it – you've got to climb on the lower shelves to get to it.'

'What sort of things *are* there in the doll's house?' asked Arrietty from the sitting-room.

'Oh, everything,' the boy told her; 'carpets and rugs and beds with mattresses, and there's a bird in a cage – not a real one, of course – and cooking pans and tables and five gilt chairs and a pot with a palm in it – a dish of plaster tarts and an imitation leg of mutton—'

Homily leaned across to Pod. 'Tell him to nail us down lightly,' she whispered. Pod stared at her and she nodded vigorously, clasping her hands.

Pod turned to the boy. 'All right,' he said, 'you nail us down. But lightly, if you see what I mean. Just a tap or two here and there . . .'

Chapter Sixteen

Then began a curious phase in their lives: borrowings beyond all dreams of borrowing – a golden age. Every night the floor was opened and treasures would appear: a real carpet for the sitting-room, a tiny coal-scuttle, a stiff little sofa with damask cushions, a double bed with a round bolster, a single ditto with a striped mattress, framed pictures instead of stamps, a kitchen stove which didn't work but which looked 'lovely' in the kitchen; there were oval tables and square tables and a little desk with one drawer; there were two maple wardrobes (one with a looking-glass) and a bureau with curved legs. Homily grew not only accustomed to the roof coming off

but even went so far as to suggest to Pod that he put the board on hinges. 'It's just the hammering I don't care for,' she explained; 'it brings down the dirt.'

When the boy brought them a grand piano Homily begged Pod to build a drawing-room. 'Next to the sitting-room,' she said, 'and we could move the store-rooms farther down. Then we could have those gilt chairs he talks about and the palm in a pot . . .' Pod, however, was a little tired of furniture removing; he was looking forward to the quiet evenings when he could doze at last beside the fire in his new red velvet chair. No sooner had he put a chest of drawers in one place when Homily, coming in and out at the door – 'to get the effect' – made

him 'try' it somewhere else. And every evening, at about his usual bedtime, the roof would fly up and more stuff would arrive. But Homily was tireless; bright-eyed and pink-cheeked, after a long day's pushing and pulling, she still would leave nothing until morning. 'Let's just *try* it,' she would beg, lifting up one end of a large doll's sideboard, so that Pod would have to lift the other; 'it won't take a minute!' But as Pod well knew, in actual fact it would be several hours before, dishevelled and aching, they finally dropped into bed. Even then Homily would sometimes hop out 'to have one last look.'

In the meantime, in payment for these riches, Arrietty would read to the boy – every afternoon in the long grass

beyond the cherry-tree. He would lie on his back and she would stand beside his shoulder and tell him when to turn the page. They were happy days to look back on afterwards, with the blue sky beyond the cherry boughs, the grasses softly stirring, and the boy's great ear listening beside her. She grew to know that ear quite well, with its curves and shadows and sunlit pinks and golds. Sometimes, as she grew bolder, she would lean against his shoulder. He was very still while she read to him and always grateful. What worlds they would explore together – strange worlds to Arrietty. She learned a lot and some of the things she learned were hard to accept. She was made to realize once and for all that this earth on which they lived turning about in space did not revolve, as she had believed, for the sake of little people. 'Not for big people either,' she reminded the boy when she saw his secret smile.

In the cool of the evening Pod would come for her – a rather weary Pod, dishevelled and dusty – to take her back for tea. And at home there would be an excited Homily and fresh delights to discover. 'Shut your eyes!' Homily would cry. 'Now open them!' and Arrietty, in a dream of joy, would see her home transformed. All kinds of surprises there were – even, one day, lace curtains at the grating, looped up with pink string.

Their only sadness was that there was no one there to see: no visitors, no casual droppers-in, no admiring cries and envious glances! What would Homily have not given for an Overmantel or a Harpsichord? Even a Rain-Barrel would have been better than no one at all. 'You write to your Uncle Hendreary,' Homily suggested, 'and tell *him*. A nice long letter, mind, and don't leave anything out!' Arrietty began the letter on the back of one of the discarded pieces of blotting-paper, but it became as she wrote it just a dull list, far too long, like a sale catalogue or the inventory of a house to let; she would have to keep jumping up to count spoons or to look up words in the dictionary, and after a while she laid it aside: there was so much else to do, so many new books to read, and so much, now, that she could talk of with the boy.

'He's been ill,' she told her mother and father; 'he's been here for the quiet and the country air. But soon he'll go back to India. Did you know,' she asked the amazed Homily, 'that the Arctic night lasts six months, and that the distance between the two poles is less than that between the two extremities of a diameter drawn through the equator?'

Yes, they were happy days and all would have been well, as Pod said afterwards, if they had stuck to borrowing from the doll's house. No one in the human household seemed to remember it was there and, consequently nothing was missed. The drawing-room, however, could not help but be a temptation: it was so seldom used nowadays; there were so many knick-knack tables which had been out of Pod's reach, and the boy, of course, could turn the key in the glass doors of the cabinet.

The silver violin he brought them first and then the silver harp; it stood no higher than Pod's shoulder and Pod restrung it with horse-hair from the sofa in the morning-room. 'A musical conversazione, that's what we could have!' cried the exulting Homily as Arrietty struck a tiny, tuneless note on a horse-hair string. 'If only,' she went on fervently, clasping her hands, 'your father would start on the drawing-room!' (She curled her hair nearly every evening nowadays and, since the house was more or less straight, she would occasionally change for dinner into a satin dress; it hung like a sack, but Homily called it 'Grecian.') 'We could use your painted ceiling,' she explained to Arrietty, 'and there are quite enough of those toy builders' bricks to make a parquet floor.' ('Parkay,' she would say. 'Par-r-r-kay . . .,' just like a Harpsichord.)

Even Great Aunt Sophy, right away upstairs in the littered grandeur of her bedroom, seemed distantly affected by a spirit of endeavour which seemed to flow, in gleeful whorls and eddies, about the staid old house. Several times lately Pod, when he went to her room, had found her out of bed. He went there nowadays not to borrow, but to rest: the room, one might almost say, had become his club; a place to which he could go 'to get away from things.' Pod was a little irked by his riches; he had never visualized, not in his wildest dreams, borrowing such as this. Homily, he felt, should call a halt; surely, now, their home was grand enough; these jewelled snuff-boxes and diamond-encrusted miniatures, these filigree vanity-cases and Dresden figurines – all, as he knew, from the drawing-room cabinet – were not really necessary: what was the good of a shepherdess nearly as tall as Arrietty or an outsize candle-snuffer? Sitting just inside the fender, where he could warm his hands at the fire, he watched Aunt Sophy hobble slowly round the room on her two sticks. 'She'll be downstairs soon, I shouldn't wonder,' he thought glumly, hardly listening to her oft-told tale about a royal luncheon aboard a Russian yacht, 'then she'll miss these things . . .'

It was not Aunt Sophy, however, who missed them first. It was Mrs Driver. Mrs Driver had never forgotten the trouble over Rosa Pickhatchet. It had not been, at the time, easy to pin-point the guilt. Even Crampfurl had felt under suspicion. 'From now on,' Mrs Driver had said, 'I'll manage on me own. No more strange maids in *this* house!' A drop of Madeira here, a pair of old stockings there, a handkerchief or so, an odd vest, or an occasional pair of gloves – these, Mrs Driver felt, were different; these were within her rights. But trinkets out of the drawing-room cabinet – that, she told herself grimly, staring at the depleted shelves, was a different story altogether!

Standing there, on that fateful day, in the spring sunshine, feather duster in hand, her little black eyes had become slits of anger and cunning. She felt tricked. It was, she calculated, as though someone, suspecting her dishonesty, were trying to catch her out. But who could it be? Crampfurl? That boy? The man who came to wind the clocks? These things had disappeared gradually, one by one: it was someone, of that she felt sure, who knew the house – and someone who wished her ill. Could it, she wondered suddenly, be the mistress herself? The old girl had been out of bed lately and walking about her room. Might she not have come downstairs in the night, poking about with her stick, snooping and spying (Mrs Driver remembered suddenly the empty Madeira bottle and the two glasses which, so often, were left on the kitchen table). Ah, thought Mrs Driver, was not this just the sort of thing she might do – the sort of thing she would cackle over, back upstairs again among her pillows, watching and waiting for Mrs Driver to report the loss? 'Everything all right downstairs, Driver?' – that's what she'd always say and she would look at Mrs Driver sideways out of those mocking old eyes of hers. 'I wouldn't put it past her!' Mrs Driver exclaimed aloud, gripping her feather duster as though it were a club. 'And a nice merry-andrew she'd look if I caught her at it – creeping about the downstairs rooms in the middle of the night. All right, my lady,' muttered Mrs Driver grimly, 'pry and potter all you want – two can play at that game!'

Chapter Seventeen

Mrs Driver was short with Crampfurl that evening; she would not sit down and drink with him as usual, but stumped about the kitchen, looking at him sideways every now and again out of the corners of her eyes. He looked uneasy – as indeed he was: there was a kind of menace in her silence, a hidden something which no one could ignore. Even Aunt Sophy had felt it when Mrs Driver brought up her wine; she heard it in the clink of the decanter against the glass as Mrs Driver set down the tray and in the rattle of the wooden rings as Mrs Driver drew the curtains; it was in the tremble of the floor-boards as Mrs Driver crossed the room and in the click of the latch as Mrs Driver closed the door. 'What's the matter with her now?' Aunt Sophy wondered vaguely as delicately, ungreedily, she poured the first glass.

The boy had felt it too. From the way Mrs Driver had stared at him as he sat hunched in the bath; from the way she soaped the loofah and the way she said: 'And now!' She had scrubbed him slowly, with a careful, angry steadiness, and all through the bathing time she did not say a word. When he was in bed she had gone through all his things, peering into cupboards and opening his drawers. She had pulled his suit-case out from under the wardrobe and found his dear dead mole and his hoard of sugar-lumps and her best potato knife. But even then she had not spoken. She had thrown the mole in the waste-paper basket and had made sharp noises with her tongue; she pocketed the potato knife and all the sugar-lumps. She had stared at him a moment before she turned the gas low – a strange stare it had been, more puzzled than accusing.

Mrs Driver slept above the scullery. She had her own back-stairs. That night she did not undress. She set the alarm clock for midnight and put it, where the tick would not disturb her, outside her door; she unbuttoned her tight shoes and crawled, grunting a little, under the eiderdown. She had 'barely closed her eyes' (as she told Crampfurl afterwards) when the clock shrilled off – chattering and rattling on its four thin legs on the bare boards of the passage-way. Mrs Driver tumbled herself out of bed and fumbled her way to the door. 'Shush,' she said to the clock as she felt for the catch, 'Shush!' and clasped it to her bosom. She stood there, in her stockinged feet, at the head of the scullery stairs: something, it seemed, had flickered below – a hint of light. Mrs Driver peered down the dark curve of the narrow stairway. Yes, there it was again – a moth-wing flutter! Candlelight – that's what it was! A moving candle – beyond the stairs, beyond the scullery, somewhere within the kitchen.

Clock in hand, Mrs Driver creaked down the stairs in her stockinged feet, panting a little in her eagerness. There seemed a sigh in the darkness, an echo of movement. And it seemed to Mrs Driver, standing there on the cold stone flags of the scullery, that this sound that was barely a sound could only mean one thing: the soft swing-to of the green baize door – that door which led out of the kitchen into the main hall beyond. Hurriedly Mrs Driver felt her way into the kitchen and fumbled for matches along the ledge above the stove; she knocked off a pepper-pot and a paper bag of cloves, and glancing quickly downwards saw a filament of light; she saw it in the second before she struck a match – a glow-worm thread, it looked like, on the floor beside her feet; it ran in an oblong shape, outlining a rough square. Mrs Driver gasped and lit the gas and the room leapt up around her: she glanced quickly at the baize door; there seemed to her startled eye a quiver of movement in it, as though it had just swung to; she ran to it and pushed it open, but the passage beyond was still and dark – no flicker of shadow nor sound of distant footfall. She let the door fall to again and watched it as it swung back, slowly, regretfully, held by its heavy spring. Yes, that was the sound she had heard from the scullery – that sighing whisper – like an indrawn breath.

Cautiously, clutching back her skirts, Mrs Driver moved towards the stove. An object lay there, something pinkish, on the floor beside the jutting board. Ah, she realized, that board – that was where the light had come from! Mrs Driver hesitated and glanced about the kitchen: everything else looked normal and just as she had left it – the plates on the dresser, the saucepans on the wall, and the row of tea-towels hanging symmetrically on their string above the stove. The pinkish object, she saw now, was a heart-shaped cachou-box – one that she knew well – from the glassed-in tray-table beside the fire-place in the drawing-room. She picked it up; it was enamel and gold and set with tiny brilliants. 'Well, I'm—' she began, and stooping swiftly with a sudden angry movement, she wrenched back the piece of floor.

And then she shrieked, loud and long. She saw movement: a running, a scrambling, a fluttering! She heard a squeaking, a jabbering, and a gasping. Little people, they looked like, with hands and feet ... and mouths opening. That's what they looked like ... but they couldn't *be* that, of course! Running here, there, and everywhere. 'Oh! oh! oh!' she shrieked and felt behind her for a chair. She clambered on to it and it wobbled

beneath her and she climbed, still shrieking, from the chair to the table . . .

And there she stood, marooned, crying and gasping, and calling out for help, until, after hours it seemed, there was a rattling at the scullery door. Crampfurl it was, roused at last by the light and the noise. 'What is it?' he called. 'Let me in!' But Mrs Driver would not leave the table. 'A nest! A nest!'' she shouted. 'Alive and squeaking!'

Crampfurl threw his weight against the door and burst open the lock. He staggered, slightly dazed, into the kitchen, his corduroy trousers pulled on over his night-shirt. 'Where?' he cried, his eyes wide beneath his tousled hair. 'What sort of a nest?'

Mrs Driver, sobbing still with fright, pointed at the floor. Crampfurl walked over in his slow, deliberate way and stared down. He saw a hole in the floor, lined and cluttered with small objects – children's toys, they looked like, bits of rubbish – that was all. 'It's nothing,' he said after a moment; 'it's that boy, that's what it is.' He stirred the contents with his foot and all the partitions fell down. 'There ain't nothing alive in there.'

'But I saw them , I tell you,' gasped Mrs Driver, 'little people like with hands – or mice dressed up . . .'

Crampfurl stared into the hole. 'Mice dressed up?' he repeated uncertainly.

'Hundreds of them,' went on Mrs Driver, 'running and squeaking. I saw them, I tell you!'

'Well, there ain't nothing there now,' said Crampfurl and he gave a final stir round with his boot.

'Then they've run away,' she cried, 'under the floor . . . up inside the walls . . . the place is alive with them.'

'Well,' said Crampfurl stolidly, 'maybe. But if you ask me, I think it's that boy – where he hides things.' His eye brightened and he went down on one knee. 'Where he's got the ferret, I shouldn't wonder.'

'Listen,' cried Mrs Driver, and there was a despairing note in her voice, 'you've got to listen. This wasn't no boy and it wasn't no ferret.' She reached for the back of the chair and lowered herself clumsily on to the floor; she came beside him to the edge of the hole. 'They had hands and faces, I tell you. Look,' she said, pointing, 'see that? It's a bed. And now I come to think of it one of 'em was in it.'

'Now you come to think of it,' said Crampfurl.

'Yes,' went on Mrs Driver firmly, 'and there's something else I come to think of. Remember that girl, Rosa Pickhatchet?'

'The one that was simple?'

'Well, simple or not, she saw one – on the drawing-room mantelpiece, with a beard.'

'One what?' asked Crampfurl.

Mrs Driver glared at him. 'What I've been telling you about – one of these – these—'

'Mice dressed up?' said Crampfurl.

'Not mice!' Mrs Driver almost shouted. 'Mice don't have beards.'

'But you said—' began Crampfurl.

'Yes, I know I said it. Not that these had beards. But what would you call them? What could they be but mice?'

'Not so loud!' whispered Crampfurl. 'You'll wake the house up.'

'They can't hear,' said Mrs Driver, 'not through the baize door.' She went to the stove and picked up the fire-tongs. 'And what if they do? We ain't done nothing. Move over,' she went on, 'and let me get at the hole.'

One by one Mrs Driver picked things out – with many shocked gasps, cries of amazement, and did-you-evers. She made two piles on the floor – one of valuables and one of what she called 'rubbish.' Curious objects dangled from the tongs: 'Would you believe it – her best lace handkerchiefs! Look, here's another . . . and another! And my big mattress needle – I knew I had one – my silver thimble, if you please, and one of hers! And look, oh my, at the wools . . . the cottons! No wonder you can never find a reel of white cotton if you want one. Potatoes . . . nuts . . . look at this, a pot of caviar – CAVIAR! No, it's too much, it really is. Doll's chairs . . . tables . . . and look at all this blotting-paper – so that's where it goes! Oh, my

goodness gracious!' she cried suddenly, her eyes staring.
'What's this?' Mrs Driver laid down the tongs and leaned
over the hole – tentatively and fearfully as though afraid
of being stung. 'It's a watch – an emerald watch – her
watch! And she's never missed it!' Her voice rose. 'And
it's going! Look, you can see by the kitchen clock!
Twenty-five past twelve!' Mrs Driver sat down suddenly
on a hard chair; her eyes were staring and her face looked
white and flabby, as though deflated. 'You know what
this means?' she said to Crampfurl.

'No?' he said.

'The police,' said Mrs Driver. 'That's what this means
– a case for the police.'

Chapter Eighteen

The boy lay, trembling a little, beneath the bed-clothes.
The screwdriver was under his mattress. He had heard
the alarm clock; he had heard Mrs Driver exclaim on the
stairs and he had run. The candle on the table beside his
bed still smelt a little and the wax must still be warm. He
lay there waiting, but they did not come upstairs. After
hours, it seemed, he heard the hall clock strike one. All
seemed quiet below, and at last he slipped out of bed and
crept along the passage to the head of the stairway. There
he sat for a while, shivering a little, and gazing
downwards into the darkened hall. There was no sound
but the steady tick of the clock and occasionally that

shuffle or whisper which might be wind, but which, as he knew, was the sound of the house itself – the sigh of the tired floors and the ache of knotted wood. So quiet it was that at last he found courage to move and to tiptoe down the staircase and along the kitchen passage. He listened awhile outside the baize door, and at length, very gently, he pushed it open. The kitchen was silent and filled with greyish darkness. He felt, as Mrs Driver had done, along the shelf for the matches and he struck a light. He saw the gaping hole in the floor and the objects piled beside it and, in the same flash, he saw a candle on the shelf. He lit it clumsily, with trembling hands. Yes, there they lay – the contents of the little home – higgledy-piggledy on the boards and the tongs lay beside them. Mrs Driver had carried away all she considered valuable and had left the 'rubbish.' And rubbish it looked thrown down like this – balls of wool, old potatoes, odd pieces of doll's furniture, match-boxes, cotton reels, crumpled squares of blotting-paper . . .

He knelt down. The 'house' itself was a shambles – partitions fallen, earth floors revealed (where Pod had dug down to give greater height to the rooms), match-sticks, an old cog-wheel, onion skins, scattered bottle-tops . . . The boy stared, blinking his eyelids and tilting the candle so that the grease ran hot on his hand. Then he got up from his knees and, crossing the kitchen on tiptoe, he closed the scullery door. He came back to the hole and, leaning down, he called softly: 'Arrietty . . . Arrietty!' After a while he called again. Something else fell hot on his hand: it was a tear from his eye. Angrily he brushed it away, and, leaning farther into the hole, he called once more. 'Pod,' he whispered. 'Homily!'

They appeared so quietly that at first, in the wavering light of the candle, he did not see them. Silent they stood,

looking up at him with scared white faces from what had
been the passage outside the store-rooms.

'Where have you been?' asked the boy.

Pod cleared his throat. 'Up at the end of the passage.
Under the clock.'

'I've got to get you out,' said the boy.

'Where to?' asked Pod.

'I don't know. What about the attic?'

'That ain't no good,' said Pod. 'I heard them talking.
They're going to get the police and a cat and the sanitary
inspector and the rat-catcher from the town hall at
Leighton Buzzard.'

They were all silent. Little eyes stared at big eyes.
'There won't be nowhere in the house that's safe,' Pod
said at last. And no one moved.

'What about the doll's house on the top shelf in the
schoolroom?' suggested the boy. 'Even a cat can't get
there.'

Homily gave a little moan of assent. 'Yes,' she said, 'the
doll's house . . .'

'No,' said Pod in the same expressionless voice, 'you
can't live on a shelf. Maybe the cat can't get up, but no

more can't you get down. You're stuck. You got to have water.'

'I'd bring you water,' said the boy; he touched the pile of 'rubbish.' 'And there are beds and things here.'

'No,' said Pod, 'a shelf ain't no good. Besides, you'll be going soon, or so they say.'

'Oh, Pod,' pleaded Homily in a husky whisper, 'there's stairs in the doll's house, and two bedrooms, and a dining-room, and a kitchen. And a bathroom,' she said.

'But it's up by the ceiling,' Pod explained wearily. 'You got to eat, haven't you,' he asked, 'and drink?'

'Yes, Pod, I know. But—'

'There ain't no buts,' said Pod. He drew a long breath. 'We got to emigrate,' he said.

'Oh,' moaned Homily softly and Arrietty began to cry.

'Now don't take on,' said Pod in a tired voice.

Arrietty had covered her face with her hands and her tears ran through her fingers; the boy, watching, saw them glisten in the candlelight. 'I'm not taking on,' she gasped, 'I'm so happy . . . happy.'

'You mean,' said the boy to Pod, but with one eye on Arrietty, 'you'll go to the badger's set?' He too felt a mounting excitement.

'Where else?' asked Pod.

'Oh, my goodness gracious!' moaned Homily, and sat down on the broken match-box chest of drawers.

'But you've got to go somewhere to-night,' said the boy. 'You've got to go somewhere before to-morrow morning.'

'Oh, my goodness gracious!' moaned Homily again.

'He's right at that,' said Pod. 'Can't cross them fields in the dark. Bad enough getting across them in daylight.'

'I know,' cried Arrietty. Her wet face glistened in the candlelight; it was alight and tremulous and she raised her arms a little as though about to fly, and she swayed as she balanced on her toe-tips. 'Let's go to the doll's house just for to-night and to-morrow' — she closed her eyes against the brightness of the vision — 'to-morrow the boy will take us — take us—' and she could not say to where.

'Take us?' cried Homily in a strange hollow voice. 'How?'

'In his pockets,' chanted Arrietty; 'won't you?' Again she swayed, with lighted upturned face.

'Yes,' he said, 'and bring the luggage up afterwards – in a fish basket.'

'Oh, my goodness!' moaned Homily.

'I'll pick all the furniture out of this pile here. Or most of it. They'll hardly notice. And anything else you want.'

'Tea,' murmured Homily. 'Enough for our lifetimes.'

'All right,' said the boy. 'I'll get a pound of tea. And coffee too if you like. And cooking pots. And matches. You'll be all right,' he said.

'But what do they eat?' wailed Homily. 'Caterpillars?'

'Now, Homily,' said Pod, 'don't be foolish. Lupy was always a good manager.'

'But Lupy isn't there,' said Homily. 'Berries. Do they eat berries? How do they cook? Out of doors?'

'Now, Homily,' said Pod, 'we'll see all that when we get there.'

'I couldn't light a fire of sticks,' said Homily, 'not in the wind. What if it rains?' she asked. 'How do they cook in the rain?'

'Now, Homily—' began Pod – he was beginning to lose patience – but Homily rushed on.

'Could you get us a couple of tins of sardines to take?' she asked the boy. 'And some salt? And some candles? And matches? And could you bring us some carpets from the doll's house?'

'Yes,' said the boy, 'I could. Of course I could. Anything you want.'

'All right,' said Homily. She still looked wild, partly because some of her hair had rolled out of the curlers, but she seemed appeased. 'How are you going to get us upstairs? Up to the schoolroom?'

The boy looked down at his pocketless night-shirt. 'I'll carry you,' he said.

'How?' asked Homily. 'In your hands?'

'Yes,' said the boy.

'I'd rather die,' said Homily. 'I'd rather stay right here and be eaten by the rat-catcher from the town hall at Leighton Buzzard.'

The boy looked round the kitchen; he seemed bewildered. 'Shall I carry you in the peg-bag?' he asked at last, seeing it hanging in its usual place on the handle of the scullery door.

'All right,' said Homily. 'Take out the pegs first.'

But she walked into it bravely enough when he laid it out on the floor. It was soft and floppy and made of woven raffia. When he picked it up Homily shrieked and clung to Pod and Arrietty. 'Oh,' she gasped as the bag swayed a little, 'oh, I can't! Stop it! Put me out! Oh! Oh!' And, clutching and slipping, they fell into a tangle at the bottom.

'Be quiet, Homily, can't you!' exclaimed Pod angrily, and held her tightly by the ankle. It was not easy to control her as he was lying on his back with his face pushed forward on his chest and one leg, held upright by the side of the bag, somewhere above his head. Arrietty climbed up, away from them, clinging to the knots of raffia, and looked out over the edge.

'Oh, I can't! I can't!' cried Homily. 'Stop it, Pod. I'm dying. Tell him to put us down.'

'Put us down,' said Pod in his patient way, 'just for a

moment. That's right. On the floor,' and, as once again the bag was placed beside the hole, they all ran out.

'Look here,' said the boy unhappily to Homily, 'you've got to try.'

'She'll try all right,' said Pod. 'Give her a breather, and take it slower, if you see what I mean.'

'All right,' agreed the boy, 'but there isn't much time. Come on,' he said nervously, 'hop in.'

'Listen!' cried Pod sharply, and froze.

The boy, looking down, saw their three upturned faces catching the light – like pebbles they looked, still and stony, against the darkness within the hole. And then in a flash they were gone – the boards were empty and the hole was bare. He leaned into it. 'Pod!' he called in a frantic whisper. 'Homily! Come back!' And then he too became frozen, stooped and rigid above the hole. The scullery door creaked open behind him.

It was Mrs Driver. She stood there silent, this time in her night-dress. Turning, the boy stared up at her. 'Hallo,' he said, uncertainly, after a moment.

She did not smile, but something lightened in her eyes – a malicious gleam, a look of triumph. She carried a candle which shone upwards on her face, streaking it strangely with light and shadow. What are you doing down here?' she asked.

He stared at her, but he did not speak.

'Answer me,' she said. 'And what are you doing with the peg-bag?'

Still he stared at her, almost stupidly. 'The peg-bag?' he repeated and looked down as though surprised to see it in his hand. 'Nothing,' he said.

'Was it you who put the watch in the hole?'

'No,' he said, staring up at her again, 'it was there already.'

'Ah,' she said and smiled, 'so you knew it was there?'

'No,' he said; 'I mean yes.'

'Do you know what you are?' asked Mrs Driver, watching him closely. 'You are a sneaking, thieving, noxious little dribbet of no-good!'

His face quivered. 'Why?' he said.

'You know why. You're a wicked, black-hearted, fribbling little pickpocket. That's what you are. And so are they. They're nasty, crafty, scampy, scurvy, squeaking little—'

'No they're not,' he put in quickly.

'And you're in league with them!' She came across to him and, taking him by the upper arm, she jerked him to his feet. 'You know what they do with thieves?' she asked.

'No,' he said.

'They lock them up. That's what they do with thieves. And that's what's going to happen to you!'

'I'm not a thief,' cried the boy, his lips trembling, 'I'm a borrower.'

'A what?' She swung him round by tightening the grip on his arm.

'A borrower,' he repeated; there were tears on his eyelids; he hoped they would not fall.

'So that's what you call it!' she exclaimed (as he himself had done – so long ago; it seemed now – that day with Arrietty).

'That's their name,' he said. 'The kind of people they are – they're Borrowers.'

'Borrowers, eh?' repeated Mrs Driver wonderingly. She laughed. 'Well, they've done all the borrowing they're ever going to do in this house!' She began to drag him towards the door.

The tears spilled over his eyelids and ran down his

cheeks. 'Don't hurt them,' he begged. 'I'll move them. I
promise. I know how.'

Mrs Driver laughed again and pushed him roughly
through the green baize door. 'They'll be moved all right,'
she said. 'Don't worry. The rat-catcher will know how.
Crampfurl's old cat will know how. So will the sanitary
inspector. And the fire-brigade, if need be. The police'll
know how, I shouldn't wonder. No need to worry about
moving them. Once you've found the nest,' she went on,
dropping her voice to a vicious whisper as they passed
Aunt Sophy's door, 'the rest is easy!'

She pushed him into the schoolroom and locked the
door and he heard the boards of the passage creak
beneath her tread as, satisfied, she moved away. He crept
into bed then, because he was cold, and cried his heart out
under the blankets.

Chapter Nineteen

'And that,' said Mrs May, laying down her crochet hook,
'is really the end.'

Kate stared at her. 'Oh, it can't be,' she gasped, 'Oh,
please . . . *please* . . .'

'The last square,' said Mrs May, smoothing it out on
her knee, 'the hundred and fiftieth. Now we can sew them
together—'

'Oh,' said Kate, breathing again, 'the quilt! I thought
you meant the story.'

'It's the end of the story too,' said Mrs May absently, 'in a way,' and she began to sort out the squares.

'But,' stammered Kate, 'you can't – I mean—' and she looked, quite suddenly, everything they had said she was – wild, self-willed, and all the rest of it. 'It's not fair,' she cried, 'it's cheating. It's—' Tears sprang to her eyes; she threw her work down on the table and darning needle after it, and she kicked the bag of wools which lay beside her on the carpet.

'Why, Kate, why?' Mrs May looked genuinely surprised.

'Something more must have happened,' cried Kate angrily. 'What about the rat-catcher? And the policeman? And the—'

'But something more did happen,' said Mrs May, 'a lot more happened. I'm going to tell you.'

'Then why did you say it was the end?'

'Because,' said Mrs May (she still looked surprised), 'he never saw them again.'

'Then how can there be more?'

'Because,' said Mrs May, 'there is more.'

Kate glared at her. 'All right,' she said, 'go on.'

Mrs May looked back at her. 'Kate,' she said after a moment, 'stories never really end. They can go on and on and on. It's just that sometimes, at a certain point, one stops telling them.'

'But not at this kind of point,' said Kate.

'Well, thread your needle,' said Mrs May, 'with grey wool, this time. And we'll sew these squares together. I'll start at the top and you can start at the bottom. First a grey square, then an emerald, then a pink, and so on—'

'Then you didn't really mean it,' said Kate irritably, trying to push the folded wool through the narrow eye of the needle, 'when you said he never saw them again?'

'But I did mean it,' said Mrs May. 'I'm telling you just what happened. He had to leave suddenly – at the end of the week – because there was a boat for India and a family who could take him. And for the three days before he left they kept him locked up in those two rooms.'

'For three days!' exclaimed Kate.

'Yes. Mrs Driver, it seemed, told Aunt Sophy that he had a cold. She wasn't unkind to him, but she was determined, you see, to keep him out of the way until she'd got rid of the Borrowers.'

'And did she?' asked Kate. 'I mean – did they all come? The policeman? And the rat-catcher? And the—'

'The sanitary inspector didn't come. At least, not while my brother was there. And they didn't have the rat-catcher from the town hall, but they had the local man. The policeman came—' Mrs May laughed. 'During those three days Mrs Driver used to give my brother a running commentary on what was going on below. She loved to grumble, and my brother, rendered harmless and shut away upstairs, became a kind of neutral. She used to carry his meals up, and, on that first morning, she brought all the doll's furniture up on the breakfast tray and made my brother climb the shelves and put it back in the doll's house. It was then she told him about the policeman. Furious he said she was. He felt almost sorry for her.'

'Why?' asked Kate.

'Because the policeman turned out to be Nellie Run-acre's son Ernie, a boy Mrs Driver had chased many a time for stealing russet apples from the tree by the gate – "A nasty, thieving, good-for-nothing dribbet of no-good," she told my brother. "Sitting down there he is now, in the kitchen, large as life with his note-book out, laughing fit to bust . . . twenty-one, he says he is now, and as cheeky as you make 'em . . .'''

'And was he,' asked Kate, round-eyed, 'a dribbet of no-good?'

'Of course not. Any more than my brother was. Ernie Runacre was a fine, upstanding young man and a credit to the police force. And he did not actually laugh at Mrs Driver when she told him her story, but he gave her what Crampfurl spoke of afterwards as "an old-fashioned look" when she described Homily in bed – "Take more water with it," it seemed to say.'

'More water with what?' asked Kate.

'The Fine Old Pale Madeira, I suppose,' said Mrs May. 'And Great Aunt Sophy had the same suspicion: she was furious when she heard that Mrs Driver had seen several little people when she herself on a full decanter had only risen to one or, at most, two. Crampfurl had to bring all the Madeira up from the cellar and stack the cases against the wall in a corner of Aunt Sophy's bedroom where, as she said, she could keep an eye on it.'

'Did they get a cat?' asked Kate.

'Yes, they did. But that wasn't much of a success either. It was Crampfurl's cat, a large yellow tom with white streaks in it. According to Mrs Driver, it had only two ideas in its head – to get out of the house or into the larder. "Talk of borrowers," Mrs Driver would say as she slammed down the fish-pie for my brother's luncheon, "that cat's a borrower, if ever there was one; borrowed the fish, that cat did, and a good half-bowl of egg sauce!" But the cat wasn't there long. The first thing the rat-catcher's terriers did was to chase it out of the house. There was a dreadful set-to, my brother said. They chased it everywhere – upstairs and downstairs, in and out all the rooms, barking their heads off. The last glimpse my brother had of the cat was streaking away through the spinney and across the fields with the terriers after it.'

Did they catch it?'

'No,' Mrs May laughed. 'It was still there when I went, a year later. A little morose, but as fit as a fiddle.'

'Tell about when *you* went.'

'Oh, I wasn't there long,' said Mrs May rather hastily, 'and after that the house was sold. My brother never went back.'

Kate stared at her suspiciously, pressing her needle against the centre of her lower lip. 'So they never caught the little people?' she said at last.

Mrs May's eyes flicked away. 'No, they never actually caught them, but' – she hesitated – 'as far as my poor brother was concerned, what they did do seemed even worse.'

'What did they do?'

Mrs May laid down her work and stared for a moment, thoughtfully, at her idle hands. 'I hated the rat-catcher,' she said suddenly.

'Why, did you know him?'

'Everybody knew him. He had a wall eye and his name was Rich William. He was also the pig-killer, and, well – he did other things as well – he had a gun, a hatchet, a spade, a pick-axe, and a contraption with bellows for smoking things out. I don't know what the smoke was exactly – poison fumes of some kind which he made himself from herbs and chemicals. I only remember the smell of it; it clung round the barns or wherever he'd been. You can imagine what my brother felt on that third day, the day he was leaving, when suddenly he smelled that smell . . .

'He was all dressed and ready to go. The bags were packed and down in the hall. Mrs Driver came and unlocked the door and took him down the passage to Aunt Sophy. He stood there, stiff and pale, in gloves and overcoat beside the curtained bed. "Seasick already?" Aunt Sophy mocked him, peering down at him over the edge of the great mattress.

'"No," he said, "it's that smell."

'Aunt Sophy lifted her nose. She sniffed. "What smell is it, Driver?"

'"It's the rat-catcher, my lady," explained Mrs Driver, reddening, "down in the kitchen."

'"What!" exclaimed Aunt Sophy, "are you smoking them out?" and she began to laugh. "Oh dear . . . oh dear!" she gasped, "but if you don't like them, Driver, the remedy's simple."

'"What is that, my lady?" asked Mrs Driver uncomfortably, and even her chins were red.

'Helpless with laughter Aunt Sophy waved a ringed hand: "Keep the bottle corked," she managed at last and motioned them weakly away. They heard her laughing still as they went on down the stairs.

'"She don't believe in them," muttered Mrs Driver, and she tightened her grip on my brother's arm. "More fool her! She'll change her tune, like enough, when I take them up afterwards, laid out in sizes, on a clean piece of newspaper . . ." and she dragged him unceremoniously across the hall.

'The clock had been moved, exposing the wainscot, and as my brother saw at once, the hole had been blocked and sealed. The front door was open as usual and the sunshine streamed in. The bags stood there beside the fibre mat, cooking a little in the golden warmth. The fruit trees beyond the bank had shed their petals and were lit with tender green, transparent in the sunlight. "Plenty of time," said Mrs Driver, glancing up at the clock, "the cab's not due 'til three-thirty—"

' "The clock's stopped," said my brother.

'Mrs Driver turned. She was wearing her hat and her best black coat, ready to take him to the station. She looked strange and tight and chapel-going – not a bit like "Driver." "So it has," she said; her jaw dropped and her cheeks became heavy and pendulous. "It's moving it," she decided after a moment. "It'll be all right," she went on, "once we get it back. Mr Frith comes on Monday," and she dragged again at his arm above the elbow.

' "Where are we going?" he asked, holding back.

' "Along to the kitchen. We've got a good ten minutes. Don't you want to see them caught?"

' "No," he said, "no!" and pulled away from her.

'Mrs Driver stared at him, smiling a little. "I do," she said; "I'd like to see 'em close. He puffs this stuff in and they come running out. At least, that's how it works with rats. But first, he says, you have to block up all the exits . . ." and her eyes followed my brother's to the hole below the wainscot.

' "How did they find it?" he asked them (puttied it looked, and with a square of brown paper pasted on crooked).

' "Rich William found it. That's his job."

' "They could unstick that," said the boy after a moment.

'Mrs Driver laughed – quite amiably for once. "Oh no they couldn't. Not now, they couldn't! Cemented, firm, that is. A great block of it, right inside, with a sheet of iron across from the front of that old stove in the outhouse. He and Crampfurl had to have the morning-room floor up to get at it. All Tuesday they was working, up till tea-time.

We aren't going to have no more capers of that kind. Not under the clock. Once you get that clock back, it can't be moved again in a hurry. Not if you want it to keep time, it can't. See where it's stood – where the floor's washed away like ?" It was then my brother saw, for the first and last time, that raised platform of unscrubbed stone. "Come on, now," said Mrs Driver and took him by the arm. "We'll hear the cab from the kitchen."

'But the kitchen, as she dragged him past the baize door, seemed a babel of sound. No approaching cab could be heard here. "Steady, steady, steady, steady, steady . . ." Crampfurl was saying, on one loud note, as he held back the rat-catcher's terriers which shrilled and panted on the leash. The policeman was there, Nellie Runacre's son Ernie. He had come out of interest and stood back from the others a little in view of his calling, with a cup of tea in his hand and his helmet pushed off his forehead. But his face was pink with boyish excitement and he stirred the teaspoon round and round. "Seeing's believing !" he said cheerfully to Mrs Driver when he saw her come in at the door. A boy from the village was there with a ferret. It kept sort of pouring out of his pocket, my brother said, and the boy kept pushing it back. Rich William himself was crouched on the floor by the hole. He had lighted something beneath a piece of sacking and the stench of its smouldering eddied about the room. He was working the bellows now, with infinite care, stooping over them – rapt and tense.

'My brother stood there as though in a dream ("Perhaps it was a dream," he said to me later – much later, after we were all grown up). He gazed round the kitchen. He saw the sunlit fruit trees through the window and a bough of the cherry-tree which stood upon the bank; he saw the empty tea-cups on the table, with spoons stuck in

them and one without a saucer; he saw, propped against
the wall close beside the baize door, the rat-catcher's
belongings – a frayed coat, patched with leather; a
bundle of rabbit snares; two sacks; a spade, a gun, and a
pick-axe . . .

'"Stand by now," Rich William was saying; there was
a rising note of excitement in his voice, but he did not turn
his head. "Stand by. Ready now to slip the dogs."

'Mrs Driver let go my brother's arm and moved
towards the hole. "Keep back," said the rat-catcher,
without turning. "Give us room—" and Mrs Driver
backed nervously towards the table. She put a chair
beside it and half raised one knee, but lowered it again
when she caught Ernie Runacre's mocking glance. "All
right, ma," he said, cocking one eyebrow, "we'll give you
a leg up when the time comes," and Mrs Driver threw
him a furious look; she snatched up the three cups from
the table and stumped away with them, angrily, in the
direction of the scullery. ". . . seemingless smutch of
something-or-other . . ." my brother heard her mutter as
she brushed past him. And at those words, suddenly, my
brother came to life . . .

'He threw a quick glance about the kitchen: the men
were absorbed; all eyes were on the rat-catcher – except
those of the village boy who was getting out his ferret.
Stealthily my brother drew off his gloves and began to
move backwards . . . slowly . . . slowly . . . towards the
green baize door; as he moved, gently stuffing his gloves
into his pocket, he kept his eyes on the group around the
hole. He paused a moment beside the rat-catcher's tools,
and stretched out a wary, groping hand; his fingers
closed at last on a wooden handle – smooth it was and
worn with wear; he glanced down quickly to make sure –
yes, it was, as he hoped, the pick-axe. He leaned back a

little and pushed – almost imperceptibly – against the door with his shoulders: it opened sweetly, in its silent way. Not one of the men had looked up. "Steady now," the rat-catcher was saying, stooping closely over the bellows, "it takes a moment like to go right through . . . there ain't much ventilation, not under a floor . . ."

'My brother slid through the barely opened door and it sighed to behind him, closing out the noise. He took a few steps on tiptoe down the dark kitchen passage and then he ran.

'There was the hall again, steeped in sunshine, with his bags beside the door. He bumped against the clock and it struck a note, a trembling note – urgent and deep. He raised the pick-axe to the height of his shoulder and aimed a sideways blow at the hole below the wainscot. The paper tore, a few crumbs of plaster fell out, and the pick-axe rebounded sharply, jarring his hands. There was indeed iron behind the cement – something immovable. Again he struck. And again and again. The wainscot above the hole became split and scratched, and the paper hung down in strips, but still the pick-axe bounced. It was no good; his hands, wet with sweat, were sliding and

slipping on the wood. He paused for breath and, looking out, he saw the cab. He saw it on the road, beyond the hedge on the far side of the orchard; soon it would reach the russet apple-tree beside the gate; soon it would turn into the drive. He glanced up at the clock. It was ticking steadily – the result, perhaps, of his knock. The sound gave him comfort and steadied his thumping heart; time, that's what he needed, a little more time. "It takes a moment like," the rat-catcher had said, "to go right through . . . there ain't much ventilation, not under a floor . . ."

'"Ventilation" – that was the word, the saving word. Pick-axe in hand my brother ran out of the door. He stumbled once on the gravel path and nearly fell; the pick-axe handle came up and struck him a sharp blow on the temple. Already, when he reached it, a thin filament of smoke was eddying out of the grating and he thought, as he ran towards it, that there was a flicker of movement against the darkness between the bars. And that was where they would be, of course, to get the air. But he did not stop to make sure. Already he heard behind him the crunch of wheels on the gravel and the sound of the horse's hoofs. He was not, as I have told you, a very strong little boy, and he was only nine (not ten, as he had boasted to Arrietty) but, with two great blows on the brickwork, he dislodged one end of the grating. It fell down sideways, slightly on a slant, hanging – it seemed – by one nail. Then he clambered up the bank and threw the pick-axe with all his might into the long grass beyond the cherry-tree. He remembered thinking as he stumbled back, sweaty and breathless, towards the cab, how that too – the loss of the pick-axe – would cause its own kind of trouble later.'

Chapter Twenty

'But,' exclaimed Kate, 'didn't he see them come out?'

'No. Mrs Driver came along then, in a flurry of annoyance, because they were late for the train. She bustled him into the cab because she wanted to get back again, she said, as fast as she could to be "in at the death." Mrs Driver was like that.'

Kate was silent a moment, looking down. 'So that *is* the end,' she said at last.

'Yes,' said Mrs May, 'in a way: or the beginning . . .'

'But' – Kate raised a worried face – 'perhaps they didn't escape through the grating? Perhaps they were caught after all?'

'Oh, they escaped all right,' said Mrs May lightly.

'But how do you know?'

'I just know,' said Mrs May.

'But how did they get across those fields? With the cows and things? And the crows?'

'They walked, of course. The Hendrearys did it. People can do anything when they have a mind to.'

'But poor Homily! She'd be so upset.'

'Yes, she was upset,' said Mrs May.

'And how would they know the way?'

'By the gas-pipe,' said Mrs May. 'There's a kind of ridge all along, through the spinney and across the fields. You see, when men dig a trench and put a pipe in it all the earth they've dug out doesn't quite fit when they've put it back. The ground looks different.'

'But poor Homily – she didn't have her tea or her furniture or her carpets or anything. Do you suppose they took anything?'

'Oh, people always grab something,' said Mrs May shortly, 'the oddest things sometimes – if you've read about shipwrecks.' She spoke hurriedly, as though she were tired of the subject. 'Do be careful, child – not grey next to pink. You'll have to unpick it.'

'But,' went on Kate in a despairing voice as she picked up the scissors, 'Homily would hate to arrive there all poor and dessitute in front of Lupy.'

'Destitute,' said Mrs May patiently, 'and Lupy wasn't there remember. Lupy never came back. And Homily would be in her element. Can't you see her? "Oh, these poor silly men . . ." she would cry and would tie on her apron at once.'

'Were they all boys?'

'Yes, Harpsichords and Clocks. And they'd spoil Arrietty dreadfully.'

'What did they eat? Did they eat caterpillars, do you think?'

'Oh, goodness, child, of course they didn't. They would have a wonderful life. Badgers' sets are almost like villages – full of passages and chambers and storehouses. They could gather hazel-nuts and beech-nuts and chest-nuts; they could gather corn – which they could store and grind into flour, just as humans do – it was all there for them: they didn't even have to plant it. They had honey. They could make elderflower tea and lime tea. They had hips and haws and blackberries and sloes and wild strawberries. The boys could fish in the stream and a minnow to them would be as big as a mackerel is to you.

They had birds' eggs – any amount of them – for custards and cakes and omelettes. You see, they would know where to look for things. And they had greens and salads, of course. Think of a salad made of those tender shoots of young hawthorn – bread and cheese we used to call it – with sorrel and dandelion and a sprinkling of thyme and wild garlic. Homily was a good cook remember. It wasn't for nothing that the Clocks had lived under the kitchen.'

'But the danger,' cried Kate; 'the weasels and the crows and the stoats and all those things?'

'Yes,' agreed Mrs May, 'of course there was danger. There's danger everywhere, but no more for them than for many of us. At least, they didn't have *wars*. And what about the early settlers in America? And those people who farm in the middle of the big game country in Africa and on the edge of the jungles in India? They get to know the habits of the animals. Even rabbits know when a fox isn't hunting; they will run quite near when he's full fed and lazing in the sun. These were boys remember; they would learn to hunt for the pot and how to protect themselves. I don't suppose it's very likely that Arrietty and Homily would wander far afield.'

'Arrietty would,' said Kate.

'Yes,' agreed Mrs May, laughing, 'I suppose Arrietty might.'

'So they'd have meat?' said Kate.

'Yes, sometimes. But Borrowers are Borrowers; not killers. I think,' said Mrs May, 'that if a stoat, say, killed a partridge they might borrow a leg!'

'And if a fox caught a rabbit they'd use the fur?'

'Yes, for rugs and things.'

'Supposing,' said Kate excitedly, 'when they had a little roast, they skinned haws and baked them, would they taste like browned potatoes?'

'Perhaps,' said Mrs May.

'But they couldn't cook in the badger's set. I suppose they cooked out of doors. How would they keep warm then in winter?'

'Do you know what I think?' said Mrs May; she laid down her work and leaned forward a little. 'I think that they didn't live in the badger's set at all. I think they used it, with all its passages and store-rooms, as a great honey-comb of an entrance hall. None but they would know the secret way through the tunnels which led at last to their home. Borrowers love passages and they love gates; and they love to live a long way from their own front doors.'

'Where *would* they live then?'

'I was wondering,' said Mrs May, 'about the gas-pipe—'

'Oh yes,' cried Kate, 'I see what you mean!'

'The soil's all soft and sandy up there. I think they'd go right through the badger's set and dig out a circular chamber, level with the gas-pipe. And off this chamber, all around it, there'd be little rooms, like cabins. And I think,' said Mrs May, 'that they'd bore three little pin-holes in the gas-pipe. One would be so tiny that you could hardly see it and that one would be always alight. The other two would have stoppers in them which, when they wanted to light the gas, they would pull out. They would light the bigger ones from the small burner. That's where they'd cook and that would give them light.'

'But would they be so clever?'

'But they are clever,' Mrs May assured her, 'very clever. Much too clever to live near a gas-pipe and not use it. They're Borrowers remember.'

'But they'd want a little air-hole?'

'Oh,' said Mrs May quickly, 'they did have one.'

'How do you know?' asked Kate.

'Because once when I was up there I smelled hot-pot.'

'Oh,' cried Kate excitedly; she twisted round and knelt up on the hassock, 'so you did go up there? So that's how you know! You saw them too!'

'No, no,' said Mrs May, drawing back a little in her chair, 'I never saw them. Never.'

'But you went up there? You know something! I can see you know!'

'Yes, I went up there.' Mrs May stared back into Kate's eager face; hesitant, she seemed, almost a little guilty. 'Well,' she conceded at last, 'I'll tell you. For what it's worth. When I went to stay in that house it was just before Aunt Sophy went into the nursing home. I knew the place was going to be sold, so I' – again Mrs May hesitated, almost shyly – 'well, I took all the furniture out of the doll's house and put it in a pillow-case and took it up there. I bought things too out of my pocket money – tea and coffee beans and salt and pepper and cloves and a great packet of lump sugar. And I took a whole lot of little pieces of silk which were over from making a patchwork quilt. And I took them some fish-bones for needles. I took the tiny thimble I had got in a Christmas pudding and a whole collection of scraps and cracker things I'd had in a chocolate box—'

'But you never saw them!'

'No. I never saw them. I sat for hours against the bank below the hawthorn hedge. It was a lovely bank, twined with twisted hawthorn roots and riddled with sandy holes and there were wood-violets and primroses and early campion. From the top of the bank you could see for miles across the fields: you could see the woods and the valleys and the twisting lanes; you could see the chimneys of the house.'

'Perhaps it was the wrong place.'

'I don't think so. Sitting there in the grass, half dreaming and watching beetles and ants, I found an oak-apple; it was smooth and polished and dry and there was a hole bored in one side of it and a slice off the top—'

'The teapot!' exclaimed Kate.

'I think so. I looked everywhere, but I couldn't find the quill spout. I called then, down all the holes – as my brother had done. But no one answered. Next day, when I went up there, the pillow-case had gone.'

'And everything in it?'

'Yes, everything. I searched the ground for yards around, in case there might be a scrap of silk or a coffee bean. But there was nothing. Of course, somebody passing might just have picked it up and carried it away. That was the day,' said Mrs May, smiling, 'that I smelled hot-pot.'

'And which was the day,' asked Kate, 'that you found Arrietty's diary?'

Mrs May laid down her work. 'Kate,' she began in a startled voice, and then, uncertainly, she smiled, 'what makes you say that?' Her cheeks had become quite pink.

'I guessed,' said Kate. 'I knew there was something – something you wouldn't tell me. Like – like reading somebody else's diary.'

'It wasn't the diary,' said Mrs May hastily, but her cheeks had become even pinker. 'It was the book called "Memoranda," the book with blank pages. That's where she'd written it. And it wasn't on that day I found it, but three weeks later – the day before I left.'

Kate sat silent, staring at Mrs May. After a while she drew a long breath. 'Then that proves it,' she said finally, 'underground chamber and all.'

'Not quite,' said Mrs May.

'Why not?' asked Kate.

'Arrietty used to make her "e's" like little half-moons with a stroke in the middle—'

'Well?' said Kate.

Mrs May laughed and took up her work again. 'My brother did too,' she said.

THE BORROWERS AFIELD

For Charlotte and Victoria

Chapter One

'WHAT HAS BEEN, MAY BE'
First recorded eclipse of the moon, 721 B.C.
[*Extract from Arrietty's Diary and Proverb Book, March 19th.*]

It was Kate who, long after she was grown up, completed the story of the borrowers. She wrote it all out, many years later, for her four children, and compiled it as you compile a case-history or a biographical novel from all kinds of evidence – things she remembered, things she had been told, and one or two things – we had better confess it – at which she just guessed. The most remarkable piece of evidence was a miniature Victorian notebook with gilt-edged pages, discovered by Kate in a gamekeeper's cottage on the Studdington estate near Leighton Buzzard, Bedfordshire.

Old Tom Goodenough, the gamekeeper, had never wanted the story put in writing, but as he had been dead now for so many years and as Kate's children were so very much alive, she thought perhaps that wherever he might be (and with a name like Goodenough it was bound to be in heaven) he would have overcome this kind of prejudice and would by now perhaps forgive her and understand. Anyway, Kate, after some thought, decided to take the risk.

When Kate had been a child herself and was living with her parents in London, an old lady shared their home (she was, I think, some kind of relation): her name was Mrs May. And it was Mrs May, on those long winter evenings beside the fire when she was teaching Kate to crochet, who had first told Kate about the borrowers.

At the time, Kate never doubted their existence – a race of tiny creatures, as like to humans as makes no matter, who live their secret lives under the floors and behind the wainscots of certain quiet old houses. It was only later that she began to wonder (and how wrong she was you will very soon be told. There were stranger happenings to come – developments more unlooked for and extraordinary than any Mrs May had dreamed of).

The original story had smacked a little of hearsay: Mrs May admitted – in fact, had been at some pains to convince Kate – that she, Mrs May, had never actually seen a borrower herself; any knowledge of such beings she had gained at second hand from her younger brother, who she admitted was a little boy with not only a vivid imagination but well known to be a tease. So there you were, Kate decided – thinking it over afterwards – you could take it or leave it.

And, truth to tell, in the year or so which followed Kate tended rather to leave it: the story of the borrowers became pushed away in the back of her mind with other childish fantasies. During this year she changed her school, made new friends, acquired a dog, took up skating, and learned to ride a bicycle. And there was no thought of 'borrowers' in Kate's mind (nor did she notice the undercurrent of excitement in Mrs May's usually calm voice) when, one morning at breakfast in early spring, Mrs May passed a letter across the table, saying: 'This will interest you, Kate, I think.'

It didn't interest Kate a bit (she was about eleven years old at the time): she read it through twice in a bewildered kind of way but could make neither head nor tail of it. It was a lawyer's letter from a firm called Jobson, Thring,

Beguid & Beguid; not only was it full of long words like 'beneficiary' and 'disentailment' but even the medium-sized words were arranged in such a manner that, to Kate, they made no sense at all (what, for instance, could 'vacant possession' mean? However much you thought about it, it could only describe a state of affairs which was manifestly quite impossible). Names there were in plenty – Studdington, Goodenough, Amberforce, Pocklinton – and quite a family of people who spelled their name 'deceased' with a small 'd.'

'Thank you very much,' Kate had said politely, passing it back.

'I thought, perhaps,' said Mrs May (and her cheeks, Kate noticed, looked slightly flushed as though with shyness), 'you might like to go down with me.'

'Go down where?' asked Kate, in her vaguest manner.

'My dear Kate,' exclaimed Mrs May, 'what was the point of showing you the letter? To Leighton Buzzard, of course.'

Leighton Buzzard? Years afterwards, when Kate described this scene to her children, she would tell them how, at these words, her heart began to bump long before her mind took in their meaning: Leighton Buzzard . . . she knew the name, of course: the name of an English country town . . . somewhere in Bedfordshire, wasn't it?

'Where Great Aunt Sophy's house was,' said Mrs May, prompting her. 'Where my brother used to say he saw the borrowers.' And before Kate could get her breath she went on, in a matter-of-fact voice: 'I have been left a little cottage, part of the Studdington estate, and,' her colour deepened as though what she was about to say now might sound slightly incredible, 'three hundred and fifty-five pounds. Enough,' she added, in happy wonderment, 'to do it up.'

Kate was silent. She stared at Mrs May, her clasped hands pressed against her middle as though to still the beating of her heart.

'Could we see the house?' she said at last, a kind of croak in her voice.

'Of course, that's why we're going.'

'I mean the big house, Aunt Sophy's house?'

'Oh, that house? Firbank Hall, it was called.' Mrs May seemed a little taken aback. 'I don't know. We could ask, perhaps; it depends of course on whoever is living there now.'

'I mean,' Kate went on, with controlled eagerness, 'even if we couldn't get inside, you could show me the grating, and Arrietty's bank; and even if they opened the front door only ever so little, you could show me where the clock was. You could kind of point with your finger, quickly . . .' and, as Mrs May still seemed to hesitate, Kate added suddenly on a note of anguish: 'You did believe in them, didn't you? Or was it' – her voice faltered – 'only a story?'

'And what if it were only a story,' said Mrs May quickly, 'so long as it was a good story? Keep your sense of wonder, child, and don't be so literal. And anything we haven't experienced for ourselves sounds like a story. All we can ever do about such things is' – she hesitated, smiling at Kate's expression – 'keep an open mind and try to sift the evidence.'

Sift the evidence? There was, Kate realized, calming down a little, a fair amount of that: even before Mrs May had spoken of such creatures, Kate had suspected their existence. How else to explain the steady, but inexplicable, disappearance of certain small objects about the house?

Not only safety-pins, needles, pencils, blotting-paper,

match-boxes, and those sort of things, but, even in Kate's short life, she had noticed that if you did not open a drawer for any length of time you never found it quite as you left it: something was always missing – your best handkerchief, your only bodkin, your carnelian heart, your lucky sixpence . . . 'But I *know* I put it in this drawer' – how often had she said these words herself, and how often had she heard them said? As for attics – 'I am absolutely certain,' Kate's mother had wailed only last week, on her knees before an open trunk searching vainly for a pair of shoe buckles, 'that I put them in this box with the ostrich-fan. They were wrapped in a piece of black wadding and I slipped them here, just below the handle . . .' And the same thing with writing-desks, sewing-baskets, button-boxes: there was never as much tea next day as you had seen in the caddy the evening before. Nor rice for that matter, nor lump sugar. Yes, Kate decided, evidence there was in plenty, if only one knew how to sift it.

'I suppose,' she remarked thoughtfully, as she began to fold up her napkin, 'some houses are more apt to have them than others.'

'Some houses,' said Mrs May, 'do not have them at all. And according to my brother,' she went on, 'it's the tidier houses, oddly enough, which attract them most. Borrowers, he used to say, are nervous people; they must know where things are kept and what each human being is likely to be doing at any hour of the day. In untidy, noisy, badly run houses, oddly enough, you can leave your belongings about with impunity – as far as borrowers are concerned, I mean.' And she gave a short laugh.

'Could borrowers live out of doors?' asked Kate suddenly.

'Not easily, no,' said Mrs May. 'They need human

beings; they live by the same things human beings live by.'

'I was thinking,' went on Kate, 'about Pod and Homily, and little Arrietty. I mean, when they were smoked out from under the floor, how do you think they managed?'

'I often wonder,' said Mrs May.

'Do you think,' asked Kate, 'that Arrietty did become the last living borrower? Like your brother said she would?'

'Yes, he said that, didn't he – the last of her race? I sincerely hope not. It was unkind of him,' Mrs May added reflectively.

'I wonder, though, how they got across those fields? Do you think they ever did find the badgers' set?'

'We can't tell. I told you about the pillow-case incident – when I took all the doll's house furniture up there in a pillow-case?'

'And you smelled something cooking? But that doesn't say our family ever got there – Pod and Homily and Arrietty. The cousins lived in the badgers' set too, didn't they – the Hendrearys? It might have been their cooking.'

'It might, of course,' said Mrs May.

Kate was silent for a while, lost in reflection; suddenly her whole face lit up and she swivelled round in her chair.

'If we do go,' she cried (and there was an awed look in her eyes as though vouchsafed by some glorious vision), 'where shall we stay? In an *inn*?'

Chapter Two

'WITHOUT PAINS, NO GAINS'
British Residency at Manipur attacked 1891
[*Extract from Arrietty's Diary and Proverb Book, March 24th.*]

But nothing turns out in fact as you have pictured it; the 'inn' was a case in point – and so, alas, was Great-aunt Sophy's house. Neither of these, to Kate, were at all as they should be:

An inn, of course, was a place you came to at night, not at three o'clock in the afternoon, preferably a rainy night – wind, too, if it could be managed; and it should, of course, be situated on a moor ('bleak,' Kate knew, was the adjective here). And there should be scullions; mine host should be gravy-stained and broad in the beam with a tousled apron pulled across his stomach; and there should be a tall, dark stranger – the one who speaks to nobody – warming thin hands before the fire. And the fire should *be* a fire – crackling and blazing, laid with an impossible size log and roaring its great heart out up the chimney. And there should be some sort of cauldron, Kate felt, somewhere about – and a couple of mastiffs, perhaps, thrown in for good measure.

But, here, were none of these things: there was a quiet-voiced young woman in a white blouse who signed them in at the desk; there was a waitress called Maureen (blonde) and one called Margaret (mousy, with pebble glasses) and an elderly waiter, the back part of whose hair did not at all match the front; the fire was not made out of logs but of bored-looking coals tirelessly licked by an abject electric flicker; and (worst of all) standing in front of it, instead of a tall dark stranger, was Mr Beguid, the lawyer (pronounced 'Be good') – plump, pink, but curiously cool-looking, with his silvery hair and steel-grey eye.

But outside Kate saw the bright spring sunshine and she liked her bedroom with its view over the market-place, its tall mahogany wardrobe, and its constant H. and C. And she knew that to-morrow they would see the house – this legendary, mysterious house which now so surprisingly had become real, built no longer of airy fantasy but, she gathered, of solid bricks and mortar, standing firmly in its own grounds not two miles along the road. Close enough, Kate realized, if only Mrs May would not talk so much with Mr Beguid, for them to have walked there after tea.

But when, next morning, they did walk there (Mrs May in her long, slightly deer-stalker-looking coat and with her rubber-tipped walking-stick made of cherry wood), Kate was disappointed; the house looked nothing at all like she had imagined it: a barrack of red brick, it appeared to her, with rows of shining windows staring blankly through her, as though they were blind.

'They've taken the creeper down,' said Mrs May (she too sounded a little surprised), but after a moment, as they stood there at the head of the drive, she rallied slightly and added on a brisker note: 'And quite right too – there's nothing like creeper for damaging brickwork,' and, as they began to walk on down the driveway, she went on to explain to Kate that this house had always been considered a particularly pure example of early Georgian architecture.

'Was it really *here*?' Kate kept asking in an incredulous voice as though Mrs May might have forgotten.

'Of course, my dear, don't be so silly. This is where the

apple-tree was, the russet apple by the gate . . . and the
third window on the left, the one with bars across, used to
be my bedroom the last few times I slept here. The night-
nursery, of course, looks out over the back. And there's
the kitchen garden. We used to jump off that wall, my
brother and I, and on to the compost heap. Ten feet high,
it's supposed to be — I remember one day Crampfurl
scolding us and measuring it with his besom.'

(Crampfurl? So there had been such a person . . .)

The front door stood open (as it must have stood, Kate
realized suddenly, years ago on that never-to-be-forgot-

ten day for Arrietty when she first saw the 'great outdoors'), and the early spring sunshine poured across the
newly whitened step into the high dark hall beyond; it
made a curtain of light through which it was hard to see.
Beside the step, Kate noticed, was an iron shoe-scraper.
Was this the one down which Arrietty had climbed? Her
heart began to beat a little faster. 'Where's the grating?'
she whispered, as Mrs May pulled the bell (they heard it
jangle far off in the dim distance, miles away it seemed).

'The grating?' said Mrs May, stepping backwards on
the gravel path and looking along the house front.

'There,' she said, with a slight nod – keeping her voice low. 'It's been repaired,' she whispered, 'but it's the same one.'

Kate wandered towards it: yes, there it was, the actual grating through which they had escaped. Pod, Homily, and little Arrietty; there was the greenish stain and a few bricks which looked newer than the others. It stood higher than she had imagined; they must have had a bit of a jump to get down. Going up to it, she stooped, trying to see inside; dank darkness, that was all. So this had been their home . . .

'Kate!' called Mrs May softly, from beside the door-step (as Pod must have called that day to Arrietty when she ran off down the path), and Kate, turning, saw suddenly a sight she recognized, something which at last was like she had imagined it – the primrose bank. Tender, blue-green blades among the faded winter grasses – sown, spattered, almost drenched they seemed – with palest gold. And the azalea bush, Kate saw, had become a tree.

After a moment Mrs May called again and Kate came back to the front door. 'We'd better ring again,' she said, and once more they heard the ghostly jangle. 'It rings near the kitchen,' explained Mrs May, in a whisper, 'just beyond the green baize door.'

('The Green Baize Door' . . . she seemed, Kate thought, to speak these words in capitals.)

At last they saw a figure through the sunbeams; it was a slatternly girl in a wet, sack-cloth apron, her bare feet in run-down sandals.

'Yes?' she said, staring at them and frowning against the sun.

Mrs May stiffened. 'I wonder,' she said, 'if I could see the owner of the house?'

'You mean Mr Dawsett-Poole?' said the girl, 'or the headmaster?' She raised her forearm, shading her eyes, a wet floor-cloth, dripping slightly, clasped in her grimy hand.

'Oh!' exclaimed Mrs May. 'Is it a school?' Kate caught her breath – that, then, explained the barracky appearance.

'Well, it always has been, hasn't it?' said the girl.

'No,' replied Mrs May, 'not always. When I was a child I used to stay here. Perhaps, then, I might speak to whoever is in charge?'

'There's only my mum,' said the girl; 'she's the caretaker. They're all away over Easter – the masters and that.'

'Well, in that case,' began Mrs May uncertainly, 'I mustn't trouble you—' and was preparing to turn away when Kate, standing her ground, addressed the girl: 'Can't we just see inside the hall?'

'Help yourself,' said the girl, looking mildly surprised, and she retreated slightly into the shadows as though to make way. 'It's okay by me.'

They stepped through the veil of sunlight into a dimmer coolness. Kate looked about her: it was wide and high and panelled and there were the stairs 'going up and up, world upon world, as Arrietty had described them' – all the same, it was nothing like she had imagined it. The floor was covered with burnished, dark green linoleum; there was a sourish smell of soapy water and the clean smell of wax.

'There's a beautiful stone floor under this,' said Mrs May, tapping the linoleum with her rubber-tipped walking-stick.

The girl stared at them curiously for a moment and then, as though bored, she turned away and disappeared

into the shadowy passage beyond the staircase, scuffling
a little in her downtrodden shoes.

Kate, about to comment, felt a touch on her arm.
'Listen,' hissed Mrs May sharply; and Kate, holding her
breath to complete the silence, heard a curious sound, a
cross between a sigh and moan. Mrs May nodded.
'That's it,' she whispered, 'the sound of the green baize
door.'

'And where was the clock?' asked Kate.

Mrs May indicated a piece of wall, now studded with a
row of coat pegs. 'There; Pod's hole must have been just
behind where that radiator is now. A radiator, they'd
have liked that . . .' She pointed to a door across the hall,
now labelled, in neat white lettering, 'Headmaster's
Study.' 'And that was the morning-room,' she said.

'Where the Overmantels lived? And Pod got the
blotting-paper?' Kate stared a moment and then, before
Mrs May could stop her, ran across and tried the handle.

'No, Kate, you mustn't. Come back.'

'It's locked,' said Kate, turning back. 'Could we just peep upstairs?' she went on. 'I'd love to see the night nursery. I could go terribly quietly . . .'

'No, Kate, come along: we must go now. We've no business to be here at all,' and Mrs May walked firmly towards the door.

'Couldn't I just peep in the kitchen window?' begged Kate at last, when they stood once again in the sunshine.

'No, Kate,' said Mrs May.

'Just to see where they lived? Where that hole was under the stove which Pod used as a chute – *please*.'

'Quickly, then,' said Mrs May; she threw a nervous glance in each direction as Kate sped off down the path.

This too was a disappointment. Kate knew where the kitchen was because of the grating, and making blinkers of her cupped hands against the reflected sunshine, she pushed her face up close against the glass. Dimly the room came into view, but it was nothing like a kitchen: shelves of bottles, gleaming retorts, heavy bench-like tables, rows of Bunsen burners: the kitchen was now a lab.

And that was that. On the way home Kate picked a very small bunch of dog-violets; there was veal and ham pie for luncheon, with salad, with the choice of plums and junket or baked jam roll; and, after luncheon, Mr Beguid arrived with car and chauffeur to take them to see the cottage.

At first Kate did not want to go: she had a secret plan of walking up to the field called Perkin's Beck and mooching about by herself, looking for badgers' sets, but when Mrs May explained to her that the field was just behind the cottage, and by the time Mr Beguid had stared long enough and pointedly enough out of the window with a bored, dry, if-this-were-my-child kind of expression on his face, Kate decided to go in the car after all, just to spite him. And it was a good thing (as she so often told her own children years afterwards) that she did: otherwise, she might never have talked to or (which was more important) made friends with – Thomas Goodenough.

Chapter Three

'WINK AT SMALL FAULTS'
Anna Seward died 1809
[*Extract from Arrietty's Diary and Proverb Book, March 25th.*]

'And about vacant possession,' Mrs May asked in the car, 'he really is going, this old man? I've forgotten his name—'

'Old Tom Goodenough? Yes, he's going all right; we've got him an almshouse. Not,' Mr Beguid added, with a short laugh, 'that he deserves it.'

'Why not?' asked Kate in her blunt way.

Mr Beguid glanced at her – a little put out, he seemed, as though the dog had spoken. 'Because,' he said, ignoring Kate and addressing Mrs May, 'he's a tiresome old humbug, that's why.' He laughed again, his complacent, short laugh. 'And the biggest liar in five counties, as they put it down in the village.'

The stone cottage stood in a field; it stood high, its back to the woods; it had a derelict look, Kate thought, as they toiled up the slope towards it, but the thatch seemed good. Beside the front door stood a water-butt leaking a little at seams and green with moss; there was slime on the brick path and a thin trickle of moisture which lost itself among the docks and thistles. Against the far end was a wooden outhouse on the walls of which Kate saw the skins of several small mammals nailed up to dry in the sun.

'I didn't realize it was quite so remote,' panted Mrs May, as Mr Beguid knocked sharply on the blistered paint of the front door. She waved her rubber-tipped

stick towards the sunken lane below the sloping field of meadow grass. 'We'll have to make some kind of path up to here.'

Kate heard a shuffling movement within and Mr Beguid, rapping again, called out impatiently: 'Come on, old Tom. Open up.'

There were footsteps and, as the door creaked open, Kate saw an old man – tall, thin, but curiously heavy about the shoulders. He carried his head sunk a little on

to his chest, and inclined sideways; and when he smiled
(as he did at once) this gave him a sly look: he had bright,
dark, strangely luminous eyes which he fixed immediately on Kate.

'Well, Tom,' said Mr Beguid briskly, 'how are you
keeping? Better, I hope. Here is Mrs May, the lady who
owns your cottage. May we come in?'

'There's naught to hide,' said the old man, backing
slightly to let them pass, but smiling only at Kate; it was,
Kate thought, as though he could not see Mr Beguid.

They filed past him into the principal room; it was
bareish but neat enough, except for a pile of wood
shavings on the stone floor and a stack of something Kate
took to be kindling beside the window embrasure. A
small fire smouldered in a blackened grate which seemed
to be half oven.

'You've tidied up a bit, I see,' said Mr Beguid, looking
about him. 'Not that it matters much. But,' he added,

speaking aside to Mrs May, and barely lowering his voice, 'before the builders come in, if I were you I'd get the whole place washed through and thoroughly fumigated.'

'I think it looks lovely,' cried Kate warmly, shocked by this want of manners, and Mrs May hastened to agree with her, addressing a friendly look towards the old man.

But old Tom gave no sign of having noticed: quietly he stood, looking down at Kate, smiling his secret smile.

'The stairs are through here,' said Mr Beguid, leading the way to a farther door; 'and here,' they heard him say, 'is the scullery.' Mrs May, about to follow, hesitated on the threshold. 'Don't you want to come, Kate, and see round the cottage?'

Kate stood stolidly where she was; she threw a quick glance at the old man, and back again to Mrs May. 'No, thanks,' she said shortly. And as Mrs May, a little surprised, followed Mr Beguid into the scullery, Kate moved towards the pile of peeled sticks. There was a short silence. 'What are you making?' Kate asked at last, a little shyly. The old man came back from his dream. 'Them?' he said in his soft voice. 'Them's sprays – for thatching.' He picked up a knife, tested the blade on his horny thumb, and pulling up a lowish stool, he sat down. 'Come you here,' he said, 'by me, and I'll show'ee.'

Kate drew up a chair beside him and watched him in silence as he cut several small lengths of the hazel sapling which at first she had taken for kindling. After a moment he said softly without looking up: 'You don't want to take no notice of him.'

'Mr Beguid?' said Kate. 'I don't. Be good! It's a silly kind of name. Compared to yours, I mean,' she added warmly; 'whatever you did wouldn't matter really with a name like Good Enough.'

The old man half turned his head in a warning gesture towards the scullery; he listened a moment and then he said: 'They're going upstairs,' and Kate, listening too, heard clumping footsteps on wooden treads. 'You know how long I bin in this cottage?' the old man asked, his head still cocked as though listening while the footsteps crossed and recrossed what must have been his bedroom. 'Nigh on eighty years,' he added after a moment. He took up a peeled sapling, grasping it firmly at either end.

'And now you've got to go?' said Kate, watching his hands as he took a firmer grip on the wood.

The old man laughed as though she had made a joke: he laughed quite silently, Kate noticed, shaking his head. 'So they make out,' he said in an amused voice, and with a twist of his two wrists he wrung the tough sapling as you wring out a wet cloth, and in the same movement doubled it back on itself. 'But I bain't going,' he added, and he threw the bent stick on the pile.

'But they wouldn't want to turn you out,' said Kate, 'not if you don't want to go, at least,' she added cautiously. 'I don't think Mrs May would.'

'Her-r-r?' he said, rolling the 'r's' and looking up at the ceiling; 'she's hand and glove with him.'

'She used to come and stay here,' Kate told him, 'when she was a child, did you know? Down at the big house. Firbank, isn't it?'

'Ay,' he said.

'Did you know her?' asked Kate curiously. 'She was called Miss Ada?'

'I knew Miss Ada all right,' said the old man, 'and her aunty. *And* her brother.' He laughed again. 'I knew the whole lot of 'em, come to that.'

As he spoke, Kate had a strange feeling; it was as though she had heard these words before, spoken by just such an old man as this and, she seemed to remember, it was in some such similar place – the sunlit window of a darkish cottage on a bright but cold spring day. She looked round wonderingly at the whitewashed walls – flaking a little they were, in a pattern she seemed to recognize; even the hollows and cracks of the worn brick floor also seemed curiously familiar – strange, because (of this she was certain) she had never been here before. She looked back at the old man, getting up courage to go a step farther. 'Did you know Crampfurl?' she asked after a moment, and before he spoke she knew what would be his answer.

'I knew Crampfurl all right,' said the old man, and he laughed again, nodding his head, enjoying some secret joke.

'And Mrs Driver, the cook?'

Here the joke became almost too much for old Tom. 'Ay,' he said, wheezing with silent laughter. 'Mrs Driver!'

and he wiped the corner of his eye with his sleeve.

'Did you know Rosa Pickhatchet?' went on Kate, 'that housemaid, the one who screamed?'

'Nay,' said old Tom, nodding and laughing. 'But I heard tell of her – screamed the house down, so they say.'

'But do you know why?' cried Kate excitedly.

He shook his head. 'No reason at all, as I can see.'

'But didn't they tell you that she saw a little man, on the drawing-room mantel-shelf, about the size of the china cupid; that she thought he was an ornament and tried to dust him with a feather duster – and suddenly he sneezed? Anyone would scream,' Kate concluded breathlessly.

'For why?' said old Tom, deftly sliding the bark from the wood as though it were a glove finger. 'They don't hurt you, borrowers don't. And they don't make no mess neither. Not like field-mice. Beats me, always has, the fuss folk'll make about a borrower, screeching and screaming and all that caper.' He ran an appreciative finger along the peeled surface. 'Smoking 'em out and them kind of games. No need for it, not with borrowers. They go quiet enough, give 'em time, once they know they've been seen. Now take field-mice—' The old man broke off to twist his stick, catching his breath with the effort.

'Don't let's,' cried Kate, 'please! I mean, tell me some more about borrowers.'

'There's naught to tell,' said the old man, tossing his stick on the pile and selecting a fresh one. 'Borrowers is as like to humans as makes no matter, and what's to tell about humans? Now you take field-mice – once one of them critturs finds a way indoors, you're done and strung up as you might say: you can't leave the place not for a couple of hours but you don't get the whole lot right down on you like a flock of starlings. Mess! And it ain't a question of getting 'em out: they've come and they've gone, if you see what I mean. Plague o' locusts ain't in it. Yes,' he went on, 'no doubt about it – in a house like this, you're apt to get more trouble from field-mice than ever you get from any borrower; in a house like this,' he repeated, 'set away like at the edge of the woods, borrowers can be company like as not.' He glanced up at the ceiling, which creaked slightly as footsteps passed and repassed in the room above. 'What you reckon they're up to?' he said.

'Measuring,' Kate said. 'Mrs May brought a yardstick. They'll be down soon,' she went on hurriedly, 'and I want to ask you something – something important. If they send me for a walk to-morrow – by myself, I mean, while they talk business, could I come up and be with you?'

'I don't see no reason why not,' said the old man, at work on his next stick. 'If you brings along a sharp knife, I'll learn you to make sprays.'

'You know,' said Kate impressively, with a glance at the ceiling, dropping her voice. 'Her brother, Mrs May's brother – or Miss Ada's or whatever you like to call her – he *saw* those borrowers down at the big house!' She paused for effect, watching his face.

'What of it?' said the old man impassively. 'You only got to keep your eyes skinned. I seen stranger things in my time than them sort of critturs – take badgers – now you come up here to-morrow and I'll tell you summat about badgers you wouldn't credit, but that I seen it with me own two eyes—'

'But have you ever seen a *borrower*?' cried Kate impatiently. 'Did you ever see any of these ones down at the big house?'

'Them as they had in the stables?'

'No, the ones who lived under the kitchen.'

'Oh, them,' he said, 'smoked out, they were. But it ain't
true—' he began, raising his face suddenly, and Kate saw
that it was a sad face when it was not smiling.

'What isn't true?'

'What they say: that I set the ferret on 'em. I wouldn't.
Not once I knew they was borrowers.'

'Oh!' exclaimed Kate, kneeling up on her chair with
excitement, 'you were the boy with the ferret?'

Old Tom looked back at her – his sideways look. 'I
were a boy,' he admitted guardedly, 'and I did have a
ferret.'

'But they did escape, didn't they?' Kate persisted
anxiously. 'Mrs May says they escaped by the grating.'

'That's right,' said old Tom, 'made off across the gravel
and up the bank.'

'But you don't know for certain,' said Kate; 'you didn't
see them go. Or *could* you see them from the window?'

'I know for certain, all right,' said old Tom. 'True
enough I saw 'em from the window, but that ain't how—'
he hesitated, looking at Kate; amused he seemed but still
wary.

'Please tell me. Please—' begged Kate.

The old man glanced upwards at the ceiling. 'You
know what he is?' he said, inclining his head.

'Mr Beguid? A lawyer.'

The old man nodded. 'That's right. And you don't
want nothing put down in writing.'

'I don't understand,' said Kate.

The old man sighed and took up his whittling knife.
'What I tells *you*, you tells *her*, and *he* puts it all down in
writing.'

'Mrs May wouldn't tell,' said Kate, 'she's—'

'She's hand in glove with him, that's what I maintain.
And it's no good telling me no different. Seemingly now,

you can't die no more where you reckons to die. And you know for why?' he said, glaring at Kate. 'Because of what's put down in writing.' And with a curiously vicious twist he doubled back his stick. Kate stared at him nonplussed. 'If I promised not to tell?' she said at last, in a timid voice.

'Promises!' exclaimed the old man; staring at Kate, he jerked a thumb towards the ceiling. 'Her-r-r great-uncle, old Sir Montague that was, *promised* me this cottage – "It's for your lifetime, Tom" he says. Promises!' he repeated angrily, and he almost spat the word. 'Promises is pie-crust.'

Kate's eyes filled with tears. 'All right,' she snapped, 'I don't care – then don't tell me!'

Tom's expression changed too, almost as violently. 'Now don't 'ee cry, little maid,' he begged, surprised and distressed.

But Kate, to her shame, could not stop; the tears ran down her cheeks and she felt the familiar hot feeling at the tip of her nose as though it were swelling. 'I was only wondering,' she gasped, fumbling for a handkerchief, 'if they were all right – and how they managed – and whether they found the badgers' set—'

'They found the badgers' set all right,' said old Tom. 'Now, don't 'ee cry, my maiden, not no more.'

'I'll stop in a minute,' Kate assured him in a stifled voice, blowing her nose.

'Now look 'ee here,' the old man went on – very upset he sounded, 'you dry your eyes and stop your weeping and old Tom'll show you summat.' Awkwardly he got up off his stool and hovered over her, drooping his shoulders like some great protective bird. 'Something you'd like. How's that, eh?'

'It's all right,' Kate said, giving a final scrub. She stuffed

away her handkerchief and smiled up at him. 'I've stopped.'

Old Tom put his hand in his pocket and then, throwing a cautious glance towards the ceiling, he seemed to change his mind: for a moment it had sounded as though the footsteps had been moving towards the stairs. 'It's all right,' whispered Kate, after listening, as he searched again and drew out a battered tin box, the kind in which pipe-smokers keep tobacco, and with his knotted fingers fumbled awkwardly with the lid; at last it was open and, breathing heavily, he turned it over and slid some object out. 'Here . . .' he said, and there on his calloused palm Kate saw the tiny book.

'Oh . . .' she breathed, staring incredulously.

'Take it up,' said old Tom, 'it won't bite you.' And, as gingerly Kate put out her hand, he added smiling: ' 'Tis Arrietty's diary.'

But Kate knew this, even before she saw the faded gilt lettering – 'Diary and Proverb Book,' and in spite of the fact that it was weather-stained and time-worn, that when she opened it the bulk of its pages slipped out from between the covers, and the ink or pencil or sap – or whatever Arrietty had used to write with – had faded to various shades of brown and sepia and a curious sickly yellow. It had opened at August the 31st, and the proverb, Kate saw, was 'Earth is the Best Shelter,' and below this the bald statement, 'Disastrous Earthquake at Charleston, U.S., 1866,' and on the page itself, in Arrietty's scratchy handwriting were three entries for the three successive years:

'Spiders in store-room.'

'Mrs D. dropped pan. Soup-leak in ceiling.'

'Talked to Spiller.'

Who was Spiller? Kate wondered. August 31st? That was after they left the big house: Spiller, she realized, must be part of the new life, the life out of doors. At random, she turned back a few pages:

'Mother bilious.'

'Threaded green beads.'

'Climbed hedge. Eggs bad.'

Climbed hedge? Arrietty must have gone birds '-nesting – and the eggs would be bad in (Kate glanced at the date) . . . yes, it was still August, and the motto for that day was 'Grasp all, lose all.'

'Where did you get this book?' Kate asked aloud in a stunned voice.

'I found it,' said old Tom.

'But where?' cried Kate.

'Here,' said old Tom, and Kate saw his eyes stray in the direction of the fire-place.

'In this house,' she exclaimed in an unbelieving voice and, staring up at his mysterious old face, Mr Beguid's unkind words came back to her suddenly, 'the biggest liar in five counties.' But here, in her hand, was the actual book; she stared down at it trying to sort out her thoughts.

'You want I should show you summat else?' he asked her, suddenly and a little pathetically, as though aware of her secret doubts. 'Come you here,' and getting up slowly

from her chair, Kate followed like a sleep-walker as he
went towards the fire-place.

The old man stooped down, and panting a little with
the effort, he dragged and tugged at the heavy wood-box;
as he shifted it aside a board fell forward with a slight
clatter and the old man, alarmed, glanced up at the
ceiling; but Kate, leaning forward, saw the board had
covered a sizeable rat-hole gouged out of the skirting and
Gothic in shape, like an opened church door.

'See?' said old Tom, after listening a moment – a little
breathless from tugging, 'goes right through to the
scullery: they'd got fire this side and water t'other. Years,
they lived here.'

Kate knelt down, staring into the hole. 'Here? In your
house?' Her voice became more and more scared and
unbelieving. 'You mean . . . Pod? And Homily? . . . And
little Arrietty?'

'Them, too,' said old Tom, 'in the end, as it were.'

'But didn't they live out of doors? That's what Arrietty
was longing to do—'

'They lived out of doors all right.' He gave a short
laugh. 'If you call it living. Or come to that, if you can call
it outdoors! But you take a look at this,' he went on
softly, with a note in his voice of thinly disguised pride,
'goes right up inside the wall, stairs they got and all
betwixt the lath and the plaster. Proper tenement, they
got here – six floors – and water on every floor. See that?'
he asked, laying his hand on a rusty pipe; 'comes down
from the cistern in the roof, that does, and goes on
through to the scullery. Tapped it, they did, in six
different places – and never a drop or a leak!'

He was silent a moment, lost in thought, before he
propped back the board again and shoved the wood-box
back into place. 'Years they lived here,' he said affection-

ately, and he sighed a little as he straightened up, dusting his hands together.

'But *who* lived here?' Kate whispered hurriedly (the footsteps above had crossed the landing and were now heard approaching the head of the stairs). 'You don't mean my ones? You said they found the badgers' set?'

'They found the badgers' set all right,' said old Tom, and gave his short laugh.

'But how do you know? Who told you?' Twittering with anxiety she followed behind him as he limped towards his stool.

Old Tom sat down, selected a stick, and with maddening deliberation tested the edge of his knife. 'She told me,' he said at last, and he cut the stick in three lengths.

'You mean you talked to Arrietty!'

He made a warning sign at her raised voice, lifting his eyebrows and jerking his head: the footsteps, Kate heard, were clumping now down the wooden treads of the stairs. 'You don't talk to that one,' he whispered, 'not while she's got a tongue to wag.'

Kate went on staring; if he had hit her on the head with a log from the log-box, she could not have appeared more stunned. 'Then she must have told you everything!' she gasped.

'Hush!' said the old man, his eye on the door.

Mrs May and Mr Beguid, it seemed, had reached the bottom of the stairs, and from the sound of their voices had turned again into the scullery for a last look round. 'Two fitted basins, at least,' Mrs May was heard saying, in a matter-of-fact tone.

'Pretty nigh on everything, I reckon,' whispered old Tom. 'She'd creep out most evenings, pretty regular.' He smiled as he spoke, glancing towards the hearth. And Kate, watching his face, suddenly saw the picture: the firelit cottage, the lonely boy at his whittling, and almost invisible in the shadows this tiny creature, seated maybe on a match-box; the fluty, monotonous voice going on and on and on . . . after a while, Kate thought, he would hardly hear it: it would merge and become part of the room's living stillness, like the simmer of the kettle or the ticking of the clock. Night after night; week after week; month after month; year, perhaps, after year . . . yes, indeed, Kate realized (staring at old Tom in the same stunned way even though, at this minute, Mrs May and Mr Beguid came back to the room talking so loudly about washbasins), Arrietty must have told Tom everything!

Chapter Four

'NO TALE LOSES IN THE TELLING'
Longfellow, American poet, died 1882; also Walt Whitman, 1891
[*Extract from Arrietty's Diary and Proverb Book, March 26th*]

And all that was needed now, she thought (as she lay that night in bed, listening to the constant gurgle in the pipes of the constant H. and C.), was for old Tom to tell *her* everything in fullest detail – as Arrietty must have told it to him. And, having gone so far, he might do this, she felt – in spite of his fear of things put down in writing. And she wouldn't tell either, she resolved staunchly – at any rate, not during his lifetime (although why he should mind so much she couldn't understand, seeing that he was known already as 'the biggest liar in five counties'). But what seemed still more hopeful was that, having shown her the little book, he had not asked for it back: she had it now in bed with her stuffed beneath her pillow and this, at any rate, was full of 'things in writing.' Not that she could understand them quite: the entries were too short, little headings, they seemed like, jotted down by Arrietty to remind herself of dates. But some of them sounded extraordinarily weird and mysterious . . . yes, she decided – suddenly inspired – that was the way to work it: she would ask old Tom to explain the headings – 'What could Arrietty have meant,' she would ask, 'by "Black men. Mother saved"?'

And this, more or less, was what did happen. While Mrs May talked business each day with Messrs Jobson, Thring, Beguid & Beguid, or argued with builders and plumbers and plumbers' mates, Kate would wander off alone across the fields and find her own way to the cottage, seeking out old Tom.

On some days (as Kate, in later years, would explain to her children) he would seem a bit 'cagey' and uninterested, but on other days a particular heading in the diary would seem to inspire him and his imagination would take wings and sail away on such swirls and eddies of miraculous memory that Kate, spellbound, could hardly believe that he had not at some time (in some other life, perhaps) been a borrower himself. And Mrs May, Kate remembered, had once said just this of her younger brother: this brother who, although three years his junior, had been known to old Tom (old Tom himself had admitted this much). Had they been friends? Great friends, perhaps? They certainly seemed birds of a feather – one famous for telling tall stories because 'he was such a tease'; the other more simply described as 'the biggest liar in five counties.' And it was this thought which, long after she was grown up, decided Kate to tell the world what was said to have happened to Pod and Homily and little Arrietty after that dreadful day when, smoked out of their house under the kitchen, they sought for refuge in the wild outdoors.

Here is her story – all 'put down in writing.' We can sift the evidence ourselves.

Chapter Five

'STEP BY STEP CLIMBS THE HILL'
Victoria Tubular Bridge, Montreal, opened 1866
[Extract from Arrietty's Diary and Proverb Book, August 25th]

Well, at first, it seems they just ran, but they ran in the
right direction – up the azalea bank, where (so many
months ago now) Arrietty had first met the boy, and
through the long grass at the top; how they got through
that, Homily used to say afterwards, she never knew –
nothing but stalks, close set. And insects: Homily had
never dreamed there could be so many different kinds of
insect – slow ones, hanging on things; fast, scuttling
ones, and ones (these were the worst) which stared at you
and did not move at once and then backed slowly, still
staring; it was as though, Homily said, they had made up
their mind to bite you and then (still malicious) changed it
out of caution. 'Wicked,' she said, 'that's what they were;
oh, wicked, wicked, wicked . . .'

As they shoved their way through the long grass, they
were choked with pollen loosened in clouds from above;

there were sharp-edged leaves, deceptively sappy and swaying, which cut their hands, gliding across the skin like the softly drawn bow of a violin but leaving blood behind; there were straw-dry, knotted stems, which caught them round the shins and ankles and which made them stumble and trip forward; often they would land on that cushiony plant with silvery, hairlike spines – spines which pricked and stung. Long grass . . . long grass . . . for ever afterwards it was Homily's nightmare.

Then, to get to the orchard, came a scramble through the privet hedge: dead leaves, below the blackened boughs of privet . . . dead leaves and rotting, desiccated berries which rose waist high as they swam their way through them, and, below the leaves, a rustling dampness. And here again were insects: things which turned over on their backs or hopped suddenly, or slyly slid away.

Across the orchard – easier going this, because the hens had fed there achieving their usual 'blasted heath' effect – a flattened surface of lava-coloured earth; and the visibility was excellent. But, if they could see, they could also be seen: the fruit trees were widely spaced, giving little cover; anyone glancing from a first-floor window in the house might well exclaim curiously: 'What's that, do you think, moving across the orchard? There by the second tree on the right – like leaves blowing. But there isn't a wind. More like something being drawn along on a thread – too steady to be birds . . .' This was the thought in Pod's mind as he urged Homily onwards. 'Oh, I can't,' she would cry. 'I must sit down! Just a moment, Pod – please!'

But he was adamant. 'You can sit down,' he'd say, gripping her below the elbow, and spinning her forward across the rubble, 'once we get to the wood. You take her other arm, Arrietty, but keep her moving !'

Once within the wood, they sank down on the side of the well-worn path, too exhausted to seek further cover. 'Oh dear . . . oh dear . . . oh dear . . .' Homily kept saying (mechanically, because she always said it), but behind her bright dark eyes in her smudged face they could see her brain was busy: and she was not hysterical, they could see that too; they could see, in other words, that Homily was 'trying.' 'There's no call for all this running,' she announced after a moment, when she could get her breath, 'nobody didn't see us go: fer all they know we're still there, trapped-like – under the floor.'

'I wouldn't be so sure,' said Arrietty, 'there was a face at the kitchen window. I saw it as we were going up the bank. A boy it looked like, with a cat or something.'

'If anyone'd seen us,' remarked Homily, 'they'd have been after us, that's what I say.'

'That's a fact,' said Pod.

'Well, which way do we go from here ?' asked Homily, gazing about among the tree-trunks. There was a long scratch across her cheek and her hair hung down in wisps.

'Well, we'd better be getting these loads sorted out first,' said Pod. 'Let's see what we've brought. What have you got in that borrowing-bag, Arrietty ?'

Arrietty opened the bag she had packed so hurriedly two days before against just this emergency; she laid out the contents on the hardened mud of the path and they looked an odd collection. There were three tin lids of varying sizes of pill bottles which fitted neatly one inside the other; a sizable piece of candle and seven wax-vestas; a change of underclothes and an extra jersey knitted by

Homily on blunted darning-needles from a much washed, unravelled sock, and last, but most treasured, her pencil from a dance programme and her Diary and Proverb Book.

'Now why did you want to cart that along?' grumbled Pod, glancing sideways at this massive tome as he laid out his own belongings. For the same reason, Arrietty thought to herself as she glanced at Pod's unpacking, that you brought along your shoemaker's needle, your hammer made from an electric bell-clapper, and a stout ball of twine: each to his hobby and the tools of the craft he loves (and hers she knew to be literature).

Besides his shoemaking equipment, Pod had brought the half nail-scissor, a thin sliver of razor-blade, ditto of child's fret-saw, an aspirin bottle with screw lid filled with water, a small twist of fuse wire, and two steel hat-pins, the shorter of which he gave to Homily. 'It'll help you up the hill,' he told her; 'we may have a bit of a climb.'

Homily had brought her knitting-needles, the rest of the unravelled sock, three pieces of lump sugar, the finger of a lady's kid glove filled with salt and pepper mixed, tied up at the neck with cotton, some broken pieces of digestive biscuit, a small tin box made for phonograph needles which now contained dry tea, a chip of soap, and her hair curlers.

Pod gazed glumly at the curious collection. 'Like as not we brought the wrong things,' he said, 'but it can't be helped now. Better pack 'em up again,' he went on, suiting the action to the word, 'and let's get going. Good idea of yours, Arrietty, the way you fitted together them tin lids. Not sure, though, we couldn't have done with a couple more—'

'We've only got to get to the badgers' set,' Arrietty

excused herself. 'I mean Aunt Lupy will have most things, won't she – like cooking utensils and such?'

'I never knew anyone as couldn't do with extra,' remarked Homily, stuffing in the remains of the sock and lashing up the neck of her bag with a length of blue embroidery silk, 'especially when they live in a badgers' set. And who's to say your Aunt Lupy's there at all?' She went on. 'I thought she got lost or something, crossing them fields out walking.'

'Well, she may be found again by now,' said Pod. 'Over a year ago, wasn't it, when she set out walking?'

'And anyway,' Arrietty pointed out, 'she wouldn't go walking with the cooking-pots.'

'I never could see,' said Homily, standing up and trying out the weight of her bag, 'nor never will, no matter what nobody tells me, what your Uncle Hendreary saw fit to marry in a stuck-up thing like that Lupy.'

'That's enough,' said Pod, 'we don't want none of that now.'

He stood up and slung his borrowing-bag on his steel hat-pin, swinging it over his shoulder. 'Now,' he asked, looking them up and down, 'sure you're both all right?'

'Not that, when put to it,' went on Homily, 'that she isn't good-hearted. It's the kind of way she does it.'

'What about your boots?' asked Pod. 'They quite comfortable?'

'Yes,' said Homily, 'for the moment,' she added.

'What about you, Arrietty?'

'I'm all right,' said Arrietty.

'Because,' said Pod, 'it's going to be a long pull. We're going to take it steady. No need to rush. But we don't want no stopping. Nor no grumbling. Understand?'

'Yes,' said Arrietty.

'And keep your eyes skinned,' Pod went on, as they all

moved off along the path. 'If you see anything, do as I do – and sharp, mind. We don't want no running every which way. We don't want no screaming.'

'I know,' said Arrietty irritably, adjusting her pack. She moved ahead as though trying to get out of earshot.

'You *think* you know,' called Pod after her. 'But you don't know nothing really; you don't know nothing about cover; nor does your mother: cover's a trained job, an art-like—'

'I know,' repeated Arrietty; 'you told me.' She glanced sideways into the shadowy depths of the brambles beside the path; she saw a great spider, hanging in space, his web was invisible: he seemed to be staring at her – she saw his eyes. Defiantly, Arrietty stared back.

'You can't tell no one in five minutes,' persisted Pod, 'things you got to learn from experience. What I told you, my girl, that day I took you out borrowing, wasn't even the A B C. I tried my best, because your mother asked me. And see where it's got us!'

'Now, Pod,' panted Homily (they were walking too fast for her), 'no need to bring up the past.'

'That's what I mean,' said Pod, 'the past *is* experience: that's all you got to learn from. You see, when it comes to borrowing—'

'But you had a lifetime of it, Pod: you was in training – Arrietty'd only been out that once—'

'That's what I *mean*,' cried Pod, and, in stubborn desperation, he stopped in his tracks for Homily to catch up, 'about cover, if only she'd known the A B C—'

'Look out!' sang Arrietty shrilly, now some way ahead.

There was a rushing clatter and a dropped shadow and a hoarse, harsh cry; and, suddenly, there was Pod – alone on the path – face to face with a large, black crow.

The bird stared, wickedly, but a little distrustfully, his cramped toes turned in slightly, his great beak just open. Frozen to stillness Pod stared back – something growing in the path, that's what he looked like – a rather peculiar kind of chunky toadstool. The great bird, very curious, turned his head sideways and tried Pod with his other eye. Pod, motionless, stared back. The crow made a murmer in its throat – a tiny bleat – and, puzzled, it moved forward. Pod let it come, a couple of sideways steps, and then – out of a still face – he spoke: 'Get back to where you was,' he said evenly, almost conversationally, and the bird seemed to hesitate. 'We don't want no nonsense from you,' Pod went on steadily; 'pigeon-toed, that's what you are! Crows is pigeon-toed, first time it struck me. Staring away like that, with one eye, and your head turned sideways . . . think it pretty, no doubt' – Pod spoke quite pleasantly – 'but it ain't, not with *that* kind of beak . . .'

The bird became still, its expression no longer curious: there was stark amazement in every line of its rigid body and, in its eye, a kind of ghastly disbelief. 'Go on! Get off with you!' shouted Pod suddenly, moving towards it. 'Shoo . . .!' And, with a distraught glance and panic-stricken croak, the great bird flapped away. Pod wiped his brow with his sleeve as Homily, white faced and still trembling, crawled out from under a foxglove leaf. 'Oh, Pod,' she gasped, 'you were brave – you were wonderful!'

'It's nothing,' said Pod, 'it's a question of keeping your nerve.'

'But the size of it!' said Homily. 'You'd never think seeing them flying they was that size!'

'Size is nothing,' said Pod, 'it's the talk that gets them.' He watched Arrietty climb out from a hollow stump and begin to brush herself down. When she looked up, he looked away. 'Well,' he said, after a moment, 'we'd better keep moving.'

Arrietty smiled; she hesitated a moment then ran across to him.

'What's that for?' asked Pod weakly, as she flung her arms round his neck. 'Oh,' cried Arrietty, hugging him, 'you deserve a medal – the way you faced up to it, I mean.'

'No, lass,' said Pod, 'you don't mean that: the way I was caught out, that's what you mean – caught out, good and proper, talking of cover.' He patted her hand. 'And, what's more, you're right: we'll face up to that one, too. You and your mother was trigger quick and I'm proud of you.' He let go her hand and swung his pack up on to his shoulders. 'But another time, remember,' he added, turning suddenly, 'not stumps. Hollow they may be but not always empty, see what I mean, and you're out of the frying-pan into the fire . . .'

On and on they went, following the path which the workmen had made when they dug out the trench for the gas-pipe. It led them through two fields of pasture land, on a gradually rising slope alongside; they could walk with perfect ease under the lowest rungs of any five-barred gate, picking a careful way across the clusters of sun-dried cattle tracks; these were crater-like but crumbling, and Homily, staggering a little beneath her load, slipped once and grazed her knee.

On the third field the gas-pipe branched away obliquely to the left, and Pod, looking ahead to where against the skyline he could just make out a stile, decided that they could safely now forsake the gas-pipe and stick to the path beside the hedge. 'Won't be so long

now,' he explained comfortingly when Homily begged to rest, 'but we got to keep going. See that stile? That's what we're aiming for and we got to make it afore sunset.'

So on they plodded and, to Homily, this last lap seemed the worst: her tired legs moved mechanically like scissors; stooping under her load, she was amazed each time she saw a foot come forward – it no longer seemed to be her foot; she wondered how it got there.

Arrietty wished they could not see the stile: their tiny steps seemed to bring it no nearer; it worked better she found to keep her eyes on the ground and then every now and again if she looked up she could see they had made progress.

But at last they reached the crest of the hill; towards the right, on the far side of the cornfield beyond the hazel hedge, lay the woods, and ahead of them, after a slight dip, rose a vast sloping field, crossed with shadow from where the sun was setting behind the trees.

On the edge of this field they stood and stared, awed by its vastness, its tilted angle against the rosy sky; on this endless sea of lengthening shadows and dreaming grassland floated an island of trees dimmed already by its long-thrown trail of dusk.

'This is it,' said Pod, after a long moment, 'Perkin's Beck.' They stood, all three of them, underneath the stile, loath to lose its shelter.

'Perkin's what?' asked Homily uneasily.

'Perkin's Beck. You know – the name of the field. This is where they live, the Hendrearies.'

'You mean,' said Homily, after a pause, 'where the badgers' set is?'

'That's right,' said Pod, staring ahead.

Homily's tired face looked yellow in the golden light; her jaw hung loose. 'But where?' she asked.

Pod waved his arm. 'Somewhere; it's in this field anyway.'

'In this field . . .' repeated Homily dully, her eyes fixed on the dim boundaries, the distant group of shadowy trees.

'Well, we got to look,' explained Pod uneasily. 'You didn't think we'd go straight to it, did you?'

'I thought you knew where it was,' said Homily. Her voice sounded husky. Arrietty, between them, stood strangely silent.

'Well, I've brought you this far. Haven't I?' said Pod. 'If the worst comes to the worst, we can camp for the night, and look round in the morning.'

'Where's the stream?' asked Arrietty. 'There's supposed to be a stream.'

'Well, there is,' said Pod, 'it flows down there, along

that distant hedge, and then comes in like – do you see ? –
across that far corner. That thicker green there – can't
you see ? – them's rushes.'

Arrietty screwed up her eyes. 'Yes,' she said uncertainly, and added : 'I'm thirsty.'

'And so am I,' said Homily ; she sat down suddenly as
though deflated. 'All the way up that hill, step after step,
hour after hour, I bin saying to meself "Never mind, the
first thing we'll do as soon as we get to that badgers' set is
sit down and have a nice cup o' tea" – it kept me going.'

'Well, we will have one,' said Pod. 'Arrietty's got the
candle.'

'And I'll tell you another thing,' went on Homily,
staring ahead, 'I couldn't walk across that there field, not
if you offered me a monkey in a cage : we'll have to go
round by the edges.'

'Well, that's just what we're going to do,' said Pod,
'you don't find no badgers' sets in the middle of a field.
We'll work round, systematic-like, bit by bit, starting out
in the morning. But we got to sleep rough to-night, that's
one thing certain. No good poking about to-night : it'll be
dark soon ; the sun's near off that hill already.'

'And there are clouds coming up,' said Arrietty, gazing
at the sunset, 'and moving fast.'

'Rain ?' cried Homily, in a stricken voice.

'Well, we'll move fast,' said Pod, slinging his pack up.
'Here, give me yours, Homily, you'll travel lighter . . .'

'Which way are we going ?' asked Arrietty.

'We'll keep along by this lower hedge,' said Pod,
setting off. 'And make towards the water. If we can't
make it before the rain comes, we'll just take any shelter.'

'What sort of shelter ?' asked Homily, stumbling after
him through the tussocky grass. 'Look out, Pod, them's
nettles !'

'I can see them,' said Pod (they were walking in a shallow ditch). 'A hole or something,' he went on. 'There's a hole there, for instance. See? Under that root.'

Homily peered at it as she came abreast. 'Oh, I couldn't go in there,' she said, 'there might be something in it.'

'Or we could go right into the hedge,' Pod called back.

'There's not much shelter in the hedge,' said Arrietty. She walked alone, on the higher ground where the grass

was shorter. 'I can see from here: it's all stems and branches.' She shivered a little in a light wind which set the leaves of the hedge plants suddenly a-tremble, clashing the drying teazles as they swung and locked together. 'It's clouding right over,' she called.

'Yes, it'll be dark soon,' said Pod, 'you'd better come down here with us; you don't want to get lost.'

'I won't get lost; I can see better from here. Look!' she called out suddenly, 'there's an old boot. Wouldn't that do?'

'An old what?' asked Homily incredulously.
'Might do,' said Pod, looking about him. 'Where is it?'
'To your left. There. In the long grass . . .'
'An old boot!' cried Homily, as she saw him set down
the borrowing-bags. 'What's the matter with you, Pod –
have you gone out of your mind?' Even as she spoke, it
began to rain, great summer drops which bounced
among the grasses.

'Take the borrowing-bags and get under that dock-leaf
– both of you – while I look.'
'An old boot . . .' repeated Homily incredulously, as
she and Arrietty crouched under the dock-leaf; she had to
raise her voice – the rain, on the swaying leaf, seemed to
clatter rather than patter. 'Hark at it!' complained
Homily. 'Come in closer, Arrietty, you'll catch your
death. Oh, my goodness me – it's running down my
back!'
'Look – he's calling to us,' said Arrietty, 'come on!'

Homily bent her neck and peered out from under the swaying leaf: there stood Pod, some yards away, barely visible among the steaming grasses, dimmed by the curtain of rain. 'A tropical scene,' Arrietty thought, remembering her *Gazetteer of the World*. She thought of man against the elements, jungle swamps, steaming forests, and Mr Livingstone she presumed . . . 'What's he want?' she heard her mother complaining. 'We can't go out in this – look at it!'

'It's coming in under-foot now,' Arrietty told her, 'can't you see? This is a ditch. Come on, we must run for it; he wants us.'

They ran, half-crouching, stunned by the pounding water. Pod pulled them up into the longer grass, snatching their borrowing-bags, gasping instructions, as they slid and slithered after him through – what Arrietty thought of as 'the bush.'

'Here it is,' said Pod. 'Get in here.'

The boot lay on its side; they had to crouch to enter. 'Oh, my goodness,' Homily kept saying. 'Oh, my goodness me . . .' and would glance fearfully about the darkness inside. 'I wonder whoever wore it.'

'Go on,' said Pod, 'get further down; it's all right.'

'No, no,' said Homily, 'I'm not going in no further: there might be something in the toe.'

'It's all right,' said Pod, 'I've looked: there's nothing but a hole in the toe.' He stacked the borrowing-bags against the inner side. 'Something to lean against,' he said.

'I wish I knew who'd wore this boot,' Homily went on, peering about uncomfortably, wiping her wet face on her wetter apron.

'What good would that do you?' Pod said, untying the strings of the largest bag.

'Whether he was clean or dirty or what,' said Homily, 'and what he died of. Suppose he died of something infectious?'

'Why suppose he died?' said Pod. 'Why shouldn't he be hale and hearty, and just had a nice wash and be sitting down to a good tea this very minute.'

'Tea?' said Homily, her face brightening. 'Where's the candle, Pod?'

'It's here,' said Pod. 'Give me a wax-vesta, Arrietty, and a medium-sized aspirin lid. We got to go careful with the tea, you know; we got to go careful with everything.'

Homily put out a finger and touched the worn leather. 'I'll give this boot a good clean out in the morning,' she said.

'It's not bad,' said Pod, taking out the half nail-scissor. 'If you ask me, we been lucky to find a boot like this. There ain't nothing to worry about: it's disinfected, all right – what with the sun and the wind and the rain, year after year of it.' He stuck the blade of the nail-scissor through an eyelet hole and lashed it firm with a bit of old bootlace.

'What are you doing that for, Papa?' asked Arrietty.

'To stand the lid on, of course,' said Pod, 'a kind of bracket over the candle; we haven't got no tripod. Now you go and fill it with water, there's a good girl – there's plenty outside . . .'

There was plenty outside: it was coming down in torrents; but the mouth of the boot faced out of the wind and there was a little dry patch before it. Arrietty filled the tin lid quite easily by tipping a large pointed fox-glove leaf towards it so the rain ran off and down the point. All about her was the steady sound of rain, and the lighted candle within the boot made the dusk seem darker: there was a smell of wildness, of space, of leaves and grasses and, as she turned away with the filled tin-lid, another smell – winy, fragrant, spicy. Arrietty took note of it to remember it for morning – it was the smell of wild strawberries.

After they had drunk their hot tea and eaten a good half of sweet, crumbly digestive biscuit, they took off their wet outer clothes and hung them out along the handle of the nail-scissor above the candle. With the old woollen sock about their three shoulders, they talked a little. '. . . Funny,' Arrietty remarked, 'to be wrapped in a sock and inside a boot.' But Pod, watching the candle flame, was worried about wastage and, when the clothes had steamed a little, he doused the flame. Tired out, they lay down at last among the borrowing-bags, cuddled together for warmth. The last sound Arrietty heard as she fell asleep was the steady drumming of the rain on the hollow leather of the boot.

Chapter Six

'SUCH IS THE TREE, SUCH IS THE FRUIT'
End of great railway strike at Peoria, Ill., 1891
[*Extract from Arrietty's Diary and Proverb Book, August 26th*]

Arrietty was the first to wake. 'Where am I!' she wondered. She felt warm – too warm, lying there between her mother and father – and when slightly she turned her head she saw three little golden suns, floating in the darkness; it was a second or two before she realized what they were, and with this knowledge memory flooded back – all that happened yesterday: the escape, the frenzied scramble across the orchard, the weary climb, the rain – the little golden suns, she realized, were the lace-holes of the boot!

Stealthily Arrietty sat up; a balmy freshness stole in upon her and, framed in the neck of the boot, she saw the bright day: grasses, softly stirring, tenderly sunlit: some were broken, where yesterday they had pushed through them dragging the borrowing-bags; there was a yellow buttercup, sticky and gleaming, it looked – like wet paint; on a tawny stalk of sorrel she saw an aphis – of a green so delicate that, against the sunlight, it looked transparent. 'Ants milk them,' Arrietty remembered, 'perhaps we could.'

She slid out from between her sleeping parents and, just as she was, with bare feet and in her vest and petticoat, she ventured out of doors.

It was a glorious day, sunlit and rain-washed – the earth breathing out its scents. 'This,' Arrietty thought, 'is what I have longed for; what I have imagined; what I knew existed – what I knew we'd have!'

She pushed through the grasses and soft drops fell on her benignly, warmed by the sun. Downhill a little way she went, towards the hedge, out of the jungle of higher grass, into the shallow ditch where, last night, the rain and darkness had combined to scare her.

There was warm mud here, between the shorter grass blades, fast-drying now in the sun; a bank rose between her and the hedge: a glorious bank, it was, filled with roots; with grasses; with tiny ferns; with small sandy holes; with violet leaves and with pale scarlet pimpernel and, here and there, a globe of deeper crimson – wild strawberries!

She climbed the bank – leisurely and happily, feeling

the warm sun through her vest, her bare feet picking their way more delicately than clumsy human feet. She gathered three strawberries heavy with juice, and ate them luxuriously, lying full-length on a steady terrace before a mouse-hole. From this bank she could see across the field, but to-day it looked different – as large as ever; as oddly tilted; but alight and alive with the early sunshine: now all the shadows ran a different way, dewy – they seemed – on the gleaming golden grass. She saw in the distance the lonely group of trees: they still seemed to float on a grassy ocean. She thought of her mother's fear of open spaces. 'But I could cross this field,' she thought, 'I could go anywhere . . .' Was this, perhaps, what Eggletina had thought? Eggletina – Uncle Hendreary's child – who, they said, had been eaten by the cat. Did enterprise, Arrietty wondered, always meet with disaster? Was it really better, as her parents had always taught her, to live in secret darkness underneath the floor?

The ants were out, she saw, and busy about their business – flurried, eager, weaving their anxious routes among the grass stems; every now and again, Arrietty noticed, waving its antennae, an ant would run up a grass stem and look around. A great contentment filled Arrietty: yes – here they were, for better or worse – there could be no going back!

Refreshed by the strawberries, she went on up the bank and into the shade of the hedge: here was sunflecked greenness and a hollowness above her. Up and up as far as she could see there were layers and storeys of green chambers, crossed and recrossed with springing branches: cathedral-like, the hedge seemed from the inside.

Arrietty put her foot on a lower branch and swung herself up into the green shadows: quite easy, it was, with branches to her hand on all sides – easier than climbing a ladder; a ladder as high as this would mean a feat of endurance, and a ladder at best was a dull thing, whereas here was variety, a changing of direction, exploration of heights unknown. Some twigs were dry and rigid, shedding curls of dusty bark; others were lissom and alive with sap: on these she would swing a little (as so often she had dreamed of swinging in that other lifetime under the floor!). 'I will come here when it is windy,' she told herself, 'when the whole hedge is alive and swaying in the wind . . .'

Up and up she went. She found an old bird's-nest, the moss inside was straw-dry. She climbed into it and lay for a while and, leaning over the edge, dropped crumbled pieces of dried moss through the tangled branches below

her; to watch them plummet between the boughs gave her, she found, an increased sense of height, a delicious giddiness which, safely in the nest, she enjoyed. But having felt this safety made climbing out and on and up seem far more dangerous. 'Suppose I fell,' thought Arrietty, 'as those bits of moss fell, skimming down through the shadowy hollows and banging and bouncing as they go?' But, as her hands closed round the friendly twigs and her toes spread a little to grip the bark, she was suddenly aware of her absolute safety – the ability (which for so long had been hidden deeply inside her) to climb. 'It's heredity,' she told herself, 'that's why borrowers' hands and feet are longer in proportion than the hands and feet of human beings; that's how my father can come down by a fold in the table-cloth; how he can climb a curtain by the bobbles; how he can swing on his name-tape from a desk to a chair, from a chair to the floor. Just because I was a girl, and not allowed to go borrowing, it doesn't say I haven't got the gift . . .'

Suddenly, raising her head, she saw the blue sky above her, through the tracery of leaves – leaves which trembled and whispered as, in her haste, she swayed their stems. Placing her foot in a fork and swinging up, she caught her petticoat on a wild rose thorn and heard it rip. She picked the thorn out of the stuff and held it in her hand (it was the size to her of a rhinoceros-horn to a human being): it was light in proportion to its bulk, but very sharp and vicious looking. 'We could use this for something,' Arrietty thought. 'I must think . . . some kind of weapon . . .' One more pull and her head and shoulders were outside the hedge; the sun fell hot on her hair, and dazzled by the brightness she screwed her eyes up as she gazed about her.

Hills and dales, valleys, fields and woods – dreaming in

the sunshine; she saw there were cows in the next field
but one. Approaching the wood, from a field on the lower
side, she saw a man with a gun – very far away, he looked,
very harmless. She saw the roof of Aunt Sophy's house
and the kitchen chimney smoking. On the turn of a
distant road, as it wound between the hedges, she saw a
milk-cart: the sunlight flashed on the metal churn and she
heard the faint fairy-like tinkle of the harness brasses.
What a world – mile upon mile, thing after thing, layer
upon layer of unimagined richness – and she might never
have seen it! She might have lived and died as so many of
her relations had done, in dusty twilight – hidden behind
a wainscot.

Coming down, she found a rhythm: a daring swing, a
letting go, and a light drop into thickly clustered leaves
which her instinct told her would act as a safety net – a
cage of lissom twigs, which sprang to hand and foot –
lightly to be caught, lightly to be let go. Such leaves
clustered more thickly towards the outside of the hedge,
not in the bare hollows within, and her passage amongst
them was almost like surf-riding – a controlled and

bouncing slither. The last bough dropped her lightly on the slope of a grassy bank, springing back into place above her head, as lightly she let it go, with a graceful elastic shiver.

Arrietty examined her hands: one was slightly grazed. 'But they'll harden up,' she told herself. Her hair stood on end and was filled with bark dust and there in her white embroidered petticoat she saw a great tear.

Hurriedly she picked three more strawberries as a peace-offering and, wrapping them in a violet leaf so as not to stain her vest, she scrambled down the bank, across the ditch, and into the clump of long grass.

Homily, at the entrance to the boot, looked worried as usual.

'Oh, Arrietty, wherever have you been? Breakfast's been ready this last twenty minutes. Your father's out of his mind!'

'Why?' asked Arrietty, surprised.

'With worrying about you – with looking for you.'

'I was quite near,' Arrietty said. 'I was only in the hedge. You could have called me.'

Homily put her finger on her lip and glanced in a fearful way from one side to another: 'You can't *call*,' she said, dropping her voice to an angry whisper. 'We're not to make any noise at all, your father says. No calling or shouting – nothing to draw attention. Danger, that's what he said there is – danger on all sides . . .'

'I don't mean you have to whisper,' Pod said, appearing suddenly from behind the boot, carrying the half nail-scissor (he had been cutting a small trail through the thickest grass). But don't you go off, Arrietty, never again, without you say just where you're going, and what for, and for how long. Understand?'

'No,' said Arrietty, uncertainly, 'I don't quite. I mean I don't always know what I'm going *for*.' (For what, for instance, had she climbed to the top of the hedge?) 'Where is all this danger? I didn't see any. Excepting three cows two fields away.'

Pod looked thoughtfully to where a sparrow-hawk hung motionless in the clear sky.

'It's everywhere,' he said, after a moment. 'Before and Behind, Above and Below.'

Chapter Seven

'PUFF AGAINST THE WIND'
Oxford and Harvard Boat Race, 1869
[*Extract from Arrietty's Diary and Proverb Book, August 27th.*]

While Homily and Arrietty were finishing breakfast, Pod got busy: he walked thoughtfully around the boot, surveying it from different angles; he would touch the leather with a practised hand, peer at it closely, and then stand back, half-closing his eyes; he removed the borrowing-bags, one by one, carefully stacking them on the grass outside, and then he crawled inside; they could hear him grunting and panting a little as he knelt, and stopped and measured – he was, they gathered, making a carefully calculated examination of seams, joins, floor space, and quality of stitching.

After a while he joined them as they sat there on the grass. 'Going to be a hot day,' he said thoughtfully, as he sat down, 'a real scorcher.' He removed his neck-tie and heaved a sigh.

'What was you looking at, Pod?' asked Homily, after a moment.

'You saw,' said Pod, 'that boot,' He was silent a moment, and then, 'That's no tramp's boot,' he said, 'nor that boot weren't made for no working man neither: that boot,' went on Pod, staring at Homily, 'is a gentleman's boot.'

'Oh,' breathed Homily in a relieved voice, half-closing her eyes and fanning her face with a limp hand, 'thank goodness for that!'

'Why, Mother,' asked Arrietty, irritated, 'what's wrong with a working man's boot? Papa's a working man, isn't he?'

Homily smiled and shook her head in a pitying way. 'It's a question,' she said, 'of quality.'

'Your mother's right there,' said Pod. 'Hand-sewn, that boot is, and as fine a bit of leather as ever I've laid me hand on.' He leaned towards Arrietty. 'And you see, lass, a gentleman's boot is well cared for, well greased and dubbined—years and years of it. If it hadn't been, don't you see, it would never have stood up — as this boot has stood up — to wind and rain and sun and frost. They pays dear for their boots, gentlemen do, but they sees they gets good value.'

'That's right,' agreed Homily, nodding her head and looking at Arrietty.

'Now, that hole in the toe,' Pod went on, 'I can patch that up with a bit of leather from the tongue. I can patch that up good and proper.'

'It's not worth the time nor the thread,' exclaimed Homily. 'I mean to say, just for a couple o' nights or a day or two; it's not as though we were going to *live* in a boot,' she pointed out, with an amused laugh.

Pod was silent a moment and then he said slowly : 'I bin thinking.'

'I mean to say,' Homily went on, 'we do know we got relations in this field and — though I wouldn't call a badgers' set a proper home, mind — at least it's some-where.'

Pod raised solemn eyes. 'Maybe,' he said, in the same grave voice, 'but all the same, I bin thinking. I bin thinking,' he went on; 'relations or no relations, they're still borrowers, ain't they ? And among human beings, for instance, who ever sees a borrower ?' He gazed round challengingly.

'Well, that boy did,' began Arrietty, 'and—'

'Ah,' said Pod, 'because you, Arrietty, who wasn't no borrower — who hadn't even learned to borrow — went up and talked to him: sought him out, shameless — knowing no better. And I told you just what would happen; hunted out, I said we'd be, by cats and rat-catchers — by policemen and all. Now was I right or wasn't I ?'

'Yes, you were right,' said Arrietty, 'but—'

'There ain't no buts,' said Pod. 'I was right. And if I was right then, I'm right now. See ? I bin thinking and what I bin thinking is right — and, this time, there ain't going to be no nonsense from you. Nor from your mother, neither.'

'There won't be no nonsense from me, Pod,' said Homily in a pious voice.

'Now,' said Pod, 'this is how it strikes me: human beings stand high and move fast; when you stand higher you can see farther — do you get me ? What I mean to say is — if, with them advantages, a human being can't never find a borrower . . . even goes as far as to say they don't believe borrowers *exist*, why should we borrowers – who

stand lower and move slower, compared to them like –
hope to do much better? Living in a house, say, with
several families – well, of course, we know each other . . .
stands to reason: we been brought up together. But come
afield, to a strange place like this and – this is how it seems
to me – borrowers is hid from borrowers.'

'Oh my—' said Homily unhappily.

'We don't move "slow" exactly,' said Arrietty.

'Compared to them, I said. Our legs move *fast* enough
– but theirs is longer: look at the ground they cover!' He
turned to Homily. 'Now don't upset yourself. I don't say
we won't find the Hendrearies – maybe we will . . . quite
soon. Or anyway before the winter—'

'The winter . . .' breathed Homily in a stricken voice.

'But we got to plan,' went on Pod, 'and act, as though
there weren't no badgers' set. Do you see what I mean?'

'Yes, Pod,' said Homily huskily.

'I bin thinking it out,' he repeated. 'Here we are, the
three of us, with what we got in the bags, two hat-pins,
and an old boot: we got to face up to it and, what's more,'
he added solemnly, 'we got to live different.'

'How different?' asked Homily.

'Cold food, for instance. No more hot tea. No coffee.
We got to keep the candle and the matches in hand for
winter. We got to look about us and see what there is.'

'Not caterpillars, Pod,' pleaded Homily, 'you promised! I couldn't never eat a caterpillar.'

'Nor you shall,' said Pod, 'not if I can help it. There's
other things, this time o'year, plenty. Now, I want you to
get up, the two of you, and see how this boot drags.'

'How do you mean?' asked Homily, mystified, but
obediently they both stood up.

'See these laces?' said Pod, 'good and strong – been
oiled, that's why . . . or tarred. Now, you each take a lace

over your shoulder and pull. Turn your back to the boot –
that's right – and just walk forward.'

Homily and Arrietty leaned on the traces and the boot
came on with a bump and a slither so fast across the
slippery grass that they stumbled and fell – they had not
expected it would be so light.

'Steady on!' cried Pod, running up beside them. 'Take
it steady, can't you? Up you get – that's the way ...
steady, steady ... that's fine. You see,' he said, when they
paused for breath, having dragged the boot to the edge of
the long grass, 'how it goes – like a bird!' Homily and
Arrietty rubbed their shoulders and said nothing; they
even smiled slightly, a pale reflection of Pod's pride and
delight. 'Now sit down, both of you. You was fine. Now,
you'll see, this is going to be good.'

He stood beaming down at them as, meekly, they sat
on the grass. 'It's like this,' he explained. 'I talked just
now of danger – to you, Arrietty – and that's because,
though brave we must be (and there's none braver than
your mother when she's put to it), we can't never be
foolhardy: we got to make our plans and we got to keep
our heads; we can't afford to waste no energy – climbing
hedges just for fun, and suchlike – and we can't afford to
take no risks. We got to make our plan and we got to stick
to it. Understand?'

'Yes,' said Arrietty, and Homily nodded her head.
'Your father's right,' she said.

'You got to have a main object,' went on Pod, 'and ours is there, ready-made – we got to find the badgers' set. Now how are we going to set about it? It's a big field – take us the best part of a day to get along one side of it, let alone have time to look down holes; and we'd be wore out, that's what we'd be. Say I went off looking by myself – well, your mother would never know a moment's peace all day long, till she had me safe back again: there's nothing bad enough for what she'd be imagining. *And* going on at you, Arrietty. Now, that's all wear and tear, and we can't afford too much of it. Folk get silly when they're fussed, if you see what I mean, and that's when accidents happen.'

'Now, my idea,' Pod went on, 'is this: we'll work our way all round this field, like I said last night, by the edges—'

'Hedges,' corrected Arrietty, under her breath, without thinking.

'I heard what you said, Arrietty,' remarked Pod quietly (he seldom grudged her superior education); 'there's hedges and edges, and I meant edges.'

'Sorry,' murmured Arrietty, blushing.

'As I was saying,' Pod went on, 'we'll work our way round, systematic-like, exploring the banks and' – he looked at Arrietty pointedly – 'hedges – and camping as we go: a day here, a day or two there, just as we feel; or depending on the holes and burrows; there'll be great bits of bank where there couldn't be no badgers' set – we can skip those, as you might say. Now you see, Homily, we couldn't do this if we had a settled home.'

'You mean,' asked Homily sharply, 'that we've got to drag the boot?'

'Well,' said Pod, 'was it heavy?'

'With all our gear in it, it would be.'

'Not over grass,' said Pod.

'And uphill !' exclaimed Homily.

'*Level* here at the bottom of the field,' corrected Pod patiently, 'as far as them rushes; then uphill at the top of the field, alongside the stream; then across – *level* again; then the last lap of all, which brings us back to the stile again, and it's downhill all the way !'

'Um-m-m,' said Homily, unconvinced.

'Well,' said Pod, 'out with it – speak your mind: I'm open to suggestions.'

'Oh, Mother—' began Arrietty in a pleading voice, and then became silent.

'Has Arrietty and me got to drag all the time ?' asked Homily.

'Now, don't be foolish,' said Pod, 'we take it in turns, of course.'

'Oh well,' sighed Homily, 'what can't be cured, needs must.'

'That's my brave old girl,' said Pod. 'Now about provender – *food*,' he explained, as Homily looked up bewildered, 'we better become vegetarian, pure and simple, one and all, and make no bones about it.'

'There won't be no bones to make,' remarked Homily grimly, 'not if we become vegetarian.'

'The nuts is coming on,' said Pod; 'nearly ripe they'll be down in that sheltered corner – milky like. Plenty of fruit – blackberries, them wild strawberries. Plenty of salad, dandelion, say, and sorrel. There's gleanings still in that cornfield t'other side of the stile. We'll manage – the thing is you got to get used to it: no hankering for boiled ham, chicken rissoles, and that kind of fodder. Now, Arrietty,' he went on, 'as you're so set on hedge-climbing, you and your mother had better go off and gather us

some nuts, how's that, eh? And I'll get down to a bit of
cobbling.' He glanced at the boot.

'Where do you find the nuts?' asked Arrietty.

'There, about half-way along' – Pod pointed to a
thickening of pale green in the hedge – 'before you get to
the water. You climb up, Arrietty, and throw 'em down,
and your mother can gather 'em up. I'll come down and
join you later: we got to dig a pit.'

'A pit? Whatever for?' asked Arrietty.

'We can't carry that weight of nuts around,' explained
Pod, 'not in a boot this size. Wherever we find provender,
we got to make a cache like, and mark it down for
winter.'

'Winter . . .' moaned Homily softly.

Nevertheless, as Arrietty helped her mother over the
rough places in the ditch, which – because it was shallow,
well drained, and fairly sheltered – could be used as a
highway, she felt closer to Homily than she had felt for
years: more like a sister, as she put it. 'Oh, look,' cried
Homily, when they saw a scarlet pimpernel; she stooped
and picked it by its hair-thin stalk. 'Int it lovely?' she said
in a tender voice; touching the fragile petals with a
work-worn finger, she tucked it into the opening of her
blouse. Arrietty found a pale-blue counterpart in the
delicate bird's-eye, and put it in her hair; and suddenly
the day began to seem like a holiday. 'Flowers made for
borrowers,' she thought.

At last they reached the nutty part of the hedge. 'Oh,
Arrietty,' exclaimed Homily, gazing up at the spreading
branches with mingled pride and fear, 'you can't never go
up there.'

But Arrietty could and would: she was delighted to
show off her climbing. In a workmanlike manner she
stripped off her jersey, hung it on a grey-green spike of

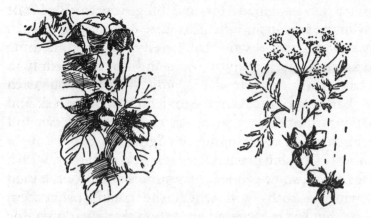

thistle, rubbed her palms together (in front of Homily she did not like to spit on them), and clambered up the bank.

Homily watched below, her two hands clasped and pressed against her heart, how the outer leaves shivered and shook as Arrietty, invisible, climbed up inside. 'Are you all right?' she kept calling. 'Oh, Arrietty, do be careful. Suppose you fell and broke your leg?' And then after a while the nuts began to come down, and poor Homily, under fire, ran this way and that, in her panting efforts to retrieve them.

Not that they came down fast enough to be really dangerous. Nut-gathering was not quite so easy as

Arrietty had imagined: for one thing, it was still a little early in the season and the nuts were not quite ripe; each was still encased in what to Arrietty looked something like a tough, green foxglove bell, and was fixed firmly to the tree. It was quite an effort, until she learned the trick of a sharp twist, for Arrietty to detach the clusters. And what was more, even to reach them was not easy: it meant climbing or swinging or edging her body along a perilously swaying branch tip (later Pod made her, with a piece of lead, some twine, and a supple dock root, a kind of swinging cosh with which she could strike them down); but she persevered, and soon there was a sizable pile in the ditch, neatly stacked up by the perspiring Homily.

'That'll do now,' Homily called out breathlessly after a while. 'No more or your poor pa will never get through with the digging,' and Arrietty, hot and dishevelled, with scratched face and smarting hands, thankfully climbed down. She flung herself full length in the speckled shade of a clump of cow-parsley and complained of feeling thirsty.

'Well, there's water farther along, so your pa says. Do you think you could walk it?'

Of course Arrietty could walk it. Tired she might be, but determined to foster this new-found spirit of adventure in her mother. She caught up her jersey and they set off along the ditch.

The sun was higher now and the ground was hotter. They came to a place where some beetles were eating a long-dead mole. 'Don't look,' said Homily, quickening her step and averting her eyes, as though it were a street accident.

But Arrietty, more practical for once, said: 'But when they've finished, perhaps we ought to have the skin. It might come in useful,' she pointed out, 'for winter.'

'Winter . . .' breathed Homily. 'You say it to torment me,' she added in a sudden spurt of temper.

The stream when they reached it seemed less a stream than a small clear pond, disturbed as they approached by several plops and spreading silvery circles as the frogs, alarmed, dived in. It meandered out of a tangled wood beyond the hedge and, crossing the corner of the field, had spread into a small marsh of cresses, mud, and deep-sunk cattle-tracks. On the farther side of the stream the field was bounded, not by a junction of hedges but by several mildewed posts hung with rusty wire slung across the water; beyond this frail barrier the shadowed tree trunks of the wood seemed to crowd and glower as though they longed to rush forward across the strip of water into the sunlit field. Arrietty saw a powdery haze of wild forget-me-not, with here and there a solitary bulrush; the dry-edged cattle-tracks were water-filled chasms criss-crossed with dikes and there was a delicious smell of fragrant slime, lightly spiced with spearmint. A sinuous feathered current of clear ripples broke the still, sky-reflecting surface of the miniature lake. It was very beautiful, Arrietty thought, and strangely exciting; she had never seen so much water before.

'Watercress!' announced Homily in a flat voice. 'We'll take a bit o' that for tea . . .'

They picked their way along the raised ridges of the cow craters whose dark pits of stagnant water reflected the cloudless sky. Arrietty, stooping over them, saw her own clear image sharply focused against the dreaming blue, but oddly tilted and somehow upside-down.

'Careful you don't fall in, Arrietty,' warned Homily, 'you only got one change, remember. You know,' she went on in an interested voice, pointing at a bulrush, 'I could have used one of those back home, under the kitchen. Just the thing for cleaning out the flues. Wonder your father never thought of it. And don't drink yet,' advised Homily, 'wait till we get where the water's running. Same with watercress, you don't want to pick it where the water's stagnant. You never know what you might get.'

At last they found a place from where it would be possible to drink: a solid piece of bark, embedded firmly in the mud yet stretching out into the stream forming a kind of landing stage or rough jetty. It was grey and nobbly and looked like a basking crocodile. Arrietty stretched her length on the corklike surface and cupping her hands took long draughts of the cool water. Homily, after some hesitation and arrangements of skirts, did the same. 'Pity,' she remarked, 'we don't have a jug nor a pail, nor some kind of bottle. We could do with some water in the boot.'

Arrietty did not reply; she was gazing happily down past the drifting surface into the depths below.

'Can vegetarians eat fish?' she asked, after a while.

'I don't rightly know,' said Homily; 'we'll have to ask your father.' Then the cook in Homily reasserted itself. 'Are there any?' she asked, a trifle hungrily.

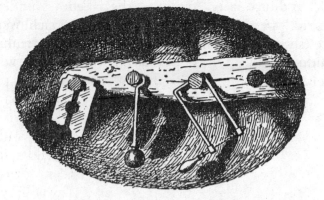

'Plenty,' Arrietty murmured dreamily, gazing down into the shifting depths: the stream, she thought, seemed to be gently breathing. 'About as long as my forearm. And some invisible things,' she added, 'like shrimps—'

'How do you mean – *invisible*?' asked Homily.

'Well,' explained Arrietty in the same absent voice, 'I mean you can see through them. And some black things,' she went on, 'like blobs of expanding velvet—'

'Leeches, I shouldn't wonder,' remarked Homily with a slight shudder, and added dubiously after a moment's thought: 'Might be all right stewed.'

'Do you think papa could make a fishing-net?' asked Arrietty.

'Your father can make anything,' asserted Homily loyally. 'No matter what – you've only got to name it.'

Arrietty lay quiet for a while, dozing she seemed on this sun-soaked piece of bark, and when at last she spoke Homily gave a startled jump – she, too, lulled for once into quietness, had begun to float away. 'Never do,' she thought, 'to drop off to sleep on a log like this: you might turn over.' And she roused herself by an inward shake and rapidly blinked her eyes.

'What did you say, Arrietty?' she asked.

'I said,' Arrietty went on after a moment in a lilting lazy voice (she spoke as though she too had been dreaming), 'couldn't we bring the boot down here? Right beside the water?'

Chapter Eight

'EVERY MAN'S HOUSE IS HIS CASTLE'
Great Fire of London began 1666
[*Extract from Arrietty's Diary and Proverb Book, September 2nd.*]

And that is just what they did do. Pod, consulted, had looked over the site, weighed the pros and cons, and rather ponderously, as though it was his own idea, decided they should move camp. They would choose a site farther along the hedge as near as was safe to the brook. 'Homily can do her washing. You got to have water,' he announced, but rather defensively as though he had only just thought of it. 'And I *might* make a fish-net, at that.'

The boot, though fully loaded, ran quite easily along the shallow ditch with all three of them in harness. The site Pod had chosen was a platform or alcove half-way up the steepish bank below the hedge.

'You want to keep fairly high,' he explained (as, to make it lighter for hauling, they unpacked the boot in the ditch), 'with rain like we had the other night and the brook so near. You got to remember,' he went on, selecting a sharp tool, 'that flood we had back home when the kitchen boiler burst.'

'What do you mean?' sniffed Homily, 'got to remember? Scalding hot, that one was, too.' She straightened her back and gazed up the slope at the site.

It was well chosen: a kind of castle, Arrietty had called it, in which they would live in the dungeons, but in their case the dungeon was more like an alcove, open to the sun and air. A large oak-tree, at one time part of the hedge, had been sawn off at the base; solid and circular, it stood above the bank where the hedge thinned, like the keep of a fortress, its roots flung out below as flying buttresses. Some of these were not quite dead and had shot forth here and there a series of suckers like miniature oak-trees. One of these saplings overhung their cave, shading its lip with sun-flecked shadow.

The underside of a large root formed the roof of their alcove and other smaller roots supported the walls and floor. These, last, Pod pointed out, would come in handy as beams and shelves.

He was busy now (while the boot still lay in the ditch) extracting some nails from the heel.

'It seems a shame,' remarked Homily as she and Arrietty sorted out belongings for earlier transportation. 'You'll loosen the whole heel.'

'What good's the heel to us?' asked Pod, perspiring with effort; 'we ain't going to wear the boot. And I need the nails,' he added firmly.

The flat top of the tree-trunk, they decided, would come in useful as a look-out, a bleaching ground for washing, and a place for drying herbs and fruit. Or for grinding corn. Pod was urged to chip out foot-holes in the bank for easier climbing. (This he did later, and for years after these foot-holes were considered by naturalists to be the work of the greater spotted woodpecker.)

'We got to dig a cache for these nuts,' remarked Pod, straightening his aching back, 'but better we get all ship-shape here first and snug for the night, as you might say. Then after the digging we can come home straight to bed.'

Seven nails, Pod decided, were enough for the moment (it was tough work extracting them). The idea had come to him when he had been mending the hole in the toe. Heretofore he had only worked on the softest of glove leathers and his little cobbler's needle was too frail to pierce the tough hide of the boot. Using the electric bell-clapper as a hammer, he had pierced (with the help of a nail) a series of matching holes – in the boot itself and the tongue which was meant to patch it; then all he had to do was to thread in some twine.

By the same token, he had made a few eyelet holes round the ankle of the boot so they could, if necessary, lash it up at night – as campers would close a tent flap.

It did not take them long to drag the empty boot up the slope, but wedging it firmly in the right position under the main root of the alcove was a tricky business and took a good deal of manoeuvring. At last it was done – and they left panting but relieved.

The boot lay on its side, sole against the rear wall and ankle facing outwards, so that if disturbed at night they could spot the intruder approaching, and when they woke in the morning they would get the early sun.

Pod drove a series of nails along one shelf-like root on the right wall of the alcove (the left wall was almost completely taken up by the boot), on which he hung his tools: the half-nail scissor, the fret-saw, the bell-clapper, and the piece of razor-blade.

Above this shelf was a sandy recess which Homily could use as a larder; it went in quite deep.

When Pod had placed the larger hat-pin in a place of strategic importance near the mouth of the alcove (the smaller one they were to keep in the boot in case, Pod said, 'of these alarms at night') they felt they had met the major demands of the moment and, though tired, they felt a pleasant sense of achievement and of effort well spent.

'Oh, my back,' exclaimed Homily, her hands in the small of it. 'Let's just sit down, Pod, for a moment and rest quietly and look at the view.' And it was worth looking at in the afternoon sunlight: they could see right across the field. A pheasant flew out of the far group of trees and whirred away to the left.

'We can't sit for long,' said Pod, after a moment; 'we got to dig that cache.'

Wearily, they collected the half nail-scissor and a borrowing-bag for anything they might see on the way, and the three of them climbed down the bank.

'Never mind,' Pod comforted Homily as they made their way along the ditch, 'we can go straight to bed after. And you haven't got no cooking,' he reminded her.

Homily was not comforted. As well as tired she realized suddenly she was feeling very hungry, but not – she reflected glumly – somehow, for nuts.

When they reached the place and Pod had removed the first sods in order to reach the soil (great shrubs these were to him, like uprooting clumps of pampas), Homily revived a little – determined to play her part: courageous helpmate, it was to-day. She had never dug before but the prospect faintly excited her. Strange things are possible in this odd world and she might (one never knew) discover a new talent.

They had to take it in turns with the half nail-scissor. ('Never mind,' Pod told them. 'I'll set to work to-morrow and rig us up a couple of spades.')

Homily screamed when she saw her first worm: it was as long as she was – even longer, she realized as the last bit wriggled free. 'Pick it up,' shouted Pod; 'it won't hurt you. You got to learn.' And before Arrietty (who was not too keen on worms herself) could volunteer to help, she saw her mother, with set face and tensed muscles, lay hold of the writhing creature and drop it some inches beyond the hole, where gratefully it writhed away among

the grasses. 'It was heavy,' Homily remarked – her only comment – as she went back to her digging; but Arrietty thought she looked a trifle pale. After her third worm, Homily became slightly truculent – she handled it with the professional casualness of an experienced snake-charmer – almost bored, she seemed. Arrietty was much impressed. It was a different story, however, when her mother dug up a centipede – then Homily not only screamed but ran, clutching her skirts, half-way up the bank, where she stood on a flat stone, almost gibbering. She only consented to rejoin them when Pod, tickling the squirming creature with the tip of the nail-scissor, sent it scuttling angrily into the 'bush.'

They carried a few nuts home for supper: these, and several wild strawberries, a leaf or two of watercress, washed down with cold water, made an adequate though dismal repast. There seemed to be something lacking; a bit of digestive biscuit would have been nice, or a good cup of hot tea. But the last piece of biscuit, Homily decided, must be kept for breakfast, and the tea (Pod had ordained) only for celebrations and emergencies.

But they slept well all the same; and felt safe, tucked away under their protecting root, with the boot laced up in front. It was a little airless, perhaps, but they were far less cramped for space because so many of their belongings could be stacked outside now in the sandy, root-filled annexe.

Chapter Nine

'AS YE SOW, SO SHALL YE REAP'
Oliver Cromwell, Protector of England, died 1658
[*Extract from Arrietty's Diary and Proverb Book, September 3rd.*]

'Now, to-day,' said Pod, at breakfast next morning, 'we'd better go gleaning. There's a harvested cornfield yonder. Nuts and fruit is all right,' he went on, 'but for winter we're going to need bread.'

'Winter?' moaned Homily. 'Aren't we supposed to be looking for the badgers' set? And,' she went on, 'who's going to grind the corn?'

'You and Arrietty, couldn't you?' said Pod, 'between two stones.'

'You'll be asking us to make fire with two sticks next,' grumbled Homily, 'and how do you think I can make bread without an oven? And what about yeast? Now, if you ask me,' she went on, 'we don't want to go gleaning and trying to make bread and all that nonsense: what we want to do is put a couple of nuts in our pockets, pick what fruit we see on the way, and have a real good look for the Hendrearies.'

'As you say,' agreed Pod, after a moment, and heaved a sigh.

They tidied away breakfast, put the more precious of their belongings inside the boot and carefully laced it up, and struck out uphill, beyond that water, along the hedge which lay at right angles to the bank in which they had passed the night.

It was a weary trapes. Their only adventure was at midday, when they rested after a frugal luncheon of rain-sodden, overripe blackberries. Homily, lying back against the bank, her drowsy eyes fixed on the space between a stone and a log, saw the ground begin to move; it streamed past the gap, in a limited but constant flow.

'Oh, my goodness, Pod,' she breathed, after watching a moment to make sure it was not an optical illusion, 'do you see what I see? There, by that log . . .' Pod, following the direction of her eyes, did not speak straight away, and when he did it was hardly above a whisper.

'Yes,' he said, seeming to hesitate, 'it's a snake.'

'Oh, my goodness . . .' breathed Homily again in a trembling voice, and Arrietty's heart began to beat wildly.

'Don't move,' whispered Pod, his eyes on the steady ripple: there seemed to be no end – the snake went on and on and on (unless it was, as Arrietty thought afterwards, that Time itself, in a moment of danger, has often been said to slow down), but just when they felt they could bear the sight not a moment longer, they saw the flick of a tail.

They all breathed again. 'What was it, Pod?' asked Homily weakly. 'An adder?'

'A grass snake, I think,' said Pod.

'Oh,' exclaimed Arrietty, with a relieved little laugh, 'they're harmless.'

Pod looked at her gravely; his currant-bunnish face seemed more doughy than usual. 'To humans,' he said slowly. 'And what's more,' he added, 'you can't talk to snakes.'

'Pity,' remarked Homily, 'that we did not bring one of the hat-pins.'

'What good would that have done?' asked Pod.

By about tea-time (rose-hips, this time: they were sick of sodden blackberries) they found, to their surprise, that

they were more than half-way along the third side of the field. There had been more walking than searching; none of the ground they had covered so far could have housed the Hendrearies, let alone a badger colony; the bank, as they made their way uphill beside the hedge, had become lower in proportion until, here where they sat drearily munching rose-hips, there was no bank at all.

'It's almost as far now,' said Pod, 'to go back the same way as we came as to keep on round. What do you say, Homily?'

'We better keep on round, then,' said Homily hoarsely, a hairy seed of a rose-hip being stuck in her throat. She began to cough. 'I thought you said you cleaned them?' she complained to Arrietty, when she could get back her breath.

'I must have missed one,' said Arrietty. 'Sorry,' and she passed her mother a new half-hip, freshly scoured; she had rather enjoyed opening the pale scarlet globes and scooping out the golden nest of close-packed seeds, and she liked the flavour of the hips themselves – they tasted, she thought, of apple-skins honeyed over with a dash of rose petal.

'Well, then,' said Pod, standing up, 'we better start moving.'

The sun was setting when they reached the fourth and last side of the field, where the hedge threw out a ragged carpet of shadow. Through a gap in the dark branches they could see a blaze of golden light on a sea of harvested stubble.

'As we're here,' suggested Pod, standing still and staring through the gap, 'and it's pretty well downhill most of the way back now, what's the harm in an ear or two of corn?'

'None,' said Homily wearily, 'if it would walk out and follow us.'

'Corn ain't heavy,' said Pod; 'wouldn't take us no time to pick up a few ears . . .'

Homily sighed. It was she who had suggested this trip, after all. In for a penny, she decided wanly, in for a pound.

'Have it your own way,' she said resignedly.

So they clambered through the hedge and into the cornfield.

And into a strange world (as it seemed to Arrietty), not like the Earth at all: the golden stubble, lit by the evening sun, stood up in rows like a blasted colourless forest; each separate bole threw its own long shadow and all the shadows, combined by the sun in one direction, lay parallel – a bizarre criss-cross of black and gold which flicked and fleckered with every footstep. Between the boles, on the dry straw-strewn earth, grew scarlet pimpernel in plenty, with here and there a ripened ear of wheat.

'Take a bit of stalk, too,' Pod advised them. 'Makes it easier to carry.'

The light was so strange in this broken, beetle-haunted

forest that, every now and again, Arrietty seemed to lose sight of her parents but, turning panic-stricken, would find them again quite close, zebra-striped with sun and shadow.

At last they could carry no more and Pod had mercy; they forgathered on their own side of the hedge, each with two bundles of wheat ears, carried head downwards by a short length of stalks. Arrietty was reminded of Crampfurl, back home in the big house, going past the grating with onions for the kitchen; they had been strung on strings and looked much like these corn giants and in something the same proportion.

'Can you manage all that?' asked Pod anxiously of Homily as she started off ahead down the hill.

'I'd sooner carry it than grind it,' retorted Homily tartly, without looking back.

'There wouldn't be no badgers' sets along this side,' panted Pod (he was carrying the heaviest load), coming abreast of Arrietty. 'Not with all the ploughing, sowing, dogs, men, horses, harrows, and what-not as there must have been—'

'Where could one be, then?' asked Arrietty, setting down her corn for a moment to rest her hands. 'We've been all round.'

'There's only one place to look now,' said Pod; 'them trees in the middle,' and standing still in the deep shadow, he gazed across the stretch of pasture land. The field looked in this light much as it had on that first day (could that only be the day before yesterday?). But from this angle they could not see the trail of dusky shadow thrown by the island of trees.

'Open ground,' said Pod, staring; 'your mother would never make it.'

'I could,' said Arrietty. 'I'd like to go . . .'

Pod was silent. 'I got to think,' he said, after a moment. 'Come on, lass. Take up your corn, else we won't get back before dark.'

They didn't. Or, rather, it was deep dusk along the ditch of their home stretch and almost dark when they came abreast of their cave. But even in the half-light there seemed something suddenly home-like and welcoming about the sight of their laced-up boot.

Homily sank down at the foot of the bank, between her bunches of corn. 'Just a breather,' she explained weakly, 'before the next pull up.'

'Take your time,' said Pod. 'I'll go ahead and undo the laces.' Panting a little, dragging his ears of corn, he started up the bank. Arrietty followed.

'Pod,' called Homily from the darkness below, without turning, 'you know what?'

'What?' asked Pod.

'It's been a long day,' said Homily; 'suppose, to-night, we made a nice cup of tea?'

'Please yourself,' said Pod, unlacing the neck of the boot and feeling cautiously inside. He raised his voice, shouting down at her: 'What you have now, you can't have later. Bring the half-scissor, Arrietty, will you? It's on a nail in the store-room.' After a moment he added impatiently: 'Hurry up. No need to take all day, it's just there to your hand.'

'It isn't,' came Arrietty's voice, after a moment.

'What do you mean – it isn't?'

'It isn't here. Everything else is, though.'

'Isn't there!' exclaimed Pod unbelievingly. 'Wait a minute, let *me* look.' Their voices sounded muffled to Homily, listening below; she wondered what the fuss was about.

'Something or someone's been mucking about in here,' she heard Pod say, after what seemed a distressed pause; and picking up her ears of wheat Homily scrambled up the bank: heavy going, she found it, in the half-light.

'Get a match, will you,' Pod was saying in a worried voice, 'and light the candle,' and Arrietty foraged in the boot to find the wax-vestas.

As the wick guttered, wavered, then rose to a steady flame, the little hollow, half-way up the bank, became illumined like a scene on a stage; strange shadows were cast on the sandy walls of the annexe. Pod and Homily and little Arrietty appeared as they passed back and forth curiously unreal, like characters in a play. There were the borrowing-bags, stacked neatly together as Pod had left them, their mouths tied up with twine; there hung the tools from their beam-like root, and, leaning beside them – as Pod had left it this morning – the purple thistle-head with which he had swept the floor. He stood there now, white-faced in the candlelight, his hand on a bare nail. 'It was here,' he was saying, tapping the nail; 'that's where I left it.'

'Oh, goodness!' exclaimed Homily, setting down her wheat ears. 'Let's just look again.' She pulled aside the borrowing-bags and felt behind them. 'And you, Arrietty,' she ordered, 'could you get round to the back of the boot?'

But it was not there, nor, they discovered suddenly, was the larger hat-pin. 'Anything but them two things,'

Pod kept on saying in a worried voice as Homily, for the third or fourth time, went through the contents of the boot. 'The smaller hat-pin's here all right,' she kept repeating, 'we still got one. You see no animal could unlace a boot—'

'But what kind of animal,' asked Pod wearily, 'would take a half nail-scissor?'

'A magpie might,' suggested Arrietty, 'if it looked kind of shiny.'

'Maybe,' said Pod. 'But what about the hat-pin? I don't see a magpie carrying the two. No,' he went on thoughtfully, 'it doesn't look to me like no magpie, nor like any other race of bird. Nor no animal neither, if it comes to that. Nor I wouldn't say it was any kind of human being. A human being, like as not, finding a hole like this smashes the whole place up. Kind of kick with their feet, human beings do out walking 'fore they touch a thing with their hands. Looks to me,' said Pod, 'like something more in the style of a borrower.'

'Oh,' cried Arrietty joyfully, 'then we've found them!'

'Found what?' asked Pod.

'The cousins . . . the Hendrearies . . .'

Pod was silent a moment. 'Maybe,' he said uneasily again.

'Maybe!' mimicked Homily, irritated. 'Who else could it be? They live in this field, don't they? Arrietty, put some water on to boil, there's a good girl; we don't want to waste the candle.'

'Now see here—' began Pod.

'But we can't fix the tin-lid,' interrupted Arrietty, 'without the ring part of the nail-scissor.'

'Oh, goodness me,' complained Homily, 'use your head and think of something! Suppose we'd never had a nail-scissor! Tie a piece of twine round an aspirin lid and hang it over the flame from a nail or a bit of root or something. What were you saying, Pod?'

'I said we got to go careful on the tea, that's all. We was only going to make tea to celebrate like, or in what you might call a case of grave emergency.'

'Well, we are, aren't we?'

'Are what?' asked Pod.

'Celebrating. Looks like we've found what we come for.'

Pod glanced uneasily towards Arrietty who, in the farther corner of the annexe, was busily knotting twine round a ridged edge of a screw-on lid. 'You don't want to go so fast, Homily,' he warned her, lowering his voice, 'nor you don't want to jump to no conclusions. Say it was one of the Hendrearies. All right then, why didn't they leave a word or sign or stay a while and wait for us? Hendreary knows our gear all right – that Proverb book of Arrietty's, say, many's the time he's seen it back home under the kitchen.'

'I don't see what you're getting at,' said Homily in a puzzled voice, watching Arrietty anxiously as gingerly she suspended the water-filled aspirin lid from a root above the candle. 'Careful,' she called out, 'you don't want to burn the twine.'

'What I'm getting at is this,' explained Pod. 'Say you look at the nail-scissor as a blade, a sword, as you might say, and the hat-pin as a spear, say, or a dagger. Well, whoever took them things has armed himself, see what I mean? And left us weaponless.'

'We got the other hat-pin,' said Homily in a troubled voice.

'Maybe,' said Pod, 'but he doesn't know that. See what I mean?'

'Yes,' whispered Homily, subdued.

'Make tea, if you like,' Pod went on, 'but I wouldn't call it a celebration. Not yet, at any rate.'

Homily glanced unhappily towards the candle: above the aspirin lid (she noticed longingly) already there rose a welcome haze of steam. 'Well,' she began, and hesitated, then suddenly she seemed to brighten, 'it comes to the same thing.'

'How do you mean?' asked Pod.

'About the tea,' explained Homily, perking up. 'Going by what you said, stealing our weapons and such – this looks to be something you might call serious. Depends how it strikes you. I mean,' she went on hurriedly, 'there's some I know as might even name it a state of grave emergency.'

'There's some as might,' agreed Pod wanly. Then, suddenly, he sprang aside, beating the air with his hands.

Arrietty screamed and Homily, for a second, thought they had both gone mad. Then she saw.

A great moth had lumbered into the alcove, attracted by the candle; it was fawn-coloured and (to Homily) hideous, drunk, and blinded with light. 'Save the tea !' she cried, panic-stricken, and seizing the purple thistle-head, beat wildly about the air. Shadows danced every way and, in their shouting and scolding, they hardly noticed a sudden, silent thickening of night swerve in on the dusk; but they felt the wind of its passing, watched the candle gutter, and saw the moth was gone.

'What was that ?' asked Arrietty at last, after an awed silence.

'It was an owl,' said Pod. He looked thoughtful.

'It ate the moth ?'

'As it would eat you,' said Pod, 'if you went mucking about after dusk. We're living and learning,' he said. 'No more candles after dark. Up with the sun and down with the sun: that's us, from now on.'

'The water's boiling, Pod,' said Homily.

'Put the tea in,' said Pod, 'and douse the light: we can drink all right in the dark,' and turning away he propped the broom handle back against the wall and, while Homily was making the tea, he tidied up the annexe, stacking the ears of wheat alongside the boot, straightening the borrowing-bags, and generally seeing all was shipshape for the night. When he had finished he crossed to the recessed shelf and ran a loving hand along his neatly hanging row of tools. Just before they doused the light, he stood for a long time, deep in thought – a quiet hand on a grimly empty nail.

Chapter Ten

'LIKE TURNS TO LIKE'
Republic declared in France, 1870
[*Extract from Arrietty's Diary and Proverb Book, September 4th.*]

They slept well and woke next morning bright and early. The sun poured slantwise into the alcove and, when Pod had unlaced it, into the neck of the boot. For breakfast Arrietty gathered six wild strawberries and Homily broke up some wheat grains with Pod's small bell-clapper which, sprinkled with water, they ate as cereal. 'And, if you're still hungry, Arrietty,' remarked Homily, 'you can get yourself a nut.' Arrietty was and did.

The programme for the day was arranged as follows: Pod, in view of last night's happening, was to make a solitary expedition across the field to the island of trees in the centre in one last bid to find the badgers' set. Homily, because of her fear of open spaces, would have to stay behind, and Arrietty, Pod said, must keep her company. 'There's plenty of jobs about the house,' he told them. 'To start with you can weather-proof one of the borrowing-bags, rub it all over hard with a bit of candle, and it'll do for carting water. Then you can take the fret-saw and saw off a few hazel-nuts for drinking out of, and while you're about it you can gather a few extra nuts and store them in the annexe, seeing as we don't have a spade. There's a nice bit o' horse-hair I saw, in the hedge going towards the stile, caught on a bramble bush; you can fetch a bit o' that along, if you feel like it, and I'll see about making a fish-net. And a bit more corn-crushing wouldn't come amiss . . .'

'Oh, come on, Pod,' protested Homily. 'Oblige you we'd like to, but we're not slaves . . .'

'Well,' said Pod, gazing thoughtfully across the ocean of tussocky grass, 'it'll take me pretty near all day – getting there, searching around, and getting back : I don't want you fretting . . .'

'I knew it would end like this,' said Homily later, in a depressed voice, as she and Arrietty were waxing the borrowing-bag. 'What did I tell you always, back home, when you wanted to emigrate ? Didn't I tell you just how it would be – draughts, moths, worms, snakes, and what not ? And you saw how it was when it rained ? What's it going to be like in winter ? You tell me that. No one can say I'm not trying,' she went on, 'and no one won't hear a word of grumble pass my lips, but you mark my words, Arrietty ; we won't none of us see another spring.' And a round tear fell on the waxed cloth and rolled away like a marble.

'What with the rat-catcher,' Arrietty pointed out, 'we wouldn't have if we'd stayed back home.'

'And I wouldn't be surprised,' Homily persisted, 'if that boy wasn't right. Remember what he said about the end of the race ? Our time is come, I shouldn't wonder. If you ask me, we're dying out.'

But she cheered up a bit when they took the bag down to the water to fill it up and a sliver of soap to wash with : the drowsy heat and the gentle stir of ripples past their landing-stage of bark seemed always to calm her ; and she even encouraged Arrietty to have a bath and let her splash about a little in the shallows. For a being so light the water was incredibly buoyant and it would not be very long, Arrietty felt, before she would learn to swim. Where she had used the soap the water went cloudy and softly translucent, the shifting colour of moonstones.

After her bath Arrietty felt refreshed and left Homily in the annexe to 'get the tea' and went on up the hedge to collect the horse-hair (not that there was anything to 'get,' Homily thought irritably, setting out a few hips and haws, some watercress, and, with the bell-clapper, she cracked a couple of nuts).

The horse-hair, caught on a bramble, was half-way up the hedge, but Arrietty, refreshed by her dip, was glad of a chance to climb. On the way down, seeking a foot-hold, she let out a tiny scream; her toes had touched, not the cool bark, but something soft and warm. She hung there, grasping the horse-hair and staring through the leaves: all was still — nothing but tangled branches, flecked with sunlight. After a second or two, in which she did not dare to move, a flicker of movement caught her eye, as though the tip of a branch had moved. Staring she saw, like a bunch of budding twigs, the shape of a brownish hand. It could not be a hand, of course, she told herself, but that's what it looked like, with tiny, calloused fingers no larger than her own. Picking up courage, she touched it with her foot and the hand grasped her toes. Screaming and struggling, she lost her balance and came tumbling through the few remaining branches on to the dead leaves below. With her had fallen a small laughing creature no taller than herself. 'That frighted you,' it said.

Arrietty stared, breathing quickly. He had a brown face, black eyes, tousled dark hair, and was dressed in what she guessed to be shabby moleskin, worn smooth side out. He seemed so soiled and earth-darkened that he matched not only the dead leaves into which they had fallen but the blackened branches as well. 'Who are you?' she asked.

'Spiller,' he said cheerfully, lying back on his elbows.

'You're filthy,' remarked Arrietty disgustedly after a
moment; she still felt breathless and very angry.

'Maybe,' he said.

'Where do you live?'

His dark eyes became sly and amused. 'Here and
there,' he said, watching her closely.

'How old are you?'

'I don't know,' he said.

'Are you a boy or a grown-up?'

'I don't know,' he said.

'Don't you ever wash?'

'No,' he said.

'Well,' said Arrietty, after an awkward silence, twisting the coarse strands of greyish horse-hair about her
wrist, 'I'd better be going—'

'To that hole in the bank?' he asked – the hint of a jeer
in his voice.

Arrietty looked startled. 'Do you know it?' When
he smiled, she noticed, his lips turned steeply upwards
at the corners making his mouth a 'V': it was the most

teasing kind of smile she had ever seen.

'Haven't you ever seen a moth before?' he asked.

'You were watching last night?' exclaimed Arrietty.

'Were it private?' he asked.

'In a way; it's our home.'

But he looked bored suddenly, turning his bright gaze away as though searching the more distant grasses. Arrietty opened her mouth to speak but he silenced her with a peremptory gesture, his eyes on the field below. Very curious, she watched him rise cautiously to his feet and then, in a single movement, spring to a branch above his head, reach for something out of sight, and drop again to the ground. The object, she saw, was a taut, dark bow strung with gut and almost as tall as he was; in the other hand he held an arrow.

Staring into the long grass he laid the arrow to the bow, the gut twanged, and the arrow was gone. There was a faint squeak.

'You've killed it,' cried Arrietty, distressed.

'I meant to,' he replied, and sprang down the bank into the field. He made his way to the tussock of grass and returned after a moment with a dead field-mouse swinging from his hand. 'You got to eat,' he explained.

Arrietty felt deeply shocked, she did not know quite why — at home, under the kitchen, they had always eaten meat; but borrowed meat from the kitchen upstairs; she had seen it raw but she had never seen it killed.

'We're vegetarians,' she said primly. He took no notice: this was just a word to Spiller, one of the noises which people made with their mouths. 'Do you want some meat?' he asked casually. 'You can have a leg.'

'I wouldn't touch it,' cried Arrietty indignantly. She rose to her feet, brushing down her skirt. 'Poor thing,' she said, referring to the field-mouse, 'and I think you're horrid,' she said, referring to him.

'Who isn't?' remarked Spiller, and reached above his head for his quiver.

'Let me look,' begged Arrietty, turning back, suddenly curious.

He passed it to her. It was made, she saw, of a glove finger – the thickish leather of a country glove; the arrows were dry pine-needles, weighted, and tipped with blackthorn.

'How do you stick the thorns to the shaft?' she asked.

'Wild-plum-gum,' sang out Spiller, all in one word.

'Wild-plum-gum?' repeated Arrietty. 'Are they poisoned?' she asked.

'No,' said Spiller, 'fair's fair. Hit or miss. They got to eat – I got to eat. And I kill 'em quicker than an owl does. Nor I don't eat so many.' It was quite a long speech for Spiller. He slung his quiver over his shoulder and turned away. 'I'm going,' he said.

Arrietty scrambled quickly down the bank. 'So am I,' she told him.

They walked along in the dry ditch together. Spiller, she noticed, as he walked glanced sharply about him: the bright black eyes were never still. Sometimes, at a slight rustle in grass or hedge, he would become motionless: there would be no tensing of muscles – he would just cease to move; on such occasions, Arrietty realized, he exactly matched his background. Once he dived into a clump of dead bracken and came out again with a struggling insect.

'Here you are,' he said, and Arrietty, staring, saw some kind of angry beetle.

'What is it?' she asked.

'A cricket. They're nice. Take it.'

'To eat?' asked Arrietty, aghast.

'Eat? No. You take it home and keep it. Sings a treat,' he added.

Arrietty hesitated. 'You carry it,' she said, without committing herself.

When they came abreast of the alcove, Arrietty looked up and saw that Homily, tired of waiting, had dozed off: she was sitting on the sunlit sand and had slumped against the boot.

'Mother,' she called softly from below, and Homily woke at once. 'Here's Spiller . . .' Arrietty went on, a trifle uncertainly.

'Here's what?' asked Homily, without interest. 'Did you get the horse-hair?'

Arrietty, glancing sideways at Spiller, saw that he was in one of his stillnesses and had become invisible. 'It's my mother,' she whispered. 'Speak to her. Go on.'

Homily, hearing a whisper, peered down, screwing her eyelids against the setting sun.

'What shall I say?' asked Spiller. Then, clearing his voice, he made an effort. 'I got a cricket,' he said. Homily screamed. It took her a moment to add the dun-coloured patches together into the shapes of face, eyes, and hands; it was to Homily as though the grass had spoken.

'Whatever is it?' she gasped. 'Oh, my goodness gracious, whatever have you got there?'

'It's a cricket,' said Spiller again, but it was not to this insect Homily referred.

'It's Spiller,' Arrietty repeated more loudly, and in an aside she whispered to Spiller: 'Drop that dead thing and come on up . . .'

Spiller not only dropped the field-mouse but a fleeting echo of some dim, half-forgotten code must have flicked his memory, and he laid aside his bow as well. Unarmed, he climbed the bank.

Homily stared at Spiller rather rudely when he stepped on to the sandy platform before the boot. She moved right forward, keeping him at bay. 'Good afternoon,' she said coldly; it was as though she spoke from the threshold.

Spiller dropped the cricket and propelled it towards her with his toe. 'Here you are,' he said. Homily screamed again, very loudly and angrily, as the cricket scuttled knee high past her skirts and made for the darker shadow behind the boot. 'It's a present, Mother,' Arrietty explained indignantly. 'It's a cricket: it sings—'

But Homily would not listen. 'How dare you! How dare you! How dare you! You naughty, dirty, unwashed

boy.' She was nearly in tears. 'How could you? You go straight out of my house this minute. Lucky,' she went on, 'that my husband's not at home, nor my brother Hendreary neither—'

'Uncle Hendreary—' began Arrietty, surprised, and, if looks could kill, Arrietty would have died.

'Take your beetle,' Homily went on to Spiller, 'and go! And never let me see you here again!' As Spiller hesitated, she added in a fury: 'Do you hear what I say?'

Spiller threw a swift look towards the rear of the boot and a somewhat pathetic one towards Arrietty. 'You better keep it,' he muttered gruffly, and dived off down the bank.

'Oh, Mother!' exclaimed Arrietty reproachfully. She stared at the 'tea' her mother had set out, and even the fact that her mother had filled the half-hips with clover honey milked from the blooms failed to comfort her. 'Poor Spiller! You were rude—'

'Well, who is he? What does he want here? Where did you find him? Forcing his way on respectable people and flinging beetles about! Wouldn't be surprised if we all woke up one day with our throats cut. Did you see the dirt! Ingrained! I wouldn't be surprised if he hadn't left a flea,' and she seized the thistle-broom and briskly swept the spot where the miserable Spiller had placed his unwelcome feet. 'I never had such an experience as this. Never. Not in all my born days. Now, that's the type,' she concluded fiercely, 'who would steal a hat-pin!'

Secretly Arrietty thought so too but she did not say so, using her tongue instead to lick a little of the honey out of the split rose-hip. She also thought, as she savoured the sun-warmed honey, that Spiller, the huntsman, would make better use of the hat-pin than either her mother or father could. She wondered why he wanted the half nail-scissor. 'Have you had your tea ?' she asked Homily after a moment.

'I've eaten a couple of wheat grains,' admitted Homily in a martyred voice. 'Now I must air the bedding.'

Arrietty smiled, gazing out across the sunlit field: the bedding was one piece of sock – poor Homily with practically no housework had little now on which to vent her energy. Well, now she'd had Spiller and it had done her good – her eyes looked brighter and her cheeks pinker. Idly, Arrietty watched a small bird picking its way amongst the grasses – no, it was too steady for a bird. 'Here comes Papa,' she said after a moment.

They ran down to meet him. 'Well ?' cried Homily eagerly, but as they drew closer, she saw by his face that the news he brought was bad. 'You didn't find it ?' she asked in a disappointed voice.

'I found it all right,' said Pod.

'What's the matter then ? Why do you look so down ? You mean – they weren't there ? You mean – they've left ?'

'They've left, all right. Or been eaten.' Pod stared unhappily.

'What can you mean, Pod ?' stammered Homily.

'It's full o' foxes,' he told them ponderously, his eyes still round with shock. 'Smells awful . . .' he added after a moment.

Chapter Eleven

'MISFORTUNES MAKE US WISE'
Louis XIV of France born 1638
[*Extract from Arrietty's Diary and Proverb Book, September 5th.*]

Homily carried on a bit that evening. It was understandable – what were they faced with now? This kind of Robinson Crusoe existence for the rest of their lives? Raw food in the summer was bad enough but in the stark cold of winter, Homily protested, it could not sustain life. Not that they had the faintest chance of surviving the winter, anyway, without some form of heat. A bit of wax candle would not last for ever. Nor would their few wax-vestas. And supposing they made a fire of sticks, it would have to be colossal – an absolute conflagration it would appear to a borrower – to keep alight at all. And the smoke of this, she pointed out, would be seen for miles. No, she concluded gloomily, they were in for it now and no two ways about it, as Pod and Arrietty would see for themselves, poor things, when the first frost came.

It was the sight of Spiller, perhaps, which had shaken Homily, confirming her worst premonitions – uncouth, unwashed, dishonest, and ill-bred, that's what she summed him up to be, everything she most detested and feared. And this was the level (as she had often warned them back home) to which borrowers must sink if ever, for their sins, they took to the great outdoors.

To make matters worse, they were awakened that night by a strange sound – a prolonged and maniac bellow, it sounded to Arrietty, as she lay there trembling, breath held and heart racing. 'What was it?' she whispered to Pod, when at last she dare speak.

The boot creaked as Pod sat up in bed. 'It's a donkey,' he said, 'but close.' After a moment he added: 'Funny – I ain't ever seen a donkey hereabouts.'

'Nor I,' whispered Arrietty. But she felt somehow relieved and was just preparing to settle down again when another sound, closer, caught her ear. 'Listen!' she said sharply, sitting up.

'You don't want to lie awake listening,' Pod grumbled, turning over and pulling after him an unfair share of the sock. 'Not at night, you don't.'

'It's in the annexe,' whispered Arrietty.

The boot creaked again as Pod sat up. 'Keep quiet, Pod, do,' grumbled Homily, who had managed to doze off.

'Quiet yourself,' said Pod, trying to concentrate. It was a small whirring sound he heard, very regular. 'You're right,' he breathed to Arrietty, 'it's in the annexe.' He threw off the sock, which Homily clutched at angrily, pulling it back about her shoulders. 'I'm going out,' he said.

'No, Pod, you don't!' implored Homily huskily. 'We're all right here, laced up. Stay quiet—'

'No, Homily, I got to see.' He felt his way along the ankle of the boot. 'Stay quiet, the two of you, I won't be long.'

'Oh dear,' exclaimed Homily in a scared voice. 'Then take the hat-pin,' she implored nervously as she saw him begin to unthread the laces. Arrietty, watching, saw the boot fall open and her father's head and shoulders appear suddenly against the night sky; there was a scrabbling, a rustling, and a skittering – and Pod's voice shouting – 'Dang you . . . dang you . . . dang you!' Then there was silence.

Arrietty crept along the ankle of the boot and put her head out into the air; the alcove was filled with bright moonlight, and every object could be plainly seen. Arrietty stepped out and looked about her. A silvery Pod stood on the lip of the alcove, staring down at the moon-drenched field.

'What was it?' called Homily from the depths of the boot.

'Danged field-mice,' called Pod, 'been at the corn.'

And Arrietty saw in that pale, friendly light that the sandy floor of the annexe was strewn with empty husks.

'Well, that's that,' said Pod, turning back and kicking the scattered husks. 'Better get the thistle,' he added, 'and sweep up the mess.'

Arrietty did so, almost dancing. Enchanted, she felt, by this friendly radiance which lent an unfamiliar magic to even the most matter-of-fact objects – such as Pod's bell-clapper hanging from its nail and the whitened stitching on the boot. When she had made three neat piles of husks she joined Pod at the lip of the alcove and they sat silent for a while on the still warm sand, listening to the night.

An owl called from the spinney beside the brook – a fluting, musical note which was answered, at great distance, by a note as haunting in a slightly higher key, weaving a shuttle of sound back and forth across the sleeping pasture, linking the sea of moonlight and the velvet shadowed woods.

'Whatever the danger,' Arrietty thought, sitting there at peace beside her father, 'whatever the difficulty, I am still glad we came!'

'What we need in this place,' said Pod at last, breaking the long silence, 'is some kind of tin.'

'Tin?' repeated Arrietty vaguely, not sure she had understood.

'Or a couple of tins. A cocoa tin would do. Or one of them they use for baccy.' He was silent awhile, and then he added: 'That pit we dug weren't deep enough; bet them danged field-mice have been at the nuts.'

'Couldn't you learn to shoot a bow and arrow?' asked Arrietty after a moment.

'Whatever for?' asked Pod.

Arrietty hesitated, then, all in a breath, she told him about Spiller: the well-sprung bow, the thorn-tipped, deadly arrows. And she described how Spiller had been watching them from the darkness when they played out their scene with the moth on the stage of the lighted alcove.

'I don't like that,' said Pod after a moment's thought, 'not neighbours watching I don't like. Can't have that, you know. Not by night nor by day neither, it ain't healthy, if you get my meaning.'

Arrietty did get his meaning. 'What we want here is some kind of shutter or door. A piece of chicken wire might do. Or that cheese-grater, perhaps – the one we had at home. It would have to be something that lets the light in, I mean,' she went on. 'We can't go back to living in the dark.'

'I got an idea,' said Pod suddenly. He stood up and, turning about, craned his neck upwards to the overhang above. The slender sapling, silvery with moonlight, leaned above their bank. Pod stared a moment at the leaves against the sky as though calculating distances; then, looking down, he kicked about the sand with his feet.

'What is it?' whispered Arrietty, thinking he had lost something.

'Ah,' said Pod, in a pleased voice, and went down on his knees, 'this 'ould do.' And he shovelled about with his hands, uncovering, after a moment, a snaking loop of tough root – seemingly endless. 'Yes,' he repeated, 'this'll do fine.'

'What for?' asked Arrietty, wildly curious.

'Get me the twine,' said Pod. 'There on that shelf, where the tools are . . .'

Arrietty, standing on tiptoe, reached her hand into the sandy recess and found the ball of twine.

'Give it here,' said Pod, 'and get me the bell-clapper.'

Arrietty watched her father tie a length of twine on to the bell-clapper and, balancing a little perilously on the very edge of their terrace, take careful aim and, with a violent effort, fling the clapper up into the branches above, it caught hold, like an anchor, among a network of twigs.

'Now, come on,' said Pod to Arrietty, breathing steadily, 'take hold and pull. Gently does it . . . steady now. Gently . . . gently . . .' and leaning together their full weight on the twine, hand over hand they drew down the stooping branch. The alcove became dark suddenly with broken shadow, cut and trembling with filtered moonlight.

'Hold on,' panted Pod, guiding the twine to the loop of root, 'while I make her fast.' He gave a grunt. 'There,' he said, and stood up, rubbing the strain out of his hands (he was flecked all over, Arrietty noticed, with trembling blobs of silver), 'get me the half-scissor. Dang it, I forgot – the fret-saw will do.'

It was hard to lay hands on the fret-saw in this sudden darkness, but at last she found it and Pod cut his halyard. 'There,' he said again in a satisfied voice. 'She's fast – and we're covered. How's that for an idea? You can let her up or down, depending on what goes on, wind, weather, and all the rest of it . . .'

He removed the bell-clapper and made the twine fast to the main branch. 'Won't keep the field-mice out, nor them kind of cattle – but,' he gave a satisfied laugh, 'there won't be no more watching.'

'It's wonderful,' said Arrietty, her face among the leaves, 'and we can still see out.'

'That's the idea,' said Pod. 'Come on now: time we got back to bed!'

As they felt their way towards the mouth of the boot, Pod tripped against a pile of wheat-husks and stumbled, coughing, into their dusty scatter. As he stood up and brushed himself down, he remarked thoughtfully: 'Spiller – you said his name was?' He was silent a moment and then added thoughtfully: 'There's a lot worse food, when you come to think of it, than a piping-hot, savoury stew made of corn-fed field-mouse.'

Chapter Twelve

'OUT OF SIGHT, OUT OF MIND'
H.M.S. *Captain* lost, 1870
[*Extract from Arrietty's Diary and Proverb Book, September 7th.*]

Homily was in a worried mood next morning. 'What's all this?' she grumbled when, a little tousled, she crept out of the boot and saw that the alcove was filled with a greenish, underwater light.

'Oh, Mother,' exclaimed Arrietty reproachfully, 'it's lovely!' A faint breeze stirred the clustered leaves which, parting and closing, let pass bright spears and arrows of dancing light. A delightful blend of mystery and gaiety (or so it seemed to Arrietty). 'Don't you see,' she went on as its inventor preserved a hurt silence, 'Papa made it: it's quick cover – lets in the light but keeps out the rain; and we can see out but they can't see in.'

'Who's they?' asked Homily.

'Anything . . . anybody passing. Spiller,' she added on a gleam of inspiration.

Homily relented. 'H'mm,' she vouchsafed in a non-committal tone, but she examined the uncovered root in the floor, noted the running clove-hitch, and ran a thoughtful finger down the taut twine.

'The thing to remember,' Pod explained earnestly, aware of her tardy approval, 'is – when you let her go – keep hold of the halyard: you don't want this here halyard ever to leave the root. See what I mean?'

Homily saw. 'But you don't want to waste the sunshine,' she pointed out, 'not while it's summer, you

don't. Soon it will be—' She shuddered slightly and
tightened her lips, unable to say the word.

'Well, winter ain't here yet,' exclaimed Pod lightly.
'Sufficient unto the day, as they say.' He was busy with
the halyard. 'Here you are – up she goes!' and, as the
twine ran squeaking under the root, the leaves flew up out
of sight and the alcove leapt into sudden sunlight.

'See what I mean?' said Pod again in a satisfied voice.

During breakfast the donkey brayed again, loud and
long, and was answered almost at once by the neigh of a
horse.

'I don't like it,' said Homily suddenly, setting down her
half hazel-shell of honey and water. Even as she spoke a
dog yelped – too close for comfort. Homily started – and
over went the honey and water, a dark stain on the sandy
floor. 'Me nerves is all to pieces,' Homily wailed,
clapping her hands to her temples and looking from side
to side with wild eyes.

'It's nothing, Mother,' Arrietty explained, irritated.
'There's a lane just below the spinney: I saw it from the
top of the hedge. It's people passing, that's all; they're
bound to pass sometimes—'

'That's right,' agreed Pod, 'you don't want to worry.
You eat up your grain—'

Homily stared distastefully at the bitten-into grain of
corn, dry and hard as a breakfast roll three days after a
picnic. 'Me teeth ain't up to it,' she said unhappily.

'According to Arrietty,' explained Pod, holding up the
spread fingers of his left hand and knocking each back in
turn, 'between us and that lane we got five barriers: the
stream down at the corner – one; them posts with rusty
wire across the stream – two; a fair-sized wood – three;
another hedge – four; and a bit o' rough grazing ground –

five.' He turned to Arrietty. 'Ain't that right, lass? You been up the hedge?'

Arrietty agreed. 'But that bit of grazing ground belongs to the lane – a kind of grass verge.'

'There you are then,' exclaimed Pod triumphantly, slapping Homily on the back, 'Common land! And someone's tethered a donkey there. What's wrong with that? Donkeys don't eat you – no more don't horses.'

'A dog might,' said Homily. 'I heard a dog.'

'And what of it?' exclaimed Pod. 'It wasn't the first time and it won't be the last. When I was a lad, down at the big house, the place was awash with setters, as you might say. Dogs is all right: you can talk to dogs.'

Homily was silent a moment, rolling the wheat grain backwards and forwards on the flat piece of slate which they used as a table.

'It's no good,' she said at last.

'What's no good?' asked Pod, dismayed.

'Going on like this,' said Homily. 'We got to do something before winter.'

'Well, we are doing something, aren't we?' said Pod. He nodded towards Arrietty. 'Like it says in her book – Rome weren't built in a day.'

'Find some kind of human habitation,' went on Homily, 'that's what we've got to do – where there's fires and pickings and proper sort of cover.' She hesitated. 'Or,' she went on in a set, determined voice, 'we got to go back home.'

There was a stunned silence. 'We got to do what?' asked Pod weakly, when he could find his voice; and Arrietty, deeply upset, breathed: 'Oh, Mother—'

'You heard me, Pod,' said Homily; 'all these hips and haws and watercress and dogs barking and foxes in the badgers' set and creeping in the night and stealing and rain coming up and nothing to cook on. You see what I mean? Back home, in the big house, it wouldn't take us no time to put a few partitions up and get kind of straight again under the kitchen. We did it once, that time the boiler burst: we can do it again.'

Pod stared across at her and when he spoke he spoke with the utmost gravity. 'You don't know what you're saying, Homily. It's not just that they'll be waiting for us; that they've got the cat, set traps, laid down poison, and all that caper: it's just that you don't *go back*, Homily, not once you've come out, you don't. And we ain't *got* a home. That's all over and done with. Like it or not, we got to go on now. See what I mean?' When Homily did not reply, he turned his grave face to Arrietty.

'I'm not saying we're not up against it; we are – right up against it. More than I like to let on. And if we don't stick together, we're finished – see? And it will be the end – like you once said, Arrietty – the end of our race! Never let me hear another word from either one of you, you or your mother, about—' with great solemnity he slightly raised his voice, stressing each word, 'going back anywhere – let alone under the floor!'

They were very impressed; they both stared back at him, unable, for the moment, to speak.

'Understand?' asked Pod sternly.

'Yes, Papa,' whispered Arrietty; and Homily swallowed, nodding her head.

'That's right,' Pod told them more gently. 'Like it says in your book, Arrietty, "A Word is enough to the Wise."'

'Now get me the horse-hair,' he went on more jovially. 'It's a nice day. And while you two clear breakfast, I'll start on the fish-net. How's that?' Homily nodded again. She did not even ask him (as on any other occasion she would immediately have) how, when they had caught the fish, he proposed that they should cook it. 'There's a nice lot of dry bark about. Do fine,' said Pod, 'for floats.'

But Pod, though good at knots, had quite a bit of trouble with the horse-hair: the long tail-strands were springy and would slide from the eye of the needle. When the chores were done, however, and Arrietty sent off to the brook with two borrowing-bags – the waxed one for water and the other for bark, Homily came to Pod's rescue and, working together, they evolved a close mesh on the spider-web principle, based on Homily's knowledge of tatting.

'What about this Spiller?' Pod asked uneasily after a while, as he sat beside Homily, watching her fingers.

Homily snorted, busy with her knots. 'Don't talk to me of that one,' she said after a moment.

'Is he a borrower, or what?' asked Pod.

'I don't know what he is,' cried Homily, 'and what's more, I don't care neither. Threw a beetle at me, that's all I know. And stole the pin and our nail-scissor.'

'You know that for sure ?' asked Pod, on a rising note.

'Sure as I'm sitting here,' said Homily. 'You ain't seen him.'

Pod was silent a moment. 'I'd like to meet him,' he said after a while, staring out across the sunlit field.

The net grew apace and the time went by almost without their noticing. Once when, each taking an end, they held the work out for inspection, a grasshopper sprang from the bank below, bullet-like, into the meshes ; and it was only after – with infinite care for the net – they had freed the struggling creature that Homily thought of luncheon.

'Goodness,' she cried, staring across the field, 'look at them shadows ! Must be after two. What can have happened to Arrietty ?'

'Playing down there with the water, I shouldn't wonder,' said Pod.

'Didn't you tell her "there and back and no dawdling" ?'

'She knows not to dawdle,' said Pod.

'That's where you're wrong, Pod, with Arrietty. With Arrietty you got to say it every time !'

'She's going on for fourteen now,' said Pod.

'No matter,' Homily told him, rising to her feet, 'she's young for her age. You always got to tell her, else she'll make excuses.'

Homily folded up the net, brushed herself down, and bustled across the annexe to the shelf above the tool rack.

'You hungry, Pod ?' (It was a rhetorical question : they were always hungry, all of them, every hour of the day. Even after meals they were hungry.)

'What is there ?' he asked.

'There's a bunch of haws, a couple of nuts, and a mildewed blackberry.'

Pod sighed. 'All right,' he said.

'But which?' asked Homily.

'The nut's more filling,' said Pod.

'But what can I do, Pod?' cried Homily unhappily. 'Any suggestions? Do you want to go and pick us a couple of wild strawberries?'

'That's an idea,' said Pod, and he moved towards the bank.

'But you got to look careful,' Homily told him, 'they've got a bit scarce now. Something's been at them. Birds maybe. Or,' she added bitterly, 'more likely that Spiller.'

'Listen!' cried Pod, raising a warning hand. He stood quite still at the edge of their cave, staring away to his left.

'What was it?' whispered Homily, after a moment.

'Voices,' said Pod.

'What kind of voices?'

'Human,' said Pod.

'Oh, my—' whispered Homily fearfully.

'Quiet,' said Pod.

They stood quite still, ears attuned. There was a faint hum of insects from the grasses below and the buzzing of a fly which had blundered into the alcove; it flew jerkily about between them and settled greedily at last on the sandy floor where at breakfast Homily had spilled the honey. Then suddenly, uncomfortably close, they heard a different sound, a sound which drove the colour from their cheeks and which filled their hearts with dread – and it was, on the face of it, a cheerful sort of sound: the sound of a human laugh.

Neither moved; frozen, they stood – pale and tense with listening. There was a pause and, nearer now, a man's voice cursed – one short, sharp word and, immediately after, they heard the yelp of a dog.

Pod stooped; swiftly, with a jerk of the wrist, he

released the halyard and, hand over steady hand, he pulled on the swaying tree: this time he used extra strength, drawing the branches lower and closer until he had stuffed the mouth of their cave with a close-knit network of twigs.

'There,' he gasped, breathing hard, 'take some getting through, that will.'

Homily, bewildered by the dappled half-light, could not make out his expression, but somehow she sensed his calm. 'Will it look all right from outside?' she asked evenly, matching her tone to his.

'Should do,' said Pod. He went up to the leaves and peered out between them, and with steady hands and sure grip tried the set of the branches. 'Now,' he said, stepping back and drawing a deep breath, 'hand me that other hat-pin.'

Then it was that a further strange thing happened. Pod put out his hand – and there at once was the hat-pin, but it had been put in his grasp too quietly and too immediately to have been put there by Homily: a shadowy third shared their dim-lit cavern, a dun-coloured creature of invisible stillness. And the hat-pin was the hat-pin they had lost.

'Spiller!' gasped Homily hoarsely.

Chapter Thirteen

'MEAT IS MUCH, BUT MANNERS ARE MORE'
New Style introduced into Britain, 1752
[*Extract from Arrietty's Diary and Proverb Book, September 11th.*]

He must have slid in with the lowering of the leaves – a shadow among shadows. Now she could see the blob of face, the tangled thatch of hair, and that he carried two borrowing-bags, one empty and one full. And the bags, Homily realized with a sinking of the heart, were the bags which that morning she had handed to Arrietty.

'What have you done with her?' Homily cried, distraught. 'What have you done with Arrietty?'

Spiller jerked his head towards the back of the alcove. 'Coming up over yon field,' he said, and his face remained quite expressionless. 'I floated her off down the current,' he added carelessly. Homily turned wild eyes towards the back of the alcove as though she might see through the sandy walls and into the field beyond: it was the field through which they had trapsed on the day of their escape.

'You what?' exclaimed Pod.

'Floated her off down the river,' said Spiller, 'in half of a soap-box,' he explained irritably, as though Pod were being dense.

Pod opened his mouth to reply, then, staring, remained silent: there was a sound of running footsteps in the ditch below; as they came abreast of the alcove and thundered past outside, the whole of the bank seemed to tremble and the bell-clapper fell off its nail – they heard the steady rasp of men's harsh breathing and the panting of a dog.

'It's all right,' said Spiller, after a tense pause, 'they cut off left, and across. Gipsies,' he added tersely, 'out rabbiting.'

'Gipsies?' echoed Pod dully, and he wiped his brow with his sleeve.

'That's right,' said Spiller, 'down there by the lane; coupla caravans.'

'Gipsies . . .' breathed Homily in a blank kind of wonderment, and for a moment she was silent – her breath held and her mouth open, listening.

'It's all right,' said Spiller, listening too, 'they gone across now, alongside the cornfield.'

'And what's this now about Arrietty?' stammered Pod.

'I told you,' said Spiller.

'Something about a soap-dish?'

'Is she all right?' implored Homily, interrupting. 'Is she safe? Tell us that—'

'She's safe,' said Spiller, 'I told you. Box, not dish,' he corrected, and glanced interestedly about the alcove. 'I slept in that boot once,' he announced conversationally, nodding his head towards it.

Homily repressed a shudder. 'Never mind that now,' she said, hurriedly dismissing the subject, 'you go on and tell us about Arrietty. This soap-dish, or box, or whatever it was. Tell us just what happened.'

It was difficult to piece the story together from Spiller's terse sentences, but at last some coherence emerged. Spiller, it seemed, owned a boat – the bottom half of an aluminium soap-case, slightly dented; in this, standing up, he would propel himself about the stream. Spiller had a summer camp (or hunting lodge) in the sloping field behind – an old blackened tea kettle it was – wedged sideways in the silt of the stream (he had several of these bases it appeared, of which, at some time, the boot had been one) – and he would borrow from the caravans, transporting the loot by water; this boat gave him a speedy getaway, and one which left no scent. Coming up against the current was slower, Spiller explained, and for this he was grateful for the hat-pin, which not only served as a sharp and pliable punt-pole, but as a harpoon as well. He became so lyrical about the hat-pin that Pod and Homily began to feel quite pleased with themselves, as though, out of the kindness of their hearts, they had achieved some benevolent gesture. Pod longed to ask to what use Spiller had put the half nail-scissor but could not bring himself to do so, fearing to strike a discordant note in so bland a state of innocent joy.

On this particular afternoon, it seemed, Spiller had been transporting two lumps of sugar, a twist of tea, three leaden hair-curlers, and one of those plain gold earrings for pierced ears known as sleepers across the wider part of the brook where, pond-like, it spread into their field, when (he told them) he had seen Arrietty at the water's edge, barefoot in the warm mud, playing some kind of game. She had a quill-like leaf of bulrush in her hand and seemed to be stalking frogs: she would steal up behind her prey, where innocently it sat basking in the sun, and – when she was close enough – she would tap the dozing creature smartly in the small of its back with her swaying length of wand; there would then be a croak, a plop, a splash – and it was one up to Arrietty. Sometimes she was seen approaching – then, of course, it was one up to the

frog. She challenged Spiller to a match, completely unaware (he said) that she had another interested spectator – the gipsies' dog, a kind of mongrel grey-hound, which stared with avid eyes from the woodland edge of the pond. Nor (he added) had she heard the crackling in the underbrush which meant that its masters were close behind.

Spiller, it seemed, had just had time to leap ashore, push Arrietty into the shallow soap-box and, with a few hurried directions about the whereabouts of the kettle, shove her off down-stream.

'But will she ever find it?' gasped Homily. 'The kettle, I mean?'

'Couldn't miss it,' said Spiller, and went on to explain that the current fetched up close against the spout, in a fethery pile-up of broken ripples – and there the soap-box always stuck. 'All she got to do,' he pointed out, 'is make fast, tip the stuff out, and walk on back up.'

'Along the ridge of the gas-pipe?' asked Pod. Spiller threw him a startled glance, shrewd but somehow closed. 'She could do,' he said shortly.

'Half a soap-box . . .' murmured Homily wonderingly, trying to picture it, '. . . hope she'll be all right.'

'She'll be all right,' said Spiller, and there b'aint no scent on the water.'

'Why didn't you get in too,' asked Pod, 'and go along with her, like?'

Spiller looked faintly uncomfortable. He rubbed his dark hand on the back of his moleskin trousers; he frowned slightly, glancing at the ceiling. 'There b'aint room for two,' he said at last, 'not with cargo.'

'You could have tipped the cargo out,' said Pod.

Spiller frowned more deeply, as though the subject bored him. 'Maybe,' he said.

'I mean,' Pod pointed out, 'there you were, weren't you? out in the open, left without cover. What's a bit of cargo compared to that?'

'Yes,' said Spiller, and added uncomfortably, referring to his boat: 'She's shallow – you ain't seen her: there b'aint room for two.'

'Oh, Pod—' cried Homily, suddenly emotional.

'Now what?' asked Pod.

'This boy,' went on Homily in ringing tones, 'this – well, anyway, there he stands!' and she threw out an arm towards Spiller.

Pod glanced at Spiller. Yes, indeed, there he stood, very embarrassed and indescribably grubby.

'He saved her life,' went on Homily, throaty with gratitude, 'at the expense of his own!'

'Not expense,' Pod pointed out after a moment, staring thoughtfully at Spiller. 'I mean he's here, isn't he?' And added reasonably in surprised afterthought: 'And she's not!'

'She will be,' said Homily, suddenly confident, 'you'll see; everything's all right. And he's welcome to the hat-pin. This boy's a hero.' Suddenly herself again, she began to bustle about. 'Now you sit here, Spiller,' she urged him hospitably, 'and rest yourself. It's a long pull up from the water. What'll you take? Could you do with a nice half a rose-hip filled with something or other? We haven't much,' she explained with a nervous laugh, 'we're newcomers, you see . . .'

Spiller put a grubby hand into a deep pocket. 'I got this,' he said, and threw down a sizable piece of something heavy which bounced juicily as it hit the slate table. Homily moved forward; curiously, she stooped. 'What is it?' she asked in an awed voice. But even as she spoke she knew: a faint gamy odour rose to her nostrils –

gamy, but deliciously savoury, and for one fleeting, glorious second she felt almost faint with greed: it was a roast haunch of—

'Meat,' said Spiller.

'What kind of meat?' asked Pod. He too looked rather glassy-eyed – an exclusive diet of hips and haws might be non-acid-forming but it certainly left corners.

'Don't tell me,' Homily protested, clapping her hands to her ears. And, as they turned towards her surprised, she looked apologetic but added eagerly: 'Let's just eat it, shall we?'

They fell to, slicing it up with the sliver of razor-blade. Spiller looked on surprised: surfeited with regular protein, he was not feeling particularly hungry. 'Lay a little by for Arrietty,' Homily kept saying, and every now and again she remembered her manners and would press Spiller to eat.

Pod, very curious, kept throwing out feelers. 'Too big for field-mouse,' he would say, chewing thoughtfully, 'yet too small for rabbit. You couldn't eat stoat . . . might be a bird, of course.'

And Homily, in a pained voice, would cry: 'Please, Pod . . .' and would turn coyly to Spiller. 'All *I* want to know is how Spiller cooks it. It's delicious and hung just right.'

But Spiller would not be drawn. 'It's easy,' he admitted once (to Homily's bewilderment: how could it be 'easy' out here in a grateless wilderness devoid of coke or coal? And, natural gratitude apart, she made more and more fuss of Spiller: she had liked him, she was convinced now, from the first).

Arrietty returned in the middle of this feast. She staggered a little when she had pushed her way through the tight-packed screen of leaves, swayed on her two feet, and sat down rather suddenly in the middle of the floor.

Homily was all concern. 'What have they done to you, Arrietty? What's the matter? Are you hurt?'

Arrietty shook her head. 'Seasick,' she said weakly, 'my head's all awhirl.' She glanced reproachfully across at Spiller. 'You spun me out in the current,' she told him accusingly. 'The thing went round and round and round and round and round and round and—'

'Now, that's enough, Arrietty,' interrupted Homily, 'or you'll have us all whirling. Spiller was very kind. You should be grateful. He gave his life for yours—'

'He didn't give his life,' explained Pod again, slightly irritated.

But Homily took no notice. 'And then came on up here with the borrowing-bags to say you were all right. You should thank him.'

'Thank you, Spiller,' said Arrietty, politely but wanly, looking up from her place on the floor.

'Now get up,' said Homily, 'that's a good girl. And come to the table. Not had a bite since breakfast – that's all that's the matter with you. We've saved you a nice piece of meat—'

'A nice piece of what?' asked Arrietty in a dazed voice, not believing her ears.

'Meat,' said Homily firmly, without looking at her.

Arrietty jumped up and came across to the table; she stared blankly down at the neat brown slices. 'But I thought we were vegetarians . . .' After a moment she raised her eyes to Spiller: there was a question in them. 'Is it—?' she began, unhappily.

Spiller shook his head quickly; it was a firm negative and settled her misgivings. 'We never ask,' put in Homily sharply, tightening her lips and creating a precedent; 'let's just call it a bit of what the gipsies caught and leave it at that.'

'Not leave it,' murmured Arrietty dreamily. Quite recovered she seemed suddenly, and arranging her skirts she joined them at the low table round which they sat picnic-wise on the floor. Tentatively she took up a slice in two fingers, took a cautious bite, then closed her eyes and almost shuddered, so welcome and downright was the flavour. '*Did* the gipsies catch it?' she asked incredulously.

'No,' said Pod, 'Spiller did.'

'I thought so,' Arrietty said. 'Thank you, Spiller,' she added. And this time her voice sounded heartfelt – alive and ringing with proper gratitude.

Chapter Fourteen

'LOOK HIGH, AND FALL LOW'
First Balloon Ascent in England, 1784
[*Extract from Arrietty's Diary and Proverb Book, September 15th.*]

Meals became different after that – different and better –
and this had something to do, Arrietty decided, with their
stolen half nail-scissor. Stolen? An unpleasant-sounding
word, seldom applied to a borrower. 'But what else can
you call it?' Homily wailed as she sat one morning on the
edge of the alcove while Pod sewed a patch on her shoe,
'or expect even? Of a poor, homeless, ignorant boy
dragged up, as they say, in the gutter—'

'Ditch, you mean,' put in Arrietty drowsily, who was
lying below on the bank.

'I mean gutter—' repeated Homily, but she looked a
little startled: she had not known Arrietty was near, 'it's a
manner of speaking. No,' she went on primly, adjusting
the hem of her skirt to hide her stockinged foot (there was
a slight hole, she had noticed, in the toe), 'you can't blame
the lad. I mean, with that sort of background, what could
he learn about ethics?'

'About whatticks?' asked Pod. Homily, poor ignorant
soul, occasionally hit on a word which surprised him and,
what surprised him still more, sometimes she hit on its
meaning.

'Ethics,' repeated Homily coolly and with perfect
confidence. 'You know what ethics are, don't you?'

'No, I don't,' Pod admitted simply, sewing away on his
patch; 'sounds to me like something you pick up in the
long grass.'

'Them's ticks,' said Homily.

'Or,' Pod went on, smoothing the neat join with a licked thumb, 'that thing that horses get from drinking too quick.'

'It's funny . . .' mused Arrietty, 'that you can't have just one.'

'One what?' asked Homily sharply.

'One ethic,' said Arrietty.

'That's where you're wrong,' snapped Homily. 'As a matter of fact there is only one. And Spiller's never learned it. One day,' she went on, 'I'm going to have a nice, quiet, friendly talk with that poor lad.'

'What about?' asked Arrietty.

Homily ignored the question: she had composed her face to a certain kind of expression and was not going to change it. '"Spiller," I'll say, "you never had a mother—"'

'How do you know he never had a mother?' asked Pod. 'He must have had,' he added reasonably, after a moment's reflection.

'Yes,' put in Arrietty, 'he did have a mother. 'That's how he knows his name.'

'How?' asked Homily, suddenly curious.

'Because his mother told him, of course! Spiller's his surname. His first name's Dreadful.'

There was a pause.

'What is it?' asked Homily then, in an awed voice.

'Dreadful!'

'Never mind,' snapped Homily, 'tell us: we're not children.'

'That's his name: Dreadful Spiller. He remembers his mother saying it one day, at table. "A Dreadful Spiller, that's what you are," she said, "aren't you?" It's about all he does remember about his mother.'

'All right,' said Homily, after a moment, composing

her features back to gentle tolerance, 'then I'll say to him'
(she smiled her sad smile), '"Dreadful," I'll say, "dear
boy, my poor orphan lad—"'

'How do you know he's orphaned?' interrupted Pod.
'Have you ever asked him if he's orphaned?'

'You can't ask Spiller things,' put in Arrietty quickly.
'Sometimes he tells you, but you can't ask him. Remember when you tried to find out how he did the cooking?
He didn't come back for two days.'

'That's right,' agreed Pod glumly, 'couple 'o days
without meat. We don't want that again in a hurry. Look
here, Homily,' he went on, turning suddenly towards her,
'better leave Spiller alone.'

'It's for his own good,' protested Homily angrily, 'and
it's *telling*, not *asking*! I was only going to say—' (again
she smiled her smile) '"Spiller, my poor lad . . ." or
"Dreadful" or whatever his name is—'

'You can't call him Dreadful, Mother,' put in Arrietty,
'not unless he asks you—'

'Well, "Spiller" then!' Homily threw up her eyes. 'But I
got to tell him.'

'Tell him what?' asked Pod, irritated.

'This *ethic*!' Homily almost shouted, 'this what we all
been brought up on! That you don't never borrow from a
borrower!'

Impatiently Pod snapped off his thread. 'He knows
that,' he said. He handed the shoe to Homily. 'Here you,
put it on.'

'Then what about the hat-pin?' persisted Homily.

'He give it back,' Pod said.

'He didn't give back the nail-scissor!'

'He skins the game with it,' said Arrietty quickly. 'And
we get the meat.'

'Skins the game?' pondered Homily. 'Well, I never.'

'That's right,' agreed Pod, 'and cuts it up. See what I mean, Homily?' He rose to his feet. 'Better leave well alone.'

Homily was struggling absent-mindedly with the laces of her shoe. 'Wonder how he does cook?' she mused aloud after a moment.

'Wonder away,' said Pod. He crossed to the shelf to replace his tools. 'No harm in that, so long as you don't ask.'

'Poor orphaned lad . . .' said Homily again. She spoke quite lightly but her eye was thoughtful.

Chapter Fifteen

'NO JOY WITHOUT ALLOY'
Columbus discovered New World, 1492
[*Extract from Arrietty's Diary and Proverb Book, September 25th.*]

The next six weeks (according to Tom Goodenough) were the happiest Arrietty ever spent out of doors. Not that they could be called halcyon exactly: they ran, of course, the usual gamut of English summer weather – days when the fields were drowned in opal mist and spiders' webs hung jewelled in the hedges; days of breathless heat and stifling closeness; thundery days with once a searing strike of lightning across the woods when Homily, terrified, had buried the razor-blade saying that 'steel attracts'; and one whole week of dismal, steady rain with scarcely a let-up, when the ditch below their bank became a roaring cataract on which Spiller, guiding his tin soap-case with uncanny speed and skill, intrepidly shot the rapids; during this week Homily and Arrietty were kept house-bound in case, Pod told them, they should slip on the mud and fall in: it would be no joke, he explained, to be swept along down the ditch to the swollen stream at the corner and on and on through the lower fields until they met the river and eventually, he concluded, be carried out to sea.

'Why not say "across to America" and have done with it?' Homily had remarked tartly, remembering Arrietty's *Gazetteer of the World*. But she got ahead with her

winter knitting, saw the men had hot drinks, and dried out poor Spiller's clothes over the candle while he huddled naked, but clean for once, in the boot. The rain never actually beat into the alcove but there was an unpleasant dampness all over everything, white mildew on the leather of the boot, and, once, a sudden crop of yellow toadstools where none had been before. Another morning, when Homily crept forth shivering to get breakfast, a silvery track of slime wound ribbon-like across the floor and, putting her hand on the tool shelf for the matches, she gave a startled scream – stuffed, the shelf was, and flowing over with a heaving mass of slug. A slug that size cannot easily be tackled by a borrower, but luckly this one shrunk up and feigned dead: once they had prized it out of its close-fitting retreat, they could bowl it over across the sandy floor and roll it away down to the bank.

After this, towards the end of September, there did come some halcyon days – about ten of them: sun and butterflies and drowsy heat; and a second burst of wild flowers. There was no end to Arrietty's amusements out of doors. She would climb down the bank, across the ditch, and into the long grass, and stretched between the stems would lie there watching. Once she became used to the habits of the insects she no longer feared them: her world, she realized, was not their world and for them hers had little interest; except, perhaps for that bug-like horror (an ethic to Pod) which, crawling sluggishly across bare skin, would bury its head and cling.

Grasshoppers would alight like prehistoric birds on the grasses above her head; strange, armour-plated creatures, but utterly harmless to such as she. The grass stems

would sway wildly beneath their sudden weight, and Arrietty, lying watchful below, would note the machine-like slicing of the mandibles as the grasshopper munched its fill.

Bees, to Arrietty, were as big as birds are to humans; and if honey-bees were pigeon-sized, a bumble-bee in weight and girth could be compared to a turkey. These too she found, if unprovoked, were harmless. A quivering bumble-bee, feeding greedily on clover, became strangely still all at once when, with gentle fingers, she stroked his fur. Benignity met with benignity: and anger, she found, was only roused through fear. Once she was nearly stung when, to tease it, she imprisoned a bee in that bloom called wild snapdragon by closing the lip with her hands. The trapped bee buzzed like a dynamo and stung, not Arrietty this time, but the enclosing calyx of the flower.

A good deal of time she would spend by the water – paddling, watching, learning to float. The frogs fought shy of her: at Arrietty's approach, they would plop away with bored bleats of distaste, their bulging eyes resigned but nervous, 'look where it comes again . . .'[1] they seemed to croak.

After bathing, before putting on her clothes, sometimes she would dress up: a skirt of violet leaves, stalks uppermost, secured about the waist with a twist of faded columbine, and, aping the fairies, a foxglove bell for a hat. This, Arrietty thought as she stared at her bright reflection in the stagnant water of a hoof crater, might look all right on gnomes, elves, brownies, pixies, and what not, but she had to admit that it looked pretty silly on a common or garden borrower: for one thing, if the lip fitted the circumference of her head, the whole thing

---

[1] Tom Thumb edition of Shakespeare's Tragedies, with foreword on the Author.

stood up too high like some kind of pinkish sausage or a very drawn-out chef's cap. Yet if, on the other hand, the lip of the bell flowed out generously in a gentle, more hat-like curve, the whole contraption slid down past her face to rest on her shoulders in a Ku-Klux-Klan effect.

And to get hold of these bells at all was not easy: foxglove plants were high. Fairies, Arrietty supposed, just flew up to them with raised chins and neatly pointed toes, trailing a wisp of gauze. Fairies did everything so gracefully: Arrietty, poor girl, had to hook down the plant with a forked stick and sit on it as heavily as she could while she plucked any bells within reach. Sometimes the plant would escape her and fly up again. But usually, by shifting her weight along the stalk, she would manage to get five or six bells – sufficient anyway to try some out for size.

Spiller, gliding by in his cleverly loaded boat, would stare with some surprise: he was not altogether approving of Arrietty's games; having spent all his life out of doors, fending for himself against nature, he had no picture of what such freedom could mean to one who had spent her childhood under a kitchen floor; frogs were just meat to Spiller; grass was 'cover'; and insects a nuisance, especially gnats; water was there to drink, not to splash in; and streams were highways which held fish. Spiller, poor harried creature, had never had time to play.

But he was a fearless borrower; that even Pod conceded; as skilful in his own way as ever Pod had been. The two gentlemen would have long discussions of an evening after supper, on the finer points of a multiplex art. Pod belonged to a more moderate school: the daily sortie and modest loot – a little here, a little there – nothing to rouse suspicion. Spiller preferred a make-hay-while-the-sun-shines technique: a swift whip-round of

whatever he could lay hands on and a quick getaway. This difference in approach was understandable, Arrietty thought, as listening she helped her mother with the dishes: Pod was a house-borrower, long established in traditional routine; whereas Spiller dealt exclusively with gipsies — here to-day and gone to-morrow — and must match his quickness with theirs.

Sometimes a whole week would elapse without their seeing Spiller, but he would leave them well stocked with cooked food: a haunch of this or that, or a little stew flavoured with wild garlic which Homily would heat over the candle. Flour, sugar, tea, butter — even bread — they had now in plenty. Spiller, in his nonchalant way, would sooner or later provide almost anything they asked for — a piece of plum-coloured velvet out of which Homily made a new skirt for Arrietty, two whole candles to augment their stub, four empty cotton-reels on which they raised their table, and, to Homily's joy, six mussel shells for plates.

Once he brought them a small glass medicine bottle, circular in shape. As he uncorked it, Spiller said: 'Know what this is?'

Homily, wry-faced, sniffed at the amber liquid. 'Some kind of hair-wash?' she asked, grimacing.

'Elder-flower wine,' Spiller told her, watching her expression. 'Good, that is.'

Homily, about to taste, suddenly changed her mind. 'When wine is in,' she told Spiller – quoting from Arrietty's *Diary and Proverb Book*, 'wit is out. Besides, I was brought up teetotal.'

'He makes it in a watering-can,' explained Spiller, 'and pours it out of the spout.'

'Who does?' asked Homily.

'Mild Eye,' said Spiller.

There was a short silence, tense with curiosity. 'And who might Mild Eye be?' asked Homily at last. Airily pinning up her back hair, she moved slightly away from Spiller and began softly to hum below her breath.

'He that had the boot,' said Spiller carelessly.

'Oh?' remarked Homily. She took up the thistle-head and began to sweep the floor – without seeming to be rude she managed to convey a gentle dismissal of the now-I-must-get-on-with-the-housework kind – 'What boot?'

'This boot,' said Spiller, and kicked the toe.

Homily stopped sweeping; she stared at Spiller. 'But this was a gentleman's boot,' she pointed out evenly.

'"Was" is right,' said Spiller.

Homily was silent a moment. 'I don't understand you,' she said at last.

'Afore Mild Eye pinched 'em,' explained Spiller.

Homily laughed. 'Mild Eye . . . Mild Eye . . . who is this Mild Eye?' she asked airily, determined not to be rattled.

'I told you,' said Spiller, 'the gipsy as took up the boots.'

'Boots?' repeated Homily, raising her eyebrows and stressing the plural.

'They was a pair. Mild Eye picked 'em up outside the scullery door . . .' Spiller jerked his head, 'that big house down yonder. Went there selling clothes-pegs and there they was, set out on the cobbles, pairs of 'em – all shapes and sizes, shined up nice, set out in the sunshine . . . brushes and all.'

'Oh,' said Homily thoughtfully – this sounded a good 'borrow,' 'and he took the lot?'

Spiller laughed. 'Not Mild Eye. Took up the pair and closed up the gap.'

'I see,' said Homily. After a moment she asked: 'And who borrowed this one? You?'

'In a manner of speaking,' said Spiller, and added, as though in part explanation: 'He's got this piebald cat.'

'What's the cat got to do with it?' asked Homily.

'A great tom comes yowling round the place one night and Mild Eye ups and heaves a boot at it – this boot.' Again Spiller kicked at the leather. 'Good and watertight this boot was afore a weasel bit into the toe. So I gets hold of her, drags her through the hedge by the laces, heaves her into the water, jumps aboard, sails downstream to the corner, brings her aground on the mud and dries her out after, up in the long grass.'

'Where we found it?' asked Homily.

'That's right,' said Spiller. He laughed. 'You should have heard old Mild Eye in the morning. Knew just where he'd heaved the boot, cussin' and swearin'. Couldn't make it out.' Spiller laughed again. 'Never passes that way,' he went on, 'but he has another look.'

Homily turned pale. 'Another look?' she repeated nervously.

Spiller shrugged. 'What's the difference? Wouldn't

think to look this side of the water. Knows where he heaved the boot, Mild Eye does: that's what he can't fathom.'

'Oh, my,' faltered Homily unhappily.

'You've no call to worry,' said Spiller. 'Anything you'm wanting?'

'A bit of something woollen, I wouldn't mind,' said Homily; 'we was cold last night in the boot.'

'Like a bit of sheep's fleece?' asked Spiller. 'There's plenty down to the lane along them brambles.'

'Anything,' agreed Homily, 'providing it's warm. And providing—' she added, suddenly struck by a horrid thought, 'it ain't a sock.' Her eyes widened. 'I don't want no sock belonging to Mild Eye.'

Spiller dined with them that night (cold boned minnow with sorrel salad). He had brought them a splendid wad of cleanish fleece and a strip of red rag off the end of a blanket. Pod, less teetotal than Homily, poured him out a half hazel-shell of elderberry wine. But Spiller would not touch it. 'I've things to do,' he told them soberly, and they guessed he was off on a trip.

'Be away long?' asked Pod casually as, just to sample it, he took a sip of wine.

'A week,' said Spiller, 'ten days, maybe . . .'

'Well,' said Pod, 'take care of yourself.' He took another sip of wine. 'It's nice,' he told Homily, proffering the hazel-shell, 'you try it.'

Homily shook her head and tightened her lips. 'We'll miss you, Spiller,' she said, batting her eyelids and ignoring Pod, 'and that's a fact—'

'Why have you got to go?' asked Arrietty suddenly.

Spiller, about to push his way through the screen of leaves, turned back to look at her.

Arrietty coloured. 'I've asked him a question,' she realized unhappily, 'now he'll disappear for weeks.' But this time Spiller seemed merely hesitant.

'Me winter clothes,' he said at last.

'Oh !' exclaimed Arrietty, raising her head – delighted. 'New ?'

Spiller nodded.

'Fur ?' asked Homily.

Spiller nodded again.

'Rabbit ?' asked Arrietty.

'Mole,' said Spiller.

There was a sudden feeling of gaiety in the candle-lit alcove: a pleasant sense of something to look forward to. All three of them smiled at Spiller and Pod raised his 'glass.' 'To Spiller's new clothes,' he said, and Spiller, suddenly embarrassed, dived quickly through the branches. But before the living curtain had stopped quivering they saw his face again; amused and shy, it poked back at them framed in leaves. 'A lady makes them,' he announced self-consciously, and quickly disappeared.

Chapter Sixteen

'EVERY TIDE HAS ITS EBB'
Burning of the Tower of London, 1841
[*Extract from Arrietty's Diary and Proverb Book, October 30th.*]

Next morning early Pod, on the edge of the alcove, summoned Arrietty from the boot. 'Come on out,' he called, 'and see this.'

Arrietty, shivering, pulled on a few clothes, and wrapping the piece of red blanket around her shoulders she crept out beside him. The sun was up and the landscape shimmered, dusted over with what, to Arrietty, looked like powdered sugar.

'This is it,' said Pod, after a moment, 'the first frost.'

Arrietty pushed her numbed fingers under her armpits, hugging the blanket closer. 'Yes,' she said soberly, and they stared in silence.

After a bit Pod cleared his throat. 'There's no call to wake your mother,' he said huskily; 'like as not, with this sun, it'll be clear in less than an hour.' He became silent again, thinking deeply. 'Thought you'd like to see it,' he said at last.

'Yes,' said Arrietty again, and added politely: 'It's pretty.'

'What we better do,' said Pod, 'is get the breakfast quietly and leave your mother sleeping. She's all right,' he went on, 'deep in that fleece.'

'I'm perished,' grumbled Homily at breakfast, her hands wrapped round a half hazel-shell filled with piping hot tea (there was less need, now they had Spiller, to economize on candles). 'It strikes right through to the marrow. You know what?' she went on.

'No,' said Pod (it was the only reply). 'What?'

'Say we went down to the caravan site and had a look round? There won't be no gipsies: when Spiller goes, it means they've moved off. Might find something,' she added, 'and in this kind of weather there ain't no sense in sitting around. What about it, Pod? We could wrap up warm.'

Arrietty was silent, watching their faces: she had learned not to urge.

Pod hesitated. Would it be poaching, he wondered – was this Spiller's preserve? 'All right,' he agreed uncertainly, after a moment.

It was not a simple expedition. Spiller having hidden his boat, they had to ferry themselves across the water on a flat piece of bark, and it was rough going when, once in the wood, they tried to follow the stream by land: both banks were thickly grown with brambles, ghastly forests of living barbed wire which tore at their hair and clothes; by the time they had scrambled through the hedge on to the stretch of grass beside the lane, they were all three dishevelled and bleeding.

Arrietty looked about her at the camping site and was depressed by what she saw: this wood through which they had scrambled now shut off the last pale gleams of sun; the shadowed grass was bruised and yellow; here

and there were odd bones, drifting feathers, bits of rag, and every now and again a stained newspaper flapped in the hedge.

'Oh dear,' muttered Homily, glancing from side to side, 'somehow, now, I don't seem to fancy that bit o' red blanket.'

'Well,' said Pod, after a pause, 'come on. We may as well take a look round . . .' And he led the way down the bank.

They poked about rather distastefully and Homily thought of fleas. Pod found an old iron saucepan without a bottom: he felt it might do for something but could not

think for what; he walked around it speculatingly and, once or twice, he tapped it sharply with the head of his hat-pin, which made a dull clang. Anyway, he decided at last as he moved away, it was no good to him here and was far too heavy to shift.

Arrietty found a disused cooking-stove: it was flung into the bank below the hedge – so sunk it was in the grasses and so thickly engrained with rust that it must have been there for years. 'You know,' she remarked to her mother, after studying it in silence, 'you could live in a stove like this.'

Homily stared. 'In that?' she exclaimed disgustedly. The stove lay tilted, partially sunk in earth; as stoves went it was a very small one, with a barred grate and a miniature oven of the kind which are built into caravans. Beside it, Arrietty noticed, lay a small pile of fragile bones.

'Not sure she isn't right,' agreed Pod, tapping the bars of the grate, 'you could have a fire in here, say, and live in the oven like.'

'Live!' exclaimed Homily. 'Be roasted alive, you mean.'

'No,' exclaimed Pod, 'needn't be a big fire. Just enough to warm the place through like. And there you'd be' – he looked at the brass latch on the door of the oven – 'safe as houses. Iron, that is,' he rapped the stove with his hat-pin; 'nothing couldn't gnaw through that.'

'Field-mice could slip through them bars,' said Homily.

'Maybe,' said Pod, 'but I wasn't thinking so much about field-mice as about' – he paused uneasily – 'stoats and foxes and them kind of cattle.'

'Oh, Pod,' exclaimed Homily, clapping her hands flat to her cheeks and making her eyes tragic, 'the things you do bring up! Why do you do it?' she implored him tearfully. 'Why? You know what it does to me!'

'Well, there are such things,' Pod pointed out stolidly. 'In this life,' he went on, 'you got to see what *is*, as you might say, and then face up to what you wish there wasn't.'

'But foxes, Pod,' protested Homily.

'Yes,' agreed Pod, 'but there they are; you can't deny 'em. See what I mean?'

'I see all right,' said Homily, eyeing the stove more kindly, 'but say you lit it, the gipsies would see the smoke.'

'And not only the gipsies,' admitted Pod, glancing

aside at the lane, 'anyone passing would see it. No,' he
sighed, as he turned to go, 'this stove ain't feasible. Pity –
because of the iron.'

The only really comforting find of the day was a piping
hot blackened potato: Arrietty found it on the site of the
gipsies' fire. The embers were still warm, and, when
stirred with a stick, a line of scarlet sparks ran snakewise
through the ash. The potato steamed when they broke it
open, and comforted they ate their fill, sitting as close as
they dared to the perilous warmth.

'Wish we could take a bit of this ash home,' Homily
remarked. 'This is how Spiller cooks, I shouldn't wonder
– borrows a bit of the gipsies' fire. What do you think,
Pod?'

Pod blew on his crumb of hot potato. 'No,' he said,
taking a bite and speaking with his mouth full, 'Spiller
cooks regular-like whether the gipsies are here or not.
Spiller's got his own method. Wish I knew what it was.'

Homily leaned forward, stirring the embers with a
charred stick. 'Say we kept this fire alight,' she suggested,
'and brought the boot down here?'

Pod glanced about uneasily. 'Too public,' he said.

'Say we put it in the hedge,' went on Homily,
'alongside that stove? What about that? Say we put it *in*
the stove?' she added suddenly, inspired but fearful.

Pod turned slowly and looked at her. 'Homily—' he
began and paused, as though stumped for words. After a
moment he laid a hand on his wife's arm and looked with
some pride towards his daughter. 'Your mother's a
wonderful woman,' he said in a moved voice. 'And never
you forget it, Arrietty.'

Then it was 'all hands to the plough': they gathered
sticks like maniacs, and wet leaves to keep up the
smoulder. Backwards and forwards they ran, up into the

hedges, along the banks, into the spinney . . . they tugged and wrenched and tripped and stumbled . . . and soon a white column of smoke spiralled up into the leaden sky.

'Oh my,' panted Homily, distressed, 'folks'll see this for miles!'

'No matter,' gasped Pod, as he pushed on a lichen-covered branch, 'they'll think it's the gipsies. Pile on some more of them leaves, Arrietty, we got to keep this going till morning.'

A sudden puff of wind blew the smoke into Homily's eyes and the tears ran down her cheeks. 'Oh my,' she exclaimed – again distressed. 'This is what we'll be doing all winter, day in, day out, till we're wore to the bone and run out of fuel. It ain't no good, Pod. See what I mean?'

And she sat down suddenly on a blackened tin-lid and wept in earnest. 'You can't spend the rest of your life,' she whimpered, 'tending an open fire.'

Pod and Arrietty had nothing to say: they knew suddenly that Homily was right: borrowers were too little and weak to create a full-sized blaze. The light was fading and the wind sharpening, a leaden wind which presaged snow.

'Better we start for home,' said Pod, at last. 'We tried anyway. Come on, now,' he urged Homily, 'dry your eyes: we'll think of something else . . .'

But they didn't think of anything else. And the weather became colder. There was no sign of Spiller and, after ten days, they ran out of meat and started (their sole source of warmth) on the last bit of candle.

'I don't know,' Homily would moan unhappily, as at night they crept under the fleece, 'what we're going to do, I'm sure. We won't see Spiller again, that's one thing certain. Dare say he's met with an accident.'

Then came the snow. Homily, tucked up in the boot, would not get up to see it. To her it presaged the end. 'I'll die here,' she announced, 'tucked up comfortable. You and father,' she told Arrietty, 'can die as you like.'

It was no good Arrietty assuring her that the field looked very pretty, that the cold seemed less severe, and that she had made a sledge of the blackened tin-lid which Pod had retrieved from the ashes: she had made her grave and was determined to lie in it.

In spite of this, and rather heartlessly, Arrietty still enjoyed her toboggan runs down the bank with a wide sweep into the ditch at the bottom. And Pod, brave soul, still went out to forage – though there was little left to eat in the hedgerows and for this little, a few remaining berries, they had to compete with the birds. Though appreciably thinner, none of them felt ill and Arrietty's snow-tanned cheeks glowed with healthy colour.

But five days later it was a different story: intense cold and a second fall of snow – snow which piled up in air-filled drifts, too light and feathery to support a matchstick, let alone a borrower. They became house-bound and, for most of the time, joined Homily in the boot. The fleece was warm but, lying there in semi-darkness, the time passed slowly and the days were very boring. Homily would revive occasionally and tell them stories of her childhood: she could be as long-winded as she liked with this audience which could not get away.

They came to an end of the food. 'There's nothing left,' announced Pod, one evening, 'but one lump of sugar and a quarter inch of candle.'

'I couldn't never eat that,' complained Homily, '– not paraffin wax.'

'No one's asking you to,' said Pod. 'And we've still that drop of elderberry wine.'

Homily sat up in bed. 'Ah!' she said, 'put the sugar in the wine and heat it up over the quarter inch of candle.'

'But, Homily,' protested Pod, surprised, 'I thought you was teetotal.'

'Grog's different,' explained Homily. 'Call me when it's ready,' and she lay down again, piously closing her eyes.

'She will have her way,' muttered Pod, aside to Arrietty. He eyed the bottle dubiously. 'There's more there than I thought there was. I hope she'll be all right . . .'

It was quite a party: so long it had been since they had lit the candle; and it was pleasant to gather round it and feel its warmth.

When at last, warmed and befuddled, they snuggled down in the fleece, a curious contentment filled Arrietty – a calmness akin to hope. Pod, she noticed, drowsed with wine, had forgotten to lace up the boot . . . well, perhaps it didn't matter – if it was their last night on earth.

Chapter Seventeen

'WHAT HEAVEN WILL, NO FROST CAN KILL'
Great Earthquake at Lisbon, 50,000 killed, 1755
[*Extract from Arrietty's Diary and Proverb Book, November 1st.*]

It was not their last night on earth: it seldom is, somehow; it was, however, their last night *in* earth.

Arrietty was the first to wake. She woke tired, as though she had slept badly, but it was only later (as she told Tom) that she remembered her dream of the earthquake. She not only woke tired but she woke cramped, and in a most uncomfortable position. There seemed more light than was usual, and then she remembered the unlaced opening. But why, she wondered, as she roused a little, did the daylight seem to come in from above, as from a half-concealed skylight? And suddenly she understood – the boot, which lay always on its side, for some extraordinary reason was standing upright. Her first thought (and it made her heart beat faster) was that her dream of an earthquake had been fact. She glanced at Pod and Homily: from what she could see of them, so enmeshed they were in fleece, they appeared to be sleeping soundly, but not, she thought, quite in the same positions as when they had gone to bed. Something had happened – she was sure of it – unless she still was dreaming.

Stealthily Arrietty sat up: although the boot was open, the air felt surprisingly warm – almost stuffy; it smelt of wood smoke and onions and of something else – a smell she could not define – could it be the scent of a human being?

Arrietty crept along the sole of the boot until she stood under the opening. Staring up she saw, instead of the sandy roof of the annexe, a curious network of wire springs and some kind of striped ceiling. They must be under some bed, she realized (she had seen this view of beds back home); but what bed? And where?

Trembling a little, but too curious not to be brave, she put her foot as high as she could into an eyelet hole and pulled herself erect on a loop of shoe-lace; another step up, a harder pull – and she found she could see out: the first thing she saw, standing close beside her – so close that she could see into it – was a second boot exactly like their own.

That was about all she could see from her present position: the bed was low, stretching up she could almost touch the springs with her hands. But she could hear things – the liquid purr of a simmering kettle, the crackle of a fire, and a deeper, more rhythmic sound – the sound of a human snore.

Arrietty hesitated: she was in half a mind to wake her parents, but, on second thoughts, she decided against it. First to find out a bit more. She unloosed a couple of lace-holes and eased out through the gap and, via the boot's instep, she walked out to the toe. Now she could really see.

As she had guessed, they were in a caravan. The boots stood under a collapsible bed which ran along one side of it's length; and facing her on the opposite side, parallel to this bed, she saw a miniature coal range very like the one in the hedge, and a light-grained overmantel. The shelves of the overmantel, she saw, were set with pieces of looking-glass and adorned with painted vases, old coronation mugs, and trails of paper flowers. Below and on each side were set-in drawers and cupboards. A kettle simmered gently on the flat of the stove and a fire glowed redly through the bars.

At right angles, across the rear end of the caravan, she saw a second bunk, built in more permanently above a locker, and the locker, she noted, thinking of cover, was not set in flush with the floor: there was space below into which, if crouching, a borrower might creep. In the bunk above the locker she saw a heaving mountain of patch-work which she knew must contain, by the sound of the snoring, a human being asleep. Beside the head of the bunk stood a watering-can, a tin mug balanced on the spout. Elderflower wine, she thought – that last night had been their undoing.

To her left, also at right angles, was the door of the caravan, the top half open to the winter sunshine; it faced, she knew, towards the shafts. A crack of sunlight ran down the latch side of this door – a crack through which, if she dared approach it, she might perhaps see out.

She hesitated. It was only a step to the crack – a yard and a half at most: the human mountain was still heaving, filling the air with sound. Lightly, Arrietty slid from the toe of the boot to the worn piece of carpet and, soundless in her stockinged feet, she tiptoed to the door. For a moment the sunlight striking brightly through the crack almost seemed to blind her, then she made out a stretch of dirty grass, sodden with melting snow, a fire smoking sulkily between two stones, and beyond that, some way distant below the hedge, she saw a familiar object – the remains of a disused stove. Her spirits rose: so they were still at the same old caravan site – they had not, as she had feared at first, been travelling in the night.

As, her nose in the crack, she stood there staring, a sudden silence behind her caused her to turn; and, having turned, she froze: the human being was sitting up in bed. He was a huge man, fully dressed, dark-skinned, and with a mass of curling hair; his eyes were screwed up, his fists stretched, and his mouth wide open in a long-drawn, groaning yawn.

Panic-stricken, she thought about cover. She glanced at the bed to her right – the bed under which she had awakened. Three strides would do it; but better to be still, that's what Pod would say: the shadowed part of the door against which she stood would seem still darker because of that opened half above, filled so brightly with winter sunshine. All Arrietty did was to move aside from the crack of light against whose brightness she might be outlined.

The human being stopped yawning and swung his legs down from the bunk and sat there a moment, pensively, admiring his stockinged feet. One of his eyes, Arrietty noticed, was dark and twinkling, the other, paler, hazel-yellow, with a strangely drooping lid. This must be Mild Eye – this great, fat, terrifying man, who sat so quietly smiling at his feet.

As Arrietty watched, the strange eyes lifted a little and the smile broadened: Mild Eye, Arrietty saw, was looking at the boots.

She caught her breath as she saw him lean forward and (a stretch of the long arm was enough) snatch them up from below the other bed. He examined them lovingly, holding them together as a pair, and then, as though struck by some discrepancy in the weight, he set one down on the floor. He shook the other gently, turning its opening towards his palm and, as nothing fell out, he put his hand inside.

The shout he gave, Arrietty thought afterwards, must have been heard for miles. He dropped the boot, which

fell on its side, and Arrietty, in an anguish of terror, saw
Homily and Pod run out and disappear between his legs
(but not, she realized, before he had glimpsed them) into
the shallow space between his bunk and the floor.

There was a horrified pause.

Arrietty was scared enough, but Mild Eye seemed even
more so: his two strange eyes bulged in a face which had
turned the colour of putty. Two tiny words hung in the
silence, a thread-thin echo, incredible to Mild Eye:
someone . . . something . . . somewhere . . . on a note of
anguish, had stammered out 'Oh dear!'

And that was controlled enough, Arrietty thought, for
what Homily must be feeling: to be woken from a deep
sleep and shaken out of the boot; to have seen those two
strange eyes staring down at her; to have heard that
thunderous shout. The space between the locker and the
floor, Arrietty calculated, could not be more than a
couple of inches; it would be impossible to stand up in
there and, although safe enough for the moment, there
they would have to stay: there seemed no possible way
out.

For herself – glued motionless against the shadows –
she was less afraid: true enough she stood face to face
with Mild Eye; but he would not see her, of this she felt
quite sure, providing she did not move: he seemed too

shaken by those half-glimpsed creatures which so inexplicably had appeared between his feet.

Stupefied, he stared for a moment longer; then awkwardly he got down on all fours and peered under the locker; as though disappointed, he got up again, found a box of matches, struck a light, and once again explored the shadows as far as the light would carry. Arrietty took advantage of his turned back to take her three strides and slip back under the bed. There was a cardboard box under here, which she could use as cover, some ends of rope, a bundle of rabbit snares, and a slimy saucer which once had contained milk.

She made her way between these objects until she reached the far end — the junction of the bed with the locker below the bunk. Peering out through the tangle of rabbit snares she saw that Mild Eye — despairing of matchlight — had armed himself with a hefty knobkerrie stick which he was now running back and forth in a business-like manner along the space between the bunk and the floor. Arrietty, her hands pressed tight against her heart, once thought she heard a strangled squeak and a muttered: 'Oh, my gracious—!'

At that moment the door of the caravan opened, there was a draught of cold air, and a wild-eyed woman looked in. Wrapped in a heavy shawl against the cold, she was carrying a basket of clothes-pegs. Arrietty, crouching among the rabbit snares, saw the wild eyes open still more wildly, and a flood of questions in some foreign tongue was aimed at Mild Eye's behind. Arrietty saw the woman's breath smoke in the clear sunshine and could hear her earrings jangle.

Mild Eye, a little shamefaced, rose to his feet; he looked very big to Arrietty and, though she could no longer see his face, his hanging hands looked helpless. He replied to the woman in the same language: he said quite a lot; sometimes his voice rose on a curious squeak of dismayed excitement.

He picked up the boot, showed it to the woman, said a lot about it, and – somewhat nervously, Arrietty noticed – he put his hand inside; he pulled out the wad of fleece, the unravelled sock, and – with some surprise because it had once been his – the strip of coloured blanket. As he showed these to the woman, who continued to jeer, his voice became almost tearful. The woman laughed then – a thin, high peal of raucous laughter. Completely heartless, Arrietty thought, completely unkind. She wanted almost for Mild Eye's sake to run out and show this doubting creature that there were such things as borrowers ('it's so awful and sad,' she once admitted to Tom Goodenough, 'to belong to a race that no sane person believes in'). But tempting as this thought was she thought better of it, and instead she edged herself out from the end of the bed into the darker space below the bunk.

And only just in time: there was a faint thud on the carpet, and there, not a foot from where she had stood, she saw the four paws of a cat – three black and one white; she saw him stretch, roll over, and rub his whiskered face on the sun-warmed carpet: he was black, she saw, with a white belly. He or she? Arrietty did not know: a fine beast anyway, sleek and heavy as cats are who hunt for themselves out of doors.

Sidling crab-wise into the shadows, her eyes on the basking cat, she felt her hand taken suddenly, held, and squeezed tight. 'Oh, thank goodness . . .' Homily breathed in her ear, 'thank heavens you're safe.'

Arrietty put a finger to her lips. 'Hush,' she whispered, barely above her breath, staring towards the cat.

'It can't get under here,' whispered Homily. Her face, Arrietty saw, looked pallid in the half-light, grey and streaked with dust. 'We're in a caravan,' she went on, determined to tell the news.

'I know,' said Arrietty, and pleaded: 'Mother, we'd better be quiet.'

Homily was silent a moment, then she said: 'He caught your father's back with that stick. The soft part,' she added reassuringly.

'Hush,' whispered Arrietty again. She could not see much from where she was, but Mild Eye, she gathered, was struggling into a coat; after a moment he stooped, and his hand came near when he felt under the settee for the bundle of rabbit snares; the woman was still out of doors busy about the fire.

After a while, her eyes growing used to the dimness, she saw her father sitting some way back, leaning against the wall. She crawled across to him, and Homily followed.

'Well, here we are,' said Pod, barely moving his lips, 'and not dead yet,' he added, with a glance at Homily.

Chapter Eighteen

'HIDDEN TROUBLES DISQUIET MOST'
Gun Powder Plot, 1605
[*Extract from Arrietty's Diary and Proverb Book, November 5th.*]

They crouched there listening, holding their breaths as Mild Eye unlatched the door, relatched it, and clumped off down the steps.

There was a pause.

'We're alone now,' remarked Homily at last in her ordinary speaking voice, 'I mean, we could get out, I shouldn't wonder, if it weren't for that cat.'

'Hush—' whispered Pod. He had heard the woman shoot some mocking question at Mild Eye and, at Mild Eye's mumbled reply, the woman had laughed her laugh. Arrietty, too, was listening.

'*He* knows we're here,' she whispered, 'but *she* won't believe him . . .'

'And that cat'll know we're here, too, soon enough,' replied Pod.

Arrietty shivered. The cat, she realized, must have been asleep on the bed, while she, Arrietty, had been standing unprotected beside the door.

Pod was silent a while, thinking deeply. 'Yes,' he said at last, 'it's a rum go: he must have come around at dusk last night, seeing after his snares . . . and there he finds his lost boot in our hollow.'

'We should have pulled down the screen,' whispered Arrietty.

'We should that,' agreed Pod.

'We didn't even lace up the boot,' went on Arrietty.

'Yes,' said Pod, and sighed. 'A bottle at night and you're out like light. That how it goes?' he asked.

'More or less,' agreed Arrietty in a whisper.

They sat waist-high in dusty trails of fluff. 'Disgusting,' remarked Homily, suppressing a sneeze. 'If I'd built this caravan,' she grumbled, 'I'd have set the bunk in flush with the floor.'

'Then thank goodness you didn't build it,' remarked Pod, as a whiskered shadow appeared between them and the light: the cat had seen them at last.

'Don't panic,' he went on calmly, as Homily gave a gasp, 'this bunk's too low, we're all right here.'

'Oh my goodness,' whispered Homily, as she saw a luminous eye. Pod squeezed her hand to silence her.

The cat, having sniffed his way along the length of the opening, lay down suddenly on its side and ogled them through the gap: quite friendly, it looked, and a little coy, as though coaxing them out to play.

'They don't *know*,' whispered Homily then, referring to cats in general.

'You keep still,' whispered Pod.

For a long time nothing much happened: the shaft of sunshine moved slowly across the worn carpet, and the cat, motionless, seemed to doze.

'Well,' whispered Homily, after a while, 'in a way, it's kind of nice to be indoors.'

Once the woman came in and fumbled in the dresser for a wooden spoon and took away the kettle; they heard her swearing as she tended the outdoor fire, and once a gust of acrid smoke blew in through the doorway, making Arrietty cough. The cat woke up at that and cocked an eye at them.

Towards midday, they smelt a savoury smell – the gamy smell of stew: it would drift towards them as the wind veered and then, tormentingly, would drift away.

Arrietty felt her mouth water.

'*Oh*, I'm hungry . . .' she sighed.

'I'm thirsty,' said Homily.

'I'm both,' said Pod. 'Now be quiet, the two of you,' he told them, 'shut your eyes and think of something else.'

'Whenever I shut my eyes,' protested Homily, 'I see a nice hot thimbleful of tea, or I think of that teapot we had back home: that oak-apple teapot, with a quill spout.'

'Well, think of it,' said Pod; 'no harm in that, if it does you good . . .'

The man came back at last. He unlatched the door and threw a couple of snared rabbits down on the carpet. He and the woman ate their meal on the steps of the caravan, using the floor as a table.

At this point the smell of food became unbearable; it drew the three borrowers out of the shadows to the very edge of their shelter: the tin plates, filled with savoury stew, were at eye level; they had a splendid view of the floury potatoes and the richly running gravy. 'Oh my . . .' muttered Homily unhappily, 'pheasant – and what a way to cook it!'

Once Mild Eye threw a morsel on the carpet. Enviously they watched the cat pounce and leisurely fall to, crunching up the bones like the hunter it was. 'Oh my . . .' muttered Homily again, 'those teeth!'

At length Mild Eye pushed aside his plate. The cat stared with interest at the pile of chewed bones to which here and there clung slivers of tender meat. Homily stared too: the plate was almost in range. 'Dare you, Pod?' she whispered.

'No,' said Pod – so loudly and firmly that the cat turned round and looked at him; gaze met gaze with curious mutual defiance; the cat's tail began slowly to swish from side to side.

'Come on', gasped Pod, as the cat crouched, and all three dodged back into the shadows in the split half-second before the pounce.

Mild Eye turned quickly. Staring, he called to the woman, pointing towards the bunk, and both man and woman stooped their heads to floor-level, gazing across the carpet . . . and gazing, it seemed to Arrietty, crouched with her parents against the back wall of the caravan, right into their faces. It seemed impossible that they could not be seen: but – 'It's all right,' Pod told them, speaking with still lips in the lightest of whispers, 'Don't panic – just you keep still.'

There was silence: even the woman now seemed uneasy – the cat, padding and peering, back and forth along the length of the locker, had aroused her curiosity. 'Don't you move,' breathed Pod again.

A sudden shadow fell across the patch of sunlight on the carpet: a third figure, Arrietty noted with surprise, loomed up behind the crouching gipsies in the doorway; someone less tall than Mild Eye. Arrietty, rigid between her parents, saw three buttons of a stained corduroy waistcoat and, as its wearer stopped, she saw a young face, and a tow-coloured head of hair. 'What's up?' asked a voice which had a crack in it.

Arrietty saw Mild Eye's expression change: it became all at once sulky and suspicious. He turned slowly and faced the speaker, but before he did so he slid his right hand inconspicuously across the floor of the caravan, pushing the two dead rabbits out of sight.

'What's up, Mild Eye?' asked the boy again. 'Looks like you'm seeing ghosties.'

Mild Eye shrugged his great shoulders. 'Maybe I am,' he said.

The boy stooped again, staring along the floor, and

Arrietty could see that, under one arm, he carried a gun. 'Wouldn't be a ferret by any chance?' he asked slily.

The woman laughed then. 'A ferret!' she exclaimed, and laughed again. 'You're the one for ferrets . . .' Pulling her shawl more tightly about her she moved away towards the fire. 'You think the cat act *kind* like that for a ferret?'

The boy stared curiously past the cat across the floor, screwing his eyelids to see beyond the pacing cat and into the shadows. 'The cat bain't acting so kind,' he remarked thoughtfully towards the fire.

'A couple of midgets he's got in there,' the woman told him, '–dressed up to kill – or so he says,' and she went off again into screams of jeering laughter.

The boy did not laugh; his expression did not change: calmly he stared at the crack below the bunk. 'Dressed up to kill . . .' he repeated and, after a moment, he added: 'Only two?'

'How many do you want?' asked the woman. 'Half a dozen? A couple's enough, ain't it?'

'What do you reckon to do with them?' asked the boy.

'Do with them?' repeated the woman, staring stupidly.

'I mean, when you catch them?'

The woman gave him a curious look, as though doubting his reason. 'But there ain't nothing there,' she told him.

'But you just said—'

The woman laughed, half angry, half bewildered. 'Mild Eye sees 'em – not me. Or so he makes out. There ain't nothing there, I tell you—'

'I seen 'em all right,' said Mild Eye. He stretched his first finger and thumb. 'This high, I'd say – a bit of a woman, it looked like, and a bit of a man.'

'Mind if I look?' asked the boy, his foot on the steps.

He laid down his gun, and Arrietty, watching, saw him put his hand in his pocket; there was a stealthiness about his movement which drove the blood from her heart. 'Oh,' she gasped, and grabbed her father's sleeve.

'What is it?' breathed Pod, leaning towards her.

'His pocket—' stammered Arrietty. 'Something alive in his pocket!'

'A ferret,' cried Homily, forgetting to whisper. 'We're finished.'

'Hush—' implored Pod. The boy had heard something; he had seated himself on the top step and was now leaning forward gazing towards them across the strip of faded carpet. At Homily's exclamation, Pod had seen his eyes widen, his face become alert.

'What's the good of whispering?' complained Homily, lowering her voice all the same. 'We're for it now. Wouldn't matter if we sang—'

'Hush—' said Pod again.

'How would you think to get 'em out?' the boy was asking, his eyes on the gap; his right hand, Arrietty saw, still feeling in his pocket.

'Easy,' explained Mild Eye; 'empty the locker and take up them boards underneath.'

'You see?' whispered Homily, almost in triumph, 'it doesn't matter what we do now!'

Pod gave up. 'Then sing,' he suggested wearily.

'Nailed down, them boards are, aren't they?' asked the boy.

'No,' said Mild Eye. 'I've had 'em out after rats; they comes out in a piece.'

The boy, his head lowered, was staring into the gap. Arrietty, from where she crouched, was looking straight into his eyes: they were thoughtful eyes, bland and blue.

'Say you catch them,' the boy went on, 'what then?'

'What then?' repeated Mild Eye, puzzled.

'What do you want to do with 'em?'

'Do with 'em? Cage 'em up. What else?'

'Cage 'em up in what?'

'In that.' Mild Eye touched the bird cage, which swung slightly. 'What else?'

('And feed us on groundsel, I shouldn't wonder,' muttered Homily below her breath.)

'You want to keep 'em?' asked the boy, his eyes on the shadowed gap.

'Keep 'em, naow! Sell 'em!' exclaimed Mild Eye.

'Fetch a pretty penny, that lot would – cage and all complete.'

'Oh, my goodness,' whimpered Homily.

'Quiet,' breathed Pod, 'better the cage than the ferret.'

'No,' thought Arrietty, 'better the ferret.'

'What would you feed 'em on?' the boy was asking; he seemed to be playing for time.

Mild Eye laughed indulgently. 'Anything. Bits o' left-overs . . .'

('You hear that?' whispered Homily, very angry.

'Well, to-day it was pheasant,' Pod reminded her; but he was glad she was angry: anger made her brave.)

Mild Eye had climbed right in now – blotting out the

sunshine. 'Move over,' he said to the boy, 'we got to get at the locker.'

The boy shifted, a token shift. 'What about the cat?' he said.

'That's right,' agreed Mild Eye, 'better have the cat out. Come on, Tiger—'

But the cat, it seemed, was as stubborn as the boy and shared his interest in borrowers: evading Mild Eye's hand, it sprang away to the bed, and (Arrietty gathered from a slight thud immediately above their heads) from the end of the bed to the locker. Mild Eye came after it: they could see his great feet close against the gap – their own dear boot was there just beside them, with the patch which Pod had sewn! It seemed incredible to see it worn, and by such a hostile foot.

'Better cart it out to the missus,' suggested the boy, as Mild Eye grabbed the cat; 'if it bain't held on to it'll only jump back in.'

('Don't you dare,' moaned Homily, just below her breath.

Pod looked amazed. 'Who are you talking to?' he asked in a whisper.

'Him – Mild Eye; the minute he leaves this caravan that boy'll be after us with the ferret.'

'Now, see here—' began Pod.

'You mark my words,' went on Homily in a panic-stricken whisper. 'I know who he is now. It's all come back to me: young Tom Goodenough. I heard speak of that one many a time back home under the kitchen. And I wouldn't be surprised if it wasn't him we saw at the window – that day we made off, remember? Proper devil he's reckoned to be with that ferret—'

'Quiet, Homily!' implored Pod.

'Why? For heaven's sake – they know we're here:

quiet or noisy – what's the difference to a ferret?')

Mild Eye swore suddenly as though the cat had scratched him. 'Cart him right out,' said the boy again, 'and see she holds him.'

'Don't fret,' said Mild Eye, 'we can shut the door.'

'That bain't no good,' said the boy; 'we can't shut the top half; we got to have light.'

On the threshold Mild Eye hesitated. 'Don't you touch nothin',' he said, and stood there a moment, waiting, before he clumped off down the steps. On the bottom rung he seemed to slip: the borrowers could hear him swearing. 'This blamed boot,' they heard him say, and something about the heel.

'You all right?' called out the boy carelessly. The answer was an oath.

'Block your ears,' whispered Homily to Arrietty. 'Oh, my goodness me, did you hear what he said?'

'Yes,' began Arrietty obligingly, 'he said—'

'Oh, you wicked, heathen girl,' cried Homily angrily, 'shame on yourself for listening!'

'Quiet, Homily,' begged Pod again.

'But you know what happened, Pod?' whispered Homily excitedly. 'The heel came off the boot! What did I tell you, up in the ditch, when you would take out them nails!' For one brief moment she forgot her fears and gave a tiny giggle.

'Look,' breathed Arrietty suddenly, and reached for her mother's hand. They looked.

The boy, leaning towards them on one elbow, his steady gaze fixed on the slit of darkness between the locker and floor, was feeling stealthily in the right-hand pocket of his coat – it was the deep, pouched pocket common to gamekeepers.

'Oh, my . . .' muttered Homily, as Pod took her hand.

'Shut your eyes,' said Pod. 'No use running and you won't know nothing: a ferret strikes quick.'

There was a pause, tense and solemn, while three small hearts beat quickly. Homily broke it.

'I've tried to be a good wife to you, Pod,' she announced tearfully, one eye screwed obediently shut, the other cautiously open.

'You've been first-rate,' said Pod, his eyes on the boy. Against the light it was hard to see, but something moved in his hand: a creature he had taken from his pocket.

'A bit sharp sometimes,' went on Homily.

'It doesn't matter now,' said Pod.

'I'm sorry, Pod,' said Homily.

'I forgive you,' said Pod absently. A deeper shadow now had fallen across the carpet: Mild Eye had come back up the steps. Pod saw the woman had sneaked up behind him, clasping the cat in her shawl.

The boy did not start or turn. 'Make for my pocket . . .' he said steadily, his eyes on the gap.

'What's that?' asked Mild Eye, surprised.

'Make for my pocket,' repeated the boy, 'do you hear what I say?' And suddenly he loosed on the carpet the thing he had held in his hand.

'Oh, my goodness—' cried Homily, clutching on to Pod.

'Whatever is it?' she went on, after a moment, both eyes suddenly open. Some kind of living creature it was, but certainly not a ferret . . . too slow . . . too angular . . . too upright . . . too—

Arrietty let out a glad cry: 'It's Spiller!'

'What?' exclaimed Homily, almost crossly – tricked, she felt, when she thought of those grave 'last words.'

'It's Spiller,' Arrietty sang out again, 'Spiller . . . Spiller . . . Spiller!'

'Looking quite ridiculous,' remarked Homily; and indeed he did look rather odd and sausage-like, stuffed out in his stiff new clothes; he would render them down gradually to a wearable suppleness.

'What are you waiting for?' asked Spiller. 'You heard what he said. Come on now. Get moving, can't you?'

'That boy?' exclaimed Homily, 'was he speaking to us?'

'Who else?' snapped Spiller. 'He don't want Mild Eye in his pocket. Come on—'

'His pocket!' exclaimed Homily in a frantic whisper. She turned to Pod. 'Now let's get this right: young Tom Goodenough wants me' – she touched her own chest – 'to run out there, right in the open, get meself over his trouser-leg, across his middle, up to his hip, and potter down all meek and mild into his pocket?'

'Not you only,' explained Pod, 'all of us.'

'He's crazy,' announced Homily firmly, tightening her lips.

'Now, see here, Homily—' began Pod.

'I'd sooner perish,' Homily asserted.

'That's just what you will do,' said Pod.

'Remember that peg-bag?' she reminded him. 'I couldn't face it, Pod. And where's he going to take us? Tell me that?'

'How should I know?' exclaimed Pod. 'Now, come on, Homily, you do what he says, there's me brave old girl ... take her by the wrist, Spiller, she's got to come ... ready Arrietty? Now for it—' and suddenly there they were, the whole group of them – out in the open.

Chapter Nineteen

'FORTUNE FAVOURS THE BRAVE'
Sherman's March to the Coast began, 1864
[Extract from Arrietty's Diary and Proverb Book, November 13th.]

The woman screeched when she saw them: she dropped the cat, and ran for her life, making hell for leather towards the main road. Mild Eye, too, was taken aback; he sat down on the bed with his feet in the air as though a contaminated flood were swirling across the carpet: the cat, unnerved by the general uproar, made a frantic leap for the overmantel, bringing down two mugs, a framed photograph, and a spray of paper rosebuds.

Pod and Arrietty made their own slithering way across the folds of trouser-leg to the rising slope of hip; but poor Spiller, pulling and pushing a protesting Homily, was picked up and dropped in. For one awful moment, attached by the wrist to Spiller, Homily dangled in air, before the boy's quick fingers gathered her up and tidied her neatly away. Only just in time – for Mild Eye, recovering, had made a sudden grab, missing her by inches ('Torn us apart, he would have,' she said later, 'like a couple of bananas!'). Deep in the pocket, she heard his angry shout of 'Four of 'em you got there. Come on: fair's fair – hand over them first two!'

They did not know what happened next: all was darkness and jumble. Some sort of struggle was going on – there was the sound of heavy breathing, muttered swear words, and the pocket swayed and bounced. Then, by the bumping, they knew the boy was running and Mild Eye, shouting behind him, was cursing his heelless boot. They

heard these shouts grow fainter, and the crackle of breaking branches as the boy crashed through a hedge.

There was no conversation in the pocket: all four of them felt too dazed. At last Pod, wedged upside-down in a corner, freed his mouth from fluff. 'You all right, Homily?' he gasped. Homily, tightly interwoven with Spiller and Arrietty, could not quite tell. Pod heard a slight squeak. 'Me leg's gone numb,' said Homily unhappily.

'Not broken, is it?' asked Pod anxiously.

'Can't feel nothing in it,' said Homily.

'Can you move it?' asked Pod.

There was a sharp exclamation from Spiller as Homily said 'No.'

'If it's the leg you're pinching,' remarked Spiller, 'stands to reason you can't move it.'

'How do you know?' asked Homily.

'Because it's mine,' he said.

The boy's steps became slower: he seemed to be going uphill; after a while he sat down. The great hand came down amongst them. Homily began to whimper, but the fingers slid past her; they were feeling for Spiller. The coat was pulled round and the pocket flap held open, so the boy could peer at them. 'You all right, Spiller?' he asked.

Spiller grunted.

'Which is Homily?' asked the boy.

'The noisy one,' said Spiller. 'I told you.'

'You all right, Homily?' asked the boy.

Homily, terrified, was silent.

The great fingers came down again, sliding their way into the pocket.

Spiller, standing now with legs apart and back supported against the upright seam, called out tersely: 'Leave 'em be.'

The fingers stopped moving. 'I wanted to see if they were all right,' said the boy.

'They're all right,' said Spiller.

'I'd like to have 'em out,' the boy went on. 'I'd like to have a look at 'em.' He peered downwards at the open pocket. 'You're not dead, are you?' he inquired anxiously. 'You bain't none of you dead?'

'How could we say, if we was?' muttered Homily irritably.

'You leave 'em be,' said Spiller again; 'it's warm in here: you don't want to bring 'em out sudden into the cold. You'll see 'em often enough,' he consoled the boy, 'once you get back home.'

The fingers withdrew and they were in the dark again; there was a rocking and the boy stood up. Pod, Homily, and Arrietty slid the length of the bottom seam of the pocket, fetching up against the opposite corner; it was full of dried breadcrumbs, jagged and hard as concrete. 'Ouch!' cried Homily, unhappily. Spiller, Arrietty noticed, though he swayed on his feet, managed to keep upright. Spiller, she guessed, had travelled by pocket before: the boy was walking again now, and the coat swayed with a more predictable rhythm. 'After a while,' Arrietty thought, 'I'll have a go at standing myself.'

Pod experimentally broke off a jagged piece of breadcrumb which, after patient sucking, slowly began to dissolve. 'I'll try a bit of that,' said Homily, holding out her hand; she had revived a little and was feeling peckish.

'Where's he taking us?' she asked Spiller after a while.

'Round the wood and over the hill.'

'Where he lives with his grandpa?'

'That's right,' admitted Spiller.

'I ain't ever heard tell much about gamekeepers,' said Homily, 'nor what they'd be apt to do with – a borrower, say. Nor what sort of boy this is neither. I mean,' she went on in a worried voice, 'my mother-in-law had an uncle once who was kept in a tin box with four holes in the lid and fed twice a day by an eye-dropper . . .'

'He ain't that sort of boy,' said Spiller.

'Whatever's an eye-dropper?' asked Pod. He took it to be some strange sort of craft or profession.

Then there was Lupy's cousin, Oggin, you remember,' went on Homily. 'They made a regular kind of world for him in the bottom of an old tin bath in the outhouse; grass, pond, and all. And they gave him a cart to ride in and a lizard for company. But the sides of the bath were good and slippery: they knew he couldn't get out . . .'

'Lupy?' repeated Spiller wonderingly. 'Wouldn't be two called that?'

'This one married my brother Hendreary,' said Homily. 'Why,' she exclaimed with sudden excitement, 'you don't say you know her!'

The pocket had stopped swaying: they heard some metallic sound and the sliding squeak of a latch.

'I know her all right,' whispered Spiller. 'She makes my winter clothes.'

'Quiet,' urged Pod; 'we've arrived.' He had heard the sound of an opening door and could smell an indoor smell.

'You know *Lupy*?' Homily persisted, unaware even that the pocket had become darker. 'But what are they doing? And where are they living – she and Hendreary? We thought they was eaten by foxes, children and all . . .'

'Quiet, Homily,' implored Pod. Strange movements seemed to be going on, doors were opening and shutting; so stealthily the boy was walking the pocket now hung still.

'Tell us, Spiller, quick,' went on Homily; but she dropped her voice to an obedient whisper. 'You must know! Where are they living now?'

Spiller hesitated – in the semi-darkness he seemed to smile.

'They're living here,' he said.

The boy now seemed to be kneeling.

As the fingers came down again, feeling amongst them, Homily let out a cry. 'It's all right,' whispered Pod, as she burrowed back among the crumbs. 'Keep your head – we got to come out some time.'

Spiller went first; he sailed away from them – nonchalantly astride a finger, without even bothering to glance back. Then it was Arrietty's turn. 'Oh my goodness me . . .' muttered Homily, 'wherever will they put her?'

Pod's turn next; but Homily went with him. She scrambled aboard at the last moment by creeping under the thumb. There was hardly time to feel sick (it was the swoosh through the empty air which Homily always dreaded), so deftly and gently they found themselves set down.

A gleam of firelight struck the tiny group as they stood beside the hearth, against a high, wooden wall: it was, they discovered later, the side of the log-box. They stood together – close and scared, controlling their longing to run. Spiller, they noticed, had disappeared.

The boy, on one knee, towered above them – a terrifying mountain of flesh. The firelight flickered on his down-turned face: they could feel the draught of his breathing.

'It's all right,' he assured them, 'you'll be all right now.' He was staring with great interest, as a collector would stare at a new-found specimen. His hand hovered above them as though he longed to touch them, to pick one of them up, to examine each more closely.

Nervously Pod cleared his throat. 'Where's Spiller?' he asked.

'He'll be back,' said the boy. After a moment he added: 'I got six altogether in there.'

'Six what?' asked Homily nervously.

'Six borrowers,' said the boy. 'I reckon I got the best collection of borrowers in two counties. And,' he added, 'me grandad ain't seen one. His eyes is sharp enough, yet he ain't ever seen a borrower.'

Pod cleared his throat again. 'He ain't supposed to,' he said.

'Some I got in there' – the boy jerked his head towards the log-box – 'I never sees neither. Scared. Some folks say you can't never tame 'em. You can give 'em the earth, 'tis said, but they'll never come out and be civil.'

'I would,' said Arrietty.

'Now you behave yourself,' snapped Homily, alarmed.

'Spiller would, too,' said Arrietty.

'Spiller's different,' replied Homily, with a nervous glance towards the boy – Spiller, she felt, was the boy's curator: the go-between of this rare collection. 'Gets so much a head, I wouldn't wonder?'

'Here he is,' said Arrietty, looking towards the corner of the log-box.

Noiselessly he had come upon them.

'She won't come out,' said Spiller to the boy.

'Oh,' exclaimed Homily, 'does he mean Lupy?'

No one answered. Spiller stood silent, looking up at the boy. The boy frowned thoughtfully; he seemed disappointed. He looked them over once more, examining each of them from head to foot as though loath to see them go; he sighed a little. 'Then take 'em in,' he said.

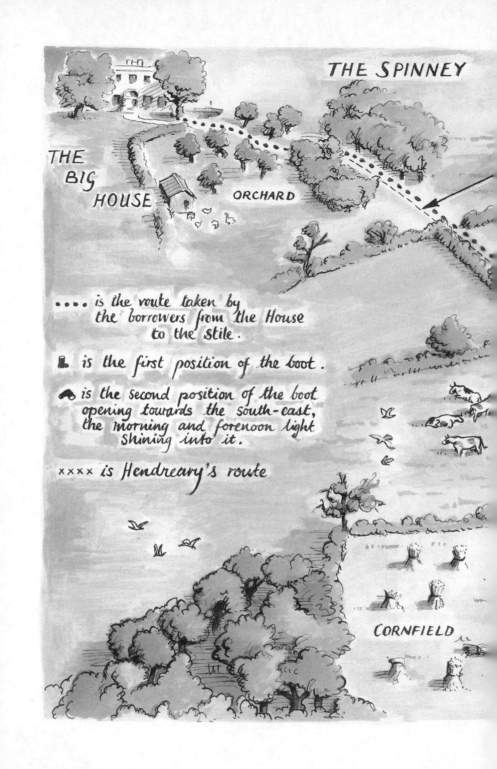

THE SPINNEY

THE BIG HOUSE

ORCHARD

.... is the route taken by the borrowers from the House to the stile.

🥾 is the first position of the boot.

👞 is the second position of the boot opening towards the south-east, the morning and forenoon light shining into it.

xxxx is Hendreary's route

CORNFIELD

THE GAS PIPE

<u>Note</u>: The borrowers followed a path made by the workmen alongside the gas pipe except for the section across the Lower Field where it ran across the field to the stile.

SPILLER'S KETTLE

N
W — E
S

THE POOL

LOWER FIELD

GYPSIES

STILE

PERKINS BECK

TOM'S COTTAGE

BADGERS' SET

Chapter Twenty

'LONG LOOKED FOR COMES AT LAST'
Vasco da Gama rounded Cape of Good Hope, 1497
[*Extract from Arrietty's Diary and Proverb Book, November 20th.*]

They filed in through the Gothic-shaped hole in the wainscot, a little nervous, a little shy. It was shadowy inside like a cave; disappointingly it felt uninhabited and smelled of dust and mice. 'Oh dear,' muttered Homily incredulously, 'is this how they live . . . ? She stopped suddenly and picked up some object from the floor. 'My goodness,' she whispered aside excitedly to Pod, 'do you know what this is?' and she brandished a whitish object under his nose.

'Yes,' said Pod, 'it's a bit of quill pipe-cleaner. Put it down, Homily, and come on, do. Spiller's waiting.'

'It's the spout of our old oak-apple tea-pot,' persisted Homily, 'that's what it is. I'd know it anywhere and it's no good telling me any different. So they *are* here . . .' she mused wonderingly as she followed Pod into the shadows to where Spiller with Arrietty stood waiting.

'We go up here,' said Spiller, and Homily saw that he stood with his hand on a ladder. Glancing up to where the rungs soared away above them into dimness, she gave a slight shudder: the ladder was made of matchsticks, neatly glued and spliced to two lengths of split cane, such as florists use to support potted plants.

'I'll go first,' said Pod. 'We better take it one at a time.'

Homily watched fearfully until she heard his voice from above.

'It's all right,' he whispered from some invisible eyrie; 'come on up.'

Homily followed, her knees trembling, and emerged at last on to the dim-lit platform beside Pod – an aerial landing stage, that was what it seemed like – which creaked a little when she stepped on it and almost seemed to sway. Below lay hollow darkness; ahead an open door. 'Oh my goodness,' she muttered, 'I do hope it's safe . . . don't look down,' she advised Arrietty, who came up next.

But Arrietty had no temptation to look down: her eyes were on the lighted doorway and the moving shadows within; she heard the faint sound of voices and a sudden high-pitched laugh.

'Come on,' said Spiller, slipping past her, and making towards the door.

Arrietty never forgot her first sight of that upstairs room: the warmth, the sudden cleanliness, the winking candlelight, and the smell of home-cooked food.

And so many voices . . . so many people . . .

Gradually, in a dazed way, she began to sort them out: that must be Aunt Lupy embracing her mother – Aunt Lupy so round and glowing, her mother so smudged and lean. Why did they cling and weep, she wondered, and squeeze each others' hands? They had never liked each other – all the world knew that. Homily had thought Lupy stuck-up because, back in the big house, Lupy had lived in the drawing-room and (she had heard it rumoured) changed for dinner at night. And Lupy despised Homily for living under the kitchen and for pronouncing parquet 'parkett.'

And here was Uncle Hendreary, his beard grown thinner, telling her father that this could not be Arrietty, and her father, with pride, telling Uncle Hendreary it could. Those must be the three boy cousins – whose names she had not caught – graduated in size but as like

as peas in a pod. And this thin, tall, fairylike creature, neither old nor young, who hovered shyly in the background with a faint uneasy smile, who was she?

Homily screamed when she saw her and clapped her hand to her mouth. 'It can't be Eggletina!'

It evidently could. Arrietty stared too, wondering if she had heard aright: Eggletina, that long lost cousin who one fine day escaped from under the floor and was never seen again? A kind of legend she had been to Arrietty and a life-long cautionary tale. Well, here she was, safe and sound, unless they all were dreaming.

And well they might be.

There was something strangely unreal about this room – furnished with doll's-house furniture of every shape and size, none of it matching or in proportion. There were chairs upholstered in rep or velvet, some of them too small to sit in and some too steep and large; there were chiffoniers which were too tall and occasional tables far too low; and a toy fire-place with coloured plaster coals and its fire-irons stuck down all-of-a-piece with the fender; there were two make-believe windows with curved pelmets and red satin curtains, each hand-painted with an imitation view – one looked out on a Swiss mountain scene, the other a Highland glen ('Eggletina did them,' Aunt Lupy boasted in her rich society voice. 'We're going to have a third when we get the curtains – a view of Lake Como from Monte S. Primo'); there were table lamps and standard lamps, flounced, festooned, and tasselled, but the light in the room, Arrietty noticed, came from humble, familiar dips like those they had made at home.

Everybody looked extraordinarily clean and Arrietty became even shyer. She threw a quick glance at her father and mother and was not reassured: none of their clothes had been washed for weeks nor, for some days, had their hands and faces. Pod's trousers had a tear in one knee and Homily's hair hung down in snakes. And here was Aunt Lupy, plump and polite, begging Homily please to take off her things in the kind of voice, Arrietty imagined, usually reserved for feather boas, opera cloaks, and freshly cleaned white kid gloves.

But Homily, who back at home had so dreaded being 'caught out' in a soiled apron, knew one worth two of that. She had, Pod and Arrietty noticed with pride, adopted her woman-tried-beyond-endurance role backed up by one called yes-I've-suffered-but-don't-let's-speak-of-it-now; she had invented a new smile, wan but brave, and had – in the same good cause – plucked the two last hair-pins out of her dust-filled hair. 'Poor dear Lupy,' she was saying, glancing wearily about, 'what a lot of furniture! Whoever helps you with the dusting?' And swaying a little, she sank on a chair.

They rushed to support her, as she hoped they might. Water was brought and they bathed her face and hands. Hendreary stood with the tears in his brotherly eyes. 'Poor valiant soul,' he muttered, shaking his head, 'your mind kind of reels when you think of what she's been through . . .'

Then, after a quick wash and brush up all round and a brisk bit of eye-wiping, they all sat down to supper. This they ate in the kitchen, which was rather a come-down except that, in here, the fire was real: a splendid cooking-range made of a large, black door-lock; they poked the fire through the keyhole, which glowed handsomely, and the smoke, they were told, went out through a series of pipes to the cottage chimney behind.

The long, white table was richly spread: it was an eighteenth-century finger-plate off some old drawing-room door – white-enamelled and painted with forget-me-nots, supported firmly on four stout pencil stubs where once the screws had been; the points of the pencils emerged slightly through the top of the table; one was copying-ink and they were warned not to touch it in case it stained their hands.

There was every kind of dish and preserve – both real

and false; pies, puddings, and bottled fruits out of season
– all cooked by Lupy, and an imitation leg of mutton and
a dish of plaster tarts borrowed from the dolls' house.
There were three real tumblers as well as acorn cups and a
couple of green glass decanters.

Talk, talk, talk . . . Arrietty, listening, felt dazed: she
saw now why they had been expected. Spiller, she
gathered, having found the alcove bootless and its
inmates flown, had salvaged their few possessions and
had run and told young Tom. Lupy felt a little faint
suddenly when they mentioned this person by name, and
had to leave the table. She sat awhile in the next room on
a frail gilt chair placed just inside the doorway – 'between
draughts' as she put it – fanning her round red face with a
lark's feather.

'Mother's like this about humans,' explained the eldest
cousin. 'It's no good telling her he's tame as anything and
wouldn't hurt a fly!'

'You never know,' said Lupy darkly, from her seat in
the doorway. 'He's nearly full grown! And that, they say,
is when they start to be dangerous . . .'

'Lupy's right,' agreed Pod, 'I'd never trust 'em meself.'

'Oh, how can you say that?' cried Arrietty. 'Look at
the way he snatched us up right out of the jaws of death!'

'Snatched you up?' screamed Lupy from the next
room. 'You mean – *with his hands?*'

Homily gave her brave little laugh, listlessly chasing a
globule of raspberry around her too slippery plate.
'Naturally . . .' She shrugged. 'It was nothing really.'

'Oh dear . . .' stammered Lupy faintly, 'oh, you poor
thing . . . imagine it! I think,' she went on, 'if you'll
excuse me a moment, I'll just go and lie down . . .' and
she heaved her weight off the tiny chair, which rocked as
she left it.

'Where did you get all this furniture, Hendreary?' asked Homily, recovering suddenly now that Lupy had gone.

'It was delivered,' her brother told her, 'in a plain white pillow-case. Someone from the big house brought it down.'

'From our house?' asked Pod.

'Stands to reason,' said Hendreary, 'It's all stuff from that doll's house, remember, they had upstairs in the school-room. Top shelf of the toy cupboard, on the right-hand side of the door.'

'Naturally I remember,' said Homily, 'seeing that some of it's mine. Pity,' she remarked aside to Arrietty, 'that we didn't keep that inventory,' she lowered her voice, 'the one you made on blotting-paper, remember.'

Arrietty nodded: there were going to be fireworks later – she could see that. She felt very tired suddenly; there seemed too much talk and the crowded room felt hot.

'Who brought it down?' Pod was asking in a surprised voice. 'Some kind of human being?'

'We reckon so,' agreed Hendreary. 'It was lying there t'other side of the bank. Soon after we got turned out of the badgers' set and had set up house in the stove—'

'What stove was that?' asked Pod. 'Not the one by the camping site?'

'That's right,' Hendreary told him; 'two years we lived there, off and on.'

'A bit too close to the gipsies for my liking,' said Pod. He cut himself a generous slice of hot boiled chestnut and spread it thickly with butter. He remembered suddenly that pile of fragile bones.

'You got to be close,' Hendreary explained, 'like it or not, when you got to borrow.'

Pod, about to bite, withdrew the chestnut: he seemed amazed. 'You borrowed from caravans?' he exclaimed. 'At your age!'

Hendreary shrugged slightly and was modestly silent.

'Well I never,' said Homily admiringly, 'there's a brother for you! You think what that means, Pod—'

'I am thinking,' said Pod. He raised his head. 'What did you do about smoke?'

'You don't have none,' Hendreary told him, 'not when you cook on gas.'

'On gas!' exclaimed Homily.

'That's right. We borrowed a bit o' gas from the gas company: they got a pipe laid all along that bank. The stove was resting on its back, like, you remember? We dug down behind through a flue, a good six weeks we spent in that tunnel. Worth it in the end, though: three pin-hole burners, we had down there.'

'How did you turn 'em on and off?' asked Pod.

'We didn't – once lit, we never let them out. Still burning they are to this day.'

'You mean that you still go back there?'

Hendreary, yawning slightly, shook his head (they had

eaten well and the room felt very close). 'Spiller lives there,' he said.

'Oh,' exclaimed Homily, 'so that's how Spiller cooked! He might have told us,' she went on, looking about in a hurt way, 'or, at any rate, asked us in—'

'He wouldn't do that,' said Hendreary. 'Once bitten, twice shy, as you might say.'

'How do you mean?' asked Homily.

'After we left the badgers' set—' began Hendreary, and broke off: slightly shamefaced, he seemed, in spite of his smile. 'Well, that stove was one of his places: he asked us in for a bite and a sup and we stayed a couple o' years—'

'Once you'd struck gas, you mean,' said Pod.

'That's right,' said Hendreary. 'We cooked and Spiller borrowed.'

'Ah!' said Pod. 'Spiller borrowed? Now I understand . . . You and me, Hendreary; we got to face up to it – we're not as young as we was. Not by a long chalk.'

'Where is Spiller now?' asked Arrietty suddenly.

'Oh, he's gone off,' said Hendreary vaguely; he seemed a little embarrassed and sat there frowning and tapping the table with a pewter spoon (one of a set of six, Homily remembered angrily: she wondered how many were left).

'Gone off where?' asked Arrietty.

'Home, I reckon,' Hendreary told her.

'But we haven't thanked him,' cried Arrietty. 'Spiller saved our lives!'

Hendreary threw off his gloom. 'Have a drop of blackberry cordial,' he suggested suddenly to Pod. 'Lupy's own make? Cheer us all up . . .'

'Not for me,' said Homily firmly, before Pod could speak. 'No good never comes of it, as we've found out to our cost.'

'But what will Spiller think?' persisted Arrietty, and there were tears in her eyes. 'We haven't even thanked him.'

Hendreary looked at her, surprised. 'Spiller? He don't hold with thanks. He's all right . . .' and he patted Arrietty's arm.

'Why didn't he stay for supper?'

'He don't ever,' Hendreary told her; 'doesn't like company. He'll cook something on his own.'

'Where?'

'In his stove.'

'But that's miles away!'

'Not for Spiller – he's used to it. Goes part way by water.'

'And it must be getting dark,' Arrietty went on unhappily.

'Now don't you fret about Spiller,' her uncle told her. 'You eat up your pie . . .'

Arrietty looked down at her plate (pink celluloid, it was, part of a tea-service which she seemed to remember); somehow she had no appetite. She raised her eyes. 'And when will he be back?' she asked anxiously.

'He don't come back much. Once a year for his new clothes. Or if young Tom sends 'im special.'

Arrietty looked thoughtful. 'He must be lonely,' she ventured at last.

'Spiller? No, I wouldn't say he was lonely. Some borrowers is made like that. Solitary. You get 'em now and again.' He glanced across the room to where his daughter, having left the table, was sitting alone by the fire. 'Eggletina's a bit like that . . . pity, but you can't do nothing about it. Them's the ones as gets this craze for humans – kind of man-eaters, they turns out to be . . .'

When Lupy returned, refreshed from her rest, it all

began again: talk, talk, talk . . . and Arrietty slipped unnoticed from the table. But, as she wandered away towards the other room, she heard it going on: talk about living arrangements; about the construction of a suite of rooms upstairs; about what pitfalls there were in this new way of life and the rules they had made to avoid such pitfalls – how you always drew the ladder up last thing at night but that it should never be moved while the men were out borrowing; that the young boys went out as learners, each in turn, but that, true to borrowing tradition, the women would stay at home; she heard her mother declining the use of the kitchen. 'Thank you, Lupy,' Homily was saying; 'it's very kind of you but we'd better begin as we mean to go on, don't you think? quite separate.'

'And so it starts again,' thought Arrietty, as entering the next room she seated herself in a stiff arm-chair. But no longer quite under the floor – up a little, they would be now, among the lath and plaster: there would be ladders instead of dusty passages, and that platform, she hoped, might do instead of her grating.

She glanced about her at the over-furnished room: the doll's-house left-overs suddenly looked silly – everything for show and nothing much for use; the false coals in the fire-place looked worn as though scrubbed too often by Lupy, and the painted view in the windows had finger-marks round the edge.

She wandered out to the dim-lit platform; this, with it's dust and shadows, had she known of such things, was something like going back-stage. The ladder was in place, she noticed – a sign that someone was out – but in this case, not so much 'out' as 'gone.' Poor Spiller . . . solitary, they had called him. 'Perhaps,' thought Arrietty self-pityingly, 'that's what's the matter with me . . .'

There was a faint light, she saw now, in the chasm below her; what at first had seemed a lessening of darkness seemed now a welcoming glow. Arrietty, her heart beating, took hold of the ladder and set her foot on the first rung. 'If I don't do it now,' she thought deperately, 'this first evening – perhaps, in the future, I should never dare again.' There seemed too many rules in Aunt Lupy's house, too many people, and the rooms seemed too dark and too hot. 'There may be compensations,' she thought, her knees trembling a little as rung after rung she started to climb down, 'but I'll have to discover them myself.'

Soon she stood once again in the dusty entrance hall; she glanced about her and then nervously she looked up; she saw the top of the ladder outlined against the light and the jagged edge of the high platform. It made her feel suddenly dizzy and more than a little afraid: suppose someone, not realizing she was below, decided to pull it up?

The faint light, she realized, came from the hole in the wainscot: the log-box, for some reason, was not laid flush against it – there might well be room to squeeze through. She would like to have one more peep at the room in which, some hours before, young Tom had set them down – to have some little knowledge, however fleeting, of this human dwelling which from now on would compose her world.

All was quiet as she stole towards the Gothic-shaped opening. The log-box, she found, was a good inch and a half away. It was easy enough to slip out and ease her tiny body along the narrow passage left between the side of the box and the wall. Again a little frightening: suppose some human being decided suddenly to shove the log-box into place. She would be squashed, she thought, and found long afterwards, glued to the wainscot, like some strange, pressed flower. For this reason she moved fast, and reaching the box's corner, she stepped out on the hearth.

She glanced about the room. She could see the rafters of the ceiling, the legs of a Windsor chair, and the underside of its seat. She saw a lighted candle on a wooden table, and, by its leg, a pile of skins on the floor – ah this, she realized, was the secret of Spiller's wardrobe.

Another kind of fur lay on the table, just beyond the candle above a piece of cloth – tawny yellow and somehow rougher. As she stared it seemed to stir. A cat? A fox? Arrietty froze to stillness, but she bravely stood her ground. Now the movement became unmistakable: a roll over and a sudden lifting up.

Arrietty gasped – a tiny sound, but it was heard.

A face looked back at her, candle-lit and drowsed with sleep, below its thatch of hair. There was a long silence. At last the boy's lips curved softly into a smile – and very young he looked after sleeping, very harmless. The arm on which he had rested his head lay loosely on the table and Arrietty, from where she stood, had seen his fingers relax. A clock was ticking somewhere above her head; the candle flame rose, still and steady, lighting the peaceful room; the coals gave a gentle shudder as they settled in the grate.

'Hallo,' said Arrietty.

'Hallo,' replied young Tom.

THE BORROWERS AFLOAT

For Guy and Sally

Chapter One

'But what do they talk about?' asked Mr Beguid, the lawyer. He spoke almost irritably as of foolish goings-on.

'They talk about the borrowers,' said Mrs May.

They stood beneath the shelter of the hedge among wet, tree-like cabbages which tumbled in the wind. Below them on this dark, dank afternoon, a lamp glowed warmly through the cottage window. 'We could have an orchard here,' she added lightly as though to change the subject.

'At our time of life,' remarked Mr Beguid, gazing still at the lighted window below them in the hollow, 'yours and mine – it's wiser to plant flowers than fruit . . .'

'You think so?' said Mrs May. She drew her ulster cape more closely about her against the eddying wind. 'But I'll leave her the cottage, you see, in my will.'

'Leave whom the cottage?'

'Kate, my niece.'

'I see,' said Mr Beguid, and he glanced again towards the lighted window behind which he knew Kate was sitting: a strange child, he thought; disconcerting – the way she gazed through one with wide unseeing eyes and yet would chatter by the hour with old Tom Goodenough, a rascally one-time gamekeeper. What could they have in common, he asked himself, this sly old man and eager, listening child? There they had been now (he glanced at his watch) for a good hour and a quarter, hunched by the window, talking, talking . . .

'Borrowers . . .' he repeated, as though troubled by the word; 'what kind of borrowers?'

'Oh, it's just a story,' said Mrs May lightly, picking her way gingerly amongst the rain-soaked cabbages towards the raised brick path; 'something we used to tell each other, my brother and I, when we stayed down here as children.'

'At Firbank Hall, you mean?'

'Yes, with great-aunt Sophy. Kate loves this story.'

'But why,' asked Mr Beguid, 'should she want to tell it to him?'

'To old Tom? Why not? As a matter of fact I believe it's the other way round: I believe he tells it to her.'

As he followed Mrs May along the worn brick path Mr Beguid became silent. He had known this family most of his life and a strange lot (he had begun to think lately) they were.

'But a story made up by you?'

'Not by me, no' – Mrs May laughed as though embarrassed – 'it was my brother, I think, who made it up. If it was made up,' she added suddenly, just above her breath.

Mr Beguid pounced on the words: 'I don't quite follow you. This story you speak of, is it something that actually happened?'

Mrs May laughed. 'Oh no, it couldn't have actually happened. Not possibly.' She began to walk on again, adding over her shoulder: 'It's just that this old man, this old Tom Goodenough, seems to know about these people.'

'What people? These cadgers?'

'Not cadgers – borrowers . . .'

'I see,' said Mr Beguid, who didn't see at all.

'We called them that,' and, turning on the path, she waited for him to catch up with her, 'or rather they called themselves that – because they had nothing of their own at all. Even their names were borrowed: the family we knew – father, mother, and child – were called Pod, Homily, and Little Arrietty.' As he came beside her she smiled: 'I think their names are rather charming.'

'Very,' he said, a little too dryly. And then, in spite of himself, he smiled back at her: always, he remembered, there had been in her manner this air of gentle mockery; even as a young man, though attracted by her prettiness, he had found her disconcerting. 'You haven't changed,' he said.

She at once became more serious: 'But you can't deny that it was a strange old house?'

'Old, yes. But no more strange than' – he looked down the slope – 'than this cottage, say.'

Mrs May laughed. 'Ah, there Kate would agree with you! She finds this cottage quite as strange as we found Firbank, neither more nor less. You know, at Firbank, my brother and I – right from the very first – had this feeling that there were other people living in the house besides the human beings.'

'But!' exclaimed Mr Beguid, exasperated, 'there can be no such things as "people" other than human beings. The terms are synonymous.'

'Other personalities then. Something far smaller than a human being but like them in all essentials – a little larger in the head, perhaps, a little longer in the hands and feet. But very small and hidden. We imagined that they lived like mice – in the wainscots, or behind the skirtings, or under the floorboards . . . and were entirely dependent on what they could filch from the great house above. Yet you couldn't call it stealing: it was a kind of garnering. On the whole they only took things that could well be spared.'

'What sort of things?' asked Mr Beguid and, suddenly feeling foolish, he sprang ahead of her to clear a trail of bramble from her path.

'Oh, all sorts of things. Any kind of food, of course, and any other small movable objects which might be useful – matchboxes, pencil ends, needles, bits of stuff... anything they could turn into tools or clothes or furniture. It was rather sad for them, we thought, because they had a sort of longing for beauty; and to make their dark little holes as charming and comfortable as the homes of human beings. My brother used to help them.' Mrs May hesitated suddenly as though embarrassed. 'Or so he said,' she concluded lamely, and for the sake of appearances she gave a little laugh.

'I see,' said Mr Beguid again. He became silent as they skirted the side of the cottage to avoid the dripping thatch. 'And where does Tom Goodenough come in?' he asked at last as she paused beside the water-butt.

She turned to face him. 'Well, it's extraordinary, isn't it? At my age – nearly seventy – to inherit this cottage and find him still here in possession?'

'Not in possession, exactly – he's the outgoing tenant.'

'I mean,' said Mrs May, 'to find him here at all. In the old days, when they were boys, he and my brother used to go rabbiting – in a way they were great companions. But that all ended – after the rumpus.'

'Oh,' said Mr Beguid, 'so there was a rumpus?' They stood together by the weather-worn front door and, intrigued against his wish, he withdrew his hand from the latch.

'There most certainly was,' exclaimed Mrs May. 'I should have thought you might have heard about it. Even the policeman was implicated – you remember Ernie Runacre? – it must have gone all over the village: the cook and the gardener got wind of these creatures and determined to smoke them out. They got in the local rat-catcher and sent up here for Tom to bring his ferret. He was a boy then, the gamekeeper's grandson – a little older than we were, but still quite young. But' – Mrs May turned suddenly towards him – 'you *must* have heard something of this?'

Mr Beguid frowned. Past rumours stirred vaguely in his memory . . . some nonsense or other at Firbank Hall; a cook with a name like Diver or Driver; things missing from the cabinet in the drawing-room . . .

'Wasn't there,' he said at last, 'some trouble about an emerald watch?'

'Yes, that's why they sent for the police.'

'But' – Mr Beguid's frown deepened – 'this woman, Diver or—'

'Driver! Yes, that was the name.'

'And this gardener – you mean to say they believed in these creatures?'

'Obviously,' said Mrs May, 'or they would not have made all this fuss.'

'What happened?' asked Mr Beguid. 'Did they catch them? No, no – I don't mean that! What I meant to say is – what did they turn out to be? Mice, I suppose?'

'I wasn't there myself at the time – so I can't say "what they turned out to be." But according to my brother they escaped out of doors through a grating – just in the nick of time: one of those ventilator things set low down in the brickwork outside. They ran away across the orchard and' – she looked around her in the half-light – 'up into these fields.'

'Were they seen to go?'

'No,' said Mrs May.

Mr Beguid glanced swiftly down the mist-enshrouded slopes: against the pallid fields the woods beyond looked dark – already wrapped in twilight.

'Squirrels,' he said, 'that's what they were, most likely.'

'Possibly,' said Mrs May. She moved away from him to where, beside the wash-house, the workmen that morning had opened up a drain. 'Wouldn't this be wide enough to take sewage?'

'Wide enough, yes,' he agreed, staring down at the earthenware sections, 'but the sanitary inspector would never allow it: all these drains run straight down to the stream. No, you'll have to have a septic tank, I'm afraid.'

'Then what was this used for?'

He nodded towards the wash-house. 'Dish-water, I suppose, from the sink.' He glanced at his watch. 'Could I give you a lift anywhere? It's getting rather late . . .'

'That's very kind of you,' said Mrs May as they moved towards the front door.

'An odd story,' remarked Mr Beguid, putting his hand to the latch.'

'Yes, very odd.'

'I mean – to go to the lengths of sending for the police. Extraordinary.'

'Yes,' agreed Mrs May, and paused to wipe her feet on a piece of torn sacking which lay beside the step.

Mr Beguid glanced at his own shoes and followed her example. 'Your brother must have been very convincing.'

'Yes, he was.'

'And very inventive.'

'Yes, according to my brother there was quite a colony of these people. He talked about another lot, cousins of the ones at Firbank, who were supposed to live in a badger's set – up here on the edge of these woods. Uncle

Hendreary and Aunt Lupy...' She looked at him sideways. 'This lot had four children.'

'According to your brother,' remarked Mr Beguid sceptically, and he reached again for the latch.

'And according to old Tom,' she laughed and lowered her voice. 'Old Tom swears that the story is true. But *he* contends that they did not live in the badger's set at all; or that, if they did, it could not have been for long. He insists that for years and years they lived up here, in the lath and plaster beside the fire-place.'

'Which fire-place?' asked Mr Beguid uneasily.

'This fire-place,' said Mrs May. As the door swung open she dropped her voice to a whisper: 'Here in this very cottage.'

'Here in this very cottage...' repeated Mr Beguid in a startled voice, and, standing aside for Mrs May to pass, he craned his neck forward to peer within without advancing across the threshold.

The quiet room seemed empty: all they could see at first was yellow lamplight spilling across the flagstones and dying embers in the grate. By the window stood a stack of hazel wands, split and trimmed for thatching, beside them a wooden arm-chair. Then Kate emerged rather suddenly from the shadows beside the fire-place. 'Hallo,' she said.

She seemed about to say more but her gaze slid past Mrs May to where Mr Beguid hovered in the doorway. 'I was looking up the chimney,' she explained.

'So I see – your face is black!'

'Is it?' said Kate, without interest. Her eyes looked very bright and she seemed to be waiting – either, thought Mrs May for Mr Beguid to shut the door and come in or for Mr Beguid to shut the door and depart.

Mrs May glanced at the empty arm-chair and then past Kate towards the door of the wash-house: 'Where's Tom?'

'Gone out to feed the pig,' said Kate. Again she hesitated, then, in a burst, she added: 'Need we go yet? It's only a step across the fields, and there's something I terribly want to show you—'

Mr Beguid glanced at his watch. 'Well, in that case—' he began.

'Yes, please don't wait for us,' interrupted Mrs May impulsively. 'As Kate says, it's only a step . . .'

'I was only going to say,' continued Mr Beguid stolidly from his neutral position on the threshold, 'that as this lane's so narrow and the ditches so full of mud I propose to drive on ahead and turn the car at the cross-roads. He began to button up his overcoat. 'Perhaps you would listen for the horn?'

'Yes, yes, indeed. Thank you . . . of course. We'll be listening . . .'

When the front door had closed and Mr Beguid had gone, Kate took Mrs May by the hand and drew her urgently towards the fire-place: 'And I've heaps to tell you. Heaps and heaps . . .'

'We weren't rude, were we?' asked Mrs May, 'I mean to Mr Beguid? We didn't shoo him off?'

'No, no, of course not. You thanked him beautifully. But look,' Kate went on, 'please look!' Loosing Mrs May's hand, she ran forward and – with much tugging and panting – dragged out the log-box from where it was jammed against the wall beside the hearth: a rat-hole was revealed in the skirting – slightly Gothic in shape. 'That's where they lived . . .' cried Kate.

Mrs May, in spite of herself, felt a curious sense of shock; staring down at it she said uneasily: 'We mustn't

be too credulous, Kate. I mean, we can't believe *quite*
everything we hear. And you know what they say about
old Tom?'

'In the village? Yes, I know what they say – "the
biggest liar in five counties." But all that started *because*
of the borrowers: at first, you see, he used to talk about
them. And that was his mistake. He thought people
would be interested. But they weren't interested – not at
all: they just didn't believe him.' Kate knelt down on the
hearth and, breathing rather heavily, she peered into the
darkness of the hole. 'There was only one other human
being, I think, who really believed in the borrowers . . .'

'Mrs Driver, you mean, the cook at Firbank?'

Kate frowned, sitting back on her heels: 'No, I don't
really think that Mrs Driver *did* believe in them. She saw
them, I know, but I don't think she trusted her eyes. No,
the one I was thinking of was Mild Eye, the gipsy. I mean,
he actually shook them out of his boot on to the floor of
his caravan. And there they were – right under his nose –
and no two ways about it. He tried to grab them, Tom,
says, but they got away. He wanted to put them in a cage
and show them for pennies at the fair. It was Tom who
rescued them. With the help of Spiller, of course.'

'Who was Spiller?' asked Mrs May – she still stared, as
though spellbound, at the rat-hole.

Kate seemed amazed: 'You haven't heard of Spiller?'
'No,' said Mrs May.

'Oh,' cried Kate, throwing her head back and half
closing her eyes, 'Spiller was wonderful!'

'I am sure he was,' said Mrs May; she pulled forward a
rush-seated chair and rather stiffly sat down on it, 'but
you and Tom have been talking for days, remember . . .
I'm a little out of touch; what was Spiller supposed to be
– a borrower?'

'He *was* a borrower,' corrected Kate, 'but rather on the
wild side – he lived in the hedgerows, and wore old
mole-skins, and didn't really wash—'

'He doesn't sound so *tremendously* wonderful.'

'Oh, but he was: Spiller ran for Tom and Tom rushed
down and rescued them; he snatched them up from
under the gipsies' noses and pushed them into his
pockets; he brought them up here – all four of them –
Spiller, Pod, Homily, and Arrietty. And he set them down
very carefully, one by one' – Kate patted the warm
flagstones – 'here, on this very spot. And then, poor
things, they ran away into the wall through that rat-hole
in the skirting' – Kate lowered her head again, trying to
peer in – 'and up a tiny ladder just inside to where the

cousins were living . . .' Kate scrambled up suddenly and, stretching one arm as far as it would go, she tapped on the plaster beside the chimney. 'The cousins' house was somewhere up here. Quite high. Two floors they had – between the lath and plaster of the wash-house and the lath and plaster of this one. They used the chimney, Tom says, and they tapped the wash-house pipes for water. Arrietty didn't like it up there: she used to creep down in the evenings to talk to young Tom. But our lot did not stay there long. Something happened, you see . . .'

'Tell me,' said Mrs May.

'Well, there isn't really time now. Mr Beguid will start hooting . . . And old Tom's the one to tell it: he seems to know everything – even what they said and did when no one else was there . . .'

'He's a born story-teller, that's why,' said Mrs May, laughing. 'And he knows people. Given a struggle for life people react very much alike – according to type, of course – whatever their size or station.' Mrs May leaned forward as though to examine the skirting. 'Even I,' she said, 'can imagine what Homily felt, homeless and destitute, faced with that dusty hole . . . And strange relations living up above who didn't know she was coming, and whom she hadn't seen for years . . .'

Chapter Two

But Mrs May was not quite right: she had underestimated their sudden sense of security – the natural joy a borrower feels when safely under cover. It is true that, as they filed in through the Gothic-shaped hole in the skirting, they had felt a little nervous, a little forlorn; this was because, at first glance, the cave-like space about them seemed disappointingly uninhabited: empty, dark, and echoing, it smelled of dust and mice . . .

'Oh dear,' Homily had muttered incredulously, 'they can't live here!'

'We go up here,' said Spiller, and Homily saw that he stood with his hand on a ladder. Glancing up to where the rungs soared away above them into dimness, she gave a slight shudder: the ladder was made of matchsticks, neatly glued and spliced to two lengths of split cane, such as florists use to support potted plants.

'I'll go first,' said Pod. 'We better take it one at a time.'

Homily watched fearfully until she heard his voice from above.

'It's all right,' he whispered from some invisible eyrie; 'come on up.'

Homily followed, her knees trembling, and emerged at last on to the dim-lit platform beside Pod – an aerial landing-stage, that was what it seemed like – which creaked a little when she stepped on it and almost seemed to sway. Below lay hollow darkness; ahead an open door. 'Oh, my goodness,' she muttered, 'I do hope it's safe . . . don't look down,' she advised Arrietty, who came up next.

But Arrietty had no temptation to look down: her eyes

were on the lighted doorway and the moving shadows within; she heard the faint sound of voices and a sudden high-pitched laugh.

'Come on,' said Spiller, slipping past, and making towards the door.

Arrietty never forgot her first sight of that upstairs room: the warmth, the sudden cleanliness, the winking candlelight, and the smell of home-cooked food.

And so many voices . . . so many people . . .

Gradually, in a dazed way, she began to sort them out: that must be Aunt Lupy embracing her mother. And here was Uncle Hendreary, his beard grown thinner, telling her father that this could not be Arrietty, and her father, with pride, telling Uncle Hendreary it could. Those must

be the three boy cousins. And this thin, tall, fair-like creature, neither old nor young, who hovered shyly in the background with a faint uneasy smile, who was she? Could it be Eggletina? Yes, she supposed it could.

Very dark it was, this strange new home, almost as dark as under the floorboards at Firbank, and lit by wax dips fixed to upturned drawing-pins (how many human dwellings must be burned down, Arrietty realized suddenly, through the carelessness of borrowers running about with lighted candles). In spite of Lupy's polishings the compartments smelled of soot and always in the background a pervading odour of cheese.

The cousins all slept in the kitchen – for warmth, Lupy explained: the ornate drawing-room was only rarely used. Outside the drawing-room was the shadowed platform with its perilous matchstick ladder leading down below.

Above this landing, high among the shadows, were the two small rooms allotted them by Lupy. There was no way up to them as yet, except by climbing hand over hand from lath to lath and scrabbling blindly for footholds, to emerge at length on a rough piece of flooring made by Hendreary from the lid of a cardboard shoe-box.

'Do those rooms good to be used,' Lupy had said (she knew Pod was a handyman), 'and we'll lend you furniture to start with.'

'To start with,' muttered Homily that first morning as, foot after hand, she followed Pod up the laths – unlike most borrowers, she was not very fond of climbing. 'What are we meant to do after?'

She dare not look down. Beneath her, she knew, was the rickety platform below which again were further depths and the matchstick ladder gleaming like a fishbone. 'Anyway,' she comforted herself, feeling clumsily for foot-holes, 'steep it may be, but at least it's a separate entrance . . . What's it like Pod?' she asked as her head emerged suddenly at floor level, through the circular trap-door – very startling it looked, as though decapitated.

'It's dry,' said Pod non-committally; he stamped about a bit on the floor as though to test it.

'Don't stamp so, Pod,' Homily complained, seeking a foothold on the quivering surface. 'It's only cardboard.'

'I know,' said Pod. 'Mustn't grumble,' he added as Homily came towards him.

'At least,' said Homily, looking about her, 'back home under the kitchen we was on solid ground . . .'

'You've lived in a boot since,' Pod reminded her, 'and you've lived in a hole in a bank. And nearly starved. And nearly frozen. And nearly been captured by the gipsies. Mustn't grumble,' he said again.

Homily looked about her. Two rooms? They were barely that: a sheet of cardboard between two sets of laths, divided by a cloth-covered book-cover, on which the words 'Pig Breeders' Annual, 1896' were stamped in tarnished gold. In this dark purple wall Hendreary had cut a door. Ceilings there were none and an eerie light came down from somewhere far above – a crack, Homily supposed, between the floorboards and the whitewashed walls of the gamekeeper's bedroom.

'Who sleeps up there,' she asked Pod, 'that boy's father?'

'Grandfather,' said Pod.

'He'll be after us, I shouldn't wonder,' said Homily, 'with traps and what-nots.'

'Yes, you've got to be quiet,' said Pod, 'especially with

gamekeepers. Out most of the day, though, and the young boy with him. Yes, it's dry,' he repeated, looking about him, 'and warm.'

'Not very,' said Homily. As she followed him through the doorway she saw that the door was hung by the canvas binding which Hendreary had not cut through. 'Soon fray, that will,' she remarked, swinging the panel to and fro, 'and then what?'

'I can stitch it,' said Pod, 'with me cobbler's thread. Easy.' He laid his hands on the great stones of the farther wall. ' 'Tis the chimney casing,' he explained; 'warm, eh?'

'Um,' said Homily, 'if you lean against it.'

'What about if we sleep here – right against the chimney?'

'What in?' asked Homily.

'They're going to lend us beds.'

'No, better keep the chimney for cooking.' Homily ran her hands across the stones and from a vertical crevice began to pick out the plaster. 'Soon get through here to the main flue . . .'

'But we're going to eat downstairs with them,' Pod explained. 'That's what's been arranged – so that it's all one cooking.'

'All one cooking and all one borrowing,' said Homily. 'There won't be no borrowing for you, Pod.'

'Rubbish,' said Pod. 'Whatever makes you say a thing like that?'

'Because,' explained Homily, 'in a cottage like this with only two human beings, a man and a boy, there aren't the pickings there were back at Firbank. You mark my words: I been talking to Lupy. Hendreary and the two elder boys can manage the lot. They won't be wanting competition.'

'Then what'll I do?' said Pod. A borrower deprived of borrowing – especially a borrower of Pod's standing? His eyes became round and blank.

'Get on with the furniture, I suppose.'

'But they're going to lend us that.'

'Lend us!' hissed Homily. 'Everything they've got was ours!'

'Now, Homily—' began Pod.

Homily dropped her voice, speaking in a breathless whisper: 'Every single blessed thing. That red velvet chair, the dresser with the painted plates, all that stuff the boy brought us from the doll's house—'

'Not the keyhole stove,' put in Pod, 'not that dining-table they've made from a door-plate. Not the—'

'The imitation leg of mutton – that was ours,' interrupted Homily, 'and the dish of plaster tarts. All the beds were ours, and the sofa. And the palm in a pot . . .'

'Now listen, Homily,' pleaded Pod, 'we've been into all that, remember. Findings keepings as they say. Far as they knew we was dead and gone – like as we might be lost at sea. The things all came to them in a plain white pillowcase delivered to the door. See what I mean? It's like as if they was left them in a will.'

'I would never have left anything to Lupy,' remarked Homily.

'Now, Homily, you've got to say they've been kind.'

'Yes,' agreed Homily, 'you've got to say it.'

Unhappily she gazed about her. The cardboard floor was scattered with lumps of fallen plaster. Absentmindedly she began to push these towards the gaps where the floor, being straight-edged, did not fit against the rough cob. They clattered hollowly down the hidden shaft into Lupy's kitchen.

'Now you've done it,' said Pod. 'And that's the kind of

noise we mustn't make, not if we value our lives. To human beings,' he went on, 'droppings and rollings means rats or squirrels. You know that as well as I do.'

'Sorry,' said Homily.

'Wait a minute,' said Pod. He had been gazing upwards towards the crack of light and now in a flash he was on the laths and climbing up towards it.

'Careful, Pod,' whispered Homily. He seemed to be pulling at some object which was hidden from Homily by the line of his body. She heard him grunting with the effort.

'It's all right,' said Pod in his normal voice, beginning to climb down again. 'There isn't no one up there. Here you are,' he went on as he landed on the floor and handed her an old bone toothbrush, slightly taller than herself. 'The first borrowing,' he announced modestly and she saw that he was pleased. 'Someone must have dropped it, up there in the bedroom, and it wedged itself in this crack between the floorboards and the wall. We can borrow from up there,' he went on, 'Easy; the wall's fallen away like or the floorboards have shrunk. Farther along it gets even wider . . . And here you are again,' he said and handed her a fair-sized cockle-shell he had pulled out from the cob. 'You go on sweeping,' he told her, 'and I'll pop up again, – might as well, while it's free of human beings . . .'

'Now, Pod, go careful . . .' Homily urged him, with a mixture of pride and anxiety. She watched him climb the laths and watched him disappear before, using the cockleshell as a dustpan, she began to sweep the floor: the bottom of a china soapdish for baths, a crocheted

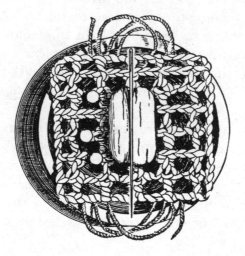

table-mat in red and yellow which would do as a carpet, a worn sliver of pale green soap with grey veins in it, a large darning-needle (slightly rusted), three aspirin tablets, a packet of pipe-cleaners, and a fair length of tarred string.

'I'm kind of hungry now,' said Pod.

Chapter Three

They climbed down the laths on to the platform –keeping well away from the edge, through Lupy's drawing-room, into the kitchen.

'Ah, here you are,' cried Lupy, in her loud, rich, aunt-like voice – very plump she looked in her dress of purple silk, and flushed from the heat of the stove. Homily, beside her, looked as thin and angular as a clothes-peg. 'We were just going to start without you.'

The door-plate table was lit by a single lamp; it was made from a silver salt shaker with a hole in the top, out of which protruded a wick. The flame burned stilly in that airless room and the porcelain table top, icily white, swam in a sea of shadow.

Eggletina, by the stove, was ladling out soup which Timmis, the younger boy, unsteadily carried round in yellow snail-shells: very pretty they looked – scoured and polished. They were rather alike – Eggletina and Timmis – Arrietty thought, quiet and pale and watchful-seeming. Hendreary and the two elder boys were already seated, tucking into their food.

'Get up, get up,' cried Lupy archly, 'when your aunt comes in,' and her two elder sons rose reluctantly and quickly sat down again. 'Harpsichord manners . . .' their expressions seemed to say. They were too young to remember those gracious days in the drawing-room of the big house – the Madeira cake, little sips of China tea, and music of an evening. Churlish and shy, they hardly ever spoke. 'They don't much like us,' Arrietty decided as she took her place at the table. Little Timmis, his hands in a cloth, brought her a shell of soup. The thin shell was piping hot and she found it hard to hold.

It was a plain meal, but wholesome: soup and boiled butter-beans with a trace of dripping – one bean each. There was none of that first evening's lavishness when Lupy had raided her store cupboards. It was as though she and Hendreary had talked things over, setting more modest standards. 'We must begin,' she had imagined Lupy saying to Hendreary in a firm, self-righteous voice, 'as we mean to go on.'

There was, however, a sparrow's egg omelette, fried in a tin lid, for Hendreary and the two boys. Lupy saw to it herself. Seasoned with thyme and a trace of wild garlic it

smelled very savoury and sizzled on the plate. 'They've
been borrowing, you see,' Lupy explained, 'out of doors
all morning. They can only get out when the front door's
open and on some days they can't get back. Three nights
Hendreary spent once in the woodshed before he got his
chance.'

Homily glanced at Pod, who had finished his bean and
whose eyes had become strangely round. 'Pod's done a
bit, too, this morning,' she remarked carelessly, 'more
high than far; but it does give you an appetite . . .'

'Borrowing?' asked Uncle Hendreary. He seemed
amazed, and his thin beard had ceased the up and down
movement which went with his eating.

'One or two things,' said Pod modestly.

'From where?' asked Hendreary, staring.

'The old man's bedroom. It's just above us . . .'

Hendreary was silent a moment and then he said:
'That's all right, Pod,' but as though it wasn't all right at
all. 'But we've got to go steady. There isn't much in this
house, not to spare like. We can't all go at it like bulls at
gates.' He took another mouthful of omelette and
consumed it slowly while Arrietty, fascinated, watched
his beard and the shadow it threw on the wall. When he
had swallowed, he said: 'I'd take it as a favour, Pod, if
you'd just leave borrowing for a while. We know the
territory, as you might say, and we work to our own
methods. Better we lend you things, for the time being.
And there's food for all, if you don't mind it plain.'

There was a long silence. The two elder boys, Arrietty
noticed, shovelling up their food, kept their eyes on their
plates. Lupy clattered about at the stove. Eggletina sat
looking at her hands, and little Timmis stared wonderingly from one to another, eyes wide in his small pale
face.

'As you wish,' said Pod slowly, as Lupy bustled back to the table.

'Homily,' said Lupy brightly, breaking the awkward silence, 'this afternoon, if you've got a moment to spare, I'd be much obliged if you'd give me a hand with Spiller's summer clothes . . .'

Homily thought of the comfortless rooms upstairs and of all she longed to do to them. 'But of course,' she told Lupy, trying to smile.

'I always get them finished,' Lupy explained, 'by early spring. Time's getting on now: to-morrow's the first of March.' And she began to clear the table. They all jumped up to help her.

'Where *is* Spiller?' asked Homily, trying to stack the snail-shells.

'Goodness knows,' said Lupy; 'off on some wild-goose chase. No one knows where Spiller is. Nor what he does for that matter. All I know is,' she went on, taking the plug out of the pipe (as they used to do at home, Arrietty remembered) to release a trickle of water, 'is that I make his moleskin suits each autumn and his white kid ones each spring and that he always comes to fetch them.'

'It's very kind of you to make his suits,' said Arrietty, watching Lupy rinse the snail-shells in a small crystal salt-cellar and standing by to dry them.

'It's only human,' said Lupy.

'Human!' exclaimed Homily, startled by the choice of word.

'Human – just short like that – means "kind,"' explained Lupy, remembering that Homily, poor dear, had had no education, being dragged up as you might say under a kitchen floor. 'It's got nothing at all to do with human beings. How could it have?'

'That's what I was wondering . . .' said Homily.

'Besides,' Lupy went on, 'he brings us things in exchange.'

'Oh, I see,' said Homily.

'He goes hunting, you see, and I smoke his meat for him – there in the chimney. Some we keep and some he takes away. What's over I make into paste with butter on the top – keeps for months that way. Birds' eggs, he brings, and berries and nuts . . . fish from the stream. I smoke the fish too, or pickle it. Some things I put down in salt . . . And if you want anything special, you tell Spiller – ahead of time, of course – and he borrows it from the gipsies. That old stove he lives in is just by their camping site. Give him time and he can get almost anything you want from the gipsies. We have a whole arm of a waterproof raincoat, got by Spiller, and very useful it was when the bees swarmed one summer . . . we all crawled inside it.'

'What bees?' asked Homily.

'Haven't I told you about the bees in the thatch? They've gone now. But that's how we got the honey, all we'd ever want, and a good, lasting wax for the candles . . .'

Homily was silent a moment – enviously silent, dazzled by Lupy's riches. Then she said, as she wiped up the last snail-shell: 'Where do these go, Lupy?'

'Into that wickerwork hair-tidy in the corner. They won't break – just take them on the tin lid and drop them in . . .'

'I must say, Lupy,' Homily remarked wonderingly as she dropped the shells one by one into the hair-tidy (it was horn-shaped with a loop to hang it on and a faded blue bow on the top), 'that you've become what they call a good manager . . .'

'For one,' agreed Lupy, laughing, 'who was brought up

in a drawing-room and never raised a hand.'

'You weren't *brought up* in a drawing-room,' Homily reminded her.'

'Oh, I don't remember those Rain-Pipe days,' said Lupy blithely; 'I married so young. Just a child . . .' And she turned suddenly to Arrietty: 'Now, what are you dreaming about, Miss-butter-wouldn't-melt-in-her-mouth?'

'I was thinking of Spiller,' said Arrietty.

'A-ha!' cried Aunt Lupy, 'she was thinking of Spiller!' And she laughed again. 'You don't want to waste precious thoughts on a ragamuffin like Spiller. You'll meet lots of nice borrowers, all in good time. Maybe, one day, you'll meet one brought up in a library: they're the best, so they say, gentlemen all, and a good cultural background.'

'I was thinking,' continued Arrietty evenly, keeping her temper, 'that I couldn't imagine Spiller dressed up in white kid.'

'It doesn't stay white long,' cried Lupy, 'of that I can assure you! It has to be white to start with because it's made from an evening glove. A ball glove, shoulder length – it's one of the few things I salvaged from the drawing-room. But he will have kid – says it's hard wearing. It stiffens up, of course, directly he gets it wet, but he soon wears it soft again. And by that time,' she added, 'It's all colours of the rainbow.'

Arrietty could imagine the colours; they would not be 'all colours of the rainbow': they would be colours without real colour, the shades which made Spiller invisible – soft fawns, pale browns, dull greens, and a kind of shadowy gun-metal. Spiller took care about 'seasoning' his clothes: he brought them to a stage where he could melt into the landscape, where one could stand beside him, almost within touching distance, and yet not see him. Spiller deceived animals as well as gipsies. Spiller deceived hawks and stoats and foxes . . . and Spiller might not wash but he had no Spiller scent: he smelled of hedgerows, and bark and grasses and of wet sun-warmed earth; he smelled of buttercups, dried cow dung, and early morning dew . . .

'When will he come?' Arrietty asked. But she ran away upstairs before anyone could tell her. She wept a little in the upstairs room, crouched down beside the soap-dish.

To talk of Spiller reminded her of out of doors and of a wild, free life she might never know again. This new-found haven among the lath and plaster might all too soon become another prison . . .

Chapter Four

It was Hendreary and the boys who carried the furniture up the laths, with Pod standing by to receive it. In this way Lupy lent them just what she wished to lend and nothing they would have chosen. Homily did not grumble, however; she had become very quiet lately as slowly she realized their predicament.

Sometimes they stayed downstairs after meals, helping generally or talking to Lupy. But they would gauge the length of these visits according to Lupy's mood: when she became flustered, blaming them for some small mishap brought on by herself, they would know it was time to go. 'We couldn't do right to-day,' they would say, sitting empty handed upstairs on Homily's old champagne corks which Lupy had unearthed for stools. They would sit by the chimney casing in the inner room to get the heat from the stones. Here Pod and Homily had a double bed, one of those from the doll's house: Arrietty slept in the outer room, the one with the entrance hole. She slept on a thickish piece of wadding, borrowed in the old days from a box of artist's pastels, and they had given her most of the bed-clothes.

'We shouldn't have come, Pod,' Homily said one evening as they sat alone upstairs.

'We had no choice,' said Pod.

'And we got to go,' she added, and sat there watching him as he stitched the sole of a boot.

'To where?' asked Pod.

Things had become a little better for Pod lately: he had filed down the rusted needle and was back at his cobbling. Hendreary had brought him the skin of a weazel, one of those nailed up by the gamekeeper to dry on the outhouse door, and he was making them all new shoes. This pleased Lupy very much and she had become a little less bossy.

'Where's Arrietty?' asked Homily suddenly.

'Downstairs, I shouldn't wonder,' said Pod.

'What does she do downstairs?'

'Tells Timmis a story and puts him to bed.'

'I know that,' said Homily, 'but why does she stay so long? I'd nearly dropped off last night when we heard her come up the laths . . .'

'I suppose they get talking,' said Pod.

Homily was silent a moment and then she said: 'I don't feel easy. I've got my feeling . . .' This was the feeling borrowers get when human beings are near; with Homily it started at the knees.

Pod glanced up towards the floorboards above them from whence came a haze of candlelight: 'It's the old man going to bed.'

'No,' said Homily, getting up, 'I'm used to that. We hear that every night.' She began to walk about. 'I think,' she said at last, 'that I'll just pop downstairs . . .'

'What for?' asked Pod.

'To see if she's there.'

'It's late,' said Pod.

'All the more reason,' said Homily.

'Where else would she be?' asked Pod.

'I don't know, Pod. I've got my feeling and I've had it once or twice lately,' she said.

Homily had grown more used to the laths: she had become more agile, even in the dark. But to-night it was very dark indeed. When she reached the landing below she felt a sense of yawning space and a draught from the depths which eddied hollowly around her; feeling her way to the drawing-room door, she kept well back from the edge of the platform.

The drawing-room too was strangely dark and so was the kitchen beyond; there was a faint glow from the keyhole fire and a rhythmic sound of breathing.

'Arrietty?' she called softly from the doorway, just above a whisper.

Hendreary gave a snort and mumbled in his sleep; she heard him turning over.

'Arrietty . . .' whispered Homily again.

'What's that?' cried Lupy, suddenly and sharply.

'It's me . . . Homily.'

'What do you want? We were all asleep. Hendreary's had a hard day . . .'

'Nothing,' faltered Homily, 'it's all right. I was looking for Arrietty . . .'

'Arrietty went upstairs hours ago,' said Lupy.

'Oh,' said Homily, and was silent a moment. The air was full of breathing. 'All right,' she said at last, 'thank you. I'm sorry . . .'

'And shut the drawing-room door on to the landing as you go out. There's a howling draught,' said Lupy.

As she felt her way back across the cluttered room, Homily saw a faint light ahead, a dim reflection from the landing. Could it come from above, she wondered, where Pod, two rooms away, was stitching? Yet it had not been there before . . .

Fearfully she stepped out on the platform. The glow, she realized, did not come from above but from somewhere far below: the matchstick ladder was still in place and she saw the top rungs quiver. After a moment's pause she summoned up the courage to peer over. Her startled eyes met those of Arrietty, who was climbing up the ladder and had nearly reached the top. Far below Homily could see the Gothic shape of the hole in the skirting: it seemed a blaze of light.

'Arrietty!' she gasped.

Arrietty did not speak. She climbed off the last rung of the ladder, put her finger to her lips, and whispered: 'I've got to draw it up. Move back.' And Homily, as though in a trance, moved out of the way as Arrietty drew the ladder up rung over rung until it teetered above her into the darkness and then, trembling a little with the effort, she eased it along and laid it against the laths.

'Well . . .' began Homily in a sort of gasp. In the half-light from below they could see each other's faces: Homily's aghast with her mouth hanging open; Arrietty's grave, her finger to her lips. 'One minute,' she whispered and went back to the edge. 'All right,' she called out softly into the space beneath; Homily heard a muffled thud, a scraping sound, the clap of wood on wood, and the light below went out.

'He's pushed back the log-box,' Arrietty whispered across the sudden darkness. 'Here, give me your hand . . . Don't worry,' she beseeched in a whisper, 'and don't take on! I was going to tell you anyway.' And supporting her shaking mother by the elbow she helped her up the laths.

Pod looked up startled. 'What's the matter?' he said as Homily sank down on the bed.

'Let me get her feet up first,' said Arrietty. She did so gently and covered her mother's legs with a folded silk handkerchief, yellowed with washing and stained with marking-ink, which Lupy had given them for a bed cover. Homily lay with her eyes closed and spoke through pale lips. 'She's been at it again,' she said.

'At what?' asked Pod. He had laid down his boot and had risen to his feet.

'Talking to humans,' said Homily.

Pod moved across and sat on the end of the bed. Homily opened her eyes. They both stared at Arrietty.

'Which ones?' asked Pod.

'Young Tom, of course,' said Homily. 'I caught her in the act. That's where she's been most evenings, I shouldn't wonder. Downstairs, they think she's up, and upstairs, we think she's down.'

'Well, you know where that gets us,' said Pod. He became very grave. 'That, my girl, back at Firbank was the start of all our troubles.'

'Talking to humans . . .' moaned Homily and a quiver passed over her face. Suddenly she sat up on one elbow and glared at Arrietty: 'You wicked thoughtless girl, how *could* you do it again!'

Arrietty stared back at them, not defiantly exactly, but as though she were unimpressed. 'But with this Tom downstairs,' she protested. 'I can't see why it matters: he knows we're here anyway. Because he put us here himself! He could get at us any minute if he really wanted to . . .'

'How could he get at us,' said Homily, 'right up here?'

'By breaking down the wall – it's only plaster.'

'Don't say such things, Arrietty,' shuddered Homily.

'But they're true,' said Arrietty. 'Anyway,' she added, 'he's going.'

'Going?' said Pod sharply.

'They're both going,' said Arrietty, 'he and his grandfather; the grandfather's going to a place called Hospital, and the boy is going to a place called Leighton Buzzard to stay with his uncle who is an ostler. What's an ostler?' she asked.

But neither of her parents replied: they were staring blankly at each other. Struck dumb, they seemed – it was rather frightening.

'We've got to tell Hendreary,' said Pod at last, 'and quickly.'

Homily nodded. Recovered from one fear to face another, she had swung her legs down from the bed.

'But it's no good waking them now,' said Pod. 'I'll go down first thing in the morning.'

'Oh, my goodness,' breathed Homily, 'all those poor children . . .'

'What's the matter?' asked Arrietty. 'What have I said?' She felt scared suddenly and gazed uncertainly from one parent to the other.

'Arrietty,' said Pod, turning towards her – his face had become very grave – 'all we've told you about human beings is true; but what we haven't told you, or haven't stressed enough maybe, is that we, the borrowers, cannot survive without them.' He drew a long deep breath. 'When they close up a house and go away it usually means the end . . .'

'No food, no fire, no clothes, no heat, no water . . .' chanted Homily, almost as though she were quoting.

'Famine . . .' said Pod.

Chapter Five

Next morning, when Hendreary heard the news, a conference was called around the door-plate. They all filed in, nervous and grave, and places were allotted them by Lupy. Arrietty was questioned again.

'Are you sure of your dates, Arrietty?'

Yes, Arrietty was sure.

'And of your facts? Quite sure: young Tom and his grandfather would leave in three days' time in a gig drawn by a grey pony called Duchess and driven by Tom's uncle, the ostler, whose name was Fred Tarabody and who lived in Leighton Buzzard and worked at the Swan Hotel – what was an ostler? she wondered again – and young Tom was worried because he had lost his ferret, although it had a bell round its neck and a collar with his name on: he had lost it two days ago down a rabbit-hole and was afraid he might have to leave without it, and even if he found it he wasn't sure they would let him take it with him.

'That's neither there nor here,' said Hendreary, drumming his fingers on the table.

They all seemed very anxious and at the same time curiously calm.

Hendreary glanced round the table. 'One, two, three, four, five, six, seven, eight, nine,' he said gloomily and began to stroke his beard.

'Pod, here,' said Homily, 'can help borrow.'

'And I could too,' put in Arrietty.

'And I could,' echoed Timmis in a sudden squeaky voice. They all turned round to look at him, except Hendreary, and Lupy stroked his hair.

'Borrow *what*?' asked Hendreary. 'No, it isn't borrowers we want; on the contrary' – he glanced across the table and Homily, meeting his eye, suddenly turned pink – 'it's something left to borrow. They won't leave a crumb behind, that boy and his grandad, not if I know 'em. We'll have to live from now on on just what we've managed to save . . .'

'For as long as it lasts,' said Lupy grimly.

'For as long as it lasts,' repeated Hendreary, 'and such as it is.' All their eyes grew wider.

'Which it won't do for ever,' said Lupy. She glanced up at her store shelves and quickly away again. She too had become rather red.

'About borrowing . . .' stammered Homily. 'I was meaning out of doors . . . the vegetable patch . . . beans and peas . . . and suchlike.'

'The birds will have that lot,' said Hendreary, 'with this house closed and the human beings gone. The birds always know in a trice . . . And what's more,' he went on, 'there's more wild things and vermin in these woods than in all the rest of the country put together – weasels, stoats, foxes, badgers, shrikes, magpies, sparrow-hawks, crows . . .'

'That's enough, Hendreary,' Pod put in quickly. 'Homily's feeling faint . . .'

'It's all right . . .' murmured Homily. She took a sip of water out of the acorn cup, and staring down at the table she rested her head on her hand.

Hendreary, carried away by the length of his list, seemed not to notice: '. . . owls, and buzzards,' he concluded in a satisfied voice. 'You've seen the skins for yourselves nailed up on the outhouse door, and the birds strung up on a thorn bush – gamekeeper's gibbet they call it. He keeps them down all right, when he's well and about. And the boy, too, takes a hand. But with them two gone . . . !' Hendreary raised his gaunt arms and cast his eyes towards the ceiling.

No one spoke. Arrietty stole a look at Timmis, whose face had become very pale.

'And when the house is closed and shuttered,' Hendreary went on again suddenly, 'how do you propose to get *out*?' He looked round the table triumphantly as one

who had made a point. Homily, her head on her hand, was silent. She had begun to regret having spoken.

'There's always ways,' murmured Pod.

Hendreary pounced on him: 'Such as?' When Pod did not reply at once Hendreary thundered on: 'The last time they went away we had a plague of field-mice . . . the whole house awash with them, upstairs and down. Now when they lock up they lock up proper. Not so much as a spider could get in!'

'Nor out,' said Lupy, nodding.

'Nor out,' agreed Hendreary and, as though exhausted by his own eloquence, he took a sip from the cup.

For a moment or two no one spoke. Then Pod cleared his throat. 'They won't be gone for ever,' he said.

Hendreary shrugged his shoulders. 'Who knows?'

'Looks to me,' said Pod, 'that they'll always need a gamekeeper. Say this one goes, another moves in like. Won't be empty long – a good house like this on the edge of the coverts, with water laid on in the wash-house . . .'

'Who knows?' said Hendreary again.

'Your problem, as I see it,' went on Pod, 'is to hold out over a period.'

'That's it,' agreed Hendreary.

'But you don't know for how long – that's your problem.'

'That's it,' agreed Hendreary.

'The farther you can stretch your food,' Pod elaborated, 'the longer you'll be able to wait . . .'

'Stands to reason,' said Lupy.

'And,' Pod went on, 'the fewer mouths you have to feed, the farther the food will stretch.'

'That's right,' agreed Hendreary.

'Now,' went on Pod, 'say there are six of you . . .'

'Nine,' said Hendreary, looking round the table, 'to be exact.'

'You don't count us,' said Pod. 'Homily, Arrietty, and me – we're moving out.' There was a stunned silence round the table as Pod, very calm, turned to Homily. 'That's right, isn't it?' he asked her.

Homily stared back at him as though he were crazy and, in despair, he nudged her with his foot. At that she swallowed hastily and began to nod her head. 'That's right . . .' she managed to stammer, blinking her eyelids.

Then pandemonium broke out: questions, suggestions, protestations, and arguments. 'You don't know what you're saying, Pod,' Hendreary kept repeating and Lupy kept on asking: 'Moving out – where to?'

'No good being hasty, Pod,' Hendreary said at last. 'The choice of course is yours, but we're all in this together, and for as long as it lasts' – he glanced around the table as though putting the words on record – 'and such as it is, what is ours is yours.'

'That's very kind of you, Hendreary,' said Pod.

'Not at all,' said Hendreary, speaking rather too smoothly; 'it stands to reason.'

'It's only human,' put in Lupy: she was very fond of this word.

'But,' went on Hendreary, as Pod remained silent, 'I see you've made up your mind.'

'That's right,' said Pod.

'In which case,' said Hendreary, 'there's nothing we can do but adjourn the meeting and wish you all good luck!'

'That's right,' said Pod.

'Good luck, Pod,' said Hendreary.

'Thanks, Hendreary,' said Pod.

'And to all three valiant souls – Pod, Homily and little Arrietty – good luck and good borrowing!'

Homily murmured something and then there was silence, an awkward silence while eyes avoided eyes. 'Come on, me old girl,' said Pod at last, and turning to Homily he helped her to her feet. 'If you'll excuse us,' he said to Lupy, who had become rather red in the face again, 'we got one or two plans to discuss.'

They all rose and Hendreary, looking worried, followed Pod to the door: 'When you think of leaving, Pod?'

'In a day or two's time,' said Pod, 'when the coast's clear down below.'

'No hurry, you know,' said Hendreary. 'And any tackle you want . . .'

'Thanks,' said Pod.

'. . . just say the word.

'I will,' said Pod. He gave a half-smile, rather shy, and went on through the door.

Chapter Six

Homily climbed the laths without speaking: she went straight to the inner room and sat down on the bed. She sat there shivering slightly and staring at her hands.

'I had to say it,' said Pod, 'and we have to do it, what's more.'

Homily nodded.

'You see how we're placed?' said Pod.

Homily nodded again.

'Any suggestions?' said Pod. 'Anything else we could do?'

'No,' said Homily, 'we've got to go. And what's more,' she added, 'we'd have had to anyway.'

'How do you make that out?' said Pod.

'I wouldn't stay here with Lupy,' declared Homily, 'not if she bribed me with molten gold, which she isn't likely to. I kept quiet, Pod, for the child's sake. A bit of young company, I thought, and a family background. I even kept quiet about the furniture . . .'

'Yes, you did,' said Pod.

'It's only,' said Homily, and again she began to shiver, 'that he went on so about the vermin . . .'

'Yes, he did go on,' said Pod.

'Better a place of our own,' said Homily.

'Yes,' agreed Pod, 'better a place of our own . . .' But he gazed round the room in a hunted kind of way, and his flat round face looked blank.

When Arrietty arrived upstairs with Timmis she looked both scared and elated.

'Oh,' said Homily, 'here you are.' And she stared rather blankly at Timmis.

'He would come,' Arrietty told her, holding him tight
by the hand.

'Well, take him along to your room. And tell him a
story or something . . .'

'All right. I will in a minute. But first I just wanted to
ask you—'

'Later,' said Pod, 'there'll be plenty of time: we'll talk
about everything later.'

'That's right,' said Homily; 'you tell Timmis a story.'

'Not about owls?' pleaded Timmis. He still looked
rather wide-eyed.

'No,' agreed Homily, 'not about owls. You ask her to
tell you about the doll's house' – she glanced at Arrietty –
'or that other place – what's it called now? – that place
with the plaster borrowers?'

But Arrietty seemed not to be listening. 'You did mean
it, didn't you?' she burst out suddenly.

Homily and Pod stared back at her, startled by her
tone. 'Of course we meant it,' said Pod.

'Oh,' cried Arrietty, 'thank goodness . . . thank goodness,' and her eyes filled suddenly with tears. 'To be out of
doors again . . . to see the sun, to—' Running forward,
she embraced them each in turn: 'It will be all right – I
know it will!' Aglow with relief and joy, she turned back
to Timmis: 'Come, Timmis, I know a lovely story – better
than the doll's house – about a whole town of houses: a
place called Little Fordham . . .'

This place, of recent years, had become a kind of legend to borrowers. How they got to know it no one could remember – perhaps a conversation overheard in some kitchen and corroborated later through dining-room or nursery – but know of it they did. Little Fordham, it appeared, was a complete model village. Solidly built, it stood out of doors in all weathers in the garden of the man who had designed it, and it covered half an acre. It had a church, with organ music laid on, a school, a row of shops, and – because it lay by a stream – its own port, shipping and custom houses. It was inhabited – or so they had heard – by a race of plaster figures, borrower size, who stood about in frozen positions; or who, wooden-faced and hopeless, rode interminably in trains. They also knew that from early morning until dusk troupes of human beings wound around and about it, removed on asphalt paths and safely enclosed by chains. They knew – as the birds knew – that these human beings would drop litter – the ends of ice-cream cones, sandwich crusts, nuts, buns, half-eaten apples. ('Not that you can live on those,' Homily would remark. 'I mean, you'd want a change . . .') But what fascinated them most about the place was the plethora of empty houses – houses to suit every taste and every size of family: detached, semi-detached, stuck together in a row, or standing comfortably each in its separate garden – houses which were solidly built and solidly roofed, set firmly in the ground and which no human being, however curious, could carelessly wrench open – as they could with doll's houses – and poke about inside. In fact, as Arrietty had heard, doors and windows were one with the structure – there were no kind of openings at all. But this was a drawback easily remedied. 'Not that they'd open up the front doors,' she explained in whispers to Timmis as they lay

curled up on Arrietty's bed; 'borrowers wouldn't be so silly; they'd burrow through the soft earth and get in underneath . . . and no human being would know they were there.'

'Go on about the trains,' whispered Timmis.

And Arrietty went on. And on. Explaining and inventing, creating another kind of life. Deep in this world she forgot the present crisis, her parents' worries, and her uncle's fears; she forgot the dusty drabness of the rooms between the laths, the hidden dangers of the woods outside, and that already she was feeling rather hungry.

Chapter Seven

'But where are we going *to*?' asked Homily for about the twentieth time. It was two days later and they were up in Arrietty's room sorting things for the journey, discarding and selecting from oddments spread round on the floor.

They could only take – Pod had been very firm about this – what Lupy described as hand luggage. She had given them for this purpose the rubberized sleeve of the waterproof raincoat, which they had cut up neatly into squares.

'I thought,' said Pod, 'we'd try first to make for that hole in the bank.'

'I don't think I'd relish that hole in the bank,' said Homily, 'not without the boot.'

'Now, Homily, we've got to go somewhere. And it's getting on for Spring.'

Homily turned and looked at him: 'Do you know the way?'

'No,' said Pod and went on folding the length of tarred string; 'we've got to ask.'

'What's the weather like now?' asked Homily.

'That's one of the things,' said Pod, 'I've asked Arrietty to find out.'

With some misgivings, but in a spirit of 'needs must,' they had sent her down the matchstick ladder to interview young Tom. 'You've got to ask him to leave us some loophole,' Pod had instructed her, 'no matter how small so long as we can get out of doors. If need be we can undo the luggage and pass the pieces through one by one. If the worst came to the worst, I wouldn't say no to a ground-floor window and something below to break the drop. But like as not they'll latch those tight and shutter them across. And tell him to leave the log-box well pulled out from the skirting. None of us can move it, not even when it's empty. A nice pickle we'd be in, and all the Hendrearys too, if he trundles off to Leighton Buzzard and leaves us shut in the wall. And tell him where we're making for – that field called Perkins Beck – but don't tell him nothing about the hole in the bank – and get him to give you a few landmarks, something to put us on our way. It's been a bit chilly indoors lately, for March: ask him if there's snow. If there's snow we're done: we've got to wait . . .'

But could they wait? he wondered now as he hung the coil of tarred string on a nail in the lath and thoughtfully took up his hat-pin. Hendreary had said in a burst of generosity: 'We're all in this together.' But Lupy had remarked afterwards, discussing their departure with Homily: 'I don't want to seem hard, Homily, but in times like these it's each one for his own. And in our place you'd say the same.' She had been very kind about giving them things – the mackintosh sleeve was a case in point – and the Christmas-pudding thimble with a ring on its tip for Homily to hang round her neck – but the store shelves, they noticed, were suddenly bare: all the food had been whisked away and hidden out of sight; and Lupy had doled out fifteen dried peas which she had said she hoped would 'last them.' These they kept upstairs, soaking in the soap-dish, and Homily would take them down three at a time to boil them on Lupy's stove.

To 'last them' for how long? Pod wondered now, as he rubbed a speck of rust off his hat-pin. Good as new, he thought, as he tested the point, pure steel and longer than he was. No, they would have to get off, he realized, the minute the coast was clear, snow or no snow . . .

'Here's someone now,' exclaimed Homily; 'it must be Arrietty.' They went to the hole and helped her on to the floor: the child looked pleased, they noticed, and flushed with the heat of the fire. In one hand she carried a long steel nail, in the other a sliver of cheese. 'We can eat this now,' she said excitedly; 'there's a lot more downstairs: he pushed it through the hole behind the log-box. There's

a slice of dry bread, some more cheese, six roasted
chestnuts, and an egg.'

'Not a hen's egg?' said Pod.

'Yes.'

'Oh my!' exclaimed Homily. 'Who's going to get it up
the laths?'

'And how are we going to cook it?' asked Pod.

Homily tossed her head: 'I'll boil it with the peas on
Lupy's stove. It's our egg: no one can say a word.'

'It's boiled already,' Arrietty told them, 'hard boiled.'

'Thank goodness for that,' exclaimed Pod. 'I'll take
down the razor-blade – we can bring it up in slices.
What's the news?' he asked Arrietty.

'Well, the weather's not bad at all,' she said; 'spring-
like, he says, when the sun's out, and pretty warm.'

'Never mind that,' said Pod; 'what about the loophole?'

'That's all right too. There's a worn-out place at the
bottom of the door – the front door, where feet have been
kicking it open, like Tom does when his arms are full of
sticks. It's shaped like an arch. But they've nailed a piece
of wood across it now to keep the field-mice out. Two

nails it's got, one on either side. This is one of them,' and she showed them the nail she had brought. 'Now all we've got to do, he says, is to swing the bit of wood up on the other nail and prop it safely, and we can all go through – underneath. After we've gone Hendreary and the cousins can knock it in again – that is if they want to.'

'Good,' said Pod, 'good.' He seemed very pleased. 'They'll want to all right because of the field-mice. And when did he say they were leaving – him and his grandpa, I mean?'

'What he said before: the day after to-morrow. But he hasn't found his ferret.'

'Good,' said Pod again: he wasn't interested in ferrets. 'And now we'd better nip down quick and get that food up the laths, or someone might see it first.'

Homily and Arrietty climbed down with him to lend a hand. They brought up the bread and cheese and the roasted chestnuts, but the egg they decided to leave. 'There's a lot of good food in a hen's egg,' Pod pointed out, 'and it's all wrapped up already, as you might say, clean and neat in its shell. We'll take that egg along with us and we'll take it just as it is.' So they rolled the egg along inside the wainscot to a shadowy corner in which they had seen shavings.

'It can wait for us there,' said Pod.

Chapter Eight

On the day the human beings moved out the borrowers kept very quiet. Sitting round the door-plate table they listened to the bangings, the bumpings, the runnings up and down stairs with interest and anxiety. They heard voices they had not heard before and sounds which they could not put a name to. They went on keeping quiet . . . long after the final bang of the front door had echoed into silence.

'You never know,' Hendreary whispered to Pod; 'they might come back for something.' But after a while the emptiness of the house below seemed to steal in upon them, seeping mysteriously through the lath and plaster – and it seemed to Pod a final kind of emptiness. 'I think it's all right now,' he ventured at last; 'suppose one of us went down to reconnoitre?'

'I'll go,' said Hendreary, rising to his feet. 'None of you move until I give the word. I want the air clear for sound . . .'

They sat in silence while he was gone. Homily stared at their three modest bundles lying by the door, strapped by Pod to his hat-pin. Lupy had lent Homily a little moleskin jacket – for which Lupy had grown too stout. Arrietty wore a scarf of Eggletina's: the tall, willowy creature had placed it round her neck, wound it three times about, but had said not a word. 'Doesn't she ever speak?' Homily had asked once, on a day when she and Lupy had been more friendly. 'Hardly ever,' Lupy had admitted, 'and never smiles. She's been like that for years, ever since that time when as a child she ran away from home.'

After a while Hendreary returned and confirmed that

the coast was clear. 'But better light your dips; it's later than I thought . . .'

One after another they scrambled down the matchstick ladder, careless now of noise. The log-box had been pulled well back from the hole and they flowed out into the room – cathedral high, it seemed to them, vast and still and echoing – but suddenly all their own: they could do anything, go anywhere. The main window was shuttered as Pod had foreseen, but a smaller, cell-like window, sunk low and deep in the wall, let in a last pale reflection of the sunset. The younger cousins and Arrietty went quite wild, running in and out of the shadows among the chair legs, exploring the cavern below the table top, the underside of which, cobweb hung, danced in the light of their dips. Discoveries were made and treasures found – under rugs, down cracks in the floor, between loose hearthstones . . . here a pin, there a matchstick; a button, an old collar-stud, a blackened farthing, a coral bead, a hook without its eye, and a broken piece of lead from a lead pencil. (Arrietty pounced on this last and pushed it into her pocket: she had had to leave her diary behind, with other non-essentials, but one never knew . . .) Then dips were set down and everybody started climbing – except for Lupy, who was too stout, and for Pod and Homily, who watched silently, standing beside the door. Hendreary tried an overcoat on a nail for the sake of what he might find in the pockets, but he had not Pod's gift for climbing fabric and had to be rescued by one of his sons from where he hung, perspiring and breathing hard, clinging to a sleeve button.

'He should have gone up by the front buttonholes,' Pod whispered to Homily; 'you can get your toes in and pull the pocket towards you, like, by folding in the stuff. You never want to make direct for a pocket . . .'

'I wish,' Homily whispered back, 'they'd stop this until we're gone.' It was the kind of occasion she would have enjoyed in an ordinary way – a glorious bargain hunt – findings keepings with no holds barred; but the shadow

of their ordeal hung over her and made such antics seem foolish.

'Now,' exclaimed Hendreary suddenly, straightening his clothes and coming towards them as though he had guessed her thought, 'we'd better test out this loophole.'

He called up his two elder sons, and together the three of them, after spitting on their hands, laid hold of the piece of wood which covered the hole in the door.

'One, two, three – hup!' intoned Hendreary, ending on a grunt. They gave a mighty heave and the slab of wood pivoted slowly, squeaking on its one nail, revealing the arch below.

Pod took his dip and peered through: grass and stones he saw for a moment and some kind of shadowy movement before a draught caught the flame and nearly blew it out. He sheltered the flame with his hand and tried again.

'Quick, Pod,' gasped Hendreary, 'this wood's heavy . . .'

Pod peered through again: no grass now, no stones – a rippling blackness, the faintest snuffle of breath and two sudden pin-points of fire, unblinking and deadly still.

'Drop the wood,' breathed Pod. He spoke without moving his lips. 'Quick,' he added under his breath as Hendreary seemed to hesitate. 'Can't you hear the bell?' And he stood there as though frozen, holding his dip steadily before him.

Down came the wood with a clap and Homily screamed. 'You saw it?' said Pod, turning. He set down his dip and wiped his brow on his sleeve: he was breathing rather heavily.

'Saw it?' cried Homily. 'In another second it would have been in here amongst us.'

Timmis began to cry and Arrietty ran to him: 'It's all right, Timmis, it's gone now. It was only an old ferret, an old tame ferret. Come, I'll tell you a story.' She took him under a rough wooden desk where she had seen an old account book. Setting it up on its outer leaves she made it into a tent. They crept inside, just the two of them, and between the sheltering pages they soon felt very cosy.

'Whatever was it?' cried Lupy, who had missed the whole occurrence.

'Like she said – a ferret,' announced Pod; 'that boy's ferret, I shouldn't wonder. If so, it'll be all round the house from now on seeking a way to get in . . .' He turned to Homily. 'There'll be no leaving here to-night,' he said.

Lupy, standing in the hearth where the ashes were still warm, sat down suddenly on an empty matchbox which gave an ominous crack. 'Nearly in amongst us,' she repeated faintly, closing her eyes against the ghastly vision. A faint cloud of wood ash rose slowly around her which she fanned away with her hand.

'Well, Pod,' said Hendreary after a pause, 'that's that.'

'How do you mean?' said Pod.

'You can't go that way. That ferret'll be round the house for weeks.'

'Yes . . .' said Pod, and was silent a moment. 'We'll have to think again.' He gazed in a worried way at the shuttered window: the smaller one was a wall aperture, glazed to give light but with the glass built in – no possibility there.

'Let's have a look at the wash-house,' he said. This door luckily had been left ajar and, dip in hand, he slid through the crack. Hendreary and Homily slid through after him, and after a while Arrietty followed. Filled with curiosity she longed to see the wash-house, as she longed to see every corner of this vast human edifice now that they had it to themselves. The chimney, she saw, in the flickering light of the dip, stood back to back with the one in the living-room; in it there stood a dingy cooking-stove; flags covered the floor. An old mangle stood in one corner; in the other a copper for boiling clothes. Against the wall, below the window, towered a stone sink. The window above the sink was heavily shuttered and rather high. The door, which led outside, was bolted in two places and had a zinc panel across the bottom reinforcing the wood.

'Nothing doing here,' said Hendreary.

'No,' agreed Pod.

They went back to the living-room. Lupy had recovered somewhat and had risen from the matchbox, leaving it slightly askew. She had brushed herself down and was packing up the borrowings preparatory to going upstairs. 'Come along, chicks,' she called to her children; 'it's nearly midnight and we'll have all day to-morrow . . .' When she saw Hendreary she said: 'I thought we might go up now and have a bite of supper.' She gave a little laugh. 'I'm a wee bit tired – what with ferrets and so on and so forth.'

Hendreary looked at Pod. 'What about you?' he said, and as Pod hesitated Hendreary turned to Lupy: 'They've had a hard day too – what with ferrets and so on and so forth – and they can't leave here to-night . . .'

'Oh?' said Lupy, and stared. She seemed slightly taken aback.

'What have we got for supper?' Hendreary asked her.

'Six boiled chestnuts' – she hesitated – 'and a smoked minnow each for you and the boys.'

'Well, perhaps we could open something,' suggested Hendreary after a moment. Again Lupy hesitated and the pause became too long. 'Why, of course—' she began in a flustered voice, but Homily interrupted.

'Thank you very much; it's very kind of you but we've got three roast chestnuts ourselves. And an egg.'

'An egg,' echoed Lupy, amazed. 'What kind of an egg?'

'A hen's egg.'

'A *hen's* egg,' echoed Lupy again as though a hen were a pterodactyl or a fabulous bird like the phoenix. 'Wherever did you get it?'

'Oh,' said Homily, 'it's just an egg we had.'

'And we'd like to stay down here a bit,' put in Pod, 'if that's all right with you.'

'Quite all right,' said Lupy stiffly. She still looked amazed about the egg. 'Come, Timmis.'

It took some minutes to round them all up. There was a lot of running back for things; chatter at the foot of the ladder; callings, scoldings, giggles, and 'take-cares.' 'One at a time,' Lupy kept saying, 'one at a time, my lambs.' But at last they were all up and their voices became more muffled as they left the echoing landing for the inner rooms beyond. Light running sounds were heard, small rollings, and the faintest of distant squeakings.

'How like mice we must sound to humans,' Arrietty realized as she listened from below. But after a while even these small patterings ceased and all became quiet and still. Arrietty turned and looked at her parents: at last they were alone.

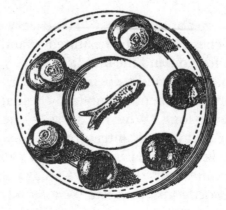

Chapter Nine

'Between the devil and the deep blue sea, that's us,' said Pod with a wan smile: he was quoting from Arrietty's diary and proverb book.

They sat grouped on the hearth where the stones were warm. The iron shovel, still too hot to sit on, lay sprawled across the ashes. Homily had pulled up the crushed match-box lid on which, with her lighter weight, she could sit comfortably. Pod and Arrietty perched on a charred stick; the three lighted dips were set between them on the ash. Shadows lay about them in the vast confines of the room and now the Hendrearys were out of earshot (sitting down to supper most likely), they felt drowned in the spreading silence.

After a while this was broken by the faint tinkle of a bell – quite close it seemed suddenly – there was a slight scratching sound and the lightest most delicate of snuffles. They all glanced wide-eyed at the door which, from where they sat, was deeply sunk in shadow.

'It can't get in, can it?' whispered Homily.

'Not a hope,' said Pod; 'let it scratch . . . we're all right here.'

All the same Arrietty threw a searching glance up the wide chimney: the stones, she thought, if the worst came to the worst, looked uneven enough to climb. Then suddenly, far, far above her, she saw a square of violet sky and in it a single star, and, for some reason, felt reassured.

'As I see it,' said Pod, 'we can't go and we can't stay.'

'And that's how I see it,' said Homily.

'Suppose,' suggested Arrietty, 'we climbed up the chimney on to the thatch?'

'And then what?' said Pod.

'I don't know,' said Arrietty.

'There we'd be,' said Pod.

'Yes, there we'd be,' agreed Homily unhappily, 'even supposing we could climb a chimney, which I doubt.'

There were a few moments' silence, then Pod said solemnly: 'Homily, there's nothing else for it . . .'

'But what?' asked Homily, raising a startled face: lit from below it looked curiously bony and was streaked

here and there with ash. And Arrietty, who guessed what was coming, gripped her two hands beneath her knees and stared fixedly down at the shovel which lay sideways across the hearth.

'But to bury our pride, that's what,' said Pod.

'How do you mean?' asked Homily weakly, but she knew quite well what he meant.

'We got to go, quite open-like, to Lupy and Hendreary and ask them to let us stay . . .'

Homily put her thin hands on either side of her thin face and stared at him dumbly.

'For the child's sake . . .' Pod pointed out gently.

The tragic eyes swivelled round to Arrietty and back again.

'A few dried peas, that's all we'd ask for,' went on Pod, very gently, 'just water to drink and a few dried peas . . .'

Still Homily did not speak.

'And we'd say they could keep the furniture in trust, like,' suggested Pod.

Homily stirred at last. 'They'd keep the furniture anyway,' she said huskily.

'Well, what about it?' asked Pod after a moment, watching her face.

Homily looked round the room in a hunted kind of way, up at the chimney then down at the ashes at their feet. At last she nodded her head. 'Should we go up now,' she suggested after a moment in a dispirited kind of voice, 'while they're all at supper, and get it over with?'

'Might as well,' said Pod. He stood up and put out a hand to Homily. 'Come on, me old girl,' he coaxed her. Homily rose slowly and Pod turned to Arrietty, Homily's hand pulled under his arm. Standing beside his wife he drew himself up to his full five inches. 'There's two kinds of courage I know of,' he said, 'possibly there's more, but your mother's got 'em all. You make a note of that, my girl, when you're writing in your diary . . .'

But Arrietty was gazing past him into the room: she was staring white-faced into the shadows beyond the log-box towards the scullery door.

'Something moved,' she whispered.

Pod turned, following the direction of her eyes. 'What like?' he asked sharply.

'Something furry . . .'

They all froze. Then Homily, with a cry, ran out from between them. Amazed and aghast they watched her scramble off the hearth and run with outstretched arms towards the shadows beyond the log-box. She seemed to be laughing – or crying – her breath coming in little gasps: 'The dear boy, the good boy ... the blessed creature!'

'It's Spiller!' cried Arrietty on a shout of joy.

She ran forward too, and they dragged him out of the shadows, pulled him on to the hearth and beside the dips where the light shone warmly on his suit of moleskins, worn now, slightly tattered, and shorter in the leg. His feet were bare and gleaming with black mud. He seemed to have grown heavier and taller. His hair was still as ragged and his pointed face as brown. They did not think to ask him where he had come from – it was enough that he was there. Spiller, it seemed to Arrietty, always materialized out of air and dissolved again as swiftly.

'Oh, Spiller!' gasped Homily, who was not supposed to like him, 'in the nick of time, the very nick of time!' And she sat down on the charred stick which flew up the farther end scattering a cloud of ash, and burst into happy tears.

'Nice to see you, Spiller,' said Pod, smiling and looking him up and down. 'Come for your summer clothes?' Spiller nodded: bright eyed, he gazed about the room, taking in the bundles strapped to the hat-pin, the pulled-out position of the log-box, the odd barenesses and rearrangements which signify human departure. But he made no comment: countrymen, such as Spiller and Pod were, do not rush into explanations; faced with whatever strange evidence they mind their manners and bide their time. 'Well, I happen to know they're not ready,' Pod went on. 'She's sewn the vest, mind, but she hasn't joined up the trousers . . .'

Spiller nodded again. His eyes sought out Arrietty who, ashamed of her first outburst, had become suddenly shy and had withdrawn behind the shovel.

'Well,' said Pod at last, looking about as though aware suddenly of strangeness in their surroundings, 'you find us in a nice sort of pickle . . .'

'Moving house?' asked Spiller casually.

'In a manner of speaking,' said Pod. And as Homily dried her eyes on her apron and began to pin up her hair he outlined the story to Spiller in a few rather fumbling words. Spiller listened with one eyebrow raised and his mocking V-shaped mouth twisted up at the corners. This was Spiller's famous expression Arrietty remembered, no matter what you were telling him.

'And so,' said Pod, shrugging his shoulders, 'you see how we're placed?'

Spiller nodded, looking thoughtful.

'Must be pretty hungry now, that ferret,' Pod went on, 'poor creature. Can't hunt with a bell: the rabbits hear him coming. Gone in a flash the rabbits are. But with our

short legs he'd be on us in a trice – bell or no bell. But how did *you* manage ?' Pod asked suddenly.

'The usual,' said Spiller.

'What usual ?'

Spiller jerked his head towards the wash-house. 'The drain, of course,' he said.

Chapter Ten

'What drain ?' asked Homily, staring.

'The one in the floor,' said Spiller as though she ought to have known. 'The sink's no good – got an S-bend. And they keep the lid on the copper.'

'I didn't see any drain in the floor . . .' said Pod.

'It's under the mangle,' explained Spiller.

'But,' went on Homily, 'I mean, do you always come by the drain ?'

'And go,' said Spiller.

'Under cover, like,' Pod pointed out to Homily, 'doesn't have to bother with the weather.'

'Or the woods,' said Homily.

'That's right,' agreed Spiller; 'you don't want to bother with the woods. Not the woods,' he repeated thoughtfully.

'Where does the drain come out ?' asked Pod.

'Down by the kettle,' said Spiller.

'What kettle ?'

'His kettle,' put in Arrietty excitedly. 'That kettle he's got by the stream . . .'

'That's right,' said Spiller.

Pod looked thoughtful. 'Do the Hendrearys know this?'

Spiller shook his head. 'Never thought to tell them,' he said.

Pod was silent a moment and then he said: 'Could anyone use this drain?'

'No reason why not,' said Spiller. 'Where you making for?'

'We don't know yet,' said Pod.

Spiller frowned and scratched his knee where the black mud, drying in the warmth of the ash, had turned to a powdery grey. 'Ever thought of the town?' he asked.

'Leighton Buzzard?'

'No,' exclaimed Spiller scornfully, 'Little Fordham.'

Had Spiller suggested a trip to the moon they could not have looked more astonished. Homily's face was a study in disbelief as though she thought Spiller was romancing. Arrietty became very still – she seemed to be holding her breath. Pod looked ponderously startled.

'So there is such a place?' he said slowly.

'Of course there is such a place,' snapped Homily; 'everyone knows that: what they don't know exactly is – *where*? And I doubt if Spiller does either.'

'Two days down the river,' said Spiller, 'if the stream's running good.'

'Oh,' said Pod.

'You mean we have to swim for it?' snapped Homily.

'I got a boat,' said Spiller.

'Oh, my goodness . . .' murmured Homily, suddenly deflated.

'Big?' asked Pod.

'Fair,' said Spiller.

'Could she take passengers?' asked Pod.

'Could do,' said Spiller.

'Oh, my goodness . . .' murmured Homily again.

'What's the matter, Homily?' asked Pod.

'Can't see myself in a boat,' said Homily, 'not on the water, I can't.'

'Well, a boat's not much good on dry land,' said Pod. 'To get something you got to risk something – that's how it goes. We got to find somewhere to live.'

'There might be something, say, in walking distance,' faltered Homily.

'Such as?'

'Well,' said Homily unhappily, throwing a quick glance at Spiller, 'say, for instance . . . Spiller's kettle.'

'Not much accommodation in a kettle,' said Pod.

'More than there was in a boot,' retorted Homily.

'Now, Homily,' said Pod, suddenly firm, 'you wouldn't be happy, not for twenty-four hours, in a kettle; and inside a week you'd be on at me night and day to find some kind of craft to get you down-stream to Little Fordham. Here you are with the chance of a good home, fresh start, and a free passage, and all you do is go on like a maniac about a drop of clean running water. Now, if it was the drain you objected to—'

Homily turned to Spiller. 'What sort of boat?' she asked nervously. 'I mean, if I could picture it like . . .'

Spiller thought a moment. 'Well,' he said, 'it's wooden.'

'Yes?' said Homily.

Spiller tried again. 'Well, it's like . . . you might say it was something like a knife-box.'

'How much like?' asked Pod.

'Very like,' said Spiller.

'In fact,' declared Homily triumphantly, 'it *is* a knife-box.'

Spiller nodded. 'That's right,' he admitted.

'Flat-bottomed?' asked Pod.

'With divisions, like, for spoons, forks, and so on?' put in Homily.

'That's right,' agreed Spiller, replying to both.

'Tarred and waxed at the seams?'

'Waxed,' said Spiller.

'Sounds all right to me,' said Pod. 'What do you say, Homily?' It sounded better to her too, Pod realized, but he saw she was not quite ready to commit herself. He turned again to Spiller. 'What do you do for power?'

'Power?'

'Got some kind of sail?'

Spiller shook his head. 'Take her down-stream, loaded – with a paddle; pole her back up-stream in ballast . . .'

'I see,' said Pod. He sounded rather impressed. 'You go often to Little Fordham?'

'Pretty regular,' said Spiller.

'I see,' said Pod again. 'Sure you could give us a lift?'

'Call back for you,' said Spiller, 'at the kettle, say. Got to go up-stream to load.'

'Load what?' asked Homily bluntly.

'The boat,' said Spiller.

'I know that,' said Homily, 'but with what?'

'Now, Homily,' put in Pod, 'that's Spiller's business. No concern of ours. Does a bit of trading up and down the river, I shouldn't wonder. Mixed cargo, eh Spiller? Nuts, birds' eggs, meat, minnows . . . that sort of tackle – more or less what he brings Lupy.'

'Depends what they're short of,' said Spiller.

'They?' exclaimed Homily.

'Now, Homily,' Pod admonished her, 'Spiller's got his customers. Stands to reason. We're not the only borrowers in the world, remember. Not by a long chalk . . .'

'But these ones at Little Fordham,' Homily pointed out. 'They say they're made of plaster?'

'That's right,' said Spiller, 'painted over. All of a piece . . . Except one,' he added.

'One live one?' asked Pod.

'That's right,' said Spiller.

'Oh, I wouldn't like that,' exclaimed Homily, 'I wouldn't like that at all: not to be the one live borrower among a lot of dummy waxworks or whatever they call themselves. Get on my nerves that would . . .'

'They don't bother him,' said Spiller, 'leastways not as much, he says, as a whole lot of live ones might.'

'Well, that's a nice friendly attitude, I must say,' snapped Homily. 'Nice kind of welcome we'll get, I can see, when we turn up there unexpected.'

'Plenty of houses,' said Spiller; 'no sort of need to live close . . .'

'And he doesn't own the place,' Pod reminded her.

'That's true,' said Homily.

'What about it, Homily?' said Pod.

'I don't mind,' said Homily, 'providing we live near the shops.'

'There's nothing in the shops,' explained Pod in a patient voice, 'or so I've heard tell, but bananas and suchlike made of plaster and all stuck down in a lump.'

'No, but it sounds nice,' said Homily, 'say you were talking to Lupy—'

'But you won't be talking to Lupy,' said Pod. 'Lupy won't even know we're gone until she wakes up to-morrow morning thinking that she's got to get us breakfast. No, Homily,' he went on earnestly, 'you don't want to make for shopping centres and all that sort of caper: better some quiet little place down by the water's edge. You won't want to be everlastingly carting water. And, say Spiller comes down pretty regular with a nice bit of cargo, you want somewhere he can tie up and unload . . . Plenty of time, once we get there, to have a look round and take our pick.'

'Take our pick . . .' Suddenly Homily felt the magic of these words: they began to work inside her – champagne bubbles of excitement welling up and up – until, at last, she flung her hands together in a sudden joyful clap. 'Oh, Pod,' she breathed, her eyes brimming as, startled by the noise, he turned sharply towards her, 'think of it – all those houses . . . we could try them *all* out if we wanted, one after another. What's to prevent us?'

'Common sense,' said Pod; he smiled at Arrietty: 'What do you say, lass? Shops or water?'

Arrietty cleared her throat. 'Down by water,' she whispered huskily, her eyes shining and her face tremulous in the dancing light of the dip. 'At least to start with . . .'

There was a short pause. Pod glanced down at his tackle strapped to the hat-pin and up at the clock on the wall. 'Getting on for half past one,' he said; 'time we had a look at this drain. What do you say, Spiller? Could you spare us a minute? And show us the ropes like?'

'Oh,' exclaimed Homily, dismayed, 'I thought Spiller was coming with us.'

'Now, Homily,' explained Pod, 'it's a long trek and he's only just arrived – he won't want to go back right away.'

'I don't see why not if his clothes aren't ready – that's what you came for, isn't it, Spiller?'

'That and other things,' said Pod; 'dare say he's brought a few oddments for Lupy.'

'That's all right,' said Spiller, 'I can tip 'em out on the floor.'

'And you will come?' cried Homily.

Spiller nodded. 'Might as well.'

Even Pod seemed slightly relieved. 'That's very civil of you, Spiller,' he said, 'very civil indeed.' He turned to Arrietty: 'Now, Arrietty, take a dip and go and fetch the egg.'

'Oh, don't let's bother with the egg,' said Homily.

Pod gave her a look. 'You go and get that egg, Arrietty. Just roll it along in front of you into the wash-house, but be careful with the light near those shavings. Homily, you bring the other two dips and I'll get the tackle . . .'

Chapter Eleven

As they filed through the crack of the door on to the stone flags of the wash-house they heard the ferret again. But Homily now felt brave. 'Scratch away,' she dared it happily, secure in their prospect of escape. But when they stood at last, grouped beneath the mangle and staring down at the drain, her new-found courage ebbed a little and she murmured: 'Oh, my goodness . . .'

Very deep and dark and well-like, it seemed, sunk below the level of the floor. The square grating which usually covered it lay beside it at an angle and in the yawning blackness she could see the reflections of their dips. A dank draught quivered round the candle flames and there was a sour smell of yellow soap, stale disinfectant, and tea leaves.

'What's that at the bottom?' she asked, peering down. 'Water?'

'Slime,' said Spiller.

'Jellied soap,' put in Pod quickly.

'And we've got to wade through that?'

'It isn't deep,' said Spiller.

'Not as though this drain was a sewer,' said Pod, trying to sound comforting and hearty. 'Beats me though,' he went on to Spiller, 'how you manage to move this grating.'

Spiller showed him. Lowering the dip, he pointed out a short length of what looked like brass curtain rod, strong but hollow, perched on a stone at the bottom of the well and leaning against the side. The top of this rod protruded slightly above the mouth of the drain. The grating, when in place, lay loosely on its worn rim of

cement. Spiller explained how, by exerting all his strength on the rod from below, he could raise one corner of the grating – as a washerwoman with a prop can raise up a clothes-line. He would then slide the base of the prop on to the raised stone in the base of the shaft, thus holding the contraption in place. Spiller would then swing himself up to the mouth of the drain on a piece of twine tied to a rung of the grating: 'only about twice my height,' he explained. The twine, Pod gathered, was a fixture. The double twist round the light iron rung was hardly noticeable from above and the length of the twine, when not in use, hung downwards into the drain. Should Spiller want to remove the grating entirely, as was the case to- day, after scrambling through the aperture raised by the rod he would pull the twine after him, fling it around one of the stays of the mangle above his head, and would drag and pull on the end. Sometimes, Spiller explained, the grating slid easily, at other times it stuck on an angle. In which event Spiller would produce a small but heavy bolt, kept specially for the purpose, which he would wind into the free end of his halyard and, climbing into the girder-like structure at the base of the mangle, would swing himself out on the bolt which, sinking under his weight, exerted a pull on the grating.

'Very ingenious,' said Pod. Dip in hand he went deeper under the mangle, examined the wet twine, pulled on the knots and finally, as though to test its weight, gave the grating a shove – it slid smoothly on the worn flagstones. 'Easier to shove than to lift,' he remarked. Arrietty, glancing upwards, saw vast shadows on the wash-house ceiling – moving and melting, advancing and receding –in the flickering light from their dips: wheels, handles, rollers, shifting spokes . . . as though, she thought, the great mangle under which they stood was silently and magically turning . . .

On the ground, beside the drain, she saw an object she recognized: the lid of an aluminium soap-box, the one in which the summer before last Spiller had spun her down the river, and from which he used to fish. It was packed now with some kind of cargo and covered with a piece of worn hide – possibly a rat skin – strapped over lid and all with lengths of knotted twine. From a hole bored in one end of the rim a second piece of twine protruded. 'I pull her up by that,' explained Spiller, following the direction of her eyes.

'I see how you get up,' said Homily unhappily, peering into the slime, 'but it's how you get down that worries me.'

'Oh, you just drop,' said Spiller. He took hold of the twine as he spoke and began to drag the tin lid away towards the door.

'It's all right, Homily,' Pod promised hurriedly, 'we'll let you down on the bolt,' and he turned quickly to Spiller. 'Where you going with that?' he asked.

Spiller, it seemed, not wishing to draw attention to the drain, was going to unpack next door. The house being free of humans and the log-box pulled out there was no need to go upstairs – he could dump what he'd brought beside the hole in the skirting.

While he was gone Pod outlined a method of procedure: '. . . if Spiller agrees,' he kept saying, courteously conceding the leadership.

Spiller did agree, or rather he raised no objections. The empty soap-box lid, lightly dangling, was lowered on to the mud: into this they dropped the egg – rolling it to the edge of the drain as though it were a giant rugby football, with a final kick from Pod to send it spinning and keep it clear of the sides. It plopped into the soap-box lid with an ominous crack. This did not matter, however, the egg being hard-boiled.

Homily, with not a few nervous exclamations, was lowered next seated astride the bolt; with one hand she clung to the twine, in the other she carried a lighted dip. When she climbed off the bolt into the lid of the soap-box the latter slid swiftly away on the slime, and Homily, for

an anxious moment, disappeared down the drain. Spiller drew her back, however, hand over hand. And there she sat behind the egg, grumbling a little, but with her candle still alight. 'Two can go in the lid,' Spiller had announced, and Arrietty (who secretly had longed to try the drop) was lowered considerably, dip in hand, in the same respectful way. She settled herself opposite her mother with the egg wobbling between them.

'You two are the light-bearers,' said Pod. 'All you've got to do is to sit quite still and – steady the egg – move the lights as we say . . .'

There was a little shuffling about in the lid and some slightly perilous balancing as Homily, who had never liked travelling – as human beings would say – back to the engine, stood up to change seats with Arrietty. 'Keep a good hold on that string,' she kept imploring Spiller as she completed this manœuvre, but soon she and Arrietty were seated again face to face, each with their candle and the egg between their knees. Arrietty was laughing.

'Now I'm going to let you go a little ways,' warned Spiller and paid out a few inches of twine. Arrietty and Homily slid smoothly under the roof of their arched tunnel, which gleamed wetly in the candlelight. Arrietty put out a finger and touched the gleaming surface: it seemed to be made of baked clay.

'Don't touch *anything*,' hissed Homily shudderingly, 'and don't breathe either – not unless you have to.'

Arrietty, lowering her dip, peered over the side at the mud. 'There's a fishbone,' she remarked, 'and a tin bottle top. And a hairpin . . .' she added on a pleased note.

'Don't even *look*,' shuddered Homily.

'A hairpin would be useful,' Arrietty pointed out.

Homily closed her eyes. 'All right,' she said, her face drawn with the effort not to mind. 'Pick it out quickly and drop it, sharp, in the bottom of the boat. And wipe your hands on my apron.'

'We can wash it in the river,' Arrietty pointed out.

Homily nodded: she was trying not to breathe.

Over Homily's shoulder Arrietty could see into the well of the drain; a bulky object was coming down the shaft: it was Pod's tackle, waterproof wrapped and strapped securely to his hat-pin. It wobbled on the mud with a slight squelch. Pod, after a while, came after it. Then came Spiller. For a moment the surface seemed to bear their weight then, knee deep, they sank in slime.

Spiller removed the length of curtain rod from the stone and set it up inconspicuously in the corner of the shaft. Before their descent he and Pod must have placed the grating above more conveniently in position: a deft pull by Spiller on the twine and they heard it clamp down into place – a dull metallic sound which echoed hollowly along the length of their tunnel. Homily gazed into the blackness ahead as though following its flight. 'Oh, my goodness,' she breathed as the sound died: she felt suddenly shut in.

'Well,' announced Pod in a cheerful voice, coming up behind them, and he placed a hand on the rim of their lid, 'we're off!'

Chapter Twelve

Spiller, they saw, to control them on a shorter length, was rolling up the towline. Not that towline was quite the right expression under the circumstances. The drain ran ahead on a slight downwards incline and Spiller functioned more as a sea anchor and used the twine as a brake.

'Here we go,' said Pod, and gave the lid a slight push. They slid ahead on the slippery scum, to be lightly checked by Spiller. The candlelight danced and shivered

on the arched roof and about the dripping walls. So thick and soapy was the scum on which they rode that Pod, behind them, seemed more to be leading his bundle than dragging it behind him. Sometimes, even, it seemed to be leading him.

'Whoa, there!' he would cry on such occasions. He was in very good spirits, and had been, Arrietty noticed, from the moment he set foot in the drain. She too felt strangely happy: here she was, with the two she held most dear, with Spiller added, making their way towards the dawn. The drain held no fears for Arrietty: leading as it did towards a life to be lived away from dust and candlelight and confining shadows – a life on which the sun would shine by day and the moon by night.

She twisted round in her seat in order to see ahead, and as she did so a great aperture opened to her left and a dank draught flattened the flame of her candle. She shielded it quickly with her hand and Homily did the same.

'That's where the pipe from the sink comes in,' said Spiller, 'and the overflow from the copper . . .'

There were other openings as they went along, drains which branched into darkness and ran away uphill. Where these joined the main drain a curious collection of flotsam and jetsam piled up over which they had to drag the soap-box lid. Arrietty and Homily got out for this to make less weight for the men. Spiller knew all these branch drains by name and the exact position of each cottage or house concerned. Arrietty began, at last, to understand the vast resources of Spiller's trading. 'Not that you get up into all of 'em,' he explained. 'I don't mind an S-bend, but where you get an S-bend you're apt to get a brass grille or suchlike in the plug hole.'

Once he said, jerking his head towards the mouth of a circular cavern: 'Holmcroft, that is . . . nothing but bath water from now on . . .' And, indeed, this cavern as they slid past it had looked cleaner than most – a shining cream-coloured porcelain, and the air from that point onwards, Arrietty noticed, smelled far less strongly of tea leaves.

Every now and again they came across small branches – of ash or holly – rammed so securely into place that they would have difficulty manœuvring round them. They were set, Arrietty noticed, at almost regular intervals. 'I can't think how these tree things get down drains, anyway,' Homily exclaimed irritably when, for about the fifth time, the soap-box was turned up sideways and eased past and she and Arrietty stood ankle deep in jetsam, shielding their dips with their hands.

'I put them there,' said Spiller, holding the boat for them to get in again. The drain at this point dropped more steeply. As Homily stepped in opposite Arrietty the soap-box lid suddenly slid away, dragging Spiller after: he slipped and skidded on the surface of the mud but miraculously he kept his balance. They fetched up in a tangle against the trunk of one of Spiller's tree-like erections and Arrietty's dip went overboard. 'So that's what they're for,' exclaimed Homily as she coaxed her own flattened wick back to brightness to give Arrietty a light.

But Spiller did not answer straight away. He pushed past the obstruction and, as they waited for Pod to catch up, he said suddenly: 'Could be . . .'

Pod looked weary when he came up to them. He was panting a little and had stripped off his jacket and slung it round his shoulders. 'The last lap's always the longest,' he pointed out.

'Would you care for a ride in the lid?' asked Homily. 'Do, Pod!'

'No, I'm better walking,' said Pod.

'Then give me your jacket,' said Homily. She folded it gently across her knees and patted it soberly as though (thought Arrietty watching) it too were tired, like Pod.

And then they were off again – an endless, monotonous vista of circular walls. Arrietty after a while began to doze: she slid forward against the egg, her head caught up on one knee. Just before she fell asleep she felt Homily slide the dip from her drooping fingers and wrap her round with Pod's coat.

When she awoke the scene was much the same: shadows sliding and flickering on the wet ceiling, Spiller's narrow face palely lit as he trudged along and the bulky shape beyond which was Pod; her mother, across the egg, smiling at her bewilderment. 'Forgotten where you were?' asked Homily.

Arrietty nodded. Her mother held a dip in either hand and the wax, Arrietty noticed, had burned very low. 'Must be nearly morning,' Arrietty remarked. She still felt very sleepy.

'Shouldn't wonder . . .' said Homily.

The walls slid by, unbroken except for arch-like thickenings at regular intervals where one length of pipe joined another. And when they spoke their voices echoed hollowly, back and forth along the tunnel.

'Aren't there any more branch drains?' Arrietty asked after a moment.

Spiller shook his head. 'No more now. Holmcroft was the last . . .'

'But that was ages ago . . . we must be nearly there.'

'Getting on,' said Spiller.

Arrietty shivered and drew Pod's coat more tightly around her shoulders: the air seemed fresher suddenly and curiously free from smell. 'Or perhaps,' she thought, 'we've grown more used to it . . .' There was no sound except for the whispering slide of the soap-box lid and the regular plop and suction of Pod's and Spiller's footsteps. But the silt seemed rather thinner: there was an occasional grating sound below the base of the tin-lid as though it rode on grit. Spiller stood still. 'Listen,' he said.

They were all quiet but could hear nothing except Pod's breathing and a faint musical drip somewhere just ahead of them. 'Better push on,' said Homily suddenly, breaking the tension; 'these dips aren't going to last for ever.'

'Quiet!' cried Spiller again. Then they heard a faint drumming sound, hardly more than a vibration.

'Whatever is it?' asked Homily.

'Can only be Holmcroft,' said Spiller. He stood rigid, with one hand raised, listening intently. 'But,' he said, turning to Pod, 'whoever'd be having a bath at this time o' night?'

Pod shook his head. 'It's morning by now,' he said; 'must be getting on for six.'

The drumming sound grew louder, less regular, more like a leaping and a banging . . .

'We've got to run for it!' cried Spiller. Towline in hand

he swung the tin-lid round and, taking the lead, flew ahead into the tunnel. Arrietty and Homily banged and rattled behind him. Dragged on the short line they swung shatteringly, thrown from wall to wall. But, panic-stricken at the thought of total darkness, each shielded the flame of her candle. Homily stretched out a free hand to Pod who caught hold of it just as his bundle bore down on him, knocking him over. He fell across it, still gripping Homily's hand, and was carried swiftly along.

'Out and up!' cried Spiller from the shadows ahead, and they saw the glistening twigs wedged tautly against the roof. 'Let the traps go!' he was shouting. 'Come on – climb!'

They each seized a branch and swung themselves up and wedged themselves tight against the ceiling. The over-turned dips lay guttering in the tin-lid and the air was filled with the sound of galloping water. In the jerking light from the dips they saw the first pearly bubbles and the racing, dancing, silvery bulk behind. And then all was choking, swirling, scented darkness.

After the first few panic-stricken seconds Arrietty found she could breathe and that the sticks still held. A mill-race of hot, scented water swilled through her clothes, piling against her at one moment, falling away the next. Sometimes it bounced above her shoulders, drenching her face and hair, at others it swirled steadily about her waist and tugged at her legs and feet. 'Hold on!' shouted Pod above the turmoil.

'Die down soon!' shouted Spiller.

'You there, Arrietty?' gasped Homily. They were all there and all breathing and, even as they realized this, the water began to drop in level and run less swiftly. Without the brightness of the dips the darkness about them seemed less opaque, as though a silvery haze rose from

the water itself, which seemed now to be running well below them and, from the sound of it, as innocent and steady as a brook.

After a while they climbed down into it and felt a smoothly running warmth about their ankles. At this level they could see a faint translucence where the surface of the water met the blackness of the walls. 'Seems lighter,' said Pod wonderingly. He seemed to perceive some shifting in the darkness where Spiller splashed and probed. 'Anything there?' he asked.

'Not a thing,' said Spiller.

Their baggage had disappeared – egg, soap-box lid, and all – swept away on the flood.

'And now what?' asked Pod dismally.

But Spiller seemed quite unworried. 'Pick it up later,' he said; 'nothing to hurt. And saves carting.'

Homily was sniffing the air. 'Sandalwood!' she exclaimed suddenly to Arrietty. 'Your father's favourite soap.'

But Arrietty, her hand on a twig to steady herself against the warm flow eddying past her ankles, did not reply: she was staring straight ahead down the incline of the drain. A bead of light hung in the darkness. For a moment she thought that, by some miraculous chance, it might be one of the dips – then she saw it was completely round and curiously steady. And mingled with the scent of sandalwood she smelled another smell – minty, grassy, mildly earthy . . .

'It's dawn,' she announced in a wondering voice; 'and what's more,' she went on, staring spellbound at the distant pearl of light, 'that's the end of the drain.'

Chapter Thirteen

The warmth from the bath water soon wore off and the rest of the walk was chilly. The circle of light grew larger and brighter as they advanced towards it until, at last, its radiance dazzled their eyes.

'The sun's out,' Arrietty decided. It was a pleasant thought, soaked to the skin as they were, and they slightly quickened their steps. The bath-water flow had sunk to the merest trickle and the drain felt gloriously clean.

Arrietty too felt somehow purged as though all traces of the old dark, dusty life had been washed away – even from their clothes. Homily had a similar thought:

'Nothing like a good, strong stream of soapy water running clean through the fabric . . . no rubbing or squeezing: all we've got to do now is lay them out to dry.'

They emerged at last, Arrietty running ahead on to a small sandy beach which fanned out sideways and down to the water in front. The mouth of the drain was set well back under the bank of the stream, which overhung it, crowned with rushes and grasses: a sheltered, windless corner on which the sun beat down, rich with the golden promise of an early summer.

'But you can never tell,' said Homily, gazing around at the weather-worn flotsam and jetsam spewed out by the drain, 'not in March . . .'

They had found Pod's bundle just within the mouth of the drain where the hat-pin had stuck in the sand. The soap-box lid had fetched up, upside-down, against a protruding root, and the egg, Arrietty discovered, had rolled right into the water: it lay in the shallows below a

fish-boning of silver ripples and seemed to have flattened out. But when they hooked it on to the dry sand they saw it was due to refraction of the water: the egg was still its old familiar shape but covered with tiny cracks. Arrietty and Spiller rolled it up the slope to where Pod was unpacking the waterlogged bundles, anxious to see if the mackintosh covering had worked. Triumphantly he laid out the contents one by one on the warm sand. 'Dry as a bone . . .' he kept saying.

Homily picked out a change of clothes for each. The jerseys, though clean, were rather worn and stretched: they were the ones she had knitted – so long ago it seemed now – on blunted darning-needles when they had lived under the kitchen at Firbank. Arrietty and Homily undressed in the mouth of the drain, but Spiller – although offered a garment of Pod's – would not bother to change. He slid off round the corner of the beach to take a look at his kettle.

When they were dressed and the wet clothes spread out to dry, Homily shelled off the top of the egg. Pod wiped down his precious piece of razor-blade, oiled to preserve it against rust, and cut them each a slice. They sat in the sunshine, eating contentedly, watching the ripples of the stream. After a while Spiller joined them. He sat just below them, steaming in the warmth, and thoughtfully eating his egg.

'Where is the kettle exactly, Spiller?' asked Arrietty.

Spiller jerked his head. 'Just round the corner.'

Pod had packed the Christmas-pudding thimble and they each had a drink of fresh water. Then they packed up the bundles again and, leaving the clothes to dry, they followed Spiller round the bend.

It was a second beach, rather more open, and the kettle lay against the bank at the far end. It lay slightly inclined, as Spiller had found it, wedged in by the twigs and branches washed by the river down-stream. It was a corner on which floating things caught up and anchored themselves against a projection of the bank. The river twisted inwards at this point, running quite swiftly just below the kettle where, Arrietty noticed, the water looked suddenly deep.

Beyond the kettle a cluster of brambles growing under the bank hung out over the water – with new leaves growing among the tawny dead ones; some of these older shoots were trailing in the water and, in the tunnel beneath them, Spiller kept his boat.

Arrietty wanted to see the boat first but Pod was examining the kettle, in the side of which where it met the base was a fair-sized circular rust-hole.

'That the way in?' asked Pod.

Spiller nodded.

Pod looked up at the top of the kettle. The lid, he noticed, was not quite in and Spiller had fixed a piece of twine to the knob in the middle of the lid and had slung it over the arched handle above.

'Come inside,' he said to Pod. 'I'll show you.'

They went inside while Arrietty and Homily waited in the sunshine. Spiller appeared again almost immediately at the rust-hole entrance, exclaiming irritably: 'Go on, get out.' And, aided by a shove from Spiller's bare foot, a mottled yellow frog leapt through the air and slithered swiftly into the stream. It was followed by two wood-lice which, as they rolled themselves up in balls, Spiller stooped down and picked up from the floor and threw lightly on to the bank above. 'Nothing else,' he remarked to Homily, grinning, and disappeared again.

Homily was silent a moment and then she whispered to Arrietty: 'Don't fancy sleeping in there to-night . . .'

'We can clean it out,' Arrietty whispered back. 'Remember the boot,' she added.

Homily nodded, rather unhappily: 'When do you think he'll get us down to Little Fordham?'

'Soon as he's been up-stream to load. He likes the
moon full . . .' Arrietty whispered.

'Why ?' whispered Homily.

'He travels mostly at night.'

'Oh,' said Homily, her expression bewildered and slightly wild.

A metallic sound attracted their attention to the top of the kettle: the lid, they saw, was wobbling on and off, raised and lowered from inside. 'According to how you want it . . .' said a voice. 'Very ingenious,' they heard a second voice reply in curiously hollow tones.

'Doesn't sound like Pod,' whispered Homily, looking startled.

'It's because they're in a kettle,' explained Arrietty.

'Oh,' said Homily again. 'I wish they'd come out.'

They came out then, even as she spoke. As Pod stepped down on the flat stone which was used as a doorstep he looked very pleased. 'See that?' he said to Homily.

Homily nodded.

'Ingenious, eh?'

Homily nodded again.

'Now,' Pod went on happily, 'we're going to take a look at Spiller's boat. What sort of shoes you got on?'

They were old ones Pod had made. 'Why?' asked Homily. 'Is it muddy?'

'Not that I know of. But if you're going aboard you don't want to slip. Better go barefoot like Arrietty . . .'

Chapter Fourteen

Although she seemed nearly aground, a runnel of ice-cold water ran between the boat and the shore; through this they waded and Spiller, at the prow, helped them to climb

aboard. Roomy but clumsy (Arrietty thought as she
scrambled in under the gaiter) but, with her flat bottom,
practically impossible to capsize. She was in fact, as
Homily had guessed, a knife-box: very long and narrow,
with symmetrical compartments for varying sizes of
cutlery.

'More what you'd call a barge,' remarked Pod, looking
about him: a wooden handle rose up inside to which, he
noticed, the gaiter had been nailed. 'Holds her firm,'

explained Spiller, tapping the roof of the canopy, 'say you
want to lift up the sides.'

The holds were empty at the moment, except for the
narrowest. In this Pod saw an amber-coloured
knitting-needle which ran the length of the vessel, a
folded square of frayed red blanket, a wafer thin butter-
knife of tarnished Georgian silver, and the handle and
blade of his old nail-scissor.

'So you've still got that?' he said.

'Comes in useful,' said Spiller. 'Careful,' he said as Pod
took it up. 'I've sharpened it up a bit.'

'Wouldn't mind this back,' said Pod a trifle enviously, 'say, one day, you got another like it.'

'Not so easy to come by,' said Spiller; and as though to change the subject he took up the butter-knife: 'Found this wedged down a crack in the side . . . does me all right for a paddle.'

'Just the thing,' said Pod – all the cracks and joins were filled in now he noticed as, regretfully, he put back the nail-scissor. 'Where did you pick up this knife-box in the first place?'

'Lying on the bottom up-stream. Full of mud when I spotted her. Bit of a job to salvage. Up by the caravans, that's where she was. Like as not someone pinched the silver and didn't want the box.'

'Like as not,' said Pod. 'So you sharpened her up?' he went on, staring again at the nail-scissor.

'That's right,' said Spiller and, stooping swiftly, he snatched up the piece of blanket. 'You take this,' he said; 'might be chilly in the kettle.'

'What about you?' said Pod.

'That's all right,' said Spiller; 'you take it!'

'Oh,' exclaimed Homily, 'it's the bit we had in the boot . . .' and then she coloured slightly. 'I think,' she added.

'That's right,' said Spiller; 'better you take it.'

'Well, thanks,' said Pod and threw it over his shoulder. He looked around again: the gaiter, he realized, was both camouflage and shelter. 'You done a good job, Spiller. I mean . . . you could live in a boat like this – come wind, say, and wet weather.'

'That's right,' agreed Spiller and he began to ease the knitting-needle out from under the gaiter, the knob emerging forward at an angle. 'Don't want to hurry you,' he said.

Homily seemed taken aback. 'You going already?' she faltered.

'Sooner he's gone, sooner he's back,' said Pod. 'Come on, Homily, all ashore now.'

'But how long does he reckon he'll be?'

'What would you put it at, Spiller?' asked Pod. 'A couple of days? Three? Four? A week?'

'May be less, may be more,' said Spiller; 'depends on the weather. Three nights from now, say, if it's moonlight . . .'

'But what if we're asleep in the kettle?' said Homily.

'That's all right, Homily, Spiller can knock.' Pod took her firmly by the elbow: 'Come on now, all ashore – you too, Arrietty.'

As Homily, with Pod's help, was lowered into the water, Arrietty jumped from the side; the wet mud, she noticed, was spangled all over with tiny footprints. They linked arms and stood well back to watch Spiller depart. He unloosed the painter and, paddle in hand, let the boat slide stern foremost from under the brambles. As it glided out into open water it became unnoticeable suddenly and somehow part of the landscape: it might have been a curl of bark or a piece of floating wood.

It was only when Spiller laid down the paddle and stood up to punt with the knitting-needle that he became at all conspicuous. They watched through the brambles as, slowly and painstakingly, leaning at each plunge on

his pole, he began to come back up-stream. As he came abreast of them they ran out from the brambies to see better. Shoes in hand they crossed the beach of the kettle and, to keep up with him, climbed round the bluff at the corner and on to the beach of the drain. There, by a tree root which came sharply into deepish water, they waved him a last good-bye.

'Wish he hadn't had to go,' said Homily, as they made their way back across the sand towards the mouth of the drain.

There lay their clothes, drying in the sun, and as they approached an irridescent cloud like a flock of birds flew off the top of the egg. 'Bluebottles!' cried Homily, running forward, then, relieved, she slackened her steps: they were not bluebottles after all, but cleanly, burnished river flies, striped with blue and gold. The egg appeared untouched but Homily blew on it hard and dusted it up with her apron because, she explained, 'You never know . . .'

Pod, poking about among the flotsam and jetsam, salvaged the circular cork which Homily had used as a seat. 'This'll just about do it,' he murmured reflectively.

'Do what?' asked Arrietty idly. A beetle had run out from where the cork had been resting and, stooping, she held it by its shell. She liked beetles: their shiny, clear-cut armour, their mechanical joints and joins. And she liked just a little to tease them: they were so easy to hold by the sharp edge of their wing casings, and so anxious to get away.

'One day you'll get bitten . . .' Homily warned her as she folded up the clothes which still, though dry, smelled faintly and pleasantly of sandalwood, 'or stung, or nipped, or whatever they do, and serve you right.'

Arrietty let the beetle go. 'They don't mind, really,' she remarked, watching the horned legs scuttle up the slope and the fine grains of dislodged sand tumbling down behind them.

'And here's a hairpin!' exclaimed Pod. It was the one Arrietty had found in the drain, clean-washed now – and gleaming. 'You know what we should do,' he went on; 'while we're here, that is?'

'What?' asked Homily.

'Come along here regular, like, every morning, and see what the drain's brought down.'

'There wouldn't be anything I'd fancy,' said Homily, folding the last garment.

'What about a gold ring? Many a gold ring, or so I've heard, gets lost down a drain . . . and you wouldn't say no to a safety-pin.'

'I'd sooner a safety-pin,' said Homily, 'living as we do now.'

They carried the bundles round the bluff on to the beach by the kettle. Homily climbed on the smooth stone which wedged the kettle at an angle and peered in through the rust-hole. A cold light shone down from above where the lid was raised by its string: the interior smelled of rust and looked very uninviting.

'What we want now, before sundown,' said Pod, 'is some good clean dried grass to sleep on. We've got the piece of blanket . . .'

He looked about for some way of climbing the bank. There was a perfect place, as though invented for borrowers, where a cluster of tangled roots hung down from the lip of the cliff which curved deeply in behind them. At some time the stream had risen and washed the roots clean of earth and they hung in festoons and clusters, elastic but safely anchored. Pod and Arrietty went up, hand over hand: there were hand-holes and footholds, seats, swings, ladders, ropes . . . It was a borrower's gymnasium and almost a disappointment to Arrietty when – so soon – they reached the top.

Here among the jade-like spears of new spring growth were pale clumps of hair-like grasses bleached to the colour of tow. Pod reaped these down with his razor-blade and Arrietty tied them into stooks. Homily, below, collected these bundles as they pushed them over the cliff edge and carried them up to the kettle.

When the floor of the kettle was well and truly lined Pod and Arrietty climbed down. Arrietty peered in through the rust-hole: the kettle now smelled of hay. The sun was sinking and the air felt slightly colder. 'What we all need now,' remarked Homily, 'is a good hot drink before bed . . .' But there was no means of making one so they got out the egg instead. There was plenty left: they each had a thickish slice, topped up by a leaf of sorrel.

Pod unpacked his length of tarred string, knotted one end securely and passed the other through the centre of the cork. He pulled it tight.

'What's that for?' asked Homily, coming beside him, wiping her hands on her apron (no washing up, thank goodness: she had carried the egg-shells down to the water's edge and had thrown them into the stream).

'Can't you guess?' asked Pod. He was trimming the cork now, breathing hard, and bevelling the edges.

'To block up the rust-hole?'

'That's right,' said Pod. 'We can pull it tight like some kind of stopper once we're all safely inside.'

Arrietty had climbed up the roots again. They could see her on top of the bank. It was breezier up there and her hair was stirring slightly in the wind. Around her the great grass blades, in gentle motion, crossed and recrossed against the darkening sky.

'She likes it out of doors . . .' said Homily fondly.

'What about you?' asked Pod.

'Well,' said Homily after a moment, 'I'm not one for insects, Pod, never was. Nor for the simple life – if there is such a thing. But to-night' – she gazed about her at the

peaceful scene – 'to-night I feel kind of all right.'

'That's the way to talk,' said Pod, scraping away with his razor-blade.

'Or it might,' said Homily, watching him, 'be partly due to that cork.'

An owl hooted somewhere in the distance, on a hollow, wobbling note . . . a liquid note, it seemed, falling musically on the dusk. But Homily's eyes widened. 'Arrietty!' she called shrilly. 'Quickly! Come on down!'

They felt snug enough in the kettle – snug and secure, with the cork pulled in and the lid let down. Homily had insisted on the latter precaution. 'We won't need to *see*,' she explained to Pod and Arrietty, 'and we get enough air down the spout.'

When they woke in the morning the sun was up and the kettle felt rather hot. But it was exciting to lift off the lid, hand over hand on the twine, and to see a cloudless sky. Pod kicked out the cork and they crawled through the rust-hole and there again was the beach . . .

They breakfasted out of doors. The egg was wearing down but there were two-thirds left to go. 'And sunshine feeds,' said Pod. After breakfast Pod went off with his hat-pin to see what had come down the drain; Homily busied herself about the kettle and laid out the blanket to air; Arrietty climbed the roots again to explore the top of the bank. 'Keep within earshot,' Pod had warned them, 'and call out now and again. We don't want accidents at this stage – not before Spiller arrives.'

'And we don't want them then,' retorted Homily. But she seemed curiously relaxed; there was nothing to do but wait – no house-work, no cooking, no borrowing, no planning. 'Might as well enjoy ourselves,' she reflected and settled herself in the sun on the piece of red blanket. To Pod and Arrietty she seemed to be dozing but this was not the case at all: Homily was busy day-dreaming about a house with front door and windows – a home of their very own. Sometimes it was small and compact, sometimes four storeys high. And what about the castle? she wondered.

For some reason the thought of the castle reminded her of Lupy: what would they be thinking now – back there in that shuttered house? That we've vanished into thin air – that's what it will seem like to them. Homily imagined Lupy's surprise, the excitement, the conjectures . . . And, smiling to herself, she half closed her eyes: never would they hit on the drain. And never, in their wildest dreams, would they think of Little Fordham . . .

Two halcyon days went by, but on the third day it rained. Clouds gathered in the morning and by afternoon there was a downpour. At first Arrietty, avid to stay outdoors, took shelter among the roots under the over-hanging bank, but soon the rain drove in on the wind and leaked down from the bank above. The roots became slippery and greasy with mud, so all three of them fled to the drain. 'I mean,' said Homily as they crouched in the entrance, 'at least from here we can see out, which is more than you can say for the kettle.'

They moved from the drain, however, when Pod heard a drumming in the distance. 'Holmcroft!' he exclaimed after listening a moment. 'Come on, get moving . . .' Homily, staring at the grey veil of rain outside, protested that, if they were in for a soaking, they might just as well have it hot as cold.

Chapter Fifteen

It was a good thing they moved, however: the stream had risen almost to the base of the bluff round which they must pass to get to the kettle. Even as it was they had to paddle. The water looked thick and brownish. The delicate ripples had become muscular and fierce and, as they hurried across the second beach, they saw great branches borne on the flood, sinking and rising as the water galloped past.

'Spiller can't travel in this . . .' moaned Homily as they changed their clothes in the kettle. She had to raise her voice against the drumming of the raindrops on the lid. Below them, almost as it might be in their cellar, they heard the thunder of the stream. But the kettle, perched on its stone and wedged against the bank, felt steady as a citadel. The spout was turned away from the wind and no drop got in through the lid. 'Double rim,' explained Pod; 'well made, these old-fashioned kettles . . .'

Banking on Spiller's arrival they had eaten the last of the egg. They felt very hungry and stared with tragic eyes through the rust-hole when, just below them, a half-loaf went by on the flood.

At last it grew dark and they pulled in the cork and prepared to go to sleep. 'Anyway,' said Pod, 'we're warm and dry. And it's bound to clear up soon . . .'

But it rained all next day. And the next. 'He'll never come in this,' moaned Homily.

'I wouldn't put it past him,' said Pod. 'That's a good solid craft that knife-box, and well covered in. The current flows in close here under those brambles. That's why he chose this corner. You mark my words, Homily, he might fetch up here any moment. Spiller's not one to be frightened by a drop of rain.'

That was the day of the banana. Pod had gone out to reconnoitre, climbing gingerly along the slippery shelf of mud beneath the brambles. The current, twisting in, was pouring steadily through Spiller's boat-house, pulling the trailing brambles in its wake: caught up in the branches where they touched the water Pod had found half a packet of sodden cigarettes, a strip of waterlogged sacking, and a whole, rather overripe banana.

Homily had screamed when he pushed it in inch by inch through the rust-hole. She did not recognize it at first and, later, as she saw what it was she began to laugh and cry at the same time.

'Steady, Homily,' said Pod, after the final push, as he peered in, grave-faced, through the rust-hole, 'get a hold on yourself.'

Homily did – almost at once. 'You should have warned us,' she protested, still gasping a little and wiping her eyes on her apron.

'I did call out,' said Pod, 'but what with the noise of the rain . . .'

They ate their fill of the banana – it was overripe already and would not last for long. Pod sliced it across, skin and all; he thus kept it decently covered. The sound of the rain made talking difficult. 'Coming down faster,' said Pod, Homily leaned forward, mouthing the words: 'Do you think he's met with an accident?'

Pod shook his head: 'He'll come when it stops. We got to have patience,' he added.

'Have what?' shouted Homily above the downpour.

'Patience,' repeated Pod.

'I can't hear you . . .'

'Patience!' roared Pod.

Rain began to come in down the spout. There was nothing for it but to sacrifice the blanket. Homily stuffed it in as tightly as she could and the kettle became very airless. 'Might go on for a month,' she grumbled.

'What?' shouted Pod.

'For a month,' repeated Homily.

'What about it?'

'The rain!' shouted Homily.

After that they gave up talking: the effort seemed hardly worth while. Instead they lay down in the layers of dried grasses and tried to go to sleep. Full-fed and in that airless warmth it did not take them long. Arrietty dreamed she was at sea in Spiller's boat: there was a gentle rocking motion which at first seemed rather pleasant and then in her dream the boat began to spin. The spinning increased and the boat became a wheel, turning . . . turning . . . She clung to the spokes, which became like straw and broke away in her grasp. She clung

to the rim, which opened outwards and seemed to fling her off, and a voice was calling again and again: 'Wake up, Arrietty, wake up . . .'

Dizzily she opened her eyes and the kettle seemed full of a whirling half-light. It was morning, she realized, and someone had pulled the blanket from the spout. Close behind her she made out the outline of Pod; he seemed in some strange way to be glued to the side of the kettle. Opposite her she perceived the form of her mother,

spreadeagled likewise in the same fixed, curious manner. She herself, half sitting, half lying, felt gripped by some dream-like force.

'We're afloat,' cried Pod, 'and spinning.' And Arrietty, besides the kettle's spin, was aware of a dipping and a swaying 'We've come adrift. We're in the current,' he went on, 'and going down-stream fast . . .'

'Oh, my . . .' moaned Homily, casting up her eyes: it was the only gesture she could make, stuck as she was like a fly to a fly-paper. But even as she spoke the speed slackened and the spinning turns slowed down, and Arrietty watched her mother slide slowly down to a sitting position on the squelching, waterlogged floor. 'Oh, my goodness . . .' Homily muttered again.

Her voice, Arrietty noticed, sounded strangely audible: the rain had stopped at last.

'I'm going to get the lid off,' said Pod. He too, as the kettle ceased turning, had fallen forward to his knees and now rose slowly, steadying himself by a hand on the side, against the swaying half-turns. 'Give me a hand with the twine, Arrietty.'

They pulled together. Water had seeped in past the cork in the rust-hole and the floor was awash with sodden grass. As they pulled they slid and slithered, but gradually the lid rose and above them they saw, at last, a circle of bright sky.

'Oh, my goodness,' Homily kept saying, and sometimes she changed it to, 'Oh, my goodness me . . .' But she helped them stack up Pod's bundles. 'We got to get out on deck, like,' Pod had insisted; 'we don't stand a chance down below.'

It was a scramble: they used the twine, they used the hat-pin, they used the banana, they used the bundles and somehow, the kettle listing steeply, they climbed out on the rim to hot sunshine and a cloudless sky. Homily sat crouched, her arms gripped tightly round the stem of the arched handle, her legs dangling below. Arrietty sat beside her holding on to the rim. To lighten the weight Pod cut the lid free and cast it overboard: they watched it float away.

'. . . seems a waste,' said Homily.

Chapter Sixteen

The kettle turned slowly as it drifted – more gently now – down-stream. The sun stood high in a brilliant sky: it was later than they had thought. The water looked muddy and yellowish after the recent storm, and in some places had overflowed the banks. To the right of them lay open fields and to the left a scrub of stunted willows and taller hazels. Above their heads golden lamb's-tails trembled against the sky and armies of rushes marched down into the water.

'Fetch up against the bank any minute now,' said Pod hopefully, watching the flow of the stream. 'One side or another,' he added; 'a kettle like this don't drift on for ever . . .'

'I should sincerely hope not,' said Homily. She had slightly relaxed her grip on the handle and, interested in spite of herself, was gazing about her.

Once they heard a bicycle bell and, some seconds later, a policeman's helmet sailed past just above the level of the bushes. 'Oh, my goodness,' muttered Homily, 'that means a footpath . . .'

'Don't worry,' said Pod. But Arrietty, glancing quickly at her father's face, saw he seemed perturbed.

'He'd only have to glance sideways,' Homily pointed out.

'It's all right,' said Pod; 'he's gone now. And he didn't.'
'What about Spiller?' Homily went on.
'What about him?'
'He'll never find us now.'
'Why not?' said Pod. 'He'll see the kettle's gone. As far as Spiller's concerned all we've got to do is bide our time,

wait quietly – wherever we happen to fetch up.'

'Suppose we don't fetch up and go on past Little Fordham?'

'Spiller'll come on past looking for us.'

'Suppose we fetch up amongst all those people?'

'What people?' asked Pod a trifle wearily. 'The plaster ones?'

'No, those human beings who swarm about on the paths.'

'Now, Homily,' said Pod, 'no good meeting trouble half way.'

'Trouble?' exclaimed Homily. 'What are we in now, I'd like to know?' She glanced down past her knees at the sodden straw below. 'And I suppose this kettle'll fill up in no time.'

'Not with the cork swollen up like it is,' said Pod. 'The wetter it gets the tighter it holds. All you got to do, Homily, is to sit there and hold on tight, and, say we come near land, get yourself ready to jump.' As he spoke he was busy making a grappling hook out of his hat-pin, twisting and knotting a length of twine about the head of the pin.

Arrietty, meanwhile, lay flat on her stomach gazing into the water below. She was perfectly happy: the cracked enamel was warm from the sun, and with one elbow crooked round the base of the handle she felt curiously safe. Once in the turgid water she saw the ghostly outline of a large fish – fanning its shadowy fins and standing backwards against the current. Sometimes there were little forests of waterweeds where blackish minnows flicked and darted. Once a water-rat swam swiftly past the kettle, almost under her nose: she called out then excitedly – as though she had seen a whale. Even Homily craned over to watch it pass, admiring the tiny air bubbles which clung like moonstones among the misted

fur. They all stood up to watch it climb out on the bank and shake itself hurriedly into a cloud of spray before it scampered away into the grasses. 'Well I never,' remarked Homily. 'Natural history,' she added reflectively.

'Then, raising her eyes, she saw the cow. It stood quite motionless above its own vast shadow, hock deep and silent in the fragrant mud. Homily stared aghast and even Arrietty felt grateful for a smoothly floating kettle and a stretch of water between. Almost impertinently safe she felt – so near and yet so far – until a sudden eddy in the current swung them in towards the bank.

'It's all right,' called Pod as Arrietty started back; 'it won't hurt you . . .'

'Oh, my goodness . . .' exclaimed Homily, making as though to climb down inside the rim. The kettle lurched.

'Steady!' cried Pod, alarmed. 'Keep her trimmed!'
And, as the kettle slid swiftly shorewards, he flung his
weight sideways, leaning out from the handle. 'Stand
by . . .' he shouted as with a vicious twist they veered
round sharply, gliding against the mud. 'Hold fast!' The
great cow backed two paces as they careered up under her
nose. She lowered her head and swayed slightly as though
embarrassed and then, sniffing the air, she clumsily
backed again.

The kettle teetered against the walls and craters of the
cow-tracks, pressed by the current's flow: a faint vibration of drumming water quivered through the iron. Then
Pod, leaning outwards, clinging with one hand to the rim,
shoved his hat-pin in against a stone: the kettle bounced
slightly turning into the current and, in a series of bumps
and quivers, began to turn away.

'Thank goodness for that, Pod . . .' cried Homily,
'thank goodness . . . thank goodness . . . Oh my, oh my,
oh my!' She sat clinging to the base of the handle, white-
faced and shaking.

'It would never hurt you,' said Pod as they glided out to
mid stream, 'not a cow wouldn't.'

'Might tread on us,' gasped Homily.

'Not once it's seen you it wouldn't.'

'And it did see us,' cried Arrietty, gazing backwards.
'It's looking at us still . . .'

Watching the cow, relaxed and relieved, they were
none of them prepared for the bump. Homily, thrown off
balance, slid forward with a cry – down through the lid
hole on to the straw below. Pod just in time caught hold
of the handle rail. Arrietty caught hold of Pod. Steadying
Arrietty, Pod turned his head: the kettle, he saw, had
fetched up against an island of sticks and branches,
plumb in the middle of the stream. Again the kettle

thrummed, banging and trembling against the obstruct-
ing sticks; little ripples rose up and broke like waves
among and around the weed-strewn, trembling mass.

'Now we are stuck,' remarked Pod, 'good and proper.'

'Get me up, Pod – do . . .' they heard Homily calling
from below.

They got her up and showed her what had happened.
Pod, peering down, saw part of a gate-post and coils of
rusted wire: on this projection a mass of rubbish was
entangled brought down by the flood, a kind of floating

island, knitted up by the current and hopelessly inter-
twined.

No good shoving with his pin: the current held them
head on and, with each successive bump, wedged them
more securely.

'It could be worse,' remarked Homily surprisingly,
when she had got her breath. She took stock of the nest-
like structure: some of the sticks, forced above water,
had already dried in the sun. The whole contraption, to
Homily, looked pleasantly like dry land. 'I mean,' she
went on, 'we could walk about on this. I wouldn't say,
really, but what I don't prefer it to the kettle . . . Better
than floating on and on and on, and ending up, as might
well be, in the Indian Ocean. Spiller could find us here
easy enough . . . plumb in the middle of the view.'

'There's something in that,' agreed Pod. He glanced up
at the banks: the stream here was wider, he noticed. On
the left bank, among the stunted willows which shrouded
the towpath, a tall hazel leaned over the water; on the
right bank the meadows came sloping down to the stream
and, beside the muddy cow-tracks, stood a sturdy clump
of ash. The tall boles, ash and hazel, stood like sentinels
one each side of the river. Yes, it was the kind of spot
Spiller would know well; the kind of place, Pod thought
to himself, to which humans might give a name. The
water on either side of the mid-stream obstruction flowed
dark and deep, scooped out by the current into pools . . .
yes, it was the kind of place, he decided – with a slight
inward tremor of his 'feeling' – where in the summer
human beings might come to bathe. Then, glancing
down-stream, he saw the bridge.

Chapter Seventeen

It was not much of a bridge – wooden, moss-grown, with a single handrail – but, in their predicament, even a modest bridge was still a bridge too many: bridges were highways, built for humans, and command long views of the river.

Homily, when he pointed it out, seemed strangely unperturbed: shading her eyes against the sunlight she gazed intently down-river. 'No human being that distance away,' she decided at last, 'could make out what's on these sticks . . .'

'You'd be surprised,' said Pod. 'They spot the movement like—'

'Not before we've spotted them. Come on, Pod, let's unload the kettle and get some stuff dried out.'

They went below and, by shifting the ballast, they got the kettle well heeled over. When they had achieved sufficient list Pod took his twine and made the handle fast to the sunken wire netting. In this way, with the kettle

held firm, they could crawl in and out through the lid hole. Soon all the gear was spread out in the warmth and, sitting in a row on a baked branch of alder, they each fell to on a slice of banana.

'This could be a lot worse,' said Homily, munching and looking about her. She was thankful for the silence and the sudden lack of motion. Down between the tangled sticks were well-like glintings of dark water, but it was quiet water and, from her high perch, far enough away to be ignored.

Arrietty, on the contrary, had taken off her shoes and stockings and was trailing her feet in the delicate ripples which played about the outer edges.

The river seemed full of voices, endless, mysterious murmurs like half-heard conversations. But conversations without pauses – breathless, steady recountings. 'She said to me, I said to her. And then . . . and then . . . and then . . .' After a while Arrietty ceased to listen as, so often, she ceased to listen to her mother when Homily, in the vein, went on and on and on. But she was aware of the sound and the deadening effect it would have on sounds made farther afield. Against this noise, she thought, something could creep up on you and, without hint or warning, suddenly be there. And then she realized that nothing can creep up on an island unless it were afloat or could swim. But, even as she thought this thought, a blue-tit flew down from above and perched beside her on a twig. It cocked its head sideways at the pale ring of banana skin which had enclosed her luncheon slice. She picked it up and threw it sideways towards him – like a quoit – and the blue-tit flew away.

Then she crept back into the nest of flotsam. Sometimes she climbed under the dry twigs on to the wet ones below. In these curious hollows, cut with sunlight and

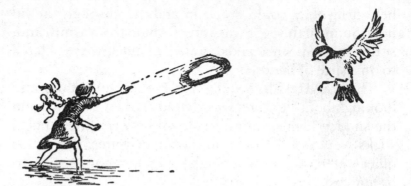

shadow, there was a vast choice of handholds and notches on which to tread. Above her a network of branches criss-crossed against the sun. Once she went right down to the shadowed water and, hanging perilously above it, saw in its blackness her pale reflected face. She found a water-snail clinging to the underside of a leaf and once, with a foot, she touched some frog's spawn, disturbing a nest of tadpoles. She tried to pull up a water-weed by the roots but, slimily, it resisted her efforts – stretching part way like a piece of elasticized rubber, then suddenly springing free.

'Where are you, Arrietty?' Homily called from above. 'Come up here where it's dry . . .'

But Arrietty seemed not to hear: she had found a hen's feather, a tuft of sheep's wool, and half a ping-pong ball which still smelled strongly of celluloid. Pleased with these borrowings she finally emerged. Her parents were suitably impressed, and Homily made a cushion of the sheep's wool, wedged it neatly in the half-ball and used it as a seat. 'And very comfortable too,' she assured them warmly, wobbling slightly on the curved base.

Once two small humans crossed the bridge, country boys of nine or ten. They dawdled and laughed and

climbed about, and threw sticks into the water. The borrowers froze, staring intently as, with backs turned, the two boys hung on the railings watching their sticks drift down-stream.

'Good thing we're up-stream,' murmured Pod from between still lips.

The sun was sinking and the river had turned to molten gold. Arrietty screwed up her eyelids against the glitter. 'Even if they saw us,' she whispered, her eyes on the bridge, 'they couldn't get at us – out here in deep water.'

'Maybe not,' said Pod, 'but the word would get around . . .'

The boys at length disappeared. But the borrowers remained still, staring at the bushes and trying to hear above the bubble of the river any sound of human beings passing along the footpath.

'I think they must have gone across the fields,' said Pod at last. 'Come on, Arrietty, give me a hand with this waterproof . . .'

Pod had been preparing a hammock bed for the night where four stout sticks lay lengthwise in a hollow: a mackintosh groundsheet, their dry clothes laid out on top, the piece of sheep's wool for a pillow and, to cover them, another groundsheet above the piece of red blanket. Snug, they would be, in a deep cocoon – protected from rain and dew and invisible from the bank.

As the flood water began to subside their island seemed to rise higher. Slimy depths were revealed among the structure, and gazing down between the sticks at the rusted wire they discovered a waterlogged shoe.

'Nothing to salvage there,' remarked Pod after a moment's thoughtful silence, 'except maybe the laces.'

Homily, who had followed them downwards, gazed wonderingly about her. It had taken courage to climb down into the depths: she had tested every foothold – some of the branches were rotten and broke away at a touch, others less securely wedged were apt to become detached and quivers and slidings took place elsewhere – like a distant disturbance in a vast erection of spillikins. Their curious island was only held together, she realized, by the inter-relation of every leaf, stick, and floating strand of weed. All the same, on the way up, she snapped off a living twig of hawthorn for the sake of the green leaf buds. 'A bit of salad, like, to eat with our supper,' she explained to Arrietty. 'You can't go on for ever just on egg and banana . . .'

Chapter Eighteen

They ate their supper on the up-stream side of the island where the ripples broke at their feet and where the kettle, tied on its side, had risen clear of the water. The level of the stream was sinking fast and the water seemed far less muddy.

It was not much of a supper: the tail end of the banana which had become rather sticky. They still felt hungry, even after they had finished off the hawthorn shoots, washing them down with draughts of cold water. They spoke wistfully of Spiller and a boat chock full of borrowings.

'Suppose we miss him?' said Homily. 'Suppose he comes in the night?'

'I'll keep watch for Spiller,' said Pod.

'Oh, Pod,' exclaimed Homily, 'you've got to have your eight hours.'

'Not to-night,' said Pod, 'nor to-morrow night. Nor any night while there's a full moon.'

'We could take it in turns,' suggested Homily.

'I'll watch to-night,' said Pod, 'and we'll see how we go.'

Homily was silent, staring down at the water. It was a dream-like evening: as the moon rose the warmth of the day still lingered on the landscape in a glow of tranquil light. Colours seemed enriched from within, vivid but softly muted.

'What's that?' said Homily suddenly, gazing down at the ripples, 'something pink . . .'

They followed the direction of her eyes. Just below the surface something wriggled, held up against the current.

'It's a worm,' said Arrietty after a moment. Homily stared at it thoughtfully. 'You said right, Pod,' she admitted after a moment. 'I have changed . . .'

'In what way?' asked Pod.

'Looking at that worm,' said Homily, 'all scoured and scrubbed, like – clean as a whistle – I was thinking.' She hesitated. 'Well, I was thinking . . . I could eat a worm like that . . .'

'What, raw?' exclaimed Pod, amazed.

'No, stewed of course,' retorted Homily crossly, 'with a bit of wild garlic.' She stared again at the water. 'What's it caught up on?'

Pod craned forward. 'I can't quite see . . .' Suddenly his face became startled and his gaze, sharply intent, slid away on a rising curve towards the bushes.

'What's the matter, Pod?' asked Homily.

He looked at her aghast – a slow stare. 'Someone's fishing,' he breathed, scarcely above his breath.

'Where?' whispered Homily.

Pod jerked his head towards the stunted willows. 'There – behind those bushes . . .'

Then Homily, raising her eyes at last, made out the

fishing line. Arrietty saw it too. Only in glimpses was it visible: not at all under water but against the surface here and there. They perceived the hair-thin shadow. As it rose it became invisible again, lost against the dimness of the willows, but they could follow its direction.

'Can't see nobody,' whispered Homily.

'Course you can't!' snapped Pod. 'A trout's got eyes, remember, just like you and me . . .'

'Not *just* like—' protested Homily.

'You don't want to show yourself,' Pod went on, 'not when you're fishing.'

'Especially if you're poaching,' put in Arrietty. Why are we whispering? she wondered. Our voices can't be heard above the voices of the river.

'That's right, lass,' said Pod, 'especially if you're poaching. And that's just what he is, I shouldn't wonder – a poacher.'

'What's a poacher?' whispered Homily.

Pod hushed her, raising his hand: 'Quiet, Homily,' and then he added aside: 'A kind of human borrower.'

'A human borrower . . .' repeated Homily in a bewildered whisper: it seemed a contradiction in terms.

'Quiet, Homily,' pleaded Pod.

'He can't hear us,' said Arrietty, 'not from the bank. Look!' she exclaimed. 'The worm's gone.'

So it had, and the line had gone too.

'Wait a minute,' said Pod; 'you'll see – he sends it down on the current.'

Straining their eyes they made out the curves of floating line and, just below the surface, the pinkness of the worm sailing before them. The worm fetched up in the same spot, just below their feet, where again it was held against the current.

Something flicked out from under the sticks below

them: there was a flurry of shadow, a swift half-turn, and most of the worm had gone.

'A fish?' whispered Arrietty.

Pod nodded.

Homily craned forward: she was becoming quite excited. 'Look, Arrietty – now you can see the hook!'

Arrietty caught just a glimpse of it and then the hook was gone.

'He felt that,' said Pod, referring to the fisherman; 'thinks he got a bite.'

'But he did get a bite,' said Arrietty.

'He got a bite but he didn't get a fish. Here it comes again . . .'

It was a new worm this time, darker in colour.

Homily shuddered: 'I wouldn't fancy that one, whichever way you cooked it.'

'Quiet, Homily,' said Pod as the worm was whisked away.

'You know,' exclaimed Homily excitedly, 'what we could do – say we had some kind of fire? We could take the fish off the hook and cook and eat it ourselves . . .'

'Say there was a fish *on* the hook,' remarked Pod, gazing soberly towards the bushes. Suddenly he gave a cry and ducked sideways, his hands across his face. 'Look out!' he yelled in a frantic voice.

It was too late: there was the hook in Homily's skirt, worm and all. They ran to her, holding her against the pull of the line while her wild shrieks echoed down the river.

'Unbutton it, Homily! Take the skirt off! Quick . . .'

But Homily couldn't or wouldn't. It might have had something to do with the fact that underneath she was wearing a very short red flannel petticoat which once had belonged to Arrietty and did not think it would look seemly, or she might quite simply just have lost her head. She clung to Pod and, dragged out of his grasp, she clung to Arrietty. Then she clung to the twigs and sticks as she was dragged past them towards the ripples.

They got her out of the water as the line for a moment went slack, and Arrietty fumbled with the small jet bead which served Homily's skirt as a button. Then the line went taut again. As Pod grabbed hold of Homily he saw out of the corner of his eye that the fisherman was standing up.

From this position, on the very edge of the bank, he could play his rod more freely: a sudden upward jerk and Homily, caught by her skirt and shrieking loudly, flew upside-down into the air with Pod and Arrietty fiercely clinging each to an arm. Then the jet button burst off, the skirt sailed away with the worm, and the borrowers, in a huddle, fell back on the sticks. The sticks sank slightly beneath the impact and rose again as gently, breaking the force of their fall.

'That was a near one,' gasped Pod, pulling his leg out of a cleft between the branches. Arrietty, who had come down on her seat, remained sitting: she seemed shaken but unhurt. Homily, crossing her arms, tenderly massaged her shoulders: she had a long graze on one cheek and a jagged tear in the red flannel petticoat. 'You all right, Homily?'

Homily nodded, and her bun unrolled slowly. White-faced and shaking she felt mechanically for hairpins: she was staring fixedly at the bank.

'And the sticks held,' said Pod, examining his grazed shin. He swung the leg slightly. 'Nothing broken,' he said. Homily took no notice: she sat, as though mesmerized, staring at the fisherman.

'It's Mild Eye,' she announced grimly after a moment.

Pod swung round, narrowing his eyes. Arrietty stood up to see better: Mild Eye, the gipsy . . . there was no mistaking the ape-like build, the heavy eyebrows, the thatch of greying hair.

'Now we'll be for it,' said Homily.

Pod was silent a moment. 'He can't get at us here,' he decided at last, 'right out in mid stream: the water's good and deep out here, on both sides of us, like.'

'He could stand in the shallows and reach,' said Homily.

'Doubt if he'd make it,' said Pod.

'He knows us and he's seen us,' said Homily in the same expressionless voice. She drew a long, quivering breath:

'And, you mark my words, he's not going to miss us again!'

There was silence except for the voices of the river. The babbling murmur, unperturbed and even, seemed suddenly alien and heartless.

'Why doesn't he move?' asked Arrietty.

'He's thinking,' said Homily.

After a moment Arrietty ventured timidly: 'Of what he's going to charge for us, and that, when he's got us in a cage?'

'Of what he's going to do next,' said Homily.

They were silent a moment, watching Mild Eye.

'Look,' said Arrietty.

'What's he up to now?' asked Pod.

'He's taking the skirt off the hook!'

'And the worm too,' said Pod. 'Look out!' he cried as the fisherman's arm flew up. There was a sudden jerk among the sticks, a shuddering series of elastic quivers. 'He's casting for us!' shouted Pod. 'Better we get under cover.'

'No,' said Homily as their island became still again; she watched the caught branch, hooked loose, bobbing away down-river. 'Say he drags this obstruction to bits, we're safer on top than below. Better we take to the kettle—'

But even as she spoke the next throw caught the cork in the rust-hole. The kettle, hooked by its stopper and tied to the sticks, resisted the drag of the rod: they clung together in silent panic as just below them branches began to slide. Then the cork bounced free and leapt away on the end of the dancing line. Their island subsided again and, unclasping each other, they moved apart, listening wide-eyed to the rhythmic gurgle of water filling the kettle.

The next throw caught a key branch, one on which they stood. They could see the hook well and truly in, and the trembling strain on the twine. Pod clambered alongside and, leaning back, tugged downwards against the pull. But strain as he might the line stayed taut and the hook as deeply embedded.

'Cut it,' cried someone above the creaking and groaning. 'Cut it . . .' the voice cried again tremulously faint, like the rippling voice of the river.

'Then give me the razor-blade,' gasped Pod. Arrietty brought it in a breathless scramble. There was a gentle twang and they all ducked down as the severed line flew free. 'Now why,' exclaimed Pod, 'didn't I think of that in the first place?'

He glanced towards the shore. Mild Eye was reeling in; the line, too light now, trailed softly on the breeze.

'He's not very pleased,' said Homily.

'No,' agreed Pod, sitting down beside her, 'he wouldn't be.'

'Don't think he's got another hook,' said Homily.

They watched Mild Eye examine the end of his line and they met his baleful glare as, angrily raising his head, he stared across the water.

'Round one to us,' said Pod.

Chapter Nineteen

They settled themselves more comfortably on the sticks, preparing for a vigil. Homily reached behind her into the bedding and pulled out the piece of red blanket. 'Look, Pod,' she said in an interested voice as she tucked it about her knees, 'what's he up to now?' They watched intently as Mild Eye, taking up his rod again, turned towards the bushes. 'You don't think he's given it up?' she added as Mild Eye, making for the towpath, disappeared from view.

'Not a hope,' said Pod, 'not Mild Eye. Not once he's seen us and knows we're here for the taking.'

'He can't get us here,' said Homily again, 'right out in deep water. And it'll be dark soon.' She seemed strangely calm.

'Maybe,' said Pod, 'but look at that moon rising. And we'll still be here in the morning.' He took up his razor-blade: 'Might as well free that kettle: it's only a weight on the sticks . . .'

Homily watched him slice through the twine and, a little sadly, they watched the kettle sink.

'Poor Spiller,' said Arrietty. 'He was kind of fond of that kettle . . .'

'Well, it served its purpose,' said Pod.

'What if we made a raft?' suggested Homily suddenly. Pod looked about at the sticks and down at the twine in his hand. 'We could do,' he said, 'but it would take a bit of time. And with him about' – he jerked his head towards the bushes – 'I reckon we're as safe here as anywhere.'

'And it's better here,' said Arrietty, 'for being seen.'

Homily, startled, turned and looked at her. 'Whatever
do you want to be seen for?'

'I was thinking of Spiller,' said Arrietty. 'With this kind
of moon and this sort of weather he'll come to-night most
likely.'

'Pretty well bound to,' agreed Pod.

'Oh dear,' said Homily, pulling the blanket around
her, 'whatever will he think? I mean, finding me like this
– in Arrietty's petticoat?'

'Nice and bright,' said Pod. 'Catch his eye nicely, that
petticoat will.'

'Not short and shrunk up like it is,' complained
Homily unhappily, 'and a great tear in the side, like.'

'It's still bright,' said Pod, 'a kind of landmark. And I'm
sorry now we sunk the kettle. He'd have seen that too.
Well, can't be helped—'

'Look!' whispered Arrietty, gazing at the bank.

There stood Mild Eye. Just beside them he seemed
now. He had walked down the towpath behind the
bushes and had emerged on the bank beside the leaning
hazel. In the clear shadowless light he seemed extraordinarily close. They could even see the pallor of his one blue
eye in contrast to the fiercely glaring black one; they
could see the joints in his fishing rod and the clothes-pegs
and coils of clothes-line in his basket, which he carried
half slung on his forearm and tilted towards them. Had it
been dry land between them four good strides would
have brought him across.

'Oh dear,' muttered Homily, 'now what?'

Mild Eye, leaning his rod against the hazel, set down
the basket from which he took two fair-sized fish strung
together by the gills. These he wrapped carefully in
several layers of dock leaves.

'Rainbow trout,' said Arrietty.

'How do you know?' asked Homily.

Arrietty blinked her eyelids. 'I just know,' she said.

'Young Tom,' said Pod; 'that's how she knows, I reckon – seeing his grandad's the gamekeeper. And that's how she knew about poachers, eh, Arrietty?'

Arrietty did not reply: she was watching Mild Eye as he returned the fish to the basket. Very carefully he seemed to be placing them, deep among the clothes-pegs. He then took up two coils of clothes-line and laid these carelessly on top.

Arrietty laughed. 'As if,' she whispered scornfully, 'they wouldn't search his basket!'

'Quiet, Arrietty,' said Homily, watching intently as Mild Eye, staring across at them, advanced to the edge of the bank. 'It's early yet to laugh . . .'

On the edge of the bank Mild Eye sat down and, his eyes still fixed on the borrowers, began to unlace his boots.

'Oh, Pod,' moaned Homily suddenly, 'you see those boots? They are the same, aren't they? I mean – to think we lived in one of them! Which was it, Pod, left or right?'

'The one with the patch,' said Pod, alert and watching. 'He won't make it,' he added thoughtfully, 'not by paddling.'

'Think of him wearing a boot patched up by you, Pod.'
'Quiet, Homily,' pleaded Pod as Mild Eye, barefoot by
now, began to roll up his trousers. 'Get ready to move
back.'

'And me getting *fond* of that boot!' exclaimed Homily just above her breath. She seemed fascinated by the pair of them, set neatly together now, on the grassy verge of the stream.

They watched as Mild Eye, a hand on the leaning hazel, lowered himself into the water. It came to just above his ankles. 'Oh, my,' muttered Homily, 'it's shallow. Better we move back——'

'Wait a minute!' said Pod. 'You watch!'

The next step took Mild Eye in to well above the knee, wetting the turn-up of his trousers. He stood, a little nonplussed, holding tight to the leaning branch of the hazel.

'Bet it's cold,' whispered Arrietty.

Mild Eye stared as though measuring the distance between them, and then he glanced back at the bank. Sliding his hand farther out along the branch he took a second step. This brought him in almost to the thigh. They saw him start as the coldness of the water seeped through his trousers to his skin. He glanced at the branch above. It was already bending: he could not with safety move farther. Then, his free arm outstretched towards them, he began to lean . . .

'Oh my——' moaned Homily as the swarthy face came nearer. The outstretched fingers had a greedy steadiness about them. Reaching, reaching . . .

'It's quite all right,' said Pod.

It was as though Mild Eye heard him. The black eye widened slightly while the blue one smoothly stared. The stream moved gently past the soaking corduroys. They could hear the gipsy's breathing.

Pod cleared his throat. 'You can't do it,' he said. Again the black eye widened and Mild Eye opened his mouth. He did not speak but his breathing became even deeper and he glanced again at the shore. Then clumsily he began to retreat, clinging to his branch, and feeling backwards with his feet for rising ground on the slimy bottom. The branch creaked ominously under his weight and, once in shallower water, he quickly let it go and splashed back unaided to the bank. He stood there dripping and gasping and staring at them heavily. There was still no expression on his face. After a while he sat down, and rather unsteadily, still staring, he rolled himself a cigarette.

Chapter Twenty

'I told you he couldn't make it,' said Pod; 'needed a good half-yard or another couple of feet . . .' He patted Homily on the arm: 'All we've got to do now is to hold out till dark. And Spiller will come for sure.'

They sat in a row on the same stick, facing up-stream. To watch Mild Eye they had to turn slightly sideways to the left.

'Look at him now,' whispered Homily. 'He's still thinking.'

'Let him think,' said Pod.

'Supposing Spiller came now?' suggested Arrietty, gazing hopefully along the water.

'He couldn't do anything,' said Pod, 'not under Mild Eye's nose. Say he did come now — he'd see we were all right, like, and he'd take cover near by until dark. Then he'd bring his boat alongside on the far side of the island and take us all aboard. That's what I reckon he'd do.'

'But it won't ever get dark,' Arrietty protested, 'not with a fu'l moon.'

'Moon or no moon,' said Pod, 'Mild Eye won't sit there all night. He'll be getting peckish soon. And as far as he calculates, he's got us all tied up, like, and safe to leave for morning. He'll come along then, soon as it's light, with all the proper tackle.'

'What is the proper tackle?' asked Homily uneasily.

'I hope,' said Pod, 'that not being here we won't never need to know.'

'How does he know we can't swim?' asked Arrietty.

'For the same reason as we know he can't: if he could've swum he'd have swum. And the same applies to us.'

'Look,' said Arrietty; 'he's standing up again . . . he's getting something out of the basket!'

They watched intently as Mild Eye, cigarette dangling out of the corner of his mouth, fumbled among the clothes-pegs.

'Oh my,' said Homily, 'see what he's doing? He's got a coil of clothes-line. Oh, I don't like this, Pod. This looks to me' – she caught her breath – 'a bit like the proper tackle.'

'Stay quiet and watch,' said Pod.

Mild Eye, cigarette in mouth, was deliberately unfolding several lengths of line which, new and stiff, hung in curious angles. Then, an end of rope in his hand, he stared at the trunk of the hazel. 'I see what he's going to do,' breathed Homily.

'Quiet, Homily – we all see. But' – Pod narrowed his eyes, watching intently as Mild Eye attached the length of rope above a branch high on the trunk of the hazel – 'I can't quite figure where it gets him . . .'

Climbing down off a curve of root Mild Eye pulled on

the rope, testing the strength of the knot. Then, turning towards them, he gazed across the river. They all turned round, following the direction of his eyes. Homily gasped: 'He's going to throw it across . . .' Instinctively she ducked as the coil of rope came sailing above their heads and landed on the opposite bank.

The slack of rope, missing their island by inches, trailed on the surface of the water. 'Wish we could get at it,' muttered Homily but, even as she spoke, the current widened the loop and carried it farther away. The main coil seemed caught in the brambles below the alder. Mild Eye had disappeared again. He emerged at last, a long way farther down the towpath almost beside the bridge.

'Can't make out what he's up to,' said Homily as Mild Eye, barefoot still, hurried across the bridge, 'throwing

that rope across. What's he going to do – walk the tightrope or something?'

'Not exactly,' said Pod; 'the other way round, like. It's a kind of overhead bridge, as you might say, and you get across by handholds. Done it myself once, from a chair back to lamp-table.'

'Well, you need both hands for that,' exclaimed Homily. 'I mean, he couldn't pick *us* up on the way. Unless he does it with his feet.'

'He doesn't need to get right across,' explained Pod – he sounded rather worried – 'he just needs something to hang on to that's a bit longer than that hazel branch, something he knows won't give way. He just wants a bit more reach, a bit more safe lean-over . . . he was pretty close to us that time he waded, remember?'

'Yes . . .' said Homily uneasily, watching as Mild Eye picked his way rather painfully along the left bank and made towards the ash-tree. 'That fields full of stubble,' she remarked unkindly, after a moment.

The rope flew up, scattering them with drops, as Mild Eye pulled it level and made it fast to the ash-tree. It quivered above them, still dripping slightly – taut, straight, and very strong-looking. 'Bear a couple of men his weight,' said Pod.

'Oh, my goodness . . .' whispered Homily.

They stared at the ash-tree: a cut end of clothes-line hung the length of the bole, still swinging slightly from Mild Eye's efforts. 'Knows how to tie a knot . . .' remarked Homily.

'Yes,' agreed Pod, looking even more glum. 'You wouldn't undo that in a hurry.'

Mild Eye took his time walking back. He paused on the bridge and stared awhile up the river as though to admire his handiwork. Confident, he seemed suddenly, and in no particular hurry.

'Can he see us from there?' asked Homily, narrowing her eyes.

'I doubt it,' said Pod, 'not if we're still. Might get a glimpse of the petticoat . . .'

'Not that it matters either way,' said Homily.

'No, it don't matter now,' said Pod. 'Come on now,' he added as Mild Eye left the bridge, and behind the bushes was starting along the towpath. 'What we better do, I reckon, is get over to the far side of the island and each of us straddle a good thick twig: something to hold on to. He may make it and he may not, but we got to keep steady now, all three of us, and take our chance. There ain't nothing else we can do.'

They each chose a thickish twig, picking the ones that seemed light enough to float and sufficiently furnished with handholds. Pod helped Homily, who was trembling so violently that she could hardly keep her balance. 'Oh, Pod,' she moaned, 'I don't know what I feel like – perched up here on my own. Wish we could all be together.'

'We'll be close enough,' said Pod. 'And maybe he won't even get within touching distance. Now you hold tight and, no matter what happens, don't you let go. Not even if you end up in the water.'

Arrietty sat on her twig as though it were a bicycle: there were two footholds and places for both hands. She felt curiously confident: if the twig broke loose, she felt, she could hold on with her hands and use her feet as paddles. 'You know,' she explained to her mother, 'like a water-beetle . . .' But Homily, who in shape was more like a water-beetle than any of them, did not seem comforted.

Pod took his seat on a knobbly branch of elder. 'And

make for this ffar bank," he said, jerking his head towards the ash-tree, 'if you find you can make for anywhere. See that piece of rope he's left dangling? Well, we might make a grab at that. Or some of those brambles where they trail down into the wateer . . . get a hold on one of them. Depends where you fetch up . . .'

They were high enough to see across the sticks of their island and Homily, from her perch, had been watching Mild Eye. 'He's coming now,' she said grimly. In her dead, expressionless voice there was a dreadful kind of calm.

They saw that this time he laid both hands on the rope and lowered himself more easily into the water. Two careful steps brought him thigh deep on his foremost leg: here he seemed to hesitate. 'Only wants that other couple of feet,' said Pod.

Mild Eye moved his foremost hand from the rope and, leaning carefully, stretched out his arm towards them. He waggled his fingers slightly, calculating distance. The rope, which had been so taut, sagged a little under his weight and the leaves of the hazel rustled. He glanced behind him, as he had done before, and seemed reassured by the lissom strength of the tree; but the light was fading and, from across where they waited, they could not see his expression. Somewhere in the dusk a cow lowed sadly and they heard a bicycle bell. If only Spiller would come . . .

Mild Eye, sliding his grasp forward, steadied himself a moment and took another step. He seemed to go in deep, but he was so close now that the height of their floating island hid him from the waistline down. They could no longer see the stretching fingers, but they heard the sticks creak and felt the movement: he was drawing their island towards him.

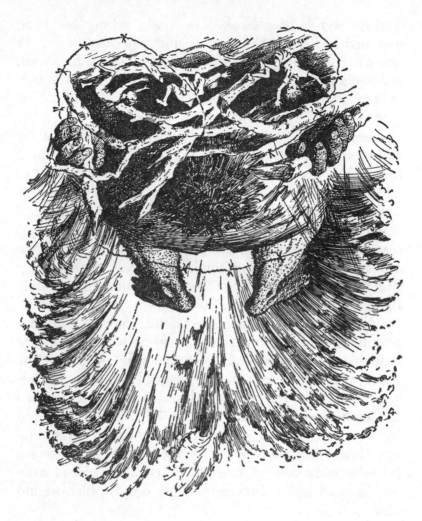

'Oh, Pod,' cried Homily as she felt the merciless pull of that unseen hand and the squeakings and scrapings below her, 'you've been so good to me. All your life you been so good. I never thought to tell you, Pod, never once – how good you've always been—'

She broke off sharply as the island lurched, caught on

the barbed wire obstruction, and, terror-stricken, clutched at her twig. There was a dull crack and two outside branches dislodged themselves slowly and bobbed away downstream.

'You all right, Homily?' called Pod.

'So far,' she gasped.

Then everything seemed to happen at once. She saw Mild Eye's expression turn to utter surprise as, lurching forward to grab their island, he pitched face downwards into the water. They went down with him in one resounding splash – or rather, as it seemed to Homily, the water rushed up to them. She had opened her mouth to scream but closed it just in time. Bubbles streamed past her face and tendrils of clinging weed. The water was icily cold but alive with noise and movement. No sooner had she let go her twig, which seemed to be dragging her down, than the hold on the sticks was released and the island rushed up again. Gasping and coughing, Homily broke surface: she saw the trees again, the rising moon, and the dim, rich evening sky. Loudly she called out for Pod.

'I'm here,' cried a choked voice from somewhere behind her. There was a sound of coughing. 'And Arrietty too. Hold tight, like I said! The island's moving . . .'

The island swung as though on a pivot, caught by one end on the wire. They were circling round in a graceful curve towards the bank of the ash-tree. Homily realized, as she grabbed for a handhold, that Mild Eye in falling had pushed on their floating sticks.

They stopped a little short of the bank and Homily could see the trailing brambles and the trunk of the ash-tree with its piece of hanging cord. She saw Pod and Arrietty had clambered down to the sticks which were nearest the shore, at which, with their backs to Homily, they seemed to be staring intently. As she made her way towards them, slipping and sliding on the wet branches, she heard Arrietty talking excitedly, clutching her father by the arm. 'It is,' she kept saying, 'it is . . .'

Pod turned as Homily approached to help her across the sticks. He seemed preoccupied and rather dazed. A long piece of weed hung down his back in a slimy kind of pigtail. 'What's the matter, Pod? You all right?'

Behind them they heard bellows of fright as Mild Eye emerging from the depths, struggled to find a foothold; Homily, alarmed, gripped Pod by the arm. 'It's all right,' he told her, 'he won't bother with us. Not again to-night at any rate . . .'

'What happened, Pod? The rope broke – or what? Or was it the tree?'

'Seemingly,' said Pod, 'it were the rope. But I can't see how. Hark at Arrietty.' He nodded towards the bank. 'She says it's Spiller's boat—'

'Where?'

'There under the brambles.'

Homily, steadying herself by clinging to Pod, peered forward. The bank was very close now – barely a foot away.

'It is, I know it is,' cried Arrietty again, 'that thing under there like a log.'

'It's like a log,' said Pod, 'because it is a log.'

'Spiller!' called Homily on a gentle rising note, peering into the brambles.

'No good,' said Pod, 'we been calling. And, say it was his boat, he'd answer. Spiller,' he called again in a vehement whisper, 'you there?'

There was no reply.

'What's that?' cried Pod, turning. A light had flashed on the opposite bank somewhere near the towpath.

'Someone's coming,' he whispered. Homily heard the sudden jangle of a bicycle and the squeak of brakes as it skidded to a stop. Mild Eye had ceased his swearing and his spitting and, though still in the water, it seemed he had ceased to move. The silence was absolute, except for the running of the river. Homily, about to speak, felt a warning grip on her arm. 'Quiet,' whispered Pod. A human being on the opposite bank was crashing through the bushes. The light flashed on again and circled about. This time it seemed more blinding, turning the dusk into darkness.

'Hallo . . . hallo . . . hallo . . . hallo . . .' said a voice. It was a young voice, both stern and gay. It was a voice which sounded familiar to Homily, though for a moment she could not put a name to it. Then she remembered that last day at Firbank, under the kitchen floor: the goings on above and the ordeal down below. It was the voice, she realized, of Mrs Driver's old enemy – Ernie Runacre, the policeman.

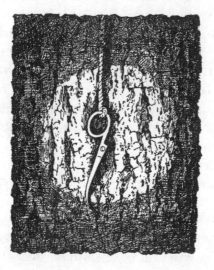

She turned to Pod. 'Quiet!' he warned her again as the circle of light trembled across the water. On the sticks – if none of them moved – he knew they would not be seen. Homily, in spite of this. gave a sudden loud gasp. 'Oh, Pod!' she exclaimed.

'Hush,' urged Pod, tightening his grip on her arm.

'It's our nail-scissor,' persisted Homily, dropping her voice to a breathy kind of whisper. 'You must look, Pod. Half way down the ash-tree . . .'

Pod swivelled his eyes round: there it hung, glittering against the bark. It seemed attached in some way to the spare end of rope which Mild Eye had left dangling.

'Then it *was* Spiller's boat,' Arrietty whispered excitedly.

'Keep quiet, can't you,' begged Pod through barely opened lips, 'till he shifts the beam of the light!'

But Ernie Runacre, on the opposite bank, seemed taken up with Mild Eye. 'Now then,' they heard him say in the same brisk, policeman's voice, 'what's going on here?' And the light beam flicked away to concentrate on the gipsy.

Pod drew a sigh of relief. 'That's better,' he said, relaxing slightly and using his normal voice.

'But where is Spiller?' fussed Homily, her teeth chattering with cold. 'Maybe he's met with an accident.'

'But that was Spiller,' put in Arrietty eagerly, 'coming down the tree with the nail-scissor. He'd have it slung by the handle on his shoulder.'

'You mean you saw him?'

'No, you don't see Spiller. Not when he doesn't want you to.'

'He'd kind of match up with the bark,' explained Pod.

'Then if you didn't see him,' said Homily after a moment, 'how can you be certain?'

'Well, you can't be certain,' agreed Pod.

Homily seemed perturbed. 'You think it was Spiller cut the rope?'

'Seemingly,' said Pod; 'shinned up the tree by that loose bit of left-over. Like I used to with my name-tape, remember?'

Homily peered at the brambles. 'Say that is his boat under there, which I doubt – why didn't he just come and fetch us?'

'Like I told you,' said Pod wearily; 'he was laying up till dark. Use your head, Homily. Spiller needs this river –it's his livelihood, like. True, he might have got us off. But – say he was spotted by Mild Eye: he'd be marked down by the gipsies from then on – boat and all. See what I mean? They'd be on the watch for him. Sometimes,' Pod went on, 'you don't talk like a borrower. You and Arrietty both – you go on at times as though you never heard about cover and suchlike, let alone about being "seen." You go on, the both of you, like a couple of human beings . . .'

'Now, Pod,' protested Homily, 'no need to get insulting.'

'But I mean it,' said Pod. 'And as far as Spiller knew we was all right here till dark. Once the hook had gone.'

They were quiet a moment, listening to the splashes across the water. Homily, caught by the sound of that brisk, familiar voice, moved away from Pod in order to hear what was happening. 'Come on now,' Ernie Runacre was saying, 'get your foot on that root. That's right. Give us your hand. Bit early, I'd say, for a dip. Wouldn't choose it myself. Sooner try me hand at a bit of fishing . . . providing, of course, I weren't too particular about the bylaws. Come on now' – he caught his breath as though to heave – 'one, two, three – hup! Well, there you are!

now, let's take a look at this basket . . .'

Homily, to get a glimpse of them, had hauled herself up
on a twig when she felt Pod's hand on her arm. 'Watch!'
she exclaimed excitedly, gripping his fingers with hers.
'He'll find that borrowed fish! That rainbow trout or
whatever it's called . . .'

'Come on now,' whispered Pod.

'Just a minute, Pod—'

'But he's waiting,' insisted Pod. 'Better we go now, he
says, while they're taken up with that basket . . . And that

light on the bank, he says, will make the river seem
darker.'

Homily turned slowly. There was Spiller's boat, bobbing alongside, with Spiller and Arrietty in the stern. She
saw their faces, pale against the shadows, lit by the rising
moon. All was quiet, except for the running of the ripples.

Dazedly she began to climb down. 'Spiller . . .' she
breathed. And, missing a foothold, she stumbled and
clung to Pod.

He supported and gently guided her down to the water.
As he helped her aboard he said: 'You and Arrietty better

get in under the canopy. Bit of a squeeze now because of the cargo, but it can't be helped . . .'

Homily hesitated, gazing dumbly at Spiller, as they met face to face in the stern. She could not, at that moment, find words to thank him, nor dare she take his hand. He seemed aloof, suddenly, and very much the captain: she just stood and looked at him until, embarrassed, he frowned and looked away. 'Come, Arrietty,' said Homily huskily and, feeling rather humbled, they crept in under the gaiter.

Chapter Twenty-One

Perched on top of the cargo, which felt very knobbly, Homily and Arrietty clung together to share their last traces of warmth. As Pod let go the painter and Spiller pushed off with his butter-knife, Homily let out a cry.

'It's all right,' Arrietty soothed her; 'see, we're in the current. It was just that one last lurch.'

The knife-box now rode smoothly on the ripples, gracefully veering with the river's twists and turns. Beyond the canopy and framed in its arch they could see Pod and Spiller in the stern. What were they talking about? Arrietty wondered. And wished very much she could hear.

'Pod'll catch his death,' muttered Homily unhappily, 'and so will we all.'

As the moon gained in brilliance the figures in the stern became silvered over. Nothing moved except Spiller's

hand on the paddle as deftly, almost carelessly, he held
the boat in the current. Once Pod laughed, and once they
heard him exclaim: 'Well, I'm danged!'

'We won't have any furniture or anything,' said
Homily after a while, 'only the clothes we stand up in –
say we were standing up, I mean. Four walls, that's all
we'll have: just four walls!'

'And windows,' said Arrietty. 'And a roof,' she added
gently.

Homily sneezed loudly. 'Say we survive,' she sniffed,
fumbling about for a handkerchief.

'Take mine,' said Arrietty, producing a sodden ball;
'yours went away with the skirt.'

Homily blew her nose and pinned up her dripping
hair; then, clinging together, they were silent awhile,
watching the figures in the stern. Homily, very tense,
seemed to be thinking. 'And your father's lost his
hacksaw,' she said at last.

'Here's papa now,' Arrietty remarked as a figure
darkened the archway. She squeezed her mother's arm:
'It will be all right. I know it will. Look, he's smiling . . .'

Pod, climbing on to the cargo, approached them on
hands and knees. 'Just thought I'd tell you,' he said to
Homily, slightly lowering his voice, 'that he's got enough
stuff in the holds he says to start us off housekeeping.'

'What sort of stuff?' asked Homily.

'Food mostly. And one or two tools and such to make
up for the nail-scissor.'

'It's clothes we're short of . . .'

'Plenty of stuff for clothes, Spiller says, down at Little
Fordham. Any amount of it: dropped gloves, handkerchiefs, scarves, jerseys, pullovers – the lot. Never a day
passes, he says, without there isn't something.'

Homily was silent. 'Pod,' she said at last, 'I never even thanked him.'

'That's all right. He don't hold with thanks.'

'But, Pod, we got to do something.'

'I been into that,' said Pod; 'there's no end to the stuff we could collect up for him once we get settled, like, in a place of our own. Say every night we whipped round quick after closing time. See what I mean?'

'Yes,' said Homily uncertainly. She could never quite visualize Little Fordham.

'Now,' said Pod, squeezing past them, 'he's got a whole lot of sheep's wool, he says, up for'ard. Better you both undress and tuck down into it. Might get a bit of sleep. We won't be there, he says, not much before dawn . . .'

'But what about you, Pod?' asked Homily.

'That's all right,' said Pod, poking about for'ard; he's lending me a suit. Here's the sheep's wool,' he said and began to pass it back.

'A suit?' echoed Homily, amazed. 'What kind of a

suit?' Mechanically she stacked up the sheep's wool. It smelled a little oily but there seemed to be plenty of it.

'Well,' said Pod, 'his summer clothes.' He sounded rather self-conscious.

'So Lupy finished them?'

'Yes, he went back for them.'

'Oh,' exclaimed Homily, 'did he tell them anything about us?'

'Not a word. You know Spiller. They did the telling. Very upset Lupy was, he says. Went on about you being the best friend she ever had. More like a sister to her, she says. Seems she's gone into mourning.'

'Mourning! Whatever for?'

'For us, I reckon,' said Pod. He smiled wanly and began to unbutton his waistcoat.

Homily was silent a moment. Then she too smiled – a little puffed up, it seemed, by the thought of Lupy in black. 'Fancy!' she said at last and, suddenly cheerful, she began to unbutton her blouse.

Arrietty, already undressed, had rolled herself into the sheep's wool. 'When did Spiller first spot us?' she asked sleepily.

'Saw us in the air,' said Pod, 'when we were on the hook.'

'Goodness . . .' murmured Arrietty. Drowsily she seemed trying to think back: 'And that's why we didn't see him.'

'And why Mild Eye didn't either. Too much going on. Spiller took his chance like a flash: slid on quick, close as he could get, and drove in under those brambles.'

'Wonder he didn't call out to us,' said Homily.

'He did,' exclaimed Pod, 'but he wasn't all that close. And what with the noise of the river—'

'Hush!' whispered Homily. 'She's dropping off . . .'

'Yes,' went on Pod, lowering his voice, 'he called all right – it was just that we didn't seem to hear him. Excepting, of course, that once.'

'When was that?' asked Homily. 'I never heard nothing.'

'That fourth throw,' whispered Pod, 'when the hook caught in our stick, remember? And I was down there pulling? Well, he yelled out then at the top of his lungs: remember a voice calling "Cut it"? Thought it was you at the time . . .'

'Me?' said Homily. In the wool-filled dimness there were faint clicking, mysterious unbuttonings . . .

'But it was Spiller,' said Pod.

'Well, I never . . .' said Homily. Her voice sounded muffled: in her modest way she was undressing under the sheep's wool and had disappeared from view. Her head emerged at last, and one thin arm with a sudden bundle of clothes. 'Anywhere we can hang these out, do you think?'

'Leave them there,' said Pod as, grunting a little, he struggled with Spiller's tunic, 'and Arrietty's too. I'll ask Spiller . . . dare say we'll manage. As I see it,' he went on, having got the tunic down past his waist and the trousers dragged up to meet it, 'in life as we live it – come this thing or that thing – there's always some way to manage. Always has been and, like as not, always will be. That's how I reckon. Maybe we could fly the clothes, like, strung out on the knitting-needle . . .'

Homily watched him in silence as he gathered the garments together. 'Maybe . . .' she said after a moment. 'Lash the point, say, and fly the knob.'

'I meant,' said Homily softly, 'what you said before; that maybe there is always some way to manage. The trouble comes, like, or so it seems to me, in whether you hit on it.'

'Yes, that's the trouble,' said Pod.

'See what I mean?'

'Yes,' said Pod. He was silent a moment, thinking this out. 'Oh, well . . .' he said at last, and turned as if to go.

'Just a minute, Pod,' pleaded Homily, raising herself on an elbow, 'let's have a look at you. No, come a bit closer. Turn round a bit . . . that's right. I wish the light was better . . .' Sitting up in her nest of fleece, she gave him a long look – it was a very gentle look for Homily. 'Yes,' she decided at last, 'white kind of suits you, Pod.'

Epilogue

In the large kitchen at Firbank Hall Crampfurl, the gardener, pushed his chair back from the table. Picking his teeth with a whittled matchstick, he stared at the embers of the stove. 'Funny . . .' he said.

Mrs Driver, the cook, who was clearing the dishes, paused in her stacking of the plates; her suspicious eyes slid sideways: 'What is?'

'Something I saw . . .'

'At market?'

'No – to-night, on the way home . . .' Crampfurl was silent a moment, staring towards the grate. 'Remember that time – last March, wasn't it – when we had the floor up?'

Mrs Driver's swarthy face seemed to darken. Tightening her lips, she clattered the plates together and, almost angrily, she threw the spoons into a dish. 'Well, what about it?'

'Kind of nest, you said it was. Mice dressed up, you said . . .'

'Oh, I never—'

'Well, you ask Ernie Runacre: he was there – nearly split his sides laughing. Mice dressed up, you said. Those were the very words. Saw them running, you said . . .'

'I swear I never.'

Crampfurl looked thoughtful: 'You've a right to deny it. But couldn't help laughing meself. I mean, there you was, perched up on that chair and—'

'That'll do.' Mrs Driver drew up a stool and sat down heavily. Leaning forward, elbows on knees, she stared into Crampfurl's face. 'Suppose I did see them – what then? What's so funny? Squeaking and squawking and running every which way . . .' Her voice rose. 'And what's more . . . now I *will* tell you something, Cramp-furl.' She paused to draw a deep breath. 'They were more like *people* than mice. Why, one of 'em even—'

Crampfurl stared back at her: 'Go on. Even what?'

'One of 'em even had its hair in curlers . . .'

She glared as she spoke, as though daring him to smile. But Crampfurl did not smile. He nodded slowly. He broke his matchstick in half and threw it into the fire. 'And yet,' he said, rising to his feet, 'if there'd been anything, we'd have found it at the time. Stands to reason – with the floor up and that hole blocked under the clock.' He yawned noisily, stretching his forearms. 'Well, I'll be getting on. Thanks for the pie . . .'

Mrs Driver did not stir. 'For all we know,' she persisted, 'they may be still about. Half the rooms being closed, like.'

'No, I wouldn't say that was likely: we been more on

the watch-out and there'd be some kind of traces. No, I got an idea they escaped – say there *was* something here in the first place.'

'There was something here all right! But what's the good of talking . . . with that Ernie Runacre splitting his sides. And' – she glanced at him sharply – 'what's changed you all of a sudden?'

'I don't say I have changed. It's just that I got thinking. Remember that scarf you was knitting – that grey one? Remember the colour of the needles?'

'Needles . . . kind of coral, wasn't they? Pinkish like . . .'

'Coral?'

'Soon tell. I've got them here.' She crossed to the dresser, pulled out a drawer, and took out a bundle of knitting-needles tied about with wool. 'These are them, these two here. More pinkish than coral. Why do you ask?'

Crampfurl took up the bundle. Curiously he turned it about. 'Had an idea they was yellow . . .'

'That's right too – fancy you remembering! I did start with yellow but I lost one: that day my niece came, remember, and we brought up tea to the hayfield?'

Crampfurl, turning the bundle, selected and drew out a needle: it was amber-coloured and slightly translucent. He measured it thoughtfully between his fingers: 'One like this, weren't it?'

'That's right. Why? You found one?'

Crampfurl shook his head: 'Not exactly.' He stared at the needle, turning it about: the same thickness, that other one, and, allowing for the part that was hidden, about the same length . . . Fragile as glass it had looked in the moonlight, with the darkened water behind, as – staring, staring – he had leaned down over the bridge.

The paddle, doubly silvered, had flashed like a fish in the stern. As the strange craft came nearer, he had caught a glimpse of the butter-knife, observed the shape of the canopy, and the barge-like depth of the hull. The set of signals flying from the mast-head seemed less like flags than miniature garments strung like washing in the breeze – a descending scale of trousers, pants, and drawers, topped gallantly (or so it had seemed) by a fluttering red-flannel petticoat – and tiny shreds of knitted stocking whipped eel-like about the mast. Some child's toy, he had thought . . . some discarded invention, abandoned and left to drift . . . Until, as the craft approached the shadow of the bridge, a face had looked up from the stern, bird's-egg pale and featureless in the moonlight, and with a mocking flick of the paddle – a fish-tail flash which broke the surface to spangles – the boat had vanished beneath him.

No, he decided, as he stood there twisting the needle, he would not tell Driver of this. Nor how, from the farther parapet, he had seen the boat emerge and had watched its course down-stream. How blackly visible it had looked against the glittering water, the mast-head garments now in fluttering silhouette . . . How it had dwindled in size until a tree shadow, flung like a shawl across the moonlit river, had absorbed it into darkness.

Crampfurl sighed and, putting the needle back with the others, he gently closed the drawer. No, he wouldn't tell Driver of this. Leastways, not to-night, he wouldn't . . .

THE BORROWERS ALOFT

This story is dedicated with love to
Tom Brunsdon and Frances Rush
and to all the children in the world who have promised
their parents never to play with gas, and who keep their
promises

Chapter One

Some people thought it strange that there should be two model villages, one so close to the other (there was a third as a matter of fact belonging to a little girl called Agnes Mercy Foster, which nobody visited, and which we need not bother about because it was not built to last).

One model village was at Fordham, called Little Fordham: it belonged to Mr Pott. Another was at Wentle-Craye, called Ballyhoggin, and belonged to Mr Platter.

It was Mr Pott who started it all, quietly and happily for his own amusement; and it was the business-like Mr Platter, for quite another reason, who copied Mr Pott.

Mr Pott was a railway-man who had lost his leg on the railway: he lost it at dusk one evening on a lonely stretch of line – not through carelessness, but when saving the life of a badger. Mr Pott had always been anxious about these creatures: the single track ran through a wood, and in the half light the badgers would trundle out, sniffing their way across the sleepers. Only at certain times of the year were they in any real danger, and that was when the early dusk (the time they liked to sally forth) coincided with the passing of the last train from Hatter's Cross. After the train passed the night would be quiet again; and foxes, hares and rabbits could cross the line with safety; and nightingales would sing in the wood.

In those early days of the railway, Mr Pott's small, lonely signal-box was almost a home from home. He had there his kettle, his oil-lamps, his plush-covered table and his broken-springed railway armchair. To while away the long hours between trains, he had his fret-saw, his stamp collection and a well-thumbed copy of the Bible which sometimes he would read aloud. Mr Pott was a good man, very kind and gentle. He loved his fellow creatures almost as much as he loved his trains. With the fret-saw he would make collecting-boxes for the Railway Benevolent Fund; these were shaped like little houses and he made them from old cigar-boxes, and no two of his houses were alike. On the first Sunday of every month Mr Pott, on his bicycle, would make a tour of the village, armed with a screwdriver and a small black bag. At each home or hostelry he would unscrew the roof of a little house and count out the contents into his bag. Sometimes he was cheated (but not often) and would mutter sadly as he rode away: 'Fox been at the eggs again.'

Occasionally, in his signal-box, Mr Pott would paint a picture, very small and detailed. He had painted two of the church, three of the vicarage, two of the post office, three of the forge and one of his own signal-box. These pictures he would give away as prizes to those who collected most for his fund.

On the night of which we speak the badger bit Mr Pott – that was the trouble. It made him lose his balance, and in that moment's delay the train wheels caught his foot. Mr Pott never saw the marks of the badger's teeth because the leg it bit was the leg they cut off. The badger itself escaped unharmed.

The Railway Benevolent were very generous. They gave Mr Pott a small lump sum and found him a cottage just outside the village, where three tall poplar-trees stood beside a stream. It was here, on a mound in his garden, that he started to build his railway.

First he bought at second hand a set of model trains. He saw them advertised in a local paper with the electric battery on which to run them. Because there was no room large enough in his tiny cottage he set up the lines in his

garden. With the help of the blacksmith he made the rails but he needed no help with the sleepers: these he cut to scale and set them firmly, as of old he had set the big ones. Once these were set he tarred them over, and when the sun was hot they smelled just right. Mr Pott would sit on the hard ground, his wooden leg stretched out before him, and close his eyes and sniff the railway smell. Lovely it was, and magic – but something was missing. Smoke, that's what it was! Yes, he badly needed some smoke – not only the tang of it, but the sight of it as well. Later, with the help of Miss Menzies of High Beech, he found a solution.

When he made his signal-box, he built it of solid brick. It was exactly like his old one, wooden stairs and all. He glazed the windows with real glass and made them to open and shut (it wasn't for nothing, he realized then, that he had kept the hinges of all the cigar-boxes passed on to him by his directors). The bricks he made from the red brick of his tumbledown pigsty; he pounded these down to a fine dust and mixed them loosely with cement. He set the mixture in a criss-cross mould which he stood on a large tin tea-tray. The mould was made of old steel corset-bones – a grill of tiny rectangles soldered by the blacksmith. With his contraption, Mr Pott could make five hundred bricks at a time. Sometimes to vary the colour he stirred in powdered ochre or a drop of cochineal. He slated the roof of his signal-box with thin flakes of actual slate, neatly trimmed to scale – these too from his ruined pigsty.

Before he put the roof on he took a lump of builder's putty. Rolling and rubbing it between his stiff old hands he made four small sausages for arms and legs and a thicker, shorter one for the body. Rolling and squeezing, he made an egg for the head and smoothed it squarely on to the shoulders. Then he pinched it here and there and carved bits out, scraping away with a horny thumb-nail.

But it wasn't very good, even as an effigy – let alone as a self-portrait. To make it more like himself he took off the leg at the knee and stuck in a match-stick. Then when the putty was hardened he painted the figure over with a decent suit of railway blue, pinked up the face, gummed on a thatch of greying hair made from that creeper called old-man's-beard, and set it up in his signal-box. There it looked much more human – and really rather frightening, standing so still and stiff and staring through the windows.

The signal-box seemed real enough though – with its outside stairway of seasoned wood, yellow lichen on the

slates, weathered bricks with their softly blended colours, windows ajar and, every now and again, the living clack of its signals.

The children of the village became rather a nuisance. They would knock on his front door and ask to see the railway. Mr Pott, once settled comfortably on the hard ground, his wooden leg stuck out before him, found it hard to rise quickly. But, being very patient, he would heave himself up and stump along to let in his callers. He would greet them civilly and conduct them down the passage, through the scullery and out into the garden. There precious building time was lost in questions, answers and general exclamation. Sometimes while they talked his cement would dry, or his soldering-iron grow cold. After a time he made the rule that they could only come at week-ends, and on Saturdays and Sundays he would leave his door ajar. On the scullery table he set a small collecting-box and the grown-ups, who now came too, were asked to pay one penny: the proceeds he sent to his Fund. The children still came free.

After he made his station, more and more people were interested and the proceeds began to mount up. The station was an exact copy of Fordham's own station, and he called it Little Fordham. The letters were picked out in white stone on a bank of growing moss. He furnished the inside before he put the roof on. In the waiting-rooms, hard dark benches, and in the station-master's office, pigeon-holes for tickets and a high wooden desk. The blacksmith (a young man called Henry who by now was deeply interested) welded him a fireplace of dark wrought iron. They burned dead moss and pine-needles to test the draught and they saw that the chimney drew.

But once the roof was on all these details were lost. There was no way to see inside except by lying down and peering through the windows, and when the platform was completed you couldn't do even this. The platform roof was edged by Mr Pott with a wooden fringe of delicate fretwork. There were cattle-pens, milk-churns; and old-fashioned station lamps in which Mr Pott could burn oil.

With Mr Pott's meticulous attention to detail and refusal to compromise with second best, the building of the station took two years and seven months. And then he started on his village.

Chapter Two

Mr Pott had never heard of Mr Platter, nor Mr Platter of Mr Pott.

Mr Platter was a builder and undertaker at Went-le-Craye, the other side of the river, of which Mr Pott's stream was a tributary. They lived quite close, as the crow flies, but far apart by road. Mr Platter had a fine, new red brick house on the main road to Bedford, with a gravel drive, and a garden which sloped to the water. He had built it himself and called it Ballyhoggin. Mr Platter had amassed a good deal of money. But people weren't dying as they used to; and when the brick factory closed down

there were fewer new inhabitants. This was because Mr Platter, building gimcrack villas for the workers, had spoiled the look of the countryside.

Some of Mr Platter's villas were left on his hands, and he would advertise them in country papers as 'suitable for elderly retired couples'. He was annoyed if, in desperation, he had to let to a bride and bridegroom : because Mr Platter was very good at arranging expensive funerals and he liked to stock-up on an older type of client. He had a tight kind of face and a pair of rimless glasses which caught the light so that you could not see his eyes. He had, however, a very polite and gentle manner; so you took the eyes on trust. 'Dear Mr Platter', the mourners said, was always 'so very kind,' and they seldom questioned his bill.

Mr Platter was small and thin but Mrs Platter was large. Both had rather mauvish faces : Mr Platter's had a violet tinge while Mrs Platter's inclined more to pink. Mrs Platter was an excellent wife and both of them worked very hard.

As villas fell vacant and funerals became scarcer, Mr Platter had time on his hands. He had never liked spare time. In order to get rid of it he took up gardening. All Mr Platter's flowers were kept like captives – firmly tied to stakes : the slightest sway or wiggle was swiftly punished – a lop here or a cut there. Very soon the plants gave in – uncomplaining as guardsmen they would stand to attention in rows. His lawns too were a sight to behold as, weed-repelled and mown in stripes, they sloped down to the river. A glimpse of Mr Platter with his weeding-tools was enough to make the slyest dandelion seed smartly change course in mid air, and it was said of a daisy plant that, realizing suddenly where it was, the pink-fringed petals turned white overnight.

Mrs Platter, for her part – and with an eye to the main road and its traffic – put up a notice which said TEAS, and she set up a stall on the grass verge for the sale of flowers and fruit. They did not do very well, however, until Mrs Platter had an inspiration and changed the wording of the notice to RIVERSIDE TEAS. Then people did stop. And once conducted to the tables behind the house they would have the 'set tea' because there was no other. This was expensive, although there was margarine instead of butter and falsely pink, oozy jam bought by Mrs Platter straight from the factory in large tin containers. She also sold soft drinks in glass bottles with marble stoppers, toy balloons and paper windmills. People kept coming and the Platters began to do well; the cyclists were glad to sit down for a while, and the motorists to take off their dust-coats and goggles and stretch their legs.

The falling-off was gradual. At first they hardly noticed it. 'Quiet Whitsun,' Mr Platter would say as they changed the position of the tables so as not to damage the lawn. He thought again about an ice-cream machine, but decided to wait: Mr Platter was a great believer in what he described as 'laying out money', but only where he saw a safe return.

Instead of this he mended up his old flat-bottomed boat and, with the aid of a shrimping net, he cleared the stream of scum. 'Boating' he wanted to add to the tea-notice; but Mrs Platter dissuaded him. There might be complaints, she thought, as with the best will in the world and a bit of pulling and pushing, you could get the boat round the nettle-infested island but that would be about all.

August Bank Holiday was a fiasco: only ten set teas sold on what Mrs Platter called 'The Saturday'; eleven on the Sunday and seven on the Monday. 'I can't make it out,' Mrs Platter kept saying, as she and Agnes Mercy threw the stale loaves into buckets for the chickens. 'Last year they were standing for tables . . .'

Agnes Mercy was fifteen now. She had grown into a large, slow, watchful girl, who seemed older than her age. This was her first job – called 'helping Mrs Platter with the teas.'

'Mrs Read's doing teas now too,' said Agnes Mercy one day, when they were cutting bread and butter.

'Mrs Read of Fordham? Mrs Read of the Crown and Anchor?' Mrs Platter seldom went to Fordham – it was what she called 'out of her way.'

'That's right,' said Agnes Mercy.

'Teas in the garden?'

Agnes Mercy nodded. 'And in the orchard. Next year they're converting the barn.'

'But what does she give them? I mean, she hasn't got a river. Does she give them strawberries?'

Agnes Mercy shook her head. 'No,' she said, 'it's because of the model railway . . .' and in her slow way, under a fire of questions, she told Mrs Platter about Mr Pott.

'A model railway . . .' remarked Mrs Platter thoughtfully, after a short reflective silence. 'Well, two can play at that game!'

Mr Platter whipped up a model railway in no time at all. There was not a moment to lose: and he laid out money in a big way. Mr Pott was a slow worker but he was several years ahead. All Mr Platter's builders were called in. A bridge was built to the island; the island was cleared of weeds; paths and turf were laid down; electric batteries installed. Mr Platter went up to London and bought two sets of the most expensive trains on the market, goods and passengers. He bought two railway stations, both exactly alike, but far more modern than the railway station at Little Fordham. Experts came down from London to install his signal-boxes and to adjust his lines and points. It was all done in less than three months.

And it worked. By the very next summer to RIVERSIDE TEAS they added the words MODEL RAILWAY.

And the people poured in.

Mr Platter had to clear a field and face it with rubble for parking the motor-cars. In addition to the set teas, it cost a shilling to cross the bridge and visit the railway. Half way through the summer the paths on the island became worn down and he refaced them with asphalt, and built a second bridge to keep people moving. And he put the price up to one and sixpence.

There was soon an asphalted car park and a special field for wagonettes, and a stone trough with running water for horses. Parties would often picnic in this field, leaving it strewn with litter.

But none of this bothered Mr Pott. He was not particularly anxious for visitors: they took up his time and disturbed his work. If he encouraged sightseers at all it was just out of loyalty to his beloved Railway Benevolent.

He took no precautions for their comfort. It was Mrs Read of the Crown and Anchor saw to that side of things, and who benefited accordingly. The whole of Mr Pott's railway could be seen from the backdoor step which led on to his garden and sightseers had to pass through his house – they were welcome, of course, as they went through the kitchen, to a glass of cool water from the tap.

When Mr Pott built his church it was an exact copy of the Norman church at Fordham, with added steeple, gravestones and all. He collected stone for over a year before he started to build. The stone-breakers helped

him, as they chipped beside the highway. So did Mr Flood, the mason. By now Mr Pott had several helpers in the village: besides Henry, the blacksmith, he had Miss Menzies of High Beech. Miss Menzies was very useful to Mr Pott, she designed Christmas cards for a living, wrote children's books and her hobbies were wood-carving, hand-weaving and barbola waxwork. She also believed in fairies.

When Mr Platter heard of the church – it took some time, because until it was finished, during visiting hours, Mr Pott swathed it in sacking – Mr Platter put up a larger one with a much higher steeple, based on Salisbury Cathedral. At a touch the windows lit up, and with the aid of a phonograph he laid on music inside. Takings had once more fallen off at Ballyhoggin, now they leapt up again.

All the same, Mr Pott was a great worry to Mr Platter – you never quite knew what he might be up to, in his gentle plodding way. When Mr Pott built two cob cottages and thatched them, Mr Platter's takings fell off for weeks. Mr Platter was forced to screen off part of his island and build, at lightning speed, a row of semi-detached villas and a public house. The same thing happened when Mr Pott built his village shop and filled the window with miniature merchandise in painted barbola work – a gift from Miss Menzies of High Beech. Immediately, of course, Mr Platter built a row of shops and a hairdresser's establishment with a striped pole.

After a while, Mr Platter found a way of spying on Mr Pott.

Chapter Three

He mended up the flat-bottomed boat, which, for lack of use, had again become waterlogged.

Between the two villages, the weed-clogged river and its twisting, deep-cleft tributaries formed an irritating network, only to be circumvented by roads to distant bridges or by clambering and wading on foot. But if, thought Mr Platter, you could force a boat through the rushes you had a short cut and could spy on Mr Pott's house through the willows by his stream.

And this he did – after business hours on summer evenings. He did not like these expeditions but felt them to be his duty. Plagued by gnats, stung by horse-flies, scratched by brambles, when he arrived back to report to Mrs Platter he was always in a very bad temper. Sometimes he got stuck in the mud and sometimes, when the river was low, he had to clamber out into slime and frog-spawn to lift the boat over hidden obstructions such as drowned logs or barbed wire. But he found a place, a little past the poplars, where, standing on the stump of a willow, he could see the whole layout of Mr Pott's model village, and be screened himself by the flicker of silvery leaves.

'You shouldn't do it, love,' Mrs Platter would say

when, panting, puce and perspiring, he sank on a bench in the garden. 'Not at your age and with your blood pressure.' But she had to agree, as she dabbed his gnat bites with ammonia or his wasp stings with dolly-blue, that taking it by and large his information was priceless. It was only due to Mr Platter's courage and endurance that they found out about the model station-master and about Mr Pott's two porters and the vicar in his cassock who stood at Mr Pott's church door. Each of these tiny figures had been modelled by Miss Menzies and dressed by her in suitable clothes which she oiled to withstand the rain.

This discovery had shaken Mr Platter. It was just before the opening of the season. 'Lifelike . . .' he kept saying, 'that's how you'd describe 'em. Madame Tussaud's isn't in it. Why any one of 'em might *speak* to you, if you see what I mean. It's enough to ruin you,' he concluded, 'and would have if I hadn't seen 'em in time.'

However, he *had* seen them in time; and soon both the model villages were inhabited. But Mr Platter's figures seemed far less real than Mr Pott's. They were hurriedly modelled, ready dressed in plaster of Paris and brightly varnished over. To make up for this they were far more varied and there were many more of them – postmen, milkmen, soldiers, sailors and boy scouts. On the steps of his church he put a bishop, surrounded by choir-boys, each of the choir-boys looked like the others, each had a hymn-book and a white plaster cassock; all had wide-open mouths.

'Now they are what I *would* call lifelike . . .' Mrs Platter used to say proudly. And the organ would boom in the church.

Then came the awful evening, long to be remembered,

when Mr Platter, returning from a boat trip, almost
stumbled as he climbed back on to the lawn. Mrs Platter,
at one of the tables, her large white cat on her lap, was
peacefully counting out the takings; the littered garden
was bathed in evening sunlight, and the sleepy birds sang
in the trees.

'Whatever's the matter?' exclaimed Mrs Platter when
she saw Mr Platter's face.

He sank down heavily in the green chair opposite,
shaking the table and dislodging a pile of half-crowns.
The cat, alarmed and filled with foreboding, streaked off
towards the shrubbery. Mr Platter stared dully at the
half-crowns as they rolled away across the greensward
but he did not stoop to pick them up. Neither did Mrs
Platter; she was staring at Mr Platter's complexion: it
looked most peculiar – a kind of greenish heliotrope, very
delicate in shade.

'Whatever's the matter? Go on, tell me! What's he
been and done now?'

Mr Platter looked back at her without any expression.
'We're done for,' he said.

'Nonsense. What he can do, we can do. And it's always

501

been like that. Remember the smoke. Now come on, tell
me!'

'Smoke,' exclaimed Mr Platter bitterly, 'that was
nothing – a bit of charred string! We soon got the hang of
the smoke. No, this is different; this is the end. We're
finished,' he added wearily.

'Why do you say that?'

Mr Platter got up from his chair and mechanically, as if
he did not know what he was doing, he picked up the
fallen half-crowns. He piled them up neatly, and pushed
the pile towards her. 'Got to look after the money now,'
he said in the same dull expressionless voice, and he
slumped again in his chair.

'Now, Sidney,' said Mrs Platter, 'this isn't like you –
you've got to show fight.'

'No good fighting,' said Mr Platter, 'where the odds are
impossible. What he's done now is plain straightforward
impossible.'

His eyes strayed to the island where, touched with
golden light among the long evening shadows, the static
plaster figures glowed dully, frozen in their attitudes –
some seeming to run, some seeming to walk, some about
to knock on doors and others simply sitting. Several
windows of the model village glowed with molten
sunlight as if they were afire. The birds hopped about
amongst the houses, seeking for crumbs dropped by the
visitors. Except for the birds, nothing moved . . . stillness
and deadness.

Mr Platter blinked. 'And I'd set my heart on a cricket
pitch,' he said huskily, 'bowler and batsmen and all.'

'Well, we still *can* have,' said Mrs Platter.

He looked at her pityingly. 'Not if they don't *play*
cricket – don't you understand? I'm *telling* you – what's
he's done now is plain, straightforward impossible.'

'What has he done then?' asked Mrs Platter in a frightened voice, infected at last by the cat's foreboding.

Mr Platter looked back at her with haggard eyes. 'He's got a lot of live ones,' he said slowly.

Chapter Four

But Miss Menzies – who believed in fairies, had seen them first. And in her girlish, excited, breathless way she had run to Mr Pott.

Mr Pott, busy with an inn-sign for his miniature Crown and Anchor, had said, 'Yes' and 'No' and 'Really'. Sometimes hearing her voice rise to fever pitch, he would exclaim 'Get away' or 'You don't mean it'. The former expression had worried Miss Menzies at first. In a puzzled way her voice would falter and her blue eyes fill with tears. But soon she learned to value this request as the ultimate expression of Mr Pott's surprise: when Mr Pott said 'Get away' she took it as a compliment and would hug her knees and laugh.

'But it's *true*!' she would protest, shaking her head. 'They're alive! They're as much alive – as you and I are, and they've moved into Vine Cottage . . . Why, you can see for yourself if you'd only look where they've even worn a path to the door!'

And Mr Pott, pincers in hand and inn-sign dangling, would glance down the slope towards his model of Vine Cottage. He would stare at the model for just long enough to please her and then, wondering what she was

talking about, he would grunt a little and return to his work. 'Well, I never did,' he would say.

Mr Pott, once she 'got started', as he put it, never dreamed of listening to Miss Menzies. Though nodding and smiling, he would make his mind a blank. It was a trick which he had learned with his late wife, who was also known as a 'talker'. And Miss Menzies spoke in such a high, strange, fanciful voice – using the oddest words and most fly-away expressions; sometimes, to his dismay, she would even recite poetry. He did not dislike her, far from it; he liked to have her about, because in her strange, leggy, loping way she always seemed girlishly happy, and her prattle, like canary song, kept him cheerful. And many a debt he owed to those restless fingers – concocting this and fashioning that: not only could they draw, paint, sew, model and wood-carve, but they could slide into places where Mr Pott's own fingers, stiffer and grubbier, got stuck or could not reach. Quick as a flash, she was; gay as a lark and steady as a rock. '. . . none of us perfect,' he'd tell himself, 'you got to have something . . .' and with her it was 'talking'.

He knew she was not young, but when she sat beside him on the rough grass, clasping her thin wrists about her bent knees, swaying back and forth, her closed eyes raised to the sun and chattering nineteen to the dozen, she seemed to Mr Pott like some kind of overgrown school-girl. And sweet eyes she had too, when they were open – that he would say – for such a long, bony face: shy eyes, which slid away when you looked too long at them – more like violets, he'd say her eyes were, than forget-me-nots. They were shining now and so were the knuckles of her long fingers clasped too tightly about her knees; even her mouse-grey silky hair had a sudden lustre.

'The great secret, you see, is never to show that you've seen them. Stillness, stillness, that's the thing – and looking obliquely and never directly. Like with bird-watching . . .'

'. . . bird-watching,' agreed Mr Pott, as Miss Menzies seemed to pause. Sometimes, to show his sympathy and disguise his lack of attention, Mr Pott would repeat the last word of Miss Menzie's last sentence; or sometimes anticipate Miss Menzies's last syllable. If Miss Menzies said: 'King and Coun—', Mr Pott would chip in, in an understanding voice, with '. . . tree'. Sometimes, being far away in mind, Mr Pott would make a mistake and Miss Menzies, referring to 'garden-produce', would find herself presented with ' . . . roller' instead, and there would be bewilderment all round.

'I can't quite really, you know, make out quite *what* they are. I mean, from the size and that, you'd say they were fairies. Now, wouldn't you?' she challenged him.

'That's right,' said Mr Pott, testing the swing of his inn-sign with a stubby finger and wondering where he had left the oil.

'But you'd be wrong, you know. This little man I saw with this sack thing on his back – he was panting. Quite out of breath, he was. Now, fairies don't pant.' As Mr Pott was silent, Miss Menzies added sharply: 'Or do they?'

'Do they what?' asked Mr Pott, watching the swing of his inn-sign and wishing it did not squeak.

'Pant!' said Miss Menzies, and waited.

Mr Pott looked troubled. What could she be talking about? 'Pant?' he repeated. Mentally, he put the word into plural, and with a glance at her face, took it out again. 'I wouldn't like to say,' he conceded cagily.

'Nor would I,' agreed Miss Menzies gaily, much to his relief. 'I mean – by and large – we know so little about fairies . . .'

'That's right,' said Mr Pott. He felt safe again.

'. . . what their habits are. I mean, whether or not they get tired or old like we do and go to bed, cook and do the housework. Or what they do about food. There's so little data. We don't even know what they . . .'

'. . . eat,' said Mr Pott.

'. . . are,' corrected Miss Menzies. 'What they are made of . . . surely not flesh and blood?'

'Surely not,' agreed Mr Pott. Then suddenly looked startled – a strange word echoed in his mind: had she said 'blood'? He laid down the inn-sign and turned to look at her. '*What* was you saying?' he asked.

Miss Menzies was away again. 'I was saying this lot couldn't be fairies – not on second thoughts and sober reflection. Why, this little fellow had a tear in his trousers and there he was – panting and puffing and toiling up the hill. There's another one in skirts – or maybe two in skirts. I can't make out how many there are: whether it's just one that keeps changing, or what it is. There was a little hand cleaning a window – rubbing and rubbing from the inside. But you couldn't see what it belonged to. White as a bluebell stalk, it looked, when you pull it out

of the earth. And about that thickness – waving and swaying. And then I found my glasses and I saw it had an elbow. I could hardly believe my eyes. There it was, a cloth in its hand and going into the corners. And yet, in a way, it seemed natural.'

'In a way,' agreed Mr Pott. But he was looking rather lost.

Chapter Five

Then began for Miss Menzies what afterwards seemed almost the happiest time of her life. She had always been a great watcher: she would watch ants in the grass, mice in the corn, spinnings of webs and buildings of nests. And she could keep very quiet, because, watching a spider plummet from a leaf, she would almost become a spider herself, and having studied the making of web after web she could have spun one herself to almost any shape, however awkward. Miss Menzies, in fact, had become quite critical of web-making.

'Oh, you silly thing . . .' she would breathe to the spider as it swayed in the air, '. . . not that leaf – it's going to fall. Try the thorn . . .'

Now, sitting on the slope, her hands about her knees, she would watch the little people, screened – as she thought – by a tall clump of thistle. And everything she saw she described to Mr Pott.

'There are three of them,' she told him some days later, 'A mother, a father and a thin little girl. Difficult to tell their ages. Sometimes I think there's a fourth . . . something or someone who comes and goes. A shadowy sort of creature. But that, of course' – she sighed happily – 'might just be my . . .'

'. . . fancy,' said Mr Pott.

'. . . imagination,' corrected Miss Menzies. 'It's strange, you know, that *you* haven't seen them !'

Mr Pott, busy brick-building, did not answer. He had decided the subject was human; village gossip of some kind, referring not to his Vine Cottage, but to the original one in Fordham.

'They've done wonders to the house,' Miss Menzies went on. 'The front door was stuck, you know. Warped, I suppose, with the rain. But he was working on it yesterday with a thing like a razor-blade. And there's another thing they've done. They've taken those curtains I made for your Crown and Anchor and put them up in Vine Cottage, so now you can't see inside. Not that I'd dare to look – you couldn't go that close, you see. And the High Street's so narrow. But isn't it exciting?'

Mr Pott grunted. Stirring his brick-dust and size, he frowned to himself and breathed rather heavily. Gossip about neighbours – he had never held with it. Nor, until now, had Miss Menzies. A talker, yes, but a lady born and bred. This wasn't like her, he thought unhappily . . . peeping in windows . . . no, it wasn't like her at all. She was on now about the station-master's coat.

'. . . she took it, you see. That's where it went. She took it for *him*, gold buttons and all, and he wears it in the evening, after sundown when the air gets chilly. I would not be at all surprised if, one day, she snapped up the vicar's cassock. It's so like a dress, you see, and would fit her perfectly. Except, of course, that might seem too obvious. They're very clever, you know. One would be bound to notice a vicar bereft of his cassock – there on the church steps for all to see. But to see the station-master you have to look right into the station. And you can't do that now; he could be without his coat for weeks and none of us any the wiser.'

Mr Pott stopped stirring to glare at Miss Menzies. She looked back in alarm at his round, angry eyes. 'But what is the matter?' she asked him uneasily, after a moment.

Mr Pott drew a deep breath. 'If you don't know,' he said, 'then I won't tell you!'

This did not seem very logical. Miss Menzies smiled

forgivingly and laid a hand on his arm. 'But there's nothing to be frightened of,' she assured him; 'they're quite all right.'

He shook his arm free and went on stirring, breathing hard and clattering with his trowel. 'There's plenty to be frightened of,' he said sternly, 'when there's gossip on the tongue. Homes ruined, I've seen, and hearts broken.'

Miss Menzies was silent a moment. 'I didn't grudge her the coat,' she said at last. Mr Pott snorted and Miss Menzies went on: 'In fact, I intend to make them some clothes myself. I thought I'd just leave the clothes about for them to find, so they'll never know where they came from . . .'

'That's better,' said Mr Pott, scraping at a brick. There was a long pause – so strangely long that Mr Pott became aware of it. Had he been a little too sharp, he wondered, and glanced sideways at Miss Menzies. With clasped knees, she sat smiling into space.

'I love them, you see,' she said softly.

After this Mr Pott let her talk again: if her interest stemmed from affection, that was another matter. Day after day he nodded and smiled, as Miss Menzies unfolded her story. The words spilled over him, soothing and gay, and slid away into the sunlight; very few caught his attention. Even on that momentous afternoon – one day in June – when, bursting with fresh news, she flung herself breathlessly beside him.

He was re-tarring a line of sleepers and, pot in one hand, brush in the other, he edged himself along the ground, his wooden leg stretched out before him. Miss Menzies, talking away, edged along to keep up with him.

'. . . and when she spoke to me,' gasped Miss Menzies, 'I was amazed, astounded! Wouldn't you have been?'

'Maybe,' said Mr Pott.

'This tiny creature – quite unafraid. Said she'd been watching me for weeks.'

'Get away,' said Mr Pott amiably. And he wiped a drop of tar off the rail. 'That's better,' he said, admiring the steely gleam . . . 'Not a trace of rust anywhere,' he thought happily.

'And now I know what they're called and everything. They're called Borrowers . . .'

'Burroughs?' said Mr Pott.

'No, Borrowers.'

'Ah, Burroughs,' said Mr Pott, stirring the tar, which stood in a can of hot water. 'Getting a bit thick,' he thought, as he raised the stick and critically watched the trickle.

'It's not their family name,' Miss Menzies went on; 'their family name is Clock. It's their racial name – the kind of creatures they are. They live like mice . . . or birds . . . on what they can find, poor things. They're an offshoot of humans, I think, and live from human left-overs. They don't own anything at all. And of course they haven't any money . . . Oh, it's perfectly all right,' said Miss Menzies, as in absent-minded sympathy Mr Pott clicked his tongue and gently shook his head. 'They wouldn't care about money. They wouldn't know what to do with it. But they have to live . . .'

'. . . and let live,' said Mr Pott brightly. He felt mildly pleased with this phrase and hoped it would fit in somewhere.

'But they *do* let live,' said Miss Menzies. 'They never take anything that matters. Except of course . . . well, I'm not sure about the station-master's overcoat. But when you come to think of it, the station-master didn't need it for warmth, did he? Being made as he is of barbola? And it wasn't his, either – I made it; come to that, I made *him*, too. So it really belongs to me. And I don't need it for warmth.'

'Not warmth,' agreed Mr Pott absently.

'These Borrowers do need warmth. They need fuel and shelter and water and they terribly need human beings. Not that they trust them. They're right, I suppose: one has only to read the papers. But it's sad, isn't it? That they can't trust us, I mean. What could be more charming for someone – like me, say – to share one's home with these little creatures? Not that I'm lonely, of course. My days' – Miss Menzies's eyes became over-bright suddenly and the gay voice hurried a little – 'are *far* too full ever to be lonely. I've so many interests, you see. I keep up with things. And I have my old dog and the two little birds. All the same, it would be nice. I know their names now – Pod, Homily and Little Arrietty. These creatures talk, you see. And just think I'd' – she laughed suddenly – 'I'd be sewing for them from morning until night. I'd make them things. I'd buy them things. I'd – oh, but you understand . . .'

'I understand,' said Mr Pott. 'I get you . . .' But he didn't understand. In a vague sort of way he felt it rather rude of Miss Menzies to refer to her new-found family of friends as 'creatures'. Down on their luck, they might be, but all the same . . . But then, of course, she did use the strangest expressions.

'And I think that's why she spoke to me,' Miss Menzies went on; 'she must have felt safe, you see. They always . . .'

'. . . know,' put in Mr Pott obligingly.

'Yes. Like animals and children and birds and . . . fairies.'

'I wouldn't commit meself about fairies,' said Mr Pott.

And, come to think of it, he would not commit himself about animals, either: he thought of the badger whose life he had rescued — if *it* had 'known' he would still have had his leg.

'They've had an awful time, poor things, really ghastly . . .' Miss Menzies gazed down the slope at the peaceful scene, the groups of miniature cottages, the smoking chimneys, the Norman church, the forge, the gleaming railway lines. 'It was wonderful, she told me, when they found this village.'

Mr Pott grunted. He shifted himself along a couple of feet and drew the tar-pot after him. Miss Menzies, lost in her dreams, did not seem to notice. Knees clasped, eyes half closed, she went on as though reciting.

'It was moonlight, she told me, the night they arrived. You can imagine it, can't you? The sharp shadows. They had heaps to carry and had to push their way up through those rushy grasses down by the water's edge. Spiller — that was the untamed one — took Arrietty round the village. He took her right inside the station, and there were those figures I made — the woman with the basket, the old man and the little girl — in a row on the seat, so still, so still . . . and just beside them the soldier with his kit-bag. They were speckled by moonlight and the fretted shadow of the station roof. They looked very real, she said, but like people under a spell or listening to music which neither she nor Spiller could hear. Arrietty too stood silent — staring and wondering at the pale moonlit faces. Until suddenly there was a rustling sound and a great black beetle ran right over them and she saw they were not alive. She doesn't mind beetles herself, she rather likes them, but this one made her scream. She said there were toadstools in the ticket office, and when they went out of the station, the field-mice were busy in the

High Street, running in and out of the shadows. And there, on the steps of the church, stood the vicar in his cassock – so silent, so still. And moonlight everywhere . . .'

'Homily, of course, fell in love with Vine Cottage. And you can't blame her – it is rather charming. But the door was stuck, warped, I suppose, by the rain, and when they opened the window it seemed to be full of something and it smelled very damp. Spiller put his hand in and – do you know? – it was filled with white grass stalks, right up to the roof. White as mushrooms, they were, through growing up in the dark. So that night they slept out of doors.

'Next day, though, she said, was lovely – bright sunshine, spring smells and the first bee. They can see things so closely, you see: every hair of the bee, the depth of the velvet, the veins on its wings and the colours vibrating. The men' – Miss Menzies laughed – 'I mean, you must call them men – soon cleared the cottage of weeds, reaping them down with a sliver of razor-blade and a kind of half nail-scissor. Then they dug out the roofs. Spiller found a chrysalis, which he gave to Arrietty. She kept it until last week. It turned out to be a red admiral. She watched it being born. But when its wings appeared and they began to see the size of it, there was absolute panic. Just in the nick of time they got it out of the front door. Its wing span would almost have filled their parlour from wall to wall. Imagine your own parlour full of butterfly and no way to let it out! When you come to think of it, it's quite fantas . . .'

'. . . tick,' added Mr Pott.

'About a week later they found your sandpile; and when they had dug up the floor they sanded it over and trod it down. Dancing and stamping like maniacs. She said it was rather fun. This was all in the very early morning. And about three weeks ago they borrowed your size. It was already mixed – when you were making that last lot of bricks, remember? Anyway, now what with sizing it over and one thing and another, she tells me, their floor has quite a good surface. They sweep it with

thistle-heads. But it's early for these, she said, the blooms are too tightly packed. The ones which come later are far more practical . . .'

But Mr Pott had heard at last. 'My sandpile . . .' he said slowly, turning to stare at her.

'Yes.' Miss Menzies laughed. 'And your size.'

'My size?' repeated Mr Pott. He was silent a moment, as though thinking this out.

'Yes,' laughed Miss Menzies, 'but so little of it – so very, very little.'

'My size . . .' repeated Mr Pott. His face grew stern, almost belligerent he seemed suddenly as he turned to Miss Menzies.

'Where are these people?' he asked.

'But I've told you!' Miss Menzies exclaimed, and as he still looked angry, she took his horny hand in both of hers as though to help him up. 'Come,' she whispered, but she was still smiling, 'come very quietly, and I'll show you!'

Chapter Six

'Stillness . . . that's the thing,' Pod whispered to Arrietty, the first time he saw Miss Menzies crouching down behind her thistle. 'They don't expect to see you, and if you're still they somehow don't. And never look at 'em direct – always look at 'em sideways like. Understand?'

'Yes, of course I understand – you've told me often enough. Stillness, stillness, quiet, quiet, creep, creep, crawl, crawl . . . What's the good of being alive?'

'Hush,' said Pod and laid a hand on her arm. Arrietty had not been herself lately. It was as though, thought Pod, she had something on her mind. But it wasn't often she was as rude as this. He decided to ignore it: getting to the awkward age – that's what it was, he wouldn't wonder.

They stood in a clump of coarse grass, shoulder high to them, with only their heads emerging. 'You see,' breathed Pod, speaking with still lips out of the corner of his mouth, 'some kind of plant or flowers, that's what we look like to her. Something in bud, maybe.'

'Supposing she decided to pick us,' suggested Arrietty irritably. Her ankles were aching and she longed to sit down; ten minutes had become quarter of an hour and still neither party had moved. An ant climbed up the grass stem beside her, waved its antennae in the air and swiftly climbed down again. A slug lay sleeping under the plantain leaf, every now and again there was a slight ripple where the frilled underside of its body appeared to caress the earth.

'It must be dreaming,' Arrietty decided, admiring the silver highlights in the lustrous gun-metal skin. 'If my father were less old-fashioned,' she thought guiltily, 'I would tell him about Miss Menzies, and then we could walk away.' But in his view and in that of her mother it was still a disgrace to be 'seen', not only a disgrace but almost a tragedy; to them it meant broken homes, wearisome treks across unexplored country and the labour of building anew. By her parents' code, to be known to exist at all put their whole way of life into jeopardy, and a borrower once 'seen' must immediately move away.

In spite of all this, in her short life of fifteen years, Arrietty herself had been 'seen' four times. What was this

longing, she wondered, which drew her so strongly to human beings? And on this – her fourth occasion of being 'seen' – actually to speak to Miss Menzies? It was reckless and stupid, no doubt, but also strangely thrilling to address and be answered by a creature of so vast a size, who yet could seem so gentle; to see the giant's eyes light up and the great mouth softly smile. Once you had done it and no dreadful disaster had followed, you were tempted to try it again. Arrietty had even gone so far as to lay in wait for Miss Menzies. Perhaps because every incident she described seemed so to delight and amaze her and – when Spiller was not there – Arrietty was often lonely.

Those first few days had been such wonderful fun! Spiller taking her on the trains – nipping into some half-empty carriage and, when the train moved, sitting so stiff and so still – pretending they too, like the rest of the passengers, were made of barbola wax. Round and round they would go, passing Vine Cottage a dozen times, and back again over the bridge. Other faces besides Mr Pott's stared down at them, and by Mr Pott's backdoor they saw rows of boots and shoes, fat legs, thin legs, stockinged legs and bare legs. They heard human laughter and human squeals of delight. It was terrifying and wonderful, but somehow, with Spiller, she felt safe.

A plume of smoke ran out behind them. The same kind of smoke which was used for the cottage chimneys, parcel string soaked in nitrate and secured in a bundle by a twist of invisible hairpin. ('Have you seen my invisible hairpins?' Miss Menzies had one day asked Mr Potts – a question which to the puzzled Mr Pott seemed an odd contradiction in terms.) In Vine Cottage, however, Pod had hooked down the smouldering bundle and had lit a real fire instead, which Homily fed with candle-grease, coal-slack and tarry lumps of cinder. On this she cooked their meals.

And it was Spiller, wild Spiller, who had helped Arrietty to make her garden and to search for plants of scarlet pimpernel, small blue-faced bird's-eyes, fern-like mosses and tiny flowering sedum. With Spiller's help she had gravelled the path and laid a lawn of moss.

Miss Menzies, behind her thistle clump, had watched this work with delight. She saw Arrietty; but Spiller, that past master of invisibility, she could never quite discern. Both still and swift, with a wild creature's instinct for cover, he could melt into any background, and disappear at will.

With Spiller too Arrietty had explored the other houses, fished for minnows and bathed in the river, screened by the towering rushes. 'Getting too tomboyish by half,' Homily had grumbled. She was nervous of Spiller's influence. 'He's not our kind really,' she would complain to Pod, in a sudden burst of ingratitude, 'even if he did save our lives.'

Standing beside her father in the grass and thinking of these things, Arrietty began to feel the burden of her secret. Had her parents searched the world over, she realized uneasily, they could not have found a more perfect place in which to settle – a complete village tailored to their size and, with so much left behind by the visitors, unusually rich in borrowings. It had been a long time since she had heard her mother sing as she sang now at her housework, or her father take up again his breathy, tuneless whistle as he pottered about the village.

There was plenty of 'cover' but they hardly needed it. There was little difference in size between themselves and the borrowers made of wax and except during visiting hours Pod could walk about the streets quite freely, providing he was ready to freeze. And there was no end to the borrowing of clothes. Homily had a hat again at last and would never leave the house without it. 'Wait,' she would say, 'while I put on my hat,' and took a fussed kind of joy in pronouncing the magic word. No, they could not be moved out now : that would be too cruel. Pod had even put a lock on the front door, complete with key. It was the lock of a pocket jewel-case belonging to Miss Menzies. He little knew to whom he owed this find – that she had dropped the case on purpose beside the clump of thistle to make the borrowing easy. And Arrietty could not tell him. Once he knew the truth (she had been through it all before), there would be worry, despair, recriminations and a pulling up of stakes.

'Oh dear, oh dear,' she breathed aloud unhappily, 'whatever should I do . . .?'

Pod glanced at her sideways. 'Sink down,' he whispered, nudging her arm. 'She's turned her head away. Sink slowly into the grasses . . .'

Arrietty was only too grateful to obey. Slowly their heads and shoulders lowered out of sight and after a moment's pause to wait and listen they crawled away among the grass stems, and taking swift cover by the churchyard wall they slid to safety through their own backdoor.

Chapter Seven

One day Miss Menzies began to talk back to Arrietty. At first her amazement had kept her silent, and confined her share of their conversations to the few leading questions which might draw Arrietty out. This for Miss Menzies was a most unusual state of affairs and could not last for long. As the summer wore on, she had garnered every detail of Arrietty's short life and a good deal of data besides. She had heard about the borrowed library of Victorian miniature books, through which Arrietty had learned to read and to gain some knowledge of the world. Miss Menzies, in her hurried, laughing, breathless way, helped to add to this knowledge. She began to tell Arrietty about her own girlhood, her parents and her family home, which she always described as 'dear Gadstone'. She spoke of London dances and of how she had hated them; of someone called 'Aubrey', her closest and dearest friend – 'my cousin, you see. We were almost brought up together. He would come to dear Gadstone for his holidays.' He and Miss Menzies would ride and talk and read poetry together. Arrietty, listening and learning about horses, wondered if there was any kind of animal which she could learn to ride. You could tame a mouse (as her cousin Eggletina had done), but a mouse was too small and too 'scuttley': you couldn't go far on a mouse. A rat? Oh no, a rat was out of the question. She doubted even if Spiller would be brave enough to train a rat. Fight one, yes – armed with Pod's old climbing-pin – Spiller was cable of that but not, she thought, of breaking a rat into harness. But what fun it would have been to go riding with Spiller, as Miss Menzies had gone riding with Aubrey.

'He married a girl called Mary Chumley-Gore,' said Miss Menzies. 'She had very thick ankles.'

'Oh . . .!' exclaimed Arrietty.

'Why do you say "Oh" in that voice?'

'I thought he might have married you!'

Miss Menzies smiled and looked down at her hands. 'So did I,' she said quietly. She was silent a moment and then she sighed. 'I suppose he knew me too well. I was almost like a sister.' She was quiet again as though thinking this out, and then she added more cheerfully: 'They were happy though, I gather; they had five children and lived in a house outside Bath.'

And Miss Menzies, even before Arrietty explained to her, understood about being 'seen'. 'You need never worry about your parents,' she assured Arrietty. 'I would never – even if you had not spoken – have looked at them directly. As far as we are concerned – and I can speak for Mr Pott – they are safe here for the rest of their lives. I would never even have looked at you directly, Arrietty, if you had not crept up and spoken to me. But even before I saw any of you I had begun to wonder – because, you see, Arrietty, your chimney sometimes smoked at quite the wrong sort of times; I only light the string for the visitors, you see, and it very soon burns out.'

'And you would never pick us up, any of us? In your hands, I mean?'

Miss Menzies gave an almost scornful laugh. 'As though I would dream of such a thing!' She sounded rather hurt.

Miss Menzies also understood about Spiller: that when he came for his brief visits, with his offerings of nuts, corn grains, hard-boiled sparrows' eggs and other delicacies, she would not see so much of Arrietty. But after Spiller had gone again, she liked to hear of their adventures.

All in all, it was a happy, glorious summer for everyone concerned.

There were scares of course. Such as the footsteps before dawn, human footsteps, but not those of the one-legged Mr Pott, when something or someone had fumb-

led at their door. And the moonlight night when the fox came, stalking silently down their village street, casting his great shadow and leaving his scent behind. The owl in the oak-tree was of course a constant source of danger. But, like most owls, he did his hunting farther afield, and once the vast shape had wafted over the river and they had heard his call on the other side of the valley, it was safe to sally forth.

Much of the borrowing was done at nights before the mice got at the scraps dropped by the visitors. Homily at first had sniffed fastidiously when presented with, say, the remains of a large ham sandwich. Pod had to persuade her to look at the thing more practically – fresh bread, pure farm butter and a clean paper bag; what had been good enough for human beings should be good enough for them. What was wrong, he asked her, with the last three grapes of a stripped bunch? You could wash them, couldn't you, in the stream? You could peel them? Or what was wrong with a caramel, wrapped up in transparent paper? Half-eaten bath-buns, he agreed, were a bit more difficult . . . but you could extract the currants, couldn't you, and collect and boil down those crusted globules of sugar?

Soon they had evolved a routine of collecting, sorting, cleaning and conserving. They used Miss Menzies's shop as a storehouse, with – unknown to Pod and Homily – her full co-operation. She had cheated a little on the furnishings, having (some years ago now) gone into the local town and bought a toy grocer's shop, complete with scales, bottles, cans, barrels and glass containers. With these, she had skilfully furnished the counter and dressed

up the windows. This little shop was a great attraction to visitors – it was a general shop and post office modelled on the one in the village – bow windows, thatched roof and all. A replica of old Mrs Purbody (slimmed down a little to flatter her) stood behind the counter inside. Miss Menzies had even reproduced the red knitted shawl which Mrs Purbody wore on her shoulders, both in summer and winter, and the crisp white apron below. Homily would borrow this apron when she worked on her sortings in the back of the shop, but would put it back punctually in time for visitors. Sometimes she washed it out, and every morning – regular as clockwork – she would dust and sweep the shop.

The trains made a good deal of noise. They very soon got used to this, however, and learned, in fact, to welcome it.

When the trains began to clatter and the smoke unfurled from the cottage chimneys, it warned them of Visiting Hours. Homily had time to take off the apron, let herself out of the shop and cross the road to her home, where she engaged herself in pleasant homely tasks until the trains stopped and all was quiet again and the garden lay dreaming and silent in the peaceful evening light.

Mr Pott, by this time, would have gone inside for his tea.

Chapter Eight

'There must be something we can do,' said Mrs Platter despairingly for about the fifth time within an hour. 'Look at the money we've sunk.'

'Sunk is the right word,' said Mr Platter.

'And it isn't as though we haven't tried.'

'Oh, we've tried hard enough,' said Mr Platter. 'And what annoys me about this Abel Pott is that he does it all without seeming to try at all. He doesn't seem to mind if people come or not. MODEL VILLAGE WITH LIVE INHABITANTS — that's what he'll put on the notice — and then we'll be finished. Finished for good and all! Better pack it in now, that's what I say, and sell out as a going concern.'

'There must be something . . .' repeated Mrs Platter stubbornly.

They sat as before at a green table on their singularly tidy lawn. On this Sunday evening it was even more singularly tidy than usual. Only five people had come that afternoon for RIVERSIDE TEAS. There had been three quite disastrous week-ends: on two of them it had rained, and on this particular Sunday there had been what local people spoke of as 'the aeronaut' – a balloon ascent from the fairground, with tea in tents, ice-cream, candy-floss and roundabouts. On Saturday people drove out to see the balloon itself (at sixpence a time to pass the rope barriers) and today in their hundreds to see the balloon go up. It had been a sad sight indeed for Mr and Mrs Platter to watch the carriages and motors stream past Ballyhoggin with never a glance nor a thought for RIVERSIDE TEAS. It had not comforted them either,

when at about three o'clock in the afternoon the balloon itself sailed silently over them, barely clearing the ilex tree which grew beside the house. They could even see 'the aeronaut', who was looking down – mockingly, it seemed – straight into the glaring eyes of Mr Platter.

'No good saying "there must be something",' he told her irritably. 'Night and day I've thought and thought and you've thought too. What with this balloon mania and Abel Pott's latest, we can't compete. That's all: it's quite simple. There isn't anything – short of stealing them.'

'What about that?' said Mrs Platter.

'About what?'

'Stealing them,' said Mrs Platter.

Mr Platter stared back at her. He opened his mouth and shut it again. 'Oh, we couldn't do that,' he managed to say at last.

'Why not?' said Mrs Platter. 'He hasn't shown them yet. Nobody knows they're there.'

'Why, it would be – I mean, it's a felony.'

'Never mind,' said Mrs Platter, 'let's commit one.'

'Oh, Mabel,' gasped Mr Platter, 'what things you do say!' But he looked slightly awestruck and admiring.

'Other people commit them,' said Mrs Platter firmly, basking in the glow of his sudden approbation. 'Why shouldn't we?'

'Yes, I see your argument,' said Mr Platter. He still looked rather dazed.

'There's got to be a first time for everything,' Mrs Platter pointed out.

'But' – he swallowed nervously – 'you go to prison for a felony. I don't mind a few extra items on a bill, I'm game for that, dear. Always was, as you well know. But this – oh, Mabel, it takes *you* to think of a thing like this!'

'Well, I said there'd be something,' acknowledged Mrs Platter modestly. 'But it's only common sense, dear. We can't afford not to.'

'You're right,' said Mr Platter; 'we're driven to it. Not a soul could blame us.'

'Not a living soul!' agreed Mrs Platter solemnly in a bravely fervent voice.

Mr Platter leaned across the table and patted her hand. 'I take my hat off to you, Mabel, for courage and initiative. You're a wonderful woman,' he said.

'Thank you, dear,' said Mrs Platter.

'And now for ways and means . . .' said Mr Platter in a suddenly business-like voice. He took off his rimless glasses and thoughtfully began polishing them. 'Tools, transport, times of day . . .'

'It's simple,' said Mrs Platter. 'You take the boat.'

'I realize that,' said Mr Platter with a kind of aloof patience. He put his rimless glasses back on his nose, returned the handkerchief to his pocket, leaned back in his chair and with the fingers of his right hand drummed lightly on the table. 'Allow me to think a while . . .'

'Of course, Sidney,' said Mrs Platter obediently, and folded her hands in her lap.

After a few moments he cleared his throat and looked across at her. 'You'll have to come with me, dear,' he said.

Mrs Platter, startled, lost all her composure. 'Oh, I couldn't do that, Sidney. You know what I'm like on the water. Couldn't you take one of the men?'

He shook his head. 'Impossible, they'd talk.'

'What about Agnes Mercy?'

'Couldn't trust her, either; it would be all over the county before the week was out. No dear, it's got to be you.'

'I *would* come with you, Sidney,' faltered Mrs Platter, 'say we went round by road. That boat's kind of small for me.'

'You can't get into his garden from the road, except by going through the house. There's a thick holly hedge on either side with no sort of gate or opening. No, dear, I've got it all worked out in my mind: the only approach is by water. Just before dawn, I'd say, when they're all asleep, and that would include Abel Pott. We shall need a good strong cardboard box, the shrimping-net and a lantern. Have we any new wicks?'

'Yes, plenty up in the attic.'

'That's where we'll have to keep them – these . . . er . . . well, whatever they are.'

'In the attic?'

'Yes, I've thought it all out, Mabel. It's the only room we always keep locked – because of the stores and that. We've got to keep them warm and dry through the winter while we get their house built. They *are* part of the stores in a manner of speaking. I'll put a couple of bolts on the door, as well as the lock, and a steel plate across the bottom. That should settle 'em. I've got to have time, you see,' Mr Platter went on earnestly, 'to think out some kind of house for them. It's got to be more like a cage than a house and yet it's got to *look* like a house, if you see what I mean. You've got to be able to see them inside and yet make it so they can't get out. It's going to take a lot of working on, Mabel.'

'You'll manage, dear,' Mrs Platter encouraged him. 'But' – she thought a moment – 'what if *he* comes here and recognizes them? Anybody can buy a ticket.'

'He wouldn't. He's so taken up with his own things that I doubt if he's ever heard of us or of Ballyhoggin or even Went-le-Craye. But say he did? What proof has he? He's been keeping them dark, hasn't he? Nobody's seen them – or the news would be all over the county. In the papers most likely. People would be going there in hundreds. No, dear, it would be his word against ours – that's all. But we've got to act quickly, Mabel, and you've got to help me. There are two weeks left to the end of the season; he may be keeping them to show next year. Or he may decide to show them at once – and then we'd be finished. You see what I mean? There's no knowing . . .'

'Yes . . .' said Mrs Platter. 'Well, what do you want me to do?'

'It's easy: you've only got to keep your head. I take the cardboard box and the lantern and you carry the shrimping-net. You follow me ashore and you tread where I tread, which you'll see by the lantern. I'll show you their house, and all you've got to do is to cover the rear side with the shrimping-net, holding it close as you can against the wall and partly over the thatch. Then I make some sort of noise at the front – they keep the front door locked now, I've found out that much. As soon as they hear me at the front door – you can mark my words – they'll go scampering, out of the back. Straight into the net. You see what I mean? Now you'll have to keep the net held tight up against the cottage wall. I'll have the cardboard box in one hand by then, and the lid in the other. When I give the word, you scoop the net up into the air, with them inside it, and tumble them into the box. I clap the lid on and that will be that.'

'Yes,' said Mrs Platter uncertainly. She thought a while and then she said: 'Do they bite?'

'I don't know that. Only seen them from a distance. But it wouldn't be much of a bite.'

'Supposing one fell out of the net or something?'

'Well, you must see they don't, Mabel, that's all. I mean, there are only three or four of 'em, all told. We can't afford any losses . . .'

'Oh, Sidney, I wish you could take one of the men. I can't even row.'

'You don't have to row. I'll row. All you have to do, Mabel, is to carry the net and follow me ashore. I'll point out their cottage and it'll be over in a minute. Before you can say Jack Robinson, we'll be back in the boat and safely home.'

'Does he keep a dog?'

'Abel Pott? No, dear, he doesn't keep a dog. It will be quite all right. Just trust me and do what I say. Like to come across to the island now and have a bit of practice on one of our own houses? You run up to the attic now and get the net and I'll get the oars and the boat-hook. Now, you've got to face up to it, Mabel,' added Mr Platter irritably, as Mrs Platter still seemed to hesitate; 'we must each do our part. Fair's fair, you know.'

Chapter Nine

The next day it began to rain and it rained on and off for ten days. Even Mr Pott had a falling-off of visitors. Not that he minded particularly; he and Miss Menzies employed themselves indoors at Mr Pott's long kitchen table – repairing, remodelling, repainting, restitching and oiling . . . The lamplight shed its gentle glow around them. While the rain poured down outside, the glue-pot bubbled on the stove and the kettle sang beside it. At last came October the first, the day when the season ended.

'Mr Pott,' said Miss Menzies, after a short but breathy silence (she was quilting an eiderdown for Homily's double bed and found the work exacting), 'I am rather worried.'

'Oh,' said Mr Pott. He was making a fence of matchsticks, glueing them delicately with the aid of pincers and a fine sable brush. 'In fact', Miss Menzies went on, 'I'm very worried indeed. Could you listen a moment?'

This direct assault took Mr Pott by surprise. 'Something wrong?' he asked.

'Yes, I think something is wrong. I haven't seen Arrietty for three days. Have you?'

'Come to think of it, no,' said Mr Pott.

'Or any of them?'

Mr Pott was silent a moment, thinking back. 'Not now you mention it – no,' he said.

'I had an appointment with her on Monday, down by the stream, but she didn't turn up. But I wasn't worried, it was raining anyway and I thought perhaps Spiller had arrived. But he hadn't, you know. I know now where he keeps his boat and it wasn't there. And then, when I passed their cottage, I saw the backdoor was open. This isn't like them, but it reassured me as I assumed they wouldn't be so careless unless they were all inside. When I passed again on my way home for tea, the door was still open. All yesterday it was open, and it was open again this morning. It's a bit . . .'

'. . . rum,' agreed Mr Pott.

'. . . odd,' said Miss Menzies – they spoke on the same instant.

'Mr Pott, dear,' went on Miss Menzies, 'after I showed them to you, so very carefully, you remember – you didn't go and stare at them or anything? You didn't frighten them?'

'No,' said Mr Pott, 'I been too busy closing up for winter. I like to see 'em, mind, but I haven't had the time.'

'And their chimney isn't smoking,' Miss Menzies went on. 'It hasn't been smoking for three days. I mean, one can't help being . . .'

'. . . worried,' said Mr Pott.

'. . . uneasy,' said Miss Menzies. She laid down her work. 'Are you still listening?' she asked.

Mr Pott tipped a matchstick with glue, breathing heavily. 'Yes, I'm thinking . . .' he said.

'I don't like to look right inside,' Miss Menzies explained. 'For one thing, you can't look in from the front because there's not room to kneel in the High Street, and you can't kneel down at the back without spoiling their garden, and the other thing is that, say they *are* inside – Pod and Homily, I mean – I'd be giving the whole game away. I've explained to you what they're like about being "seen"? If they hadn't gone already, they'd go then because I'd "seen" them. And we would be out of the frying-pan into the fire . . .'

Mr Pott nodded; he was rather new to borrowers and depended on Miss Menzies for his data – she had, he felt – through months of study, somehow got the whole thing taped. 'Have you counted the people?' he suggested at last.

'Our people? Yes, I thought of that – and I've been through every one twice. A hundred and seven, and those two being mended. That's right, isn't it? And I've examined them all very carefully one by one and been through every railway carriage and everything. No, they're either in their house or they've gone right away. You're sure you didn't frighten them? Even by accident?'

'I've told you,' said Mr Pott. Very deliberately, he gave her a look, laid down his tools and went to the drawer in the table.

'What are you going to do?' asked Miss Menzies, aware that he had a plan.

'Find my screwdriver,' said Mr Pott. 'The roof of Vine Cottage comes off in a piece. It was so we could make the two floors – remember?'

'But you can't do that – supposing they *are* inside. It would be fatal!'

'We've got to take the risk,' said Mr Pott. 'Just get your coat on now and find the umbrella.'

Miss Menzies did as she was told; relieved, she felt suddenly, to surrender the leadership. Her father, she thought, would have acted just like this. And so, of course, would have Aubrey.

Obediently she followed him into the rain and held the umbrella while he went to work. Mr Pott took up a careful position within the High Street and Miss Menzies (feet awkwardly placed to avoid damage) teetered slightly above Church Lane and the back garden. Stooping anxiously they towered above the house.

Several deft turns of the screwdriver and a good deal of grunting soon loosened the soaking thatch. Lid-like, it came off in a piece. 'Bone dry inside,' remarked Mr Pott as he laid it aside.

They saw Pod and Homily's bedroom – a little bare it looked, in spite of the three pieces of doll's-house furniture which once Miss Menzies had bought and left about to be borrowed. The bed, with its handkerchief sheets, looked tousled as though they had left it hurriedly. Pod's working-coat, carefully folded, lay on a chair and his best suit hung on a safety-pin coat-hanger suspended against the wall; while Homily's day clothes were neatly ranged on two rails at the foot of the bed.

There was a feeling of deadness and desertion – no sound but the thrum of the rain as it pattered on the soaked umbrella.

Miss Menzies looked aghast. 'But this is dreadful – they've gone in their night clothes! What could have happened? It's like the *Marie Celeste*—'

'Nothing's been inside,' said Mr Pott, staring down, screwdriver in hand, 'no animal marks, no signs of what you'd call a scuffle . . . Well, we better see what's below. As far as I remember this floor comes out all in a piece with the stairs. Better get a box for the furniture.'

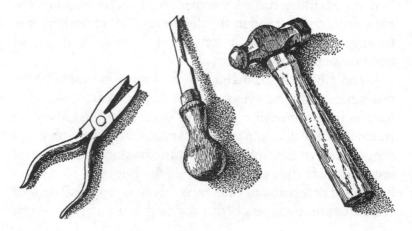

'The furniture!' thought Miss Menzies as she squelched back to the house, picking her way with great Gulliver-like strides over walls and railway lines, streets and alleyways. Just beside the churchyard her foot slipped on the mud, and to save herself she caught hold of the steeple; beautifully built, it held firm, but a bell rang faintly inside: a small, sad, ghostly protest. No; 'the furniture', she realized, was too grand an expression for the contents of that little room. If she had known she would have bought them more things, or left more about for them to borrow. She knew how clever they were at contriving but it takes time, she realized, to furnish a whole house from left-overs. She found a box at last and picked her way back to Mr Pott.

He had lifted out the bedroom floor with the ladder stairway attached and was gazing into the parlour. Neat but bare, Miss Menzies saw again: the usual match-box chest of drawers, a wood-block for a table, bottle-lid cooking-pots beside the hearth and Arrietty's truckle-bed pushed away in a corner; it was the deeper half of a velvet-lined case which must once have contained a large cigar-holder. She wondered where they had found it – perhaps Spiller had brought it to them? Here too the bedclothes had been thrown back hurriedly and Arrietty's day clothes lay neatly folded on a pill-box at the foot.

'I can't bear it,' said Miss Menzies in a stifled voice, feeling for her handkerchief. 'It's all right,' she went on hurriedly, wiping her eyes, 'I'm not going to break down. But what can we do? It's no good going to the police – they would only laugh at us in a polite kind of way and secretly think we were crazy. I know because of what happened when I saw that fairy. People would be polite to one's face, but . . .'

'I wouldn't know about fairies,' said Mr Pott, staring disconsolately into the gutted house, 'but *these* I seen with my own two eyes.'

'I am so glad and thankful that you did see them!' exclaimed Miss Menzies warmly, 'or where should I be now?' For once, it was almost a conversation.

'Well, we'll pack up these things,' said Mr Pott, suiting the action to the word, 'and set the roof back. Got to keep the place dry.'

'Yes,' said Miss Menzies, 'at least we can do that. Just in case . . .' her voice faltered and her fingers trembled a little, as carefully she took up the wardrobe. It had no hooks inside, she noticed – toymakers never quite completed things – so she laid it flat and packed it like a box with the little piles of clothes. The cheap piece of looking-glass flashed suddenly in a watery beam of sunlight and she saw the rain had stopped.

'Are we doing right?' she asked suddenly. 'I mean, shouldn't we leave it all as we found it? Supposing quite unexpectedly they did come back?'

Mr Pott looked thoughtful. 'Well,' he said, 'seeing as we got the place all opened up like, I thought maybe I'd make a few alterations.'

Miss Menzies, struggling with the rusty catch of Mr Pott's umbrella, paused to stare at him. 'You mean – make the whole place more comfortable?'

'That's what I do mean,' said Mr Pott. 'Do the whole thing over like – give them a proper cooking-stove, running water and all.'

'Running water! Could you do that?'

'Easy,' said Mr Pott.

The umbrella shut with a snap, showering them with drops, but Miss Menzies seemed not to notice. 'And I could furnish it,' she exclaimed; 'carpets, beds, chairs, everything . . .'

'You got to do something,' said Mr Pott, eyeing her tear-marked face, 'to keep your mind off.'

'Yes, yes, of course,' said Miss Menzies.

'But don't be too hopeful about their coming back, you got to keep ready to face the worst. Say they had a fright and ran off on their own accord: that's one thing. Like as not, once the fright's over, they'd come back. But, say, they were *took*. Well, that's another matter altogether – whoever it was that took them, took them to *keep* them, see what I mean?'

'*Whoever?*' repeated Miss Menzies wonderingly.

'See this,' said Mr Pott, moving aside his wooden leg and pointing with his screwdriver to a soggy patch in the High Street. 'That's a human footprint – and it's neither mine nor yours; the pavement's broken all along and the bridge is cracked as though someone has stood on it. Neither you nor me would do that, now would we?'

'No,' said Miss Menzies faintly. 'But', she went on wonderingly, 'no one except you and I knew of their existence.'

'Or so we thought,' said Mr Pott.

'I see,' said Miss Menzies, and was silent a moment.

Then she said slowly: 'I am thinking now, whether they laugh at us or not, I must report this loss to the police. It would stake our claim. In case', she went on, 'they should turn up somewhere else.'

Mr Pott looked thoughtful. 'Might be wise,' he said.

Chapter Ten

At first they lay very still in the corner of the cardboard box, recovering from the shock. Since the lid had been removed they were aware of vastness and of great, white,
sloping ceilings. Two dormer windows, high in the tent-like walls, let in a coldish light. The edges of the box obscured the floor.

Arrietty felt very bruised and shaken: she glanced at her mother, who lay back limply, in her long white nightgown, her eyes still doggedly closed, and knew that,
for the present, Homily had given up. She glanced at her father, who was leaning forward lost in thought, his hands limply on his knees, sat and noticed that he alone had managed to snatch up a garment – a patched pair of

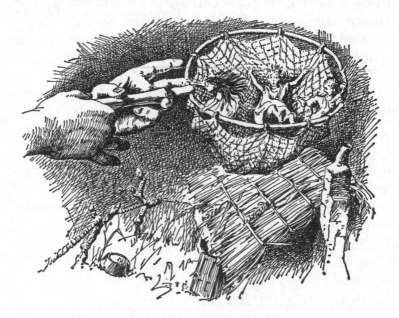

working trousers which he had pulled on over his nightshirt.

Shivering a little in her thin cambric nightgown, she crept towards him, and crouching beside him laid her cheek against his shoulder. He did not speak but his arm came loosely about her, and he patted her gently in an absent-minded way.

'Who are they?' she whispered huskily. 'What happened, Papa?'

'I don't rightly know,' he said.

'It was all so quick – like an earthquake . . .'

'That's right,' he said.

'Mother won't speak,' whispered Arrietty.

'I don't blame her,' said Pod.

'But she's all right, I think,' Arrietty went on; 'it's just her nerves . . .'

'We'd better take a look at her,' said Pod. They crawled towards her on their knees across the washed-out blanket with which the box was lined. For some reason – perhaps their old instinct for cover – neither as yet had dared stand upright.

'How are you feeling, Homily?' asked Pod.

'Just off dead,' she muttered faintly through barely moving lips. Dreadful she looked – lying so straight and so still.

'Anything broken?' asked Pod.

'Everything,' she moaned. But when anxiously he tried to feel the stick-like arms and fragile outstretched legs, she sat up suddenly and exclaimed crossly: 'Don't, Pod,' and began to pin up her hair. She then sank back again, and in a faint voice murmured: 'Where am I?' and with a loose, almost tragic gesture, flung the back of her hand on her brow.

'Well, we could all ask ourselves *that*,' said Pod. 'We're

in some kind of room in some kind of human house.' He glanced up at the distant windows. 'We're in an attic; that's where we are. Take a look . . .'

'I couldn't,' said Homily, and shivered.

'And we're alone,' said Pod.

'We won't be for long,' said Homily, 'I've got my "feeling", and I've got it pretty sharp.'

'She's right,' said Arrietty, and gripped her father's shoulder. 'Listen!'

With beating hearts and raised faces they crouched together tensely in the corner of the box – there were footsteps below them on the stairs.

Arrietty sprang up wildly but her father caught her by the arm. 'Steady, girl, what are you after?'

'Cover,' gasped Arrietty, as the footsteps became less muffled. 'There must be somewhere . . . Come on, quick, let's hide!'

'No good,' said Pod; 'they know we're here. There'd only be searchings and pokings and sticks and pullings-out; your mother couldn't stand it. No, better we stay dead quiet.'

'But we don't know what they'll do to us,' Arrietty almost sobbed. 'We can't just be here and let them!'

Homily suddenly sat up and took Arrietty in her arms. 'Hush, girl, hush,' she whispered, strangely calm all at once. 'Your father's right. There's nothing we can do.'

The footsteps grew louder as though the stairs were now uncarpeted, and there was a creaking of wooden treads. The borrowers clung more tightly together. Pod, face raised, was listening intently.

'That's good,' he breathed in Arrietty's ear. 'I like to hear that – gives us plenty of warning – they can't burst in on us unexpected like.'

Arrietty, still sobbing below her breath, clung to her

mother's waist – never had she been more terrified. 'Hush, girl, hush . . .' Homily kept saying.

The footsteps now had reached the landing. There was heavy breathing outside the door, the clink of keys and the tinkle of china. There was the thud of a drawn bolt; and then another, and a key squeaked and turned in the lock.

'Careful,' said a voice; 'you're spilling it!'

Then the floorboards creaked and trembled as the two

pairs of footsteps approached. A great plate loomed suddenly over them, and behind the plate, a face. Extraordinary it looked – pink and powdered, with piled-up golden hair, on each side of this face two jet earrings dangled towards them. Down it came, closer, closer – until they could see each purple vein in the powdered bloom of the cheeks and each pale eyelash of the staring light-blue eyes; and the plate was set down on the floor.

Another face appeared hanging beside the first – tighter and lighter, with rimless glasses, blank and pale with light. A saucer swung sharply towards them and was set down beside the plate.

The pinkish mouth of the first face opened suddenly and some words came tumbling out. 'Think they're all right, dear?' it said – on a warm gust of breath which ruffled Homily's hair.

From the other face they saw the rimless glasses removed suddenly, polished and put back again. Scared as he was, Pod could not help thinking: 'I could use those for something, and that great silk handkerchief, too.' 'Bit out of shape,' the thinner mouth replied; 'you bumped them a bit in the box.'

'What about a drop of brandy in their milk, dear?' the pink mouth suggested. 'Have you got your hip flask?'

The rimless glasses receded, disappeared for a moment and there was the clink of metal on china. Pod, in some message to Homily, tightened his grip on her hand. Quite strongly, she squeezed his back as the first voice said: 'That's enough, Sidney, you don't want to overdo it.'

Again the two faces loomed over them, staring, staring . . .

'Look at their little faces – hands, hair, feet and everything. What *are* they, do you think, Sidney?'

'They're a find, that's what they are! They're a goldmine! Come, dear, they won't eat while we're here.'

'Suppose I picked one up?'

'No, Mabel, they shouldn't be handled.' (Again Pod squeezed Homily's hand.)

'How do you know?'

'It stands to reason – we haven't got them here as pets. Leave them be now, Mabel – and let's see how they settle. We can come back a bit later on.'

Chapter Eleven

'Mabel and Sidney,' said Arrietty, as the footsteps died away. She seemed quite calm suddenly.

'What do you mean?' asked Pod.

'Those are their names,' said Arrietty lightly. 'Didn't you listen when they were talking?'

'Yes, I heard them say that we mustn't be handled and they would put a drop of brandy in our milk . . .'

'As though we were cats or something!' muttered Homily.

But suddenly they all felt relieved; the moment of terror had passed – at least they had seen their captors.

'If you ask me,' said Pod, 'I'd say they were not too bright. Clever enough maybe, in their way – but not what you'd rightly call "bright".'

'Mabel and Sidney?' said Arrietty. She laughed suddenly and walked to the edge of the box.

Pod smiled at her tone. 'Yes, them,' he said.

'Food,' announced Arrietty, looking out over the box edge. 'I'm terribly hungry, aren't you?'

'I couldn't touch a thing!' said Homily. But after a moment she seemed to change her mind. 'What *is* there?' she asked faintly.

'I can't quite recognize it from here,' Arrietty told her, leaning over.

'Wait a moment,' said Pod, 'something's just come to me – something important, and it's come to me like a flash. Come back here, Arrietty, sit down beside your mother – the food won't run away.'

When both were seated, waiting expectantly, Pod coughed to clear his throat. 'We don't want to underrate our position,' he began. 'I been thinking it over and I don't want to frighten you like – but our position is bad, it's very bad indeed.' He paused, and Homily took Arrietty's hand in both of hers and patted it reassuringly, but her eyes were on Pod's face. 'No borrower,' Pod went on, 'at least none that I've ever heard tell of – has lived in the absolute power of a set of human beings. The absolute power!' he repeated, gravely, looking from one scared face to the other. 'Borrowers have been "seen" – we've been "seen" ourselves – borrowers have been starved out or chased away – but I never heard tell of this sort of caper – not ever in the whole of my life. Have you, Homily?'

Homily moistened her lips. 'No,' she whispered. Arrietty looked very grave.

'Well, unless we can hit on some sensible way of escape that's what's going to happen to us. We're going to live out our lives in the absolute power of a set of human beings. The absolute power . . .' he repeated again slowly as though to brand the phrase on their minds. There was an awed silence, until Pod spoke again. 'Now, who is the captain of our little ship?'

'You are, Pod,' said Homily huskily.

'Yes, I am. And I'm going to ask a lot of you both – and I'm going to make rules as we go – depending on what's needed. The first rule, of course, is obedience . . .'

'That's right,' nodded Homily, squeezing Arrietty's hand.

'. . . And the second rule – this is the thing that came to me – is: we must none of us speak a word.'

'Now, Pod . . .' began Homily reasonably, aware of her own limitations.

Arrietty saw the point. 'He means to Mabel and Sidney.'

Pod smiled again at her tone, albeit rather wryly. 'Yes, them,' he said. 'Never let 'em know we can speak. Because' – he struck his left palm with two fingers of his right to emphasize his meaning – 'if they don't think we can speak, they'll think we don't understand. Just as they are with animals. And if they think we don't understand, they'll talk before us. *Now* do you get my meaning?'

Homily nodded several times in quick succession: she felt very proud of Pod.

'Well,' he went on in a more relaxed tone, 'let's take a look at this food, and after we've eaten we're going to begin a tour of this room – explore every crack and cranny of it from floor to ceiling. May take us several days . . .'

Arrietty helped her mother to her feet. Pod, at the box edge, swung a leg and lightly dropped to the floor. Then he turned to help Homily. Arrietty followed and made at once for the plate.

'Cold rice pudding,' she said, walking round it, 'a bit of mince, cold cabbage, bread' – she put out a finger to touch something black, she sucked the finger – 'and half a pickled walnut.'

'Careful, Arrietty,' warned Homily, 'it may be poisoned.'

'I wouldn't reckon so,' said Pod. 'Seems like they want us alive. Wish I knew for why.'

'But how are we supposed to drink this milk?' complained Homily.

'Well, take it up in your hands, like.'

Homily knelt down and cupped her hands. Her face became very milky but as she drank the reviving warmth seemed to flow through her veins, and her spirits lifted. 'Brandy,' she said. 'Back home at Firbank they kept it in the morning room and those Overmantels used to—'

'Now, Homily,' said Pod, 'this is no time for gossip. And that was whisky.'

'Something anyway, and dead drunk they used to be – or so they say – every time the bailiff came in to do the accounts. What's the mince like, Arrietty?'

'It's good,' she replied, licking her fingers.

Chapter Twelve

'Now', said Pod some time later when they had finished eating, 'we better start on the room.'

He looked upwards. In each sharply sloping wall was set a dormer window, at what seemed a dizzy height; the windows were casement-latched and each had a vertical bolt. Above each was a naked curtain rail, hung with rusted rings. Through one window Pod could see the bough of an ilex-tree tossing in the wind.

'It's odd', Arrietty remarked, 'how from starting under the floor we seem to get higher and higher . . .'

'And it isn't natural', put in Homily quickly, 'for borrowers to get high. Never leads to no good. Look at those Overmantels, for instance, back in the morning room at Firbank. Stuck up they were, through living high. Never so much as give you good day, say you were on the floor. It was as though they couldn't see you. Those windows are no good,' she remarked, 'doubt if even a human being could reach up there. Wonder how they clean them?'

'They'd stand on a chair,' said Pod.

'What about the gas-fire?' Homily suggested.

'No hope there,' said Pod, 'it's soldered into the chimney surround.'

It was a small iron gas-fire, with a separate ring – on which, in a pan, stood a battered glue-pot.

'What about the door?' said Arrietty. 'Suppose we cut a piece out of the bottom?'

'What with?' asked Pod, who was still examining the fireplace.

'We might find something,' said Arrietty, looking about her.

There were plenty of objects in the room. Beside the fireplace stood a dressmaker's dummy, upholstered in a dark green rep: it was shaped like an hourglass, had a knob for a head and below the swelling hips a kind of wire-frame petticoat – a support for the fitting of skirts. It stood on three curved legs with swivel wheels. Its dark green bosom was stuck with pins and on one shoulder, in a row, three threaded needles. Arrietty had a strange thought: did human beings look like this, she wondered, without their clothes? Were they, unlike the borrowers, perhaps not made of flesh and blood at all? Come to think of it, as 'Mabel' had put down the plate, there had been a kind of creaking; and it stood to reason that, to keep such bulk erect, there must surely be some hidden form of scaffolding.

Above the mantel-shelf, on either side, were swivel gas-brackets of tarnished brass. From one hung a length of measuring tape, marked in inches. On the shelf itself she saw the edge of a chipped saucer, the blades of what must be a pair of cutting-out scissors, and a large iron horseshoe propped upside down.

At right angles to the fireplace, pulled out from the

sloping wall, she saw a treadle sewing-machine; it was like one she remembered at Firbank. Above the sewing-machine, hanging on a nail, were the inner tube of a bicycle tyre and a bunch of raffia. There were two trunks, several piles of magazines and some broken slatted chairs. Between the trunks, leaning at an angle, was the shrimping-net which had achieved their capture. Homily glanced at the bamboo handle and, shuddering, averted her eyes.

On the other side of the room, a fair-sized kitchen table was pushed against the wall, and beside it a ladder-back chair. The table was piled with various neat stacks of plates and saucers, and other things which from floor level were difficult to recognize.

On the floor, beyond the chair and immediately below the window, stood a solid box of walnut veneer, inlaid with tarnished brass. The veneer was cracked and peeling. 'It's a dressing-case,' said Pod, who had seen something like it at Firbank, 'or one of those folding writing-desks. No, it isn't though,' he went on as he walked round to the far side, 'it's got a handle . . .'

'It's a musical-box,' said Arrietty.

After a moment of seeming stuck, the handle wound quite easily. They could turn it as one turned an old-fashioned mangle, though the upward swing at its highest limit was difficult to control. Homily could manage, though, with her long wrists and arms; she was a little taller than Pod. There was a grinding sound from within the box and suddenly the tune tinkled out. It was fairylike and charming, but somehow a little sad. It ended very abruptly.

'Oh, play it again!' cried Arrietty.

'No, that's enough,' said Pod, 'we've got to get on.' He was staring towards the table.

'Just once,' pleaded Arrietty.

'All right,' he said, 'but hurry up. We haven't got all day . . .'

And while they played their encore he stood in the middle of the room, gazing thoughtfully at the table top.

When at last they came beside him, he said: 'It's worth while getting up there!'

'Don't see quite how you could,' said Homily.

'Quiet,' said Pod, 'I'm getting it . . .'

Obediently they stood silent, watching the direction of his eyes as he gauged the height of the ladder-back chair, and then, turning his back on it, glanced up at the raffia on the opposite wall, took in the position of the pins in the bosom of the dressmaker's dummy, and turned back again to the table. Homily and Arrietty held their breaths, aware some great issue was at stake.

'Easy,' said Pod at last, 'child's play,' and, smiling, he rubbed his hands: it always cheered him to solve a

professional problem. 'Some good stuff up there, I shouldn't wonder.'

'But what good can it do us?' asked Homily, 'seeing there's no way out?'

'Well, you never know,' said Pod. 'Anyway,' he went on briskly, 'keeps your hands in and your mind off.'

Chapter Thirteen

The next two or three days established their daily routine. At about nine o'clock each morning Mr or Mrs Platter – or both – would arrive with their food. They would air the attic, clear away the dirty plates and generally set the borrowers up for the day. Mrs Platter, to Homily's fury, persisted with the cat treatment: a saucer of milk, a bowl of water and a baking tin of ashes, set out daily beside their food on a clean sheet of newspaper.

Towards evening, at between six and seven o'clock, the process was repeated and was called 'putting them to bed'. It was dark by then and sometimes they would have dozed off – to be woken suddenly by the scrape of a match and the flare of a roaring gas-jet. It was one of Pod's rules that, however active they might be between whiles, the Platters' arrival should always find them once again in their box. The footsteps on the stairs gave them plenty of warning. 'And never let them know we can climb.'

The morning food seemed to consist of the remains of the Platters' breakfast; the evening food, the remains of the Platers' midday meal, was slightly more interesting. Anything they left on the plate was never served up again. 'After all,' they had heard Mr Platter say, 'there are no books about them, no way to find out what they live on except by trial and error. We must try them out with a bit of this and that, and we'll soon see what agrees.'

Except on the rare occasions when Mr or Mrs Platter decided to do a repairing job on the attic or to stagger upstairs with trays of china or cutlery to be put away for the winter, the hours between meals were their own.

They were very active hours. On that first afternoon Pod, with the aid of a bent pin and a knotted strand of raffia, achieved the ascent of the table, and once safely esconced, showed Arrietty how to follow. Later, he said, they would make a raffia ladder.

Gradually they worked their way through various cardboard boxes; some contained teaspoons and cutlery; some contained paper windmills, others toy balloons. There were boxes of nails and assorted screws and there was a small square biscuit-tin without a lid, filled with a jumble of keys. There was a tottering pile of pink-stained strawberry baskets and there were sets of neatly packed ice-cream cones, hermetically sealed in transparent grease-proof paper.

There were two drawers in the table, one of which was not quite closed. They squeezed through the crack, and in the half light saw it was full of tools. Pod's leg went down between a spanner and a screwdriver, in extricating which he rolled the screwdriver over and struck Arrietty on the ankle. Although neither injury was serious, they decided the drawer was a dangerous place and put it out of bounds.

By the fourth day the operation was complete: they had learned the position and possible use of every object

in the room. They had even succeeded in opening the lid
of the musical-box, in a vain hope of changing the tune. It
slid up quite easily on a brass arm which, clinking into a
locked position, held the lid in place. It closed, rather

faster but almost as easily, by pressure on a knob. They could not change the tune, however; the brass cylinders, spiked with an odd pattern of steel prickles, were too heavy for them to lift, and they could only look longingly at the five unknown tunes on the equally heavy cylinders ranged at the back of the box. But with each new discovery – such as the steel backing of the lower part of the door and the dizzy height of the dormer windows from which the sloping walls slid steeply away – their hopes grew fainter: there still seemed no way of escape.

Pod spent more and more of his time just sitting and thinking. Arrietty, tired of the musical-box, had discovered on the magazine pile several tattered copies of the *Illustrated London News*. She would drag them one at a time under the table, and turning over the vast sail-like pages would walk about on them listlessly, looking at the pictures and sometimes reading aloud.

'You see nobody knows where we are,' Pod would exclaim, breaking a dreary silence, 'not even Spiller.'

'And not even Miss Menzies . . .' Arrietty would think to herself, staring unhappily at a half-page diagram of a dam to be built on the lower reaches of the Nile.

As the mornings became chillier Homily tore some strips off the worn blanket and she and Arrietty fashioned themselves sarong-like skirts and pointed shawls to draw round their shoulders.

Seeing this, the Platters decided to light the gas-fire and would leave it burning low. The borrowers were glad, because, although sometimes the air grew dry and stuffy, they were able to toast up scraps of the duller foods and make their meals more appetizing.

One day Mrs Platter bustled in and, looking very purposeful, went to the closed drawer of the table. Watching her from their box in the corner as she pulled out some of the contents they saw it contained rags and rolls of old stuff, neatly tied round with tape. She unrolled a piece of yellowed flannel and, taking up the cutting-out scissors, came and stared down on them with narrowed, thoughtful eyes.

They stared back nervously at the waving scissor blades. Was she going to snip and snap and tailor them to size? But no – with a little creaking and much heavy breathing, she kneeled down on the floor and, spreading the stuff doubled before her, cut out three combination garments, each one all of a piece, with magyar sleeves and legs. These she seamed up on the sewing-machine, 'tutting' to herself under her breath when the wheel stuck or the thread parted. When her thimble rolled away under the treadle of the sewing-machine they noted its position: a drinking-cup at last!

Breathing hard, and with the aid of a bone crochet-hook, Mrs Platter turned the garments inside out. 'There you are,' she said, and threw them into the box. They lay there stiffly like little headless effigies. None of the borrowers moved.

'You can put them on yourselves, can't you?' said Mrs Platter at last. The borrowers stared back at her, with wide, unblinking eyes, until, after waiting a moment, she turned and went away.

They were terrible garments, stiff and shapeless, fitting nowhere at all. But at least they were warm; and Homily could now rinse out their own clothes in the bowl of drinking water and hang them before the gas-fire to dry. 'Thank heavens, I can't see myself,' she remarked grimly, as she gazed incredulously at Pod.

'Thank goodness you can't,' he replied, smiling, and he turned rather quickly away.

Chapter Fourteen

As the weeks went by they learned gradually of the reason for their capture and the use to which they would be put. As well as the construction of the cage-like house on the island, Mr and Mrs Platter – assured of vast takings at last – were installing a turnstile in place of the gate to the drive.

One side of their cage-house, they learned, was to be made of thick plate-glass, exposing their home life to view. 'Good and heavy' the glass would have to be – Mr Platter had insisted, describing the 'layout' to Mrs Platter – nothing the borrowers could break; and fixed in a slot so the Platters could raise it for cleaning. The furniture was to be fixed to the floor and set in such a way that there should be nothing behind which they might hide.

'You know those cages at the Zoo with sleeping-quarters at the back, where you wait and wait, and the animal never comes out? Well, we don't want anything like that. Can't have people asking for their money back . . .'

Mrs Platter had agreed. She saw the whole project in her mind's eye and thought Mr Platter very far-seeing and wonderful. 'And you've got to set the cage,' he went on earnestly, 'or house, or whatever we decide to call it, in a bed of cement. You can't have them burrowing.'

No, that wouldn't do, Mrs Platter had agreed again. And as Mr Platter went ahead with the construction of the house, Mrs Platter, they learned, had arranged with a seamstress to make them an entirely new wardrobe. She had taken away their own clothes to serve as patterns for size. Homily was very intrigued by Mrs Platter's descrip-

tion to Mr Platter of a green dress 'with a hint of a bustle –
like my purple plaid, you remember?' 'Wish I could *see*
her purple plaid,' Homily kept worrying, 'just so as to get
the idea . . .'

But Pod's thoughts were set on graver matters. Every
conversation overheard brought day by day an increasing
awareness of their fate: to live out the rest of their lives
under a barrage of human eyes – a constant, unremitting
state of being 'seen'. Flesh and blood could not stand it,
he thought; they would shrivel up under these stares –
that's what would happen – they would waste away and
die. And people would watch them even on their
deathbeds – they would watch, with necks craned and
shoulders jostling – while Pod stroked the dying Homily's brow or Homily stroked the dying Pod's. No, he
decided grimly, from now on there could be but one
thought governing their lives – a burning resolve to
escape: to escape while they were still in the attic; to
escape before spring. Cost what it might, he realized, they

must never be taken alive to that house with a wall of glass!

For these reasons, as the winter wore on, he became irritated by Homily's fussings over details such as the ash-pan and Arrietty's unheeding preoccupation with the *Illustrated London News*.

Chapter Fifteen

During this period (mid November to December) several projects were planned and attempted. Pod had succeeded in drawing out four nails which secured a patch of mended floorboard below the kitchen table. 'They don't walk here, you see,' he explained to his wife and child, 'and it's in shadow like.' These four stout nails he replaced with slimmer ones from the tin box on the table. The finer nails could be lifted out with ease and the three of them together could move the boards aside. Below they found the familiar joists and crossbeams, with a film of dust which lay – ankle-deep to them – on the ceiling plaster of the room below. ('Reminds me of the time when we first moved in under the floor at Firbank,' said Homily. 'I thought sometimes we would never get it straight, but we did.')

But Pod's project was nothing to do with home-making – he was seeking a way which might lead them to the lath and plaster walls of the room immediately below. If they could achieve this, he thought, there was nothing to stop them climbing down through the whole depth of the house, with the help of the laths within the walls: mice did it, rats did it; and as he pointed out, risky and toilsome as it was, they had done it several times themselves. ('We were younger then, Pod,' Homily reminded him nervously, but she seemed quite willing to try.)

It was no good, however; the attic was in the roof and the roof was set fairly and squarely on the brickwork of the main house, bedded and held in some mixture like cement. There was no way down to the laths.

Pod's next idea was one of breaking a small hole in the plaster of the ceiling below, and with the aid of the swinging ladder made of raffia, descend without cover into whatever room it might turn out to be.

'At least,' he said, 'we'd be one floor down, the window will be lower and the door unlocked . . .' First, though, he decided to borrow a packing-needle from the tool drawer and make a peephole. This, too, was hazardous: not only might the ceiling crack but there was bound to be some small fall of plaster on to the floor below. They decided to risk it, however; borrowers' eyes are particularly sharp: they could manage with a very small hole.

When at last they had made the hole and to their startled gaze the room below sprang to view; it turned out to be Mr and Mrs Platter's bedroom. There was a large brass bed, a very pink, shiny eiderdown, a Turkey carpet, a wash-hand-stand with two sets of flowered china, a dressing-table and a cat-basket. And what was still more alarming, Mrs Platter was having her afternoon's rest. It was an extraordinary sight to see her vast bulk from this angle, propped against the pillows. Very peaceful and unconcerned she looked, reading a home journal – leisurely turning the pages and eating butterscotch from a round tin. The cat lay on the eiderdown at her feet. A powdery film of ceiling plaster had settled in a ring on the pinkness of the eiderdown just beside the cat. This, Pod realized thankfully, would be swiftly shaken off when Mrs Platter arose.

Trembling and silent the borrowers backed away from their peephole, and noiselessly felt their way through the blanketing dust to the exit in the floorboards. Silently they lifted the small plank into place and gingerly dropped back the nails.

'Phew! . . .' said Pod, sinking back, as they reached their box in the corner. He wiped his brow on his sleeve, 'didn't expect to see that!' He looked very shaken.

'Nor did I,' said Homily. She thought a while. 'But it might be useful.'

'Might,' agreed Pod uncertainly.

The next attempt concerned the window – the one through which they could see the waving branch of the ilex. This branch was their only link with out of doors. 'Wind's in the east today,' Mrs Platter would sometimes say as she opened the casements to air the attic – this she achieved by standing on a chair – and the borrowers took note of what she said, and by the streaming of the leaves in one direction or another could roughly foretell the weather: 'wind in the east' meant snow.

When the flakes piled up on the outer sill they liked to watch them dance and scurry, but were thankful for the gas-fire. This was early January and not the most auspicious weather for Pod's study of the window, but they had no time to lose.

Homily, on occasion, was apt to discourage him. 'Say we did get it open, where would we be? On the roof! And you can see how steep it is by the slope of these ceilings. I mean, we're better in here than on the roof, Pod. I'm game in most things, but if you think I'm going to make a jump for that branch, you'll have to think again.'

'You couldn't make a jump for that branch, Homily,' Pod would tell her patiently, 'it's yards and yards away. And what's more, it's never still. No, it's not the branch I'm thinking of . . .'

'What are you thinking of, then?'

'Of where we are,' said Pod, 'that's what I want to find out. You might *see* something from the roof. You've heard them talk – about Little Fordham and that. And about the river. I'd like just to know where we *are*.'

'What good does that do us,' retorted Homily, 'if we can't get out, anyway?'

Pod turned and looked at her. 'We've got to keep trying,' he explained.

'I know, Pod,' admitted Homily quickly. She glanced towards the table, under which, as usual, Arrietty was immersed in the *Illustrated London News*, 'and we both want to help you. I mean, we did make the raffia ladder. Just tell us what to do.'

'There isn't much you *can* do,' said Pod, 'at least not at the moment. What foxes me about this window is that, to free the latch you have to turn the handle of the catch upwards. See what I mean? The same with that vertical bolt – you've got to pull it out of its socket *upwards*. Now say to open the window you had to turn the handle of the catch downwards – that would be easy! We could fling a piece of twine or something over, swing our weight on the twine like and the catch would slide up free.'

'Yes,' said Homily thoughtfully, staring at the window. 'Yes, I see what you mean.' They were silent a moment – both thinking hard. 'What about that curtain rod?' asked Homily at last.

'The curtain rod? I don't quite get you . . .'

'Is it fast in the wall?'

Pod screwed up his eyes. 'Pretty fast, I'd say, it's brass. And with those brackets . . .'

'Could you get a bit of twine over the curtain rod?'

'Over the curtain rod?'

'Yes, and use it like a pulley.'

A change came over Pod's face. 'Homily,' he said, 'that's it! Here am I – been weeks on the problem . . . and you hit on the answer first time . . .'

'It's nothing,' said Homily, smiling.

Pod gave his orders; and swiftly they all went to work: the ball of twine and a small key to be carried to the table and up to the topmost box (this to bring Pod, sideways on, to within easier throwing distance of the curtain rod); the horseshoe to be knocked from the mantel-shelf to the floor; and to be dragged to a spot beside the musical-box, and immediately below the window; several patient swinging throws by Pod from the box pile on the table of the key attached to the twine, aimed at the wall above the curtain rod, which stood out slightly on its twin brass brackets (and suddenly there had been the welcome clatter of the key against the glass and the key falling swiftly as Arrietty paid out the twine – down past the window, past the sill, to Homily on the floor, beside the horseshoe); the removal of the key by Homily and the knotting of the raffia ladder to the twine to be wound back again by Arrietty, to bring the head of the ladder even with the window catch; the tying, by Homily, of the base of the swinging ladder to the horseshoe on the floor; the twine to be pulled taut and made fast by Arrietty to a table leg; the descent of Pod to the floor.

It was wonderful. The ladder rose tautly from the horseshoe, straight up the centre join of the casement windows to the catch, held firmly by the twine around the curtain rod.

Up the raffia ladder went Pod, watched by Arrietty and Homily from the floor. When on a level with the window catch, he hooked the first rung over the curtain rail, making – for a few essential moments – the ladder independent of the twine. Arrietty, beside the table leg, paying out several inches from the ball, enabling Pod to knot the twine about the iron handle of the catch. Pod then descending to the floor from the table leg and bringing the ball directly below the window.

'So far, so good,' he said. 'Now we've all got to pull on the twine. You behind Arrietty, Homily, and I'll bring up the rear.'

Obediently they did as he said. With a twist of twine tug-of-war-like around each tiny fist, they leaned backwards into the room, panting and straining and digging in their heels. Slowly, steadily the handle of the latch moved upward and the hammer-shaped head dipped down in a sliding half-circle, until at last it left one casement free.

'We've done it,' said Pod. 'You can let go now. That's the first stage.' They all stood rubbing their hands and feeling very happy. 'Now for the bolt,' Pod went on. And the whole performance was repeated; more efficiently, this time – more swiftly. The small bolt, easy in its groove, lifted gently and hung above its socket. 'The window's open,' cried Pod. 'There's nothing holding it now except for the snow on the sill!'

'And we could brush that off – if, say, we went up the ladder,' said Homily. 'And I'd like to see the view.'

'You can see the view in a minute,' said Pod, 'but what we mustn't touch is that snow. You don't want Mabel and Sidney coming upstairs and finding we've been at the window. At least, not yet awhile . . . What we must do now, and do quickly, is shut it up again. How do you feel, Homily? Like to rest a moment?'

'No, I'm all right,' she said.

'Then we better get going,' said Pod.

Chapter Sixteen

Under Pod's direction, and with one or two small
mistakes on the parts of Homily and Arrietty, the process
was reversed and the latch and bolt made fast again. But
not before – as Pod had promised – all three had climbed
the ladder in solemn file, and rubbing the misted breath
from the glass, had stared out over the landscape. They
had seen, so far below them, the dazzling slope of Mr
Platter's lawn, the snake-like river, black as a whiplash,
curving away into the distance; they had seen the snow-
covered roofs of Fordham – and beside a far loop of the
stream the three tall poplars, which as they knew marked
the site of Little Fordham. They looked very far away –
even, thought Homily, as the crow flies . . .

They did not talk much after they had seen these things. They felt overawed by the distance, the height and the whiteness. On Pod's orders they set about storing the tackle below the floorboard, where, though safely hidden, it would always be ready to hand. 'We'll practise that window job again tomorrow,' said Pod, 'and every other day from now on.'

As they worked the wind rose again and the underside of the ilex leaves showed grey as the grey sky. Before dusk it began to snow again. When they had set back the board and replaced the nails, they crept up close to the gas-fire and sat there thinking, as the daylight drained from the room. There still seemed no way of escape. 'We're too high,' Homily kept saying. 'Never does and never has done borrowers any good to be high . . .'

At last the footsteps of Mrs Platter on the stairs drove them back to their box. When the match scraped and the gas-jet flared they saw the room again and the blackness of the window with the snow piled high on the outer sill. The line of white rose softly as they watched it with each descending snowflake.

'Terrible weather,' muttered Mrs Platter to herself, as she set down their plate and their saucer. She stared at them anxiously as they lay huddled in the box and turned up the gas-fire a little before she went away. And they were left as always to eat by themselves in the dark.

Chapter Seventeen

The snow and frost and leaden cold continued into early February. Until one morning they woke to soft rain and the pale clouds running in the sky. The leaves of the ilex branch, enamelled and shining, streamed black against the grey and showed no silvery glimpse of underside. 'Wind's in the south,' announced Pod that morning in the satisfied voice of an experienced weather prophet. 'We're likely to have a thaw.'

In the past weeks they had employed their time as best they could. Against the weight of snow on the sill they had practised the raising of the latch and had brought the process to a fine art. Mr and Mrs Platter, they gathered, had been held up on the building of the cage-house, but

the borrowers' clothes had arrived, laid out between layers of tissue-paper in a cardboard dress-box. It took them no time at all to get the lid off and with infinite care and cunning to examine the contents and in secret to try them on. The seamstress had nimbler fingers than those of Mrs Platter and had worked in far finer materials. There was a grey suit for Pod with – instead of a shirt – a curious kind of dicky with the collar and tie painted on; there was a pleated and ruched dress for Arrietty with two pinafores to keep it clean. Homily, although ready to grumble, took to her green dress with its 'hint of a bustle', and would wear it sometimes to a moment of danger – the dread sound of footsteps on the stairs.

To Pod these goings-on seemed frivolous and childish. Had they forgotten, he wondered, their immediate danger and the fate which day by day became closer as the weather cleared and Mr Platter worked away on the house? He did not reproach them, however. Let them have their little bit of happiness, he decided, in face of misery to come.

But he became very 'down'. Better they all should be dead, he told them one day, than in lifelong public captivity; and he would sit and stare into space.

He became so 'down' that Homily and Arrietty grew frightened. They stopped dressing up and conferred together in corners. They tried to liven him with little jokes and anecdotes; they saved him all the titbits from the food. But Pod seemed to have lost his appetite. Even when they reminded him that spring was in the air and soon it would be March – 'and something always happens to us in March' – he evinced no interest. 'Something *will* happen to us in March,' was all he said before retreating again into silence.

One day Arrietty came beside him as he sat there, dully

thinking, in the corner of the box. She took his hand. 'I have an idea,' she said.

He made an effort to smile and gently squeezed her hand. 'There isn't anything,' he said; 'we've got to face it, lass.'

'But there is something,' Arrietty persisted. 'Do listen, Papa. I've thought of the very thing!'

'Have you, my girl?' he said gently, and, smiling a little, he stroked back the hair from her cheek.

'Yes,' said Arrietty, 'we could make a balloon.'

'A what?' he exclaimed. And Homily, who had been toasting up a sliver of bacon at the gas-fire, came across to them, drawn by the sharpness of his tone.

'We needn't even make it!' Arrietty hurried on. 'There are heaps of balloons in those boxes and we have all those strawberry baskets, and there are diagrams and everything . . .' She pulled his hand. 'Come and look at this copy of the *Illustrated London News*.'

There was a three-page spread in the *Illustrated London News* – with diagrams, photographs and an expert article, set out comprehensively in columns, on the lately revived sport of free ballooning.

Pod could count and add up, but he could not read, so Arrietty, walking about on the page, read the article aloud. He listened attentively, trying to take it in. 'Let's have that again, lass,' he would say, frowning with his effort to understand.

'Well, move, Mother – please,' Arrietty would say, because Homily, weak from standing, had suddenly sat down on the page. 'You're on the piece about wind velocity . . .'

Homily kept muttering phrases like: 'Oh, my goodness – oh, my goodness gracious me . . .' as the full implica-

tions of their plan began to dawn on her. She looked strained and a little wild, but awake now to their desperate plight, was resigned to a lesser evil.

'I've got that,' Pod would say at last, after several repetitions of a paragraph concerning something described as 'the canopy or envelope'. 'Now let's have that bit about the valve line and the load ring. It's up near the top of the second column.' And he and Arrietty would walk up the page again and patiently, clearly, although stumbling now and again on the big words, Arrietty would read aloud.

In the tool drawer, no longer out of bounds, they had found the stub of a lead pencil. Pod extracted the lead and sharpened it to a fine point, for Arrietty to underline key headings and to make lists.

At last, on the third day of concentrated homework, Pod announced: 'I'm there!'

He was a changed man suddenly; what had once seemed a ridiculous flight of fancy on the part of Arrietty could now become sober fact, and he was practical enough to see it.

The first job was swiftly to dismantle the shrimping-net. On this, in more senses than one, would hang all their hopes of success. Homily, with a cut-down morsel of fret-saw blade, taken from a box in the tool drawer, was to cut the knots which secured the net to the frame. Pod would then saw up the frame into several portable lengths and take off the bamboo handle.

'That whole shrimping-net's got to disappear', Pod explained, 'as though it had never existed. We can't have them seeing the frame with the netting part cut away. Once it's in pieces, like, we can hide it under the floor.'

It took less time than they had foreseen and as they laid back the floorboard and dropped the nails into place, Pod – who was not often given to philosophizing – said: 'Funny, when you come to think of it, that this old net we were caught in should turn out to be our salvation.'

That night, when they went to bed, they felt tired but a good deal happier. Pod for some time lay awake, thinking another great test lay before them on the morrow. Could the balloon be filled from the gas-jet? There was a real danger in meddling with gas, he realized uneasily; even adult human beings had met with accidents, let alone disobedient children. He had warned Arrietty about gas in the days when they lived at Firbank, and she, good girl, had respected his advice and had understood the peril. He would of course take every precaution: first the window must be opened wide and the cock of the gas-fire shut off, and the fire allowed to cool down until not a spot of red remained. There was plenty of pressure in the gas-jet; even this very evening, when Mrs Platter had first lit it, he remembered how fiercely it had roared; she had always – he had noticed – to turn it a fraction lower. The ascent to the mantel-shelf could be made via the dummy. It was no use worrying, he decided at last, they were bound to have this try-out and to abide by the result. All the same, it was a long time – several hours it seemed – before Pod fell asleep.

Chapter Eighteen

The balloon filled perfectly. Lashed around the nozzle of the gas-jet and anchored to the horseshoe on the floor by a separate piece of twine, it first swelled slightly in a limp mass which hung loosely down against the burner and then – to their startled joy – suddenly shot upright and went on swelling. Bigger and bigger it grew – until it became a vast, tight globe of a rich translucent purple. Then Pod, firmly perched among the ornate scrollwork of the bracket, leaned sideways and turned off the gas.

As though making a tourniquet, he tied the neck of the balloon above the nozzle and undid the lashing just below. The balloon leapt free almost with a jump but was

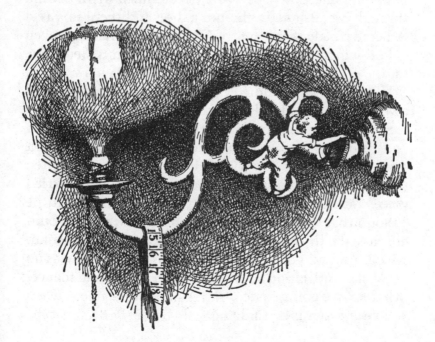

brought up short by the tethering string which Pod had anchored to the horseshoe.

Homily and Arrietty on the floor beside the horseshoe let out their 'Aaahs' and 'Ohs' . . . and Arrietty ran forward and, seizing the string, tried her weight on it. She swung a little to and fro as the balloon bumped against the ceiling.

'Gently!' cried Pod from the bosom of the dummy. He was climbing down slowly on carefully set footholds of pins. When he reached the caged part below the dummy's hips he swung down more quickly from one wire rung to another.

'Now, we'll all three take hold,' he told them, running to grasp the string. 'Pull', he cried, 'as hard as you can. Hand over hand!'

Hand over hand they pulled and swung and slowly the balloon came down. A swift double turn of the twine through a nail-hole in the horseshoe and there it was – tethered beside them, gently swaying and twisting.

Pod wiped his brow on his sleeve. 'It's too small,' he said.

'Too small!' exclaimed Homily. She felt dwarfed and awed by the great bobbing purple mass. But it gave her a feeling of delightful power to push it and make it sway; and a sideways stroke of her fingers would send it into a spin.

'Of course it's too small,' explained Pod in a worried voice. 'We shouldn't be able to pull it down like that. A balloon that size might take Arrietty alone, but it would not take the three of us – not with the net and the basket added. And we got to have ballast too.'

'Well,' said Homily, after a short, dismayed silence, 'what are we going to do?'

'I've got to think,' said Pod.

'Suppose we all stopped eating and thinned down a bit?' suggested Homily.

'That wouldn't be any good. And you're thin enough already.' Pod seemed very worried. 'No, I've got to think.'

'There is a bigger balloon,' said Arrietty. 'It's in a box by itself. At least, it looked bigger to me.'

'Well, let's take a look,' said Pod, but he did not sound very hopeful.

It did seem bigger and was covered with shrivelled white markings. 'I think it's some kind of lettering,' Arrietty remarked, turning over the box-lid. 'Yes, it says here: "Printed to your own specification" – I wonder what it means . . .'

'I don't care what it means,' exclaimed Pod, 'so long as there's room for a lot of it. Yes, it's bigger,' he went on, 'a good deal bigger, and it's heavier. Yes, this balloon may just do us nicely. Might as well try it at once, now we've got the fire off and the window open.'

'What shall we do with this one?' asked Homily from the floor. She tapped it sharply so that it trembled and spun.

'We better burst it,' said Pod on his way down from the table via the raffia ladder which swung on bent pins from the chair back, 'and hide the remains. Nothing much else that we *can* do.'

He burst it with a pin. The report seemed deafening and the balloon, deflating, jumped about like a mad thing; Homily screamed and ran for safety into the wire cage below the dummy. There was a terrible smell of gas.

'Didn't think it would make such a noise,' said Pod, pin in hand and looking rather startled. 'Never mind, with the window open – the smell will soon wear off.'

The new balloon was more cumbersome to climb with

and Pod had to rest a while on the mantel-shelf before he
tackled the gas-jet.

'Like me to come up and help you, Papa?' Arrietty
called out from the floor.

'No,' he said, 'I'll be all right in a minute. Just let me get
my breath . . .'

The heavier balloon remained limp for longer; until,
almost as though groaning under the effort, it raised itself
upright and slowly began to fill. 'Oh,' breathed Arrietty,
'it's going to be a lovely colour . . .' It was a deep fuschia

pink, becoming each moment – as the rubber swelled –
more delicately pale. As it swayed a little on the gas-jet
white lettering began to appear. STOP! was the first
word, with an exclamation mark after it. Arrietty,
reading the word aloud, hoped it was not an omen. Below
STOP came the word BALLYHOGGIN, and below that
again in slightly smaller print: 'World Famous Model
Village and Riverside Teas.'

The balloon was growing larger and larger. Homily
looked alarmed. 'Careful, Pod,' she begged; 'whatever
you do, don't burst it!'

'It can go a bit more yet,' said Pod. They watched anxiously until at last Pod, in a glow of pink shadow from the swaying monster above him, said: 'That's about it,' and leaning sideways to the wall, sharply turned off the gas. Climbing back, he took up the tape-measure which still hung from the gas-bracket and measured the height of the letter 'i' in 'Riverside Teas'. 'A good three inches,' he said, 'that gives us something to check by the next time we inflate.' He now spoke more often in current balloon-ing terms and had acquired quite a fair-sized vocabulary concerning such things as flying ballast, rip lines, trail ropes or grapnel hooks.

This time the balloon, soaring to the ceiling, half lifted the horseshoe and dragged it along the floor. With great presence of mind Homily sat down on the horseshoe while Arrietty leapt for the string.

'That looks more like it,' said Pod as he climbed once again down the bosom of the dummy. As he started down excitedly his foot slipped on a pin, but leaning sideways he pushed the pin back in again almost to the head and made the foothold secure. But for the rest of the climb he controlled his eagerness and took the stages more slowly. By the time he reached the floor, in spite of the cold air from the window, he looked very hot and dishevelled.

'Any give on the line?' he asked Arrietty as he waited to recover his breath.

'No,' gasped Arrietty. Then they all three pulled together but the balloon merely twisted on the ceiling as though held there by a magnet.

'That's enough,' said Pod, after they had all three lifted their feet from the floor and had swung about awhile, still with no effect on the balloon. 'Let her go. I've got to think again.'

They were quiet while he did so, but watched anxiously as he paced about frowning with concentration. Once he untethered the balloon from the horseshoe and, tow-line in hand, walked it about on the ceiling. It bumped a little but followed him obediently as he sketched out its course from the floor.

'Time's getting on, Pod,' Homily said at last.

'I know,' he said.

'I mean,' Homily went on in a worried voice. 'How are we going to get it down? I'm thinking of Mabel and Sidney. We've got to get it down before supper, Pod.'

'I know that,' he said. He walked the balloon across the room until he stood below the lip of the table. 'What we need is some kind of winch – some kind of worm and worm-wheel.' He stared up at the knob of the tool-drawer.

'Worm and worm-wheel . . .' said Homily in a mystified voice. '*Worm?*' she repeated incredulously.

Arrietty, up to date now with almost every aspect of free ballooning, including the use of winches, laughed and said: 'It's a thing that takes the weight – supposing, say, you were turning a handle. Like the—' she stopped abruptly, struck by a sudden thought. 'Papa!' she called out excitedly, 'what about the musical-box?'

'The musical-box?' he repeated blankly. Then, as Arrietty nodded, a light dawned and his whole expression changed. 'That's it!' he exclaimed. 'You've hit it. That's our winch-handle, weight, cylinder, worm and wheel and all!'

Chapter Nineteen

In no time at all they had the musical box open and Pod, standing on an upturned match-box, was staring down at the works. 'We've got a problem,' he said, as they scrambled up beside him. 'I'll solve it, mind, but I've got to find the right tool. It's those teeth,' he pointed out.

Gazing into the works, they saw he meant a row of metal points suspended downwards from a bar, these were the strikers which, brushing the cylinder as it turned, rang from each prickle one tinkling note of the tune. 'You've got to have those teeth out, or they'd mess up the tow-line. If they're welded in it's going to be difficult, but looks to me as though they're all in a piece held in by those screws.'

'It looks to me like that too,' said Arrietty, leaning forward to see better.

'Well, we'll soon have those screws out,' said Pod.

While he climbed once again to the tool drawer, Homily and Arrietty played one last tune. 'Pity we never heard the others,' said Arrietty, 'and we never shall hear them now.'

'If we get out of here alive,' said Homily, 'I don't care if I never see or hear any kind of musical box again in the whole of the rest of my life!'

'Well, you are going to get out of here alive,' remarked Pod in a grimly determined voice. He had come back amongst them with the smallest screwdriver he could find; even then it was as tall as himself. He walked out on the bar and, feet apart, holding the handle at chest level, took his position above the screw and set the edge into the slot. After a short resistance the screw turned easily as

Pod revolved the handle. 'Light as watch screws,' he remarked as he loosened the others. 'It's well made, this musical-box.'

Soon they could lift out the row of spiked teeth and make fast the tow-line to the cylinder. It swayed loosely as the balloon above it surged against the ceiling. 'Now', said Pod, 'I'll take the first turn and we'll see how it goes . . .'

Arrietty and Homily held their breaths as he grasped the handle of the musical-box and slowly began to turn. The line tautened and became dead straight. Slowly and steadily, as Pod put more effort into his turning, the balloon started down towards them. They watched it anxiously, with upturned faces and aching necks, until at last – swaying and pulling slightly at its moorings – it was brought within their reach.

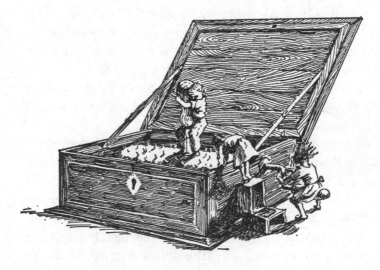

'What about that?' said Pod in a satisfied voice. But he looked very white and tired.

'What do we do now?' asked Homily.

'We deflate it,' he said.

'Let the gas out,' explained Arrietty as Homily still looked blank.

'We've to find some kind of platform', announced Pod, 'to set across the top of this musical-box, something we can walk about on . . .' He looked about the room. Under the gas-ring, on which stood the empty glue-pot, was a small oblong of scorched tin, used to protect the boards of the floor. 'That'll do us,' said Pod.

All three were very tired by now, but they managed to slide the strip of tin from below the gas-ring and hoist it across the opened top of the musical-box. From this platform Pod could handle the neck of the balloon and

begin to untie the knot. 'You and Arrietty keep your
distance,' he advised Homily. 'Better go under the table.
No knowing what this balloon might do.'

What it did, when released from the knotted twine,
was to sail off sideways into the air and, descending
slowly, to bump along the floor. With each bump the
smell of gas became stronger. It seemed to Arrietty, as she
watched it from under the table, that the balloon was
dying in jerks. At last the envelope lay still and empty and
Arrietty and Homily emerged from under the table and
stood looking down at it with Pod.

'What a day!' said Homily. 'And we've still got to close
the window . . .'

'It's been a worth-while day,' said Pod.

But by the time they had gone through the elaborate
process of closing up the window and had hidden all
traces of the recent experiment below the floorboard,
they were utterly worn out. It was not yet dusk before

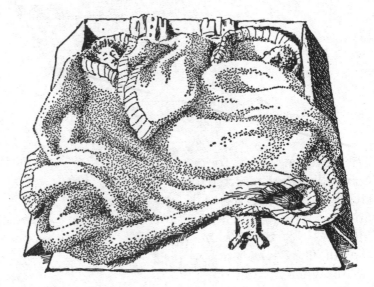

they crept wearily into their blanket-lined box and stretched their aching limbs.

By the time Mr and Mrs Platter brought their supper all three were lost to the world in a deep, exhausted sleep. They did not hear Mrs Platter exclaim because the fire was out. Nor did they see Mr Platter sniffing delicately and peering about the room, and complaining that 'You ought to be more careful, Mabel – there's a wicked smell of gas.'

Mrs Platter, very indignant, protested her innocence. 'It was you who lit the gas-fire this morning, Sidney.'

'No, that was yesterday,' he said. And as each knew the other (when caught out in misdoing) to have little regard for truth, they disbelieved each other and came to no conclusion.

'Anyhow', Mrs Platter summed up at last, 'the weather's too mild now for gas-fires . . .' And they never lit it again.

Chapter Twenty

The next ten days were confined to serious experiment, controlled and directed by Pod. 'We want to go at it steady now,' he explained. 'Keep to a programme, like, and not try too much at a time. It's a big undertaking, Homily – you don't want to rush it. "Step by step climbs the hill"!'

'But when do they open, Pod?'

'Riverside Teas? April the first, if the cage-house is finished.'

'I'll wager it's finished now. And we're getting well into March . . .'

'You're wrong, Homily. They've not delivered the plate-glass, nor the handle to lift it up with. And something went wrong with the drainage. They had a flood, remember? Didn't you listen when they were talking?'

'Not if they're talking about the cage-house I don't listen,' said Homily. 'It gives me the creeps to hear them. Once they start on about the cage-house, I go right under the blanket.'

During these busy ten days Pod and Arrietty walked about so much on the open pages of the *Illustrated London News* that the print became quite blurred. They had to discard the idea of a valve at the top of the canopy, to be controlled from below by a line which passed through the open neck into the basket because, as Pod explained to Arrietty, of the nature of the canopy. He touched the diagram with his foot. 'With this kind of fabric balloon you *can* have the valve line through the neck . . . but rubber's like elastic, squeezes the gas out . . . we'd all be gassed in less than ten minutes if we left the neck open like they do.'

He was disappointed about this because he had already invented a way to insert a control valve where it should be – in the top of the canopy, and had practised on the smaller balloons, of which they had an endless supply.

In the meantime, as Homily with a needle ground down by Pod worked on the shaping of the net, he and Arrietty studied 'equilibrium and weight disposal'. A series of loops was made in the tow-line on which, once the balloon was inflated, they would hang up various objects – a strawberry basket, the half-shaped net, a couple of keys, a hollow curtain ring, a tear-off roll of one-and-sixpenny entrance tickets to Ballyhoggin, and lastly they would swing on the line themselves. There came a day when they achieved a perfect balance. Half a dozen one-and-sixpenny entrance tickets, torn off by Arrietty, would raise the balloon two feet; and one small luggage key, hooked on by Pod, would bring it down with a bump.

Still, they could find no way of controlling the gas through the neck. They could go up, but not down. Untying what he called 'the guard knot' at the neck – or even loosening the guard knot – would, Pod thought, be a little too risky. The gas might rush out in a burst (as they had seen it do so often by now) and the whole contraption – balloon, basket, ballast and aeronauts – would drop like a stone to the earth. 'We can't risk that, you know,' Pod said to Arrietty. 'What we need is some sort of valve or lever . . .' and for the tenth time that day he climbed back into the tool-drawer.

Arrietty joined Homily in her corner by the box to help her with the load-ring. The net was shaping up nicely and Homily, instructed by Pod and Arrietty, had threaded in and made secure the piece of slightly heavier cord which, as it encircled the balloon round its fullest circumference, was suitably called 'the equator'. She was now attaching the load-ring which, when the balloon was netted, would encircle the neck and from which they would hang the basket. They had used the hollow curtain ring, whose weight was now known and tested. 'It's lovely, Mamma! You are clever . . .'

'It's easy,' said Homily, 'once you've got the hang of it. It's no harder than tatting.'

'You've shaped it so beautifully.'

'Well, your father did the calculations . . .'

'I've got it!' cried Pod from the tool-drawer. He had been very quiet for a very long while and now emerged slowly with a long cylindrical object almost as tall as himself, which he carefully stowed on the table. 'Or so I believe,' he added, as he climbed up after it by means of the repair kit. In his hand was a small length of fretsaw blade.

Arrietty ran excitedly across the room and swiftly climbed up to join him. The long object turned out to be a topless fountain-pen, with an ink-encrusted nib, one prong of which was broken. Pod had already unscrewed the pen and taken it apart, and the nib end now lay on the table attached to its worm-like rubber tube, with the empty shaft beside it.

'I cut the shaft off here,' said Pod, 'about an inch and a half from the top, just above the filling lever; then I'll cut off the closed end of this inner tube – but right at the end, like – so it sticks out a good inch and a half beyond the cut-off end of the pen casing. May be more. Now' – he went on, speaking cheerfully but rather ponderously, as though giving a lesson (a 'do-it-yourself' lesson, thought Arrietty, remembering the Household Hints section in her Diary and Proverb Book) – 'we screw the whole thing together again and what do we get? We get a capless fountain-pen with the top of its shaft cut off and an extra bit of tube. Do you follow me?'

'So far,' said Arrietty.

'Then,' said Pod, 'we unscrew the nib . . .'

'Can you?' asked Arrietty.

'Of course,' said Pod; 'they're always changing nibs. I'll show you.' He took up the pen and, straddling the shaft, he gripped it firmly between his legs, and taking the nib in both hands, he quickly unscrewed it at chest level.

'Now,' he said as he laid the nib aside, 'we have a circular hole where that nib was – leading straight into the rubber tube. Take a look . . .'

Arrietty peered down the shaft. 'Yes,' she said.

'Well, there you are,' said Pod.

But where? Arrietty wanted to say; instead she said, more politely: 'I don't think I quite . . .'

'Well,' said Pod in a patient voice as though slightly dashed by her slowness, 'we insert the nib end into the neck of the balloon – after inflation of course, and just below the guard knot. We whip it around with a good firm lashing of twine. I take hold of the filling lever and pull it down sideways at right angles to the pen shaft. That's the working position, with the gas safely shut off. We then untie the guard knot. And there we are: with the cut-off pen shaft and rubber tube hanging down into the basket.' He paused. 'Are you with me? Never mind,' he went on confidently, 'you'll see it as I do it. Now' – he drew a long satisfied breath – 'standing in the basket, I reach up my hand to the filling lever and I close it down slowly towards the shaft and the gas flows out through the tube. Feel,' he went on happily, 'the lever's quite loose,' and with one foot on the pen to steady it, he worked the filling lever gently up and down. Arrietty tried it, too. Worn with use, it slid easily.

'Then,' said Pod, 'I raise the lever back up so it stands out again at right angles – and the gas is now shut off.'

'It's wonderful,' said Arrietty, but suddenly she thought of something. 'What about all that gas coming down straight into the basket?'

'We leave it behind!' cried Pod. 'Don't you see, girl – the gas is rising all the time and rising faster than the balloon's descending? I thought of that: that's why I wanted that bit of extra tube; we can turn the tube-end upwards, sideways – where we like; but whichever way we turn it the gas'll be rushing upwards and we'll be dropping away from it. See what I mean? Come to think of it, we could bend the tube upwards to start with and clip it to the shaft of the pen. No reason why not.'

He was silent a moment, thinking this over.

'And there won't be all that much gas – not once I've sorted out the lever. You only let it out by degrees . . .'

During the next few days, which were very exciting, Arrietty often thought of Spiller – how deft he would have been at adjusting the net as the envelope filled at the gas-jet. This was Homily's and Arrietty's job – tiresome pullings by hand or with bone crochet hook, while Pod controlled the intake of gas; the netted canopy would slowly swell above them until the letter 'I' in RIVERSIDE TEAS had achieved its right proportion. The 'equator' of the net, as Pod told them, must bisect the envelope exactly for the load-ring to hang straight and keep the basket level.

Arrietty wished Spiller could have seen the first attachment of the basket by raffia bridles to the load-ring. This took place on the platform of the musical-box, with the basket at this stage weighted down with keys.

And on that first free flight up to the ceiling when Pod, all his attention on the fountain-pen lever, had brought them down so gently, Spiller – Arrietty knew – would have prevented Homily from making the fatal mistake of jumping out of the basket as soon as it touched the floor. At terrifying speed, Pod and Arrietty had shot aloft again, hitting the ceiling with a force which nearly threw them out of the basket, while Homily – in tears – wrung her hands below them. It took a long time to descend, even with the valve wide open, and Pod was very shaken.

'You must remember, Homily,' he told her gravely when, anchored once more to the musical-box, the balloon was slowly deflating, 'you weigh as much as a couple of Gladstone-bag keys and a roll and a half of tickets. No passenger must ever attempt to leave the car or basket until the envelope is completely collapsed.' He looked very serious. 'We were lucky to have a ceiling. Suppose we'd been out of doors – do you know what would have happened?'

'No,' whispered Homily huskily, drying her cheeks with the back of her trembling hand and giving a final sniff.

'Arrietty and me would've shot up to twenty thousand feet and that would have been the end of us . . .'

'Oh dear . . .' muttered Homily.

'At that great height,' said Pod, 'the gas would expand so quickly that it would burst the canopy.' He stared at her accusingly. 'Unless, of course, we'd had the presence of mind to open the valve and keep it open on the whole rush up. Even then, when we did begin to descend, we'd descend too quickly. We'd have to throw everything overboard – ballast, equipment, clothes, food, perhaps even one of the passengers—'

'Oh no!' gasped Homily.

'And in spite of all this,' Pod concluded, 'we'd probably crash just the same!'

Homily remained silent, and after watching her face for a moment, Pod said more gently:

'This isn't a joy-ride, Homily.'

'I know that,' she retorted with feeling.

Chapter Twenty-One

But it did seem a joy-ride to Arrietty when – on 28th March, having opened the window for the last time and left it open, they drifted slowly out into the pale spring sunshine.

The moment of actual departure had come with a shock of surprise, depending as it did on wind and weather. The night before they had gone to bed as usual, and this morning, before Mabel and Sidney had brought their breakfast, Pod, studying the ilex branch, had announced that this was The Day.

It had seemed quite unreal to Arrietty and it still seemed unreal to her now. Their passage was so dream-like and silent . . . At one moment they were in the room, which seemed now almost to smell of their captivity, and the next moment – free as thistledown – they sailed softly into a vast ocean of landscape, undulating into distance and brushed with the green veil of spring.

There was a smell of sweet damp earth and for a moment the smell of something frying in Mrs Platter's kitchen. There were myriad tiny sounds – a bicycle bell, the sound of a horse's hoofs and a man's voice growling 'Giddup . . .' Then suddenly they heard Mrs Platter calling to Mr Platter from a window: 'Put on your coat, dear, if you're going to stay out long . . .' And, looking down at the gravel path below them, they saw Mr Platter, tool-bag in hand, on his way to the island. He looked a strange shape from above – head down between his shoulders and feet twinkling in and out as he hurried towards his objective.

'He's going to work on the cage-house,' said Homily.

They saw with a kind of distant curiosity the whole layout of Mr Platter's model village, and the river twisting away beyond it to the three distant poplars which marked what Pod now referred to as their L.Z.[1]

During the last few days he had taken to using abbreviations of ballooning terms, referring to the musical-box as the T.O.P.[2] They were now, with the gleaming slates of roof just below them, feeling their way towards a convenient C.A.[3]

Strangely enough, after their many trial trips up and down from the ceiling, the basket felt quite home-like and familiar. Arrietty, whose job was 'ballast', glanced at her father, who stood looking rapt and interested – but not too preoccupied – with his hand on the lever of the cut-off fountain-pen. Homily, although a little pale, was matter-of-factly adjusting the coiled line of the grapnel, one spike of which had slid below the level of the basket. 'Might just catch in something,' she murmured. The grapnel consisted of two large open safety-pins, securely wired back to back. Pod, who for days had been studying the trend of the ilex leaves, remarked: 'Wind's all right but not enough of it . . .' as very gently, as though waltzing, they twisted above the roof. Pod, looking ahead, had his eye on the ilex.

'A couple of tickets now, Arrietty,' he said; 'takes a few minutes to feel the effect . . .'

She tore them off and dropped them overboard. They fluttered gently and ran a little on the slates on the roof and then lay still.

'Let's give her two more,' said Pod. And within a few seconds, staring at the ilex-tree as slowly it loomed nearer, he added: 'Better make it three . . .'

---

[1] Landing Zone.   [2] Take off Point.   [3] Chosen Altitude.

'We've had six shillings' worth already,' Arrietty protested.

'All right,' said Pod, as the balloon began to lift, 'let's leave it at that.'

'But I've done it now,' she said.

They sailed over the ilex-tree with plenty of height to spare and the balloon still went on rising. Homily gazed down as the ground receded.

'Careful, Pod,' she said.

'It's all right,' he told them, 'I'm bringing her down.' And in spite of the upturned tube they smelled a slight smell of gas.

Even from this height the noises were quite distinct. They heard Mr Platter hammering at the cage-house and, although the railway looked so distant, the sound of a shunting train. As they swept down rather faster than Pod had bargained for, they found themselves carried beyond the confines of Mr Platter's garden and drifting – on a descending spiral – above the main road. A farm cart crawled slowly beneath them on the broad sunlit stretch which, curving ribbon-like into the distance, looked frayed along one side by the shadows thrown from the hedges and from the spindly wayside woods. There was a woman on the shafts of the farm cart and a man asleep in the back.

'We're heading away from our L.Z.' said Pod. 'Better give her three more tickets – there's less wind down here than above . . .'

As the balloon began to lift they passed over one of Mr Platter's lately built villas in which someone was practising the piano – a stream of metallic notes flowed up and about them. And a dog began to bark.

They began to rise quite swiftly – on the three legitimate tickets – and an extra one-and-sixpennyworth thrown down by Arrietty. She did it on an impulse and knew at once that it was wrong. Their very lives depended on obedience to the pilot, and how could the pilot navigate if she cheated on commands? She felt very guilty as the balloon continued to rise. They were passing over a field of cows which, second by second, as she stared down at them, were becoming steadily smaller; all the same, a tremulous 'Moo' surged up to them through the quiet air and eddied about their ears. She could hear a lark singing – and over a spreading cherry orchard she smelled the sticky scent of sun-warmed buds and blossoms. 'It's more like mid April', Arrietty thought, 'than the 28th of March.'

'Spiller would have liked this,' she said aloud.

'Maybe,' said Homily rather grimly.

'When I grow up I think I'll marry Spiller . . .'

'Spiller!' exclaimed Homily in an astounded voice.

'What's wrong with him?' asked Arrietty.

'There's nothing exactly wrong with him,' admitted Homily grudgingly. 'I mean if you tidied him up a bit . . . But where do you imagine you'd live? He's always on the move.'

'I'd be on the move too,' said Arrietty.

Homily stared at her. 'Whatever will you think of to say next? And what a place to choose to say it in. Marry Spiller! Did you hear that, Pod?'

'Yes, I heard,' he said.

The balloon was still rising.

'He likes the out-of-doors, you see,' said Arrietty, 'and I like it, too.'

'Marry *Spiller* . . .' Homily repeated to herself – she could not get over it.

'And if we were always on the move, we'd be freer to come and see you more often . . .'

'So it's got to "we"!' said Homily.

'. . . and I couldn't do that', Arrietty went on, 'if I married into a family with a set house the other side of Bedfordshire—'

'But you're only sixteen!' exclaimed Homily.

'Seventeen – nearly,' said Arrietty. She was silent a moment and then she said, 'I think I ought to tell him—'

'Pod!' exclaimed Homily, 'do you hear? It must be the height or something, but this child's gone out of her senses!'

'I'm trying to find the wind,' said Pod, staring steadily upwards to where a slight film of mist appeared to drift towards the sun.

'You see,' Arrietty went on quietly (she had been thinking of her talks with Miss Menzies and of those blue eyes full of tears), 'he's so shy and he goes about so much, he might never think of asking me. And one day he might get tired of being lonely and marry some' – Arrietty hesitated – 'some *terribly nice* kind of borrower with very fat legs . . .'

'There isn't such a thing as a borrower with fat legs,' exclaimed Homily, 'except perhaps your Aunt Lupy. Not that I've actually ever seen her legs . . .' she added thoughtfully, gazing upwards as though following the direction of Pod's eyes. Then she snapped back again to the subject. 'What nonsense you do talk, Arrietty,' she said, 'I can't imagine what sort of rubbish you must have been reading in that *Illustrated London News*. Why, you and Spiller are more like brother and sister!'

Arrietty was just about going to say – but she couldn't quite find the words – that this seemed quite a good kind of trial run for what was after all a lifelong companionship, when something came between them and the sun and a sudden chill struck the basket. The top of the envelope had melted into mist and the earth below them disappeared from sight.

They stared at each other. Nothing else existed now except the familiar juice-stained basket, hung in a limbo of whiteness, and their three rather frightened selves.

'It's all right,' said Pod, 'we're in a cloud. I'll let out a little gas . . .'

They were silent while he did so, staring intently at his steady hand on the lever – it hardly seemed to move.

'Not too much,' he explained in a quiet conversational voice. 'The condensation on the net will help us : there's a lot of weight in water. And I think we've found the wind !'

Chapter Twenty-Two

They were in sunshine again quite suddenly and cruising smoothly and softly on a gentle breeze towards their still distant L.Z.

'Shouldn't wonder,' remarked Pod cheerfully, 'if we hadn't hit on our right C.A. at last.'

Homily shivered. 'I didn't like that at all.'

'Nor did I,' agreed Arrietty. There was no sense of wind in the basket and she turned up her face to the sun, basking gratefully in the suddenly restored warmth.

They passed over a group of cottages set about a small, squat church. Three people with baskets were grouped about a shop, and they heard a sudden peal of very hearty laughter. In a back garden they saw a woman with her

back to them, hanging washing on a line; it hung quite limply.

'Not much wind down there,' remarked Pod.

'Not all that much up here,' retorted Homily.

They stared down in silence for a while.

'I wonder why no one ever looks up,' Arrietty exclaimed suddenly.

'Human beings don't look up much,' said Pod. 'Too full of their own concerns.' He thought a moment. 'Unless, maybe, they hear a sudden loud noise . . or see a flash or something. They don't have to keep their eyes open like borrowers do.'

'Or birds,' said Arrietty, 'or mice . . .'

'Or anything that's hunted,' said Pod.

'Isn't there anything that hunts human beings?' Arrietty asked.

'Not that I know of,' said Pod. 'Might do 'em a bit of good if there were. Show 'em what it feels like, for once.' He was silent a moment and then said: 'Some say they hunt each other—'

'Oh no!' exclaimed Homily, shocked. (Strictly brought up in the borrowers' code of one-for-all and all-for-one, it was as though he had accused the human race of cannibalism.) 'You shouldn't say such things, Pod – no kind of creature could be as bad as that!'

'I've heard it said!' he persisted stolidly. 'Sometimes singly and sometimes one lot against another lot!'

'All of them human beings?' Homily exclaimed incredulously.

Pod nodded. 'Yes,' he said, 'all of them human beings.'

Horrified but fascinated, Homily stared down below at a man on a bicycle, as though unable to grasp such depravity. He looked quite ordinary – almost like a borrower from here – and wobbled slightly on the lower slopes of what appeared to be a hill. She stared incredulously until the rider turned into the lower gate of the churchyard.

There was a sudden smell of Irish stew, followed by a whiff of coffee.

'Must be getting on for midday,' said Pod, and as he spoke the church clock struck twelve.

'I don't like these eddies,' said Pod some time later, as the balloon once again on a downward spiral curved away from the river; 'something to do with the ground warming up and that bit of hill over there.'

'Would anybody like something to eat?' suggested Homily suddenly. There were slivers of ham, a crumbly knob of cheese, a few grains of cold rice pudding and a long segment of orange on which to quench their thirst.

'Better wait awhile,' said Pod, his hand on the valve. The balloon was moving downwards.

'I don't see why,' said Homily; 'it must be long past one.'

'I know,' said Pod, 'but it's better we hold off, if we can. We may have to jettison the rations, and you can't do that once you've eaten them.'

'I don't know what you mean,' complained Homily.

'Throw the food overboard,' explained Arrietty, who, on Pod's orders, had torn off several more tickets.

'You see,' said Pod, 'what with one thing and another, I've let out a good deal of gas.'

Homily was silent. After a while she said: 'I don't like the way we keep turning round; first the church is on our right, the next it's run round to the left. I mean, you don't know where you are, not for two minutes together.'

'It'll be all right,' said Pod, 'once we've hit the wind. Let go another two,' he added to Arrietty.

It was just enough; they rose gently and, held on a steady current, moved slowly towards the stream.

'Now,' said Pod, 'if we keep on this, we're all right.' He stared ahead to where, speckled by the sunshine, the poplar-trees loomed nearer. 'We're going nicely now.'

'You mean we might hit Little Fordham?'

'Not unlikely,' said Pod.

'If you ask me,' exclaimed Homily, screwing up her eyes against the afternoon sun, 'the whole thing's hit or miss!'

'Not altogether,' said Pod, and he let out a little more gas. 'We bring her down slowly, gradually losing altitude. Once we're in reach of the ground we steady her with the trail rope. Acts like a kind of brake. And directly I give her the word, Arrietty releases the grapnel.'

Homily was silent again. Impressed, but still rather anxious, she stared steadily ahead. The river swam gently towards them until and at last it came directly below. The light wind seemed to follow the river's course as it curved ahead into distance. The poplars now seemed to beckon as they swayed and stirred in the breeze, and their long shadows – even longer by now – were stretching directly towards them. They sailed as though drawn on a string.

Pod let out more gas. 'Better uncoil the trail rope,' he said to Arrietty.

'Already?'

'Yes,' said Pod, 'you got to be prepared . . .'

The ground swayed slowly up towards them. A clump of oak-trees seemed to move aside and they saw just ahead and slightly tilted a bird's-eye view of their long lost Little Fordham.

'You wouldn't credit it!' breathed Homily as, enraptured, they stared ahead.

They could see the railway lines glinting in the sunshine, the weathercock flashing on the church steeple, the uneven roofs along the narrow High Street and the crooked chimney of their own dear home. They saw the garden front of Mr Pott's thatched cottage, and beyond the dark green of the holly hedge a stretch of sunlit lane. A tweed-clad figure strode along it, in a loose-limbed, youthful way. They knew it was Miss Menzies – going home to tea. And Mr Pott, thought Arrietty, would have gone inside for his.

The balloon was sinking fast.

'Careful, Pod!' urged Homily, 'or you'll have us in the river!'

As swiftly the balloon sank down, a veil-like something suddenly appeared along the edge of the garden. As they swam down they saw it to be a line of strong wire fencing girding the bank of the river. Mr Pott had taken precautions and his treasures were now caged in.

'Time, too!' said Homily grimly. Then suddenly she shrieked and clung to the sides of the basket as the stream rushed up towards them.

'Get ready the grapnel!' shouted Pod. But even as he spoke the basket had hit the water and, tilted sideways in a flurry of spray, they were dragged along the surface. All three were thrown off balance and, knee-deep in rushing water, they clung to raffia bridles while the envelope surged on ahead. Pod just managed to close the valve as Arrietty, clinging on with one hand, tried with the other to free the grapnel. But Homily, in a panic and before anyone could stop her, threw out the knob of cheese. The balloon shot violently upwards, accompanied by Homily's screams, and then – just as violently – snapped back to a sickening halt. The roll of tickets shot up between them and sailed down into the water. Except for their grasp on the bridles the occupants would have followed; they were thrown up into the air, where they hung for a moment before tumbling back into the basket: a safety-pin of the grapnel had caught in the wire of the fence. The trembling, creakings, twistings and strainings seemed enough to uproot the fence, and Pod, looking downwards as he clung to the reopened valve lever, saw the barb of the safety-pin slide.

'That won't hold for long,' he gasped.

The quivering basket was held at a terrifying tilt – almost pulled apart, it seemed, between the force of the upward surge and the drag of the grapnel below. The gas was escaping too slowly – it was clearly a race against time.

There was a steady stream of water from the dripping basket. Their three backs were braced against the tilted floor and their feet against one side. As, white-faced, they

all stared downwards they could hear each other's breathing. The angle of the opened pin was slowly growing wider.

Pod took a sudden resolve. 'Get hold of the trail rope,' he said to Arrietty, 'and pass it over to me. I'm going down the grapnel-line and taking the trail rope with me.'

'Oh, Pod!' cried Homily miserably, 'suppose we shot up without you!'

He took no notice. 'Quick!' he urged. And, as Arrietty pulled up the length of dripping twine, he took one end in his hand and swung over the edge of the basket on to the line of the grapnel. He slid away below them in one swift downward run, his elbow encircling the trail rope. They watched him steady himself on the top of the fence and climb down a couple of meshes. They watched his swift one-handed movements as he passed the trail rope through the mesh and made fast with a double turn.

Then his small square face turned up towards them.

'Get a hold on the bridles,' he called, 'there's going to be a bit of a jerk . . .' He shifted himself a few meshes sideways, from where he could watch the pin.

It slid free with a metallic ping, even sooner than they had expected, and was flung out in a quivering arch which, whiplike, thrashed the air. The balloon shot up in a frenzied leap but was held by the knotted twine. It seemed frustrated as it strained above them, as though striving to tear itself free. Arrietty and Homily clung together, half laughing and half crying, in a wild access of relief. He had moored them just in time.

'You'll be all right now,' Pod called up cheerfully; 'nothing to do but wait,' and after staring a moment reflectively, he began to climb down the fence.

'Where are you going, Pod?' Homily cried out shrilly.

He paused and looked up again. 'Thought I'd take a

look at the house – our chimney's smoking, seems like there's someone inside.'

'But what about us?' cried Homily.

'You'll come down slowly, as the envelope deflates, and then you can climb down the fence. I'll be back,' he added.

'Of all the things,' exclaimed Homily, 'to go away and leave us!'

'What do you want me to do?' asked Pod. 'Just stand down below and watch? I won't be long and – say it's Spiller – he's likely to give us a hand. You're all right,' he went on. 'Take a pull on the trail rope as the balloon comes down, that'll bring you alongside.'

'Of all the things!' exclaimed Homily again incredulously, as Pod went on climbing down.

Chapter Twenty-Three

The door of Vine Cottage was unlocked and Pod pushed it open. A fire was burning in an unfamiliar grate and Spiller lay asleep on the floor. As Pod entered he scrambled to his feet. They stared at each other. Spiller's pointed face looked tired and his eyes a little sunken.

Pod smiled slowly. 'Hallo,' he said.

'Hallo', said Spiller, and without any change of expression he stooped and picked some nutshells from the floor and threw them on to the fire. It was a new floor, Pod noticed, of honey-coloured wood, with a woven mat beside the fireplace.

'Been away quite a while,' remarked Spiller casually, staring at the blaze. The changed fireplace, Pod noticed, now incorporated a small iron cooking-stove.

'Yes,' he said, looking about the room, 'we've been all winter in an attic.'

Spiller nodded.

'*You* know,' said Pod, 'a room at the top of a human house.'

Spiller nodded again and kicked a piece of fallen nutshell back into the grate. It flared up brightly with a cheerful crackle.

'We couldn't get out,' said Pod.

'Ah,' said Spiller non-committally.

'So we made a balloon,' went on Pod, 'and we sailed it out of the window.' Spiller looked up sharply, suddenly alert. 'Arrietty and Homily are in it now. It's caught on the wire fence.'

Spiller's puzzled glance darted towards the window and as swiftly darted away again: the fence was not visible from here.

'Some kind of boat?' he said at last.

'In a manner of speaking,' Pod smiled. 'Care to see it?' he added carelessly.

Something flashed in Spiller's face — a spark which was swiftly quenched. 'Might as well,' he conceded.

'May interest you,' said Pod, a note of pride in his voice. He glanced once more about the room.

'They've done the house up,' he remarked.

Spiller nodded. 'Running water and all . . .'

'Running water!' exclaimed Pod.

'That's right,' said Spiller, edging towards the door.

Pod stared at the piping above the sink but he made no move to inspect it. Tables and floor were strewn with Spiller's borrowings: sparrows' eggs and eggshells, nuts, grain and, laid out on a dandelion leaf, six rather shrivelled smoked minnows.

'Been staying here?' he said.

'On and off,' said Spiller, teetering on the threshold.

Again Pod's eyes travelled about the room: the general style of it emerged, in spite of Spiller's clutter – plain chairs, scrubbable tables, wooden dresser, painted plates, hand-woven rugs, all very Rossetti-ish and practical.

'Smells of humans,' he remarked.

'Does a bit,' agreed Spiller.

'We might just tidy round,' Pod suggested, 'wouldn't take us a minute.' As though in apology, he added: 'It's first impressions with her, if you get my meaning. Always has been. And—' he broke off abruptly as a sharp sound split the silence.

'What's that?' said Spiller, as eye met startled eye.

'It's the balloon,' cried Pod, and, suddenly white-faced, he stared in a stunned way at the window. 'They've burst it,' he exclaimed and, pushing past Spiller, he dashed out through the door.

Homily and Arrietty, shaken but unharmed, were clinging to the wires. The basket dangled emptily and the envelope, in tatters, seemed threaded into the fence; the net now looked like a bird's nest.

'We got it down lovely,' Pod heard Homily gasping, as hand over hand, he and Spiller climbed up the mesh of the fence.

'Stay where you are,' Pod called out.

'Came down like a dream, Pod,' Homily kept on crying. 'Came down like a bird . . .'

'All right,' called Pod, 'just you stay quiet where you are.'

'Then the wind changed', persisted Homily, half sobbing but still at the top of her voice, 'and swung us round sideways . . . against that jagged wire . . . But she came down lovely, Pod, light as thistledown. Didn't she, Arrietty?'

But Arrietty, too proud to be rescued, was well on her way to the ground. Spiller climbed swiftly towards her and they met in a circle of mesh. 'You're on the wrong side,' said Spiller.

'I know, I can soon climb through.' There were tears in her eyes, her cheeks were crimson and her hair blew about in wisps.

'Like a hand?' said Spiller.

'No, thank you. I'm quite all right,' and avoiding his curious gaze, she hurriedly went on down. 'How stupid, how stupid,' she exclaimed aloud when she felt herself out of earshot. She was almost in tears: it should never have been like this: he would never understand the balloon without having seen it inflated, and mere words could never make clear all they had gone through to make it and the extent of their dizzy success. There was nothing to show for this now but a stained old strawberry basket, some shreds of shrivelled rubber and a tangled bunch of string. A few moments earlier she and her mother had been bringing it down so beautifully. After the first flurry of panic Homily had had one of her sudden calms. Perhaps it was the realization of being home again; the sight of their unchanged village at peace in the afternoon light; and the filament of smoke which rose up unexpectedly from the chimney of Vine Cottage, a drifting pennant of welcome which showed the house was inhabited and that the fire had only just been lit. Not lit by Miss Menzies, who had long since passed out of sight; nor Pod, who had not yet reached the house, so they guessed it must be Spiller. They had suddenly felt among friends again and, proud of their great achievement, they had longed to show off their prowess. In a business-like manner they had coiled up the ropes, stacked the tackle and made the basket shipshape. They had wrung out their wet clothes and Homily had redone her hair. Then, methodically and calmly, they had set to work, following Pod's instructions.

'It's too bad,' Arrietty exclaimed, looking upwards, as she reached the last rung of the wire: there was her father helping Homily with footholds, and Spiller of course at the top of the fence busily engaged in examining the wreckage. Very dispirited, she stepped off the wire, drew down a plantain leaf by it's tip, and flinging herself along it's springy length she lay there glumly, staring upwards, her hands behind her head.

Homily too seemed very upset when, steered by Pod, she eventually reached the ground. 'It was nothing we did,' she kept saying, 'it was just a change of wind.'

'I know, I know,' he consoled her; 'forget it now – it served it's purpose and there's a surprise for you up at the house. You and Arrietty go on ahead while Spiller and I do the salvage . . .'

When Homily saw the house she became a different creature: it was as though, thought Arrietty, watching her mother's expression, Homily had walked into paradise. There were a few stunned moments of quiet incredulous joy before excitement broke loose and she ran like a mad thing from room to room, exploring, touching, adjusting and endlessly exclaiming. 'They've divided the upstairs into two, there's a little room for you, Arrietty. Look at this sink, I ask you, Arrietty! Water in the tap and all! And what's that thing on the ceiling?'

'It's a bulb from a hand torch of some kind,' said Arrietty, after a moment's study. And beside the backdoor, in a kind of lean-to shed, they found the great square battery.

'So we've got electric light . . .' breathed Homily, slowly backing away, 'better not touch it', she went on, in an awestruck and frightened voice, 'until your father comes. Now help me clear up Spiller's clobber,' she continued excitedly; 'I pity any unfortunate creature who ever keeps house for *him* . . .' But her eyes were alight and shining. She hung up her new dress beside the fire to dry and, delighted to find them again, she changed into old clothes. Arrietty, who for some reason still felt dispirited, found she had grown out of hers.

'I look ridiculous in this,' she said unhappily, trying to pull down her jersey.

'Well, who's to see you,' Homily retorted, 'except your father and Spiller?'

Panting and straining, she worked away, clearing and stacking and altering the positions of the furniture. Soon nothing was where it had been originally and the room looked rather odd.

'You can't do *much* with a kitchen-living-room,' Homily remarked when, panting a little, she surveyed the general post, 'and I'm still not sure about that dresser.'

'What about it?' said Arrietty, who was longing to sit down.

'That it wouldn't be better where it was.'

'Can't we leave the men to do it?' said Arrietty. 'They'll be back soon – for supper.'

'That's just the point,' said Homily, 'If we move it at all we must do it now, before I start on the cooking. It looks dreadful there,' she went on crossly. 'Spoils the whole look of the room. Now come on, Arrietty – it won't take us a minute.'

With the dresser back in its old position the other things looked out of place. 'Now that table could go here,' Homily suggested, 'if we move this chest of drawers. You take one end, Arrietty . . .'

There were several more reshuffles before she seemed content. 'A lot of trouble,' she admitted happily, as she surveyed the final result, 'but worth it in the end. It looks a lot better now, doesn't it, Arrietty? It suddenly looks kind of *right*.'

'Yes,' said Arrietty dryly, 'because everything's back where it was.'

'What do you mean?' exclaimed Homily.

'Where it was before we started,' said Arrietty.

'Nonsense,' snapped Homily crossly, but she looked about her uncertainly. 'Why – that stool was under the window! But we can't waste time arguing now: those men will be back any moment and I haven't started the soup. Run down to the stream now, there's a good girl, and get me a few leaves of watercress . . .'

Chapter Twenty-Four

Later that night when – having eaten and cleared away – the four of them sat round the fire, Arrietty began to feel a little annoyed with Spiller. Balloon crazy – that's what he seemed to have become; and all within a few short hours. No eyes, no ears, nor thoughts for anyone or anything except for those boring shreds of shrivelled rubber, now safely stored with the other trappings in the back of the village shop. He had listened, of course, at supper when Arrietty, hoping to interest him, had tried to recount their adventures, but if she paused even for a moment the bright dark glance would fly again to Pod and again, in his tense, dry way he would ply Pod with questions: 'Oiled silk instead of rubber next time for the canopy? The silk would be easy to borrow – and Mr Pott would have the oil . . .' Questions on wind velocity, trail ropes, moorings, grapnels, inflation – there seemed no end to these nor to his curiosity which, for some masculine reason Arrietty could not fathom, could only be satisfied by Pod. Any timid contribution on the part of Arrietty seemed to slide across his mind unheard. 'And I know as much about it as anybody,' she told herself crossly, as she huddled in the shadows. 'More in fact. It was I who had to teach Papa.' She stared in a bored way about the firelit room: the drawn curtains, plates glinting on the dresser, the general air of peace and comfort. Even this, in a way, they owed entirely to her: it was she who had had the courage to speak to Miss Menzies – and, in the course of this friendship, describe their habits and needs. How cosy they all looked in their ignorance, sitting smugly around the fire. Leaning forward suddenly, right into the fire-light, she said: 'Papa, would you listen, please?'

'Don't see why not,' replied Pod, smiling slightly at the eager, firelit face and the breathless tone of her voice.

'It's something I've got to tell you. I couldn't once. But I can now . . .' As she spoke her heart began to beat a little faster: even Spiller, she saw, was paying attention. 'It's about this house; it's about why they made these things for us; it's about how they knew what we wanted . . .'

'What *we* wanted . . . ?' repeated Pod.

'Yes, or why do you think they did it?'

Pod took his time. 'I wouldn't know for *why* they did it', he said at last, 'any more than I'd know for *why* they built that church or the railway. Reckon they're furnish-ing all these houses . . . one by one, like.'

'No,' exclaimed Arrietty, and her voice trembled slightly, 'you're wrong, Papa. They've only furnished one house and that's our house – because they know all about us and they like us and they want us to stay here!'

There was a short, stunned silence. Then Homily muttered: 'Oh, my goodness . . .' under her breath.

Spiller, still as stone, stared unblinkingly, and Pod said

slowly: 'Explain what you mean, Arrietty. How do they know about us?'

'I told her,' said Arrietty.

'Her-r?' repeated Pod slowly, rolling his r-rs in the country way, his custom when deeply moved.

'Miss Menzies,' said Arrietty; 'the tall one with the long hands, who hid behind the thistle.'

'Oh, my goodness . . .' muttered Homily again.

'It's all right, Mother,' Arrietty assured her earnestly. 'There's nothing to be frightened of. You'll be safe here, safer than you've ever been – in the whole of all your life. They'll look after us, and protect us and take care of us – for ever and ever and ever. She promised me.'

Homily, though trembling, looked slightly reassured.

'What does your father think?' she asked faintly, and stared across at Pod. Arrietty too wheeled round towards him. 'Don't say anything, Papa, not yet, please . . . please! Not until I've told you everything, then' – at the sight of his expression she lost her nerve, and finished lamely – 'then you're practically sure to see.'

'See what?' said Pod.

'That it's quite all right.'

'Go on, then,' he said.

Hurriedly, almost pleadingly, Arrietty gave them the facts. She described her friendship with Miss Menzies right from the very beginning. She described Miss Menzies's character, her loyalty, her charity, her gifts, her imagination and her courage. She even told them about dear Gadstone and about Aubrey, Miss Menzies's 'best friend' (Homily shook her head there, and clicked her tongue. 'Sad when that happens,' she said musingly. 'It was like that with my younger sister, Milligram; Milli never married neither. She took to collecting dead flies' wings, making them into fans and suchlike. And pretty they looked, in certain lights, all colours of the rainbow . . .'), and went on to describe all she had learned from Miss Menzies concerning Mr Pott: how kind he was, and how gentle, and so skilled in making-do and invention that he might be a borrower himself.

'That's right,' Spiller said suddenly at this juncture. He spoke so feelingly that Arrietty, looking across at him, felt something stir in her memory.

'Was *he* the borrower you once told us about – the one you said lived here alone?'

Spiller smiled slyly. 'That's right,' he admitted; 'learn a lot from him, *any* borrower could.'

'Not when everything's laid on', said Pod, 'and there's nothing left to borrow. Go on, Arrietty,' he said, as she suddenly seemed lost in thought.

'Well, that's all. At least all I can think of now.'

'It's enough,' said Pod. He stared across at her, his arms folded, his expression very grave. 'You shouldn't have done it,' he said quietly, 'no matter what it's given us.'

'Listen, Pod,' Homily put in quickly, 'she has done it and she can't undo it now, however much you scold her. I mean' – she glanced about the firelit room, at the winking plates on the dresser, the tap above the sink, the unlit globe in the ceiling – 'we've a lot to be thankful for.'

'It all smells of humans,' said Pod.

'That'll wear off, Pod.'

'Will it?' he said.

Arrietty, suddenly out of patience, jumped up from her stool by the fire, 'I just don't know what any of you do want,' she exclaimed unhappily. 'I thought you might be pleased or proud of me or something. Mother's always longed for a house like this!' and fumbling at the latch, she opened the door, and ran out into the moonlight.

There was silence in the room after she had gone. No one moved until a stool squeaked slightly, as Spiller rose to his feet.

'Where are you off to?' asked Pod casually.

'Just to take a look at my moorings.'

'But you'll come back here to sleep?' said Homily; very hospitable, she felt suddenly, surrounded by new-found amenities.

'Thanks,' said Spiller.

'I'll come with you,' said Pod.

'No need,' said Spiller.

'I'd like the air,' said Pod.

Arrietty, in the shadow of the house, saw them go by in the moonlight. As they passed out of sight, into darkness, she heard her father say: '. . . depends how you look at it.' Look at what, she wondered? Suddenly Arrietty felt left out of things: her father and mother had their house, Spiller had his boat, Miss Menzies had Mr Pott and his village, Mr Pott had Miss Menzies and his railway, but what was left for her? She reached out and took hold of a dandelion stalk the size of a lamp-post which had grown beside the house to the height of her bedroom window. On a sudden impulse she snapped the stalk in half: the silver seeds scattered madly into the moonlight and the juice ran out on her hands. For a moment she stood there watching until the silky spikes, righting themselves, had floated into darkness, and then, suddenly feeling cold, she turned and went inside.

Homily still sat where they had left her, dreaming by the fire. But she had swept the hearth and lighted a dip, which shed its glow from the table. Arrietty, with a sudden pang, saw her mother's deep content.

'Would you like to live here always?' she asked as she drew up a stool to the fire.

'Yes,' said Homily, 'now we've got it comfortable. Why? Wouldn't you?'

'I don't know,' said Arrietty. 'All those people in the summer. All the dust and noise . . .'

'Yes,' said Homily, 'you've got to keep on sweeping. But there's always something,' she added, 'and at least we've got running water.'

'And being cooped up during visiting hours . . .'

'I don't mind that,' said Homily; 'there's plenty to do in the house and I've been cooped up all my life. That's your lot, like, say you're born a borrower.'

Arrietty was silent a moment. 'It would never be Spiller's lot,' she said at last.

'Oh, him!' exclaimed Homily impatiently. 'I've never known nothing about those out-of-door ones. A race apart, my father used to say. Or house-borrowers just gone wild . . .'

'Where have they gone?'

'They're all over the place, I shouldn't wonder, hidden away in the rabbit holes and hedges.'

'I mean my father and Spiller.'

'Oh, them. Down to the stream to see to his moorings. And if I was you, Arrietty,' Homily went on more earnestly, 'I'd get to bed before your father comes in – your bed's all ready, new sheets and everything, *and*' – her voice almost broken with pride – 'under the quilt, there's a little silken eiderdown!'

'They're coming now,' said Arrietty. 'I can hear them.'

'Well, just say good night and run off,' urged Homily anxiously. As the latch clicked she dropped her voice to a whisper: 'I think you've upset him a bit with that talk about Miss – Miss—'

'Menzies,' said Arrietty.

Chapter Twenty-Five

There was a strange aura about Pod when he entered the room with Spiller: it was more than a night-breath of leaves and grasses and a moon-cold tang of water; it was a strength and a stillness, Arrietty thought when she went to kiss him good night, but he seemed very far away. He received her kiss without a word and mechanically pecked at her ear but, as she went off towards the stairs, he suddenly called her back.

'Just a minute, Arrietty. Sit down, Spiller,' he said. He drew up a chair and once more they encircled the fire.

'What's the matter, Pod?' asked Homily. She put out a nervous arm and drew Arrietty closer beside her. 'Is it something you've seen?'

'I haven't seen nothing,' said Pod, 'only moon on the water, a couple of bats and this telltale smoke from our chimney.'

'Then let the child go to bed, it's been a long day.'

'I been thinking,' said Pod.

'It seems more like two days,' Homily went on, 'I mean, now you begin to look back on it.' And suddenly, incredibly, it seemed to her, that on this very morning they had wakened still as prisoners and here they were – home again and united about a hearth! Not the same hearth, a better hearth and a home beyond their dreams. 'You take the dip now,' she said to Arrietty, 'and get yourself into bed. Spiller can sleep down here. Take a drop of water up if you like to have a wash: there's plenty in the tap—'

'It won't do,' said Pod suddenly.

They all turned and looked at him. 'What won't do?' faltered Homily.

Pod waved an arm. 'All this. None of it will do. Not one bit of it. And Spiller agrees with me.'

Arrietty's glance flew across to Spiller: she noticed the closed look, the set gleam and the curt, unsmiling nod.

'What could you be meaning, Pod?' Homily moistened her lips. 'You couldn't be meaning this house?'

'That's just what I do mean,' said Pod.

'But you haven't really seen it, Pod,' Homily protested. 'You've never tried the switch, yet. Nor the tap either. You haven't even seen upstairs. You should see what they've done at the top of the landing, how Arrietty's room opens out of ours, like—'

'Wouldn't make no difference,' said Pod.

'But you liked it here, Pod,' Homily reminded him, 'before that attic lot took us away. You was whistling again and singing as you worked, like you did in the old days at Firbank. Wasn't he, Arrietty?'

'I didn't know then,' said Pod, 'the thing that we all know now – that these humans knew we was here.'

'I see,' said Homily unhappily, and stared into the fire. Arrietty, looking down at her, saw Homily's hunched shoulders and the sudden empty look of her loosely hanging hands.

She turned again to her father. 'These ones are different,' she assured him; 'they're not like Mabel and Sidney: they're tame, you see. I tamed Miss Menzies myself.'

'They're never tamed,' said Pod. 'One day they'll break out – one day, when you least expect it.'

'Not Miss Menzies,' protested Arrietty loyally.

Pod leaned forward. 'They don't mean it,' he explained, 'they just does it. It isn't their fault. In that they're pretty much like the rest of us: none of us means harm – we just does it.'

'You never did no harm, Pod,' protested Homily warmly.

'Not knowingly,' he conceded. He looked across at his daughter. 'Nor did Arrietty mean harm when she spoke to that Miss. But she did harm – she kept us deceived, like: she saw us planning away and not knowing – working away in our ignorance. And it didn't make her happy; now, did it, lass?'

'No,' Arrietty admitted, 'but all the same—'

'All right, all right,' Pod interrupted; he spoke quite quietly and still without reproach. 'I see how it was.' He sighed, and looked down at his hands.

'And she saw us, before we saw her,' Arrietty pointed out.

'I'd seen her,' said Pod.

'But you didn't know that she'd seen you.'

'You could have told me,' said Pod. He spoke so gently that the tears welled up in Arrietty's eyes. 'I'm sorry,' she gasped.

He did not speak for a moment and then he said: 'I'd have planned different, you see.'

'It wasn't Miss Menzies fault that Mabel and Sidney took us.'

'I know that,' said Pod, 'but knowing different, I'd have planned different. We'd have been gone by then, and safely hidden away.'

'Gone? Where to?' exclaimed Homily.

'Plenty of places,' said Pod. 'Spiller knows of a mill – not far from here, is it, Spiller? – with one old human. Never sees a soul except for flour carters. And short-sighted at that. That's more the place for us, Homily.'

Homily was silent: she seemed to be thinking hard. Although her hands were gripped in her lap, her shoulders had straightened again.

'She loves us,' said Arrietty. 'Miss Menzies really loves us, Papa.'

He sighed. 'I don't see for why. But maybe she does. Like they do their pets – their cats and dogs and birds and such. Like your cousin Eggletina had that baby mouse, bringing it up by hand, teaching it tricks and such, and rubbing its coat up with velvet. But it ran away in the end, back to the other mice. And your Uncle Hendreary's second boy once had a cockroach. Fat as butter, it grew, in a cage he made out of a tea-strainer. But your mother never thought it was happy. Never a hungry moment that cockroach had, but that strainer was still a cage.'

'I see what you mean,' said Arrietty uncertainly.

'Spiller sees,' said Pod.

Arrietty glanced across at Spiller: the pointed face was still but the eyes were wild and bright. So wildly bright, they seemed to Arrietty, that she quickly looked away.

'You wouldn't see Spiller in a house like this,' said Pod, 'with everything all done for him and a lady human being watching through the window.'

'She doesn't,' exclaimed Arrietty hotly, 'she wouldn't!'

'As good as,' said Pod. 'And sooner or later the word gets around once humans know where you are – or where you're to be found at certain times of day, like. And there's always one they wants to tell, and that one tells another. And that Mabel and Sidney, finding us gone, where do you think they'll look? Here, of course. And I'll tell you for why: they'll think this lot stole us back.'

'But now we've got the fence,' Arrietty reminded him.

'Yes,' said Pod, 'they've wired us in nice now, like chickens in a hen-run. But what's even worse,' he went on, 'it's only a question of time before one of us gets caught out by a visitor. Day after day, they come in their hundreds, and all eyes, as you might say. No, Homily, it isn't taps and switches that count. Nor dressers and eiderdowns neither. You can pay too high for a bit of soft living, as we found out that time with Lupy. It's making your own way that counts and being easy in your mind, and I wouldn't never be easy here.'

There was silence for a moment. Homily touched the fire with a rusty nail which Spiller had used as a poker, and the slack flared up with a sudden brightness, lighting the walls and ceiling and the ring of thoughtful faces. 'Well, what are we going to do?' Homily asked at last.

'We're going,' said Pod.

'When?' asked Homily.

Pod turned to Spiller. 'Your boat's in ballast, ain't it?' Spiller nodded. 'Well, as soon as we've got it loaded.'

'Where are we going to?' asked Homily, in a tone of blank bewilderment. How many times, she wondered now, had she heard herself ask this question?

'To where we belong,' said Pod.

'Where's that?' asked Homily.

'You know as well as I do,' said Pod, 'some place that's quiet-like and secret, which humans couldn't find.'

'You mean that mill?'

'That's what I reckon,' said Pod. 'And I'm going by Spiller – no human ain't never seen *him*. We got timber, water, sacks, grain, and what food the old man eats. We got outdoors as well as in. And, say Spiller here keeps the boat trim, there's nothing to stop us punting up here of an evening for a quick borrow round, like. Am I right, Spiller?'

Spiller nodded, and again there was silence. 'But you don't mean tonight, Pod?' Homily said at last: she suddenly looked very tired.

He shook his head. 'Nor tomorrow neither. We'll be some days loading, and better we take our time. If we play it careful and put this fire out, they've no call to think we're back. Weather's fair now and getting warmer. No need to rush it. I'll take a look at the site first and plan out the stuff we need . . .' He rose stiffly, and stretched his arms. 'What we need now,' he said, stifling a yawn, 'is bed. And a good twelve hours of it.' Crossing the room, he took a plate from the shelf and slowly, methodically, he scooped up the ashes to cover the glowing slack.

As the room became darker, Homily said suddenly: 'Couldn't we try out the light?'

'The electric?' said Pod.

'Just once,' she pleaded.

'Don't see why not,' he said, and went to the switch by the door. Homily blew out the dips and, as almost explosively the room sprang to brightness, she covered her eyes with her hands. Arrietty, blinking hard, gazed interestedly about her: white and shadowless, the room stared starkly back. 'Oh, I don't like it,' she said.

'No more do I,' said Homily.

'But you see what I mean, Papa,' Arrietty pointed out as though still seeking some acknowledgement, 'we could never have done this by ourselves!'

'And you'll see what *I* mean,' he said quietly, 'when you get to be a little older.'

'What has age got to do with it?' she replied.

Pod's glance flickered across to Spiller and back again to Arrietty. Very thoughtful he looked, as though carefully choosing his words. 'Well, it's like this,' he said, 'if you can try to get my meaning: say, one day, you had a little place of your own. A little family maybe – supposing, like, you'd picked up a good borrower. D'you think you'd go making up to humans? Never,' he said, and shook his head. 'And I'll tell you for why: you wouldn't want to do nothing to put that family in danger. Nor that borrower either. See what I mean?'

'Yes,' said Arrietty. She felt confused: and glad

suddenly that, facing Pod, she stood with her back to Spiller.

'You won't always have us to look after you,' Pod went on, 'and I tell you now there's nothing never been gained by borrowers talking to humans. No matter how they seem, or what they say, or which things they promise you. It's never been worth the risk.'

Arrietty was silent.

'And Spiller agrees with me,' said Pod.

Homily, watching from her corner by the fireside, saw the tears well up in Arrietty's eyes and saw Arrietty swallow. 'That's enough for tonight, Pod,' she said quickly. 'Let's put out the light now and get ourselves to bed.'

'Let her just promise us,' said Pod, 'here under the electric, that she'll never do it again.'

'No need to promise, Pod – she understands. Like she did about the gas. Let's get to bed now.'

'I promise,' said Arrietty suddenly. She spoke quite loudly and clearly, and then she burst into tears.

'Now there's no need for that, Arrietty,' said Pod, going quickly towards her as Homily rose to her feet. 'No need to cry, lass, we was speaking for your own good, like.'

'I know,' gasped Arrietty from between her fingers.

'What's the matter, then? Tell us, Arrietty. Is it about the mill?'

'No, no,' she sobbed, 'I was thinking about Miss Menzies . . .'

'What about her?' said Homily.

'Now I've promised,' gasped Arrietty, 'there'll be no one to tell her. She'll never know we escaped. She'll never know about Mabel and Sidney. She'll never know about the balloon. She'll never know we came back. She'll never know anything. All her life she'll be wondering. And lying awake in the nights . . .'

Above Arrietty's bowed head, Pod and Homily exchanged looks: neither seemed to know what to say.

'I didn't promise,' said Spiller suddenly, in his harshest, most corncrakey voice. They all turned and looked at him, and Arrietty took her hands from her face.

'You,' she exclaimed, staring. Spiller looked back at her, rubbing his ear with his sleeve. 'You mean,' she went on, forgetting, in her amazement, her tear-stained cheeks and her usual shyness of Spiller, 'that *you'd* come back

and tell her? You who've never been seen! You who're so crazy about cover! You who never even speak!'

He nodded curtly, looking straight back at her, his eyes alert and steady. Homily broke the silence. 'He'd do it for *you*, dear,' she said gently. And then, for some reason, she suddenly felt annoyed. 'But I've got to try and like him,' she excused herself irritably. 'I've really got to try.' As she saw the disbelief on Arrietty's face change slowly to joyous surprise, she turned aside to Pod, and said brusquely: 'Put the light out now, for goodness' sake. And let's all get to bed.'

Stories never really end. They can go on and on – and on: it is just that at some point or another (as Mrs May once said to Kate) the teller ceases to tell them. With this last move towards a more hidden life, I come to the end of all I've really learned about borrowers. Without human witnesses there would be guess-work instead of evidence, and as far as I know (though you may have heard differently) no human has seen them again.

The story still goes on but it is your turn now to tell it. Much will continue to happen – things about which your guess will be just as true as mine. Arrietty will marry Spiller of course (we all know that), and they will have a fine adventurous life – far freer than that of her parents. Pod and Homily will be amazed at the distance 'these children' travel by boat and by the house they build among the tree-roots in the river bank – rooms upon rooms, with overhanging terraces; and their own secret well of spring water. Homily will grow anxious if they stay away too long, although messages will come downstream pretty regularly in the form of skeleton leaves, rare grasses, or flower petals of certain colours – each with its own coded meaning. But as the years go by and Pod, growing older, climbs less easily and tires more quickly – she will become fonder and fonder of Spiller, who will care for them both to the end.

What I do know for certain is that Mr and Mrs Platter cut their losses at Ballyhoggin and went to live near Mrs Platter's married daughter in London. Their last known address was 'Arundel', 105B Lower East Sheen Road, Surbiton.

Miss Menzies and Mr Pott stayed quietly where they

were. When Mr Pott grew frailer, Miss Menzies decided to cook for him. As in everything she undertook, she became very good at it. Mr Pott was touched and grateful. As time went by he forgot his small, secret longings for steak-and-kidney pudding and grew to like her Bœuf à la Bourgignonne.

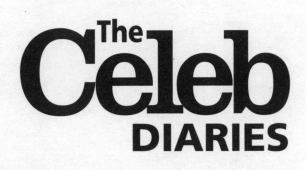

The Celeb DIARIES

THE SENSATIONAL INSIDE STORY OF THE CELEBRITY DECADE

MARK FRITH

EBURY
PRESS

1 3 5 7 9 10 8 6 4 2

Published in 2008 by Ebury Press, an imprint of Ebury Publishing
A Random House Group Company

The Random House Group Limited Reg. No. 954009

Addresses for companies within the Random House Group
can be found at www.randomhouse.co.uk

A CIP catalogue record for this book
is available from the British Library

The Random House Group Limited supports The Forest Stewardship
Council (FSC), the leading international forest certification
organisation. All our titles that are printed on Greenpeace approved
FSC certified paper carry the FSC logo. Our paper procurement
policy can be found at www.rbooks.co.uk/environment

Mixed Sources
Product group from well-managed
forests and other controlled sources
www.fsc.org Cert no. TT-COC-2139
© 1996 Forest Stewardship Council

FSC

Designed and set by seagulls.net

Printed and bound in Great Britain by Clays Ltd, St Ives PLC

HB ISBN 9780091927981
EXPORT ONLY TPB ISBN 9780091928285

To buy books by your favourite authors and register for offers visit
www.rbooks.co.uk

To Victoria Beckham, who saved *Heat* magazine.

And probably now really regrets it.

Contents

Introduction

Celebrities. I've been writing about them for eight years solid and I still don't understand them. I often would have meetings with the *Heat* team that would end with me shaking my head and saying the words, 'They're all MAD! The lot of them!' There is no group of people on God's earth more infuriating, ego-driven, contradictory, pampered, spoilt and downright ridiculous than celebrities. And for eight years I was caught up in their madness.

When I was a kid, magazines – and the people in them – were the centre of my life. I'd buy four or five a week, subsidised (although only just) by the worst-paid paper round in Sheffield (£2.50 a week for five morning shifts. I'm not joking!) There's just something about magazines. They were everything to me. My favourite was *Smash Hits* and I cherished every single page: pored over each one, consumed every word, examined every picture before turning the page and getting upset cos that meant I was two pages nearer the end. I loved that they were produced by people who were passionate about their subject. I loved how the journalists who wrote for them crafted each sentence with skill and humour. On my paper round I'd dawdle as I read all the magazines (and the *Sun*'s gossip column) in such detail that the good people of Woodseats in Sheffield would either get the wrong paper or the right one far too late. I became obsessed. I read everything: free newspapers, leaflets on buses, my grandma's copy of *Woman's Own* magazine, *everything*.

I never, as a painfully shy lad growing up in Yorkshire, *ever* thought I would actually get to work at a magazine. Why ever would I? And anyway, I was too shy to speak to anyone so there were practical problems there. The careers teacher at my rough comprehensive school told me only out-going people became journalists.

But still, I told everyone who asked that I was going to work for a magazine one day. They didn't believe it and I didn't believe it but I didn't have any better answers. For five years, from the age of 13 to 18, I kept telling people I was going to work at a magazine but did absolutely nothing about it. Then, in autumn 1988 during my first week at the Polytechnic Of East London, I plucked up the courage to go along to the offices of the Student Union magazine, asked them if they wanted a pop music column and they said they did. My confidence gradually increased: I ended up editing it and then one day, in the launderette, I saw an advert for a job at *Smash Hits* ...

I loved working at a pop magazine. Music was my thing and it was easy for me to write about it. *Smash Hits* led to *Sky* magazine and I was suddenly reliving my student magazine days doing a magazine for hedonistic (or pretend hedonistic) college kids. Then, in autumn 1997, I was approached about a new magazine, *Heat*, that was being lined up for launch. *Heat* magazine was intended to be a serious, wordy look at the world of entertainment.

We launched with a huge fanfare on 1 February 1999. We knew by week three that *Heat* had flopped. Big time. Why? Good question. It wasn't a bad magazine but it was probably the wrong magazine. That year, 1999, was all about Posh and Becks' wedding and Posh and Becks' wedding was all about gossip, glamour and fashion. Those were the three reasons this event was interesting, but also there were other famous people out there who were becoming interesting for similar reasons. In spring 2000, the publishers Emap relaunched *Heat* as a magazine about these celebrities, with me in charge. This book begins as I'm handed the reins and hurtles through a time when celebrity got bigger, more democratic and a lot more controversial. It's one hell of a roller coaster ride.

Originally I never wanted to do magazines about 'celebrities', as music magazines were my thing, but somehow I ended up doing this. And, as people took me into their confidence, allowed me in the dressing rooms or photo studios or parties, I saw the madness of it all at close hand. And it fascinated me – I'm intrigued by how people relate to each other, how they fall for each other and fall out. The world of celebrity is the new human zoo and I loved watching it all.

I'm very proud of the fact that I managed to not get sucked in by it, to take it seriously or believe *I* was famous simply because I wrote about famous people. None of these famous people you read about here became my friends. I do happen to have two friends that are quite famous but I only know them because my girlfriend went to school with them. I promised them I wouldn't mention either in the book (they're both really boring anyway).

So why do the book? I, more than perhaps anyone else, have had a front-row seat for the celebrity decade. I wanted to document that. I can't deny I was inspired by Piers Morgan's brilliant book *The Insider* because I was. I read it on holiday in the summer of 2005 and thought to myself that one day I'd document my time at a magazine in the way he documented his time at a newspaper, never thinking I'd actually get a chance to do it. But, as you'll see from reading the book, my attitude to life is pretty different to his and the magazine world is a completely different environment from the newspaper world: far less brutal, far more relaxed (a little too relaxed at times). Like him I made mistakes – including one doozy in late 2007 – but when you have to make hundreds of different decisions a week you don't get everything right.

So, this *is* the story of The Celebrity Decade, as it will come to be known, told by a lad from Yorkshire watching it all from close quarters. But it's also the story of a magazine: the people who graced its pages and the characters who created it. Cos magazines are great.

Three days before I wrote this introduction I was in a newsagent's near my home with my two-year-old son. He likes our newsagent's for two very good reasons. Firstly it has three steps leading up to it and he loves climbing steps. Secondly the newsagent's has magazines in it. So, on Sunday he climbed the steps and ran – ran! – over to where the kids' magazines were, handily laid out at kid height. There he surveyed the scene, spied the *Teletubbies* magazine and pulled it out of the selection. 'Okay, you can have it. But I need to take it over to the man because I have to pay for it.' I try and take it out of his hand but he gives it a short tug towards him. 'Danny …' He starts sobbing. 'I need to …' He isn't letting go. 'All right!'

I wander over to the counter, without the magazine, and explain to them what's happening.

'Hi, sorry, my son has a magazine that I'd like to pay for. It's £1.99, can I just give you the money for it now, because he won't let me bring it to the counter and …' As I say the word 'he' I look down to see my son. He is lying on the floor, painstakingly examining every bit of the opening page of the magazine before turning the page and doing the same again on the next one.

Like I say, there's just something about magazines …

Prologue

Wednesday 12 July 2006

I've done some pretty stupid things in my time editing this magazine, but this has to be the most stupid.

In fact, I can't believe we're going to go through with this.

It's 4 p.m., Wednesday afternoon. In three days' time the biggest celebrity wedding since Posh and Becks takes place. Cheryl Tweedy, Girls Aloud's feisty, mouthy ex-reality TV star and singer, is marrying one of the richest young men in Britain: England and Chelsea footballer Ashley Cole. It's a huge wedding and like all huge weddings it has to be bought up, exclusively, by … *OK* magazine.

The all-important preparations are being made over the next few days. Us cheeky kids from *Heat* are not allowed in, naturally.

So I've told the team that we're going to gatecrash.

Publicly *Heat* magazine, because we're cooler than all the other celeb mags, hates the whole magazine wedding thing. I, Lucie, Hannah, Julian and the gang give endless interviews to celebrity 'talking heads' TV shows about how cheesy we think these weddings are, how sad we think it is that someone's big day is sullied by security guards who frisk you wherever you go and confiscate your cameras, about how really it's just about money and nothing to do with love and commitment and tradition.

In private, of course, we're all obsessed by the spectacle and I'm sure some of the *Heat* staff would love to work as part of a celebrity wedding reporting team.

So, what we attempt to do on our pages is to get the story behind the event. Find out what really happens behind the scenes.

I'll admit it, we do face a few problems when we attempt to cover a wedding we have no access to.

We have no pictures of the dress.

We have no pictures of the ceremony.

We won't be able to run an interview with the happy couple.

The other disadvantage we have (and this is a biggie) is that we have to print the magazine before the actual wedding happens. But look as though we've printed it after it happened. Yes, I know what you're thinking: 'That's ridiculous.' You're right, of course.

It's especially a problem if, say, you don't even know where the wedding is.

And we don't.

We need to find out where it is – and quickly. There's only one man for the job. Unfortunately he is unavailable, so we're sending Daniel Fulvio instead ...

How to explain Daniel Fulvio? He's in his early twenties, eccentric, laughs all the time, is nervous around authority but at other times (especially when he's had a drink) is the life and soul of the party. He's hard-working, intense and one hell of a character. And now he's been given the challenge of his career so far: to infiltrate the preparations for Cheryl Tweedy and Ashley Cole's wedding. He mustn't fail.

So, we know that Dan will be out of the office tomorrow roaming the countryside trying to find this wedding. But as we leave the office for the evening we're not quite sure which direction he'll be heading in.

Then, late this evening, my phone buzzed with a text. It's Dan. He's certain he knows where the wedding will be.

'Mark, heard it from several good sources that it's Highclere House in Berkshire. Off there first thing tomorrow morning. Over and out.'

Here we go.

Thursday 13 July

I get to the office at 9 as usual. Hannah's already in, working hard at it.

'He's got a hangover.'

'Who's got a hangover?'

'La Fulvio!'

She's laughing now. Good start – but he'll be fine.

He calls us from Paddington station. He's waiting for a train to Newbury (the nearest station to the hotel) and – because time is tight – he's trying to stand-up his hunch on his way over there.

'So I called them and tried to do my best premiership football-player voice to the girl who answered. I said, "I'm coming to Cheryl and Ashley's wedding this Saturday and I've just received the invite. Could you give me directions?" I could hear the guy speak to someone else. "I've got a guy on the phone asking about Cheryl and Ashley's wedding. What should I tell him?" That confirms it! I'm sure we've got the place!'

I'm really not so sure the phone call told us anything but he seems convinced. Anyway, time's running out. We've got to go for this.

An hour or so later we get another call. He's arrived. And there's a huge white marquee in the centre of the hotel's grounds.

BINGO!

Dan spies vans unloading stuff into the marquee – then follows the staff as they carry stuff out of them. Despite wearing a fluorescent green T-shirt with Tinkabelle performing a strip tease on it, Dan manages to fool the team into believing that he's an event-organiser.

Bloody hell. He's in!

The phone calls keep coming, each one more clandestine and in more hushed tones than the last.

'This tent is vast. It's huge – the size of a football pitch – and a dozen men are busy unpacking boxes and sound-testing a DJ box – pumping eardrum-shattering dance music. There is dry ice and a massive lighting rig. Wa-hey!'

Fulvio gets very excited at times. He raises his voice at the end of the call; he can't help himself.

His final sentence is triumphant.

'They're preparing for the wedding reception of the century in here!'

I listen in as Hannah tries to get him off the line.

'Be careful,' she shouts down the phone. 'Call me again when you can.'

The next time we hear from him is 20 minutes later. He's since been chucked out of the main marquee by the person testing the sound – noooo!

Hmm, maybe that T-shirt he's wearing was a give-away. Memo to self: put a LOT more thought into the journalist's outfit next time (if there ever is a next time. Not sure my nerves can cope with this).

Anyway, then he went into the kitchens. He got chucked out of there too …

The phone rings again. 'A woman with a clipboard saw me go in. I told her I was Cheryl's PA and that I was there to make sure everything was going according to plan for Saturday. She exchanged glances with this woman next to her and told me I'd need to speak to Cheryl about all of that.'

He's still not got anything that really stands up, of course, but we are beginning to banish any doubts we've had.

Because of the rumours we've heard, because of the marquee (and the sheer size of the thing), because of their attempts to chuck us out we are now convinced this is the place.

As editor, I have to make a decision and dramatically swing into action.

'Russ, we need some aerial shots of Highclere House as soon as possible – first thing tomorrow by the latest. Great epic shots showing the house and the marquee. It's huge, we really need to get the size and the scale of this event on to the page.'

We've asked Dan to look around a bit more – so he does. He checks out the portaloos and finds a tiny ornate chapel the house has onsite. That's where the ceremony will take place, of course! This all adds up perfectly. Making notes all the time he now has everything he needs: pages and pages of information.

This will be great. A proper news story. And it will look brilliant.

I call him again.

'Dan, you can come back to the office. We've got the perfect piece. I can see it now – BEHIND THE SCENES AT THE CELEBRITY WEDDING OF THE DECADE!'

Today was a great day.

Friday 14 July

By lunchtime the feature is complete. The aerial shots of the venue look incredible, we've loads of information – everything from what food they'll be eating to the fact that in the men's portaloos the soap is black pepper and ginseng while in the ladies' it's mandarin and grapefruit. It's a proper news job.

However, at just after three, less than two hours before we finish work for the week, Hannah receives a troubling phone call.

A paparazzi photographer friend of hers tells her there's a lot of movement near a venue called Wrotham Park in Hertfordshire.

A convoy of cars with blacked-out windows has just sped into the grounds and other paps are on their way. They think Ashley Cole is in one of the cars. I call Dan over to my desk and let him know.

Dan – his face now as white as a sheet – phones Wrotham Park up. 'They say there's no wedding taking place this weekend.'

'Well, they would, wouldn't they!' I say.

'Yes. I guess.'

At just after five o'clock Deputy News Editor Charlotte gets a call from a showbiz reporter contact at the *Sun* saying that he's received an inventory and schedule detailing all the plans of the big day and that it is happening at … yep, Wrotham Park.

Hannah holds her head in her hands.

'I saw the DJ set up, the food being prepared,' stammers Dan. 'The staff even admitted it.'

'Dan. Did anyone actually say to you that this was the venue of Cheryl's wedding?'

'No. But I mentioned her name to two different people and they didn't bat an eyelid when I did. They didn't flinch. Except …'

'Go on?'

'The woman in the kitchens did give another woman a funny look.'

'So if this wasn't Cheryl and Ashley's wedding, what was it?'

'That's the thing! It was a wedding. It was huge and posh and DJs were setting up.'

I raise my voice.

'Are we *really* to believe that this whole event at Highclere House has been arranged just to put *us* off the scent. It must have cost a fortune! The marquee, all that food. That's the bit I don't get!'

Come on, Mark. What to do? I've summoned Al, our Creative Director, back from the pub. All mentions of Highclere House have now been stripped out and we've kept the copy as vague as possible. I've no idea what else we can do.

It's not a great piece but it's a piece. No one will die if we get it wrong (except perhaps Dan).

But I have to face facts. This is a disaster. A total cock-up. *Heat* magazine, the most talked-about magazine of the last ten years, the one that transformed itself from Britain's biggest flop to an award-winning, world-famous, magazine-publishing sensation has just infiltrated THE WRONG BLOODY WEDDING.

Or even, possibly, not a wedding at all.

Dan feels terrible but it's as much my fault.

We all so much wanted to believe that we'd spoilt *OK*'s big exclusive of the year.

'Don't worry,' I say as he heads out of the office. 'You'll look back at this and laugh. One day.'

Saturday 15 July

This morning is like waking up with a hangover. I'm trying to piece together the events of yesterday by reading through the newspapers and surfing the web.

Here's what I can make out:

1. Highclere House *was* the original venue for the Cole/Tweedy wedding but they cancelled it months ago.
2. To protect *OK*'s exclusive the organisers decided Highclere may be a good decoy so they asked the venue not to deny the event was happening – which explains why the team were like they were with Dan.
3. What Dan infiltrated was a corporate event, bizarrely, not a wedding. That event is already over – the marquee is being dismantled this morning.
4. The actual Cole/Tweedy wedding ceremony has already taken place – it was yesterday.
5. The reception and party take place today – at Wrotham Park.
6. We've been had – good and proper.

It was never meant to be like this. When I was starting out in magazines it was all very straightforward. Pop group releases record. Record gets to number one. Keen, young reporter goes along and interviews said pop group. Interview gets written up. People read it.

Somehow, I've ended up in a position where I'm asking journalists to break into people's weddings, getting screamed at down the phone by TV presenters, printing half-naked pictures of the Prime Minister and nearly getting run over by film stars. How the hell did I get here?

Welcome to the life a celebrity magazine editor. Trust me, there's never a dull moment.

PART ONE

Hot

CHAPTER ONE

Posh to
the rescue

NEW LOOK!

Royle Family win Baftas. Plus: Cannes & Liz Hurley

This week's hottest celebrity news
£1.25 – Every Thursday · 20 - 26 May 2000

heat

EXCLUSIVE!

"My doctor
says I should
be nine stone"

Posh
Spice

answers
all the
rumours

Posh on David…

Posh on Brooklyn…

Posh on her weight…

Issue 66

CHAPTER ONE
Posh to the rescue!
December 1999 – May 2000

Wednesday 8 December

I couldn't get home fast enough tonight. It's been a really mad day. I've got a lot of thinking to do. It all started with a very odd lunch.

Sue Hawken has been my boss for the majority of my adult life. And I was summoned to see her at short notice. Great, I thought, that'll be more bad news.

I sat in Bertorelli's on Frith Street in Soho playing with the breadsticks, wondering, to be honest, if she might be about to fire me. It's all been going so badly recently.

Heat – this bloody magazine I am meant to be editing – is the biggest (and most public) flop in the history of British magazines. We launched on 1 February as a smart, serious, wordy entertainment magazine aimed mostly at men. To say it hasn't gone well would be an understatement. It's been a disaster. We put out 300,000 copies of the first issue and sold about 70,000 of them. Since then things have gone from bad to worse. Now we're only selling half of that.

It doesn't help that I'm listed in the magazine as Editor but I'm not actually in charge. For the last year I've always had an Editorial Director above me and I've played deputy. Of course *I* want to run this magazine. I've got loads of ideas, enthusiasm and I just want my chance. But today, as I wait for Sue to arrive at the restaurant, it dawns on me that the game is probably up. It's over. They're going to fire me.

Sue arrives. Short, smartly dressed but serious to the point of scary, Sue Hawken has always frightened the life out of me: a foot shorter she may be but her blunt manner can bring me and anyone down to size. She's also not one for small talk. She sits down, asks me how things are going with the magazine and I automatically launch fully into defensive mode. I tell her about how the bad sales have affected me – the virtually sleepless nights, three in the last week – how I have a vision of the magazine that isn't getting through, about what *Heat* could be and what needs to be done.

'I understand that it's been rotten. It hasn't *exactly* been a barrel of laughs for the board either,' was her response.

A fair comment I suppose. Is this it then? Is this the moment she fires me? If she is going to do it she'll do it straightaway: no fanfare, no build-up, straight in there.

She opens the bottle of mineral water and pours herself a glass.

'I've got something to tell you, Mark.'

My mouth goes completely dry. I looked her in the eye (not something I find easy at the best of times, but being confronted with the big boss? Bloody terrifying!)

'David Davies is moving off *Heat*.'

I'm not being fired! Thank God. Come on, Mark, compose yourself.

'Oh. Right.'

'We want you to be in charge. Properly this time. But the magazine needs radical change.'

Even better! This can't be happening.

I'm beaming, of course. But the 'radical change' bit is a little unnerving. I've got plenty of ideas, yes, but I'm not sure if I'm really the radical type.

'Don't see this as a magazine for you any more. This is going to be more a magazine for your girlfriend.'

'It's going to be a magazine for women?'

'Correct.'

'O-kaay.'

I really try to process all of this. Really really try.

I know about women's magazines. I don't read them, obviously, they're for women but I know all about them. Yes, women's magazines: horoscopes and fashion tips and problem pages and real-life stories about falling in love with the guy who burgled your house and pictures of blokes with their tops off and MAKE-UP! Lots and lots of make-up.

I know about women's magazine editors too. They're all women! Glamorous, fashion-obsessed women. I'm a bloke. A gangly, some would unkindly say 'lanky', six foot four and a half (the half is important) tall bloke. I am not glamorous (if the clothes I'm wearing in any way suit me, which is unlikely, it's because my girlfriend Gaby has persuaded me not to buy it in the grey). A bloke. Editing a women's magazine. For women! What the hell are they playing at?

'Mark!'

'Uh-huh?'

'Are you listening?'

'Yes! Of course!'

'We need sales over 100,000 every week by the end of June or we'll close it. I'm not going to lie to you. Think about it tonight and Louise will speak to you tomorrow. You'll be reporting to her from now on if you decide to do this.'

And we hadn't even ordered our food yet.

Taken at face value, of course, this is exactly what I've been waiting for. Dreaming of. *Dying* for. The chance to run things. I love magazines, love everything about them. Love the way they grab you with an enticing front page. Love the way that reading one makes you feel like you're part of a special club that no one else is part of. I am obsessed.

But my passion for the job might not be enough. Can *Heat* be saved or is this just a great big poisoned chalice? Am I the one who'll go down with the ship, the editor who steered a multi-million-pound launch into the abyss?

Oh well, not a bad day all in all. There's still the thorny issue of me not being a woman but at least I didn't get fired.

Well, not yet anyway.

Thursday 9 December

Got up extra early this morning – 7.15 – and started making notes, bowl of Special K in one hand, pen in the other. I'm a morning person, which is lucky because I've got a meeting that I need to do lots of preparation for.

I pace around the flat. I live in Primrose Hill, an area becoming increasingly trendy with more and more celebrities coming to live here all the time.

Jude Law and Sadie Frost live two streets away with their kids in a huge house on a grotty street with uneven pavements and litter blowing everywhere.

Kate Moss lives five minutes away. She's always going round to Sadie 'n' Jude's and I often see them in the local minimarket, Shepherd's, picking junk food off the shelves and talking really loudly between themselves, too loudly, almost as if they need to get noticed all the time.

Just round the corner is Supernova Heights, Noel Gallagher's home for years. He's just sold it to Davinia Taylor, best friend of Kate 'n' Sadie, ex-girlfriend of Ryan Giggs and daughter of a multi-millionaire paper-mill owner.

Two minutes away is Liam and Patsy's old place. The graffiti's still there, and you'll often see Japanese girls posing and taking photos of each other outside.

Then, just ten minutes up the road, lives Ewan McGregor, one of the biggest movie stars of his generation.

I LOVE it.

I've lived here for a year with Gaby. I met her at work – she was the pretty girl in the next office. These days she works in interior design but sadly she can't do much with our place. We're in a rented flat with bare walls that are caked with dust. We don't hoover and the place is a mess. The least glamorous flat in London's most glam-orous area.

Downstairs lives one of my heroes, an American record producer called Stephen Hague, who's probably best known for producing 'West End Girls' for the Pet Shop Boys. He came up and introduced himself on our first day in the flat.

'Hi, I'm Stephen from downstairs ...'

'Oh my God, you're Stephen Hague!'

'Yeah. Listen, there appears to be water pouring through our ceiling.'

You know the hole on the side of a bath that lets water out if it goes over a certain level? Well, ours didn't have one. It's a disgrace! You'd expect Primrose Hill baths to come with their own entourage, each one scooping out excess amounts of water. Ours didn't even have an overflow.

(They say you should never meet your heroes. Is this kind of thing the reason why?)

Anyway, I made notes for an hour at home then for another 15 minutes on a packed tube into work just off Oxford Street. Trying to concentrate isn't easy when someone's paper is rubbing up against your face and someone else is standing on your foot. Also I can't help thinking back to the one previous time I met Louise Matthews and what an utter disaster it was.

Back in 1995 when the once-great *Smash Hits* was, to use one of its own phrases, going down the dumper, I was dragged in front of the board of Emap, the company I've worked for since I was 20 years old.

Smash Hits was embarking on yet another reinvention and I was the poor sod leading it. And there I was, in my nicely ironed shirt, just 24, achingly shy and telling the board of this huge publishing company that even though it was a pop music magazine, movie stars were the future of *Smash Hits*.

It was a stupid idea, of course, but the men in the room just wanted me to do SOMETHING and all of them murmured in positive tones. Louise Matthews was the only woman in the room that day and she didn't do any murmuring at all. In fact – if I remember correctly – she chewed gum and gave me a look throughout the presentation that basically said 'you're an idiot'. I probably was.

Hopefully, I thought, today she'll be a little nicer. Or at least a little more restrained.

In a small room at the back of the editorial office (two chairs, no table), Louise told me the plan: I am going to disappear for a few weeks into a small redesign room on a different floor to the *Heat* office with Lottie, our Art Editor. We are to completely reinvent the magazine. Ian Birch, the man whose job it is to oversee all the women's magazines in the company, is going to work with us to make sure we stay on track. Then Ian, Louise and I will come up with a strategy to save the magazine. And then Louise reiterated the closure plan …

'Remember, if we don't get to 100,000 every week we are dead.'
'Do you know what, Sue said something like that to me yesterday.' She laughed.
'You're getting the message?'
'Kind of.'

It's clear that what everyone says about Louise is true – she doesn't mess about. Less scary than Sue, Louise gets her way by gentle persuasion, encouragement and infectious enthusiasm.

We started throwing around ideas and at last I had a chance to have my say: about how excited I was to finally be in charge, that I'd been spending my evenings manically typing up ideas for how the magazine could look ... everything. She seems to approve of the way I'm thinking about it all. Thank God. Whatever she thinks, the truth is I've either got six months to make this work, or me and the entire *Heat* team will be picking up our P45s.

Tuesday 4 January 2000

Met with Ian Birch today in the foyer of the Berners Hotel round the corner from the office. Originally from Northern Ireland – with lilting accent still intact – Birchy is a tough, demanding guy who has edited some of the biggest and best magazines in the world. He has high standards.

I showed him my vision for the new-look *Heat* in written form. I want *Heat* to be a different kind of magazine, purposely the opposite of all the dull, fawning mags with cheesy stars that are already out there. This can be different.

This magazine was not a music magazine, not a TV magazine, not a film magazine, not a combination of the three. It was to be about celebs, the breed of people who could be famous for being in any of those three worlds or maybe even none of them. They were just famous. You'd recognise them if you saw them on the bus but often you wouldn't be able to quite place them.

To make it absolutely clear, for myself as much as Ian, I wrote our vision up in point form – it is to become the new magazine's manifesto:

* We're going to be the cool celebrity magazine for women.
* We'll be really funny.
* We'll have lots of exclusive interviews – and ask the questions people really want to see asked.
* We won't take celebrities that seriously.
* We'll take risks.
* No one can be boring in our magazine.

And then I showed him the latest issue, the one I and the team had finished putting together last week.

'But this is none of those things!' says Birchy, hardly able to keep his face straight.

He's right – the latest issue is drab and sooo boring.

Johnny Vaughan is on the cover, pulling his jacket collar up over his chin and grimacing.

Over the page are some tedious industry stories about people you've never heard of.

A few pages later a techy article about the latest bit of kit from Japan.

Then Johnny bloody Vaughan going on about himself over three pages.

And finally, 40 pages – 40 pages! – of TV listings with hardly any pictures.

It's obvious we have a mountain to climb.

It was a good session today, but I am convinced Ian doesn't think I can do this.

But then why would he? I'm not sure I can do it myself! I didn't tell him that, of course, but the fact is none of us have much confidence that we can pull this off. On the other hand, this is the sort of challenge I've been waiting for for years. I've been whinging all this time to Gaby at home that I want to actually be in charge and now I am, so I can't argue. I'll give it my very best shot. That's all anyone can ask. And anyway, I've got to stay positive.

Monday 21 February

After a frustrating month of research and team-rearranging we've finally started revamping the mag. We're in a small room just off someone else's office. Formerly a store cupboard, our den is about six feet by ten, has no windows and is unbelievably hot, even in February. And this is our home for the next six weeks. Ian pops in on the first day. He tells me, not that I didn't know, that I'm going to need a lot of help with the fashion and beauty content. Luckily he's found someone who can: Julian Linley, the brilliant and instinctive Deputy Editor at *More* magazine who's clearly destined for big things. I dare say they're putting him in with me for when I mess up. Maybe it should bother me that someone else is being given such a huge section of *my* magazine but the truth is it's a relief because I've got so much on my plate. In fact, I'm pathetically grateful.

Tuesday 22 February

Although I'm in my little store cupboard cooking up ideas, I'm still overseeing the magazine office. And we've got another problem. Because we're the most famous flop in the history of British magazines, no one will give us an interview. No one we want anyway. Because of this we've resigned ourselves to buying in interviews from other magazines and agencies. There's not many good ones about but this week, at least, we're running a juicy one: Noel Gallagher. I bloody love the Gallagher brothers. Until Oasis came along every guitar band was the same: too cool for their own good, monosyllabic in interviews and really really boring. It's a badge of honour to be moronic when you're in an indie band, it seems. No use AT ALL when you're running a magazine like ours. Oasis have changed all that – they bitch, they argue, they shout their mouths off and, in 'our' interview, Noel does this more than ever before.

The interview particularly dwells on the brothers' relationship with Robbie Williams. When Robbie left Take That three years ago he latched on to Oasis. Although he was in a cheesy boy band Robbie really wanted to be in an indie band. Oasis, more specifically. Within days of leaving Take That he drove his car, loaded down with champagne, on to the Glastonbury site and spent the next three days partying with his heroes. Soon after, the friendship cooled off, but the two parties have never discussed why. Until this piece.

'I've never been his friend!' says Noel, clearly riled. 'He was Liam's friend. Liam used to invite him to the gigs and stuff like that. I've been in dressing rooms with him but I wouldn't even consider him to be a friend of mine.'

The journalist, really onto something now, asks why.

'Why? Because he was in Take That! He's a fat dancer from Take That. Somebody who danced for a living! Stick to what you're good at, that's what I always say.'

Half with the new mag in mind, I've run that quote as the headline. It looks great on the page, a real result.

Wednesday 23 February

Our bought-in interview is being talked about everywhere. It's had a real impact. Robbie's not happy. He sent a wreath of white roses and lilies with a card to the showbiz desk at the *Sun*. The card read: 'To Noel Gallagher, RIP. Heard your latest album, with deepest sympathy. Robbie Williams.'

What a bitch! I love it when celebrities do stuff like this.

Monday 28 February

Jesus, now Liam's getting involved. This morning *The Big Breakfast* ran an interview where he says he'd break Williams' nose if he bumped into him. What have we started?

Friday 3 March

Most of the office is hungover this morning. It was the Brit Awards last night, the usual parade of show-offs, nearly there dresses (Liz Hurley, you've caused this) and stunts. I love the Brits; it's so ridiculous. And this year, a feud we created dominated the whole night. Robbie Williams came onstage and challenged Liam to a fight! 'So, anybody like to see me fight Liam?' he shouted to huge applause and cheering. 'Would you pay to come and see it? Liam, a hundred grand of your money and a hundred grand of my money. We'll get in a ring and we'll have a fight and you can all watch it on TV.'

Of course, everyone lapped it up. And the by-product of it all is that everyone's been running stories about our interview as a result.

This is incredible stuff. A magazine no one talks about suddenly getting acres of press. It's unnerving though – you get used to no one talking about your magazine so when they do you feel like you're put up there to be shot at. That's the only downside, though, because this sort of thing is great for business.

Friday 31 March

Gradually we're getting somewhere. With the fashion and beauty coverage being originated elsewhere I've been concentrating on the stuff I *can* do. Lottie's design is exceptional – fresh, uncluttered and very different to anything else on the market. Day-by-day, page-by-page we've been inventing the new-look *Heat*:

✳ Pacey, colourful interviews with headlines that shout out at you.
✳ Sets of photos with arrows that point stuff out and sarcastic captions that deride the very people we're celebrating.

✳ Pages and pages of designer shoes and bags with information on how to get hold of high-street copies for a fraction of the price – the idea is that the reader can look as good as the celebrities, but without spending all that money.

It's loud, anarchic and completely different to all the boring kiss-arse celebrity magazines already out there. I'm starting to feel really good about it. But there's still loads to do.

Tuesday 11 April

Five weeks to go until our first new-look magazine comes on sale. We urgently need a cover star. One that will triple our sales. Yeah, right. I've been thinking hard about all the potential options. In our position we don't have many.

While we were desperately trying to be a cool music, film and TV magazine last year, there was one huge event in the celebrity world, one single event that made 'celebrity' a far bigger deal than it ever was before.

The wedding of David Beckham and Victoria Adams had everything: glamour, opulence (it was rumoured to have cost two million quid!), a real kitsch, over-the-top, quality (at one point in the reception, the bride and groom sat on thrones). Also, because the event was bought up exclusively by *OK* magazine, we could all share in the fun. This was the world of celebrity as we'd never seen it before: up close and with us as part of it. We saw them cut the cake, laugh with their friends, walk up the aisle. We even saw the exact moment they became man and wife. We also learnt – and became hooked by – Victoria's story. It was fairytale stuff: dumpy, awkward teenager reinvents herself, becomes a pop star and marries her Prince Charming. Victoria was Miss Average made good and we'd followed her story through the media every step of the way: cheering for her, being pleased for her and fascinated that she'd stayed so normal. I remember being so struck by all of this at the time: how complete her reinvention was, how fascinating it must be if you were the age she was when she started and weren't happy about how you looked. Victoria is the story of the day. She has to be on the cover of our big relaunch issue. She is exactly the sort of person our new *Heat* readers will want to read about.

Only one problem – and it's a biggie. I'll have to convince her fearsome publicist Caroline McAteer that Victoria really should be on the cover of a magazine that no one is buying and everyone thinks is an embarrassing disaster at a time when she has nothing to promote. For free. We haven't got any money!

I need to get her on the phone first – and today, despite three attempts, I can't even do that.

Thursday 13 April
Two more messages left with Caroline today, one email and a fax. Nothing.

Tuesday 18 April
Made the last couple of appointments to our new-look team today. We've got a great set of section heads:

There's Julian: brilliant on features and fashion. Every few months he assigns part of the office wall to be his 'New Season' wall, full of pictures torn out of fashion magazines of how he wants to dress over the next few months.

Lottie is in charge of the design: prim and proper on the outside, but after a couple of drinks she comes out of her shell a bit. Okay, a lot. Very serious about what she does; there's been a few tears in our little bunker but it's only because she cares so much (that and the fact there's no windows, it's unbearably hot and is, in fact, merely a cupboard).

Dom – a former teen-magazine editor bussed in to make things operate a little more smoothly. A fearless interviewer, he loves the jokes and piss-taking of office life.

And there's Boyd. How do you describe Boyd? Me and Dom rescued him from a dull desk job at the Press Association and he's eternally grateful. Our 'TV coordinator', he's discerning, a great people person and seems to be able to make friends with every TV star he meets.

Slowly, as we all gel, we're forming a solid team spirit. Music gets cranked up in the office, silly pictures get stuck on the wall (usually animals wearing clothing, mass-murderers, polar bears kissing or naked men). In an average visit the suits will screw their noses up at at least five things they see or hear. Good. They're lucky we don't lock the doors.

Wednesday 19 April

Still no response from Caroline McAteer. But I will not be beaten.

Tuesday 25 April

I've been bugging Caroline McAteer for two whole weeks now. When I call she either sounds busy and 'will call me back' or I just get deflected by her assistant. Emails don't get replies. It's the classic brush-off. I'm becoming annoying so have left her alone for the past couple of days. Then today – finally – she agrees to see me. Tomorrow. Oh shit.

Wednesday 26 April

They say that Hollywood has the hardest-to-please publicists in the world and they're mostly right. It's always tough dealing with the LA PRs – abrupt, paranoid and impossible to get hold of, my time spent speaking to them at previous magazines has always been miserable. I'd often have to stay late in the office, dial them up in LA and – if they deigned to speak to me – spend half an hour promising their rubbish, unknown clients a feature before being told, after 30 minutes of small talk, that no I *can't* have an interview with Jennifer Aniston.

UK-based PRs are different: tough but essentially friendly characters who genuinely seem to like working with journalists.

Barbara Charone was born in the US, once a music journalist and has spent years protecting Madonna while also being jocular, down-to-earth and great company.

Gary Farrow is an incredible operator – his clients (and in his time he's worked with everyone from Jonathan Ross to George Michael) are all well served by his no-bullshit approach and strong relationships with all the UK tabloids.

Then there's Caroline McAteer.

Small, Irish, hard as nails, Caroline McAteer doesn't see eye to eye with most journalists. Most of the time, I get on with her. I've never wanted a scrap (whereas loads of tabloid hacks want nothing but), and I've been nice to her and on occasion even made her laugh. But still, getting Victoria Beckham on to the cover, whichever way you look at it, is a tough thing to ask.

I traipsed up Tottenham Court Road this morning to her office above Dreams ('the bed superstore'), with a pile of A3 boards on which we'd mounted dummy spreads for our new-look mag: the Star Style spreads with pieces about Versace and Dolce & Gabbana, our immaculate new beauty pages, articles about celebrity hangouts and hotels around the world, the five new must-visit boutiques in London. Yes, that's right; I chose all the pages shopping addict Victoria Beckham would be most likely to warm to! But also these are the pages that showed Caroline the brave new world we were soon to be in. A world miles away from the blokey magazine we'd been producing before.

I was shown into a tiny office at the back of the building; five minutes later she joined me.

'This better be good, you've been bugging me enough about it.'

She was right, it'd better. I launched into my spiel using the boards as props. I hadn't written down a word of what I was going to say, but had been living and breathing these pages so deeply I could talk for England about all of them. Apart from the fashion pages, of course. Then I was bluffing. Boy, was I bluffing.

I finished my presentation sweating from talking too quickly about fashion labels I know nothing about and hadn't even *heard* of two hours ago (Julian gave me a crash-course in high-end fashion before I left the office). After name-dropping Marc Jacobs and Dolce & Gabbana and God-alone knows who else (did I pronounce all the names correctly? Nooo, of course not, but I said them quickly so I was fine) I slumped on to a chair, the boards dropped to the floor and I grabbed my glass of water and gulped it down.

'So,' I say struggling to get my breath back, 'whaddaya think?'

'Really good. Really cool. I love the product pages.'

I beam.

'Thank you.'

This is in the bag. Heh-heh. Slam dunk!

'So ...'

I inhale.

'... when can we do the interview?' I grin my chirpiest grin.

'She's not doing any interviews.'

I let out a weird, high-pitched sound. '*WHAT?*'

'She's got nothing to promote. In August she will, but not now.'

No use. I need her now. I can't think of anyone else who can get us above 100,000 copies. I start to get desperate.

'Just ten minutes on the phone! We don't even need a shoot!' I'm begging now. I look pathetic.

'Mark – sorry. It's just not the right time.'

She begins to stand up. Is the meeting over already?

'But you like the new look! She'll love the new look.'

'Stop asking me! We'll talk again in a few months. I'm sorry, Mark. The magazine does look great though.'

No time for pride now, I decide. Copies of that day's papers are on the table and I pick one up …

'Okay, what about all these ridiculous stories in the tabloids? The stories you keep saying are lies? Surely,' my voice goes up a few octaves at this point, '… *surely* she needs to put the record straight about these, otherwise people will think they're all true!'

Silence.

Caroline curls her lip, looks up at me and …

'Actually, she probably would do something like that.'

I hold out a clammy hand.

'Deal!'

She smiles.

'Okay, deal. I'll call you tomorrow.'

I retained my composure until I got into the shaky, poky little lift that took me back downstairs, then punched the air. This interview, if it's good, could help us get the sales we want. I ran all the way back to the office to tell Louise and Ian.

'My God!' said Ian, in his typically infectious excited way.

'Mark, that's *amazing*,' said Louise.

We've never interviewed *anyone* very famous before really and now we've got the most famous person in Britain all to ourselves. I better not blow this.

Thursday 11 May

I'm sitting with Caroline in the reception of a posh accountants' office in Manchester waiting for David and Victoria to emerge from a meeting. Oh, to be a fly on the wall in *that* room. Me being here is the last throw of the dice for the magazine I have put everything into for the last year and a half. So today needs to go well …

After half an hour Posh pretend-staggers out of the meeting, earlier than either of us were expecting her to – they've clearly let her leave early cos she was getting bored.

'Thank God for that!' she says when she sees us.

'Enjoyed that, did you?'

'Yeah …'

Her face is full of sarcasm as she looks over her shoulder as the men and women in suits wander out.

'… loved it!'

She's in off-duty mode and you can tell that by the way she acts (like a kid who's been let off double maths, which in a way she just has been) and the way she looks: leisurewear, no make-up and baseball cap (bad hair day, clearly).

I like Posh and not just because she might well be about to save my career. I like her because she's funny and smart and sussed and doesn't take any shit. She's an interviewer's dream. And today, luckily, she's on top form and for nearly an hour and a half happily puts the record straight about various nonsense stories that have appeared in the tabloids over the last few months. But, as I hoped it would, the interview then strays into all sorts of other juicy areas: who she hates on TV, bitchy comments about other celebs. It's fantastic stuff. The revelations just kept coming: how her doctor has told her she is underweight and is worried about her and how she was once told that she'd never be able to conceive.

I feared she'd clam up when the conversation moved on to all the anorexia rumours – the opposite was true. With Caroline sitting silently at the back of the room, Victoria – slowly and cautiously – gave her side of the story to me.

'I did look bloody awful. There are pictures [from around the time of the anorexia rumours] that I looked at and cried.'

'How much do you weigh now?'

'Seven and a half stone.'

'And did your doctor say that was normal for your height?'

'No. I should be about eight and a half or nine stone [she's 5' 6"]. But you know, who is totally happy with their body?'

The interview ended only when David came back from Boots – brilliantly, Victoria had sent him to buy a couple of things for her. There's a weird tension between these two, you can see it straightaway.

Stuff she says seems to embarrass him constantly. He gets niggled by her just being her – as they stand together in front of me he bristles. He is very serious: seems to have a set way of doing things and doesn't have the casual, easy, frivolous attitude to life most footballers have. Whereas she is the opposite of that – naturally awkward, she deflects that by being girly and silly. She was like that today. She hated the accountants' meeting – moaning about it throughout our time together – and talking to us is her idea of light relief. Most famous people hate interviews; I think Victoria sees it as time for a gossip. An outlet. In fact she talked so much that the two of them were going to be late leaving for their next appointment. David headed off to the ground floor reception to wait. And wait. And wait!

He phoned her.

She didn't answer.

Eventually she, Caroline and I got in the lift and as we only had one floor to go we pressed the next button down. It actually only took us to the mezzanine level and we piled out only to see David Beckham looking up at us, with a look of total despair. He screwed his face up as if to say 'duh' and watched us eventually make our way to the ground floor.

Something just doesn't quite ring true about this so-called perfect romance: it all seems very unbalanced.

Her last motion before rushing through the door is to put her shades on. I stood in the foyer and watched them walk out to the car – it's all rather like something out of a film. A single paparazzi photographer steps forward to get a shot. She pulls the cap down even further. Office girls over the road stop and stare. And then they are gone.

I can't quite believe it all happened, can't believe how good a story she's given me either. I'm euphoric.

Friday 12 May

My last day in the office for a fortnight and I'm working late. It's just me and the cleaner. I've written up the interview, painstakingly divided it into two – first rule of magazines: why let something run in one issue when it could be a two-parter – then started work on the cover. The cover will be finished by Lottie and Ian Birch on Monday but I want to establish the cover wording this evening. Up until now, desperate for sales, we've squeezed four or five stories on to the average cover. On this one we let our star dominate. Apart from a small sell at the top of the cover about the Baftas this will be all about Posh ...

EXCLUSIVE!
'My doctor says I should be nine stone'
Posh Spice answers all the rumours

Then along the bottom of the cover we go into more detail about what the interview covers.

Posh on David ...
Posh on Brooklyn ...
Posh on her weight ...

It's all or nothing. We hope that the appetite for the couple who are coming to epitomise this new decadent, moneyed celebrity world can save the magazine. We haven't gone through the 100,000 barrier yet – in fact the sales are at pretty similar levels to the ones I inherited – and if we don't with this we're finished. I head off on holiday not knowing if I'll have a magazine to edit in a week's time. I look back over my shoulder as I leave the office.

I might never be back.

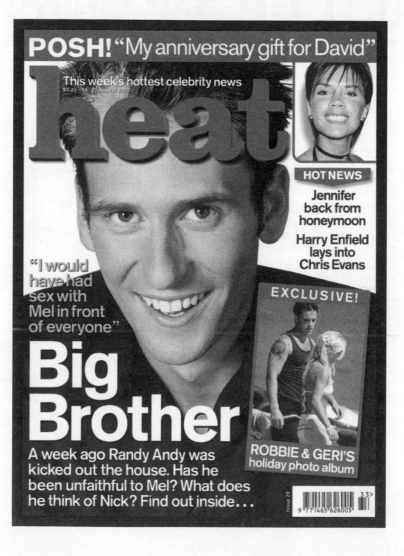

POSH! "My anniversary gift for David"

This week's hottest celebrity news
£1.25 19–25 August 2000

heat

HOT NEWS

Jennifer back from honeymoon

Harry Enfield lays into Chris Evans

"I would have had sex with Mel in front of everyone"

Big Brother

A week ago Randy Andy was kicked out the house. Has he been unfaithful to Mel? What does he think of Nick? Find out inside…

EXCLUSIVE!

ROBBIE & GERI'S holiday photo album

Issue 79

9 771465 626005

33>

CHAPTER TWO
Big Brother –
it'll never work
May – September 2000

Friday 19 May

Aah, a relaxing holiday in the Greek Islands. Well, that's the idea.

This place is perfect: a small villa down a dirt track in the middle of nowhere. Just Gaby and me. And a pile of newspapers.

Being a magazine junkie I've managed to find a newsagent's somehow. I'm sad (I know this because Gaby keeps telling me I am – she can't abide the tabloids and certainly can't understand why anyone would want to read one when you're in a different country). But today I'm glad I went: I proudly returned from the shop with a copy of yesterday's *Sun*. Emap has supplied them with quotes from my interview and they've gone big on it. And in return, there, at the bottom of the article, is the reason we give them the stuff: a two-inch high thumbnail cover of *Heat*. Sharon Ring – an ex-editor of *OK*, now editor of a doomed Emap travel magazine called *Escape Routes* – has loads of contacts in the tabloid world so she's been calling them, gauging their interest in our exclusive before making sure (and this bit is vital) that the all-important cover picture appears on any coverage. That's what it's all about. Without the cover everyone will think this is an interview Posh has done for the *Sun* and that would be a disaster – for her (Posh has had such a hard time from the tabloids recently that she wants nothing to do with them) and for us. But it's there, it's huge (well, two inches high) and there's no doubt that this is a plug for our magazine.

I obsess about the article all afternoon. I'd set myself a target of 50 lengths in the villa's outdoor pool today and ended up doing nearly 80: I'm working out in my mind what this means for us. If 1 per cent of the people reading the *Sun* then decide to buy the magazine, that's 40,000 extra sales. Which would take us from our usual 80,000 to 120,000. Then there's part two of the interview, which should keep us over 100,000. But we won't know anything until I get back. I'm meant to be relaxing – it's my first holiday in nearly a year after all – but the stress of not knowing is starting to get to me a bit.

Monday 22 May

Happy Birthday to me! A landmark event, my 30th birthday, but the weather was not up to much, so today we just walked along the beach dodging the intermittent rain showers. I'm getting increasingly anxious about this week's issue, can't talk about anything else. Think Gaby wants to dump me.

Monday 29 May

Is a holiday actually a holiday if you end it more stressed than when you started it? A week ago I was a mildly concerned editor of a magazine; now, on the flight home, I'm a paranoid, anxiety-ridden fool who fiddles with strips of paper until they're in bits and just keeps shaking his head all the time. Fine in the privacy of my own flat but on a packed plane home I look deranged. The kind of person who you'd want to be sat well away from. Back in work tomorrow: D-Day.

Tuesday 30 May

Back in the office and I can't find a single soul who'll tell me if they know any sales information. What if it's a disaster and they're locked in a meeting deciding how and when to fold the magazine? It's early afternoon before the boss comes in – I'm sitting at my desk and look up as Louise walks through the door. 'It's 170,000. We might just have a hit on our hands.'

I freeze.

I can't quite believe this!

This isn't happening.

Louise is so matter of fact – with good news and bad – that sometimes you can't quite take it in. She also has utter confidence in everything she does. I, however, as I've shown to my possibly soon-to-be-ex-girlfriend, think most decisions I make are wrong. In this case, the pessimism makes the news twice as exciting. One by one people stop working, nudge each other and look over. Without thinking I get everyone together. It's not like they don't know anything's going on. I say a few words: telling the section heads, designers, subs and picture researchers who've stuck with me all this time how proud I am about what we've achieved with this issue but telling them (as I have to) that it's only one week's sale and there's a long way to go yet.

There are smiles where, for as long as I can remember, there have mainly been frowns. Someone buys half a dozen bottles of champagne. Executives I've never met before come in and slap me on the back. 'I always knew it could be done,' says one of them. Well, I'm glad you did!

Rushed home to tell Gaby the news. It's as much a relief for her as it is for me – we've had to deal with all sorts of worrying scenarios: that I'd have to go freelance and we'd have to cut our spending. That I'd be sacked and be out of work. What a relief.

Wednesday 31 May

I'm a born worrier and today – with a feeling of genuine euphoria around the office – is clearly not the day to remind people there's a long way to go. In fact, when I try it gets a bad reaction. So I shut myself into a meeting room and make notes, ideas about what we do next. The challenge we've been set is simple – sales have to be over 100,000 every week. Now we've done Posh, what on earth are we going to do next?

Monday 5 June

We're putting a real emphasis on news at the moment. News meetings are a really important part of our week now and the Monday morning one is vital.

We keep the numbers down but everyone plays their part.

News Editor Mat came from indie-music land – the *NME*. Passionate, eager to please and with great contacts. A truly lovely man.

We've just recruited Dan Wakeford from the *Sun* and he's fantastic, young and keen to impress. This is only his third week in the job but already he's doing well. While I was on holiday he shoved a copy of *Heat* into Tom Cruise's hands while he was walking along the street and got a snapper to take a shot – it really does look like Tom's carrying the magazine. And that was only Dan's fourth day in the office! He's a great talent.

Then there's Clara, our Picture Editor. I first met Clara when she sold pictures for an agency and would come from office to office selling her wares. Fiery, a tough negotiator and hard work, frankly –

needs reining in at times, but you'd rather have her on your side than on theirs.

Our Chief Sub is Julie – she makes sure we keep to our deadlines. Slightly older than most of the team but younger than all of us in spirit. A party girl, she can drink anyone under the table. Energetic and very popular – her background in high-frequency titles is essential.

Buzzing about our Beckham sale the meeting is dominated by what we can get on her next.

'We need more Posh stuff, something every week,' I say.

'Every week?' Mat raises his eyes to the ceiling but I know he's up for the challenge.

Dan has news. 'We'll get the first shots of her new look for the single in a few weeks, I spoke to Caroline yesterday.'

Ah, Caroline.

'Dan, let's keep her happy. Give her what she wants.'

'Okay, what else?'

Clara shows me some pictures.

'Julia Roberts throwing her shoes at Brad Pitt.'

'I'm sorry?'

She's winding me up.

'Okay, they're making a film! Still good, let's do a spread on these. Mat, what else?'

'This new TV show, a cartoon. There's a storyline where Britney's trying to pull Prince William.'

There's a real energy in these meetings now. We have a laugh too – very important for the morale and the atmosphere in the office. This isn't rocket science. But it feels right, and it's productive. Let's hope it continues.

More sales came in today. Our two Posh covers both sold well over 100,000. But based on very early figures, the one after, with a cobbled piece about Madonna on the front, sold bang on 100,000. We can't fall below that figure. Our closure threat is still there – if we don't deliver every week we're still in trouble.

Today we were offered a Robbie interview by a journalist who'd been commissioned by an Australian magazine. Only one problem: she's not sure if she's meant to be selling it on as she can't remember what kind of contract she signed. Robbie is such a big deal now that his management company usually want to have a say in where his interviews run – in Britain, where he couldn't be any *more* famous, they don't want him appearing anywhere. They think he's over-exposed and people will get fed up of him, so no one in the UK gets interviews. But in Australia – where he isn't as famous – the management and record company need him everywhere.

However, this journalist needs the money and she's prepared to sell it to us for a fee. And we're desperate. This 100,000 thing is addictive – all I can see in my mind is next week's cover and the words:

ROBBIE – EXCLUSIVE INTERVIEW

We need this. We're probably not supposed to do it, but I don't feel I've got much of an alternative.

I email her and tell her she has her deal, but decide not to tell anyone else how this came about. The thought of such a big interview is huge, it's exciting, but the guilt is pretty sizeable too – if the contract does preclude her selling it on we could get into trouble and she could too. But we have nothing else because no one will give us a damn thing.

Thursday 8 June

Thursday is *Heat*'s press day and the biggest day of the week. The main job of the day is getting the cover done. Essentially, it's me, Lottie, and my bosses Louise and Ian peering at a screen. Other members of the team walk past from time to time to pass comment, slag off the cover star's outfit or, occasionally, say 'who's that?' (always slightly worrying, that last one).

The Robbie cover looks really exciting and leads off with a quote about Nicole Appleton who was engaged to Robbie a couple of years before and is now going out with his mortal enemy – Liam Gallagher. It's incredible stuff … that he was never in love with Nicole, how he's often tempted to take drugs, how much he misses Take That. Reading it, I conclude that Robbie fancies the journalist, because he's flirting with her throughout and telling her everything – either that or he's just so relaxed in the knowledge that no one will ever read it outside of Australia that he feels he can say anything he wants. If he does think that, he's being very naive, as some fan site is bound to put it on the web in a matter of weeks. We're selling it in a suitably hard fashion:

SENSATIONAL INTERVIEW
Robbie!
'I've never been in love. Engaged? Yeah, but ...
that doesn't really mean anything does it?'

As with the Posh piece I've divided the interview into two and sent it off to the printers with a mouth-watering plug at the end – Robbie will talk openly about how he wants to become a dad and (most enticing of all) he'll tell *Heat*'s 100,000 (or so) readers which pop star he secretly fancies. This is dynamite. They'll be gagging for part two!

Tuesday 13 June

This afternoon we got a legal letter from Robbie's lawyers. They say we haven't the right to print the interview and are suing us. Oh shit. I've had a couple of legal letters before but this is scary and there's no room for compromise. Tonight I have just one thought on my mind:

'We're being sued. We're being sued.'

As an editor you never get used to the idea of being sued. It's rotten – the first time it happens and the hundredth. The feeling of doom when your PA walks over and puts three or four pages of A4 face down on your desk. All my PAs throughout the years have given me the same look as they do it: that mixture of sympathy and 'boy, are *you* in the shit now'. You know it's a legal letter from their look. You can also make out through the paper that densely typed text, with the official bit in bold type at the top of the letter and the bits in inverted commas where they quote the words from your article that seemed so smart and funny when you wrote it but now seem reckless and ridiculous. 'Great,' you think, 'this is going to cost my bosses, the very ones I'm supposed to be impressing, a HUGE amount of money.' Lawyers' letters are one of the few things that can get a good editor fired: it shows a lack of judgement, embarrasses the whole company and can cost a fortune they hadn't budgeted for (lots of companies do have budgets for legal costs but they always assume it won't be spent and it can go on something nicer instead).

The more a magazine pushes the boundaries – and, after all, two parts of the *Heat* philosophy are 'we won't take celebrities that seriously' and 'we'll take risks' – the more this sort of thing will happen.

I went home tonight feeling truly sick. I know that this won't be the only time a celebrity will come after us. Better get used to it.

The really sickening thing about today? Robbie's lawyers won't let me run my beloved part two.

Wednesday 14 June

Our main mission for today is to try and overturn Robbie's ban on part two of 'our' interview.

I'm trying everything. At the other end of the phone, our lawyer Richard bats away every pathetic attempt I make.

'Just say to them there's no point in stopping part two because the worst bits have already run in part one.'

'But they say you shouldn't have run any of it.'

'Hmm. How about we only run some of it.'

'They won't go for that.'

'I know, offer Robbie some money for his charity, then they'll let us print it.'

He's really not sure but agrees to give it a go.

Two hours later he calls back.

'Robbie wants to thank you for the money ...'

Yes!

'... He says the charity will be very grateful ...'

I am a genius!

'... But you still can't run it.'

Oh great. Our next cover: gone. Also, and this hurts, the 100,000 readers we've managed to get to read the magazine are now going to feel let down by us because we can't provide them with something we promised.

A thoroughly depressing day – and still no cover for the next issue.

Thursday 15 June

Press day. Everything has to leave the office by the end of today – if it doesn't we risk not having the magazine on sale next Tuesday. The team arrived at work this morning to see me there pacing around the office like some demented zoo animal. I've had an idea – just cos we're not allowed to put part two of the interview on the cover doesn't mean we can't put Robbie on there. So we have done! With Kylie, the pop star he was about to reveal he fancied.

Everyone piles in to the cuttings cupboard – filing cabinets full of articles and interviews and news stories all cut out (badly) from news-papers. Mat Smith, our brilliant News Editor who deserves far more challenging assignments than this one, finds a quote from Robbie saying how much he likes Kylie: 'She's gorgeous and frail, I feel like I want to protect her and keep her under my wing.'

Our junior news guy Paul Croughton – several hours later – finds one from Kylie about Robbie. 'I think he's well fanciable,' the quote goes. 'It might happen. He's very cute.'

Put them together and … BINGO! The same story as the one we're not allowed to run!

Today, we've had a real 'Eureka!' moment. Since the Posh inter-view – and the increased pressures on me to maintain that 100,000+ sale – I've been constantly frustrated by the brick wall we're up against. No one big gives us interviews, no one big (in Robbie's case) even wants us to have second-hand interviews. Yet the tabloids (who don't get them either) sell millions a day by being clever, cheeky even. It's that attitude that *Heat* needs. Why wait around for scraps when we can get in there, roll up our sleeves and get what we want, what our read-ers what. A tabloid, but in magazine form. It's more expensive than a paper, sure, but the pictures are in glossy colour, the ink doesn't come off in your hands and you're not ashamed to read it on the train.

Today, we delivered the kind of magazine we wanted by being clever and cheeky and without having to butter up famous people and the team of people around them. I can't face doing that every single week. It is soul-destroying and rarely works anyway. Getting an inter-view with a million-selling singer or top Hollywood star, week in week out, would involve doing all of the following:

1. Suck up to a PR. This could take several months.
2. Promise the PR the world – copy-approved interviews, retouched photos, the lot.
3. Arrive at the interview, discover that famous person will only discuss how great it was to work with their latest co-star, and not their boyfriend/girlfriend, person they're having an affair with, their famous friends, money, houses, the drugs they take or the partying (i.e. anything interesting).
4. Eventually manage to persuade the star to give you a bit of 'colour'

– some piece of gossip that they think is amazingly revelatory but is actually the same anecdote they trot out in every interview.

5. Get it all approved, put the words together with the retouched pictures (where the celeb no longer looks like them or even human) and then put the magazine on sale.

That is what incredibly famous people (and their agents and publicists) will put magazine editors through every day of the week if they're allowed to.

But readers are now getting bored with all that, they realise that they're not getting to see the real person and they're aware that, essentially, this is someone selling product with the least possible bit of effort on their part. Sales of glossy mags are falling because people want something a bit real. Tabloid papers have done it for years but now there's an appetite among magazine readers for this too.

Quotes given when celebs are not on their guard or don't have PRs breathing down their necks is what we want.

This way we can deliver the stories people really want even if we don't get an interview. Readers want their magazines fast, pacey and unapproved now – they don't want retouched photos and bland copy-approved interviews any more. They don't believe them.

I think the tables may have turned. Maybe now we can call the shots.

Wednesday 28 June

Another great day. The marketing team burst into a news meeting with some fantastic news – both Robbie issues (the one with him on his own and the one with him and Kylie) sold over 100,000. We still stand a chance of survival – the average sale from mid-May to now is just over 100,000. The team are working long hours, fuelled by adrenalin and the occasional glass of management champagne (they LOVE us now!)

Friday 14 July

Today ten people have gone into something called the Big Brother house. I've been hearing about the Dutch version of this show for several months now and I have to be honest: the whole thing unnerves me. Foreign TV has always been more out there than ours – Chris Tarrant has got several series out of what mad Japanese people put themselves through for fame – but this seems to be taking an odder, darker turn. The stuff I hear about the show makes it sound wilfully cruel: people are locked in a house for nine weeks, they don't know what time of day it is, they're woken up in the middle of the night by some shadowy figure called Big Brother. Weird. Its arrival on Dutch TV was met with criticism from a media concerned about the effect on the contestants. I'm not sure either. Plus, the hype is unbearable. We've run a few bits on the UK version of the show but I'm sceptical. 'Let's not go overboard on this,' I told the TV team yesterday, leading from the front as always. 'Just because the rest of Europe's gone mad for it doesn't mean Britain will. This could well be a huge flop.'

Tuesday 18 July
The first episode of *Big Brother* – covering the first few days that the contestants have been in the house – went out on Channel 4 this evening. The show began with the housemates wheeling their suitcases along a path into this characterless box. So far, so dull. But within minutes they were arguing, engaging in power struggles and taking their clothes off. I realised halfway through that I know nothing and it will be huge. In fact it's amazing. There's nothing like watching how people interact, flirt, get annoyed and cope under pressure. It's a little unsettling too: voyeuristic with a real sense that you're seeing something you shouldn't.

Wednesday 19 July
Boyd came over with the news that 3.7 million people watched last night's show – huge for Channel 4. I look like an idiot in the office. Might have to reverse my opinion about covering it in the mag.

Friday 28 July
In Edinburgh for the weekend with Gaby but it hasn't gone to plan. The plane was delayed and my plans to watch the first *Big Brother* 'eviction' show have been wrecked (yep, I'm now addicted). Our taxi pulled up at the hotel about 20 minutes before the end of the show, we checked in and dashed up to the room just in time to see sloaney Sada evicted. The scenes are incredible – scary even. Davina McCall is standing in front of a baying crowd – some of whom have placards for God's sake! – as some poor woman prepares to come up out of a TV house

she's been locked in for two weeks. This is proper edgy TV, the sort of thing that scares you. The power of the show has hit me tonight. It's extreme but exciting and absolutely fascinating: what if someone in that crowd starts throwing things? Could someone rush the barriers and grab hold of a contestant they don't like? I can't stop thinking about it.

Thursday 3 August

Tonight, two of the contestants on *Big Brother* have snogged. Brilliant! Now we've got a TV programme! Andy (bit big for his boots) and Mel (far more streetwise, if a little self-conscious) kissed at just after 9 p.m. this evening. He's clearly into her; she's not that into him. 'You shouldn't have done that,' she said while grinning, 'you couldn't handle me in the real world.'

Andy, clearly not ready to retreat, replied with a rather smug, 'I'm willing to give it a try.'

Then they got interrupted. Booooo!

Friday 4 August

The snog. The snog! The office can talk about nothing but the snog. They're obsessed. In the middle of the office Clara and her picture team are in full swing …

'She's just playing with him! He's putty in her hands.'

'Rubbish, she's just playing it cool because the cameras are on her.'

'We'll see – it won't last two minutes outside, betcha.'

I know why they're so gripped as well – for all the great dramas or incredible fly-on-the-wall documentaries, TV has never seen this real-ness. We've never been there when someone falls for someone or even just decide they fancy them. And now we are. It's like the *OK* cover of the Beckham wedding: what people loved about that magazine was that they, the reader, could be there when the two of them became man and wife. But this TV show is even better, because now we can be there when people kiss for the first time. *Heat*, I have decided, should be the magazine that's there at the most important moments of a celebrity's life: when they fall in love (or lust), split up or are in despair. We can be the magazine equivalent of a reality TV show, a soap opera but about real people who just happen to be famous. I think I knew this all anyway, but *Big Brother* has crystallised every-thing for me. Suddenly everything seems so obviously clear.

If we're discussing it in the office chances are hundreds of thousands of other people are gossiping about 'Randy Andy' and Mel, too. Does she like him or was she just being kind? Was he forcing himself on her to try and avoid eviction, by suggesting to the people at home that something more would happen if they kept him in? If he did think that, it didn't work. Tonight he is the second *Big Brother* evictee. And Mel isn't that bothered. She already has her eye on shy Irish housemate Tom ...

Thursday 10 August
As is our Thursday tradition, the inner cabal is convened and we design the cover, But this week I'm having a minor panic. The semi-finished design has a photoshoot we did with Randy Andy on it – and I'm grabbing people from around the office to have a look. 'Okay,' I'd say pointing at it, 'but is he actually famous? I mean, I know he's on telly but he's not a celebrity is he?'

I've agonised over this. It seems the weirdest thing – I get that the show's huge but here's someone – an ordinary guy who's been locked in a house for a few weeks – who's not really a celebrity at all, but he's on our cover. Well, he is a celebrity, sort of. But he's not a film star, and he doesn't make records ... First rule of celebrity magazines: put a celebrity on the cover, stupid!

Julian, thinking instinctively as usual, reckons it's a great idea: 'Everyone's talking about him in the office – don't worry about it.'

Louise is freaked out by it – she just doesn't get *Big Brother* and thinks we're going 'too far, too soon'. Still, we've gone with it.

Tuesday 15 August
Spent the evening at the BBC. Because of the magazine's ever-increasing profile quite a few of us are getting asked to be on TV shows and I encourage anyone asked to say yes. It's essentially free advertising – and if we don't say yes to sitting on some TV sofa our rivals probably will.

Tonight I was asked to be on a show called *Liquid News* and I jumped at the chance. I love *Liquid News* and have been hoping for a while that I'd get asked to be on. A daily round-up of the latest entertainment news, the show is most notable for its presenter: a large, wry, some would say sarcy, gay, *Eurovision*-obsessed guy called Christopher

Price. The show looks like a normal news bulletin – guy in a suit sits behind a desk, cueing in reporter-fronted news items. But all the reports are about the world of celebrity and Price treats the ridiculous characters of that world with the disdain they require. It's a great show and I am flattered to be asked on it, even if it takes up much of my evening (it goes out live at 7 p.m.). In many ways it's a companion to what *Heat* does, the moving picture version of our funny, sarcy take on showbiz. Today's other guest was our current cover star Randy Andy and (ridiculously) I felt really star-struck. Of all the people you meet in this job why the *hell* am I star-struck about a guy who isn't famous and has just been filmed in a house doing bugger all for a few weeks? No idea. But I was. It's pathetic. Show went well and they asked me back on.

Wednesday 16 August

Interviewed Jamie Theakston this morning for our next cover. An ex-kids' TV presenter who's just recently gravitated to bigger things, he's being hounded by the tabloids at the moment – he wanted to be interviewed outside of central London because he's being followed by the paparazzi day and night, so we met at the Cobden Club, a grand, showy private members' bar – all drapes and secret alcoves – frequented by the ultra-cool West London brigade. You think the Groucho Club/Soho House lot are cool? The West London bunch look down on that crowd. Too many suits and expense accounts for the Notting Hill bunch, the clientele here are ten years younger and would rather die than wear trainers you can actually buy in Britain. They wear jeans that fall beneath your arse (on purpose), grow silly little beards and greet each other with complicated handshakes. It's like I've wandered into an alien world, Planet Stupidly Cool.

Theakston's nervous and cagey from the moment I shake hands with him – although that's not that surprising. The last few occasions he's been written about haven't gone well. One tabloid journo concluded he was an egomaniac ('for 20 minutes all Jamie did was talk about himself' the piece said – surely the point of interviews?), his relatively new relationship with a very famous, older woman (Joely Richardson) has been pulled apart and – worst of all – an ex-girlfriend apparently told a gossip columnist that he had a small penis! Whoops. This has led to all sorts of hassle for him: he's been joked about by his friend Sara Cox on the radio, opinion columnists have mocked him and, on one particularly memorable day, a lorry driver shouted 'pencil dick' at him as he walked down the street. With his mum!

I'm genuinely shocked. 'That actually happened?'

'Yep,' he says looking mortified, 'then I had to explain the whole thing to her because she doesn't read those newspapers.'

So no wonder he's so nervy – although he opens up a bit, he won't talk about exes, is overly formal and uptight about certain 'hot spots', so answers end up sounding over-rehearsed and naff (having a child would be 'a blessing' he 'reveals' at one point. 'I'm sure the birth of my first child will be a huge defining moment in my life').

Eventually, though, I do get him to open up when I ask about Joely because he is so loved up: how he had to miss a big Euro 2000 match because she'd hurt her leg, about the sacrifices he makes for her. He feels he can trust us and he's right. *Heat* is gradually getting to be known as the safe enclave of celebdom – battered and bruised by the tabloids? Come to *Heat* and we'll be nicer to you. I like that approach. It feels right for me. It doesn't come easily to me, being mean. Anyway, Theakston's a nice guy and he appreciates that we're giving him a fair hearing. In fact he's so relaxed that a shot we hoped he'd pose for but assumed he'd refuse to do – of him at a urinal, a reference to willy-gate – he's quite happy to do. Increasingly people like him like us – because we're the good guys.

Thursday 17 August

It's insane the effect a TV show can have on an office of people. Granted, it doesn't take much to put the *Heat* team off their work but today is extreme. After becoming aware of his manipulating ways the housemates confronted *Big Brother*'s bad guy Nick Bateman and, prompted by this, the show's producers chucked him out! We watched this unfold on the Internet – live footage is streamed 24/7 but the system keeps crashing so we only watch a few minutes at a time before it happens again and we have to reboot the computer. But gradually the entire office wandered over to the poor designer's computer, people from other parts of the building even dropping in. Somehow, this all feels like a big cultural event and we've all found ourselves stopping work to get our voyeuristic kicks from the pictures. I remember, at primary school, loads of us gathering around the big school telly to watch the shuttle take-off. Surely some bloke wheeling a suitcase out of a house can't have the same must-see effect? But, weirdly, it does. This is the world of celebrity, 21st-century style.

I convened an emergency meeting in the hallway.

'So he's gone?' I ask Julian.

'Yeah, the press team just called.'

'He's going to have to go into hiding, isn't he? The whole nation hates him, don't they?'

Everyone shrugs. We've no idea if this guy – because of his actions on a TV show – has just gone and ruined his entire life. Yes it's just a TV programme, but right now *Big Brother* feels like the centre of our world. I've cleared six pages for the Nasty Nick departure story, and I've just called up the marketing department suggesting they print 50,000 extra copies next week.

Tuesday 22 August

The Randy Andy issue has been a huge seller for us – over 150,000. The Nasty Nick one will surpass that, I'm sure. The definition of celebrity has just widened.

Anyone is now a celebrity. We've been the first to realise this and it's something that is helping us immensely. No one else has picked up on it. The papers are dismissing it as a minority Channel 4 show and aren't covering it. The other magazines are run by people who are – frankly – too old and just don't get it (which is crazy, especially as these offices will be packed full of twenty-something junior writers and designers who will be talking about nothing else). *Big Brother* is where we can really make ourselves stand out from the competition. And, rather brilliantly, there's an endless supply of new faces for us to cover too. It could have been invented for us.

Monday 4 September

Next week is the final of *Big Brother* and we're compiling a special preview issue. We sat around thinking of ideas and, half-joking, I suggested starting a helpline for *Big Brother* obsessives who can't face life without it. I've become convinced it's a great idea: a German radio station did one when Take That split up and it's kind of the same. We've persuaded Phillip Hodson, the Agony Uncle on the eighties Saturday morning kids' TV show *Going Live*, to man a phoneline for five hours the day after the final and we'll plug it in the new issue.

Thursday 7 September

Put the issue to bed, with the phoneline number printed in huge 48-point type on a really prominent page. Other people aren't as keen as I am: in fact, it's become known as 'Mark's helpline' in the office as I'm the only one who thinks it's a good idea. Not so sure myself any more.

Friday 15 September

The *Big Brother* final! Buoyed by some great sales and fascinated by the programme, we are going to work late, probably until about 3 a.m., putting together an end-of-series souvenir issue – the first 30 pages is full of interviews, analysis and pictures of the best moments. Craig, the amiable scouser, won. The media went *Big Brother* crazy – our PRs received seven or eight requests for interviews with me! I only had time to do one – a TV interview for an American TV channel. When I got there they didn't seem interested in who I thought would win, my opinions on the final three or anything. They were just obsessed by my STUPID helpline idea. It really is not an idea that stands up that well to examination: 'Do you really think your readers will need counselling when a TV programme ends?' No, we did it as a joke. 'What are you trying to say about people who watch this TV programme?' Nothing, it was a joke. And so on. The papers have even been writing about it. We're going to look like idiots.

Saturday 16 September

Slept badly last night. I wasn't going to have a great night's sleep anyway as I didn't get home until 4 a.m. but I woke up at 10 a.m. just as the helpline opened. In the cold light of day it seems like such a dumb idea. I have visions of idiots phoning up lovely Phillip Hodson and being rude to him or just putting the phone down. The PR for the show rings to say that 10 million watched the final part of last night's show. And 7.7 million of them voted. Bloody hell!

Monday 18 September

How early can you call a counsellor? Do they sleep in? Get up early? I managed to hold out calling Phillip Hodson until, ooh, five past nine. Incredible news: 2,000 people called our helpline. As he was the only person manning the phone for the five hours the line was open, he could only answer just under 100 of them. But the response was astonishing – I was expecting prank-callers, piss-takers and the occasional media enquiry but what we got was real emotion. One girl phoned in in tears because she loved Craig, who won, but felt let down when she read a taboid interview that made him sound like a bit of a love-rat. One softly spoken woman told Phillip that Nasty Nick was haunting her dreams night after night and she didn't know what to do. Several said the series ending made them realise they didn't have enough friends and decided to try and meet more or join clubs and societies. Many rang in just to say they felt silly being upset about a TV show ending – you and me both!

This really has been an incredible success. Lots of people laughed when they knew we were doing it – *I* didn't even take it that seriously. But this show has somehow affected people's lives. It is truly involving TV – and I can't pretend I am any different from some of the people calling the helpline.

But it's now three days since the show ended and I'm missing it – nothing to watch on TV, hurriedly making plans to fill up spare evenings. I made the mistake of telling Julie this. What was I thinking – with a perma-glint in her eye she relishes any chance to take the piss: 'Is that helpline of yours still open? Maybe you should give it a ring?'

Cheers.

Tuesday 26 September
Now *Big Brother*'s over, Gaby and I have been able to get away for a bit. Nothing to watch on telly any more anyway so the Algarve – still boiling hot at this time of year – is the perfect place. It's certainly been a less-stressed holiday than the last one. We fly home tomorrow and I feel nicely refreshed. Even better, this morning I got my first work text of the trip – from Lottie, who won the battle to tell me the good news – the end-of-series *Big Brother* souvenir issue has sold over 200,000 copies, the first issue to do that many. I can die a happy man.

Wednesday 27 September
Woke up at 5.30 a.m. in a total panic. *Big Brother*. It's finished. What the hell are we going to fill our pages with now?

CHAPTER THREE
Geri wants my children
October 2000 – September 2001

Wednesday 18 October

Thank God for the Spice Girls. Thank God for Caroline McAteer. I spent all day backstage at *Top Of The Pops*, smuggled in as part of the Spice Girls entourage. *Top Of The Pops* has a rule that only their own magazine's journalists are allowed in so I have signed in as a friend of the band. I'm here to write an access-all-areas piece and, God, it's exhausting.

Mel B's gorgeous daughter Phoenix Chi is running around from person to person asking for food. 'Have you got any chips?' she'd say. 'No, sorry Phoenix.' Then on to the next person: 'Have you got any chips?' When they say no she moves on to the next. Kids are *shameless*.

Posh spends all her time posing, preening, asking if she looks all right and popping back into their dressing room endlessly. Her mum's there too. 'Mum, how does this look?' 'You look fine.' 'Really?' 'Yes! Fine, gorgeous.' She then heads over to the mirror and shakes her head as she fiddles with her outfit then her hair.

Emma is lovely (Emma is always lovely – friendly, polite, an absolute dream).

Then there's Mel C.

Mel C isn't really speaking to me, which isn't ideal when you're supposed to be interviewing her. Since *Big Brother* ended we've gone Spice Girls crazy. Scared silly about our sales falling off now the show's over, we've been covering everything they do, no matter how tenuous: who's put on weight, who's lost weight, who's bought a new dress. We're a celebrity magazine after all: we can get away with this sort of stuff. Particularly of interest, though, has been Mel's love life. Earlier this year the (completely incorrect) tabloid story was that she was a lesbian – she was very close to her female assistant and the two holidayed together. Since the rumours died down she's gone man-mad: there was a fling with Robbie Williams, an affair with one of the boys in Five and now a new man, a guy called Dan who's in a band called Tomcat, who is here, skulking in the shadows. The team with the Spice Girls are doing everything they can to keep me away from him. No, you can't speak to him. No, you can't take photos. In fact, it becomes patently obvious that she doesn't really want me here at all.

'Ah, *Heat* magazine!' she says with a fake cheesy grin. 'I'm not talking to you.'

'Aww, come on Mel! Don't be like that! How's the new bloke?'

'Get lost.'

She grabs Dan's hand and wanders off.

I decide to follow them. It's my journalistic duty. Some would call it stalking but that's patently not true – after all, I'm with the band. For the next five minutes I wander down corridors, ducking out of the way when she looks over her shoulder.

Eventually I find them through a side door, snogging each other's faces off. Ten minutes later they're down a different corridor doing the same.

Okay, Mel. We get the idea. You're not a lesbian. Don't shove it down our throat (or his).

Once she's onstage I manage to escape Caroline's clutches for ten minutes and grab Dan. He's like a love-sick puppy, looking wistfully at Mel C as she throws shapes for the camera. 'She acts really hard when she's up there but she's not, you know. She's dead soft.'

Mel comes offstage and eyes me with huge suspicion. I know she saw me talking to him. She steers him away from me for the rest of the day.

Tuesday 31 October

Robbie and Liam are still at each other's throats. Tonight was the *Q* Awards at the Park Lane Hotel and they were both there. While most other music awards shows have got dull and corporate, the *Q* Awards is still an unruly, drunken bear pit. Drinks are thrown, people get into scraps and – because it's not televised – they say and do whatever they want. This is the off-duty awards and anything goes.

Sitting in the basement after the award ceremony had taken place there was a sudden commotion two tables away. Liam had been taunting Robbie all night and Robbie – surrounded by his own entourage and four security guards – didn't seem that bothered. Until, that is, Gallagher started chanting insults about Kylie. Then Robbie got more and more agitated.

Liam was drunk but that's no excuse for being purposely vile.

As she walked a few yards in front of him he shouted the immortal words, 'Get your tits out, you lesbian!'

I couldn't believe this was happening – there was Liam Gallagher screaming in Kylie's direction. Suddenly everyone around us felt incredibly uncomfortable. Robbie glares at him. But Liam isn't finished.

'Yeah … and write your own songs.'

At this point, Robbie saw red. He walked over to Liam, fists clenched by his side. Then, just yards away, he unclenched his fists and did a swift about turn, just yards from Liam's table. Part of me was disappointed. Is that bad? Feuds sell magazines and fights make for good picture spreads.

Tuesday 14 November

Today Dominic Smith interviewed Kelly Brook. Kelly Brook isn't happy and really doesn't want to do the interview and I don't blame her. But she has to – she's in a play in London called *Eye Contact* and the contract she's signed says she has to do magazine interviews. Whereas some celebs hate magazines because of some perceived slight or because they didn't pump up their ego enough, Kelly Brook probably hates us because one week last autumn we paid a journalist to watch every minute of *The Big Breakfast* – the show she was presenting – and write down every mistake she made. Every fluff, every mispronounced name, everything. The article had a huge effect on her – it led to an endless stream of tabloid criticism, industry speculation and, eventually, she was removed from the show. We didn't make the decision to fire her – the show's producers did – but we are still partly responsible. How responsible she thinks we are we were about to find out …

Dom was the right man for the job. A tough, persistent interviewer he loves challenges like this. Any other journalist would be nervous as they're heading out to do an interview this contentious, Dom just grabbed his tape recorder and off he went. I wait in the office for news and when I get some it seems Dom's charmed the pants off her. She has a bit of a rant (quite rightly) about what we did. 'It was a delicate situation,' she told Dom, 'I'd just started my first TV job and I didn't really need that.'

Dom – who opposed the original piece anyway – is sympathetic and gets real raw emotion out of her. She knows it was my idea so gives Dom an easy ride. If she ever bumps into me, I don't think I'll get off so lightly.

Saturday 18 November

Catherine Zeta-Jones and Micheal Douglas marry in New York. A photographer sneaks into the wedding posing as a waiter and sells the pictures to *Hello* magazine, in spite of the happy couple's exclusive deal with *OK* magazine. The shit's really going to hit the fan now.

Friday 22 December

Madonna married Guy Ritchie at a remote castle in Scotland today. It's just three days before Christmas but still the local village is packed with journalists and photographers, all standing outside the gates to the castle freezing and getting bugger all. One photographer, fed up with the cold and with his agency screaming down the phone at him, hides in a piano inside the chapel so he can get some exclusive pictures of the ceremony. Sadly he was discovered a few hours before the vows. It's a sign of how big the whole celebrity thing is now, that the wedding becomes such a circus.

Tuesday 2 January 2001

First day back and we've only got four days to do the issue. Today's news meeting is vitally important.

I'm trying to get the meeting started but Dan and Clara are distracted – they're poring over some photographs.

'You won't believe these.'

'Dan, try me … Jesus!'

There, before my very eyes, is pop singer Billie (a mere 18) sitting on the knee of Chris Evans (34).

'Dan, tell me they're joking. This is a wind up.'

'Nope, he's just bought her a Ferrari. Delivered it to her just before Christmas.'

'Billie can't drive!'

'Correct.'

The consensus of the meeting – and the *Heat* office generally – can be summed up in one sentence: dirty old man.

This relationship isn't going anywhere.

Wednesday 24 January

The big TV show at the moment is ITV's *Popstars*. The show features a series of singers going through a prolonged audition to become part of a pop band. Star of the show at the moment is a Glaswegian student called Darius. Darius is an over-the-top show-off whose animated cover versions have become cult viewing. ITV have tipped us off that he's getting the boot in Saturday's show (the series is pre-recorded) so today we interviewed him. He is now far more modest but still thinks he's going to have a number one record. We're putting him straight on the cover next Tuesday.

Saturday 27 January

So glad we've got Darius for Tuesday's cover. ITV said his final show was going to be good and they weren't wrong. His performance of Britney Spears' '...Baby One More Time' is preposterous: full of exaggerated gestures and odd quirks. He is a true *Heat* character: funny, memorable and everyone's talking about him. No one has picked up on him other than us – the competition has been left well behind.

Thursday 15 February

Another great day: at midday we announced our latest sales figures for the six months between July and December last year. Our average sale was 172,311 copies! The *Guardian* have asked me to write a piece about how well we've done – it's a great opportunity to show off. 'We've got a brilliant, loyal team working hard every single day,' I wrote. 'The management have been nothing short of inspirational' (what a creep!) before building up to the truly self-satisfied, 'There's no bigger thrill than seeing people reading *Heat* on buses, raving about it to their friends, talking about it on the radio, writing about us in the papers.'

I look really smug in the picture too. People are going to hate us.

Tuesday 20 February

Lunch with Kris Thykier today. Kris is the MD at Freud Communications, one of the biggest PR companies around. He arrives at Chez Gérard with the last *Heat* in his sweaty palm. He looks angry.

'What the hell are you doing?'

Always a good start.

'What do you mean?'

'You've printed a picture of one of my clients' houses.'

He opens the magazine at a story about Geri Halliwell. There, clear as anything, is her house. There's no street name but the number of the house is clear.

'There's burglers in London right now targeting rich people. You can't do this.'

'But there's no street name on it! Kris, it'll be fine.'

Eventually he calms down. Of course it'll be fine. PR people worry too much.

Monday 26 February

Oh my God. Just got back from the Brit Awards and no one is talking about the performances or who won what. They're talking about Geri bloody Halliwell, who debuted her new body on the show. There's nothing of her! She looks like she's down to about seven stone, and she clearly wanted to show off all her hard work (short skirt, gold bra top, boots and nothing else) and it's the most gobsmacking transformation I've ever seen. I liked the chunky Geri – clearly Geri didn't!

Tuesday 27 February

Birchy rushes into the office first thing. 'Geri Halliwell! It's a cover, surely!' I love Birchy. He's as amused by the scandal, the weight loss, the weight gain and the who-said-what-to-whom as I am. He's right, of course. He's always right.

'We won't get an interview in time,' I tell him, 'if at all.'

'Doesn't matter!' he says without a second's hesitation. 'Put her on the cover anyway.'

So we have done. Our Fashion Editor Ellie is blown away by her new look – 'Is that really her?' she said to me when I show the pictures, '*the* Geri Halliwell?' and is given the piece to write. It's our girliest cover yet – unashamedly interested in one woman's body. It feels kind of voyeuristic – we analyse every sinew, every bump on her body. 'Geri's Amazing New Look!' reads the breathless coverline. 'New body, new hair – how did she do that?'

Wednesday 28 February

Spent today in Brighton at Zoë Ball's house.

In decades past, journalists and famous people would spend days together, sometimes weeks, to get a decent interview. They'd go round their houses, go on tour with them, ring them for follow-up chats after the main interview had been done. Hell, many of them even slept together. These days most famous people will give you an hour of their time for an interview (if you're lucky), and a small percentage (growing for *Heat* because our sales are getting pretty high) will give you a photoshoot. Zoë sees it the old-fashioned way, which is why I spent all day with her today.

I got off the train at Brighton station just after 11, met up with our photographer Paul Rider who drove his mini down from London for the occasion: a mini packed with cameras, photographic umbrella, various other photographic paraphernalia, plus an assistant, make-up artist and hair person. I squeezed into the back and we headed out of Brighton towards Hove and immediately got lost. So we rang Zoë (celebrities letting journalists have their phone number – there's something that doesn't happen very often), she passed the phone to Norman (aka Fatboy Slim aka Zoë's husband) and he gave us directions. Which was useful because we were hopelessly, pathetically lost …

I tell Norman where we are …

'You've gone too far! Turn around.'

'Okay, we're heading back to Brighton.'

'Can you see a sign on your right that says No Entry?'

'Er, yep.'

'That has a winding lane just beyond it?'

'Yessss.'

'Go down there.'

'There' is the most exclusive road on the Sussex coast. A row of eight huge beach-front houses, each with their own bit of beach. Paul

McCartney owns one, Nick Berry – possibly the biggest TV actor of the moment, thanks to his starring role in *Heartbeat* – another, and Norman and Zoë? Well, they own two. Of course.

'Okay, we're going down the lane now.'

'Now can you see a balding bloke waving manically at you?'

And there he was. Norman Cook, superstar DJ, one of the ten richest musicians of the last year, waving his long bronzed arms above his head.

We'd made it.

Norman helped us with our bags and walked us into the house to meet Zoë. Just two and a half months after giving birth to baby Woody she's in great shape and doesn't look that tired, a situation that may be helped by a woman called Jackie, Woody's nanny. Also present are Norman's gooey-eyed parents and two people known as 'The Dusters'. They wear matching outfits and carry about the business with all the zeal and purpose of someone involved in major renovation work. In actual fact all they're doing is dusting. They come to the house to do this twice a week, every week of the year. Life of a celebrity, eh? You can have dusters on the payroll and everything!

However, if any house in all of Christendom needed over 100 dusts a year it's this one. It's not just two houses stuck together: it's two big, wide houses stuck together – so corridors go from east to west and stretch as far as the eye can see.

I ask for a tour – as if I was going to take no for an answer. First stop, the staircase and the display of hundreds of acid-house smileys. Smileys on mugs, smiley badges, smiley stickers. Miles of smileys.

Zoë leads us upstairs. 'Do you want to see the bar?'

Sure, what visit to a person's house is complete without a visit to the bar?

This one is vast – as big as the main bar at your average village pub. It has a huge neon sign (that reads 'Norm's Bar'), real optics to get real measures and, naturally, a pole. A great big, slippery, glistening pole. For pole-dancing.

Next is the balcony, with giant hot tub. 'I'd suggest doing the interview in the hot tub,' says Zoë, completely seriously, 'but it's raining.'

I didn't get to see either Zoë and Norm's bedroom or Woody's but I did see the kitchen (reassuringly messy) and the bathrooms.

Which leaves just the beach. The private beach. There's no garden here but, frankly, when you have your own piece of Brighton beach (or rather two pieces of beach, one comes with each house after all) that really doesn't matter.

The tour over, we headed to the upstairs lounge for the interview. Zoë appreciates the sit down – she's adjusting to having a child around, is doing extensive press for her new show and has just got her period so the chance to relax and chat for an hour or so is perfect for her.

I love Zoë. As nice as many famous people are it's often a real battle to get to see the real them. Spend five minutes in Zoë Ball's company and you get to see the real her. She is a hyperactive bundle of insecurities and is constantly in a panic about a million different things: what people think of her, her figure, saying the wrong thing. The last one is fascinating: normally people who are worried about saying the wrong thing and upsetting people are insular and bland. Zoë just shoots her mouth off all the time. If she meets someone and they're an arsehole to her she'll tell you as soon as they're out of the door – forgetting for a second that you'll print it and that she'll have to work with them again at some point in the future. Get her on the subject of the Spice Girls, say, and she's scathing: she'll tell you about the time she interviewed them and how one of them threw completely uncalled-for diva strops. Then she'll wonder why that person is funny with her the next time they speak.

Anyway, today there's no stopping her: she doesn't give a damn about Billie and Chris Evans, thinks his behaviour towards Geri Halliwell was 'appalling' before saying that the only reason Geri Halliwell got the figure she had at the Brits is because she 'doesn't eat'.

She's candid beyond belief, even telling me the story of how she and Norman nearly had sex a few hours after the birth when she was still high on the epidural. 'He climbed into bed with me and we're like, "Oh my God, what are we doing?" – getting a bit amorous. Then the nurse came in and we were like teenage kids getting caught out.'

She's great copy, gossipy, indiscreet and just fun. I adore her. I ended up spending several hours with her and Norman and headed back to London exhilarated, having made my first ever famous friend. It'll be holidays to Ibiza and nights out clubbing at Ministry before I know it, guaranteed.

Monday 5 March

There's something about editing a magazine that turns mild-mannered individuals into rabidly competitive sub-humans. For the last few months we've made all the news in the world of publishing – because of our incredible rising sales, because we instigated the Liam/Robbie war and because it seems we now have a direct line to the Beckhams (we wish!) This week, though, someone is threatening our top-dog status and I don't like it one single bit. Conde Nast, the high-end home of classy mags like *Vogue* and *GQ*, are launching a new magazine called *Glamour*. Some of their team used to work here and we like them but its very existence bugs me. Jealously I know they'll steal loads of our limelight and probably some of our sales. Their big, hugely expensive launch party is tomorrow. I'm invited but I can't face it. Going will mean spending all night telling them through gritted teeth how great their magazine is, which isn't going to happen. My competitive spirit won't let me go. I'm afraid that, even worse, I just want to rain on their parade.

Opposite the party venue in Leicester Square is a vast disused club called Sound. The place is gutted these days but their focal point remains – a 30-foot high screen stuck to the front. I asked the marketing team how much it would cost to hire it for the night tomorrow, and it's dirt cheap! I've had an evil idea, but we needed to execute it quickly. We've found a designer with a free hour and set him to work ...

Tuesday 6 March

Tonight I spent the evening outside a party I was meant to be at, taking pictures of a 30-foot tall screen. *Glamour*'s USP is that it's handbag sized. The jury is out on whether this is a bold move or an expensive folly. We hired the screen and got an ad together – this week's *Heat* cover accompanied by the words 'Size Does Matter'.

It looks incredible. Every taxi arriving at the party pulls up in front of it – people point and laugh at the advert. I know it's petty but to me it's hilarious.

Sunday 18 March

The band formed by the TV show *Popstars* – Hear'say – go straight in at number one, with their first single 'Pure and Simple' selling more copies in one week than any other record. Weird.

Tuesday 20 March
Police say Geri Halliwell's home was burgled on Sunday night. She came back from holiday yesterday to discover that her place had been broken into, obscene messages had been daubed on her walls, milk and Ribena sprayed everwhere (!) and that stuff had been stolen.

I feel terrible. Even if this isn't our fault – and I maintain that we made sure Geri's address was unidentifiable when we ran the picture – some people will still blame us.

Thursday 29 March
Called Geri's PR team to request an interview.

Their response is pretty blunt: 'No way.'

I'm not surprised, but feign surprise anyway: 'What? Why?'

'You know why – you printed a photo of her front door in your magazine.'

'Aw, come on!'

'Mark, it's a no.'

Tuesday 10 April
The *Daily Mirror* are claiming that Chris Evans and Billie Piper are now engaged! The paper says he proposed in Paris last week (on 1 April in fact, Evans' 35th birthday). The couple are holed up in his holiday home in Portugal, so aren't commenting. What is it about famous people that they have to do everything on fast forward? It's great for us obviously (always something to report – never a dull day!) but what is it about them that makes them want to do everything so bloody quickly? Slow down!

Wednesday 11 April
Geri Halliwell's record company have announced the release date for her next single. Now they'll do it. Ring the PR.

'So, erm, there's a release date for the single now.'

'Mark, she won't do an interview with you.'

Can't some people just forgive and forget?

Monday 23 April

Here's a turn-up for the books – Geri's PR is now phoning *me*.

'You know you wanted an interview with Geri?'

'A-ha.'

'Would it be a cover?'

Celebrities. They'll do anything for a front cover. Even talk to the magazine that may have got them burgled.

We have our interview.

Wednesday 25 April

Today – at last – was Geri Halliwell interview day. A day I never thought would come. By rights she should hate us. But she does have a single to promote, she's desperate to match the Spice Girls and get to number one with her comeback solo single – a version of The Weather Girls' camp classic 'It's Raining Men' – and being on our cover the week of release will help hugely.

Geri's doing a day of foreign press at St Martins Lane Hotel in central London and has hired the suite on the top floor. Pristine, white and elegant, it's one of those suites that is so posh that you don't want to touch a thing for fear that it might break. I've always liked Geri: smart, quotable, a proper celebrity. And today – maybe cos she feels she needs to butter me up, maybe cos for some reason I've become strangely irresistible to women for the day – Geri likes me ...

After waiting an hour, she walks into the suite wearing shades, dragging her shih-tzu dog Harry and trailed by her entourage.

I love entourages – they're hilarious. They're the things that keep famous people from experiencing the real world. The more you want to be kept away from normal people, the larger the entourage. Part protection, part ego, you can tell a lot about an entourage.

Geri's is bijou, but entertaining: first up is her female personal assistant/best friend who videos everything she says and does. Then there's her press officer, Simon. An affable chap who just wants every-thing to go smoothly but gets tetchy when things run late. He checks his watch a lot. Then there's her head of international press. As we're gatecrashing a day of overseas press she resents my presence and wants to whisk Geri away from me from the moment we meet. They can go and take a running jump as far as I'm concerned.

I've been kept waiting for an hour but she's worth the wait, and is flirty from the off …

'So, you're the man from *Heat*,' she says. 'Well, I need to eat before the interview. If I don't eat now I'll have to eat you.'

She carries on like this throughout the entire interview: chastising me, touching my knee. I'm sure I'm being seduced into giving her a good write-up but she's good at it. And she's not finished yet …

I ask for a quick photo with her and she dutifully stands at my side. She looks up to me and smiles.

'Hi.'

'Er, hi.'

'This could look a little weird.'

I peer down at her.

'Yes, well …'

Geri Halliwell is making me stutter.

'You see we really need a photo, so …'

The PR is still fiddling with the camera.

'You're really tall.'

'Er, yep.'

'How tall are you?' she whispers.

'Um, six foot five.'

'You'd be really good father material.'

I gulp.

The photo set-up looks ludicrous. She's five foot not-very-much and I'm six foot five. As the guy taking the picture gets his camera ready she looks up at me. 'This is going to look stupid,' she concludes. 'How about I sit on your shoulders?' And so she does. With PRs flapping around, journalists being kept waiting in a room, here I am standing in a suite at a London hotel with Britain's most talked-about pop star's thighs wrapped around my neck. Tough job this.

Sunday 6 May

The celebrity world is in shock – Chris Evans has married Billie. The wedding took place at the Little Church of the West in Las Vegas (Noel Gallagher and Meg Mathews got married there a few years ago). Weddings there cost about 65 dollars for the basic hire of the church but the happy couple seemed to have chosen the pricier package – it included a video of their day, ten glossy photographs, a bouquet of flowers for her and a buttonhole for him. The whole event was very dressed down, however. He wore striped trousers and a green shirt, she wore a white cotton blouse, pink sarong and – my favourite detail – flip-flops.

Told you it wouldn't last.

Friday 25 May

Big Brother 2 kicked off today with a new set of housemates going into the show. This lot seem even better than last year's: some of the personalities are quirkier, there's a greater chance of sparks. I particularly like the look of one girl called Helen Adams, a sweet dizzy Welsh girl with a smiley positive demeanour. The production team speak about her in glowing terms: she's so excited to be alive, never mind be on the biggest TV show in Britain.

The press team very kindly slipped us the photos of the contestants in advance – we got them emailed over this afternoon. We also got a really heavy contract where I have to promise that no one else will see the photos until the show airs. I ignore it and get everyone to gather around Clara's computer where we look at the pictures one by one. Anarchy. Every photo provokes a huge reaction.

First comes Paul: young, moderately good looking with spiky hair.

'Gay!' shouts Julian.

'Gay!' shouts Polly, our new recruit from *Elle* magazine. It's fair to say Polly feels liberated to be outside of fashion-mag land, a world she's been trying to escape from for months. (Paul isn't actually gay, I point out, but they're not listening.)

Next is Penny, a late-thirty-something English teacher

'Too old,' screams Polly. 'Next! Come on!'

Then there's Dean, a thirty-something guy from Birmingham.

'Too old!' shouts Polly again. If Polly had her way the maximum age limit of *Big Brother* contestants would be 19.

'Gay!' shouts Julian, for good measure. (Dean isn't gay either.)

'Gay and too old!' hollers Polly.

You get the idea. Sorry Channel 4. Will keep them to myself next time (yeah, right).

Wednesday 6 June

Gradually, week by week, we're becoming talked about. People like our sense of humour, the way we write about celebrities. Today saw a huge break-through in our profile – in the opening titles of her new cookery show Nigella Lawson reads *Heat* while lying on a sofa. The episode is all about 'Guilty Pleasures'. That's what we've become: a fun, entertaining way of spending the time. This five-second clip of Nigella flicking through our pages will do us so much good.

Friday 20 July

Big Brother is obsessing the office again. As amazing as the first series was, we didn't really see much in the way of romance. This year we have. Sweet Helen has paired up with Paul who, early in the series, managed to prise himself away from the clutches of English teacher Penny (who's persistence got her evicted early on). *Big Brother* has been canny – the other week they conspired to get Paul and Helen together for a date. There's only one problem – she has a boyfriend. The conversations between the two fledgling lovebirds are fascinating – she's hesitant around him because of the boyfriend, and he doesn't want to do anything that will get him beaten up when he leaves the house. Their conversations are full of sexual tension, guilt, tenderness and, at times, excruciating awkwardness. It's as complicated as any relationship being formed in a student bar or workplace or nightclub. It's real. These are normal people figuring out what they want, and both seem unaware of the cameras. Tonight, though, the romance ended when the two of them went up against each other in the public vote and Paul was evicted. Helen's tears, as she gazed out of the window in the direction Paul had left, were heartbreaking. (Memo to self: It is only a TV show, I repeat, it is only a TV show).

Friday 27 July

It's the final of *Big Brother* and I'm laid up in bed with a ridiculous virus. The finals are becoming such a big deal now they really should be declared national holidays. Davina McCall starts tonight's show by saying hello to everyone who's having a *Big Brother* party as they watch the show. The *Heat* team – as well as working terribly, terribly hard – have their own party in the office which involves each of them dressing up as a different housemate. Polly found a blonde wig and put on fake tan to become Helen. Dan wore a tight-fitting top and put on a ridiculous pout to be Josh, the house's campest contestant. Brian, a sweet-natured Ryanair Trolley Dolly, wins.

Monday 13 August

I'm out of the office for a couple of weeks redesigning the mag again. It's been more than a year since we overhauled *Heat* and it's looking a little tired already. It's fine for monthly magazines, they can go for years without changing a thing, but we do 52 of these a year so we need to keep things looking fresh. In my absence Dominic Smith is in charge. Unflappable and experienced, he is ruling the roost expertly. Dom rings first thing with an idea for next week's cover …

'Helen and Paul want to do an interview with us.'

Great! Well, do it. It will sell loads.

'They want paying. Their agents said so.'

I am utterly speechless. That sweet lovely couple, who lived ordinary lives and had ordinary jobs and just happened to end up in a house that's filmed for a TV show, have gone and got themselves *agents*. Not just any agents – but the same company that represents Davina and Dermot. And they want a few thousand quid for their first interview.

Both of them intend to give at least some of the money to charity but still! *Heat* don't pay people! It's a ridiculous idea. But we really want this cover. The idea of these people having advisors and PRs and people to do their dry cleaning seems ludicrous but that is what's happening now. It's partly our fault, of course – if we make it clear there's a demand for them, they'll charge. Julian is doing the deal tonight.

Wednesday 15 August

A crazy day. We did our Helen and Paul shoot this afternoon and we now know how big a deal all this *Big Brother* stuff really is.

We sent a car for them, which picked them both up from Paul's mum and dad's in Reading. Julian called me from the shoot just before Helen and Paul were due to arrive there.

'They've just called me from the car – they're being trailed by paparazzi photographers! I've told them to lie down with blankets over their heads and come out of the car separately.'

This is madness. This is what people do for Madonna!

Half an hour later I get another call. It's Julian again.

'They're here now but you'll never guess what's just happened! A photographer from the *News of the World* has just tried to break into the shoot. He shimmied up the drainpipe and tried to get in through the window.'

The team are loving this. We've gone through a long period of people not giving a damn about us, so to have this attention is fantastic.

Thursday 16 August

Our latest sales were announced today – we now sell over 235,000 copies a week.

Tuesday 11 September

It's not often that I go out to lunch but today I did. Paige (our Reviews Editor) and I went to the nearby Berners Hotel to catch up on various things. We got back a little after two and were surprised to see the entire team gathered round the small TV screen above the news desk. A plane had crashed into one of the two World Trade Center towers in downtown New York. Then a second crashes into the other.

It's truly shocking and we all feel numb. Rapidly I come to the conclusion every other boss in the world must be coming to. No work today. Not that there's anything to report. The news channels have switched to rolling footage from New York, the evening papers have nothing but World Trade Center stuff and, most noticeably, there are no pictures of celebrities coming through. All the New York agencies have dispatched their paparazzi photographers to the site – snappers used to getting snatched pictures of Sharon Stone getting her groceries are now taking pictures of grim desperation.

Wednesday 12 September

There are no DJs on the radio today. The papers have dropped their gossip pages. The world feels different to how it was 48 hours ago. And still no pictures.

At half 11 Clara calls me over. 'Britney pictures, just in.'

Great! Britney. Britney will always bail us out.

I virtually run over to Clara's desk to look at them. It's Britney, just off a plane at Sydney Airport, in pieces. 'Her brother's in New York – she hadn't managed to get hold of him when this was taken.'

Her brother is fine but she didn't know it at that moment. Intrusive? Undoubtedly. But we need to run *something*.

Thursday 13 September

Still no DJs, still no gossip pages, still no pictures. Added to that are a glut of media think pieces about the role of celebrity, post the World Trade Center disaster. In a nutshell they're saying we're finished, 'the new seriousness' post 9/11 means that no one will want celebrities any more, there's no room, these days, for that kind of trivial stuff they say. We've finished this week's magazine– there's an interview with Kylie that, in the absence of any news, has become our cover feature. Everyone's writing us off, the celebrity world is dead, apparently, and we've got nothing to put in the magazine. Just as we announce record figures, the whole thing looks like it's about to go into reverse. Next week we'll get early sales on this issue. Don't think I'll come in that day. The game's well and truly up.

CHAPTER FOUR
Thank God for Kylie

September – December 2001

Tuesday 18 September

This morning, on my way into work through Celebrity Central, I did my usual routine. In fact, I've done this every Tuesday for a year and a half since I was put in charge of *Heat*. I walk down the road, over the train track, down the hill, over the zebra crossing, then past two newsagents', the one by the road and the one in the tube station. As I walk past newsagent number one my pace slows, I look over my left shoulder and glance at the row of newly released celebrity magazines. Then on to newsagent number two. Here I stop altogether, peering through the glass into the shop. I'm doing what I do every week: rating the opposition, seeing who's brought in what exclusive and checking out how good our cover looks on the news-stand. Most weeks I beam, proud of how good we've made ourselves look, smug that we've beaten our rivals to the big interview of the week again. Today, at newsagent one and again at newsagent two, I wince. Anything about celebrities seems inappropriate this week. We're surrounded by newspapers reporting the incredible stories of death or survival and, increasingly, of grief. Our 'happy happy' stance looks even weirder as in both newsagents' we're next to *Hello* magazine who have forgone their usual cover diet of royalty or bland – but glammed up – Hollywood movie stars for an image of the Twin Towers on fire. I stand at the second newsagent's for longer than I normally would and watch as customers come and go. There seem to be more than normal and, without exception, they walk past the papers and, without giving *Hello* a second glance, pick up either *Heat* or *OK* or *Now*. I watched for ten minutes. In my head everything about the world was changing – that's certainly what our critics were saying – but not much about these women seems to have changed. Although I'm sure they're truly shocked by what has happened, their concerns are clearly still the same: will they get to work on time? Will their money last until the next pay packet? It's just that now more than ever they needed entertainment, a diversion from the horrors of the latest news bulletin. They want something frivolous, something to lose themselves in, something glamorous. And, based on what I saw, today they want a celebrity magazine.

Friday 21 September

Louise came in this morning with some early figures.

'Kylie issue looks like it's going to be huge, one of the biggest sellers of the year.'

What is it about Kylie? For three decades now she's been providing people with frothy, diversionary entertainment. She's number one in both the singles and album charts ('Can't Get You Out Of My Head' is the pop record of the year) and now she's selling us huge numbers of magazines in a week when they shouldn't be selling at all. No one provides escapism quite like Kylie Minogue.

Thursday 27 September

To the Hard Rock Café for the launch of a new TV programme called *Pop Idol*. It's a reinvention of the classic music audition show and looks fantastic. At the launch they showed a video of some of the good auditionees and some of the crap ones. And then there's Gareth Gates. Gates is a young – very young – lad from Yorkshire with a chronic stammer. It takes him several attempts to get his name out when the judges ask him. But when he sings the stammer goes – he sings like an angel.

As we leave the launch there's considerable debate about what we've just seen. For me, it was uncomfortable viewing.

'I think that's cruel. He clearly has no chance of being a singer. He's too nervous to speak! It'll kill him, poor lad.'

Polly Hudson, Queen Of Strong Opinions, agrees.

'Yeah, it's not fair. Imagine him singing on a live show.'

Boyd thinks otherwise. 'But he's fine when he sings! And anyway, they'll look after him.'

'It's cruel though, isn't it?' I ask. 'Putting someone through something, on TV, that will cause them so much stress.'

We're all agreed it will be a huge success, though.

'I WANT TO KNOW WHAT WILL HAPPEN TO HIIIIIM!' screams Polly at the Hyde Park Corner traffic.

Hooked. Already!

Sunday 14 October

Out shopping with Gaby at Brent Cross, I stop off at the local WHSmith, as is my Sunday tradition …

'Can you never give it a rest?'

'Huh?'

'Newspapers! Magazines!'

'It's my job! If I read them all now, inside the shop, that means I won't have to buy them so they won't clutter up the flat.'

She seems quite happy with this option. WHSmith, here I come …

Sara Cox, the Radio 1 breakfast show DJ, is on honeymoon with her new husband, a DJ called Jon Carter. Today, the *Sunday People* have run some pictures that invade her privacy to a ridiculous extent. The pictures show the couple in the grounds of their private villa in the Seychelles, getting in and out of their jacuzzi. In most of the shots the couple are naked, their genitals covered by the paper's art department (Sara is shown topless in several, however). It's really odd – the laws of privacy clearly state that you can't run photos taken on private property. It's a stupid, reckless move that is so obviously going to get them into trouble. I fold the paper up, put it back on the rack and wander off. 'Rather them than me,' I think, 'that's going to cause someone a load of hassle.'

Watching TV this evening and … Good God, Darius is back! ITV have just shown him making it through to the next stage of *Pop Idol*. His performances are still corny but the rendition he gave of Seal's 'Future Love Paradise' in this weekend's show was too good to see him chucked out. He's got to be back on our cover next week: everyone loves an underdog and Darius is just so good at it!

Monday 15 October

Without fail a huge Sunday newspaper exclusive leads to *a lot* of activity in magazine land the next day. Not only are we talking obsessively about it (usually around the news desk, the central point of the office and manned by the loudest people in the building, Dan and Polly, who are more than happy to engage a crowd of people in conversation about the latest scandal) but also Monday morning is the time when picture agencies try and sell second rights to whatever was the big set from that weekend's papers. Obviously it's the Sara Cox pictures we're offered early this morning and obviously I turned them down. An hour later the phone rings. It's Sara Cox's gravel-voiced agent, Melanie Coupland. And she's livid.

'I've been told you're buying these photos.'

'Of course we're not. It's obvious to me and anyone who looks at them that they're a flagrant invasion of privacy.'

'So why the HELL are you running with them.'

I've never spoken to this woman in my life and now she's screaming down the phone at me, accusing me of lying.

'Melanie, we are *not* running these pictures!'

'I've got it on good authority that you are.'

Hard to know where to go with this one. I decide to go down the repetition road. With extra indignation thrown in for good measure.

'Well, we're not!'

Journalists are often kept away from agents and it often frustrates the hell out of us – PRs feel like go-betweens at times, and you feel that only the people closest to them (the agents) can provide you with the answers that you want. But today I'm pretty glad I don't have to speak to agents all the time.

After ten minutes I calm her down, but she still doesn't believe me. Back in the firing line, and I've done nothing to warrant it. Went home in a bad, bad mood.

Tuesday 23 October

Sales continue to boom post 9/11, the world of celebrity seems to be getting bigger than ever and (surprisingly to all of us, particularly Louise who *still* doesn't get the appeal of the show at all) anything to do with *Big Brother* is big business even though the show ended months ago. Notable, then, that in this boom time the editor of the *Daily Mirror*, Piers Morgan, takes to the stage at an event in Belfast this evening to bemoan the growing celeb culture. 'Is my journalistic career going to depend on whether I can persuade some halfwit from Wales called Helen to take my company's £250,000 and reveal in sizzlingly tedious details that she's even more stupid than we first feared?' Morgan goes on to say that celebrity culture is on the way out: 'I hear secretaries talking about anthrax and Al Qaeda, not *EastEnders*.' He's wrong, of course: they're talking about anthrax *and* *EastEnders*. But the newspapers moving back to the serious stuff is a) understandable, they are 'news'papers after all and b) brilliant for us. Leave Helen to us, Piers, we'll have your sales.

Wednesday 24 October

The legend that is Barbara Charone – all five foot nothing of PR expertise – hosted a dinner tonight for Cher. It was impeccable PR – Cher was taken round to meet everyone in the room, chat (she's a charmer, as happy to talk about you as she is herself) and have her picture taken with you. I found myself staring at her throughout our blissful three and a half minutes together – really staring, observing every line and dimple. And I'm glad I did because while doing so, I made a brilliant discovery: Cher has no philtrum! You know, the bit between the bottom of your nose and the middle of your top lip. The bit that goes in. Well, hers doesn't go in! All the surgery, you see! Rather than get a cab back to Celebrity Central I walk home, full of my brilliant journalistic discovery. Cher: no philtrum! I'll be dining out on this for months.

Thursday 25 October

'Let me get this right,' says Julie, 'you met Cher and you didn't ask her about Tom Cruise.'

'Or the surgery,' says Jo Carnegie.

No one in the office seems in the slightest bit interested that Cher doesn't have a philtrum.

They think I'm a rubbish journalist. They're probably quite right.

Tuesday 6 November

Sales are increasing but we're still not being talked about enough. There's an interview in this week's issue that may be about to change all of that.

Boyd has just interviewed Frank Skinner. The conversation got on to the subject of relationships – Frank has just split up with Caroline Feraday, his girlfriend of a year, and as Feraday was considerably younger than he was Boyd asks why he always seems to go out with much younger women.

'The thing is,' he replies, 'there aren't many good older properties on the market. All the good ones have been snapped up by the time they're 25. There are single women in their thirties knocking around but they're all rough as arseholes so they're not really on the list at the moment.'

Is he joking? Who knows? But the papers will love this.

Wednesday 7 November

The papers are full of the Frank Skinner story. It's a funny thing with comedians – they can say the most inappropriate, outrageous things onstage (and loads of them do) and get away with it, but in print it just doesn't wash. Why is that? Why is something regarded as inoffensive in one context but when said by the same person in a different one it's out of order? He's clearly joking here – well, at least I hope he is – but the papers (and especially the Wednesday columnists) don't get it at all.

Thursday 8 November

I love Elton John: funny, smart, mouthy. The perfect celebrity. And today we find out he reads *Heat*. Clara beckoned me over just before five. 'Mark, look at these. We're famous!' There, on the screen of her Mac, is Elton, coming out of a newsagent's in Chelsea. Just behind him is the poor unfortunate newsagent struggling to carry a huge plastic bag full of what must be 20 or 30 magazines. On top, visible through the plastic, is that week's *Heat*. An amazing moment that I mark in the only way you should mark a moment like this: I phoned my mum.

Friday 9 November

Our biggest mailbag so far. Well, I say mailbag – it's all emails these days. Anyway, the Frank Skinner interview is causing a rumpus and I'm really not surprised. As the average age of the *Heat* reader is 25 years old his comments about how 'all the good ones have been snapped up by the time they're 25' has really struck a nerve, never mind what he said about women over 30.

There's so many of them that we dedicated almost the entire letters page to him.

Excuse me, Mr Skinner, but I would just like to set the record straight for all those single women over 25. We are simply making sure we do not end up with a man as opinionated as you.
Sam, by email

and

Mr Skinner, next time you label someone as 'rough', I suggest you take a look in the mirror, you haddock!
Jenny, by email

and

Frank Skinner's autobiography is a great read. In it he says he could only pull ugly birds until he was famous. Well, I must be really ugly because I'm a big fan of his and have met him a few times and he didn't offer to sleep with me!
Debbie, by email

Monday 12 November

Some nice pictures of Ewan McGregor with his new baby arrive in the office. His PR, Ciara Parkes, hears we've got them and threatens that he will have nothing to do with us if we run them. We replied by offering to drop all shots that show the baby's face. This is pretty generous of us – we don't have to do this at all; in fact, most other publications wouldn't do it. The child would be unidentifiable and no one would have any need to be upset about anything. But they're not interested. They say they'll still have nothing to do with us even if we don't show the baby's face. That's a pretty hollow threat anyway – McGregor, in common with most film stars, has nothing to do with us anyway, never gives us interviews, never does anything with us. Also, they were walking down a public street where anyone could see them. It's become a case of 'Damned if you do, damned if you don't'. If we're not help-ing our case by hiding the baby's face then let's not hide it – they're being pretty confrontational about it, which helps me make my deci-sion. I really don't appreciate it when people are like that with my team. I've decided to run the pictures. We'll go to press with them at the end of the week.

Tuesday 13 November

We're really overdoing the cute thing with Gareth Gates now. Today we ran pictures of him in his school classroom: chewing on his pencil, looking dreamily at the blackboard. This is extreme bias, but we don't care. None of the other contenders get a look in, we're Gareth obsessed!

I overhear the girls on the picture desk discuss him.

'Look at his spiky hair ...'

'He's got such a sweet grin!'

'Oh, look at him there!'

Oh deary me.

Monday 19 November

At ten to seven this evening, just before leaving the office, I received a fax from Ciara Parkes. She was the one at the end of the phone asking us not run the pictures of Ewan McGregor and his new baby. She was the one who turned down our – completely fair – compro-mise of running the photos with the child's face obscured. Clearly aware her tactics hadn't worked and that we were running the photos anyway she decides to get in a pre-emptive strike. The fax – sent to several big newspapers and magazines – reads really oddly.

> *I am writing to you with a request. Recently my client, Ewan McGregor and his wife Eve, have had a second daughter who seems to have attracted a huge amount of attention from the paparazzi.*
>
> *Ewan would like to take this opportunity to politely ask that while he realises that doing the job he has chosen will attract press attention, it is not something he wants for his children. In the past, generally the press have behaved responsibly but recent events*

have prompted him to reiterate his vehemence in his wish to protect his daughters from photographers.

I am writing to ask you to respect his and his family's wishes and not publish pictures of his children. There will be publications that will not adhere to this request and I would like to make it clear that those that don't will not be included in any promotional activity pertaining to any of Ewan's future films.

We would like to thank you for you [sic] *co-operation in advance,*
Ciara Parkes
Publicist to Ewan McGregor

What's the point? They've made their case, not been prepared to settle for our compromise and sent us this, knowing full well our magazine – with the pictures – will be on the news-stands of Britain in just a few hours' time. And, again, there's that hollow 'you won't get any interviews' bit. Why?

Tuesday 20 November
The issue goes on sale. All is calm. Weird.

Tuesday 27 November
More controversial pictures. Well, Chris Moyles thinks so. I've known Moyles for five years – at a previous magazine I made him one of our 'Faces Of '97' when he was just starting out. It was the first time he'd been written about in a high-profile publication and he was pretty grateful (although, in his modest way, he reckoned he thoroughly deserved the accolade and probably much more beside). Despite his cocky exterior Moyles is a lovely guy – funny, personable, close to his family (whom he worships), loyal to his friends and a real charmer. He never forgot his first mention and tries to plug my magazines whenever he can. Today, though, he thinks *Heat* has overstepped the mark. Moyles, overweight for much of his life, is on a serious health kick. He's hired a personal trainer and he's embarking on twice-weekly workout sessions. Only fair, then, that we print some pictures in today's magazine showing just how hard he works out – all the stretches, the ball-throwing ...

He is not happy. I tuned in to his radio show just after four to hear him gearing up for a rant.

'This week's *Heat* magazine – Jesus Christ! They decide to hide in some bushes, take photos of me and print them with the clever-arse headline "Chris Moyles does some exercise!"'

He's shouting now.

'Listen to this: "He went a bit red in the face but soon recovered and stepped up the pace again by throwing – and catching – a yellow ball." Think that's easy, do you? Well, you try it!'

My phone rings.

'Chris wants to speak to you on air.'

'Oh, great.'

'Stay there, he'll be with you in a minute.'

What do I do? Turn my phone off? Probably shouldn't piss him off even more. Why do I give my phone number to famous people? I skulk into the TV room, where we do all our phone interviews.

'Mark, you're on air in ten seconds.'

Suddenly I'm live to the nation.

'Oi, Frith! You think that's easy, you try it! This Thursday morning, you're coming with us.'

Oh, brilliant.

After another five minutes of barracking he plays a record and he's finished with me. His assistant comes on the line and tells me where to meet them. This is no joke. I've not run since school. I don't do exercise beyond the odd length at the swimming pool. I HAVE NOTHING TO WEAR!

I emerge from the TV room to huge cheers from the team.

Then I spend the next hour fielding email after email. Everyone listens to Chris Moyles, it seems. Mark Ellen, the launch editor of *Q* magazine and a *Heat* staffer from the dark days, is the first. 'Brilliant banter just then! Brilliant!'

Banter? He ripped the piss out of me for half an hour!

Then others arrive:

'You can't buy that kind of publicity,' said one.

'Everyone knows about *Heat* now,' said another.

'So many people will be buying the magazine next week to see how you get on!'

Wednesday 28 November

Usually, my last words to my team as I head out of the door for the evening are cheery ones. I'm a cheery soul, really. On a typical day it would be something like 'See you tomorrow!' or 'Watch yourself on that bike! There's some nutters out there!' Today it was less cheery. 'I want to die ... where do I get tracksuit bottoms from around here then?'

Ellie, fashion guru for all occasions, even this one, points me in the direction of a sports shop in Covent Garden. I buy running bottoms, tracksuit top and fetching (well, so I reckon) Fila hat. I look at myself in the mirror. I actually almost look the part. Which is a good job because I'm bringing a photographer with me tomorrow. This might not be a complete disaster.

Thursday 29 November

Up bright and early. The meeting place is handy for me – the top of Primrose Hill itself, slap bang in the middle of Celebrity Central. I arrive first. Within minutes Personal Trainer Janie is there. Then Moyles's producer Will. Then his sidekick Comedy Dave. Then Production Assistant Lizzie (in full make-up, because she knows she's going to have her photo taken). But no Moyles. We ring him. No answer. We ring him again. Still no answer. Someone is dispatched to his house nearby and they beat on the door for ten minutes. No answer. And so, bizarrely, his entire team work up a sweat for an hour round Primrose Hill minus the reason we're doing it in the first place. Chris Moyles – what a lightweight.

Friday 30 November

Summoned to the Radio 1 studios to go on Moyles's show. Feeling really smug.

'So where were you?'

'No one called me!'

'Yes we did!'

'Well ... hmph.'

He's sulking. He sulks even more when Personal Trainer Janie tells him – and the millions listening – that I was 'really good – real promise'.

Typically, though, I didn't have the last laugh. Unbeknownst to me Radio 1 had their own photographer hiding incognito in the bushes, just as we had done two weeks earlier, to take photos of me flailing around a park at eight in the morning. Game, set and match. But like the email said the other day, you can't buy publicity like this.

Monday 3 December

Today the shit hit the fan.

The new issue of *Arena* landed on my desk first thing. *Arena* is Emap's men's fashion magazine and since we bought it from another company three years ago it's struggled to get decent sales.

To combat this they've recently given the editor's job to Anthony Noguera, the former *FHM* editor. The success of *Heat* must be real competition and likely to grab the attention of the Emap top brass – 'not a real magazine', is what he apparently tells anyone who's prepared to listen. Up to now any dislike had been kept to himself or his inner circle, his editorial team and acolytes who worship the ground he walks on.

The cover star of his new issue is my good friend Ewan McGregor. Conducted just a couple of weeks ago – in the midst of the fuss about our photos – McGregor is damning about *Heat*, the paparazzi and the celebrity culture we're both part of. At one point – and here's something to show the relatives – he appears to wish me dead.

'I knew that *Heat* magazine had got photographs of me and my kids,' he says at one point in the printed interview, 'and even though I went to them personally – or as personally as I would go because I don't trust myself not to lose my rag – they published them anyway. I wonder how the editors of these pieces of shit will feel on their deathbeds that their only contribution to humanity is to steal other people's privacy. What arseholes!'

There it is, in black and white: 'those pieces of shit'.

Management go into meltdown. They confront Noguera about the article – he denies he saw it and promises them it went in unread by him. It's an appalling state of affairs. I considered resigning there and then, but if I do it will just look stroppy and it will be me that loses out. No job and with my magazine known as a 'piece of shit' as my epitaph.

Not a good day.

Tuesday 4 December

Met John Noel for lunch. Noel is the agent *du jour*. He's got Davina McCall on his books along with Dermot O'Leary – two of the hottest stars of the moment thanks to the mega success that is *Big Brother*. Noel is hugely important to us. If he likes us we get access to those two before anyone else. Or instead of anyone else. He also signs up loads of the *Big Brother* evictees, the lifeblood of the magazine this past summer (alongside Kylie and Posh Spice – who still sells for us no matter what we do on her, no matter how tenuous the story). So this is an important lunch. Katherine Lister, Noel's ultra-canny in-house PR, comes along too, as does Julian.

John guides us to our table, seating us by the window at not a very nice table, despite the fact that the restaurant is almost completely empty. Julian and I are left with a good view of a grotty piece of pavement. What the hell's going on? Noel seems distracted and starts looking at his watch all the time. It's thoroughly unnerving. We order the food but John's still distracted and quite frankly I begin to wonder why we were there at all. Then, out of the corner of my eye, I see a mad-looking bloke amble down the street. The kind of bloke you'd swerve to avoid. He has a neck brace and naff clothes and he heads straight for us. Oh, great. Why do I always get the nutter? He rushes over to the window by where we're sitting, stares at us, then starts licking the window. What the hell?

Oh, great, I thought, now he's coming in ...

The guy walks through the door, grabs Katherine and starts snogging her and introduces himself to us as Avid Merrion, *Heat*'s number one fan. Then he goes. 'That's Leigh,' whispers Katherine, 'John's new signing.' What a weird bloke, I think to myself on the way back to the office. And how odd that he walked past when we were there. I say this to Julian.

'It was a set-up! Don't you realise!'

Julian Linley may well be my faithful deputy, but at times he really does despair.

'Don't you get it? He put us by the window, told that guy what time to walk past, got him to do his act ... it was all a set-up so that we know who he is.'

Sometimes I can be really thick.

'Oh. Oh, right. Yeah, yeah, of course, I knew that.'

Monday 10 December

I've taken on a new PA, Sal. Today wasn't her finest day. Don't get me wrong, she's great – hard-working, affable, loves *Heat*. What she isn't good at, so I found out at 11.36 this morning, is knowing who anyone is in the world of magazines.

'Mark!' she shouts across the open plan office. 'It's Alison, Richard Desmond's PA. She wants you to come in and see him.'

She then gives me her best 'beats me' shrug. The rest of the team stared at me with open mouths.

How to explain Richard Desmond? Here goes: he's in his early fifties, got a taste for the world of magazines when he sold advertising after school. He then went on to publish the UK edition of *Penthouse* and eventually various other porn magazines (Desmond disputes the word porn, saying that porn is illegal, his magazines don't feature anything illegal and that what he publishes are 'adult' magazines). Anyway, he also owns several 'adult' TV channels (The Fantasy Channel, Red Hot) and the far more respectable *OK* magazine. *OK* is the Don of celebrity magazines, one of the most profitable – if not the most profitable – of all the magazines on the UK news-stands. And it's *OK* that he wants to meet with me about. On Thursday.

After I put down the phone I took Sal into the TV room, gradually getting known around the office as the telling-off room. Been rude to a PR on the phone? Let's go into the TV room. Failed to book enough freelancers so we're here until BLOODY TEN O'CLOCK THREE NIGHTS IN A ROW! The TV room, please.

So me and Sal have a little chat, in the TV room, about being discreet and stuff like that. She takes it very well.

'Oh God, I'm so sorry! I've never heard of him!'

'Sal … it's fine. You had no reason to have heard of him.'

'I know who he is now!'

'Good, good. Now, we're going to have a new system from now on. You get a call, you ring through to me, you tell me who it is and then I tell you whether I'll take it.'

'Cool … sorry.'

My mind's racing about Thursday, I'm not really listening to what she's saying.

'Sorry, say that again?'

'I was just saying that's cool. And that I'm sorry. Again.'
Silence.
'Mark?'
'Yeah.'
'You're not going to leave, are you?'
'Sal … I don't know.'

Catherine ZJ gets a bizarre makeover

This week's hottest celebrity news
£1.45   16 – 22 February 2002

heat

REVEALED: MUSIC'S BIGGEST EARNERS

PLUS!
30 BEST MOMENTS OF POP IDOL

END OF SERIES SOUVENIR ISSUE!

Issue 155

"Yes! I did it!"

● First magazine interview with the winner
● Relive Will's emotional victory!
● Secret stuff you **DIDN'T** see on TV

CHAPTER FIVE
Gareth's going to walk it
December 2001 – May 2002

Thursday 13 December

Someone attempting to poach you is supposed to be one of the pinnacles of your time in a profession. It's meant to put an extra spring in your step, make you think you're king of the world, a chance to lord it up over everyone else. Not me. It just makes me feel really guilty.

So, at 8.57 a.m. this morning, when I arrived at Ludgate House, 245 Blackfriars Road, the home of Express Newspapers (proprietor R. Desmond), why did I try and keep my head down so no one could see me? Why did I say the words 'Richard' and 'Desmond' to the receptionist as though I was some ventriloquist, muttering through clenched teeth?

Well, there's several reasons.

One: someone already has the job I was about to be interviewed for (that's quite a good first reason in my book).

Two: I could have been recognised by anyone (which will make the situation referred to in Reason One a whole load trickier).

Three: because Emap has stuck by me through thick and thin (more thin than thick in recent years, to be frank). I felt like I was betraying them by even being here. By entertaining the idea of working for another company.

Other than that … bring it on!

So there I am: jacket collar up, leaning in towards the receptionist (who leans back with a totally reasonable 'what the hell are you *doing*, lanky boy' look on her face. I'm speaking to her through clenched teeth when Desmond himself walks through the door. Nervous though I am, I spring into Mr Operator mode.

'Richard!'

'Mark ...'

So there he was – taller than I expected, full of presence with an unwavering eye contact.

We walked over to the lifts – I'd always been told that he had his own private lift but today, at least, he was more than happy to use the regular one. We made small talk and went up to his floor where all hope of me going through this incognito failed – to get to his office we needed to leave the lift then walk through the offices housing one of his newspapers. There weren't loads of people in – or if they were they were in meetings – but there were enough. Everyone else would hide away the editor from the rival company who they were trying to poach; Desmond wanted to show me off.

His office is vast. A huge, long thing with views of the Thames, a seating area with table and chairs at one end, private office with computer and phone at the other. And in the middle, something I've never seen in any other company boss's office – a full drum kit. Desmond is a keen drummer, plays in a band at charity dos – and staff in adjacent offices regularly hear him bash the hell out of them during the working day.

We sit down. His butler arrives. He has his own butler.

'Tea, sir?'

'Lovely, thank you. Er, normal tea, please ... erm ... milk, no sugar.'

A butler. A proper butler in formal get-up with a silver tray. A butler who – according to legend – delivers a banana to Desmond twice a day, at 11 a.m. and 5 p.m. Twice a day he comes in, lifts up the lid of his silver salver and offers his boss one of his two daily bananas. Brilliant. *I* want a butler.

Then down to business, although business in the more informal area to the left of the drum kit. With us is Paul Ashford, a softly spoken guy known as Desmond's right-hand man and billed officially as his Editorial Director. This means he's the guy who acts as a go-between between Richard and the editorial teams. Although, as he was about to prove, Richard Desmond doesn't seem to need a go-between ...

'How can we improve *OK*, then?'

Here we go. How do I answer the question without giving away all my trade secrets, while at the same time at least showing some kind of interest?

'Well, erm, I think it's doing pretty well. I think you could make it a little newsier, though.'

'News doesn't work for *OK*, we've tried.'

I start burbling on about the need to 'own' the celebrity magazine market, shutting others out and spending whatever it takes to get a dominant position.

He seems impressed. The tea arrives. I reach over to pour mine and the butler stops me and I let him do the honours. I may have just offended the butler.

When he's left, Desmond leans in.

'What I want to know is this – what do we have to do to get you over here, how much will it cost us and how quickly can we do it.'

He leans back.

I stutter. Again.

'Well, erm, well … I think that's jumping the gun somewhat. I'll need to think about it.'

'Fine, you think. Take your time.'

He leans back and lights a cigar.

Right. So he wants me to think now!

'Richard, I'm sorry, I just can't give you an answer now. I need to think about it.'

He'd been charm personified to me – nothing like as scary as I thought. But, of course, that was because he wanted me to do the job, so, of course, he was going to be. I knew, deep down, that I didn't want it.

I told him I'd call tomorrow. I think he saw this as a brush-off but was still unfailingly polite as he walked me to the lift, back through the now packed (it's an hour later and the working day has properly begun) editorial office.

Walking through reception I became convinced I was being watched by Nic McCarthy, the current editor of *OK*. I couldn't be 100 per cent sure it was her and felt far too guilty to look back. Instead, as I did when I arrived, I pulled the collar of my jacket up to my chin and kept my head down.

Friday 14 December

Spent most of this morning plucking up the courage to call Desmond. By 11.30 I thought 'sod it' and went into the TV room to make the call, notes in front of me mapping what I was going to say.

✳ Was lovely to meet you.
✳ I'm happy where I am at the moment.
✳ I'll have to decline your very kind offer.

All bland stuff.

I pick up the phone and dial his PA Alison, hoping, praying that it goes to voicemail. One ring, two rings – she's about to answer, I can feel it – three rings – DON'T ANSWER THE PHONE! – a fourth, then Alison's voice asking me to leave a message. Thank you, I will.

Saturday 15 December

I tell friends about Thursday. They're incredulous I didn't ask about the wage. 'You idiot!' says one. 'It could have been double what you're earning.' I should've done, of course. I think turning down the job without asking about the money makes me sound principled. They think I'm a fool. But then it's not the first time.

Monday 17 December

I was a guest on *Liquid News* again tonight, with Jenny Éclair, the maverick comedienne. Tradition has it that the guests (tonight, that's just me and her) gather in the green room to be briefed by one of the production team, usually a lovely guy called Andrew. Mid-briefing, Éclair decides this is her opportunity to get changed for the show. So she does. As Andrew briefs us, she takes her top off in front of us, pulls on a glam new one and straightens it. In the fine tradition of awkward British males we carry on talking regardless. Then the jeans come off, revealing a pair of skimpy, black lace knickers. Andrew manfully carries on the briefing as Jenny stands up in front of us and eases herself into her leather trousers. So this is what they mean by the racy world of television?

Wednesday 23 January 2002

On *Liquid News* again tonight. The fans of the show are up in arms that I'm on so much – bombarding the BBC's message boards with complaints every time I'm announced! Sod 'em, I love it. And they pay me. Christopher, the show's presenter, did an interview today where as well as going on – at length – about his beloved *Eurovision*, the journalist asked why I was on so much. His answer was the kind of thing that could easily give a boy an ego.

'It's very hard to find news commentators who can talk about everything – film, music, drug overdoses – and he is the best at giving a credible answer about sometimes what is a fluffy, silly story. And he's quite attractive!'

Wednesday 30 January

It's just seven weeks since I turned down Richard Desmond's offer of the *OK* editorship and today *OK* has hit the news-stands with a new, free magazine attached to its centre pages, promoted on the cover with the words 'two magazines for the price of one'. The new, free magazine is called *Hot Stars* – and it looks a little familiar. The logo is similar to ours, they use the same colours and a not-dissimilar font. It has news, followed by a picture section, followed by celeb-related fashion and beauty. It looks like a bootleg version of *Heat* and I flick through it with a mix of anger and amusement. It's flattering, of course, but has been cynically invented to get us out of the celebrity magazine market, to close us down.

I never did hear back from Desmond when I left him that message, never even gave a thought to how me turning him down affected him. But now I know. His reaction, clearly, is to try and punish me for saying no. *Heat* is too successful and too high profile for him to stomach. We're getting sales and advertising money he feels is rightly his and he's doing all he can to put me out of a job. This is a business decision but, I reckon, it's also personal, aimed at me. I've called our lawyers and arranged a meeting for tomorrow.

Thursday 31 January

Never been in a lawyer's office before. But earlier today, along with Emap's Head of Legal Affairs, Louise and I met with our lawyers, Farrers. It makes no sense to me or Louise but they tell us there's nothing we can do about *Hot Stars*. You can't really copyright design, they tell us. If it was exactly the same and we could prove that thousands of *Heat* readers had bought this thinking it was our magazine, we'd have a chance. But we can't, especially as it's contained within another magazine. Our lawyers think Desmond has been clever, that he's made enough tweaks and changes to our design to make it just different enough. There's nothing we can do, other than fight them on the news-stands every week. That's what I must do.

Saturday 2 February

Darius was knocked out of *Pop Idol* this evening but he did brilliantly, finishing third. Next weekend's final is between Gareth and Will Young – a posh southerner and the most perfect contrast to Gareth you could imagine.

Tuesday 5 February

At the *Empire* Film Awards tonight, special guest Ewan McGregor passed just yards in front of me but, luckily, he didn't recognise me. As he mentioned in *Arena*, he finds it very difficult to control himself face to face. Luckily he didn't get the chance to not control himself in front of me …

Friday 8 February

Pop Idol ends tomorrow and the hype is getting bigger and bigger. I was asked to go on a TV show called *Pop Idol Extra*, the ITV2 sister show of the main programme, and met, for the first time, Will Young. Will seems very unhappy about some of the attention he's had in the press, not ideal if you're in a contest like this one! I pointed this out to him on air and, as the closing credits are about to run, I turned to him and said: 'Will, I do not think you are ready to be the nation's *Pop Idol*.'

Of course, I'm saying this because Gareth is going to walk tomorrow's final and I will look so cool and on-the-money when he does.

I am a complete genius.

Saturday 9 February

Bugger. Will has won *Pop Idol*.

Spent all of this evening in the office doing a special end-of-series issue of the magazine. We shot both of the final two punching the air and did up two covers, one with Gareth, one with Will. Both have the same coverline:

'YES! I DID IT!'

We had to send both to the printers yesterday and called them tonight to tell them which to print. Convinced it was going to be Gareth's cover we would be bringing out we spent hours on his cover and hardly any time on Will's. Fortunately, it looks half-decent. Except for the fact that it has a complete and utter twat on the front.

Polly, not one for keeping her feelings to herself, isn't happy.

'It's clearly a fix! Obviously!'

'Polly, it's not, be quiet.'

'Fix! Fix! Fix!'

Michelle Davies, one of the few Will supporters in the office, is over the moon. I want to slink off home. Who says the good guy always wins?

Monday 11 February

Still angry about the whole *Hot Stars* thing. Our lawyers told us to keep watching what *Hot Stars* do but there doesn't seem to be much we can achieve. As part of the legal process our team suggested Louise sent the editor a letter laying out our objections in a formal for-the-record manner, so that if there is litigation in the future we've made it clear we objected all along. That's as much as we can do. Today we got a reply.

> *Dear Louise*
> *Thank you very much for your letter and for letting me know all about your magazine,* Heat. *I've never seen your magazine before but went out today and bought a copy and it really is not bad. Congratulations and keep up the good work.*
> *Yours Sincerely,*
> **Martin Smith**
> *Editor,* Hot Stars.

Cheeky bastard. And he'll clearly pinch anything – look, he's virtually nicked *my own name*.

Thursday 14 February

At midday we announced our latest sales figures for the final six months of last year – up 106.2 per cent (the .2 bit is very important) to an average of over 355,000 copies a week. Wow. A lot of the trade press today focuses on the incredible rises in sales of weeklies – *Now* magazine, the one I have in my sights, is now above 500,000 a week – and the falls in sales for some of the glossy, monthly magazines. *Vogue*, for example – the home of ultra-skinny models and kiss-arse interviews – has fallen below 200,000, which is terrible for them. *Vogue*'s Publishing Director is quick out of the blocks, blaming 9/11 – yet we know that our sales went up after it. Excuses, excuses.

Friday 15 February

Our sales figures have even made their way into the broadsheet newspapers' news pages. The *Independent* today run a story titled 'Things far from *OK* as Desmond feels the *Heat*'. Their sales are down by 17 per cent, despite their tricks. I hope he reads it.

Thursday 21 February

Last night was the Brit Awards, and we were invited by Mastercard to sit on their table. What I didn't know, until I got there, was that I was sitting on the next table to Nic McCarthy – Editor of *OK* magazine.

We managed to avoid each other for most of the evening but, fortified by a couple of drinks, McCarthy came over to say hello.

'Mark, I'm Nic. Listen I know you came to see Richard, it's not a problem.'

So maybe it was her I saw that day. What the hell do I say now?

'Nic, the whole thing was ridiculous. I was intrigued, I knew it was the wrong thing to do straightaway.'

'It's fine! Seriously, I'd have done the same.'

'It's not fine, though, is it? I went to see someone about a magazine job, a magazine that already had an editor.'

As brave of her as it is to speak to me, she looks like a beaten woman. It can't be much fun doing a job when you know the boss wants someone else.

On the way home I picked up the *Evening Standard*, the local London paper. Their main media story was headlined '*Heat* Of The Moment' – it's a follow-up piece to last week's sales figures and it's a bitchy – sometimes aggressive – piece where all the celebrity magazine editors (me plus the editors of *Now*, *Hello* and *Hot Stars*) pile in and slag each other off.

I describe *OK* and *Hello* as 'naff' and call *Hot Stars* 'rubbish – I don't know how the team behind it can look at their CVs without shame.' That's told them!

Arrive to an email from Louise. 'The Chief Exec wants you to stop slagging off other editors in magazine interviews. He says there's no need, makes you look bad.'

That's told me.

Sunday 17 March

Today there's a huge piece about *Heat* in the *New York Times*. 'Star-crazy magazine charms London.' It's a new high and certainly impresses Gaby's American relatives who are over in the country this weekend.

I'm thrilled because a) I adore the *New York Times*, b) what we do is getting known in the States, which I never expected and is truly humbling, and c) the piece interviews half a dozen well-regarded Cool Britainians, among them Fashion Designer Matthew Williamson and Alice Rawsthorn, director of the Design Museum, a long-time champion of the mag. Williamson is particularly emphatic in his praise: 'I love it, it's like candy, I need a fix.'

The only detractor is called Carl Templar, a Creative Director.

'The trouble is that it's a summary of where England is right now – obsessed with minor celebrity. It's not just *Heat*, it's caused other publications to follow, so now everyone is obsessing over the same celebrities. And if you ask why someone is famous, no one can really tell you.'

He's right in that we have created this club of people who are more famous for being famous (or, rather, for being in *Heat* magazine) than a specific talent, like Jordan, for example, who's known as a glamour model, but the readers can't get enough of her. But that's great – it means they're ours, our playthings. The *New York Times* laud us being funny and silly ('Gen X irreverence' they call it) and this week's coverlines bear that out: a piece about Brooklyn Beckham's third birthday titled 'Jelly! Famous guests! Chicken nuggets!' while one about a Calvin Klein model had the coverline 'HUNKY MODEL TRAVIS: WHAT'S *REALLY* IN HIS PANTS?'

We're flying at the moment. Why, all of New York now knows who we are.

Monday 25 March

Clara calls me over to the picture desk.

'Look at these!'

She has some pictures of Nicole Kidman and they're already drawing a crowd.

'I *love* them!' says Julian. 'Put them on the cover, go on!'

The photos are of Nicole Kidman – of all the big Hollywood stars of the day, she's the most secretive and coy – visiting a portable toilet at an indie film festival. Photos like this – where we debunk celebrities, make people realise they're just like you or me – are perfect for *Heat*. Julian's right: they're going on the cover.

Friday 5 April

Tonight I DJed at the *New Woman* Beauty Awards. Well, I'm cheap. The event is a beano for the beauty industry and helps *New Woman* pull in loads of lucrative beauty advertising. To make it seem more glam the organisers invite a smattering of celebs. There was one woman who's face I knew but who's name still escapes me. I think she was a children's TV presenter. She appeared to start the evening drunk before getting even drunker. And, for reasons that can only be explained by her drunkenness, throughout this process she had me in her sights. From time to time she'd dance towards me, pointing her finger, then dance back, often tripping up before rejoining her friends. I busied myself looking through records, pretending to cue them up, stuff that I'd seen proper DJs do. But I was doing it to avoid her. Then she started blowing me kisses before deciding to play her ace card. Again she broke away from the friends. Again she edged over to me. But this time, as she did, she grabbed the strap of her dress that was resting on her right-hand shoulder and pulled it quickly down. Yes, a children's TV presenter was flashing me – standing in front of me, tonnes of famous people and the entire UK beauty industry with her right breast proudly hanging out of her dress. Her friends quickly grabbed her and bundled her off the dance floor. Half an hour later, as my triumphant DJ set came to a close, I made a hasty exit.

Monday 22 April

A terribly sad day. I got a call from my friend Douglas just after work to say that Christopher Price had been found dead at his home. He was just 34. Over the last year and a half I've become a regular guest on *Liquid News* and loved it. The celebrity world is – at heart – a preposterous one, full of ego, money and ridiculous behaviour. Christopher – he hated being called Chris – was able to puncture that ridiculousness with a perfectly judged withering comment or look.

I can't pretend I was Christopher's friend but I'd always stay on set to talk to him after the show. He was interested in the magazine, what we thought about various things. He'd occasionally say that I should try being a guest presenter on the show; I'd tell him he was being ridiculous. The ease that he did the job with didn't come to many people, I said. To be yourself plus be funny, calm while juggling guests, outside broadcasts and someone screaming in your ear can't be easy. He made it look *effortless*.

The BBC loved him, had just given him a quarter of a million quid two-year deal and had lined up a role for him on the BBC's coverage of next month's *Eurovision Song Contest* (it would have been his dream job). The place is in shock: throughout the evening I got calls from people who'd been in the office when the team were told. Richard Bacon had been due to present tonight's show (Christopher has been off work with terrible headaches) and told me about the tears and the disbelief of the team. I can well believe it: the team is large but close, both physically – it's a ridiculously cramped office – and emotionally. Tonight's show was cancelled as a mark of respect. Tomorrow they're airing a tribute. The production team are arriving at 11.30 to film my bit.

Tuesday 23 April
Filmed Christopher's tribute show this morning and the programme was shown this evening. In just a few hours the team had recorded tributes and recollections from 40 or 50 friends, colleagues and guests.

Saddest bits were the contributions from two people Christopher was particularly close to. Reporter Alex Stanger has recently been sent on a sabbatical to the show's LA office so was away when he died – her grief at his death, combined with her sadness at being out of the country in his final few weeks, was obvious. She was crying throughout her satellite link-up tribute.

Then, at the end of the show, Christopher's best friend, reporter Robert Nisbet broke down on camera as he spoke.

'Someone earlier today asked me to sum up Christopher's best radio or TV moment,' Robert's voice cracks. 'I said to them that his best moments were off-screen, not on the radio or on TV. He was a fantastic friend.'

The two had known each other for nearly ten years. When Christopher fell ill the previous week it was Robert who rang him each day to see how he was. By Monday he was so worried that he went round to Christopher's house to find him dead. The inquest verdict will tell us how he died next month.

Friday 26 April

Met up with Simon Cowell and Pete Waterman this morning at the ITV building on Gray's Inn Road. It's the first time I've seem them since Will Young's surprise *Pop Idol* victory and all three of us are still raging about the result. The conversation began in the meeting room, carried on in the lift and reached a peak on the pavement outside the building where we've had to relocate so smoking addict Cowell could have a desperately needed fag. Waterman, who seems to spend his entire life getting heated about something, is the angriest of the lot. The conversation gets particularly heated when he alleges – to anyone who'll listen – that the result was due to some kind of middle-class conspiracy against the nation's proletariat.

Cowell is far more philosophical. 'Pete, calm down!'

'Simon,' counters Waterman, 'I don't feel very calm.'

Simon ploughs on in between drags on his cigarette. 'It's not the end of the story. Gareth will end up the bigger star, trust me.'

Wednesday 8 May

Tonight at the PPA Awards we won Magazine Of The Year and I won Editor Of The Year – the two biggest awards of the night. Surreal. It's usually weighty or arty magazines that win these awards, not celebrity weeklies. It doesn't get much better than this. And now we can put the words 'Magazine Of The Year' on our cover for the next 12 months.

Friday 10 May

Vanity Fair name-checks us in their 'Who's Hot, Who's Not' feature (we're hot, by the way).

Tuesday 14 May

Our features team spent all morning trying to pull off an interview with Will Young. It's a nightmare.

Features Editor Michelle Davies has been very patient with his PR team, more patient than I'd be.

'He'll do it but he won't talk about various things,' she says to me after one long conversation.

'But we're giving him a cover! What's his problem?'

Something's going on here. We've given the guy loads of coverage since he won, yet he doesn't seem to want to spend time in our company.

Interviewed Simon Cowell onstage at an ITV conference this afternoon. Offstage he's his usual candid self – especially when I tell him what's happened this morning. 'Why do you think Will Young seems to hate you and me?' he tells me. 'It must be because we supported Gareth!'

So it's a grudge? This could get interesting.

Thursday 16 May

Since Christopher died *Liquid News* has been hosted by a variety of stand-in presenters. Today I'm asked to present one. I have no presenting experience. At all. I'm doing it in 15 days' time. What a stupid thing to agree to.

Wednesday 22 May

Today's my 32nd birthday and I celebrated by reading a brilliantly snotty piece about my forthcoming *Liquid News* appearance on the *Guardian* website. I can't help but ask myself if the writer – a guy called Matt Wells – thinks he should have been asked to do the show instead of me.

> *The* Heat *magazine editor and showbusiness pundit, Mark Frith, is adding a new string to his ever-expanding bow with a stint as a television presenter.*
>
> *Frith is to present an edition of* Liquid News, *the BBC Choice entertainment show on which he regularly appeared as a guest when it was fronted by the late Christopher Price.*

He will make his first appearance on the programme on 31 May. Frith has not presented a live television show before. [All right, all right! Can people stop going on about this!]

Frith has relentlessly plugged his magazine by appearing on virtually every television programme that will have him [miaow!] *and encouraging members of his team to do the same.*

The strategy was a success when his magazine was in danger of being closed down; however barely a 'Top Ten' (TV show) goes by without an appearance from Frith, Boyd Hilton, Polly Hudson or Dan Wakeford.

He's correct of course – I do encourage the team to go on TV or radio. I've even sent some of them off on a course on how to come across well on air. But the idea we should somehow stop now we're popular is, of course, ridiculous. That kind of exposure will help us get even bigger.

I can't rule out the the option that Matt Wells is possibly, just possibly, jealous. Although, to be frank, I'm so bloody nervous about this thing, if he asked I'd probably let him do it. What have I done? As he rightly says, I *have* never presented a live television show before.

Saturday 25 May
Christopher Price's memorial this afternoon was a big camp affair held at a chi-chi restaurant called Mezzo on Wardour Street. Friends and work colleagues spoke and past *Eurovision Song Contest* stars performed. The most memorable bit for me was a simple, straightforward gallery of photos that were shown on a big screen: because I'd only seen him at work, in a suit, on set behind a big news desk, the pictures of him out clubbing, dancing, caning it in a big way were fantastic. Life-affirming. He lived every minute to the full – the huge smile on his face said it all. I left with just one thought: mustn't waste a single moment.

Monday 27 May
Today Jordan gave birth to a son, Harvey. The baby was two weeks overdue. She's not with the baby's dad any more – a footballer called Dwight Yorke – but he came over for the birth. This will be a big

story for us and I begin to sketch out ideas on how this could look in the magazine.

Tuesday 28 May

Jordan left hospital today and the scenes were ridiculous. She's done a huge exclusive deal with *OK*, which meant she had to hide her poor child head to toe in a blanket as she left. Even more ridiculous than that were the scenes as she made her way to the car. She was surrounded by four – four! – security guards who escorted her and Harvey as they walked through the photographers.

Thursday 30 May

Tomorrow is D-Day. The day I present my own half-hour TV programme. Live. I have been given no training, have no idea how anything works and have just been told to get to the BBC at 10 a.m. the following day to go through the ropes. The show doesn't start until 7 p.m. but I'll need all nine hours to prepare. This is ridiculous. I want out.

Is **James** two-timing **Kylie**?

This week's hottest celebrity news

£1.45 (Canary Islands 3.00Eur, Spain 3.70Eur) **7 – 13 September 2002**

heat

MAGAZINE OF THE YEAR!

EXCLUSIVE!

Posh & Becks'
Baby
Number 2!

First with loads of
inside information!

Issue 184

**MTV
AWARDS**
See ALL the
best (& worst!)
dresses inside

I'M A CELEBRITY
Get Me Out Of Here!

OH! MY! GOD!
The MADDEST
moments so far

CHAPTER SIX
Getting desperate
May – October 2002

Friday 31 May

Awful night's sleep. Eventually dropped off at about 3.30 a.m. after telling myself – repeatedly – that I had to see today like a training course, the sort of thing I get sent on by work from time to time. I've been on all sorts – team-building ones, ones on giving speeches – over the years. I had to see today as a one-day training course in how to present my own TV show.

The first few hours were fine: here's the script, rewrite it how you want, you do this at this point, speak to this person over here at this point, fine. I concentrated really hard and it all sank in.

But with three hours to go the drama really starts. I did my run-through in the studio, put on my (one and only) suit, went into make-up and then met the guests. I've struck lucky with them: Colin Murray, the Radio 1 DJ, and Shovell, jovial percussionist from M People. Both are veterans at this and both can talk and talk and talk (I have a sneaking suspicion that this is the reason they've been booked for my show. There sure as hell will be no awkward gaps with these two around). They are also both aware it's my first show and promise to be gentle.

The *Liquid News* studio is also home to the *60 Seconds* news bulletin that precedes our show. As it finishes, the cameras swing round from filming them to point at me, the continuity announcer says my name, the opening titles roll, then we're on!

I'm as nervous as hell, but decide a huge beaming (some would say freaky) smile will make amends. Fluffing a big intro? Big grin? Pronouncing a name wrong? Grin. I almost manage to pull it off. I LOVE the interviewing bits, am not so sure about some of the reading aspects, but it goes quickly and well. I turn to the guests near the end and tell them about how this has been my *Jim'll Fix It* moment, a once-in-a-lifetime, never-to-be-repeated experience. The end titles run and we're off. I breathe an enormous sigh of relief, the like of which I've never breathed before. There, done it. Presented a TV show.

Thursday 6 June

Jade Goody is becoming the star of this year's *Big Brother*. This evening Channel 4 show footage of her having a conversation with Spencer – who Polly and half the office have the major hots for – and she's clearly stupid but charming with it. She thinks East Anglia (or East Angular as she calls it) is abroad and that Cambridge is in London. She's not bright but she is entertaining.

Friday 7 June

Received an email from Chris Wilson, *Liquid News* Series Editor.

> *Hi Mark,*
>
> *Hope you're well. Thanks again for last Friday. First-rate stuff.*
>
> *Okay, here's the thing. I just wanted to sound you out a bit.*
>
> *How would you feel about doing the show more often? Like – a lot more often?*
>
> *As you know we're looking at various options for the future – but you did really well on Friday.*
>
> *Just after a tentative steer at the moment – but be really interested to get a feeling for what you might think.*
>
> *Feel free to give me a bell to discuss if you wish. Or you might just want to laugh derisively in my face.*
>
> *Cheers,* **Chris**

I've arranged to meet him next Wednesday.

Wednesday 12 June

Chris seems keen for me to present *Liquid News* five nights a week but seems perplexed when I tell him I won't leave *Heat*.

'I can do both!' I announce.

'No, you can't.'

'Why not?'

'You just can't.'

'Finish at *Heat* at five-ish, head over to the BBC, present a quick show, then home. Perfect.'

He thinks I'm insane.

Wednesday 19 June

The coroner investigating Christopher Price's death announced today that he'd been killed by heart failure caused by a very rare brain disease called meningoencephalitis, similar, apparently to meningitis. According to the BBC website the disease causes the lining of the brain to swell and it may well have spread from an ear infection. It's gone on the record as death by natural causes.

For the friends and family it has been another heartbreaking day.

Wednesday 3 July

Away in the Greek Islands with Gaby for a week. Bliss. In a lovely remote villa that has the added advantage of a shop onsite; and a woman who works there brings us lunch every day. And this time I've made it clear: no work calls.

Although having said that, there is one call I want. I check my phone every half hour to make sure it's working. Put it on a table where I know – just know – it won't lose reception. But nothing.

Then, at half past six in the evening, it rings. It's Chris Wilson.

'Gaby, I need to take this phone call.'

'I know, you've been going on about it for three days.'

Yes, I had mentioned it. I went upstairs for some privacy.

As I expected the BBC are saying no to me doing the show as well as editing the magazine but they want me to do one day a week – a special Friday show – and stand-in slots when the main presenters are away. I go back downstairs.

'Gaby – I'm a TV presenter!'

She doesn't look as excited about it as me. She'll regret that when I'm presenting *Newsnight* in a year's time.

Wednesday 10 July

The cult of Jade is growing by the day. This morning I dispatched Dan Wakeford and Polly Hudson to Bermondsey, south-east London to interview Jade's mum, Jackiey.

Jackiey has already become a cult figure in our readers' minds after just one TV appearance – a five-minute interview on *Big Brother*'s sister show *Big Brother's Little Brother*.

Jackiey is, and I can say this with utter confidence, a character. She brought Jade up as a single parent and, because of a motorbike accident when Jade was just five, has only the use of her right arm. Jackiey is also an out lesbian. She smokes like a chimney and has one of the gruffest voices I've ever heard (male *or* female). As I say, she's a character.

The two of them – Polly especially – are a little nervous about heading over to Jackiey's house. The Goodys live in a very rough area and Jackiey doesn't even know the pair of them are coming.

We hear nothing for three hours. Then suddenly, they return. And they smell of dope.

Dan's triumphant.

'We got the interview and these pictures too!'

They show me them: Jackiey, Dan and Polly all posing away in Jackiey's backyard.

'Only thing is she wouldn't let us do the interview until at least one of us had smoked some of her dope.'

He's not giving away exactly who put themselves through the, ahem, ultimate sacrifice.

'And she made me read all these X-rated sex texts that her girl-friend had sent to her phone! They were absolutely filthy! We've had a brilliant time!'

Just another day in the life of *Heat* magazine …

Friday 26 July

The third *Big Brother* came to a close tonight. Although it's won by a girl called Kate Lawler – a hard-partying IT helpdesk girl from Beckenham in Kent – Jade, who eventually came fourth, has been the real star of the show. Unsophisticated and definitely not that bright, Jade survived accusations of bullying (against Sophie, a smarter, prettier girl who entered the house a few weeks in) to make it to the final day. We desperately wanted her on the cover, I've been telling this to anyone who'll listen for days now. People are asking me why we are so interested in her and not, say, Gwyneth Paltrow or Nicole Kidman (the big movie stars of the day). The answer I give is that people can relate to Jade and they can't relate to big Hollywood movie stars.

Interview Gwyneth Paltrow and all she'll want to tell you is how great her latest director was. Interview Jade from Bermondsey and you'll know all about her body issues, her men issues, career issues, normal stuff that every woman of that age worries about. People can relate to her. Which is why the *Heat* team spent much of this evening bidding – against our two biggest competitors: *OK*, the glossy mag with deep, deep pockets, and *Now*, the odd, old-fashioned celebrity mag – for the first interview with her. The winning offer – that we were part of, alongside the *News of the World* – was six figures, seven or eight times the yearly salary she earned as a dental assistant pre-*Big Brother*. It's worth it – we'll sell big with Jade on our cover.

Sunday 28 July

Today, in the *News of the World*, Jordan has revealed that her son is blind.

His sight had failed to develop in the womb and there's no surgery that can correct it. For someone who we're used to seeing pouting or sticking out her chest or getting ridiculously drunk it's a real shock to see her in this kind of context. The interview is, as you'd expect, emotional and full of soul-searching. 'I was shattered. I burst into tears. I asked if I was the cause – was my lifestyle responsible for Harvey's blindness?'

This is a theme the other papers' later editions take up and will clearly be something that will get a lot of comment over the next few days. Can someone who drinks heavily (drinks to excess on occasion) cause damage to their unborn child's sight? Jordan says she's been told it's not the case but this won't stop certain other papers using this information as a way of punishing her and her lifestyle.

Sunday 11 August

Another Sunday, another *News of the World* exclusive on Jordan. She has cancer.

It's a rare type, called leiomyosarcoma, and was found in her hand. The lump was removed at a hospital near her home a few days ago and she's going through tests now to see if it has spread to any other part of her body. The Jordan story is becoming like a modern-day Greek Tragedy: hard partying glamour model hit by life-changing bad luck. In public too, although, of course, if she sells a story that becomes her decision.

Tuesday 20 August

We put Jade on the cover for the second week in a row today – really getting our value for money out of this deal. We're getting a lot of negative mail about her, though; a lot of people *really* don't like her.

Friday 23 August

The announcement that I'm to be a regular presenter of *Liquid News* was made today. I'll be co-hosting with an Australian comedienne called Julia Morris, another regular guest on the show. I'm particularly thrilled that the story has made its way on to Teletext, so thrilled in fact that I decided to take a photograph of my story from the TV screen.

I am aware this looks a little odd.

Thursday 29 August

Bugger. We don't have a cover. Arggggh!

We've been covering the Jordan story for several weeks now but this week that's all gone a bit quiet. There's nothing happening with Jade (for once) so she's out of the running too.

So we are left with one option. But it is a risk.

Some of the papers are reporting that Victoria Beckham – very heavily pregnant with her second child – will give birth by Caesarean section this Sunday, 1 September. Reporting on the birth after it's happened will be impossible for next Tuesday's magazine. *Heat* – in common with most of the other celebrity magazines – prints on a Saturday so the story would appear in the issue after next, the one on sale on Tuesday 10 September. That's ten days after the rumoured birth – way too late. The tabloids, TV and radio will have covered the story in endless detail by then.

So why, goes my thinking, can't we go to press with a cover saying they've had the baby now because when we come out on Tuesday it will be true?

Julian can think of one very good reason.

'We know nothing about the baby! Nothing! How can we write an article about the birth of a baby we know nothing about?'

'We know loads!' I counter pathetically. 'We know, erm, where it will be born, when it will be born, erm ... the fact that she's having it by Caesarean.'

'Who the father is?' chips in one of the subs.

'Yes! Who the father is … all right, you're taking the piss now.'

But this barracking from the team was nothing compared to what I was about to face. Every Thursday at midday, without fail, Louise comes into the office, sees the front cover and tells us (in her typically blunt fashion) what she thinks of it. She doesn't hold back. And here I am about to show her a front-page story about something that hasn't happened yet!

EXCLUSIVE!
Posh & Becks: Baby Number 2!
First with loads of inside information!

Suddenly I'm embarrassed by all those exclamation marks. And everything else about it.

Louise stares at it for a few seconds.

'She's had the baby?'

'Err, no. She's having it on Sunday.'

'Let's go in here for a minute.'

The rest of our Thursday cover panel, Julian and Mark Taylor, our fantastic (and patient) new Art Director, look at each other in bemusement as Louise and I walk off to the TV room, the telling-off room. And now, irony of ironies, I'm about to be told off myself.

'What if something happens during the birth? Something goes wrong? And you're there on Tuesday with "Ooh, here's a baby".'

'Well, I guess we'll have to pulp it.'

'Do you know how much that costs? Tens of thousands of pounds, possibly even hundreds.'

'We have nothing else.'

She gave me that 'You're an idiot' look again. The one she gave me all those years ago on the day we met.

Sunday 1 September

Why do I put myself through this? Today I can't be too far away from *Sky News* – Gaby not happy *at all* – and it's not until I see a beaming David Beckham speak to reporters outside the Portland Hospital that I'm able to relax.

'You're always nervous having children, but it's the most beautiful thing in the world.'

Nervous? Tell me about being nervous! I'll give you 'nervous'! Never again.

Tuesday 10 September

Today I was asked to go on a celebrity edition of *The Weakest Link*. Because of my appearances on *Liquid News* it seems I am now deemed a 'celebrity'. I tried to explain to them that I *wasn't* a celebrity but they weren't having any of it. They've got great people lined up: Jarvis Cocker from Pulp, Mo Mowlam and a couple of members of the So Solid Crew. Like an idiot I say yes.

Sunday 13 October

Drama. Jordan has given an interview to today's *News of the World* where she says that she had an affair with nice clean-cut Gareth Gates earlier this year when she was six months pregnant. It seems bizarre – he is a shy, awkward guy with a stutter and she is a ballsy motormouth. If she is lying, this will come back at her in a pretty big way. But then why would she lie? Through a combination of boob jobs, high-profile relationships and the like, she's incredibly famous anyway. The quotes certainly seem pretty believable. 'I can't deny our affair any longer. We kept our love secret for a number of reasons – but mainly because Gareth was under pressure from his management to stay squeaky clean. Clearly that wasn't a problem for me!'

Monday 14 October

Gareth has come straight out with a denial. In the *Daily Mirror* he is pretty damning of Jordan's claims.

'It's a total mystery to me why Jordan has made up a story about us,' he says. 'The fact is I've only ever met her once at the *Elle* style awards.'

The quote sounds a little fake, a bit cleaned-up – as though it came from the keyboard of a PR rather than from Gates's mouth – but still this is what his camp is saying and they're standing by it.

This is fascinating. Clearly one of them is lying and one of them will end up looking incredibly stupid – there's no halfway house here. Either they did or they didn't. Time for a team meeting.

'So what do we think?'

'She's lying! She's doing it just to get attention,' says one of the news team.

Julian's calmer about the whole thing: 'Okay, but a young lad like that, Jordan's probably his fantasy! I'm not saying I believe her necessarily but it's not as weird as it sounds.'

Jo Carnegie, our new Deputy Features Editor, can't get over the six months pregnant aspect of the story.

'So they were doing it when she was three months away from having a baby! That's the bit that seems weird to me. Them *doing it* when she's that pregnant.'

Generally the team seem to believe Gareth but the story is just too good to trot out a dull denial. Jordan's adamant, Gareth's very unlikely to sue (well, it would be unusual). Gareth's people are saying no to an interview (although Michelle Davies from our features team is on their case and won't be giving up anytime soon). It's early in the week but we've drafted the coverlines anyway. They're suitably over the top – everyone's going to have this story on their covers next week so we have to make sure ours really stand out.

THE TRUTH – ONLY IN HEAT
Gareth & Jordan's affair!
* What really happened?
* Secret meeting at fashion party

It's a risk but if I've called this right I'll look good. If I've called it wrong I'll look stupid. Of course, all I have to do now is find out what actually happened …

←Location's **Phil & Kirstie:** Property, partners & partying!

↘Are **Britney & Justin** giving love another chance?

This week's hottest celebrity news

£1.45 (Canary Islands €3.00, Spain €2.70) 5 – 11 April 2003

heat

MAGAZINE OF THE YEAR!

Issue 213

PHIL & LISA'S **Real-life split**

NICOLE's chicken fillets!

J-LO's **cellulite!**

GERI's TitTape!

OH NO!

The MORTIFYING photos they didn't want you to see — AND THERE'S 20 MORE INSIDE!

J-Lo & Ben **OSCAR snog-fest!** **PLUS** Frocks! Gossip!

Oooh!

MARTINE vs JENNY KITTEN The BIGGEST showbiz fight of the year

CHAPTER SEVEN
Chicken fillets and cellulite
October 2002 – July 2003

Tuesday 22 October

The things I put myself through …

Today I filmed the 'celebrity' edition of *The Weakest Link*.

As I was sitting in my dressing room I attempted to look on the positive side. It'll be fine as I'm not even remotely famous, I thought. Anne will have nothing to pick on me about and I'll proceed through the contest unnoticed until getting voted off in a respectable mid-placed slot.

When I signed up to do this, the people who were going to be on it alongside me were pretty impressive: Jarvis Cocker, Mo Mowlam and members of the So Solid Crew.

By the time I arrived there just after midday today the line-up had become me, Edwina Currie, one of Bucks Fizz, the bloke who runs marathons in silly outfits for charity and Terry Christian. Are they really going to let this go on air? Apparently so. In this lot's company I *am* actually quite famous.

The drill is this: after extensive make-up, contestants are herded into a green room where we're all shown chatting. Then we're introduced one by one by the warm-up guy, before running through a dummy round.

I was awful in the warm-up round and got everything wrong. Pitiful. This, I decided, was going to be a disaster.

The filming begins, proper. I'm awful in the first round too but luckily Gay Rights campaigner Peter Tatchell (I know, I know, A-list stuff!) is even worse than me and gets chucked off.

Then I start to relax. Enjoy it even. Before I know it I've made it through to the fourth round with hardly any votes to be chucked off and with Anne leaving me alone. This is great.

Clearly thinking that I'm not going to go anywhere soon, the production team decide that I should be brought into the show in some way. But not in the way I expected.

'Mark!'

Uh-oh. Here goes.

'You're very handsome.'

'Thank you, Anne.' Where's she going with this?

'I can see I'm going to have to keep my eye on you.'

She fancies me! The Queen Of Mean, the woman who's horrible to everyone, has got the hots for me!

It doesn't stop there – when Terry bloody Christian is being mean to me, she steps in to defend me. She teases me about my lisp (she's flirting with me! I recognise that behaviour anywhere!) At one point she appears to ask me out. When Edwina Currie also says she fancies me – Jesus, what's going on here? – she gets all territorial.

'Edwina, get lost. I saw him first.'

I'm loving this. The attention, the fact that I'm getting some questions right, the fact that Edwina and I managed to get Terry bloody Christian and a man who once ran the London Marathon in a full suit of armour voted off despite being the two best players.

Then, before I know it, it's down to the final two. Me and Edwina versus Anne. The deciding question is about my home town.

'Which 1997 film, set in Sheffield, was released in China under the title *Six Naked Pigs*?'

I knew it before she even said the bit about China. I'm from Sheffield. There aren't too many films set there.

'*The Full Monty*, Anne.'

'Mark, you are the strongest link. You go home with £10,500 for the charity of your choice. Edwina, you go home with nothing.'

Get me! I'm the strongest link.

Saw Terry Christian after the show, not much love lost there. I didn't see Anne Robinson. Of course, I fully expected it to be all congratulatory champagne and caviar in her dressing room but she buggered off straightaway. Conventional wisdom would have it that she does this to maintain her Queen Of Mean mystique, that her persona simply will not allow her to make small talk with the contestants. I tend to favour the view that she simply doesn't want to have anything to do with us rabble. No matter – I'VE BLOODY WON *THE WEAKEST LINK*!

Wednesday 23 October

Ulrika Jonsson has a book out this week and the tabloids have become obsessed by one story – the revelation that she was raped by a well-known TV presenter. The story has stepped up a gear today when the Channel 5 presenter Matthew Wright named (by mistake) *This Morning* host John Leslie as the perpetrator live on air. If it isn't him, Wright, the production company and Channel 5 could be facing a huge libel action

Thursday 24 October

Most of the papers name Leslie today in conjunction with the TV gaff. I spent most of the afternoon consulting with our legal team and we have decided to name him too. There's no strength in numbers with this, though – if we're wrong we could all get sued.

Tuesday 12 November

Anne Robinson is obsessed with me, clearly. Today we interviewed her to promote the new series of *The Weakest Link* and I asked the writer who's doing it, Chris Longridge, to throw in a few extra questions, not intended for the magazine, about my appearance.

Well, you would, wouldn't you?

We understand you met our editor recently.
Oh gosh, yes. I forgot all my harshness because I didn't know he was going to be so dazzlingly good-looking.
Oh please ...
I did give him a bit of stick about his Rs though. I thought it would be amusing to hear him doing sentences like 'Round and round the ragged rock ...'
But you made up for it?
I did. I decided he was far too good-looking for me to be rude to. I'm not sure they're going to pay me for that episode. He caught me unawares and I temporarily forgot myself.
You asked him out, didn't you?

I think I did. I'm already feeling embarrassed. My attitude towards him was most unprofessional.

And what does your husband think about all of this?
He hasn't seen it yet, thank God.

But you're quite flirtatious anyway when you're not being mean.
Yes, I adore men, and I particularly like good-looking, tall, twinkly men like Mark.

Wednesday 11 December

Yesterday we put Jade on the cover for the fifth time this year. Today, the torrent of abusive mail begins ...

> *Dear* Heat,
>   *Just as the painful memory of She Who Is Not Famous (Jade) fades, you insist on putting her on your cover repeatedly. Why? Bring back week after week of Posh covers, all is forgiven.*
> ***Francesca, by email***

And here's another one ...

> *Dear Mark,*
>   *What's going on at Heat Towers? Your magazine's obsession with Jade simply eludes me. I'd had enough of the Posh Spice non-stories and then when she's finally off the pages you stick Jade in her place.*
> ***Lola, by email***

This happens every time we put Jade in the magazine. Hundreds and hundreds of emails just slagging her off. Yet they always sell well. People, genuinely, either love her or hate her, there's no grey area.

At first these emails perturbed me – receiving them after we'd done our first Jade cover (which cost us a fair bit) was unnerving. Had I just wasted stacks of money on someone all our readers hated? But gradually I saw the pattern. Jade + hate mail = huge sales. Posh has a similar effect (although not quite as many emails). These people provoke a reaction – good or bad. I can't imagine anyone having any kind of reaction to Nicole Kidman, say, or Gwyneth Paltrow.

Tuesday 17 December

Jordan wins 'Most Ludicrous Person In Showbiz' category in *Heat* readers' poll – our readers clearly think she's lying about sleeping with Gareth Gates. We get more mail about him than anyone else, much of it obsessive. It's not surprising that many of them should leap to his defence and vote for her in this way.

Tuesday 7 January 2003

Today we run an interview with Jordan – she is *still* insisting that she had sex with Gareth Gates. Why doesn't she give it a rest?

Thursday 9 January

I'm at the BBC about to begin recording *Liquid News* when some truly preposterous pictures of Leslie Ash with ridiculously inflated lips get emailed to me – clearly a lip implant gone wrong. We've just finished this week's magazine but I'm adamant these have to go in. I ring Julian.

'Have you seen these pictures?'

'It's just incredible! We're getting emails from the readers already about them.'

The picture has made its way into some of the evening newspapers (and some websites too) and our readers have responded with considerable gusto.

'Hello *Heat*! Leslie Ash looks like a guppy fish I saw on a school visit to our local aquarium when I was seven years old,' said one. 'It scared the life out of me then and it scares the life out of me now. Please make it stop.'

'Dear *Heat*, my kids are huge fans of *The Tweenies* and as I watched this afternoon's show with them I tried to decide which of them Leslie Ash looks most like. I think it's Fizz.'

I love our readers. They're genuinely sussed and funny (and, it has to be said, pretty quick off the mark too).

Tuesday 14 January

Today we've run our Leslie Ash piece with *that* picture filling an entire page.

Rachel Eling has written the piece. Although based in our fashion team, Rachel has been making a name for herself in other areas of the magazine recently, particularly with a section called What Were You Thinking?

What Were You Thinking? has swiftly become the readers' favourite item, if our surveys are to be believed. The idea is simple: very famous people wearing very horrible dresses at premieres or parties or fashion shows have their outfit ridiculed in print by Rachel. Because she has fashion credibility, Rachel can dissect the picture with authority. And, because these people have chosen to wear these outfits or listened to a stylist when they really shouldn't have, we conclude (fairly, I think) that it is all their fault and really they should expect public ridicule. As the weeks have gone on her copy has become more withering and despairing. Now we've given her the ultimate What Were You Thinking? assignment: Leslie Ash.

The piece begins in style:

Clang! That was the sound that rang through Britain last week as six million forks were dropped during the opener of the new series of BBC1's Merseybeat. *As Leslie Ash made her debut in the police drama, it wasn't her shiny new badge we were all looking at – we could barely tear our eyes away from her mouth. The country was united in its cry of, 'What the hell has happened to Leslie Ash's lips?'*

Then the piece goes into satirical territory. We've taken inspiration from some of the ideas readers have been sending in – we've had a couple of hundred emails already, in less than a week – and compiled a side-bar on the main article entitled 'What Does She Look Like?' featuring pictures of Fizz from *The Tweenies*, a Canary Rockfish, Jar Jar Binks, Jack Nicholson as The Joker in the late eighties *Batman* movie and Janice from *The Muppets*.

I read the piece through three times before it went off – are we being just a little too cruel? In the end I decided that we had to go with it because it was completely in sync with what our readers were thinking.

In offices, colleges and front rooms right now people are discussing this picture – and they're not being kind. To be different from all the boring monthlies we have to tell it like it is, we have to talk how our readers talk and we have to be real. This magazine isn't aspirational magazine publishing: this is conversation fodder. And, I tell myself for the tenth time this week, it was her decision to do this …

Friday 17 January
Well, it seems we haven't been mean enough to Leslie Ash. If I was ever worried that we'd gone too far the emails we're getting this week would reassure me. Apparently, our readers want more …

> *Her new and improved face has clearly frightened the casting agents of* Merseybeat *into giving her a job. Do the producers not have eyes? Or has she been hired for the 'Oh. My. God' factor? Does she not have a mirror? Send her one, and send her the number of a decent surgeon too.*
> *Marc, Haworth, West Yorkshire*

> *I was unable to follow the plot of the opening episode of* Merseybeat *as I was mesmerised by Leslie Ash's huge gob. How the other actors kept a straight face when she obviously couldn't is beyond me.*
> *Sophie, Preston*

Sunday 19 January
News has been coming through this week that Zoë Ball has been having an affair with a little-known DJ called Dan Peppe. I'm stunned. From what I saw that day in Brighton – and what other people tell me – she and Norman are a strong, strong couple.

Monday 20 January
We start looking into the Zoë Ball affair story and come across a friend of Peppe's who is happy speaking to us but also wants to stay anonymous. The story they have is rather different to the one the papers are putting out there – they say that instead of it being a new relationship that only began last December it's actually been going on for six months. We've spoken to this friend several times on the phone – painstakingly working towards confirming that he is who he says he is

(and he is) while trying to stand-up all he says (not easy). I have concerns – from what they're saying they do seem to know Peppe and be believeable, but when I speak to Zoë's agent we just get stonewalled.

Thursday 23 January

Today Zoë Ball released a statement saying that her relationship with Norman Cook is over. It's so terribly sad.

Thursday 30 January

After much soul-searching I put the Dan Peppe/Zoë Ball secret six-month affair revelations on the cover. We're selling the whole thing quite hard and I've combined our findings with the words from Zoë's press statement. And, because it's pretty irresistible, I've sold the press statement words as though they were an interview.

For the first time …
ZOË SPEAKS OUT!
* She's been seeing new boyfriend for six months.
* It's all over with Norman.

It looks like an interview. I want it to look like an interview. Well, it kind of is an interview – she's said these words to someone so … doesn't that make it an interview?

Anyway, the cover looks great like this. This is the one we have to put out.

We're on really friendly terms. Zoë and I will be fine.

Friday 31 January

We've had a tip-off that Madonna is pregnant with her third child at the age of 44. We've looked into it and it all seems to stand up – the contact is a relative of someone who has been involved in her pre-natal treatment – and we've done loads of checks. One person we haven't called is Barbara Charone – aka BC – Madonna's publicist. The reason for that is simple – we're pretty sure of our sources and journalists sometimes get paranoid that if you tell a PR you have it they then give it to everyone else too. That's not BC's style, but we won't take the risk. This is our story – ours to own, ours exclusively – and I am damned if anyone else is going to get it too. I don't know BC well enough to know whether she would do this (I'm sure she wouldn't) but I don't want to risk it.

Tuesday 4 February

Today we are running with our Madonna pregnancy story on the cover.

Within hours the phone is ringing. It's BC.

'Your story is rubbish,' she tells me firmly.

'BC, we're pretty confident of our sources.'

'I'm telling you, your story is rubbish.'

She doesn't sound angry. Worse, her words are cool, calm and therefore twice as deadly.

'And I'm particularly offended you didn't let me know you were going to run it. We've got the whole world's media on the phone – the least you could have done is given me the courtesy of tipping me off. We have to deal with all of this shit because of a stupid, untrue story you've run.'

She's not messing about. Barbara Charone would not have called me – and given me both barrels in this way – if it was true. She'll have spoken to Madonna. Hell, BC would probably have found out Madonna was pregnant before Madonna did, that's how on the case she is.

By 5 p.m. our nightmare has escalated. To punish us, and to keep the world's press away, BC has put out a press release. To EVERY-ONE. The press release says our story is nonsense and, what's more, that Madonna herself will be putting in an official complaint to the Press Complaints Commission.

When I say she's put this press release out to everybody I really do mean everybody – the first I know it exists is when it's the top story on *E! Online*, an American website. And not just any American website – for my money the most trusted entertainment site of the moment and certainly one of the most widely read. This is an unmitigated disaster.

Wednesday 5 February

The Press Complaints Commission story is everywhere on the web, thanks to BC putting it out to the Press Association and Reuters this morning. In fact, there are probably now people on *the moon* who know we printed an untrue story about Madonna being pregnant. Very few newspapers in the UK have mentioned it, though. There's an unwritten rule that (out of loyalty to your fellow publications) you don't report another newspaper or magazine's mistakes. 'There but for the grace of God', and all that. The one publication that has gone big on it, though, is the *Daily Mirror*. And they're on our side, big time.

The *Daily Mirror* has, for a while, seen itself as the poor relation when it comes to Madonna stories. Because she's after the big numbers and a close relationship with one team who she feels she can trust, Charone mostly chooses the *Sun* as the home for her Madonna stories and interviews. This, understandably, makes the *Daily Mirror* angry. Today their anger spilled over.

On a page lead near the front of the paper, the 3am showbiz team wrote a witty, sarcy piece that made me feel a whole lot better.

MADONNA DENIES SHE'S PREGNANT AGAIN
It must be true then ...
*It's one of our favourite games. Madonna is denying rumours she
is pregnant which can only mean one thing – she's up the duff.*

The piece distils ours – giving the basic facts and evidence – then proceeds to list the previous true stories that were, at some point, denied by Madonna's US publicist Liz Rosenberg.

It ends in style ...

So what do we make of yesterday's denials?
Well, we don't believe a word of it!

This piece – seemingly *very* confident in what it's saying – has completely thrown me. Surely the woman who was adamantly telling me our story was nonsense was telling me the truth? I don't know what to think any more.

Thursday 6 February
Charone's threat to get the Press Complaints Commision involved was no joke. This morning we receive a letter from them. Enclosed is

Me with Posh, minutes after she gave me the interview that saved *Heat* magazine

© HEAT

Sada, the UK's first ever *Big Brother* evictee, July 2000. Madness ensues

ENDEMOL

The kiss – Andy and Mel make *Big Brother* history with the first ever snog

'Security!' Emma Bunton decides the best way to deal with people who've broken in to *Top of the Pops* is to ignore them

DEAN FREEMAN

Me, Cher and Julian Linley
(Cher's the one in the middle)

A triumphant moment as *Heat*
favourite Gareth Gates beats
Will Young to win *Pop Idol* ... oops

Me lying on a bed
with Darius, Simon
Cowell and Pete
Waterman – and I
don't even drink!

One more time – Darius gives
it some on *Popstars* in 2000

Who says journalists are spiteful? Trying to bugger up *Glamour's* launch party in 2001

'Feel the burn lanky boy!' Working out with Chris Moyles' team (minus Chris Moyles)

Jade leaves the house after coming fourth in *Big Brother* 2002. Five years later she made the mistake of going back in

What a poser! The *Liquid News* days with my first TV wife the faaaaabulous Julia Morris

Me with Geri Halliwell on my shoulders, St Martin's Lane Hotel, 2001

Minutes before beating an all-star cast to win a 'Celebrity' *Weakest Link*

'Mmm, still not quite right.' Leslie Ash shows off her lips

Posh and Becks put on a show of unity during Loosgate. It fooled no one

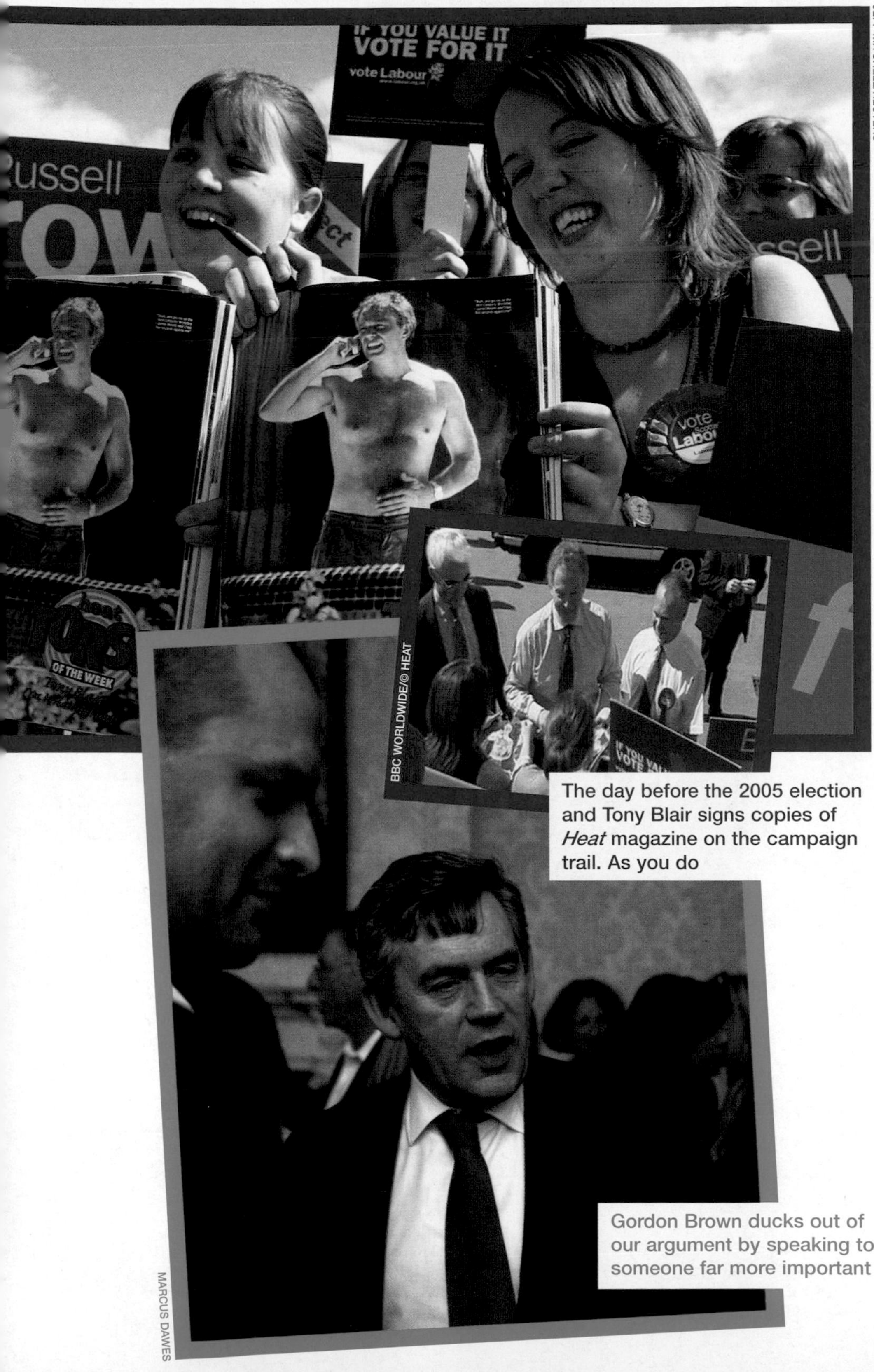

IF YOU VALUE IT
VOTE FOR IT
vote Labour

vote Labour

The day before the 2005 election and Tony Blair signs copies of *Heat* magazine on the campaign trail. As you do

Gordon Brown ducks out of our argument by speaking to someone far more important

GABY KAY

GOODBYE 2004

... and good riddance. Five days after the tsunami hit, there's not a lot to celebrate in the Maldives

X17

Jude Law and the nanny, before the affair that killed his relationship with Sienna Miller

an email sent from Charone to them – stating yet again that Madonna is not pregnant (a fact she says has been confirmed to her by Madonna's manager Caresse Henry and her American publicist Liz Rosenberg). Buoyed up by the *Daily Mirror* article, I am becoming highly sceptical of everyone involved from Madonna's camp. As with Ewan McGregor, we get nothing at all from Madonna ever so I have no incentive to concede on this one. I don't like to fall out with people but with this story I'm not about to concede that we're wrong unless I'm 100 per cent convinced that we are.

Monday 10 February

Zoë Ball isn't my friend any more. Today this was in my in-box:

> *Hello Mr Frith*
>
> *Just wanted to say how sad I was to see Heat when I arrived back from abroad yesterday. I always thought we had quite a good working relationship. Norman and I have always been fans and always made time to talk to you.*
>
> *In fact you're just another scummy publication with no scruples. I object to the fact that you made out I gave an interview – clever magazine 'exclusive' tricks – and that you have written complete nonsense about my relationship with Daniel Peppe, facts that you could have quite easily checked with Vivienne. Frankly it is no one else's business what is going on in my life but I appreciate that it will be written about and shit made up but you've got no excuse, Mark.*
>
> *I really would appreciate some kind of apology, otherwise I can promise you Norman and I will never speak to your magazine again. Not that it will be much of a loss as you make it all up anyway.*
>
> *From **Zoë Ball***

I've read this through again and again. She's right, of course, that we over-heated the story but seems, in the email, to be asking for some special treatment because we know each other. It's much more difficult to do a story on someone you like, someone you get on with. But do them you must. Clearly this whole thing has been a huge shock to

Zoë and Norman. But they are famous, they are in the public eye and there is going to be interest in what they do. Deep down she must realise that. I guess it's just a shock coming from me. She's surprised – and disappointed – that I can be as tabloid as the rest of them.

We're getting this reaction a lot at the moment. For decades magazines have been seen as soft in comparison to the 'hard-as-nails' red-top newspapers – the place to go to promote your latest film or perfume or whatever, where you can be welcomed by writers (possibly personally chosen by you!) who will say lovely things about you, adore you and not ask any tough questions. The photos of you will be retouched – so you look perfect in every one – and you can even choose which one goes on the cover. Increasingly readers see through all of this, and want something a bit more real. Having good news stories – that celebrities don't want us to print – doesn't have to be just the domain of newspapers; there's no reason magazines shouldn't run them too. For some people – long able to rely on us to print pretty much what they wanted – this isn't great news. *Heat* is no longer the good guy.

For me, though, all that matters is the readers. Too many editors forget this but it's something I've put at the front of my mind in everything I've done at *Heat*. The readers are all that matters – what they want to read about is all that matters. If that means forgoing lovely holidays with the Ball family in some lovely Ibizan hideaway, so be it.

Not that they ever asked.

Tuesday 11 February

After thinking about it overnight I have decided to reply to Zoë – but where to begin? Despite the chummy 'Hello Mr Frith' bit the email is pretty angry. I've started by admitting that we were cheeky in turning her statement into an interview (but that she did say it all) and that we had the information from the Peppe camp on good authority. Hit send.

Later, during her live XFM radio show, she replies, by email again.

Hello Mr Frith
  Much appreciated. Sorry to rant, it's just getting to me now.
Take care.
  Zoë xx

Huh? What a difference a day makes ...

Wednesday 12 February

I have composed my reply to the Press Complaints Commission on the Madonna thing. My letter is pretty desperate: I say that Madonna's camp have denied stuff before that turns out to be true, and that's why I didn't put it to them. I also question whether Madonna is really in any 'distress' because of our piece as their letter suggested.

'I would dispute that this story caused any distress to Madonna,' I write. 'She's written about every hour of every day. Do we know for certain the story has caused stress to Madonna?'

It's not a bad letter – although it makes me sound like a stroppy, contradictory prick – but really I'm fighting a losing battle here. If Madonna isn't pregnant, we need to apologise. I've sent off the letter and I'm not hugely looking forward to their reply.

Thursday 13 February

New sales figures released today show us breaking through the half a million barrier for the first time – but as our rise in circulation is half what it was in percentage terms last time, some commentators seem to see this as the end of our huge upwards surge. There's no pleasing some people.

Friday 14 February

It never rains but it pours – a piece in today's *Daily Telegraph* tears into us in a pretty major way. They say success has gone to our heads and even quote one anonymous 'showbusiness PR' who hammers home that point:

'People get dizzy with their own success. You just get to a point where you feel indestructible.' The same PR is scathing about us following the tabloid trend of being more intrusive into celebs' private lives.

Talking of PRs, the PCC replied today batting back my arguments about our Madonna story. We've told them we'll apologise in the next possible issue.

Wednesday 19 February

Now Zoë Ball's husband hates me. He and Zoë are back together and we've run a piece about it in our latest issue. We've made the point –

quite fairly – that despite this surprise reconciliation, Zoë still isn't wearing her wedding ring.

This morning Sal beckoned me over to her phone as she was going through the messages left overnight for us.

'Mark. I think you should listen to this.'

'Who is it?'

'He says he's Norman Cook. It certainly sounds like him. By the way, he's drunk.'

He certainly is. I hold the phone close to my ear so I can hear what he says. It's not easy.

'This is a message for the editor … why are you writing all this stuff about us? Zoë says you and her are friends so why all this … crap? I know that no one wants to hear this but the truth is we're really happy and we'd be even happier if everyone just left us alone.'

There's a long pause while he thinks of what to say next. In that few seconds his mood seems to lighten somewhat.

'Sorry I have to ring up and say this … it's just that we're really happy and no one seems to want to hear that. Anyway … this is Angry from Brighton signing off … bye bye.'

Sunday 23 February

Went to the Baftas for some light relief tonight. It's been a good year for the British film industry and the crowds were huge. Gaby and I somehow ended up getting in one of the chauffeur-driven cars meant for the film talent so we arrived at the party in style and the flashbulbs went off as we stepped out of the car – boy, were those photographers disappointed when they saw who it was. The autograph-hunters weren't that impressed either, apart from one who beckoned me over to him. Huh?

I couldn't hear what he was saying so I edged over to where he was standing – with autograph book and pen in his hand.

I get close to him.

'Jonny! Jonny! Can I have your autograph?'

On occasion my slight resemblance to Angelina Jolie's ex-husband Jonny Lee Miller has been commented on. I don't see it myself – he's about a foot shorter than me and even more good-looking (if such a thing is possible). I really do look nothing like him.

'I'm not him!' I say as I stumble off.

'Gaby!' I say, catching her up. 'He thought I was Jonny Lee Miller.' Gaby gives me her well-practised 'as if' look.

The do passed off otherwise uneventfully, except for the brilliant moment when Richard Desmond walked straight past me, blanking me completely. Nice to see you too.

Wednesday 26 February

Wednesday is *Now* magazine day. The battle for leadership in the celebrity market is becoming a two-horse race and so it's them – and their editor Jane Ennis – that have become our biggest rivals. Every Wednesday we get the new issue of their magazine, crowd round it and rip it to shreds. (Not literally.)

It doesn't deserve it, of course, because it's pretty good but the rivalry between the two of us is such that you have to do it.

Today, though, I've come to the conclusion that they have completely lost it.

Their new cover is radical to say the least.

It has three huge pictures – one of Lisa Kudrow (Phoebe in *Friends*) one of *GMTV* host Fiona Phillips and one of Nicole Kidman. They all look awful – pale, tired and wearing little or no make-up.

The headline is huge – and vicious.

ROUGH!
Even stars have bad days

Julian's the first to see it: 'What the hell ...'

Mark Taylor, our Art Director, can't quite believe it either.

'Why bring out a magazine where the people on the cover look bad? I don't get it.'

Me neither. The celebrity weeklies are changing the rules of how magazines are made but still one is surely sacrosanct – the rule that people have to look good on covers.

The crowd round Mark's desk grew and I addressed them en masse.

'I confidently predict,' everyone turns to look at me, 'that this issue of *Now* will be a total flop.'

A little cheer goes up, even a polite ripple of applause. I love being right all the time.

Wednesday 5 March

Shit. Early figures indicate that the 'Rough!' issue of *Now* magazine was a huge seller. Possibly as high as 700,000.

Liz Martin, our brilliant marketing manager, came up to give me the good news.

'Liz, stop winding me up. All three of those women look awful.'

'People like that! It makes them feel better about themselves.'

'Is there any way these figures are wrong?'

'We'll know more in a week. But I don't think so.'

Tuesday 11 March

The following appears on the letters page in today's magazine:

MADONNA NOT PREGNANT
Madonna's representatives have said that, contrary to our report in the 8 February issue, she is not pregnant. We are happy to set the record straight.

Not so convinced about the 'happy' bit. I don't feel very happy today. Oh well, that means it's all concluded now. The deed is done. Madonna 1, *Heat* 0.

Wednesday 12 March

We now know more about *Now*'s sale. And it was even bigger than we thought. Latest estimates put it at 730,000.

That cover has changed everything in the celebrity magazine market. It shows that readers want their celebs to look awful rather than good. *Heat* need a piece of the action. I've sent the picture desk off to find as many pictures as they can of famous people looking awful. Now *this* is fun!

Thursday 20 March

Good piece about us in *Press Gazette* today, the printed media's trade magazine. We've had a lot of negative press recently so it's great to have something positive for a change.

The article has been written by Janice Turner, a long-term supporter of *Heat*. She was writing about us when no one else was and, as a former editor herself (of *Real* and *That's Life* magazines) I respect her opinion. This week she's writing about Richard Desmond's new celebrity magazine (yes, there's another one) called (wait for it ...) *New*. It's awful, but it's only 60p so might take sales away from us, she reckons. She uses the piece to take a look at the entire celebrity magazine world including *New*, *Now*, us and our new sister magazine *Closer*, which Turner sees as an older, frumpier version of *Heat*. She's very complimentary about us, and it puts a real spring in my step after a month and a half of bad news.

> *Emap must be pleased that* Closer *has not affected its brilliant sister title,* Heat. *At first, skimming through, I wondered whether it had lost its edge. The opening pages are so-so. What's this obsession with Jade from* Big Brother? *Why was its J-Lo bum story 100 per cent gag-free?*
>
> *But* Heat*'s strength goes beyond getting the hottest set of snaps. From the picture captions to the TV listings blurbs there is a coherence; a bubbling, infectious enjoyment of the new, a solid understanding of its restless, metropolitan reader.*
>
> *Perhaps only the teen titles are more powered by tiny shifts in the zeitgeist. But with editor Mark Frith – who knows complacency could be fatal –* Heat *is well placed to survive any market crash.*

Tuesday 25 March

Our two-week search for pictures of famous people looking terrible has paid off! Ah, if only my old college professors could see me now, how proud they'd be.

Anyway, Clara and the team have chosen really well and today they took me through the 23 pictures they'd chosen for the feature. Standing around Clara's computer this afternoon, she showed me, one by one, the most mortifying pictures of celebrities that have ever been taken. Put it this way, it was eye-opening ...

'Okay, here's Nicole Kidman and you can see her chicken fillet.'

'Her what?'

'Chicken fillet! You know, padding that women put down their front to make their boobs bigger.'

'Never heard of them. I had no idea. You mean you ...'

Clara gives me a withering look, and ploughs on.

'Jennifer Lopez with cellulite.'

Jennifer Lopez is the glamour girl of the moment – hit albums, huge films, a hunky boyfriend (Ben Affleck). And last week she's just gone up a further notch on the fame ladder by wearing the most talked-about dress at the Oscars. And here she is, in *our* magazine, with a large patch of rather *un*glamorous cellulite on her right thigh.

'Right, very good. What's next?'

'Geri Halliwell's tit tape.'

'Geri Halliwell's what?'

'Tit tape!'

Clara's despairing of me now.

'If you want to go out for a night in a nice dress, no bra, this attaches the dress to your chest so you don't fall out. Everyone wears it, it's just that you're not meant to ever see it. But here you can.'

What an informative day!

And so on. There's Cat Deeley with veiny feet, Holly Valance with a spotty chin, Penelope Cruz with a double chin and Britney Spears with lopsided nipples.

Forty minutes later I've seen all 23 pictures, all brilliant, that will ensure we fall out with another 23 famous people, no doubt. But it is a great feature and I bet the readers will love it.

Thursday 27 March

Saw the finished embarrassing photos feature today. Looks amazing. We've slaved over the coverlines – no, really – and it looks wonderfully commercial.

Nicole's chicken fillets!
J-Lo's cellulite!
Geri's TitTape!
OH NO!
The MORTIFYING photos they didn't want you to see –
AND THERE'S 20 MORE INSIDE!

Tuesday 8 April

The letters page in this week's issue is full of reaction to last week's cover and they love it.

There's the occasional dissenting voice that says we're being too mean but most love it, many say they're fed up of seeing 'perfect' – looking celebrities all the time and they like the fact that these pictures proved they were normal people, that at last they looked real.

We've printed a handful:

Heat, you've just made my (and half the population of Britain's) day. Oh, how I revelled in absolute glee at Nicole's chicken fillets, Mad Mariah's un-tanned hands and Ms Hurley's manky feet. They're just like us (apart from the fact that we don't have millions of pounds in the bank). I do have a problem with you insulting the 'not that large really' Martine McCutcheon's size. By insulting her, you insulted about 99 per cent of British females. But still the 20 gross-looking celebs was well worth the pain that was caused to me after your beastly insult to the lovely Ms McCutcheon.
Nia, Cardiff

and

How brilliant was your article 'It's A Disaster?' I cannot stop laughing at the TitTapeTM calamity of Ms Geri Halliwell. I keep looking at it when I really should be working, and giggling like a naughty schoolgirl. How did she get it sooooooo wrong? Still, it's great to know there is hope for us civilians.
Donna, Leeds

The sales are huge too – nearly 600,000. Time to plan the next one.

'Right Clara – Stars Without Make-up! I need 20 pictures in two weeks' time!'

She raises her eyes to the ceiling. But I know she'll do a great job.

Thursday 24 April

If it ain't broke, don't fix it! Today's press day on our next embarrassing pictures cover. Glam stars without their slap – there's Kylie,

Britney and, just in case things weren't bad enough between us, Zoë Ball. The coverline may seem slightly familiar.

Zoë!

Kylie!

Britney!

STARS WITHOUT MAKE-UP!

18 pictures they really don't want you to see

This is *easy*.

So we nicked another magazine's idea? Twice! So what. We've interpreted it in a far more direct way.

The weird thing is that since their huge sales for 'Rough!', *Now* haven't followed it up with a second 'glam stars looking awful' cover.

My philosophy is simple: if something sells well, commission a similar cover straightaway. Make sure the concept is slightly different (so people don't feel it's exactly the same as the thing they bought three weeks ago) but, whatever you do, don't feel you need to reinvent the wheel every single week. If it ain't broke …

Wednesday 7 May

Tonight we won Magazine Of The Year at the PPA Awards for the second year in a row – this year, though, we shared it with *Glamour* magazine which is completely fair: Jo Elvin and the team have made it a huge success (she's gutted to share it, though: you can tell by her face as she went to the stage to collect it). Jane Ennis from *Now* also won an award – the Editor Of The Year trophy I won for the past two years. It's her first ever PPA award and she does an excited little dance as she runs – literally, runs – to the stage.

Thursday 15 May

Ewan McGregor went back on the attack today. He gave an interview where he described *Heat* as a 'dirty piece of shit'. Lovely.

McGregor's travelling the country with Texas singer Sharleen Spiteri promoting the Children's Hospice Association Of Scotland. When one reporter – from a London radio station called LBC – asked Spiteri about having her photo taken by paparazzi while pregnant she named us as one of the publications who printed it. This was McGregor's cue. As if he needed one.

He told the reporter that *Heat* was 'a dirty, filthy piece of shit … I'd like to put that on record. People shouldn't buy it because it sucks.' Warming to his theme he tore into the paparazzi trade.

'They don't have the right to intrude on people's lives. They shouldn't be shot, but they should be severely beaten up.'

Within minutes we had the BBC ringing up for a comment. We politely declined. When, later on, it became big news on the radio I send an email to the team.

'You're probably all aware of Ewan McGregor's comments about *Heat* that he made earlier today. As tough as it is to hear this sort of thing about the magazine we work for we have to remember this – we don't do this magazine for Ewan McGregor. We do it for the half a million plus people who love the magazine. Don't ever forget that.'

People don't seem much happier after the email and I don't blame them – they're all going to go home this evening to boyfriends, girl-friends, mums, dads – whatever – who'll ask them about the Ewan McGregor interview and they'll probably have to defend what we do to all of them.

Friday 4 July

For several months now, with the Jordan story never really cleared up, Michelle Davies has been trying to bag an interview with Gareth Gates. It has taken her a lot of time and patience, and finally today they've said yes.

The Gareth Gates interview is the one all our readers now want to read. Jordan's not backing down in saying she slept with him, while he is keeping schtum – other than the wishy-washy press statement his team issued when the story first emerged. Next week we'll interview him, exclusively. This could be good – we've had a rotten few months. We need something to make us feel a little happier about ourselves …

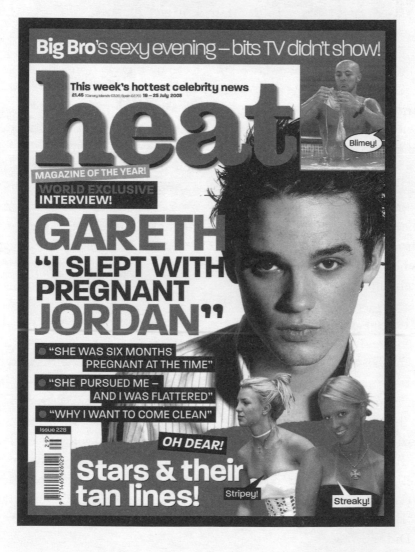

CHAPTER EIGHT
Gareth comes clean
July 2003 – March 2004

Monday 7 July

The Gareth Gates interview went better than any of us could ever have hoped.

This was a huge moment for Michelle. A former sub-editor, I know that she felt she'd been in a career rut until we gave her a job on our features desk. Since being given that opportunity she has really made the most of her chance – fiercely ambitious and not afraid to occasionally rub people up the wrong way with her ultra-direct manner, in interview situations Michelle shows a very different side. Patient and serious, yet an expert in the art of cajoling, her manner is exactly what this assignment needed.

The interview took place at Gareth's management company and, as she predicted before she left the office, it wasn't easy. So much of the interviewing skill is about patience and persistence – too many journalists rush in to ask follow-up questions when the interviewee hasn't finished their previous answer. So determined was Michelle to get the answers she was convinced she could get, she let him talk, allowing him all the time he needed. Gareth's – still chronic – stutter, plus his uncertainty about what he was saying, meant this took a long time. But when it came it was everything we wanted and more.

On whether he was involved with Jordan:

'I did have a brief relationship with her.'

Did they have sex?

'Yes.'

Was it a long relationship?

'It was brief. But relationships are so private, I don't want to go into details.'

Why come clean now?

'I had no intention of saying anything, but I was bemused by the fact that she went to the press. A relationship is private. I'd never do that.'

According to rumours going round she was pregnant at the time – was she?

'Yeah, she was. I was very naive. I was a 17-year-old who had moved from Bradford to London and she pursued me. I'll be honest with you – it was flattering at the time, the fact that she was chasing me.'

Michelle rang me from the interview to tell me what had happened. She was breathless with excitement, understandably.

My next call was from Gareth's head of PR, Julian Henry, boss of Henry's House. I've known Julian since I was a cub reporter at *Smash Hits*. He took me on my first-ever plane journey at the age of 20, to Germany where I interviewed Lisa Stansfield, the pop star of the day. Smiley, balding, with a sideline as the singer in a pop group (moderately big in Japan – I'm not joking), Julian is brilliant at his job but way too nice for the sordid world of PR. A lovely lovely man, who, today, is really not very happy.

At. All.

Until the interview began, Julian didn't know Gareth had slept with Jordan. In fact Julian had been given the impression – for an entire year, since the stories first appeared – that he definitely had *not* slept with her. Gareth had told him this, indeed several people in the team behind Gareth had told him this. So he was fuming – upset that he had not been told the whole truth, upset that he hadn't been able to 'PR-manage' (the phrase of the day) this situation in the way he wanted to.

'You got a good interview then?' he asked.

'Yes! Fantastic, Michelle did a great job.'

'She did, but listen, he's going to have to give an interview to the *Sun* as well.'

'No he's not.' He cannot do this.

'Yes he will. We've had to deny it to them for months, so now it turns out to be true they'll need to run it too.'

In the history of the reborn *Heat*, this has to be our biggest exclusive so far, the biggest celebrity story of the year. No way is it about to be handed over to the *Sun*.

PRs – and Julian is certainly not alone in this – fear the *Sun* more than anything or anyone else. Rile them, so the theory goes, and all your artists are finished and you with it. Julian has a lot to lose – the company that bears his name, Henry's House, handles PR for all of Simon Fuller's artists (several ex-Spice Girls, Will Young and many others) and some heavyweight corporate clients too, Coca-Cola among them. And on this story, because his client hasn't kept him in the loop, he's in danger of looking a prize chump.

In reality no story is going to get you blacklisted for ever, though a few might temporarily; it's just the fear of it that keeps the PR community in line. It's the unknown: how bad will their revenge stories be? Will it lose me accounts? Will they ring up the people who pay my wages?

We talked round and round the issue for at least an hour. Julian was blunt – if I won't say yes to handing over our interview for the *Sun* to run whenever they want, he will arrange for them to sit in a room with Gareth where they'll get the story from him direct. I've precious few cards to play in these sort of circumstances and – although he wasn't due to do any more interviews for a week – Gareth's PR team can give out interviews to whoever, whenever. There is no contract between us – no exclusivity, no nothing.

Whichever way you look at it, we're at this guy's mercy.

But throughout the course of the call I become quite angry – this is a genuine exclusive and we'd worked hard for it. No one else has this story and I'm damned if we're going to lose it to save a PR's back. And anger, as I was about to find out, can get you a long way.

'So Julian, what you're effectively saying is that any publication can have their exclusive taken away from them if that's what the PR decides? Think carefully about the precedent you're going to set with your answer.'

'You've still got your exclusive. You're the only magazine that's got an interview.'

'We got this through hard work. Hard work setting up the interview, hard work getting him to fess up. We are *not* giving that away!'

'Okay … I'll ring you back.'

Five minutes later he's on the phone again. He's adamant but open to a possible compromise. With the Victoria Beckham publicity from three years ago still fresh in my mind I suggest to him that we do give the *Sun* some quotes but they can't run them until the day our interview comes out – and with a two-inch high *Heat* front cover and a credit that makes it clear this is an interview from *Heat* magazine.

At 7.30 p.m, two hours after he first called, he agrees. Which is great for us because we'd have wanted to do this kind of PR link-up anyway.

Tuesday 8 July

As much as I feel I can trust Julian Henry, I was relieved to wake up this morning and see that the *Sun* haven't run with our story today. You're never really sure if someone is going to stick to what they've agreed. Maybe we will be able to keep this story to ourselves after all.

I've decided to bring forward the publication of the interview by a week anyway – it will be our cover feature next Tuesday. Fascinated to know how Jordan will react.

Wednesday 9 July

On Monday I made my debut appearance in the *Guardian*'s 100 Most Influential People In The Media poll. I'm over the moon about it – the list is full of industry heavyweights and hoary old broadsheet newspaper editors. I'm the first celebrity weekly editor to ever make it in there, a fact that hasn't gone unnoticed by one particular hoary old broadsheet newspaper editor, Andrew Neil. Writing in his *Evening Standard* column, the *Sunday Times* boss thinks it's a scandal I'm in there.

'The *Guardian*'s annual list of the most influential people in the British media is always good for a few guffaws, but this year's top 100 will have readers splitting their sides,' he wrote. 'Nobody could quarrel with Greg Dyke and Rupert Murdoch taking first and second places respectively. But what is the editor of *Heat* magazine doing at 88 when the editor of *The Economist*, probably the most important weekly magazine in the world, doesn't even make the list? "*Heat* is cool," says one of the panellists who made the selection. Oh yeah? Which one will still be around in 20 years' time?'

I love the fact that Neil thinks I shouldn't be in there. It makes me even happier to be listed. Anything that causes him a few more heart palpitations is good for me.

Thursday 10 July

Sent the Gareth cover off to the printers today – looks incredible.

The cover shot is of him looking mean and moody (and, under-standably, sheepish) – the lines aren't subtle.

WORLD EXCLUSIVE INTERVIEW!
GARETH: 'I SLEPT WITH PREGNANT JORDAN'
* 'She was six months pregnant at the time'
* 'She pursued me – and I was flattered'
* 'Why I want to come clean'

Louise questions the 'World' bit of World Exclusive.

'No one knows who he is outside of the UK!' she says, not unfairly.

'Yeah, but it makes it more exciting, doesn't it.'

'Are you sure about this?'

'It's the wow factor, isn't it?'

It is ridiculous, of course, but in magazines it does you no harm to be overenthusiastic. And, also, I'm just so excited about this that I need it to go the extra mile.

Speaking of which, today the interview became a two-parter – this bit is but a taster. Utterly shameless. I love it!

Monday 14 July

Went to the premiere of (the excellent) *Pirates Of The Caribbean* tonight (Gaby's a big Orlando Bloom fan). On the way home I bought the first edition of tomorrow's *Sun*. The top third of the cover is – as arranged – our story.

GARETH CONFESSES
'I DID sleep with Jordan'
See page 3

Great! There's our two-inch high cover, two further plugs and nearly four million people who will know about our story come the morning. I sink into the seat in the back of the cab a very happy man.

'Four million people will see this,' I tell Gaby.

'Darling, that's fantastic.'

'Gaby – four million people!'

'All right! I get the idea!'

This was a hard-won battle. We'll get a huge sale, the tabloids won't be too hacked off – and Julian Henry still has a job. So everyone's happy.

Tuesday 15 July

The issue's out and it's flying, you can tell. Jordan – never one to stay quiet – has come out to say her bit. She's over the moon about the interview – and feels vindicated at last. It can't be much fun spending nine months with everyone thinking you're a liar – on top of all the other shit she has to deal with.

'Obviously it is no surprise to me,' she told the pack of reporters waiting outside her house. 'He has lied to an awful lot of people. Nothing has changed and I don't wish to say any more because all the details will be in the book,' she said.

Bless her. Any chance for a quick plug.

Tuesday 12 August

The new ABC figures are announced this Thursday. *Now*'s figures must be good – because in this morning's *Financial Times* they interviewed Jane Ennis and she is really giving it some. Reading it you realise pretty quickly that Jane is clearly one editor who hasn't been told to shut up by *her* Chief Executive …

She has always had this thing about us copying her magazine. She's utterly obsessed about the subject and today she gives it another go.

'Sometimes I feel I'm driving in a Formula One race,' she says rather grandly, 'taking all the risks on the curves, and everyone is just slipping on behind me.'

Thursday 14 August

Ennis was right to be pleased: the figures released today for the first six months of the year show them up 3.6 per cent. To just above 590,000. But we went up 18 per cent to over 565,000. We're closing on them. And fast.

Sunday 21 September

Newspapers today report trouble in the Beckhams' marriage.

Heat has been receiving these kind of reports for a while. Since the couple moved to Spain an entire industry has set up over there – there's photographers, 'stringers' (freelance journalists who report gossip told to them by waiters, taxi drivers, doormen or whoever has come into contact with the couple) and all are ready, at a moment's notice, to file to us for cold, hard cash. We're hearing from them that Victoria's not happy out there since David's move to Real Madrid (although based on what we've seen she's hardly ever there) and that when she is there David would rather be on his own. None of it surprises me – what I saw that day three years ago made me convinced that he sometimes just wishes she wasn't there.

Today's stories finally put into print some of the rumours we'd been hearing. The piece, in later editions of the *News of the World*, alleges that they're close to a spilt, that the move to Madrid has destroyed their relationship and that they barely see each other.

Monday 22 September

Heat gets sent – very early on a Monday morning – a denial from the Beckham camp, just 24 hours after the *News of the World* story appeared. 'Contrary to newspaper reports,' it reads, 'our marriage is not in crisis. We are extremely happy together as a family. Our only difficulty has been finding a house in Madrid that meets our needs.' A-ha. Clearly the PR team have been ready for just this kind of story, hence the speediness of the rebuttal. They know all is not right and they're ready to quash things as soon as they can. Very ready.

Sunday 28 September

Another Sunday, another David Beckham story. This morning's *News of the World* goes one step further than last week's did. They allege that he's been out on the town with a 'stunning brunette' twice in a week. Posh was out of the country of both occasions. No denial this time, which is very telling. A lack of denial is often as strong as an admission. Fascinating.

Tuesday 28 October

Just got back from the National TV Awards at the Royal Albert Hall. Spend half the evening being harangued by a very drunk Jessie Wallace, the hottest thing on TV at the moment thanks to her starring role in *EastEnders* as mouthy, out-of-control Kat Slater.

I don't know where they got their inspiration from.

'I'm fat am I?' she says while lurching towards me. 'You said I was fat!'

We've never said anything of the sort. What's she going on about?

There's only one thing a journalist should do in this situation: run off and hide.

Tuesday 4 November

We've brought in a new regular feature called 'The Embarrassment!' Originally known as 'Oh, The Embarrassment!', we lost the 'Oh' bit because the team, en masse, thought it looked 'a bit stupid'. 'The Embarrassment' sits within a pull-out section called *Scandal* which is our rather pathetic attempt to do to *OK* what they did to us with *Hot Stars*. If they can be 'two magazines for the price of one' we can bloody well have 'two magazines for the price of one' as well. It's a poor attempt, frankly: whereas *Hot Stars* is an extra 96-page pull-out, ours is a mere 12 pages. And I bet no one ever pulls it out. Still, the content is good (celebrities pictured doing embarrassing things) but there's a bit we struggle with every single week and that's 'The Embarrassment'. It's meant to be a series of pictures of one embarrassing incident – i.e., someone falling over in frame-by-frame detail. In one picture they stumble! In the next they fall to the ground! In the next they're picking up all their shopping from the floor! Something like that. The problem, we've discovered, is that famous people don't fall to the ground in public that often. And if they do, there don't seem to be photographers catching the moment. So, we usually end up running pictures of minor celebs getting parking tickets. (Celeb leaves car on double yellow lines! Traffic Warden gives them a ticket! Celeb comes back to car and angrily rips ticket from the windscreen!) It's really not working. Today, though, we've got a passable set of pictures of Chris Moyles where he appears to be picking his nose. Not a classic but they'll do, and we'll run them in next Tuesday's issue.

Tuesday 11 November

Chris Moyles has seen the nose-picking pictures and he's not happy. This afternoon, with Radio 1 blasting out in the *Heat* office, he goes off on one, live on air.

'How dare they! I used to love *Heat* magazine, these days it's rubbish, just rubbish. I don't pick my nose, you can see from the pictures that I'm not picking my nose, I'm rubbing it! How dare they! Mark Frith, you don't know what you're doing.'

Work in the office comes to a halt. Everyone stops and looks at me. I go bright red. For me this is humiliating – being slagged off by a DJ as my entire team listen in. I don't like this one bit. Also, as I'm all too aware, Moyles' ratings are at an all-time high at the moment – the self-proclaimed Saviour Of Radio 1 has millions listening to his show every day. Most of our readers – and potential readers – will be listening to this.

I went into the TV room to speak to Aled Haydn-Jones, one of Chris's production team on the phone. I was so rude.

'Tell Chris this won't be forgotten. Get him to stop talking about this now.'

I don't know what came over me. I don't think I was that bothered about it going out on air, but I was concerned about the team hearing it.

Moyles comes out of the record and Aled tells him and the listeners about the conversation he'd just had with me. After conducting a straw poll of the team, he begins to simmer down. The Chris Moyles and *Heat* magazine love-in is now officially over. Who knows if we will ever make up?

Monday 8 December

Victoria Wood is making a show about the diet industry. She's clearly got a bee in her bonnet about celebrity magazines and how they deal with the subject of weight and dieting which is why, today, she decided to phone one of our picture team. I'm fine getting the flack for what we do in the magazine but for a junior member of the team to get it – and be recorded on tape! – is hugely unfair.

Wood was filming with Johnny Vegas in a cake shop and rang our picture desk to suggest we got down there with a photographer. For some reason we still can't quite fathom, she appeared to be pretending to be someone else.

'I've just seen Johnny Vegas and Victoria Wood in a cake shop,' she said in a slightly hysterical manner. 'He's buying some cakes and I'm worried about what he's about to do with them.'

Mariana didn't know what to think, other than that she needed to get her off the phone as soon as possible. It was clearly a set-up to somehow show that we were obsessed with photos of overweight famous people eating. (Not true. *Anyone* eating in a particularly graphic way can be entertaining. They don't have to be overweight. But I wasn't about to have that particular discussion with Wood today.)

Tuesday 9 December

Victoria Wood's production team has emailed Mariana – not me – asking for permission to run the conversation between Wood and her. It's the sort of desperate email TV people send all the time when they're trying to get you to do something you'd be crazy to agree to do.

> *To: Mariana*
> *Importance: High*
>   *We are making a two-part documentary about diets and the slimming industry due for transmission in early January.*
>   *Victoria decided on impulse to do a lighthearted sequence with you on the phone while she was waiting to do her interview with Johnny Vegas. I can remind you of your conversation if you want me to but basically Victoria says she's just seen Johnny Vegas and Victoria Wood together and would you like to send a photographer along?*
>   *You're very patient and have a think about it and then we get on with the rest of the programme. It's just a lovely funny sequence.*
>   *To finalise the paperwork, I need you to sign a release form or respond to this email please. If you have any queries you can give me a call on 07710...*

I was furious.

Winding up a member of the team who's doing their job then trying to, in a sly way, get them to hand over their rights is not on. That's before we get on to the whole business of someone pretending to be someone else.

Unsurprisingly, we tell them to sod off.

Tuesday 16 December

Today we publish our Christmas double issue, the traditional *Heat* way to end the year. We've had higher sales than ever before this year. With that comes greater notoriety. The Victoria Wood incident is just one example of how we're starting to rile people; Ewan McGregor's outburst is another. Even our own fans occasionally have a go.

Ricky Gervais has always been incredibly supportive of *Heat* – he reads the magazine, likes it (he says that his scathing attitude towards the world of celebrity isn't that different to our own – and he's also obsessed with reality TV) and is particularly grateful of the early support we gave *The Office* – Boyd wrote about the show more favourably than any other UK journalist when it began – something Ricky has never forgotten.

But now even Gervais is taking the piss. Every year we get sent (or rather ask for) Christmas cards from a whole bunch of famous people.

Gervais's arrived late, but in just enough time to get into today's issue. It read as follows:

> *To* Heat *Magazine*
> *Dear people in charge of fame, Merry Xmas*
> *Love **Ricky Gervais***
>
> *PS I have a picture of a celebrity with a pimple. If you magnify it you could fill a couple of pages. Do I get any money?*

As he handed it to me, Boyd said, 'I guess you'll want to take the PS out?'

I laughed. 'It's fine, I love it.'

And I do. If we are getting notorious for what we do, that's no bad thing. We can't take it too seriously.

Wednesday 24 December

One of the big shows of the Christmas period is on TV tonight: *The Real Beckhams.* It's a fly-on-the-wall documentary about life with Britain's most famous couple. With all their money and fame you'd think they'd be the happiest people in the world. But whenever Victoria spoke, Becks seemed to be really annoyed. The tension I saw that day in Manchester is still there; it just seems David can't deal with it any more.

Saturday 3 January 2004

Britney Spears got married today. In Vegas, To someone she barely knows. Apparently they got drunk in her hotel room and decided to do it on a whim. Britney's always seemed very in control of her life, very disciplined, so this is odd.

Monday 5 January

The first day back after the Christmas and New Year break is the same in any office. People are full of stories of what they've done and where they've been (and what they've heard).

Even though it was two weeks ago we're all still talking about the Posh and Becks documentary. The Beckhams have always been a *Heat* office obsession but a rumoured marriage breakdown is even more exciting – it's like we've all grown bored of 'the perfect relationship' and now we need some tension and conflict to keep us interested.

I love magazine offices at times like these – they're full of buzz and indiscreet gossip and laughter all the time. Thanks to the papers' insatiable interest, every day brings a new thing for us to get excited about. Usually someone loud like Polly Hudson on the news team or Jo Carnegie on features will read something in the paper, then someone else at that desk would join in the conversation, then other people from around the office would come over and have their say.

Both Jo and Polly have become vitally important members of the *Heat* team, not just for their writing (although they are both exceptional writers and interviewers) but also for what they bring to the office. Opinionated, incredibly loud, dead funny and with often unconventional views, they help push the magazine into a different sphere. The reputation we're beginning to get for being caustic, sarcastic and larger than life comes from the two of them more than anyone else. No one else has a Jo or a Polly. No one else – frankly – could put up with them!

Today the conversation is still about the documentary …

'Did you see the way she looked at him – OH MY GOD!'

'… and when she started taking the piss out of him! His face!'

And so on. Ideas for pieces come from these sorts of conversations all the time, whole features just created there and then.

'Write it down!' I'd say. 'Don't just talk about it – WRITE IT DOWN!'

It's days like these that I'm glad I don't have my own office, away from all the jokes and gossip. Most editors do, and I did in previous jobs, but it was a mistake and now I sit in the middle of the team so I can be aware of all that's going on. It means you're never left out, means that if two people on the picture desk are having a row you can speak to them about it later, means that a conversation the Features Editor is having where she's promising too much can be quickly sorted with a wave of the arms. Office life – there's nothing like it.

Monday 26 January

Series three of the insanely popular *I'm A Celebrity, Get Me Out Of Here!* kicks off this evening and they've pulled off a major coup: they've signed up Jordan. She won't have come cheap but she'll be worth it.

Thursday 29 January

Another glowing piece by Janice Turner in today's *Press Gazette*. As *Press Gazette* is the trade magazine of the journalism world, anything positive (or negative) written there really gets noticed. Turner is becoming a very important figure in our world – she likes us so much and supports us so completely that her columns are great for us as a team, advertisers we want to attract and those rivals whose nose we want to thoroughly rub in it. Today's column is particularly timely – we're just two weeks away from releasing new figures that, I hope, will show that we're virtually neck and neck with *Now*, still number one in the weekly celebrity market. The piece is ostensibly about the men's market, comparing the two new men's mags, *Zoo* and *Nuts*. *Zoo*, like

Heat, is an Emap magazine, *Nuts* – like *Now* – is an IPC magazine. This is Turner's cue for a punchy overview about the celebrity market.

'These two launches reveal differences in corporate culture between IPC (*Nuts*) and Emap (*Zoo* weekly). It's like *Now* v *Heat*: the former a diligent, all-boxes-ticked, competent job, the latter fizzing and surprising, with a stick of rock thoroughness so that a DVD review on page 102 is as funny as the opening spread.'

For Turner – herself a respected former magazine editor – to notice the nuances, the cleverness, notice that we'd gone the extra mile is important. For her to do it so enthusiastically, in such a public forum and at such a crucial time was pretty amazing. I took the article to the office photocopier, enlarged that paragraph then put the enlarged version through the copier again so it ended up even bigger. Then I took it home and stuck it up in the kitchen. I know I'm sad, but I can retire happy.

Monday 9 February

I'm A Celebrity, Get Me Out Of Here! finished tonight. Jordan (who is supposed to have a boyfriend) has got it together with ex-teen-pin-up Peter Andre. Good for them. At least it will stop her going on about Gareth Gates for a while.

Thursday 12 February

The latest sales figures were released today – and although we're not far behind we still haven't beaten *Now*. Between July and December last year we sold an average of 566,731 copies a week, Now sold 592,076.

Monday 8 March

The Oscars are the big story of the week and we've got an incredible exclusive from it – private pictures of Jude Law, girlfriend and mum getting ready for the ceremony. They're incredible: in one a half-naked Jude's getting dressed, in others new girlfriend Sienna and Jude's mum are pictured arm-in-arm (the first time they've ever been shown together). Jude took the pictures for a website and the website have happily given them to us – deals like this happen all the time. Because so many people read us now people are tripping over themselves to give us stuff because we reach so many people and our readership are cool and young. This is a fantastic plug for them.

We laid out the pictures straightaway. It's a lovely spread and I've sold it in a way that pushes the exclusivity of this – we're the only magazine that's got them and I'm going to shout about it.

JUDE
'MY OSCAR DAY DIARY'
EXCLUSIVE! His private record of the event.

Superb. Popped it off to the printers. Job done.

Friday 12 March

Oh dear, what a dreadful evening.

We finished the final pages of the issue at four-ish. It's a great issue, the Jude piece being the highlight, obviously. Feeling pretty chuffed, Gabs and I headed out for the evening to our friend Richard's house in Chiswick.

When an issue is finished and the week is done it's time to properly relax. I can easily forget about work when the week ends – and tonight I was quite happy to leave my mobile in my jacket pocket as we trooped upstairs to watch TV after dinner.

At just after midnight we went to leave. I picked up my jacket, checked the time on my phone and discovered I had a missed a call and a voicemail message.

'Mark, I'm Jude Law's lawyer. I believe you're about to print some photographs we've not authorised you to run. Can you call me as soon as possible.'

Oh shit. It's gone midnight, I'm in the middle of nowhere and I've got a heavyweight lawyer who I've never spoken to before ringing my mobile.

My first reaction is anger – how the hell does he have my number? Who on earth has given it to him?

In the car, it's freezing. I zip up my huge jacket, pull up the hood and clutch my phone, shivering in the passenger seat as Gaby drives.

'Who was the message?'

'Um, Jude Law's lawyer.'

'What?'

'Yep, I think they want to stop the magazine coming out.'

'How did he get your number?'

'I have no idea. Right. I need to think.'

We've decided to spend the night at Gaby's parents' house in Ealing just ten minutes away, rather than a 40-minute trek to Celeb Central.

Even then, it was gone half past midnight before we got home. My thinking session wasn't much use but I do know one thing: I wouldn't sleep tonight unless I called. So I did. It rings and rings and then goes to voicemail.

Shit. What do I say?

'Hi. You want to stop my magazine coming out. The magazine I sweat blood about every stinking week! Well, you can't. Go on, take a running jump.'

No, too aggressive.

'How dare you ring me this late! And who gave you my number?'

No, too confrontational. And aggressive. And I'm becoming obsessed by how he got my number now.

I settled for the non-commital approach.

'Hello, it's Mark Frith at *Heat* returning your call. Give me a call when you get this message.'

I fully expect him to call back straightaway. If he's that keen to get the magazine stopped, he will, I conclude. Even if it is quarter to one in the morning.

It's now half one and I can't sleep. Someone I've never met, who shouldn't even have my number, wants to stop my magazine coming out. I'm seething. And tomorrow is going to be no fun at all.

(Blimey! What will **BRAD** say?)

JEN & MATT's REAL-LIFE kiss!

This week's hottest celebrity news
£1.50 (Canary Islands €3.25, Spain €3.00) **24 – 30 April 2004**

heat

MAGAZINE OF THE YEAR!

REBECCA
reveals
EVERYTHING
about Becks

PLUS IS **POSH** CRACKING UP?

"PHONE SEX AS WELL AS TEXT SEX"

"MARRIAGE WAS IN TROUBLE BEFORE ME"

"GETTING SAUCY IN MUSEUM"

Issue 267

CORRIE'S TINA
on splitting with one
co-star... then dating another

HER FIRST INTERVIEW!

9 771465 626036

CHAPTER NINE
Falling out with the Beckhams

March – August 2004

Saturday 13 March

After a rotten night's sleep I wake up at about 7.30. I have calls to make – to Nick Folland, Emap's Head Of Legal Affairs for the company, and to Julian Pike, the lawyer assigned to *Heat* at Farrers, the well-regarded legal firm.

Funny how lawyers' formality and by-the-book approach is a pain in the arse when you're trying to get a big, spicy story into the magazine on press day, yet that's just the thing you need at quarter to eight on a Saturday morning when you feel your whole world is crashing around you.

Nick Folland – reassuring and kind – was the first person I spoke to. He advised me to wait until the lawyer called and then to explain patiently (!) that we'd run the pictures in good faith (a website had happily given us them, knew what we were doing with them and we'd credited them and their charity, promised as part of the deal). He then wanted me to call Julian Pike.

Julian Pike – business-like but sympathetic to what I was going through – wanted to know a little more about the situation but offered the same words of wisdom. 'Don't say too much,' was another bit of advice, albeit one I've been getting all my life.

So I waited and waited. Gaby and her family were out so it was just me, pacing around their huge, empty house.

I decided to be prepared, ready for when the call came. I put the lawyer's name and number into my phone so I knew it was him when he rang. Then I placed a pen and paper at the side of the phone.

Nine a.m. came and went. No call.

Became obsessed again about how he'd got hold of my number.

Nine-thirty came and went. Still no call. Jesus, what time do lawyers sleep in till?

Amused myself by changing the name of the lawyer in my phone to 'The Devil' so that when the phone rang it would come up as 'The Devil Is Calling'.

Heh heh. I'm sooooo funny.

Then, with the lawyer's advice front of mind, I wrote the words 'Don't Say Too Much' in big letters at the top of the piece of paper.

And as I was writing the final word, my phone lit up.

THE DEVIL IS CALLING.

Phone rings once.

I sit down and pick up my pen.

Phone rings a second time.

Huge deep breath.

Phone rings a third time. Don't Say Too Much. Don't Say Too Much.

'Hello.'

'Can I speak to Mark Frith, please?'

'Speaking.'

'Mark, it's Jude Law's lawyer again. We've reason to believe you're planning to run some photographs that you don't have permission to run.'

I gulped.

'Erm, well ... that's, er, not my understanding of the situation. We, um, ran these in good faith ...'

'I can assure you that you don't have permission to run those pictures. When does the magazine print?'

'It already has. We print the magazine in two sections. This section printed in the early hours of Friday morning.'

Silence.

'It's important that you know two hours ago we sent your company a letter asking you to not print these pictures. You will need to make your lawyer aware of this.'

This is how Nick and Julian said it would go. Now is the time to get out of this phone call. But that would be too easy, wouldn't it? No, I have to go and spoil things.

'Can I ask how you got hold of my number?'

Silence. This was not the sort of question he was expecting.

'People know your phone number.'

I was seething now.

'Well, I think we better finish this here,' I say. My voice is now all over the place.

'Oh, okay. You'll tell your legal team about the letter.'

'Yes. Goodbye.'

I throw the phone down and lie back on the bed.

I feel completely stitched up. Photos we've been given permission to run causing me all this stress. Angry lawyers ringing me up on my private phone number. And I'm made to feel guilty, all because some film star presumably thinks he's above appearing in a celebrity magazine, a magazine bought by the people who pay to watch his films, who pay his wages.

That's my weekend ruined.

Monday 15 March

Went into work to discover the legal letter sent two days earlier. Passed it on to the lawyers. The lawyers tell me they already have one. Great.

Tuesday 16 March

The issue of *Heat* with the Jude Law pictures in went on sale today. The world didn't stop turning, but I'm sure his lawyers are preparing their next move.

Thursday 18 March

Good God.

I nearly got run over by Jude Law's car today.

I'm not kidding.

At about half past eight I walked through the streets of Celebrity Central on my way to work as normal.

Same route, same everything. Turned right out of the house, crossed over the road, turned left and headed down the hill.

As normal.

Then, just as I was beginning to cross the road, a car hurtled around the corner. I quickly took two steps back.

Standing on the kerb I watched, petrified, as the black 4x4 went by in front of me. There, in the driver's seat, was Jude Law.

What the hell?

Did he see me? Did he recognise me? Did he know I was the guy currently in battle with his legal team? Of course not, I decided. How could he? He's hardly the sort of person who sits around watching *Liquid News* of an evening. He's got films to make, bouffant-style hair to comb. He didn't know it was me, so this was purely a coincidence – wasn't it?

Tuesday 23 March

Jude Law is clearly still angry with us, even though none of this is our fault. He's got his legal team to send further letters and although we have pointed them (quite rightly) in the direction of the website that gave us the photographs, they're still not satisfied. We could fight this and rack up considerable costs ourselves or give him the apology he wants, to him and to the two people (one his assistant, one his US publicist) that physically took most of the photographs. We have reluctantly agreed. It will appear in next Tuesday's issue.

Tuesday 30 March

Today we printed our apology to Jude and friends.

> *JUDE LAW, BEN JACKSON AND SIMON HALLS –*
> *APOLOGY*
> *In last week's issue of* Heat *Magazine we published two pages of photographs of Jude Law under the headline: Jude 'My Oscar Day Diary' Exclusive, his private record of the event. Pics by Jude Law.'*
>
> *We wish to point out that the photographs were in fact taken by Ben Jackson and Simon Halls and that neither Jude, Ben nor Simon consented or agreed to publication of the pictures in* Heat *magazine or any other magazine. We apologise to all concerned.*

The most telling bit of this, to my mind, is the 'neither Jude, Ben nor Simon consented or agreed to publication of the pictures in *Heat* magazine or any other magazine' bit. They wanted to give these pictures to this website and to be seen to support a charity but being in a magazine that was also supporting the charity was not what they wanted. There's a huge amount of snobbishness about magazines and celebrity magazines in particular. But we must be the real bane of people like Law because they can't control us. And these people want control. At all times.

Sunday 4 April

Bombshell. The *News of the World* is reporting that David Beckham has been having an affair with his Spanish translator Rebecca Loos. It's incredible stuff – especially the allegations that the affair has been going on for a while and that they'd been sending each other filthy text messages as recently as last month, six months after the affair began last autumn.

The best bit about the article is the transcript of the text messages between the two. This was no 'honey trap' on Loos' behalf: Beckham is more than happy to out-filth her in the messages. In fact the thing that's most striking about the text exchanges is how sexually compatible the couple appear. The exchange is explicit and intended to arouse the other person using thorough knowledge of each other's preferences and shared memories of the sex they've had together. Throughout the texts (and there's several) there's an intense desire to turn the other person on. That's all they care about.

The sexual relationship appears to have taken place mainly (or possibly only) last September. The texts appear to have been exchanged in recent weeks. The fact that they've all been recorded and are recent seems to indicate that they may have been initiated by Loos or a member of her team with an eye on a possible kiss and tell, the perfect kind of proof a newspaper needs before going into print. But the gap between affair and texts doesn't devalue the story, it actually heightens it – it makes it apparent that these two are able to reignite their passion for each other instantaneously, through these texts, because the chemistry between them is so great. It could be that these texts, and the circumstances around them being exchanged so long after the physical relationship, is the aspect of the whole thing that hurts Victoria the most: their very existence paints such a pessimistic picture of her marriage.

This evening David is let off football duties to fly to France where his wife is currently on a ski holiday.

Monday 5 April

There's no point doing a magazine this week.

I may as well just record the conversations in the office and print all of them. The Monday morning news meeting is effectively cancelled today. There's too much Beckham scandal to discuss.

'He doesn't fancy his wife any more!' shouts Jo. 'I've known it for ages. She's too skinny, too pre-occupied with herself. Not attractive.'

'You can just see the appeal of this other woman,' says Hannah. 'She's good-looking, clearly adored David, made a fuss over him. Who wouldn't be flattered?'

Others find it all very depressing: 'If they can't make it work, who can?' asks one.

This is a popular view in the office. This marriage has been sold to us as the perfect relationship. We all know, deep down, that no such thing exists, yet we need to believe. Because of the romantic wedding, the lovey-dovey photoshoots and the interviews they gave about each other, we felt that, at last, this was a couple who had got it all right – and that he, especially, wasn't prone to the wandering eye that afflicts many footballers. We admired his restraint, how the love of a good woman kept him faithful. Now we all feel let down. Maybe we were just wrong to believe. They're only normal human beings after all.

Tuesday 6 April

Jonathan Ross is really really angry. It's 11 o'clock in the morning and he is shouting at me down the phone. Really shouting. We've just printed some (really sweet) photos of him and his son flying toy planes on Hampstead Heath and he's not happy about it. We're allowed to – the shots were taken in a public place and although we're asked to show caution in what we do or don't print when it comes to kids, the Ross family happily pose everywhere – they have their pictures taken at premieres together, they've even posed inside their home for *Hello* magazine before. So I wasn't worried until he phoned, leaving his mobile number (memo to famous people: don't give journalists your mobile number) and I called him back. I've met him before and he's been fine, but today he's off on one. This is one of those moments where you hold the phone a considerable distance from your ear ...

'I cannot believe you've printed these. Give me one reason why I shouldn't call the Press Council? One reason?'

I explain, patiently, that we've received (and published) lots of pictures of him and his son (and daughters) at various dos. And anyway, the only shot that shows his son's face shows him from the side and is blurred, making him unidentifiable.

'Don't care. You shouldn't have printed these.'

I hear him begin to flick through the pages of the magazine at the other end of the phone, then he starts to read bits of the copy to me.

'You say here "what a great dad" – I don't care if you think I'm a good dad or not. You've not given me a single reason not to go to the Press Council.'

I don't have the heart to tell him that the Press Council doesn't exist and hasn't for years. The whole thing is crazy – if he did take us to the Press Complaints Commission – the modern equivalent of the Press Council – he wouldn't have a leg to stand on because he happily poses with his family at every premiere going.

I apologise, tell him we realise he doesn't want pictures of his kids appearing anywhere ever again and pass on the message to the team.

I *am* genuinely sorry about it too – he may have posed with the kids in the past but if he doesn't want them pictured any more we will, of course, honour that. We'll leave his kids to get on with their lives in total privacy.

An hour later, Suzi Aplin, Jonathan Ross's Executive Producer, sends me a text. 'I'm so sorry about all of that, I really tried to talk him out of it but he wouldn't hear it.' I've known Suzi for years – she seems a little embarrassed by it all.

Wednesday 7 April

The first pictures from the Victoria and David Beckham's impromptu holiday in the French Alps arrived in the office this afternoon. We all gathered round Clara's computer as she took us through them one at a time.

They put on one hell of a show – laughing, joking, even giving each other piggybacks, but the fake display only lasts until the door of their villa closes on the photographers. The press pack being what it is these days, our reporters and photographers are everywhere. We get to hear about, or see, everything. There's way too much stuff to print. My favourite bit? Word, from one of the press pack watching their every move, is that as soon as David walks through the door after flying in to see his wife, before he or she say a word to each other, she strolls up to him and slaps him hard in the face.

Monday 19 April

It's clear, now, the route the Beckhams have chosen to take on the media storm: deny and keep on denying. It's brazen, but it might just work. And they're still putting on one hell of a show – arriving at a party for their management company, 19, they were pawing at each other all the way up the red carpet. It's all too try-hard – and he looks absolutely mortified.

Tuesday 27 April

We've printed the pictures of the Beckhams from outside the party and accompanied it with a comment article from Max Clifford where he questions the team behind the Beckhams. The team have largely kept quiet up until now but this perceived slight is just too much for them and a woman called Charlotte Hickson, who works at 19 – sadly *Heat*'s friend Caroline McAteer is no longer our main contact – sends me an arsey email. She wants to know why we chose to quote Clifford (working currently as Loos publicist) and says that she finds it 'offensive' that we chose to do so.

I have replied in a robust manner – they can't really control what we write, they aren't commenting themselves, yet we still have pages to fill, etc., etc. I may even have told her that I wouldn't dream of telling her how to do her job. But things are clearly changing between us and Camp Beckham. From that day in summer 2000 to now there's been a sea change. Then, when we corrected a tabloid story, we were part of the solution. Now we are part of the problem. One of 'them'. The *Heat*/Beckhams love affair is now well and truly over. They may be heading for a split, but we have already divorced.

Sunday 2 May

We're up in Liverpool this weekend for a family do. We checked into the hotel yesterday evening. Checking in to a hotel is a whole different ball game in this job as the receptionist was about to find out.

'Wake-up call?'

'No thanks.' (It's a Sunday. Show me a journalist who's up early on a Sunday.)

'Newspapers?'

I look at Gaby. Her eyes go up to the ceiling. She knows what's coming next.

'Erm, yep. *Sunday Times* ...'

Gaby's fine at this point. She loves the magazines.

'... the *Observer* ...'

Ditto.

'... *News of the World*, *Sunday Mirror*, *Sunday People* ...'

Gaby starts shaking her head, looks around to see if anyone's listening and then shakes her head a bit more.

It's not embarrassment about the titles I've chosen, more that this wealth of newsprint being sent to our room, in her mind, implies to the outside world (or rather anyone who happens to be passing by reception at that moment) that I'd rather read tabloid scandal than pay attention to her. Not true, of course. I have to do this for my job and, anyway, I'll have probably scanned them all by the time she wakes up.

She's not appeased. This is public humiliation on a grand scale and in the lift up to the room I get it in the neck.

'Do you really need that many?'

At least she's laughing.

'What if there's a good story in one I hadn't got? Huh?'

She shakes her head.

Conveniently proving my point, this morning's *Sunday People* (the paper I'd probably be most likely to drop from my order) has – for once – a really good exclusive.

Leslie Grantham – Dirty Den in *EastEnders* – has exposed himself to women over the Internet and sent some lurid messages. All of this from his *EastEnders* dressing room, via a laptop and computer-mounted webcam. And, if that's not bad enough, some of the exchanges he's had with women involve him dishing the dirt on his co-stars, among them Jessie Wallace, Shane Richie and Wendy Richard. For someone as famous as him to do this is utter madness – completely stupid – and now he's been caught out by a journalist posing as an ordinary member of the public. It was only a matter of time before this happened, surely he must have known that?

I show Gaby the front page.

'See! This is why I need to get these!'

She does that raised eyebrow thing again.

Friday 21 May

Watching *Friday Night With Jonathan Ross*. He's talking about a recent family visit to Alton Towers and illustrates the tale with a load of pictures that get flashed up on the screen. The photos show his kids, clearly identifiable and broadcast to four million people.

Friday 28 May

Big Brother 5 began today – one of the contestants has had a sex change! The bookies reckon he/she won't last five minutes because viewers will just find the whole thing a little weird (or, possibly, that it's too much of a gimmick).

Thursday 17 June

There's been a huge mass brawl in the Big Brother house this evening and it was really unpleasant stuff. Two of the housemates – Michelle and Emma – have been locked up in a side room (known as the *Big Brother* bedsit) since last Friday and tonight they were let back into the main house. Unbeknownst to the rest of the house, Michelle and Emma have been able to listen to everything the others have been saying about them. So, they went back into the house this evening keen to settle a few scores and – because they've all been fuelled by a not inconsiderable amount of alcohol – a fight erupted which eventually led to security guards coming into the house and taking away two of the main protagonists. Channel 4's sister digital channel E4 wisely cut the footage at the point security came in but not before we'd seen people being pushed about, threats being made and, at one point, a tray being thrown at someone's head. Tonight was the night *Big Brother* lost its innocence.

Monday 12 July

The *Media Guardian* published their 100 Most Influential People In The Media supplement today and I'm up to number 52. The write-up is glowing and I couldn't be happier.

'In terms of influence on other sections of the media – from print to TV, radio and the Internet – *Heat*'s influence is unrivalled. It has also overtaken *FHM* as Emap's biggest profit-maker.'

Andrew Neil has kept his huge mouth shut this time.

Friday 6 August

Nadia Almada (she of the sex change) won *Big Brother* this evening. Shows you how much I know – I thought she'd have been out weeks ago. It was an incredible moment, especially as Nadia (formerly Jorge) had kept her secret quiet from the other housemates for the show's entire run.

Tuesday 10 August

Today Lucie Cave interviewed Nadia. Hers is the most gobsmacking story we've printed so far. You can say what you like about the world of celebrity, but the people in it certainly throw up some fantastic stories. Our team have the inquisitiveness and interest in what makes people tick to seek out the great stories – it's what's helping us get such a reputation at the moment, what helps us to make it so high up the *Guardian*'s list.

Lucie is certainly at the forefront of this growing reputation. I've known her for more than ten years since she came in to do a week's work experience at *Smash Hits*. She was still in her teens, but made it her business even back then to get involved in all aspects of magazine life. She wanted to know everything.

Her interest in how people think and why they act the way they do makes her the person all her friends go to for advice and problem-olving – I sit opposite her in the office, I know these things – but also makes her a great interviewer, a skill she honed during a successful spell as a presenter on kids' TV. She is also fearless, despite being tiny, just five feet tall ('and half an inch' as she'll tell anyone who'll listen).

Lucie, naturally, asks Nadia how she came to realise she needed the operation and about the aftermath. She knew she was different from an early age:

'I still remember it so clearly. I was about five years old and we were living in Madeira. My mum had some nail varnish and I decided to paint my nails red. My father gave me a big slap and made me feel like it was a bad thing. But I knew there was something different and I was never going to be like my brothers.'

There were tears when Lucie asked about how she felt as she came round from the actual sex-change operation.

'It was beautiful but I was in a huge amount of pain. I had a big nappy thing strapped around me really tightly and I was bruised for ages. In the weeks before, I sent my mum pictures of me dressed as a woman so she could get used to the idea. To start with she was a bit worried about what other people would say but then my brother came over with his girlfriend and they could see how happy I was and that I had friends around me.'

Wednesday 11 August

Oh great, now the nicest person in the world hates me.

In yesterday's issue we printed a spread of photographs from a calendar put together by the PDSA, the charity that helps sick animals. It was a quiet week last week (apart from Nadia, *nothing* is happening in the world of celebrity) so we resorted to that fall-back option: pictures of cute animals.

The calendar features some well-known pet owners posing with their dogs. Jay Kay from Jamiroquai is on there with his Alsatians Titan and Lugar, an actor called Jeremy Edwards is happily posing with his pet Mollie and a guy called Ben Fogle – most famous for being the guy who held things together on the BBC's remote island reality TV experiment *Castaway* – is there with his dog Inca.

All good. Except that we failed to spot that Inca was wearing a tag around his neck emblazoned with his owner's phone number. Which is why we've just printed three-quarters of a million magazines with Ben Fogle's mobile number in it.

Our new Editorial Assistant Bronagh took his call this morning. She leaves me a yellow Post-it note with this message written on it:

'Ben Fogle called, can you ring him back? He says you've got the number.'

Ha ha. Good start – the anger that comes through just from that message makes me realise this isn't going to be much fun. What makes it even worse is that before becoming famous on TV he worked on a magazine picture desk, probably spotting things like this and ensuring they didn't make their way into print. He will think that we are complete idiots.

I imagine it takes a lot to make Ben Fogle unhappy. Since he rose to prominence in 2000 he's made loads of appearances on nicey-nice TV shows, being charming and sweet. Middle-aged women adore him – he's like the perfect son-in-law. Their daughters like him too – he's the guy your mum would be most pleased to have brought round for Sunday lunch.

However – and there's no getting away from this – the nicest man on TV is about to completely, utterly, unequivocally (and rightly) bollock me.

I open up the magazine at the feature in question, read off the number and tap it in to the phone. It goes straight to voicemail so I leave him my mobile number for him to call back on (I have his, it's only fair he has mine. It's a small gesture of goodwill that almost certainly won't go any way to making amends. Not in the slightest).

He calls back half an hour later.

My God, he's angry.

'I just can't understand how you let this run? What's wrong with your picture desk that they didn't spot it?'

'Well, Ben,' I say, 'we feel very let down that the calendar people didn't spot this ...'

'Not their fault. They weren't about to print this, you were. On the actual calendar they got rid of it. I've worked on picture desks before and I'd be mortified if I let this past. Outrageous.'

Of course, there's nothing I can do to appease him, nothing that can make the situation better. I just have to sit and take this.

'I've already had nearly 100 messages from people I've never met. Luckily they're being nice, but today – on a day I really need to use my phone – I have to keep it switched off and later on I'll have to change my number. The first thing I know about this is when one of your readers phoned me yesterday!'

We're only three-quarters of the way through the year but we seem to be falling out with everyone. Sales are slightly wobbly at the moment and a lot of people are getting pissed off by what we do: Jude, Jonathan Ross and now Ben Fogle, the nicest person on television, a person who, I'd imagine, doesn't fall out with *anyone*.

If things like this keep happening, our goodwill is going to dry up completely. We're not going to be nice to everyone but it would be good if *some* people liked us. We need access, but slowly that's ebbing away. For the first time since 9/11 I'm fearful about what happens next with the magazine and where we're going. We've so much incredible success, is the only way down?

20% OFF EVERYTHING AT **KNICKERBOX!**

NADIA'S TEARFUL CONFESSION
"WHY I BECAME A PROSTITUTE"
PLUS HER SPECIAL MESSAGE TO YOU!

This week's hottest celebrity news
£1.50 (€3.25) 6 – 12 November 2004

heat

NATIONAL TV AWARDS
EXCLUSIVE PICS & GOSSIP

BRITAIN'S BEST CELEB MAG

KATE
7½ STONE

THEY NEED FEEDING!

NICOLE
8 STONE

MARY–KATE
6½ STONE

SHOCK REPORT:
YOU ARE TOO THIN!

The diet mad stars who've gone too far

FIRST PICS!
BRIAN & "NEW GIRLFRIEND"
PLUS! Brian talks about Kerry split

Issue 295

9 771465 626036

CHAPTER TEN
Bring on the skinny celebs
August 2004 – January 2005

Friday 13 August

It's been a rubbish six months for everyone but we're so used to sales increases – and hefty ones at that – that today is tough. After nearly five years of constant sales rises, today's ABC figures show that we're down 5 per cent on last year. I had to get up in front of the team and accentuate the positive: we're still ahead of *OK* magazine; *Now* are having a tough time as well. But still there's lots of questions from the team and I answer them the best I can. They are particularly concerned that our sales are down despite the Posh and Becks drama happening in the six months covered by the figures – I explain that with a story like that people can learn about it anywhere and everywhere. It's on the radio, there are hour-long documentaries about it on TV, you can read about it on countless constantly updated websites, it's in the *News of the World*, then in the *Sun* and the *Mirror*, then in all the broadsheets too.

These figures show that, in the months and years ahead, things could be getting tougher. Celebrity is such big business now that everyone wants a bit of it. It's everywhere.

Sunday 19 September

Britney Spears got married for the second time in a year last night. Her new husband is a dancer called Kevin Federline, who has two kids from a previous relationship. They got married in the back garden of Kevin's tailor's home (!) in California.

The bride wore a white, strapless gown with a huge veil and a tiara. The groom wore a tux. Proving that – in typical Britney style – it wasn't an entirely classy affair, the food at the reception consisted of ribs, chicken wings and mini cheeseburgers and – get this – all 30 guests took home a goody bag. Yep, a goody bag. The kind of thing journalists get from a tacky launch party – each one contained a pair of Gap jeans, some sweets, a pair of Nike shoe laces and a key ring with an image of the newly-weds on.

Guests were also banned from bringing cameras as *People* magazine had paid a million dollars for the exclusive rights to cover the event.

Monday 20 September

Oh dear. Looks like *People* magazine might have wasted their money. In-the-know US website Drudge Report is saying that the couple never filed a marriage licence so because of that the wedding was fake (and staged to put the press off the scent – a real wedding will be staged next month, they say). The couple say they haven't had a chance to file the licence but will the following week. These days, nothing's ever straightforward in Spears-land.

Friday 24 September

In trouble again. This time with our old friend Will Young.

We've just printed some pictures of Young walking down the street with his young nephew. For reasons best known to themselves, our readers are still obsessed by him (to the detriment of Gareth Gates whose career has stalled over recent months – see, Simon Cowell isn't right about *everything*).

Unlike the Ross family, Young's young relatives have never put themselves in front of the camera so we pixilated the lad's face so he was unidentifiable.

Responsible journalism. As always.

Will's still not happy, though, and his lawyers have written a letter to the agency that supplied us with the photo and one to us, as the magazine that put them out into the public domain. We've violated his privacy, they say, and subjected Young's nephew to embarrassment. Often we have no response to a letter like this, but this time we do. We've replied with a strong letter informing them that we've done nothing wrong and that we have clearly protected the nephew's anonymity by pixilating the shot. I don't expect they'll pursue things after reading this.

Tuesday 5 October
A news reporter called Charlotte Ward has recently joined us and today she's written a story about Kate Lawler, the winner of *Big Brother* in 2002. Lawler is looking painfully thin these days, losing at least a stone and a half in a matter of months. Her boyfriend's concerned and so he bloody well should be – new photos we've got our hands on show that her breast bone is clearly visible. The pictures are horrible, actually, upsetting and utterly mystifying. Why do this when it makes her look so ill? The copy is very spiky. Before she joined us Charlotte had her own column at a local newspaper, so was encouraged to voice her opinions. This she's carried into the *Heat* office – she has a no-bullshit approach to meetings, speaks up if she thinks something I'm doing is wrong and her writing has plenty of character. She wasn't holding back here.

The piece ends with a right-to-reply from Lawler followed by Charlotte's verdict on what she'd said.

'I do recognise you need a balance between being fit and not over-doing it,' Kate told Heat. *'But I still love burgers and chips.'*
Hmm, might be a good idea to eat a few more of them.

Because the main picture we use, taken the other day at an awards show, all skin and bones, is so grim, we buried the story away on page 37 of the magazine.

Friday 22 October
Tonight's Emap's annual awards ceremony – an excuse for the team to dress up and get drunk, basically. We won two awards and were Highly Commended in four other categories, an impressive result. Clara won Picture Editor Of The Year and our brilliant Marketing Manager Kelly Logan won an award too. Twenty minutes after the awards ended I said my goodbyes and went home. No magazine team wants the editor hanging around while they party. Another great night for *Heat*, though.

Tuesday 26 October
Julian's come up with an idea for a cover story and I hate it. I feel bad saying this because we see eye to eye on most things and he has a fantastic commercial sense. But this one, for me, simply won't sell.

Since Charlotte wrote her piece about Kate Lawler we've had other pictures of celebrities who've lost loads of weight come into the office. The trend seems to be most prevalent in the States, but a couple of British stars are also included.

Julian wants us to do a cover story on this story – and print three or four of the most shocking pictures on the front page. My view is that the pictures are so unpleasant that it will just put people off buying us and I tell him this. He's not happy but he'll just have to live with it.

Can ill-looking people sell copies of magazines? I think not. Now, though, I've got to find an alternative.

Wednesday 27 October

Right, so there *is* no bloody alternative. There's bits happening this week: our old friend Nadia has just revealed she used to be a prostitute, but *News of the World* broke the story last Sunday so it will be an old story by next week. There's some nice new pictures of Brian McFadden – who's just ditched his wife, Kerry Katona – with his rumoured new girlfriend, Australian singer Delta Goodrem. But these are a classic second sell – good as a cover drop-in but not much use as the main cover story.

Need to find something else – and quick. Can't have celebrity skeletons on the cover.

Thursday 28 October

There's nothing else. And Julian, utterly convinced his story is the right thing to do, has now gone and mocked up his own cover.

'I've done next week's cover for you.'

'Oh. Right. Good … ah, has it got thin people on it?'

'Just look at it and then tell me what you think.'

'Julian, it won't sell! Where is it?'

'Over on this screen.'

When Julian's excited about a story you know it. He's passionate about what he does beyond all belief – jumping up and down in a state of complete delirium when he finds a story he likes. He will also fight for something until you say no again and again. This time he didn't even stop at that …

We walk over to the art department.

'Okay, here goes.'

The cover flashes up. It is unlike any other celebrity cover I've seen – so radical the thought of it going on the news-stands of Britain scares the life out of me.

SHOCK REPORT:
YOU ARE TOO THIN!
The diet mad stars who've gone <u>too</u> far

The cover features three stars, each with their approximate weight – in stones – beneath their name. Just above them, Julian has written an emotive sub-sell:

THEY NEED FEEDING!
KATE 7½ STONE
NICOLE 8 STONE
MARY-KATE 6½ STONE

For me this is a huge risk. Today I received early figures from our last couple of issues – they show that sales are down slightly on last year. Now, every issue is crucial as we must stop this decline. My instinct says this won't sell but we have nothing else. Also, I'm intrigued by his determination. He's *obsessed* by this cover ...

Now it's time to write the piece – Julian works on an opening paragraph that makes clear our opinion on the subject. It's strong stuff, unlike anything a (fun, light-hearted) celebrity magazine has done before.

> *They've got money, looks and fabulous careers but some of the world's biggest celebrities are risking their happiness and well-being every day.*

Then, each picture has a small box attached identifying the stars' weight before they slimmed, their weight now and the reasons for it.

The main copy goes on ...

As the scales plummet and their hip bones jut still further, problems such as anaemia, infertility, lethargy, osteoporosis, constipation and a weakened immune system could become serious health issues for these stars.

Skinny people appear on the cover of – and inside – women's glossy magazines every single month. Often retouched – so they look less pale – these magazines celebrate these unhealthy figures. Now we're putting skinny pictures on the cover ourselves it's essential that we make our position clear, make it clear we think extreme dieting is no way to live your life.

I'm satisfied we've done that.

Now let's see if anyone buys it.

Friday 5 November

How bizarre. Charles our Film Editor forwarded me a story from a gossip website called Holy Moly today. The story is ridiculous – but hilarious.

POOR THE MARK FRITH

My EMAP moles tell me that at the incestuous bout of backslap-pery EMAP Awards last week (presented by Jack Dee) Heat were up for a few gongs, including best mag etc.

Mark Frith sat at his table with a list of all the awards they were nominated for and with increasing frustration, scribbled out each category they'd failed to win as it was announced.

In the end, they only won best photography, ostensibly for the photoshoot where Eamonn Holmes and Fiona Phillips were made over as the White Stripes.

Britain's best celebrity journalist (puts on sincere face) Mark's anger boiled over, he got up from the table and stormed off to go home early, declaring the evening 'an absolute shower of shit'.

I may be a lot of things but I'm certainly not one of life's 'stormers'. In fact if my memory serves me right I strolled very happily out of the place. There was no list of nominees (they don't announce nominees in advance of the actual awards), we won two awards and there wasn't one for Best Photography. Other than that, spot on.

Sunday 7 November

A strangely familiar story in the media pages of today's *Observer*:

> *FEELING THE* HEAT
> *Pity poor Mark Frith, the multi-award-winning editor of* Heat *who was reduced to the status of an also-ran at Emap's internal awards ceremony. These occasions owe as much to office politics as they do to editorial excellence, so perhaps Frith shouldn't have been too surprised to walk away with just one gong, despite being nominated in many categories. Apparently not. As celebrity host Jack Dee doled out the awards to other titles, Frith scribbled each off his list in frustration. Finally, after* Heat *had been awarded the consolation prize 'best photoshoot', he stormed off, declaring the evening 'an absolute shower of shit'. Hell hath no fury like an editor scorned.*

Now things are getting a bit serious. A story on a website is one thing, a story in a newspaper that hundreds of thousands of people read is quite another. In the media section too – a section specifically aimed at people like my workmates, employers and – most importantly – future employers. Anyone thinking of giving me a job at some point in the future would read this and quite properly conclude that I was a sulky, arrogant egomaniac who storms out of any event where he's not given exactly what he wants. I've always wanted to sue someone – after all, it's been done to me enough times – and always promised myself that I would if lies were printed about me and now here's my chance. Bring it on!

Monday 8 November

My spoilsport bosses say I'm not to sue. They think it would inflame relations between the *Observer* and us and that the diplomatic route is the best option.

I met up with Sarah Ewing, who heads up the PR strategy for Emap.

'I want to sue them. Please let me sue them.'

'Mark, I'll draft a letter to them and you see what you think.'

'I want to sue them.'

'Mark, shut up.'

I think I may have finally lost it. I am now turning into the sort of person who would storm out of something.

Tuesday 9 November

Early sales are in for the skinny issue – it sold really well, nearly 600,000. For the first time in ages we're up on last year. This could really help reverse our year-on-year decline.

Wednesday 10 November

Sarah Ewing has drafted a strong letter to James Robinson at the *Observer* who wrote the diary piece, making it clear I didn't storm off nor refer to the evening as 'a shower of shit'. In it we request an apology this coming Sunday. It's a very formal letter until the final paragraph, which is brilliant and scathing:

'Mark was upset to find out that it was you who were responsible for writing the piece, or rather lifting the piece – without credit – from another source (see below).'

Sarah then attached the original Holy Moly piece to the bottom of the email, as forwarded by Charles.

Thursday 11 November

James Robinson received the email today and has already replied.

He is hugely offended that anyone would think for a second that he'd nicked someone else's gossip …

'I would like to make it clear that we do not lift stories from websites, as you suggest. As you know, journalists go to great lengths to protect the identity of their sources but I can assure you that I was tipped off about the awards ceremony by someone who claimed to have been present. I was astonished to discover that the information I was given may have come from a website. I fear I may have been misled.'

Then, in a generous final paragraph, he apologises and promises to print a correction the following Sunday.

I feel happier. He knows he messed up (done it enough times myself, I know how he feels). The real villain in this is the as-yet-unidentified person who took it upon themselves to lie about me.

Sunday 14 November

The apology appears in today's *Observer*. It appears right at the bottom of the page, of course, but is prominent enough. And sincere.

> *POOR MARKS*
> *Last week we were guilty of an embarrassing howler when we claimed* Heat *editor Mark Frith stormed out of Emap's internal awards after his title failed to repeat last year's stellar perform-ance. In fact he stayed with his entire team and tells us he had an enjoyable evening. We're happy to set the record straight. Sincerest apologies, Mark.*

Sunday 28 November

UKTV G2, the rather excellent home of recent classic TV, is launching a new series called *The People's Poll 1954 vs 2004*, a huge survey comparing life now with 50 years ago. They've launched the show with a series of one-page adverts in today's newspapers using the line 'Are you more '54 or '04?'

The image used for 1954 was a Bible. The image used for 2004 was a copy of *Heat*. We always said we were the celebrity bible, now we've proved it. Another fine moment.

Tuesday 30 November

Boyd Hilton has become one of our key writers and today we are running a fantastic interview he got with Elton John in Vegas last week. Elton is a real hero of Boyd's but that doesn't stop him asking him some tough questions and really digging on certain subjects.

As incredible as Elton's career is, what *Heat* readers are most interested in are his famous friends. Elton John has, certainly for the past decade, maybe even for his entire career, been a key, central figure in his (and our) world: people want to work with him or get advice from him or go to his parties. What Elton thinks of them matters. Which is why this interview will be picked over in record companies and management offices all over town.

On the Beckhams, Elton is more open than the couple themselves have been about the whole Rebecca Loos thing. Eight months on neither of them have admitted anything did happen, but Elton – who has been close to them for years – appears to admit it for them.

'Things went wrong when he first went to Real Madrid. If you live six months in a hotel room in Madrid – or anywhere – it's going to drive you crazy. They should have put a statement out saying something like: "Every marriage has its ups and downs and we're just going through a down phase at the moment." But they just denied it and kept denying it, and there obviously were problems ... which now they seem to have sorted out.'

Boyd also asks about Robbie Williams who, in his recent book *Feel*, implied that Elton 'kidnapped' him when he turned up at John's house asking for help.

'We didn't really kidnap him ... well, maybe we did. We were so worried. We got him into a treatment centre. The thing about Robbie is that he doesn't seem to enjoy his career and his life.'

Best of all, though, is Elton's thoughts on George Michael. Boyd asks Elton if he's still friendly with George, and the answer he gives is surprising and candid.

'George is in a strange place. I thought *Patience* was good, but considering it's been a long time in the making it was a bit disappointing. He's one of the most talented people I've ever met and certainly one of the best singers I've ever heard. And I love him as a friend so I have to be careful what I say. So all I would say to George is: you should get out more.'

And when Boyd asks him what he means by that, his reply is far from 'careful'.

'It upsets me because he won't perform live, for example. He's quite happy just being at home all the time and I think that's a waste of talent. But it's his life, not mine. There seems to be a deep-rooted unhappiness in his life and it shows on the album.'

Boyd has done a fantastic job and this is all pretty sensational stuff.

Tuesday 7 December

The biggest show on TV this week is *The X Factor* – the show is absolutely gigantic, a huge hit. We're getting loads of mail about the show's presenter Kate Thornton. Our readers really don't like her. As an example of their feelings towards her we have printed two letters in today's issue.

> *Will someone please tell Kate Thornton to stop shouting? She's like The X Factor's strict schoolmistress and makes watching the show very difficult. We're still pining for Ant & Dec, so why does she have to make things worse by being so stressy and annoying?*
> *Penny, by email*

> *How aggressive was Kate Thornton on* The X Factor *when Rowetta was voted off the show? 'This is your final warning, Rowetta – go back to your group.' She's so bossy! Please bring back Ant & Dec, or even Davina McCall – at least they're warm, funny and have a laugh with the contestants without treating them all like little kids.*
> *Sofia, by email*

Late this afternoon one of our writers spoke to Kate who is convinced we've made up the letters to get at her. Sorry, Kate, but some people really aren't that keen on you.

Wednesday 8 December

Had a Post-it note left on my desk this morning with the chilling words 'Andy Stephens wants to send you an email'. Stephens is George Michael's manager. So, he's read the Elton interview then! Fearful that we're being sued – although the interview was checked over by a lawyer before we went into print – I called him straightaway. (Actually, to be honest, an extreme lack of patience is probably the real reason I phoned straightaway.)

Whatever, I was pretty unsure of what kind of reaction I was going to get.

'Andy – Mark Frith at *Heat*.'

'Mark, thanks for calling. George is very upset about Elton's comments and he's written you an email. He wants you to print it in the next issue.'

'Andy, we'd be more than happy.'

'Good. There are a few conditions – we need this printed on the letters page and in full. George wrote this himself at home last night, it's really important that you print every word.'

'Of course … erm, Andy? Can I ask you one thing? You're saying George Michael actually wrote this himself.'

'Yes. Of course.'

'Right. Wow. Thank you.'

I gave him my email address and we say goodbye.

Now, no matter what success we've had, no matter how many awards we've won, George Michael writing to our letters page is up there with our greatest moments.

The email comes through 20 minutes later.

Dear Heat *magazine,*

Much as I am saddened to have to write this letter in full view of the general public, I feel I have no choice but to defend myself (and my partner Kenny, in a way) from some of the comments Elton made in Heat *magazine a couple of weeks ago.*

Let me start by saying that I will always be grateful to Elton for the inspiration that he gave me as a child, and that will never change. These songs are still dear to me 30 years on. But having said that, in order that my fans do not take Elton's 'observations' about my life too seriously, or worry about the 'strange place' I'm in these days, I think that it's time to set the record straight about my friendship with Sir Elton John, and how he may have come to such negative conclusions about my life.

Elton John knows very little about George Michael, and that's a fact. Contrary to the public's impression, we have spoken rarely in the last ten years, and what would probably surprise most people is that we have never discussed my private life. Ever.

Those really close to me, straight or gay, would tell you that I am not secretive at all in terms of my sexuality. In fact the phrase 'too much information' comes to mind occasionally, but with Elton it was never like that.

Sadly, I was always aware that Elton's circle of friends was the busiest rumour mill in town, and that respect for my privacy was not exactly guaranteed.

So, we never became genuinely close, which is very sad. And to this day, most of what Elton thinks he knows about my life is pretty much limited to the gossip he hears on what you would call the 'gay grapevine', which, as you can imagine, is lovely stuff.

Other than that, he knows that I don't like to tour, that I smoke too much pot, and that my albums still have a habit of going to number one. In other words, he knows as much as most of my fans do. What he doesn't know is that I have rarely been as happy and confident as I am today, thanks to my partner Kenny and the continued support of my fans.

If I stay at home too much, if anything it is because I am too contented right now.

I have travelled the world many times and, at 41, I think I have earned the right to a quiet life, which I truly love, and maybe Elton just can't relate to that. After all, he tours incessantly, he is a great artist and loves to play live.

We are totally different in that sense. He makes millions playing those old classics day in and day out, whereas my drive and passion is still about the future, and the songs I have yet to write for the public. And much as I am saddened that he would feel the need to criticise my album (which is, of course, in my humble opinion, a classic!), I am far more surprised that Elton seems to have forgotten me calling him a few months back to tell him that my American royalties from Patience *would be donated entirely to the Elton John AIDS Foundation.*

Yours Sincerely, **George Michael**

I read it with an ever-widening grin on my face. This is dynamite. Two huge stars, who everyone assumed were best mates, are having a huge spat through the pages of OUR magazine.

It's all great but the best bits are George's constant digs at Elton's age and his own recent success. I read through it again and translated the words in my own mind into what I think he really means.

'I will always be grateful to Elton for the inspiration he gave me as a child' (i.e., when you were most famous I was just a little kid).

'Those songs are still dear to me 30 years on' (ditto).

'My albums still have a habit of going to number one' (and yours don't, sunshine!)

'He makes millions playing those old classics day in day out' (fantastic use of the phrase 'old classics' – that's George putting Elton firmly in the category of rock dinosaur).

I rushed it over to Hannah, our News Editor. This is perfect timing – we're about to go to press on our Christmas double issue and we need a story for an empty spread we have.

'Hannah, you know that gap we have? Filled it.'

I hand over the print-out. She shakes her head then puts her hand over her mouth as she reads it.

'There's a slight problem, though. I've said it will only go on the letters page.'

'They won't mind! Anyway, this is too good to waste.'

Hannah's from the *News of the World* – she's had to hide down corridors, skulk around hotel foyers and expose cheating boyfriends and girlfriends. She has no fear. She's bloody tough, despite her sweet exterior. Putting something on a different page doesn't concern her but I'm pretty keen to keep everyone happy. We've had so many celebrities fall out with us in the last few months, to have at least one being our friend would be a good thing. But still, the news pages is, obviously, where it should be. Decisions, decisions …

Hannah wrote up a small story to explain the background to it all – and then we printed the email in full in her news section. We designed it to look like a letter by adding a signature we found on the Internet to the bottom (okay, so it's cheating a little, but emails don't look great on the page). But I have pushed my agreement with Andy Stephens a little too far.

Tuesday 14 December
The Christmas double issue came on sale today, featuring George Michael's letter.

Just before lunch the email from Andy Stephens pops up.
Luckily, he's happy.
Mostly.

Mark,
    Saw the piece in full as promised. Thank you.
Andy

    PS Don't ever be tempted into a career in forgery. The signature is crap!

Wednesday 15 December

The papers love the feud story, understandably. The *Daily Mail*'s headline is 'George gives "gossip" Elton a handbagging' while the *Daily Mirror* go with the more direct 'Slag! Slag!' Our Reviews Editor Paige, back in her native Australia for the Christmas break, calls to tell me it's even been a big story in her local paper the *Adelaide Advertiser*. We put all the news stories together for a self-congratulatory page that we'll run in the next issue.

    'Hannah, I've got a headline in mind: "Elton vs George: World's Press Reacts!" Do you think that's over the top?'

    'Yes.'

    'Oh ...'

    'That's a good thing!'

    It is over the top. It's all over the top. But today we're kingpins: all our rivals will be jealous of us and we want to shout about it.

    And George Michael knows we exist!

Thursday 16 December

No matter how well things are going there's always Ricky Gervais to put you in your place. In all the fuss about the George Michael drama I'd forgotten the other notable item from the Christmas double issue – another insulting Christmas card from Ricky Gervais – until the boss came up to me today and asked if it was really the sort of thing we should be printing.

To all Heat *readers,*
  May you find happiness and something better to do with your time in the New Year.
  Love, **Ricky Gervais**

Cheers, Ricky.
  Happy Christmas.

Sunday 26 December

Things are so flat out all the time at work that we've got into the habit of spending Christmas away. To be able to fly away somewhere hot after the nightmare of Christmas deadlines (often finishing two issues in the same week) is fantastic. It's one of the things that helps keep me sane.

This year we've chosen the Maldives but suddenly – on day two – it's all taken a less-than-relaxing turn. It's our second morning here and waves are lapping up against our villa with real ferocity. Then there's a knock at the door. One of the hotel staff is there, smiling that obedient smile people who work in hotels have fixed on their face, despite having difficulty standing upright in the wind. 'Sir! Madam! All the guests need to gather in reception!'

The hotel management have just told us that there are some high waves throughout the Indian Ocean, floods in the Maldives capital Male and in other areas too. We've been told to stay here, in the reception area, and that going back to the villas would be dangerous. A staircase that was previously attached to one of the villas has just been washed away. A whole part of the island is now inaccessible because the path leading to it is no more. And, as the morning has progressed, rumours have started to spread – whole islands destroyed, bodies being washed up on beaches. We have nothing to do but sit and talk: complete strangers conversing and empathising with each other. We realise that here, in this reception area, we have to bond to stay sane. I've also just realised that Ruby Wax is staying on our island. Bet she's going to be over the moon at being trapped – literally – with a journalist.

Thursday 30 December

The weirdest 72 hours of my life. We spent it trying to contact friends and relatives to tell them we're safe from the disaster that has claimed the lives of hundreds of thousands. As more news comes in Gaby and I realise how lucky we've been and become increasingly fearful about aftershocks.

There's not much to cheer any of us, not even watching Ruby Wax doing some amazingly elaborate stretching exercises on – not at the side of, but actually on – her lounger. She's as fascinated and amused at being stuck on a island with me as I am at being stuck with her. 'Hey, want a picture of my cellulite?' she shouts whenever she sees me.

Today is the bleakest day so far. CNN are predicting a possible second tsunami. We ran to the TV room. The Indian authorities were advising people to head for high ground because of expectations of an earthquake near Australia which would cause a tsunami, possibly even on the same scale as the first. We all stared at the screen.

Ruby Wax – a woman who can think of a gag for every situation – no longer had any. She was shaking. Utterly petrified. 'Ed, can I have a word with you outside.' Ruby and her husband, the TV director Ed Bye, left the room but we all could still hear them and it wasn't pleasant.

'Ed, how can we get off this island? There must be a way, what can we do? Ed, I don't care how we do it, we're going. Ed, what do we do?'

I stayed in the TV room watching the news develop, feeling like it was only a matter of time.

The first tsunami we knew nothing about, ignorance was bliss. This next one … Jesus. I feel hollow, panic-stricken and devoid of energy. All you can do is hope. And look around the island – where's the highest roof top? Surely there's somewhere higher? It's pointless, of course. If a big wave strikes, we've had it.

I don't drink but today I want to start.

Saturday 1 January 2005

Happy New Year.

The island have tried their best to arrange a celebration but no one is in a celebratory mood. Although the rumoured second tsunami never struck (or hasn't yet) we're all just hoping for the best. For Ruby the holiday had to come to an end. She'd been through too much, too publicly, and she retired to the family villa yesterday, not even coming out for the New Year 'party'. She eventually – after loads of phone calls and unimaginable expense – managed to get off the island today. In fact, gradually, everyone has left and no one new has arrived.

Sunday 2 January

We now have our very own private island, a peace only disturbed by the phone calls from mum still wanting to know why we aren't leaving. I've told her it is safer to stay than go through the capital, which was badly hit, or take a plane that would involve us changing in Sri Lanka, hit by death and disease. In this oddly still paradise, the real world seems far away. And I'm quite happy to stay away from it for as long as I can. Tomorrow, sadly, we have to leave.

Monday 3 January

Back home. The capital, Male, seemed calm as we passed through. Caught up on some more news footage when we arrived back, finally seeing the coverage as our relatives would have done, through British eyes. The latest figures say that more than 250,000 people are either dead or missing. And now I need to go to work and write about celebrities.

PART TWO
Hotter

Michelle McManus loses
5½ STONE!

THEN

NOW!

FIRST PICS!

This week's hottest celebrity news
£1.50 (€3.25 excl. ROI) 23 – 29 April 2005

heat

BRITNEY'S
BABY
NEWS!

SHE'S SO
HAPPY!

CHARLOTTE?

Which do
men prefer?

SKINNY
OR
CURVY?

Heat Poll:
We ask 100 blokes
(many of them famous)

OR POSH?

ISSUE 318

CHAPTER ELEVEN
If it ain't broke...
January – May 2005

Tuesday 4 January

Back at work. Lucky to be alive.

New things to worry about now. I've been in charge for five years, five incredible years. We've gone from 60,000 copies a week to over half a million. I still want to be the number one magazine (but with *Now* as strong as ever, that may have to stay a pipe dream) and I like the fact that I still have that desire after half a decade.

The nagging worry? The best may be in the past. I've got people advising me left, right and centre to get out while I'm on top. But it's tricky when you love a job as much as I do.

Now, where were we ...

Saturday 8 January

It's been a quiet first few days back, luckily. But today, just when our latest issue is at the printers, Brad Pitt and Jennifer Aniston have announced they're splitting up after four and a half years of marriage. This afternoon they released a joint statement through Brad's publicist.

'We would like to announce that after seven years together we have decided to formally separate.

'For those who follow these sorts of things, we would like to explain that our separation is not the result of any speculation reported by the tabloid media – this decision is the result of much thoughtful consideration.

'We happily remain committed and caring friends with great love and admiration for one another.

'We ask in advance for your kindness and sensitivity in the coming months.'

I love the 'for those who follow these sorts of things' bit. A fantastic Jude Law-style sentence admonishing anyone who picks up a celebrity magazine. It's their way of dismissing every tabloid or magazine story without going into any detail on whether they're true or not. This is a huge story for us – even more so than with Victoria and David, the pair seemed like another perfect couple.

Tuesday 11 January
The big American celebrity magazines – usually out on a Wednesday or a Thursday – have come out a day early this week to get news of the break-up to their readers sooner. *US* Magazine devoted 31 pages to the split, *People* – who broke the news on their website on Saturday – a 'mere' 12. Interestingly, both publications have sidebars titled 'The Angelina Factor' – with heavy speculation that Brad had an affair with co-star Angelina Jolie while filming the movie *Mr and Mrs Smith*.

Wednesday 12 January
With the huge wealth of material linking her to the marriage split Angelina Jolie has reportedly denied any involvement in their break-up.

Tuesday 18 January
The papers are reporting that Kate Moss is dating Babyshambles singer Pete Doherty. The pair met at her 31st birthday party at the weekend and he certainly fits into her bad-boy boyfriend mould – he was chucked out of his last band after failing to kick his crack cocaine and heroin habits.

Thursday 17 February
The champagne's back out in the office – after a poor set of results last August our sales are up again, helped hugely by our Nadia exclusives, the skinny cover last autumn and by the publicity around us when the George Michael/Elton John story broke. The figures we're releasing today show that we sold an average of 552,000 copies every week last year.

Monday 21 February
Our yearly three weeks out of the office begins today. We're going to be thinking up new ideas and today we came up with the first of them:

a gratuitous picture of a topless bloke called 'Torso Of The Week'. Very *Heat*.

Tuesday 1 March

Still out of the office working on new ideas. The new issue landed on my desk this morning and Julian – who is in charge for the three weeks I'm away – has done a great job. Looking at it I realise how much has changed in the celebrity world. A nice interview with Robbie Williams – even if what he says is quite revelatory – is no longer enough. Our readers are obsessed with all the body image stuff and want more of it – this kind of coverage is emotive and involving. It's been a steep learning curve for me, I have no experience of anything to do with this kind of stuff. I've had to learn what our readers want, why they want it and when. We always could do this magazine without access and that's even more the case now – celebrities are our playthings and we feel we can say whatever we want about them, and particularly their bodies, as long as the readers agree with us. The readers have strong views all the time – they shout and scream at the TV, point out every bulge and fold as they look at pictures in a newspaper or magazine, so now – truly – we are looking at the celebrity world the way they do. Questioning, criticising, analysing – this is how our readers see celebrities. Being responsible at the same time? That's the tricky part. And on the subject of these shrinking stars, we're making our opinion clear.

The cover of this new issue – on sale today – is another controversial one:

Teri Hatcher
Nicole Richie
Jessica Simpson
THEY'RE SKIN & BONES!

We're shocked on a daily basis by some of the pictures coming out of the States. Their young female celebs seem to be involved in some sick battle of under-nourishment if these pictures are anything to go by. Jutting shoulder bones, visible ribs, arms that look like they might break, the standard figure now is skeletal.

We've not done a skinny cover since the high-selling one last autumn – I feel we should do them when the pictures are there and the right experts are available to comment on them.

Looking at the cover this afternoon, as it sat on my desk, it's very unpleasant viewing. I'm not alone in thinking this. But also, it is what every magazine cover should be – compulsively engaging. On my way home I went into a big WHSmiths and looked at our cover sitting among the hundreds of other magazines. The covers are a mass of bland smiley faces that all merge into one – all white teeth and glossy hair. You don't notice any of them. Then there's ours: a car-crash cover of ribs and bones, a cover that instantly makes you react. It's a cover you can't ignore. It has your attention. Instantly.

Saturday 26 March

Amid huge hype, *Doctor Who* returns to British screens tonight, starring Christopher Eccleston and Billie Piper. In the first episode the doctor is seen reading a copy of *Heat*. Yet more fantastic publicity.

Tuesday 29 March

That utter bastard Darren Day has walked out on his girlfriend Suzanne Shaw and their young baby. To mark the occasion – and to acknowledge our bewilderment that anyone would ever want to go out with him in the first place – today we've printed The Darren Day Pledge that we're asking all our readers to sign and send back to us at the office.

Among other things we're asking all our readers to pledge that they will never accept a drink from him, never get engaged to him ('no matter how big and expensive the ring is') and finally to repeat the mantra 'being a mad old spinster with lots of cats is better than falling for Darren Day' three times a day for ever.

Tuesday 5 April

The sale for the Skin & Bones issue was huge; the mail bag was pretty big too. And still the pictures keep coming – and now more and more of the British stars are falling victim.

Jo Carnegie has been working on a piece about the trend this week – she's got a great panel of people together (from doctors to personal trainers to healthy-looking celebrities) all warning people against excessive weight loss. Jo is keen to make sure the piece clearly gets across our view on the subject. Celebrities, she says, are setting a dangerous precedent for young women who will do anything to look just like them.

I particularly like her closing paragraph.

'Just in case they (the skinny stars) have completely lost the plot, here are a few basic facts which we hope they can bring themselves to swallow: 1. Being able to count your ribs is not normal; 2. Boobs, bums and thighs are womanly and sexy; 3. Food is tasty.'

Monday 11 April

Jo received a phone call today from the mother of one of our readers. The daughter had food issues and her weight had dropped in recent months, yet the mum had been prevented from talking about the subject because the daughter simply wouldn't discuss what was happening.

The other week her daughter had come into the kitchen where her mum was, a copy of *Heat* in her hands. She was fighting back tears as she approached and showed her the cover feature.

'Mum, do I look like these women?'

Her mum told her she did.

Apparently this conversation led to some others and, a few days on, the daughter was beginning to improve her eating and get healthier. At points, Jo found it difficult to hear what the mother was saying because she was crying so much.

I'd love people to think we had loads of phone calls like this. We didn't. We had one. But we did get lots of letters from people thanking us for pushing forward a view that doesn't advocate major weight loss. We also, to be fair, got loads of letters from people reminding us that being overweight is also unhealthy. They are right, of course, but we are not advocating that either. We are simply on the side of our readers, raising the subjects they wanted raised and, crucially, helping them feel better about themselves. That's the key to high sales and reader loyalty. Simple as.

Tuesday 19 April

We're on a mission now. The skinny covers are really engaging people and selling well. Last week we commissioned a survey that asked the question: Which do men prefer – skinny vs curvy?

It's fine us pushing a positive 'extreme dieting isn't attractive' view but if all our readers sit at home and assume men will only fancy them if they look like skeletons then that's all gone to waste.

We commissioned a research company to go and interview 100 men aged between 18 and 30 – the results are overwhelming with 85 per cent preferring the curvier woman.

With the pervading fashion magazine (and fashion industry) ethos of 'skeletal is best', this verdict, in fact this whole feature, feels really radical. Loads and loads of blokes are coming out and saying that they fancy women who are healthy-looking and who enjoy eating. A 28-year-old guy called Marcus, after being shown a picture of a very thin Teri Hatcher, told our researchers, 'If she was my wife, I'd take her to Pizza Hut!' A 21-year-old lifeguard called Samuel – where do they find these people? – agrees: 'They look like they eat too little and exercise too much.'

These skinny covers sell very well for us. But that's not the reason we began doing them. All of us, every single one, became appalled by the photographs we've been seeing coming out of the States. We all know people who look at these pictures and think that this is the way to live your life – that dramatic weight loss is healthy, attractive and desirable. It's not.

Why can't women with normal size 14 or 16 figures find anything to wear in high-street fashion stores? Why is no one of the average size represented in fashion shoots or modelling campaigns or on the catwalk? What message is all of this sending out?

Wednesday 20 April

One of our journalists, Isabel Mohan, interviewed Zoë Ball this morning. She came straight over to me when she got back into the office.

'She wanted me to pass a message on to you. She says she's sorry about what happened back then, she went crazy for a bit and wants you to know she's better and more together now.'

We've not spoken since we fell out but it's great to get the message, clearing the air. However, she really has nothing to apologise for – us turning a statement sent to everyone into an 'Exclusive Interview' was completely out of order. One of the sweetest people I've met through the course of my career, it's the mark of the woman that she was the one breaking the ice. Based on what I've read of Isabel's interview this afternoon she's clearly got things back on track with Norman and sounds happier than ever. Good. This is a woman who deserves every bit of her happiness.

Monday 25 April

If the mail we're receiving is anything to go on, the readers love 'Torso Of The Week'.

Jo, in a typically perverse moment, has chosen an unusual candidate for next week's torso.

She comes over to me in the middle of the morning in fits of giggles, several members of the picture team following her.

'I – okay, we – have decided that Tony Blair should be the next "Torso Of The Week".'

Silence.

'What do you think?'

The four of them, now all giggling, look at me with a pleading 'oh go on!' look on their face.

'Are you being serious?'

'Yes!' they chime.

'It's for election week! Go on, it'll be hilarious!'

'Where the hell are we going to find a topless photograph of the Prime Minister?'

They all look at Jo and nod towards something she's holding behind her back.

'Ta-*daaa!*'

There it is. A colour printout of the leader of our country, on holiday, speaking on his mobile phone, dressed in just navy blue shorts, rubbing his bare stomach.

He is, to be frank, virtually naked.

He also looks bloody amazing.

For a Prime Minister.

'Shit, we've got to do this.'

The four of them cheer, high-five each other and run off to the design department.

It is a brilliant idea. It feels edgy, is funny and takes guts – no other magazine would dare do it.

I see Jo go from desk to desk telling everyone about her victory.

'Tony Blair's going to be "Torso Of The Week". I love it,' then laughing hysterically.

She's becoming like my crazy alterego. Whereas I, being the boss, have to be sensible, she can be as out-there as she likes, dreaming up daft or just plain stupid ideas that she falls in love with and then sells to me with a crazy passion. She's loud and brash at times, but we need her badly. She may be a nutter, but she's our nutter and we love her.

And this could well be her finest moment.

Wednesday 27 April

Many years ago I worked for a student union and several people I know from those days now work for, or are involved in, the Labour Party. One of them rang me up this morning.

'So what are you doing to support Blair next week then?'

'I'm sorry? We're not doing anything to *support* him, but we are doing him in "Torso Of The Week".'

He starts laughing.

'Brilliant, brilliant! I'll let his team know. Gotta go.'

His team? What team?

Like he'd be interested in us, the week before an election.

Thursday 28 April

Today there was a second call, from a different friend connected to the Labour Party.

'What have you got planned for the election week issue?'

'Not you as well! Well, we've got Tony Blair in "Torso Of The Week" so that's a full page but that's all.'

'Okay, great. And will that be on the cover?'

'No! We're a celebrity magazine! He's Tony Blair!'

'Hmm. I think you should.'

'I'll think about it.'

'And will there be some kind of "Vote Labour" message within the piece?'

'No, there won't!'

This is crazy.

What I thought were merely friendly phone calls are clearly something more than that. We are being canvassed!

It's dawning on me what's happening here.

Bizarrely, what *Heat* does and thinks is suddenly important to Tony Blair's team. Much is made of the influence newspapers – particularly the *Sun* – have on voters during the week of an election and the two main parties have spent considerable time and energy in the last few years courting the editors of the big popular newspapers.

But this is different. Clearly there are people in and around government who believe that what *we* do could influence our readers.

This is madness.

The call came at the right time, though. Today is the day we design the cover and the excitement about the Blair page in the office is huge. Our PR team, headed up by an ex-editor of the *Sun*, Stuart Higgins, when told about this got very excited. 'People are going to love this, they're going to go crazy for it.'

It ends up in the top left-hand corner of the cover. And after a long debate between myself, Jo and Louise – who can't stand Blair and is a little anxious about what we're about to do – we have decided on the words that go with the naked picture of him.

TONY GETS OUR VOTE!

The line is, of course, insinuation, and a little bit nudge-nudge. It alludes to his attractiveness and great physique in the photo. It's the right coverline for *Heat*'s take on the world. But it is also *exactly* the sort of thing Blair's team would hope for, a clear message that we are supporting Tony Blair in next week's election. Would I have chosen this line anyway or have I allowed myself to be completely and utterly spun?

Friday 29 April

With all the Blair madness of the last few days I've not had a chance to go through the most recent sets of pictures coming into the office.

Clara's team now receive thousands of photos every day. Going through them sends them half-crazy, especially as picture agencies are happy to send you any old rubbish, including pictures of celebrities we'd never be interested in for a second and sometimes even – yuck – real people!

The set that stands out by a mile this week, though, were taken in Rome over the last two days. Wednesday's pictures show Katie Holmes (26) holding hands with Tom Cruise (42). Thursday's pictures show them snogging. They go straight into the last available pages of this week's issue, over three pages. Being *Heat*, we have well and truly failed to restrain ourselves from mentioning how much taller she is than him …

Monday 2 May

The Blair issue is back from the printers. Now I'm worried. In all the excitement about the picture I'm not sure we made enough enquiries about the legality of the shot. It had been run once before – in a newspaper ages ago – but that's not the point. If this picture had been taken of him on private property he may have a real issue with us running it. People around him may know about and be fine with it but he might not.

Too late now; it's on sale tomorrow. But after falling out with film stars, TV presenters and singers, is our own Prime Minister about to come after us? I could really do with not falling out with the Prime Minister too.

Skinny celebs pile on the pounds (at last!)

RACHEL

ALICIA

This week's hottest celebrity news

£1.50 (€3.25 excl ROI) 28 May – 3 June 2005

heat

WORLD EXCLUSIVE

Kylie: 'I WILL beat this'

NEW BIG BROTHER HOUSE!
SEE IT HERE FIRST

THIS WEEK...
5p FROM EVERY HEAT GOES TO
breakthrough
breast cancer

ISSUE 323

9 771465 626036

CHAPTER TWELVE
Tears in the office
May – November 2005

Tuesday 3 May

Well, if Tony Blair didn't know about his debut on *Heat*'s 'prestigious' 'Torso Of The Week' page he does today. It's everywhere. The *Sun* ran it, even the *Daily Telegraph*. 'Just what do the good ladies of *Heat* magazine think they are up to?' ask the *Telegraph*, before going on to point out that the person in the photo, taken a year ago, looks nothing like the Tony Blair currently pounding the campaign trail. 'Old Tony don't look like that no more. The Kit Kats and the stress have seen to that. So *Heat* may reckon him torso of the week – but it ain't this week, girls, believe us.'

Wednesday 4 May

Unsurprisingly, my two Labour Party supporter friends LOVE me. One of them – a member of a well-regarded PR team – goes to work on milking it for all it's worth.

Late afternoon today he called me – so excited he could barely speak. Blair has seen the magazine and loved it. Sally Morgan, one of Blair's close inner cabal, called the Prime Minister yesterday when she saw the magazine. Apparently he was bemused, but thrilled.

Less thrilled was Alastair Campbell. With the team at 10 Downing Street in a state of high amusement about the picture, one of them had mentioned it to Campbell at the end of a phone conversation. Their excited babble fell on deaf ears – Campbell wasn't amused by the piece and certainly didn't like the idea of people fawning over his boss in such a way.

'How ridiculous,' he told the person at the other end of the phone. 'Why the hell are the press making such a fuss over this? Who cares?'

'Basically,' the woman told my friend after the conversation with Campbell, 'he's jealous. He can't stand the attention Tony's getting over this, about his physique. He's as jealous as hell.'

This evening, the BBC ran footage of Tony Blair's final day of campaigning. He was shown in the marginal constituency of Dumfries and Galloway, going along a line of supporters, saying hello and shaking hands. Then, two-thirds of the way along the line, two twenty-something women each hold out a copy of *Heat*, folded open at Blair's torso picture. With a huge Alastair Campbell-defying grin on his face, he happily signed them both.

Thursday 5 May

Today was Polling Day – and I've been catching up on the mail we've received in the office about the Blair torso picture. I was expecting the vast majority of it to be pretty scathing: how dare we bring politics into the magazine, we know it was just a stunt, put properly sexy celebrities back on 'Torso Of The Week', that sort of thing. But there just aren't those kind of emails. Most of them, in fact, are pretty damn lustful.

In reference to Heat's *'Torso Of The Week': Tony Blair … you're sick! And now you've left my mind in a disturbed and confused state. Must. Not. Fancy. Prime. Minister. Must. Not. Fancy. Prime. Minister. Must. Not. Fancy. Prime. Minister …*
Nancy, Leeds

Tony Blair's torso – if ever there was a reason to vote Labour, this was it. And the Government were worried no one was going to turn out? Note to the other party leaders: please don't follow in Tony's footsteps. Please, God, no.
Kath, by email

Oh my God, I just fancied Tony Blair. Eww!
Kelly, by email

Friday 6 May

Blair won a third term last night, albeit with a severely reduced majority. I have taken this as our cue to print a number of the letters we've received about him in next week's issue under the headline:

It's *Heat* wot won it!

a pastiche of a famous *Sun* front page the day after John Major had won the 1992 campaign, partly thanks to an anti-Neil Kinnock front page they ran on the day of the Major vs Kinnock election.

Tuesday 10 May
Renée Zellweger got married last night to a guy she's only been seeing for four months, the country singer Kenny Chesney. Totally bewildering. Zellweger always struck me as a very grounded woman – who the hell gets married that quickly?

Tuesday 17 May
Having my lunch in the office when *Sky News* flash up the story that Kylie Minogue has been diagnosed with breast cancer. All those in the office stopped what they were doing and crowded around the TV. Some of them were in tears.

As the afternoon went on, the news didn't feel any less shocking. Many of us – myself included – have met Kylie, some have met other members of her family. But even if we haven't, a story regarding a healthy young celebrity becoming ill is the type to hit you hard. This thing doesn't happen to young stars, and planning coverage about this seems really surreal.

I went to see Louise to ask her if it's okay for us to put a circle on every cover saying that 5p from each sale goes to Breakthrough Breast Cancer. She okays it immediately without a thought. (Behind the scenes, of course, she will now have to tell the money men and women at the company what she's done without checking with them previously. But Louise, supportive to the hilt for us, can also be pretty ruthless with those above us, so I can't see that being too much of a problem.)

Monday 23 May
Tom Cruise sure is excited about dating Katie Holmes. He was on *Oprah* in the States this afternoon and at one point began jumping on her sofa. Poor Tom Cruise – he may simply be excited about finding a (young, sexy, tall) new girlfriend, but unfortunately, because people are highly suspicious of his beliefs and way of living his life,

loads of people are just going to assume he's gone completely and utterly bonkers.

Tuesday 24 May

Oh God, now I'm having to defend Tom Cruise. To the entire office.

Often, news meetings get hijacked by lively debate about the topic of the day. Today we spend 20 minutes – 20 minutes! – on a heated Cruise/Oprah debate.

'Oh dear,' says Julian, flicking through some photos, 'he really has lost it, hasn't he?'

I protest.

'Well, I think it's sweet! He's in love and he's excited!'

'He's crazy!' says Hannah. 'Look at him.'

'This is how people feel inside when they meet someone new and he just wants to show it, that's all.'

'Really?' asks Hannah.

'Really. Also, I'm so bloody bored with film stars who do nothing. Bland interviews, boring boring boring.'

They look at me like I'm mad. They do that if I go off on one.

Number of people who think it's really sweet: one (me).

Number of people who think he's insane: lots (everybody else, in fact).

Thursday 26 May

It's not often that I take half of press day off but today there's a good reason. Gaby is pregnant! This morning we went for our first scan. Because we live in Celebrity Central we have decided that the only possible option is to have the scan at the clinic attached to The Hospital of St John & St Elizabeth. Kate Moss has had a baby here, Heather Mills, too. Even David Baddiel's wife! All the stars. I came back to the office straight after to tell the team. Today I am walking on air.

Friday 17 June

Katie and Tom are now engaged. As much as I like their (very public) romance this is daft. Why so quick? What is he trying to prove?

He proposed at the Eiffel Tower early this morning, highly inconvenient for us as it's our press day, giving us an hour to turn the story around.

I convened an emergency news meeting, always exciting these, and started to plan our coverage.

'So – pictures. Clara, what is there?'

'Nothing.'

A woman of few words, as always.

'Great. Charlotte – anything?'

'One quote, that's all.'

At times like these, magazines and newspapers use American stringers. It's early, so America is still asleep.

This is a crap meeting.

'Right, Clara – you can get us a picture of the Eiffel Tower?'

'What, just any picture?'

'Yes.'

'Of course.'

'Well, at least we have that … thanks everyone, this has been a huge success.'

What was I expecting? He's only just proposed.

I've cleared one page on the flatplan. Charlotte has somehow pulled together 150 words and we've run the headline big:

9 weeks after meeting, Tom & Katie get ENGAGED!

Clara arrives with the Eiffel Tower picture. It's all we have. Designing the page, a stock shot of the Eiffel Tower, probably taken years ago, is our main picture.

'Mark, this was taken years ago. There's no Tom or Katie in this shot.'

No one can do withering quite like Clara Massie.

'I know! It's fine, trust me, I have an idea.'

Twenty minutes later and the page is ready to go but with a couple of changes. There's an arrow pointing to the top of the tower, where people would stand to get the best view of Paris. That's probably where Tom proposed. Maybe.

The arrow says:

IT'S TOM & KATIE!

Then there's a huge stamp on the page that says

EXCLUSIVE FIRST PICTURE!

Well, made me laugh.

Thursday 30 June

Six of our last 12 covers have led on the whole skinny debate. It's a trend that's not gone unnoticed, I realise today.

The *Guardian* – a newspaper that has rarely written about us other than in their media section – have today run a large article on the subject, entitled 'The *Heat* is On'. The writer, Emily Wilson, praises our covers, although is critical of some aspects of what we do.

'Is *Heat*'s anti-skinny campaign a symptom of some growing backlash against the West's twisted worship of women with a body mass index of 10 or less?' she asks. 'It may actually do some good. One ought to hate *Heat* and its very modern freak show – but it is hard to summon up real anger. *Heat* levels the playing field a little for all the non-reconstructed, non-styled, not airbrushed women out there.'

At last people get it. When we started down this road we made a choice – forgo the generic, bland, retouched cover that everyone else does, and put in its place articles and pictures that make you feel better about yourself. Look awful in the morning? Don't worry, Gwyneth and Nicole do, too. Don't have the earnings/genes to be a skinny? Don't worry, they all look bloody awful. Don't go to the gym for the twentieth night in a row, stay in and enjoy yourself instead. Eat chocolate. Enjoy life.

Others preach self-denial, restraint, extreme discipline (and expensive gym memberships). *Heat* magazine, in June 2005, aims to preach contentment, enjoyment of life and remind people of the undeniable fact that the grass is never greener on the starvation side.

Amen.

Tuesday 5 July

There's loads of stories around at the moment about Kerry Katona and her drug intake – *News of the World*, for instance, are very publicly saying she's taken cocaine. We're running an interview with her this week and she's adamant that the stories are lies. 'The only drug I have ever taken is nicotine,' she tells our journalist Simon Gage. Well, that's sorted that out then.

Monday 11 July

In the current issue we've printed some new pictures of Jude Law and Sienna Miller. Big mistake. I was out of the office when they were chosen and sent off to the printers and the team should never have even bought them. The photographer was clearly standing on Law's driveway when they were taken.

'It's obvious, look! That's why he's so angry.'

The member of the picture team who did the deal for them disagrees.

'Nah, he's angry because the photographer has caught him carrying Sienna's handbag.'

'Look, it's clearly his driveway. Private property! That's out of bounds for us.'

Sure enough, this afternoon we get a legal letter. I've only just got over the last Jude Law drama. Not sure I can cope with this.

Tuesday 12 July

Overnight, our lawyer that handled our last Jude Law escapade has begun to sift through this one. And the news really isn't good at all.

I came in today to an email with his findings.

'I get the feeling Law wants blood,' he wrote. 'He's unlikely to give up without getting something. This is not a pretty one to fight, either in the courts or before the PCC. The snapper has plainly stepped over the mark on all fronts and not just the front drive to Law's house.'

We've really messed up this time and any email that mentions 'court', 'the PCC' and that someone 'wants blood' on the same page is really not good at all.

So far in my career I've managed to avoid having to go to court and I'm rather proud of it. Now, though, thanks to my old adversaries Jude Law and his legal team, it seems I could end up there.

We've had a few good months, a really good run. Now, it seems, we've hit the buffers yet again. Great.

Sunday 17 July

Today, the *Sunday Mirror* has run a story alleging that Jude Law has been having an affair with his kids' nanny.

The nanny, a woman called Daisy Wright, has given the paper an interview and it's fantastic stuff: all about how the two of them (plus one of Jude's children) went to a concert, how Jude and the nanny got drunk, then ended up in bed together before – and here's the most shocking bit – the child, who was having a bad dream, came into the bedroom and saw them there together.

Jude Law is (or was) dating Sienna Miller. No comment from either of them yet.

Monday 18 July

This is fascinating – Jude Law has issued a public apology to Sienna Miller.

No one does this sort of thing usually. Affairs are either hushed up or if they do get made public the people responsible deny it or won't talk about it. So this is a shock. Especially as movie stars never usually say anything about anything.

My guess is that Sienna – currently staying schtum on the whole thing – has either made him do it, or – more likely – Jude, thinking he's probably going to lose her, reckons this is his only hope. I don't think he does have a hope.

The statement was issued first thing this morning and is brief but does the job.

'I just want to say I am deeply ashamed and upset that I've hurt Sienna and the people most close to us.

'There is no defence for my actions which I sincerely regret.'

Tuesday 19 July

Sienna has dumped Jude.

Got an email from our lawyer. In the subject line he's written the words 'Jude "no wonder I like my privacy" Law'.

'It may be that the events over the weekend will dampen Mr Law's enthusiasm for pushing forward his complaint … it may be that he has more important things on his mind than being snapped in the dead of night by a pap.'

Tuesday 26 July
Still no word from Jude's lawyers. We're in the clear.

Wednesday 27 July
I have just seen the most gobsmacking set of pictures to ever arrive in the *Heat* office. Shots of the Beckhams and another couple enjoying dinner outside a restaurant in Seville. And, as clear as anything, you can make out David Beckham playing footsie with the woman opposite. With Victoria sat at his side. In fact, footsie is too soft a word – Becks (in sandals) is easing his big toe very precisely inside the bottom of the woman's jeans and rubbing it against her heel. To survive all they have – with their marriage just about intact – and then to do this is reckless in the extreme. Astonishing. The cruel bit of seeing a set of pictures you love is the bidding war. The photos are sent electronically to every celebrity magazine and then you bid. You phone the agency with your offer. Then your rival does the same – this keeps going until all but one drop out. In 2000 nothing would ever go above £5,000. Now it could keep going to £100,000. No joke. If you're reading this and you're not a paparazzi photographer you're in the wrong job. Trust me. Luckily no one saw the little game of footsie we spotted and they were ours for a bargain. We've run them across a spread and dropped them in on the cover.

Friday 5 August
People are telling me that *Heat* is in the UK fashion industry's bad books. Nothing concrete, just a sense that some elements are pissed off with us over our criticism of the fashion world's stick-thin obsession. Today, the first fashion editor of note goes into print with her feelings on the subject.

Hadley Freeman, Fashion Editor of the *Guardian*, has written a long article for today's paper.

THE LEARNING CURVE
Shock news! Thin is no longer in. Hadley Freeman looks at how
fashion has finally embraced a fuller shape.

Using our skinny features as evidence, Freeman reckons there has been a 'long overdue shift in the fashion industry away from knees that protrude from legs like vinyl albums, toothpick limbs and cheek-bones of such sharpness you could slice cheese on them.' However, the fashion industry, she says 'insists on using underweight teenagers to advertise clothes for middle-aged women'. Referring to *Heat*, Freeman notes 'this gentle easing up in the fashion industry coincides with the media's reaction against the wretched standards of slimness in Hollywood'.

I'd love to think we were having an effect but the 'curvier' models she says are now appearing in catwalk shows (she gives the example of Roland Mouret) still look pretty thin to me. I'm not sure the fashion industry is shifting that much, despite what this reasoned, well-written piece says. We shall see ...

Tuesday 16 August
One of the pleasing things about working at Heat Towers in the last year has been seeing the development of a journalist called Jordan Paramor. Jordan was my PA/Editorial Assistant at *Smash Hits* and she combined her job with some of the most rampant partying I've ever seen in a magazine employee.

Every day she was hungover, but that, over time, became so closely incorporated into her DNA that it didn't affect her work at all. She always looks back on that time with total embarrassment, thinks she was rubbish at her job and I spend much of my time telling her she wasn't and that, now she's successfully working with me in a writing and interviewing capacity, she's pretty good at that too.

Jordan just won't hear it. To the outside world she is über-confident – a reputation enhanced by her 1,000 words a minute conversational style – but she finds being confident tricky at times. She's talented, though, and her confidence is increasing by the day. Mainly because she works hard at what she does, is very good at crafting questions and, being the friendly type, all who meet her like her a lot.

This week we've given her a tough assignment: *Heat*'s first inter-view with the much-maligned Kate Thornton since we printed all those letters about her presenting technique.

After a few soft questions to ease her way into the interview, halfway through Jordan bites the bullet and asks about the letters. 'They did give me a hard time and I think criticism hurts most when you think, "Actually, they've got a point". I almost wanted to write back to every-one and go "But I had to be bossy. I had to control Rowetta!"'

She's taken this well; I'm pleasantly surprised. Now let's see how this year's series – starting in a week and a half – goes.

Tuesday 23 August

Got a call this morning from a PR for a theme park. Jonathan Ross and his family were there the previous day and the park's photogra-pher took some photos of them. Do *Heat* want them?

I tell the PR – who I like enormously and trust – that there's been a mistake, that there's no way Jonathan Ross would ever want a picture of his kids in *Heat*. 'No, he knows they're going to you. He's fine with it.'

The photos have just arrived: Jonathan, David Walliams and Jonathan's three kids all posing in front of the park's central feature. Another one with him and kids on a ride. Now, I'm fully aware – as is the whole world – of how some of these visits work. Many of the parks and attractions do it – bus celebs in, put them up in the nicest hotel room around, treat them like VIPs and hopefully get them to pose for a few pictures that plug their attraction. I don't know whether this was the case for this visit, but I can't help but feel a bit peeved that when it suits him Ross wants us to publish his family photos. To make a point – and because we always love a good set of free pictures – we'll run them all.

Tuesday 6 September

Running some new pictures of Kate Hudson – in the shots we've been sent she looks a lot thinner than usual. It's a great cover.

Thursday 15 September

The front page of today's *Daily Mirror* shows Kate Moss appearing to snort cocaine. Under the headline 'Cocaine Kate', Moss is pictured at a Babyshambles recording session (she's still dating the band's lead singer Pete Doherty) taking the drug – the accompanying article alleges that she snorted five lines in 40 minutes. The rest of the media go into meltdown but I've really no idea why – the idea that a famous person takes cocaine doesn't surprise me. Yes, it's a good story, but surprising? I don't think so. *Heat* won't be running anything on it.

Friday 16 September
After just 18 weeks of marriage, Renée Zellweger has filed for divorce from husband Kenny Chesney. They have spent just 15 days together since their wedding back in May.

Wednesday 21 September
In the last 24 hours Kate Moss has been dropped from two high-profile advertising campaigns: Chanel and H&M.

Thursday 22 September
This evening – presumably because she doesn't want to lose any more contracts – Kate Moss has finally issued a statement: 'I take full responsibility for my actions. I also accept that there are various personal issues that I need to address and have started taking the difficult, yet necessary, steps to resolve them,' she said. 'I want to apologise to all of the people I have let down because of my behaviour which has reflected badly on my family, friends, co-workers, business associates and others.'

Although the papers are bashing her, her boyfriend seems to be getting even greater criticism. He's a loser, basically, with a long history of antisocial behaviour and drug charges. But she won't dump him.

I find it difficult to cover this story – it's so grim, they're both a bit tawdry and our readers have little interest and even less sympathy. They won't be able to *begin* to identify with these two. The team are bemused by my attitude but I'm sticking to my guns: our readers are not interested in this horrible couple.

Wednesday 19 October
Met up with my friend Leesa in a Pizza Express just round the corner from BBC Radio.

There, at a table by the door, is that children's TV presenter and disco flasher. She smiles brightly at me ... then suddenly it hits her where she knows me from. She looks panicked, goes bright red and suddenly finds the menu on the table very, very interesting.

I spared her further blushes by smiling back and walking quickly to the other side of the restaurant.

Tuesday 1 November
This week we've run a brilliant story about Sharon Osbourne. We've always loved the Osbournes – they have all the trappings of the perfect moneyed Hollywood lifestyle but have retained a down-to-earth no-bullshit approach. We love that. In a showbiz world of fakery and pretend they provide a much-needed dose of reality – and the whole family have had a lot of fun mocking others for their pretensions. But in the last couple of years it's become clear that Sharon herself is becoming a bit showbiz. There's no better example of this than our story. For last week's National TV Awards Sharon was nominated for an award that she knew she was going to win. But she didn't show, which made no sense to us. She was in the country and would have loved an opportunity to lord it up in front Simon Cowell, who she beat to the award. Weird. So we investigated further – and the reason she didn't go is brilliant. Earlier in the week a hairdresser had mucked up her hair colouring. She was distraught and decided she wasn't going to the ceremony. Then she had a change of heart, deciding the opportunity to showboat in front of Cowell was too great. Different hairdressers were called in and they all tried to sort it out. The resulting do – ruby red with blonde streaks – didn't work either and, eventually, she threw in the towel. We have printed the whole grisly tale in full. She'll be fine about – her view will be 'if you can't take it, don't give it out'. Bound to be.

Wednesday 2 November
Bump into Sharon's PR, Gary Farrow, in The Ivy. 'Sharon's not happy.' Suddenly fear for my life: journalists who've upset Sharon in the past have often been cut off from the Osbourne camp entirely. Others, delightfully, have received faeces in the post (in a nicely presented box, apparently, but still: faeces is faeces. Great. This will be

a nice story to tell the grandchildren). 'It was a story about hair! Can't you calm her down?' He promises to try.

Monday 7 November

The news breaks that Kate Hudson is suing us over the skinny pictures we printed two months ago. Her lawyers say the photos 'suggested that she had an eating disorder that was so grave and serious that she was wasting away, to the extreme concern of her mother and family'. I believe we implied nothing of the sort. Louise's PA Anita emailed me at 11.30 to tell me she'd received a lawyer's letter. 'It's here in my office when you want to collect it.' Luckily, she's kept it from Louise for now. Not sure she can take another legal letter.

Then, an hour after the first email, Anita sends another. 'Now it's on the Radio 1 news!'

Oh, fantastic. Won't be able to keep this from the boss now.

Thursday 10 November

Press day and I get a call on my direct line. No one ever rings my direct line. No one has the number. Usually I answer with the words 'Hello, wrong number!' in my chirpiest voice. Today it's a very serious-sounding posho from the *Sunday Telegraph* called Rebecca Tyrrel.

'Can I speak to Mark, please?'

'Speaking.'

'Mark Frith?'

'Yup.'

Get to the point, I'm thinking, it's bloody press day.

'Mark Frith, the editor?'

'Yeeeees.'

She sounds utterly taken back by the fact that I'm answering my own phone. I love that. Makes me seem a bit 'man of the people'.

Anyway, once we've established that I'm me and she's her she tells me she's doing a story for that weekend's paper about the whole skinny thing and would I give her a quote about Kate Hudson suing us.

Talk about being put on the spot.

Now, from what I recall from all my legal seminars (and I've been forced to go to loads in recent years for some strange reason involving us being sued every two minutes) I do know you're not meant to comment at times like these. So I didn't. Not easy when you like talking as much as I do.

'Erm, well, it will have to be a no comment.'

I apologised and put the phone down, realising that I'd just been party to a conversation between the two most confused-sounding people in the world – one surprised that anyone's ringing him and the other surprised that anyone is taking her call.

However, job done. I didn't give her a quote, so she won't have a piece to write. Heh heh heh. Yet again I have shown complete brilliance in the art of being an editor.

Sunday 13 November

So there we were, Gaby and I, in Waitrose this lunchtime. I was queuing at the till, she was going off around the supermarket collecting all the things we'd forgotten (i.e., everything) and I decided to see what nice posh Rebecca Tyrrel had decided to write about instead of writing about us getting sued by Kate Hudson.

Turning to page 17 of the main paper I get my answer – she's decided to write about us getting sued by Kate Hudson.

Actually, she's done more than that. She's constructed a huge argument that basically alleges that we are evil.

It's a big piece – an entire colour page. The *Sunday Telegraph* has relaunched recently under the editorship of Sarah Sands and her aim has been to make the paper (famously staid and old in its readership) younger and more female-friendly which, I guess, is why they're so interested in us.

I know from the headline and sell that this is going to be eventful.

TRULY SHOCKING: MODELS WEIGH LESS THAN NORMAL PEOPLE
Of course they do, writes Rebecca Tyrrel, it's their job. So why are gossip magazines obsessed with the so-called celebrity 'skeleton brigade'?

This piece is hysterical – in both senses of the word. One of its central points appears to be that famous women have to look like skeletons because the camera adds ten pounds and that we are only embarking on this campaign to get publicity (untrue, we're doing it for the same reason we do everything – because our readers will be interested in it).

But the most incredible part of the article is a cameo appearance from Alexandra Shulman, editor of *Vogue* magazine, a woman who has done more than most to promote the thinner frame through its many appearances in her magazine.

Bemoaning our concern about celebrities who look like they're on the verge of death, Shulman embarks on a bit of a rant.

'This is about knocking them down,' she begins. 'It'll be moles next and they'll say they're worried about skin cancer.'

Then to the final paragraph. And it's a goody.

Asked if she reads *Heat*, Shulman says no. 'I used to,' she splutters, 'but I think we are all a bit over that.'

There it is. In black and white. The singularly most condescending, snobbish thing an editor has ever said about another editor's magazine.

Nothing could illustrate more how much magazines like ours have changed the landscape of British publishing and the effect this has had on the old guard. Those editors pushing a diet of the same old skinny models and celebrities, while failing on so many occasions to question the industry that supports them, are feeling the pressure. The irony of what she says, of course, is that in recent years our sales have begun to dwarf hers. Far from being 'all over that', it's magazines like *Vogue* that are getting left behind. We overtook their sales three years ago and haven't looked back. Two years ago we were selling double what they were; now it's nearly three times what they're doing.

Sunday 20 November

The British Society Of Magazine Editors is an organisation that enables editors to meet with other editors at social events, talks and the like. The centrepiece of the BSME calendar is their awards, being held tomorrow evening at a very posh hotel on Park Lane. I realised as I was putting my (only) Black Tie ensemble together ready for the do that my new arch-nemesis Alexandra Shulman will also be there – we're both nominated for awards. This could be *very* interesting.

How Preston proposed to Chantelle **FULL STORY– ONLY IN HEAT**

FISHY!
POSH GETS A TROUT POUT!

This week's hottest celebrity news
£1.55 (at 3.25 excl RO) €2.90 Spain & Canary Islands) 22 – 28 April 2006

heat

ISSUE 369

WORLD EXCLUSIVE!
● "Harvey kicks me"
● "He weighs 6st – and wears 16-year -old's trousers"

JORDAN

The sad truth about living with my Harvey

La Fulvio's finest moment –
being molested by a Spice
Girl, Summer 2007

In happier days – Amy
wows the Grammys

The moment we knew all
wasn't well on Planet Britney.
Things were to get even worse

Well, he sure looks pretty happy. Pete wins *Big Brother* 7 (and three weeks later dumps Nikki)

Jade Goody goes on a PR charm offensive after 2007's *Celebrity Big Brother*

NEWS 24x7 EXCLUSIVE Jade: Wont keep any of prize money

David Walliams swims the channel with the *Heat* logo on his arse

speedo
heat

Breaking my no-alcohol rule after
winning the Mark Boxer Award, the
biggest award in British magazines

A busy executive often needs to lean, which is where Julie Emery comes in handy

Ah, so young! Julian Linley and me in the old Mappin House office (note essential vitamins)

Michelle Davies

Boyd

Louise

Julian

Clara

Julie Emery

Polly

Dan W

Lucie

Ellie

The team at *Heat*

Cover star for the day – my departure commemorated in true *Heat* style

CHAPTER THIRTEEN
Jordan spills the beans
November 2005 – June 2006

Tuesday 22 November

As much as I hate getting dressed up in the whole Black Tie garb (actually a suit I've had for 15 years with a bow tie that just about matches it), awards ceremonies have been pretty good for us over recent years.

Last night at the BSME Awards, Jane Johnson, editor of *Heat*'s sister magazine *Closer*, decided to plonk herself next to me.

Two things you need to know about Jane Johnson:

1. She's on the BSME committee so is privy to loads of information about the awards, most notably, who won what.
2. It appears that, in certain circumstances, she can't keep a secret.

'It's going to be a good night for you.'

'Jane – shut up.'

'Are you sure you're ready for this?'

'Jane!'

'I'm not giving anything away, just saying I think this could be a good night for you.'

I was nominated in just one category – Editor Of The Year, Entertainment Magazines. I didn't think I was going to win, being up against the editor of *NME*, a magazine enjoying something of a renaissance in reputation and relevance. But, clearly, if you listen to big-mouth Johnson, I'm a shoe-in!

As the nominees in my category were announced I began to prepare myself: I attempt to straighten my tie, brush imaginary crumbs off my jacket and generally aim to look the part.

I then glance over at Jane, smile at her and nod knowingly.

She gives me a 'what are you doing, you're weird' look (a look I've seen a lot in my life). I look away, perplexed. 'She's decided to play it cool,' I conclude. 'About time too.'

Piers Morgan – now a celebrity rather than someone who writes about celebrities after the huge success of his book *The Insider* – is presenting the awards.

Here we go, prepare yourself Frith.

Breathe in, breathe out, breathe in, breathe out …

'And the winner of the British Society Of Magazine Editors award for Editor Of The Year, Entertainment Magazines is …'

Here we go, we have lift off! COME ON!

'… Conor McNicholas from the *NME*!'

Uh?

I look at Jane.

'Uh?'

'I didn't say it was that award!'

'But I'm only nominated for … oh, never mind.'

So, this was all a wind-up. Something for her amusement. She's using her position as a committee member to mess with my mind.

Well, thanks a bloody bundle.

I launch into a sulk. She gives it a rest.

For, like, *two minutes*.

Then …

'You getting ready?

I ignore her.

Another award passes. She asks me again.

The fourth time she asks me I stick my fingers in my ears. The seventh I stick the palm of my hand up and put it in her direction, doing the whole 'talk to the hand' thing I've seen people do on *Jerry Springer*.

There's just two awards left now. The final one is the Editor's Editor Of The Year award, an award voted for by all the members of the society to recognise achievement in that year. I won this one in 2001 but I'm not nominated for it this year.

The penultimate one, and the one coming up in a minute, is the Mark Boxer Award – named after the truly exceptional editor, writer and cartoonist – that recognises special achievement in magazines. Industry veterans win this award, people who've been in the business for a long time. It's the BSME equivalent of the lifetime achievement awards you see at things like the Oscars and the Baftas, you know the ones, won by the sort of people who have to be helped onstage. The winners here are a few years younger and a little more mobile than that, but you get the idea.

'Our winner,' announces *GQ* editor Dylan Jones, Morgan's co-host for the evening, 'was born in Sheffield in 1970 …'

'What a weird coincidence,' I think to myself, '*I* was born in Sheffield in 1970 too.'

Then, of course, it dawns on me as they're reading through the list – they're talking about me.

Am I really that old?

Never mind …

'I've bloody won.'

This knocks me sideways – the biggest award in magazine publishing and I've won it. I can barely function but I'm together enough to make a very special detour as I walk towards – and then again back from – the stage. I decide to walk past the table Alexandra Shulman, sadly not an award winner tonight, is sitting at. I don't glance over, but I'm glad I did it. Tonight is my night.

I never stay around at these things for long but this evening I feel I should, although I just want to go home and show Gaby this incredible award, mine for a year, a vast rosebowl-type affair with all the winners' names on the side.

Jane, the opposite of me when it comes to partying, wouldn't let me leave anyway. Which is why, at gone 11 p.m. on a Monday evening – a work night! I *ask* you! – I'm being photographed by Jane Johnson drinking champagne out of a huge rose bowl at a hotel in Park Lane.

'But I don't drink,' I keep saying to her.

'Never mind, turn sideways, I need a better shot.'

'But …'

'Shut up and keep drinking.'

People come up to me, either to say congratulations or to remind me that I don't drink.

At 11.30 I head for home.

Gaby is over the moon for me. The proud girlfriend side of her is made up for me, aware of the magnitude of the compliment. The interior designer side of her, though, isn't best pleased.

'It's so big! It's doesn't really go with any of the rooms.'

'Gaby, it is going … there!'

I plonk it in the middle of the coffee table.

'We can use it as a fruit bowl!'

'Okay, it can stay.'

She grins at me, then gives me the biggest hug an eight-month baby bump allows.

This morning I got a text from Louise first thing. She – and Chief Executive Paul Keenan – have had to go abroad for a board meeting, but she's made up for me.

In my reply, I told her it's equally her award. It really is. To have a boss like her, for so long, who allows me to do what I want to do, with regular bits of smart, thoughtful advice thrown in, is one of the best things about this job. She, at times, has to deal with the crap – explaining to the board why we occasionally get sued, juggling business stuff (she gets us the investment and tools we need without fail, no matter what the odds stacked against her). She's a genius and I'm beyond lucky to have her. I try and tell her as much in the reply, without, of course, embarrassing both of us too much.

My reverie is interrupted by the arrival of Jane and the photos last night. Luckily, my consumption of alcohol extended to no more than a few sips but if anything was to give me a hangover it would be this.

These are, essentially, pictures of a bald man looking stupid drinking booze out of a huge bowl.

Thank God the world will never see them.

Thursday 15 December

Danny Joseph Frith was born at 9.53 a.m. this morning. He's beautiful, like his mother. I think I'll take a few days off.

Tuesday 3 January 2006

A lot to catch up on today, after being out of the office for three weeks. Heard a brilliant story from one of my two Labour party insider friends.

Just before Christmas, Tony Blair's team at 10 Downing Street had held their annual Christmas raffle. Basically, they put various prizes up on offer, so that other members of the team can win them. One of the prizes, won by a female member of his team, was a framed, signed version of ... his 'Torso Of The Week' image.

Blair's always been portrayed as a showbiz Prime Minister but this is something else. Here's a man comfortable with his celebrity status, even – you could argue – loving it a bit too much. It's clear now that the Prime Minister, under the cosh because of his involvement in the Iraq War, is enjoying being appreciated for his looks and (based on the mail we got from readers) considerable sex appeal. It must be a pleasant diversion from the reality of his life, his day-to-day hassle. And it's great for us. But it is still a little odd – and pure, *pure* show-biz. In January 2006, it seems even the Prime Minister has signed up to *Heat*'s celebrity world.

Wednesday 11 January

Jesus Christ. Sometimes I wonder about the world *Heat* have helped create. Received an email from a PR today that has the headline 'Foot Reading At The Oscars'.

You *would* read an email like that, wouldn't you?

'When we study the stars on Oscar Night, we love to analyse their outfits.'

Fair enough. That's an understandable first line of a press release. But then ...

'Jane Sheehan is the UK's leading foot reader, and she likes to analyse their feet! She can tell a lot about a person's personality, physical and emotional health. The interest is not only in what their feet say about their personality and health (and what they may be hiding from the public) but also in studying if their personality matches that of the character they play in their current or past movies.'

This is becoming the finest email I have ever received.

'The Oscars are less than eight weeks away, so if you are planning your Oscars feature now, brief your photographer to get close-up to some celebrity feet and give me a call to tap into Jane's knowledge.'

Wednesday 1 February

Today, Marcus Rich (my boss for periods of my time here at the company) took me into a room to tell me that tomorrow the *Guardian* will be announcing the closure of *Smash Hits* magazine. Although I knew it had – in common with most teenage magazines – been struggling for a while, this is still a shock. *Smash Hits* was my route into magazines. It was my favourite magazine as a teenager and the day I got a job there was the best day of my young life. As I'm an ex-*Smash Hits* editor who can handle himself on TV and radio, I've been pushed forward as Emap's representative for any interviews that need doing. Before I left Marcus's office I suggested an idea to him: how about we put together a 'Best Of *Smash Hits*' book that we release in time for Christmas? He's got other stuff on his mind at the moment, understandably, but seems keen.

Sunday 5 February

India Knight wrote about the demise of *Smash Hits* in her *Sunday Times* column. I love India Knight anyway, but I didn't realise quite how perceptive she is until today.

'I hope some clever person – possibly Mark Frith, once editor of *Smash Hits* – puts together a fat *Jackie*-style annual of the best bits of *Smash Hits* in time for next Christmas,' she writes in her column. 'Ideally with a foreword by Paul "Whacky Thumbs Aloft" McCartney.'

This is brilliant! Emap have to do it now.

Thursday 9 February

Shocking pictures arrive in the office of Britney driving a car with her five-month-old son Sean Preston on her lap. She's not wearing a seatbelt. Charlotte Ward spoke to The Royal Society for the Prevention of Accidents who were, understandably, disgusted.

'A child can be thrown through the windscreen from a car travelling at just 5 mph. Britney is a role model and should be setting a better example.'

The pictures are so impossible to comprehend – and what we're saying about her is so scathing – I began to panic slightly. This doesn't add up. No one would truly do this, would they? I look at the photos again, really closely. Some show her with Sean on her lap when the car isn't moving. Others are close-ups of Britney with one hand on the wheel and the other around her son – but how can we prove she is actually moving at that time? There's no video footage.

Our lawyer is pretty convinced we're fine but wants the money shot, the one that will prove the car is moving. As soon as I finished our call I went over to the picture department to Russ, our new Picture Director.

'Russ, I know we're pretty sure of this but I need a shot where the car is clearly moving …'

Five minutes later he calls me over.

'How about this?'

There it is. The proof. A Malibu highway with Britney's car in the foreground and, although it's not very busy, you can clearly make out three other cars all moving in the same direction.

I go through the necessary checklist with Russ.

'Russ, I know this sounds stupid but we have to be very careful here. This is clearly a highway, that car is clearly moving?'

He thinks I've gone nuts.

'Yeeees,' he says with a look that clearly says 'he's lost it'.

'It's a road – and those are cars,' he says, slowly so I understand.

He's right, I'm right, we're going to do the story. We were right all along. It's just that – and I'm not just saying this as a new dad – it still seems too horrific to contemplate. One medium-sized push on the brakes and that child could be dead.

Friday 10 February

Complete confirmation – if we still needed such a thing – about the incident came through from the Spears camp overnight. They've issued a statement admitting Britney drove with Sean on her lap. The tone of it, though, is very interesting …

'Today I had a horrifying, frightful encounter with the paparazzi while I was with my baby.

'Because of a recent incident when I was trapped in my car without my baby by a throng of paparazzi, I was terrified that this time the physically aggressive paparazzi would put both me and my baby in danger.

'I instinctively took measures to get my baby and me out of harm's way, but the paparazzi continued to stalk us and took photos of us which were sold … I love my child and would do anything to protect him.'

I first saw the statement when I got in at nine this morning. It's tough for us to be able to fit too much in on a Friday (we print at the very end of the day so we have to be quick) but I'm determined to get this in the magazine.

It's a robust – and clever – defence but full of holes. After a brief office discussion we've decided to print the statement with certain bits circled and our comments.

I sent Hannah off with the statement. She's gone in on it pretty hard but she's right.

Where Britney's statement says she was 'terrified' we point out (quite rightly) that 'In the shots of Britney driving away she looks calm and collected – not terrified as she claims', whereas her claim that 'I instinctively took measures to get my baby and me out of harm's way' is met by our assertion that 'Sean was more in harm's way on Britney's lap than in the back.' Our response to her final line ('I love my child and would do anything to protect him') is suitably withering: 'Except put him in a car seat, eh Britney?'

We have gone in hard on her. But now I'm a parent a story like this seems even more shocking and incomprehensible than it would have done before. Our cards will be marked with the Britney camp – we'll never get an interview with her in the future now. But I feel this is right.

Tuesday 18 April

We ran an interview with Jordan today. The interview focused largely on Harvey, now three and a half years old. Whereas most celebrities are protective of their kids, it's in Jordan's interest to be very public about them. She makes an absolute fortune from posing with them for endless covers of *OK* magazine.

So in our interview she speaks a lot about him – particularly his food intake and weight. Although it can't be much fun at times the answers Jordan gives to Lucie are often filled with humour and shows she doesn't take life too seriously.

'He's six stone and he's only three and a half so that is heavy. If I want a cuddle, I have to drag him on my lap or ask Pete to plonk him there. Sometimes I ask, "Can I have a cuddle?" and he says, "No." Then I say, "Do you love Mummy?" and he says, "No." Then I say "Do you love Daddy?" and he'll say, "No." But when I say, "Do you love cake?" he instantly says, "Yes."'

Sunday 7 May

Rumours in the Sunday papers that Paul McCartney and Heather Mills McCartney are living in separate homes and that their marriage is over. Mills McCartney has spoken to the *Sunday People* to rebuff them, in pretty firm terms. 'It's hilarious. Of course we are together. Paul and I are still very much together. Paul and I are together 100 per cent.'

Sunday 14 May

But she wanted to have babies with *me*! Geri Halliwell gives birth to Bluebell Madonna Halliwell; the baby weighs just 5 lbs 12 oz. See Geri, that's what happens when you make babies with short men!

Tuesday 16 May

Met with Darryn Lyons for lunch. Lyons is the boss of Big Pictures, a leading paparazzi agency. He wanted to meet with me but I still had to go and see him, at a restaurant (Smiths of Smithfields) round the corner from his office.

Lyons is the sort of person who would hope to be described as 'larger than life'. In person he's pretty small but well built and gets himself noticed with his crazy hair colouring.

My suspicion is he once went to an exotic zoo, saw a cockatoo and thought 'Right, that's how to get noticed!' Today his hair is big and pink. He looks ridiculous, but he does get noticed. And in business that's no bad thing.

We order. He tells me about the weekend he's just had – although an Aussie by birth he seems to be on a never-ending mission to infiltrate English high society and has been playing for his regular polo team alongside a whole series of toffs. He wants me to go and watch him play. I make all the right noises but know I never will.

Then, eventually, after banging on about the polo, he gets down to business.

'Listen Mark, you must get invited to loads of different events.'

'God, loads, yeh.'

'And you won't be able to go to most of them.'

'No. Way too many.'

'How about we come to a deal whereby we go on your behalf so everything's covered.'

'Right. And you'll only give the stuff to us?'

'Well, no.'

'Right, so you're suggesting a system where we get you into loads of events and you sell the pictures on?'

No wonder he wanted to meet with me. We argue the toss for the rest of the meal.

'I don't see what's in it for me, Darryn.'

'It means everything is covered. You have a photographer everywhere.'

'Which you then sell on!'

He just doesn't understand why I won't go for this.

The meal ends and we go our separate ways – him by foot to the office, me in a cab. My cab drives past him so I see him stomping off down the street in one hell of a huff.

You've got to admire his cheek, but still, did he *really* think I'd hand over all of *Heat*'s access just like that?

Darryn Lyons is clearly an ambitious man, though, and I feel this may not be the last time I get an offer from him.

Wednesday 17 May

Paul McCartney and Heather Mills McCartney have announced they're splitting up after just four years of marriage. Her words just ten days ago appear to have been less than completely honest. And it's all the fault of the press, apparently. In their joint statement they lay the blame at the press's door.

'Our parting is amicable and both of us still care about each other very much but have found it increasingly difficult to maintain a normal relationship with constant intrusion into our private lives.'

What nonsense. Who has ever split up because of the press? Famous people split up for exactly the same reasons non-famous people split up. They argue all the time or they've given up working at it or they fancy someone else. No one splits up because of the press. It's a pathetic attempt to blame other people – they really should take some responsibility for their own actions. And they'll probably have to – this divorce could be very public and very brutal.

In other news: we have a Robbie Williams interview at last! Six years after he sued us, Robbie has invited us down to a training session for a charity football event taking place at the end of May. Robbie really wants to plug the cause – Unicef, a charity he's supported for many years – and has decided the best way to do that is to talk to *Heat*. He's probably right – latest figures show that we are now read by over two million people (for every copy we sell, another three people will get to read it). We send Lucie down – she's going to be the ball girl for the day (the things we put her through!) We'll get the photos back tomorrow and turn round the article quickly for next week.

Thursday 18 May
Lucie's day with Robbie went way better than we could ever have hoped. As well as being Ball Girl ('nice legs' were Robbie's first words to her after she changed into her 'age 13' kit), she served the celebrity footballers food and limbered up with them. At 11 a.m. the photos arrived ...

There's Lucie doing press-ups with Robbie and Gordon Ramsay. Her – in waitress uniform – offering a plate of pastries to Robbie Williams. And one of her crouching down on all fours as Robbie Williams rubs his groin against her backside.

The pictures have drawn quite a crowd around Russ's computer.
'Erm, Lucie ...'
'Yeah.'
'Have you seen this?'
'Oh God! Forgot about that.'
'Are you sure you're fine with us running a picture that appears to show Robbie Williams shagging you on a football pitch?'
She studies it and pulls a face.
'It's funny, run it.'
A cheer goes up.
The piece is designed and the subs team show me the final proof. The main picture is one of Lucie standing in between Gordon and Robbie. Both are holding a football against her head. The caption reads, 'The boys enjoyed rubbing their balls on Lucie's face.'
Here we go again.
'Er, Lucie. There's something else I need to show you ...'

Friday 19 May
Last night *Big Brother* began its seventh series. There's a lot of pressure on a show like this to keep reinventing itself, to push boundaries

and to shock. It's done all three with one of this year's contestants: Pete Bennett. Pete is 24, lives in Brighton and has battled Tourette's syndrome all his life. High anxiety and stress make his condition worse, causing bouts of mania and hyperactivity. So, as you can imagine, going into a reality TV show watched by millions in front of a live audience would cause a certain amount of high anxiety and it does. As each contestant walks into the house one by one they're confronted by this seemingly out-of-control guy with tics who shouts the word 'Wankers' at them. They're nervous enough already: this you'd think would be enough to send them over the edge. But they deal with this pretty damn well – asking him questions, showing a huge amount of interest in him and his condition and, after a couple of hours in the house (sorry, I just can't break my addiction to live *Big Brother* streaming), he has calmed down and seems to be beginning to enjoy his new life. He is suddenly less manic and there is less swearing.

I don't believe for a second that Endemol have brought Pete into the show to educate people about disability, I'm sure they've done it to get headlines and to provide compelling TV, but they may – just may – be able to open people's eyes a little bit.

Also of interest this year are Nikki, a Veruca Salt-type spoilt little madam, and Grace, a mouthy, posh girl who – based on early evidence – is intent on keeping her head down for the first few weeks.

Wednesday 24 May

Take That have just reformed (minus Robbie) and I spent the evening backstage at their Wembley Arena concert. A substantial part of my adult life has been spent at Take That concerts. When I was editor of *Smash Hits*, Take That were our biggest cover stars and you needed to show your face at their gigs. Over time, though, I began to become a real fan. Their shows were on a bigger scale than any UK pop band before them and were dramatic, exciting, colourful and edgy. Being back here – 12 years on – is fascinating in that not very much has changed. They're escorted around the backstage area by the same security guard that tried to keep our writers out of their dressing rooms in the *Smash Hits* days, the fans are the same ones as before, just more than a decade older and with a babysitter they need to get back by 11 o'clock for.

Jason comes over to talk to us – Jason's a very intense, thought-ful guy. He didn't get much of a chance to sing solos or play on the classic TT records and that still rankles. This is an opportunity for him to come to the fore a bit more. But being a pop star again is taking its toll.

'I'm knackered! I've forgotten how much energy you need for a show like this.'

A grinning Howard comes over to shake hands too.

'A bit less crazy than when I last saw you!' he says.

It is, but only a little. The fans don't camp out outside their homes any more or wait for them at airports with the band's symbol painted on their cheeks because they're that bit older and have families and/or jobs. But they still scream – my God, they scream – and when the band walk through the crowd they get their crotches grabbed and their cheeks kissed as much as ever. Must be bloody awful.

No wonder Howard's smiling so much.

Tuesday 30 May

In this week's issue we're running a story that says Britney and Kevin are about to split. We have very good sources so I've given it a full spread near the front of the magazine.

BRITNEY TO DUMP KEV – FOR GOOD
Star signs divorce papers after
secret meeting with her family

We've heard that her family flew her from New York to LA to sign divorce papers that they had pre-written – they're not that keen on Kevin and think she'd be better off as a single mum.

Tuesday 13 June

Another Britney story this week. We've heard – and run – that Kevin is threatening to lift the lid on their marriage as soon as the divorce is final. At the end of the day we hear that their lawyer – an Irish guy called Paul Tweed – is unhappy with us again. Fired up by the driving story and having seen the divorce coverage, we're now heading for a legal battle with the biggest celebrity in the Western world.

We pick **32** great
bikinis & swimsuits

This week's hottest celebrity news

£1.55 (€3.25 excl ROI: €2.90 Spain & Canary Islands) 24 – 30 June 2006

heat

BRITNEY
BURSTS INTO
TEARS ON US TV

**WORLD
CUP WIVES**
FASHION SPECIAL

COLEEN!

POSH!

CHERYL!

THE OFFICIAL
BIG BROTHER
MAG!

PLUS!
**Glyn's
funniest
moments**

ISSUE 378

EXCLUSIVE
TO HEAT

Their best
**OUTFITS,
BAGS,
SHOES &
SHADES**

THE FALL OF
GRACE

**The FULL behind-the-
scenes story of that
INCREDIBLE eviction**

CHAPTER FOURTEEN
It'll never work

June – September 2006

Wednesday 14 June

Had a big planning meeting with the suits today: this has to be a huge summer for us. *OK* magazine is stronger than ever and we've got to combat them somehow – especially as they have the big celebrity event of the year, the wedding of Cheryl Tweedy and Ashley Cole. I grandly tell Louise that she has nothing to worry about: we'll do a great spoiler for the wedding coverage and we'll really deliver something exceptional on *Big Brother*. Clearly I have no idea what the hell either of those two things mean but it sounds good. Now to work …

Thursday 15 June

Luckily for us, it genuinely is all starting to kick off on *Big Brother*. Grace Adams-Short is this year's hate figure and she's the biggest *Big Brother* baddy so far. Yes, even worse than Nasty Nick. Posh but street-wise, Grace is an unappetising mix of bitchiness and public school head-girl attitude. She's horrible. This week she's up for eviction and we're working late tomorrow night to cover the occasion. Whereas usually we'd run an interview with the evictee, this week we're certain it will be Grace and have concluded, reasonably I think, that no one will want to know what this horrendous woman thinks about anything. Instead we're planning a triumphant 'The Fall Of Grace' cover.

We've done all sorts of covers before: people looking great, people looking awful, people looking thin, people looking fat. We've broken loads of the rules about what works and what doesn't, but this may be one step too far.

We are about to put someone on the cover who NONE of our readers like.

First rule of magazines: only put people on the cover your readers like. It's so obvious it barely needs saying. But we're about to ignore this.

Time to speak to Louise.

'Erm, Louise, there's something you need to know.'

'Right.'

'We're about to put someone on the cover of the magazine who none of our readers like.'

'Fine.'

'You're fine with that?'

'If you feel it's right.'

I love conversations like this. Getting your boss to sign up to something you're about to do means it's two people's fault if it all goes wrong!

Friday 16 June

Another crazy *Big Brother* day.

Our planning for tonight was something else. We had a reporter in the crowd to see the reaction when she came out. We smuggled another into the studio where she was interviewed. Then we had photographers outside the gates taking pictures of the crowd as they arrived.

The security was suffocating. So scared were Channel 4 that something was going to happen because Grace is so hated, they were taking no chances. Everyone was being searched, officials were patrolling the crowds and the banners were so offensive, in many cases, that they had to be checked at the gate – and were, in many cases, being confiscated. The banners are a large part of our coverage – this cover feature was only going to work if the article inside communicated the extent of the crowd's rage towards this woman and their happiness when she's gone.

Our photographer called at six o'clock. Russ took the call.

'They're now confiscating *all* the banners before the crowd get anywhere near the house. He's got nothing.'

'Okay, get him to move way down the road. We need him to reach them before they reach security.'

'They don't want him there. They think that us printing pictures of the banners is incitement.'

'He needs to escape the security guards. And quickly.'

The message is passed on and the photographer moves to a position a quarter of a mile from the actual Big Brother house. Now he's got too much choice. The banners come along thick and fast – their slogans are angry and aggressive.

There's the one with the picture of the Yorkshire Terrier next to the picture of her and the slogan 'Spot The Difference?'

Then there's '16/6/6 (the three sixes are highlighted) The spawn of Satan is out.'

Worst of all, and using her own 'babe' catchphrase against her, is 'Grace babe. The only pig in the city'.

I see the pictures as they come through with Hannah.

'Hannah, the question is this, are our reporters even safe there?'

Jo Hoare, one of our fashion team who managed to get a ticket for tonight's show, has been positioned in the crowd outside the house. She calls in.

'It's really scary. The entire crowd are chanting "Get Grace Out!" Her mum just approached one group of people and screamed, at the top of her voice, "Shut your mouths" at them. Security led her away and she looked like she was about to burst into tears.'

All for a TV show. My fears when I watched that first eviction back in the summer 2000 could well be realised tonight.

I just hope those security guards have done their searches properly.

At 9.22 p.m. it's announced that Grace is being evicted with 87.9 per cent of the eviction vote, the second highest ever. But there's one surprise left – just before leaving, Grace grabs a glass of water and throws it directly in the face of Susie, the woman who put her up for eviction. She then calls Susie a moose and heads up the stairs to the outside world and to boos like I've never heard before.

We worked until two in the morning collecting stories, quotes and pictures and end up with a five-page piece that sums up the madness of the night.

Should I find this so exciting? Should I get a thrill from the aggression, the threat of violence, the angry exchanges? What is this programme doing to me, to us? It's involving – as always – but what are we involved in? How much further can it go?

Friday 14 July

Oh great. Nikki Grahame, the deranged but entertaining *Big Brother* contestant, has been evicted. Without her and Grace it could get very dull indeed.

Isabel Mohan sends me a text as her eviction is announced.

'Oh no! *Big Brother* is over!'

Now that's all we need.

Tuesday 18 July

The Britney legal situation is rumbling on. We have no reason to believe that these two aren't heading for imminent divorce. The only indication they're not is Britney's lawyer, Paul Tweed, who is after blood. Today he's got the UK version of *National Enquirer* to apologise for running a similar story to ours. The apology is pretty full on …

> *In the 5th and 12th June issues of the UK* Enquirer, *we published articles under the headlines 'Britney Marriage Is Over' and 'Britney and Kevin: And Now Their Divorce'.*
>
> *Contrary to what our articles might have suggested, we now accept that their marriage is not over and they are not getting divorced.*
>
> *These allegations are untrue and we now accept Britney's position that the statements are without foundation. We apologise for any distress caused.*

Tweed sees the *National Enquirer* apology as a major scalp – and he gives a triumphant interview to the BBC's website who have gone big on it. This is a 'rare if not unprecedented gesture' he says. 'The couple are very satisfied with the *Enquirer*'s prompt and good faith response.'

The BBC piece runs one chilling line for us.

'Mr Tweed added that legal proceedings were going ahead against a number of other newspapers and magazines.'

They're coming after us. They may take their time but they're certainly coming after us.

Thursday 3 August

A truly shocking story. Last night, during a fashion show in Uruguay, a 22-year-old model called Luisel Ramos collapsed seconds after leaving the catwalk. She died shortly after. Early reports say she died of heart failure while one Latin website is quoting her father as saying that she hadn't eaten for several days.

This event is truly tragic but will also be seen as deeply symbolic. She died at a fashion show. She had been modelling at that fashion show. Someone somewhere decided this woman was fit and able to model last night, despite being so malnourished that she was close to death. Hopefully this will lead to some kind of change in how this industry works.

Monday 14 August

Jonathan Ross is having another trip to a theme park and we've been offered the pictures. Again all the kids will be in them, posing for the cameras on rides, in front of the attractions … unbelievable.

Saturday 19 August

Last night Pete Bennett won *Big Brother* and it's big news. Although the constant swearing was shocking at first, after a while we got used to him. Then we all fell in love with him and a sweet (but mismatched) romance with mad Nikki took his fame to another level. When she was evicted he was distraught – and people saw the sweet, sensitive side of the manic guy who shouted 'WANKERS!' every few minutes.

We were in the office until three last night putting together our coverage. But while the rest of the team can have a lie-in I was on the phone from early this morning to Pete and Nikki's agent trying to do a deal for the first joint interview.

The whole world of *Big Brother* contestants and agents is fascinating. Since Helen and Paul in series two, *Big Brother* housemates have been big business. Agents aren't interested in them because they're going to be the next big Saturday night TV presenter or end up doing the Radio 1 breakfast show one day: they're interested in them because that week (and, if they're lucky, the next week too) our readers want to read about them. Magazines will pay large amounts of money for the exclusives and agents can help them get that money.

For the agents this is a way to make a quick buck – and some will be pleasantly surprised that the housemates stay famous for longer than just a few weeks.

So, last night, as usual, various agents contacted Channel 4 to let them know who they were interested in. Then, this morning, after a few hours' sleep, the finalists met with the agents one by one. It's a fascinating process – the housemates wait in their room or in their hotel's restaurant and the agents come in one at a time to flatter them, tell them which magazines they have good links with and generally promise them the world. Clever housemates see through the last part, realise that their fame will probably be just fleeting and sign with whoever can get them the best deals now.

Pete – wisely – likes the look of John Noel Management and signs with them. John Noel Management have a long-held connection to *Big Brother*. Davina McCall, Dermot O'Leary and Russell Brand (all *BB* presenters) are on their roster and many ex-housemates from Helen and Paul onwards have signed with them. JNM tend to have plans for housemates above and beyond the mag-deal money – and will stick with a client long-term or as long as both feel the situation is working out.

The other advantage for Pete in going with John Noel Management is that they've already signed Nikki, so will be able to negotiate joint deals, unencumbered by different agents.

I've put myself in charge of the negotiations for *Heat*. We have one huge problem: *OK* magazine. They'll have way more money than us.

At 10.30 a.m. I put in my first call to Katherine Lister, John Noel's brilliant in-house press-liaison person. Now the bidding will begin and I'm hoping that it will start quite low. It doesn't.

'Katherine! Look what we have to offer, we're a cool magazine, the pictures will look great and in *OK* they'd look cheesy.'

I flick through that day's edition of the *Sun* as we're talking.

'I'm looking at pictures of him now. We need to play down this over-the-top persona, we know that at heart he's a sensitive, thoughtful bloke. Let's get that across.'

I flick to the next page, a piece about an ex-*Big Brother* contestant called Chantelle who's getting married next Friday. 'Oh. And I tell you another reason why you have to go with us. *OK* have got the Preston and Chantelle wedding for next week's cover. They don't even want Pete and Nikki.'

'Silence.

'They do. They're fine to hold it for a week or just do it inside and not have it on their cover.'

'So you're prepared for your big new signings to do a deal where they won't be the cover? Come on, go with us.'

'Okay, we'll do it with you.'

She wanted to all along, of course, but she (and John, one of the sharpest managers around) will have had a set idea of the amount we should pay. And I've paid it.

Katherine knows that covers are all that matters and we'll do this well.

Monday 21 August

It's 10 a.m. and the contract is sitting on my desk. Louise isn't in today so I call her.

'We're paying quite a lot for this – are you sure it will sell?' She asks me.

'Yes.'

'Lots and lots of copies?'

'Yes.'

'Over 700,000 copies?'

'Yes … No! We've never had an issue that sells over 700,000!'

'Not until this one.'

Oh, the irony. Seven years ago we were battling to sell 100,000. Now it's 700,000 that's in our sights.

This afternoon we convened a visual meeting and decided to base the shoot on some classic, iconic celebrity images. There's a great one of John and Yoko, sprawled across the floor, one of Sarah Jessica Parker sitting on the lap of Chris Noth (Big, from *Sex And The City*) and, best of all, an amazing Liam and Patsy shot with her kissing his cheek as he looks into the lens. This is the one we have in mind for the cover. We shoot on Wednesday.

Thursday 24 August

The team have done a great job and the pictures look exactly how we wanted them to. Pete and Nikki seem so into each other, and the cover shot – Pete looking straight ahead, Nikki cupping his face and kissing his left cheek – proves just how much Nikki adores him. She's properly hooked. Him? We'll see. There's one odd shot in the set – the two of them are leaning against a wall in a classic, attitude-heavy rock 'n' roll pose. But for the shot Pete has purposely hitched his T-shirt up and hooked it into his belt so the camera can clearly see the plastic cherries stuck on to the front of the belt. It doesn't ruin the shot but is noticeable – we're happy with it going in, but it makes you wonder what it is about this belt that makes him so proud of it.

I've cleared the whole cover below the logo for the story and really built up an iconic feel with the coverlines – they may just be ex-*Big Brother* housemates, but this week they're the most famous people in Britain, so we won't do this half-heartedly.

> **Pete: 'People tell me it won't work.**
> **I just think, "Oh shut up"'**
> **Nikki: 'I can't argue with him.**
> **He makes me feel calm'**
> **WORLD EXCLUSIVE**
> **PETE & NIKKI**
> **Their only joint interview**
> **Their only joint photoshoot**

Yep, the World Exclusive bit is back. They'll be cacking themselves with excitement in Papua New Guinea. And this time, Louise doesn't even question it.

'700,000 here we come,' she says.

She's usually right, but this time she may be being a little over-optimistic.

Tuesday 29 August

Hannah Perry has built up a really good relationship with Pete's mum, Anne. We're going to need a stream of Pete and Nikki stories over the next few weeks and, with limited resources (thanks to our over-spending), we need to use every contact we can.

But we may not need any other contacts.

It's becoming apparent that Pete tells his mum everything. And I mean everything.

It's 11 a.m. and it's time for the weekly news meeting, a day late because of the bank holiday weekend.

Hannah handed out her list of potential stories.

'Right, Hannah, off you go.'

'Okay, first story, Pete and Nikki have had sex ...'

'I beg your pardon?'

'They had sex. On Saturday night.'

'How do we *know* this?'

'His mum told me.'

I look around the room.

I see a mixture of bewilderment and utter amusement.

'He tells his mum every time he has sex?'

Hannah looks through her notes.

'I'm not sure about every time but he has this time.'

Good God.

Just before leaving the office for the day I sketched out how the cover will look. All of the area above the logo (a 2 by 12-inch space) is filled with the words ...

EXCLUSIVE!
Pete & Nikki
'We've done it! We've had sex!'

That's a new one.

Friday 1 September

Early sales came in for the first Pete and Nikki cover today. It was huge. And, as always, Louise's prediction came true. Not only will it be above 700,000: it could be as high as 720,000.

'Hannah!' I shout across the office. 'We need more Pete and Nikki stories!'

Friday 8 September

Hannah Perry truly is the first with all the news.

'Pete's had enough of Nikki and he's going to dump her this weekend.'

'Great. Let's run it!'

Hannah gives me her best 'Are you stupid?' look.

'No! He's got to do it first.'

'Oh right, of course … erm, Hannah?'

'Yeah?'

'She has no idea?'

'No.'

'And you do?'

'Yep.'

WHY DOESN'T LINDSAY LOHAN WEAR KNICKERS?

POSH EXCLUSIVE!
'David's better-looking than me'

This week's hottest celebrity news

£1.65 (€3.30 excl ROI, €2.90 Spain & Canary Islands) 23 – 29 September 2006

heat

You know it, baby!

HIS ONLY INTERVIEW

Pete: 'Why I finished with Nikki'

'THE REAL REASON WE'VE SPLIT'

'HOW I ENDED IT – FOR GOOD'

PLUS! NIKKI'S REACTION TO THE SHOCK NEWS

ISSUE 391
3.8

CHAPTER FIFTEEN
Poor poor Nikki

September – October 2006

Monday 11 September

'What do you mean he hasn't finished with her?'

'He said he just couldn't do it.'

Is it wrong to be selfish at times like these? Is it wrong to suddenly pipe up and say the words, 'Hannah, that's all well and good but we don't have a cover this week until he does.'

Oh, sod it.

'Hannah, that's all well and good but we don't have a cover this week until he does!'

'Pardon?'

'Nothing.'

So there I was, over the weekend, thinking that this week would be a breeze. A doddle. No cover to prepare because Pete would finish with Nikki, then tell us all about it, then it would sell in huge numbers and we could all go home early.

'He might do it tonight, apparently.'

'How sure? 50–50?'

'About that. I think he's scared of her!'

Well, you would be. Nikki thinks she's met her Prince Charming here: she's going to be heartbroken.

She's had a rotten life has Nikki. She's suffered from anorexia since she was eight and spent several years in and out of institutions – she'd put on weight when she was in there then lose it all again once she'd left so would have to be re-admitted. Between the ages of eight and 15 she attempted suicide twice. Then, on Boxing Day nine years ago, Nikki's mum received a phone call that said Nikki, at that point in hospital and weighing less than five stone, could have just 15 minutes to live.

She pulled through and from age 16 onwards she began to get healthier and less insular. She made new friends, went to college and then became a TV star on *Big Brother*. And now this.

What effect will tonight (or whenever he does it) have on her life? What happens next?

Tuesday 12 September
Guess what? He's not done it ...

Wednesday 13 September
Pete finished with Nikki in a phone call last night.

'He's done it!' says Hannah as I arrive at work.

Thursday 14 September
We've signed Pete up for an exclusive interview and photoshoot tomorrow morning. The cost is high but this is a proper exclusive.

Friday 15 September
Time was getting tight on this week's issue so Hannah had to do the interview first thing this morning. Pete is clearly traumatised, either at the scale of what he's just gone and done or the fact that he's now agreed to talk about it.

The weird thing about the interview, of course, is that we kind of know what he's going to say. Because we've been finding out about it as the days have gone on, we know loads about he feels about Nikki, the relationship and the split – way more than poor old Nikki does, certainly. But here is his chance to fill in the gaps.

It's a good interview: Pete is very open with Hannah. Over the weeks it's pretty obvious that the fairytale story they'd both hoped for just wasn't going to happen. Pete said Nikki had been rude to his friends, he didn't like how she treated a waiter in a restaurant they went to together and how her stroppy TV persona wasn't an act. The pair had appeared on Jonathan Ross's chat show together and Nikki was upset by the way Pete had spoken about her on the show (although he can't remember saying much at all). When they got home they had a huge row. Nikki said Pete wasn't a good boyfriend and didn't pay her enough attention. At that point he decided that was it. The gap between now and then was the time it took to pluck up the necessary courage to do the deed (this bit we certainly knew). In the end he did it on Wednesday night on the phone: 'I didn't want to do it face to face because I didn't know how she'd be – when I'm with her, I'm quite weak. I told her I thought it would be better to be just friends.'

Nikki took it as well as she could, it seems. 'She was really calm and said she didn't want to put any pressure on me and that she'd always be there for me. She was really nice about it and she didn't cry.'

I know it will be a fascinating story for our readers and yet again we clear the whole space beneath the logo for it.

HIS ONLY INTERVIEW
Pete: 'Why I Finished With Nikki'
'THE REAL REASON WE'VE SPLIT'
'HOW I ENDED IT – FOR GOOD'

That night I go home and think a lot about the piece. On TV Nikki doesn't look fragile – quite the opposite. She's loud and confident, possibly too confident. But her background indicates she is very fragile. And we're about to go into print with revelations that could deeply affect her.

By midnight I've convinced myself we're doing the right thing: it's a fantastic story, if we didn't do it someone else would and a break-up is a break-up. It's crap whether two people know about it or two million. I'm reassured by the back-up she has in her life – a close family, a good management team – and this makes me happier about running it. But still, it's another example of the ways magazines like us can affect people's lives.

Monday 18 September

Met up with Gary Barlow for the first time in nearly ten years. So much of my twenties was spent at *Smash Hits*, a lot of it interviewing the band or watching them in concert or (on one memorable occasion) being refused interview access and booking myself into the same hotel as them so I could follow them around for the day. There's no stalking today – Barlow has just been given a huge advance by a publisher for a book and as part of the deal he has to do interviews. *Heat* are one of a chosen few.

On the way over I thought about how weird it would be to see him again, about how great the difference between him then and him now would be. But no, he seemed exactly the same – affable enough but keen to maintain his distance. Awkward in his role as a famous person. The interesting story, of course, is what happened between our last two meetings and I'll try to put as much of that in my piece as I can.

When everything fell apart post-Take That, Gary – always a big eater – found solace in food.

'I thought, "Well, no one needs to see me now, so I can eat what I like."'

He'd also – at his lowest point – smoked 15 spliffs a day, well, 14½ because 'I'd usually save half of the last one to smoke the next morning before I got out of bed.'

Everything fell apart, except, he says, his relationship (he's been married for seven years to Dawn, a dancer) which was unaffected by all his troubles. I'm not sure I totally believe this bit, but if so that makes them the most resilient, adaptable couple in Christendom. Which they may well be. Anyway, they're certainly still together now, have two young children and he's made it through a period that would finish many people off. Take That are huge again – I couldn't be happier for him, but still don't feel I really know the guy even after all our meetings.

Tuesday 19 September
The Pete cover is out and there's already a backlash.

Throughout the day Clare Hepworth, my acting Editorial Assistant, has been keeping me supplied with readers' letters. They're not great reading for Pete.

Pete's been very harsh about Nikki. I think they are both insecure people, which he knows, but he still chose to run her down in his interview. Couldn't he have been kinder and not mentioned all the awful things Nikki had said and done? I am shocked at Pete's

shallowness. I never thought he would be so narrow-minded as to speak like that about someone he cared for.
Sa, by email

I have to say I'm very disappointed in the way Pete handled his split from Nikki. Over the phone! Not very manly.
Laura, Co. Wicklow

Wednesday 20 September

The evening news is reporting that Richard Hammond, the *Top Gear* presenter, has had a near-fatal accident after a driving stunt went wrong. Hammond was attempting to beat the UK land speed record in a jet-powered car when a tyre blew and the car flipped into the air. His condition is critical, but the doctors believe that the fact he regained consciousness so soon after the accident is a good sign.

Thursday 21 September

Dan managed to doorstep Nikki today. She's not saying very much – understandably – but he did get a couple of lines out of her. Everything in Nikki's life is dramatic but today we'll allow her a few overdramatic moments. 'I'm distraught and destroyed,' she announced outside her flat. 'I can't believe he couldn't tell me the reasons why he wanted to finish with me.'

Pete clearly gave her a soft-soap explanation for why they were through on the phone and it's only through reading our magazine that she found out the real reasons why. Heartbreaking for her, an incredible exclusive for us.

Her mother (and best friend) Sue is even more direct.

'She's too good for him, far too good for him. Let him go back to his smelly friends. Anyway, I've heard that he's got someone else.'

Indeed he has. Thanks to Pete's mum (again) we know he's going out with a girl called Cherry who he met before *Big Brother* and dated briefly before she broke his heart. Because he was pining for her throughout *Big Brother* – and after – he would often wear something to show the world he was thinking of her – a plastic belt with cherries on.

It's hard not to be cynical about Bennett's motives. This now looks like a planned operation by him and his mum to get as much money in as short a time as possible. Maybe I'm in a minority here but I do believe the relationship with Nikki was real. He was holding a torch for this girl Cherry, but in a lovelorn way, an I'm-still-thinking-of-her-but-it-will-never-happen-between-us type way. But certainly there is now a huge difference between the early days of *Big Brother* (where ex-housemates didn't earn much or if they did it went straight to charity) and the vast sums at play now. And with money at stake, I guess, people can become a lot smarter and more strategic than most people are. And that goes for their mums too …

Friday 29 September

Today we interviewed Kerry Katona for the first time since she told us she didn't take drugs. Since then she's admitted that she does, and has done for years – coincidentally this revelation came out when she had a book to promote. Strange that. For Lucie Cave – five feet tall, but fearless – this is a chance to question her about her denial.

Lucie is properly, genuinely annoyed on the readers' behalf. We were lied to, and we happily printed the lie (because we trusted Kerry) which means that now *we* look like idiots. We need to confront her because we need to show our readers that we weren't happy about being lied to. If we don't confront her about it how can they trust us in the future? After all, it was the readers she was lying to at the end of the day.

When Lucie arrived at the shoot she saw a very different Katona to the bubbly, anarchic motormouth who won *I'm A Celebrity, Get Me Out Of Here!* Here was a woman who seemed beaten down by life: pregnant (for a third time) with a child fathered by an ex-minicab driver called Mark Croft ('ex' because he doesn't appear to have done as much minicab-driving since moving in with Kerry). He was at the shoot – following Kerry around, sitting in on the interview and even interrupting at points. But that wasn't the worst thing he did. The worst thing he did was to ask Bronagh, formerly my PA, now part of the fashion team, to go and fetch him some food. Bad move. I know what Bronagh's like. He's lucky she didn't lamp him.

When the time comes for the interview itself, despite Lucie's best efforts, she and Kerry aren't alone. Mark is there and an agent is in tow too. But she won't be put off from asking what she needs to ask …

Lucie asks Kerry why she lied.

'Why am I going to tell you when I can't even admit I have a problem to myself?'

'But,' Lucie suggests, 'people now think you denied it to save the story for the book.'

'I hadn't decided to say anything then.'

Lucie persists: but you were asked outright and you still lied.

'My heart was racing. If that interview had been face to face you would have been able to tell. When I put the phone down, I thought, "Why are you lying?" But at the time I didn't even know I had a problem with drugs, so why am I going to tell someone else I have?'

Are we being too cynical here? It wouldn't be surprising if we were. The *Heat* team are not a cynical lot – we love the world we cover; we glory in it. But increasingly I'm seeing a lot of game-playing in our world – game-playing that is being initiated for one reason: money. It's so widespread that it's difficult to take anything at face value or believe what we're told. I'm seeing it in lots of different circumstances: there's the *Big Brother* contestant who knows not to give anything away at the post-eviction press conference for fear of scuppering a big money exclusive deal. Often we're warned off certain topics when we're interviewing Jordan (for free) as she promotes her latest range only to see her talk about them (for cash) in the next week's *OK*. Then there's the confessional book, where suddenly people remember that, oh yes, they did take drugs. We have to fight against this. We have to keep asking the tough questions and get them answered. But there's going to be more of this 'only doing it for the cash' approach and I'm already seeing some of our access disappear and the quality of it being reduced. The stars, the agents are getting too clever. And if some of them – not all – had their way we'd just get the scraps.

Lucie's Kerry piece ends with Katona getting dressed for the shoot and talking aloud as she looks at herself in the mirror.

'Look at me – I'm 26, divorced, got two kids, a stepchild and I'm pregnant again ...'

Luckily, she then laughs.

Monday 9 October

Britney's lawyers are back on our case. It was only a matter of time. They want an apology in the next edition clearly stating – twice, for some reason – that the allegations that the marriage is over are untrue and for this to appear in a prominent part of the magazine. (They'll get it at the bottom of the letters page and like it!)

Thursday 12 October

We've written back, letting them know that – reluctantly – we will print the apology in our next issue if that's what they insist.

Monday 16 October

Nothing back from Britney's lawyers. They've now missed the issue their apology was due to go into and it will have to go into the next one.

Wednesday 18 October

Still nothing from Camp Britney. That's another issue they've missed going into. What is going on? We're offering them an apology and a cheque and they won't get back to us.

Wednesday 25 October

A story that Kate Thornton is being dumped as presenter of *The X Factor* has appeared in the *Sun* today and is immediately denied. We interviewed her this evening (at an All Saints gig) and she's not very happy. 'It wasn't nice to see that story. I would've preferred for it not to have run, but I've worked in the press so I know how it works.'

Thornton certainly has worked in the press – formerly a showbiz reporter at the *Mirror*, Kate then went on to edit *Smash Hits* after me. Her stint in charge there was different than mine to say the least – she ruffled lots of feathers and was a tough, at times autocratic, boss. I know she's a fighter but maybe she has a tendency to fight a little too hard.

Thursday 26 October

The Kate Thornton story won't go away. A source at ITV has told us, 'Kate's only chance of coming back to the show is as a contestant.'

Ouch! Well, that's it, then, she's gone. She's about to be fired. And it seems the one person who doesn't appear to know that is Kate herself.

Tuesday 31 October

Each year, *Heat* is one of the sponsors of the National TV Awards and for our cash we get an area at the after-show party, which we deck out with a different TV-related theme. We then take photos of all the (famous) partygoers in the area which could be anything from a beauty salon to a pub to an *EastEnders*-style market. Tonight the theme was a wedding reception. We got Simon Cowell (as a groom) to pretend to get married to Louis Walsh (more than happy to be the bride), then Pete and Nikki (who are on good-ish terms again it seems) to also pretend to be married. This night proves what I've always hoped (and suspected) – famous people will do anything for *Heat* magazine.

Also there tonight was Kate Thornton. It was brave of her to show up in the midst of all the rumours. The place was swarming with tabloid journalists but she was fortified by two different things:

1. Drink. She's had a couple.
2. Simon Cowell had just given an interview in the press room after collecting the award for *The X Factor* and Kate has, for some reason, interpreted what he said as conclusive proof that she would definitely be doing the next series. He said nothing of the sort, of course, choosing instead to go with a non-conclusive series of statements: 'I have no plans to replace anyone' and 'We haven't even spoken about next year yet.'

Tripping into the *Heat* area she was jubilant. An hour later when I see her again she is less happy, having had to fend off an endless stream of journos less convinced than her that she'll be back for next year's series. It's a bad time to approach her for a chat, but approach her we must.

Time to bring on Daniel Fulvio.

La Fulvio, fast becoming *Heat*'s roving reporter, approaches Thornton (there with her boyfriend, musician and DJ Darren Emerson) but doesn't tell them who he is. He also doesn't declare that he has a tape recorder in his jacket pocket that's going to record every word.

'Kate! How are you dealing with the rumours?'

She sighs.

'There are no rumours any more. Simon clearly stated in the press conference that everything's fine.'

'You must be relieved.'

'Well, I knew everything was fine anyway but ...'

At this point Thornton spies a bright yellow light in Fulvio's jacket pocket.

'Are you taping this?'

'Errr ...'

'You are! You're taping this! Listen, I used to be an editor, I know all about the PCC code, you are not allowed to tape interviews without the other person willingly being interviewed. Call yourself a journalist? Who's your editor? Where are you from?'

'My editor's Mark Frith. I'm from *Heat*.'

'Oh good God, no.'

She's right, of course. We should have let her know at the beginning.

Kate insists Dan hands over the tape. Her boyfriend goes one step further (okay, half a dozen steps further) and threatens to smash the tape recorder and tape. It's a bit of a scene.

Dan beats a hasty retreat.

As he does, Kate's boyfriend gives her a reassuring hug and they wander off to the other side of the party to calm down.

After a short while Darren Emerson decides it's time to take her home and leads her out of the venue to a car.

I stayed until midnight. As cheeky as Dan was, in reality she said nothing other than the same anodyne quotes she'd been giving out all evening so it's unlikely we'd get in trouble if we did print them (and we won't print them, well, not at the moment anyway). He was just doing his job, although, admittedly, pushing it a bit. All right, a lot.

In the cab on the way home I found myself mulling it all over in my mind. We were once the magazine everyone would kill to be in: we now seem to be winding a few of those people (and others) up. In fact, these days, *Heat* seems to do *nothing* but wind people up. Does the world of celebrity hate us that much? As a team we are pushing things more – and I have tough decisions to make every day about how we conduct ourselves. We were right to push Kerry – the readers could make up their own minds when they read what she said. But with Kate we broke a rule and were (quite fairly) given a hard time by her and her boyfriend. Increasingly there are a lot of tough calls to make. This job doesn't get any easier and the moral dilemmas I'm facing now are clearly greater than they ever were before.

CHAPTER SIXTEEN
And it was all going so well
November 2006 – January 2007

Wednesday 1 November

First thing this morning – with the events of the night still fresh in our mind – we told ITV what happened last night. We're important to them, so having one of their key presenters screaming at a writer of ours is bad public relations, however you look at it, but the Kate issue is a sensitive one. Still, they promise we'll get a statement, just for us, tomorrow.

Thursday 2 November

The X Factor's publicist, Ben Webster, sent me the email this morning. It contains the statement and a further note.

'Mark, can I reiterate how sorry Kate is that she's caused any offence. This was not her intention and she wholeheartedly apologises.'

The statement is interesting. Yet again it fails to rule out the possibility that she will leave. There's even talk of 'new shows' – shows other than *The X Factor* …

'Kate is a fantastic presenter and we're in the middle of an incredibly successful third series of *The X Factor*. Her talent in running a major live studio show is unprecedented and we look forward to continuing to work with her – we are already in talks about new shows for 2007. ITV executives have not had any discussions with any agents or talent concerning the presenter role on the next run of *The X Factor*, in fact there have been no detailed discussions about series four at all.'

She's leaving. They may not know who will take over – and may not even, as they state, have had advanced discussions with talent – but make no bones about it, they've decided she's going. Otherwise the statement would say 'We want Kate back – in fact we've just signed her up for another year.' And it doesn't.

Monday 6 November

Dan calls me over first thing.

'Our friend Will Young – he's been at it again.'

Last Friday there was a huge charity event in South Africa called Unite Of The Stars. Our colleagues at *Heat* South Africa – our one and only foreign edition – were pretty taken aback by his diva-like behaviour – banning photographers from using their flash at the event's press conference and refusing to pose with the other stars on the bill. At one point things nearly came to blows when one of the other singers performing at the concert – a guy called Jacques Terre'Blanche – confronted Young in person in the foyer of the Hilton Hotel in Durban and called him an 'arrogant dick' in front of Young's entire entourage.

Monday 13 November

Britney and Kevin are separating. Yep, you heard right. So what the hell was that lawyer stuff all about then? We've had to live with the threat of a major court case for over six bloody months, to find out that our sources were right all along. I'm completely, and justifiably, livid.

Wednesday 15 November

I'm not the only one who's angry about the Britney run-around. Our woes (wasted time, wasted lawyer time and expense) are nothing compared to those of an Irish newspaper called the *Sunday Independent*. They printed similar allegations to us as part of an interview with Spears but Britney's lawyers came after them before us – and they were about to run an apology.

It's very rare for lawyers to go into print with their feelings about court cases – no matter how angry they get, they manage to button it. Not this one. The *Sunday Independent*'s lawyer is a guy called Simon McAleese – he's been defending the newspaper in this case for months: dealing with the letters, replying umpteen times and having all the hassle that comes with that. All that and he's now found out they *are* splitting up.

'She's [Spears] trying to get money,' he told the Irish broadcaster RTE today. 'It was plainly bloody obvious that her marriage was on the rocks when the interview took place. She is a Hollywood airhead.

Why should my clients have to pay for her bubble-headed rubbish? We're fed up. Her gaffe has been blown. It's a shame we're dealing with ludicrous drivel like this as it can be costly.'

Like I say – he's angry. (I especially love the swearing.)

After a brief email correspondence with our lawyer Julian Pike – who knows McAleese and is pretty damn pissed off himself – we have decided not to pursue the Spears camp for all the trouble they've caused us. There's nothing to gain, reckons Julian, and Simon has already said the sort of things we'd like to say.

Today – after so much aggro – I'm just glad it's all over.

Thursday 16 November

Yesterday a Brazilian model called Ana Carolina Reston died at the age of 21. She had been in hospital for three weeks suffering from a kidney malfunction caused by anorexia and bulimia nervosa. Newspaper reports say that in her later life she was living on a diet of just apples and tomatoes. This tragic story has yet again focused attention on the extremes that some models go to to get what is, in their mind, an ideal figure.

Friday 17 November

The ex-newsreader Jan Leeming is currently in *I'm A Celebrity, Get Me Out Of Here!* and today her son has sent me an annoyed email. He works in the office downstairs from the *Heat* team selling advertising and he's demanding to know why we haven't been after him for his story.

> *Hi Mark,*
> *Just thought I'd email you as I'm a bit surprised your journalistic team haven't been in touch with me yet regarding my mother's performance in the jungle ...*
> *If you want one of your guys to speak to me, I'm just downstairs*
> *Cheers, J*

It's not only famous people that enjoy the limelight, it appears – their families do too ...

Monday 27 November

For the last year and a bit Julian Linley has been off working on another project. Today, he's back with plans for a *Heat* website. It's amazing to have him back, he's a bloody genius.

Tuesday 28 November

We've run an interview with Vernon Kay who makes a public appeal (through our magazine!) to other TV presenters *not* to accept *The X Factor* job if offered it – out of loyalty to Kate Thornton.

'It's totally out of order, all this rumour mill stuff about Kate being replaced. I think it's absolutely disgusting. I have not been offered it, no one's mentioned it to me and I hope that no one ever mentions it to anyone else.'

Tuesday 5 December

Rumours are flying around that Mel B is pregnant with Eddie Murphy's baby. In an interview with a Dutch TV show today Murphy has confirmed that she is pregnant. But then, when asked further about their future plans as a couple, Murphy goes on to say that the child may not be his.

'We're not together any more. And I don't know whose child that is, until it comes out and has a blood test. You shouldn't jump to conclusions, sir.'

Love the use of the word 'it'. What an idiot.

Thursday 7 December

Mel B released an angry statement today in response to Eddie Murphy's claims that the child is not actually his.

We get 100 press releases every day into the office. They tend to get thrown in the recycling bin straightaway or passed from desk to desk trying – in vain – to find someone who will be interested in their contents.

Today, though, we all want to read this. It is *brilliant*.

Thursday 7th December
STATEMENT
MELANIE BROWN

I am obviously upset and distressed at some of the comments made by Eddie Murphy to the media. I have no idea why anybody would want to conduct themselves in this kind of manner about such a personal matter in such a public way. My main concern is for the well being of my daughter Phoenix and of course the baby. I was astonished about what Eddie said – there is absolutely no question that Eddie is the father.

Wednesday 3 January 2007

Big Brother is still huge business for magazines like us. Although the main event is still clearly the ever-growing summer run, *Celebrity Big Brother* (which runs for four or so weeks every January) also gives us a decent boost in sales. Tonight the fifth run kicks off – the line-up isn't that promising but we've been tipped off that Jade Goody and family are set to arrive a few days in. This, of course, raises the question of what is and what isn't a celebrity. Is Jade, having been on *Big Brother* already, more of a celebrity than her other co-housemates? It certainly feels like she is. Is her mum? It will all be very interesting.

Tuesday 9 January

It's emerged that poor Harvey, Jordan's son, has been in hospital after suffering severe burns in a domestic accident. 'Harvey got into an empty bath in his clothes and turned the hot tap on, which scalded his leg,' explained Jordan. How or why we don't know. Someone also, in the ensuing panic, tried to pull the trousers off him, removing sections of skin as they did. Jordan's camp is remaining schtum on who was responsible.

Monday 15 January

Celebrity Big Brother is in the news when three housemates (Jade Goody, Danielle Lloyd and Jo O'Meara) aim what appears to be racially motivated abuse at Shilpa Shetty, a Bollywood actress. Events unfolded after a row about chicken – some of the housemates believe Shilpa undercooked it, which caused Jade to be ill. Their attitude towards Shilpa is patronising, antagonistic and at times aggressive. Three white women appearing to gang up on one Asian woman (while the other housemates shamefully decide to not get involved) is uncomfortable viewing.

By the end of the day 200 viewers have complained to either TV watchdog Ofcom or Channel 4.

Tuesday 16 January

Another (bigger) row about the chicken. Jade is shown referring to Shilpa as 'Shilpa Fuckawallah' and 'Shilpa Poppadom'. The row is even more aggressive, yet Jade seems utterly unaware of what she's doing – I watch her on my TV snarling and shouting as though no one would ever witness it. We've started to get an avalanche of emails threatening to boycott *Heat* if we feature any of the three in the magazine.

The row has made its way on to the main television news – during the day we have *Sky News* on permanently on the TV screen above where Boyd and the TV team sit.

At times I just stare at it and wonder what this huge event that now everyone is talking about means for us. When the news channels run out of new stuff to report they get the media commentators and observers in. It's now constant coverage.

Today, every half hour or so, I looked up at the screen to see commentators predicting the end of *Big Brother* and the whole celebrity culture. Our world. Our magazine. My job.

By the end of the day 7,600 complaints have been received by Ofcom and Channel 4.

Wednesday 17 January

Loads more letters, and I've forced myself to read them all. The strength of feeling is unlike anything we've ever experienced. Here's just a selection …

> *Dear Editors,*
>
> *I feel let down that I was a regular subscriber to your magazine that has idolised Jade Goody.*
>
> *Her ill-treatment of Shilpa, and encouragement of Danielle to do the same is reminiscent of her treatment of Sophie, whom she bullied incessantly for no fathomable reason in* Big Brother *five*

years ago. I hope the British press realise that the majority of the public buy their publications in spite of Jade being on the front cover, NOT because of it and shall be most grateful if you distance yourself from this most hated Briton who has brought more shame to the country with her ignorance and nastiness.

In future I will NOT BUY ANY MAGAZINE that has any Jade story on the cover. I will not be wrong to say that my thoughts will be reflected by many of your regular subscribers.

*Yours sincerely, **J Bandyopadhyay***

Dear Sir,

Please note that I am a loyal weekly reader of your magazines (mainly: More, Grazia, Closer *and* Heat*). I have decided that in light of what has gone on in the Big Brother house, I will no longer buy your magazine, if it features any of the three bullies / racists in the house (Jade, Danielle & Jo), on the front cover of your magazine. This is because I do not support this type of behaviour.*

I think that these girls are perfect candidates for the BNP party! They will probably get approached as soon as they come out of the house. Perhaps they are already members?

Many Thanks,

Mrs S McArdle

… and so on. The subject has been raised in the House of Commons and effigies of Jade are being burned on the streets of Patna in Eastern India.

Sky News is barely covering anything else – and the fact that Gordon Brown is over in India at the moment amplifies it all to an even greater extent.

Now every time I look up from my computer screen I see *Sky News* reporting live from India. I can see flames, groups of chanting people, each new bit of footage and each new development convincing me that this whole celebrity thing could be irreparably tainted by this incredible series of events. And there's nothing we can do about it – it's all being played out on this huge scale, out of our hands.

The number of complaints now exceeds 22,000.

Thursday 18 January

The Perfume Shop and Debenhams have both removed Jade's perfume Shh... from their shelves today. There have now been over 45,000 complaints to the two organisations. I have to cover the story everyone's talking about – we're working on an issue where the main coverline is 'The Fall of Jade'.

Friday 19 January

The *Sun*'s front page is 'Evict Face Of Hate' which features pictures of a snarling Jade. She will be evicted tonight – with a record percentage for *Celebrity Big Brother* I'd imagine.

Which leaves me with a yet another dilemma.

Normally, we'd be the first in line to sign up the latest *Big Brother* evictee. But Jade seems to be a no-go area.

For a start, no one likes her any more (and not in the boo-hiss baddie way they didn't like Grace – put simply, they now see Jade as a racist) plus, and this bit is clear, we've been put on notice by our readers that if we run an interview with Jade they will boycott us in large numbers.

So we should steer clear.

Obviously.

So why did I, at 11 a.m. this morning, ask Lucie to put in a call to Jade's agent asking about the possibility of an interview?

Two reasons.

One: The magazine is selling poorly at the moment and we need a sales lift.

Two: It is against my instinct as an editor to put anything on our cover other than the biggest story of the week. This week – and for the foreseeable future – the readers want to read about Jade. No one else. They will also – most of them – want to read an interview with her. They'll want to know why she did what she did, how much she apologises, they'll want to pore over the photos, look into her eyes for signs of remorse and tears. But are we brave enough to do it?

This evening we were due to work until very late to cover Jade's eviction as it happened, but I had a few hours off between the end of work and our night shift. I spent the few hours at the Electric Cinema, in the dark, trying to concentrate on *The Last King Of Scotland*, having paranoid thoughts about what could happen if we *were* to run an interview with Jade. Would our readers boycott us? Would there be protests outside the building? Would my team be safe? Would I – and my family – be safe? Surely these thoughts seem over the top – but tensions are so heightened I've no idea what the reaction will be.

I called Lucie from the car as I headed from Notting Hill into the *Heat* office to prepare for covering the eviction. There's been no three hours off for her; she's been on the phone to Jade's people again and I need an update.

'Obviously they've not spoken to her because she's still in the house but they're going to advise her to do an interview with us. If they suggest it she'll do it. We need to pay her, though.'

'Absolutely not. We can't be seen to pay her.'

'It won't go to her; we'll send it directly to a charity but they want to still believe Jade has some value – and they want a charity to bene-fit from all that's happened. They mentioned 20 grand.'

'Tell them we're keen, because I don't want anyone else to have this. But at the same time, the way I'm feeling now, I'll pull this at the end of the week if it doesn't feel right. Don't tell them that bit.'

'Okay. I'll tell them I've spoken to you and that we definitely want it, yeah?'

'It all depends on how she is in the exit interview, doesn't it? If she shows total remorse and regret we may run this. Anything less than that and we won't. I'll make a final decision tomorrow – what happens tonight will have a big effect on my decision.'

Seven of us watched the eviction in the office and we finished our Fall Of Jade cover story. Jade was evicted last night with a vote of 82 per cent.

When she left she was met by Davina McCall – and no crowd. Channel 4 had rightly concluded that the chances of someone climb-ing over the barrier or throwing something were just too great, and that despite a security presence, it was their only option.

The interview was superb. People often give Davina a hard time for being too soft (she certainly was with Grace) but mostly I think she judges it perfectly. Last night, she got it spot on. Most notable were the exchanges after Jade was shown a montage of her actions over the past week – her screaming and shouting, the abuse towards Shilpa, the front pages and the burning effigies …

Davina: So, what have you got to say, now you've seen that footage of yourself?

Jade: I am not a racist person, but looking at that film I can see why it's had the impact that it's had, because I look like a complete and utter nasty, small ... One of those people that I actually don't like myself. A person that I turn my nose up at.

Davina: What would you say to anyone watching who would say you were a racist?

Jade: That I am not a racist. And I sincerely, with my hand on my heart, apologise to anyone I've offended. That was not meant in the way that it was shown. I meant no actual hate or nasty ... I can't dignify myself in that respect, because that video footage of myself is nasty.

Davina: But this brings me on to [the observation] that it would seem there was bullying going on ...

Jade: The bullying side of things ... again, I wouldn't say I'm a bully. Yes, I am outspoken, as everybody knows. And yeah, I do speak my mind. But the thing with that is, there were two other people who happened to be girls who thought the same, and I happen to get on extremely well with those girls. So we were just talking among ourselves about it. So I can see why it looks like bullying, because we're talking about one particular person.

Davina: I think if you saw it back, it would make you feel uncomfortable too ...

Jade: I'm not sitting here saying that video was great to watch and I feel great about myself as I watch it. I'm a mum, I'm 25 and I've got two children. And in all honesty, I'm disgusted in myself for witnessing what I just saw, because I don't approve of any of my actions. I'm not going to sit here and defend myself. I am sincerely sorry to anyone that I've offended out there and in here.

Davina: Have you learnt anything from this time in the house?

Jade: Yes. I've learnt that just because someone doesn't argue the same way as you and they might not raise their temper as much as you, and they don't say the same things as you do or they might be from a different culture or have had a different life that

doesn't mean they're fake or not genuine. And now I'm embar-
rassed and disgusted with myself.

The issue went to the printers, and with her the main story of what is a very striking cover – *Heat*'s biggest icon, trashed on the front page of the magazine that helped make her.

THE FALL OF JADE
The FULL behind-the-scenes story
of the week that wrecked her career

It's clearly not backing her, clearly highly critical of her, but will these wannabe boycotters care about that? When they say they'll boycott ANYTHING with Jade on the cover, do they means this sort of thing too?

Is this Cameron's rebound fling?

This week's hottest celebrity news

£1.65 3 – 9 February 2007

heat

KERRY'S **HUGE** BABY BUMP!

LEMME OUT!

- **"Yes, I have had death threats"**
- **"I've put my kids in terrible danger"**
- **"I'll stack shelves for a living"**

JADE RECEIVED NO PAYMENT FOR THIS INTERVIEW

JADE

THE MOST SHOCKING CELEBRITY INTERVIEW YOU WILL EVER READ

CHAPTER SEVENTEEN
Risking it all for Jade

January – April 2007

Saturday 20 January

We were in the office until 1.30 a.m. last night and I think we've dealt with a difficult situation well – it's a good piece. I bought a photocopy home with me and I've been reading it again. It's too late to change anything but I just want to go through it once more, quietly, away from all the madness.

Received a phone call from Lucie at about half three this afternoon. Jade has just called her but made Lucie promise she doesn't tell anyone (including her agent) that she'd called. Lucie decides telling me doesn't count – it has some kind of logic and anyway, face it, the chances of Lucie not calling me to tell me are nil. The two know each other well but Lucie is shocked by how Jade is.

'Didn't sound like her. He voice was quiet – and Jade is never quiet – really hesitant.'

'What did she say?'

'That she was in a hotel and no one had found her there yet, but that they were going to have to move to another one this evening when it's dark.'

Her speech, Lucie said, was painfully slow and filled with utter paranoia – she can't go back to her house because photographers are outside. She's also heard from a relative that someone has smashed windows there. She's received hate mail at her home, is getting abusive text messages and phone calls. It's not safe to see her kids and she has to go to a different hotel every night for the foreseeable future. But many hotels won't even let her stay. The ones that do prefer it if she enters and leaves by a back door – they say it's for her own safety and to avoid too much attention (she agrees with that) but

I can't help thinking that this is good for them too – who wants the world to know that you've got Jade Goody staying with you?

Monday 22 January

Meet with all the senior members of my team one by one to decide whether we should run an interview with Jade. All but one (my deputy Jo) say yes. Jo was the first person I spoke to and thinks it's the wrong thing to do. She feels very strongly about it.

As Editor I have a huge dilemma – do I not feature the biggest story we have ever had because people are threatening to boycott the magazine? What would be the reaction if we did run this? Obviously the piece we have in mind is highly critical of Jade and her cronies but this correspondence is so militant that – if what they say is correct – they will walk past our cover if we feature her in any way at all. And won't come back. I then talked about it with the rest of the team. Endlessly. They're talking about nothing else so think it's natural to run it on the cover. But I'm left with questions: will we lose thousands of sales? Will the magazine suffer long term?

I've decided that we should take the risk and do the interview. A time and venue are arranged – it's going to be this Thursday. We are paying for it, but every penny is going to charity (management, Jade and *Heat* were in total agreement on this – in fact there was never a chance that wouldn't be the case).

Tuesday 23 January

The cover of *Now* (still our biggest rival for sales) reads 'We All Hate You, Jade'. A pathetic, shameful coverline – it's depressing that some-one feels they have to sink to that level. Jane Ennis even appeared on ITV's *News At Ten* proudly showing it off. Shame on her.

Thursday 25 January

Lucie interviewed Jade today. It's incredible stuff. She told her she doesn't feel she can ever go home because someone smashed her windows. She's scared to walk down the street. Then she told her about she's now got a neighbour going through all her post to weed out the death threats. She's also become addicted to reading posts about herself on Internet message boards: the other day she read one person saying they wanted to beat her up, another said they wanted to glass her. She has a security guard with her 24 hours a day – he sleeps in the room next door. It's the portrait of a life ruined – utterly ruined – by her actions on a reality TV show. Lucie was taken aback by how utterly broken Jade seemed. The members of the picture team who were also there described it as the most depressing shoot they'd been part of. All of them know, though, that it's a great story. *The* story.

Friday 26 January

Despite calls for a ban on size zero models at the forthcoming London Fashion Week which begins in two weeks' time, various papers are this morning reporting that they now *won't* be banned, and that they will leave the decision about who models and who doesn't to the discretion of the individual fashion houses. In the light of what happened with the two models that died last year this is a hopelessly out-of-step decision.

Sunday 28 January

Tonight was the final of *Celebrity Big Brother* – Shilpa won by a huge margin, as expected. To endure the abuse she received from Jade and friends and stick things out was admirable and she acted with immense dignity and people rewarded that with their vote. The whole evening, though, is muted. One of the TV highlights of the year is now a damp squib.

Tuesday 30 January

The Jade interview issue went on sale today. Some of the mail we got as the day progressed is still very critical. Several simply didn't believe our assertion (prominently displayed on the cover) that we didn't pay her a penny. 'Jade and *Heat*,' wrote one, 'you're both liars. She isn't really sorry and you gave her money.'

Others can't even begin to understand how we can be in the same room as her, take her picture, have a conversation with her. They ask me how I sleep at night (badly at the moment, thank you). But the major-ity have sympathy, mainly because of how the situation is affecting the lives of Jade's kids (the mum they don't really care about, but seeing it through the eyes of her innocent children makes them care a lot).

Wednesday 31 January

The *Guardian* get completely the wrong end of the stick and decide that we are paying Jade for the interview. Emap are forced to issue a statement to clarify what we're doing.

'Jade received no payment for this interview. *Heat* is currently looking at a range of charities that will benefit from a substantial but undisclosed donation equivalent to the payment she would have received for such an exclusive interview given the circumstances.'

Monday 5 February

Vogue editor Alexandra Shulman has written a piece for today's *Daily Mail* about London Fashion Week refusing to ban size zero models. Her piece is the most high-profile acceptance yet about the influence images of underweight models like the ones in her magazine have.

'The argument that seeing preternaturally thin models inspires young women to starve themselves in order to emulate these girls is a valid one.'

Yet she's not prepared, it seems, to do much to change that situation.

'Fashion shows and fashion photographs are there to show clothes in their best possible light and to make us dream of them and want to own them. And, annoying as it is, the majority of us feel that clothes look better on slim women. If I started to photograph all our shoots on size 14 women (and remember the camera lies – it piles on the pounds) would everyone want to look like them? I think not.'

Wednesday 7 February

The Jade issue has sold in huge numbers – nearly 650,000. We're triumphant about it – pleased that we covered the story of the day in the right way. This has been tough – but what won out was the simple *Heat* philosophy: it's all about what the readers want. And, this week, they wanted to read about this woman and how her life was in tatters. I do have one lingering thought, though: what if those prospective boycotters followed through with their promise? What if they were regular readers who will never come back? At this stage I just don't know. Today is a good day but the future looks uncertain. The concept of celebrity could well be tainted – and us with it.

Sunday 11 February
Ah, but today is a good day.

This month's *Observer Woman* magazine is a special:

THE 50 MEN WHO REALLY
UNDERSTAND WOMEN

I'm at number 34 below George Clooney, the inventor of the pill and Manolo Blahnik (I know, outrageous! Who, in their right mind, would put me below them?) but ahead of Christian Louboutin, creator of the TV series *Sex And The City*, Darren Star and the world-renowned gynaecologist/obstetrician Yehudi Gordon (whose hospital, St John & St Elizabeth, delivered our son). I love being in the list and know that this gives me bragging rights for, ooh, the rest of my life. Gaby loves it too and proceeds to tell everyone she knows that her boyfriend is a big girl.

Friday 23 February
Received an invite today to a British Society Of Magazine Editors drinks reception at 11 Downing Street in April. Excellent news. Will be fantastic to snoop around the place.

Wednesday 7 March
Hannah calls me this evening with some news.

'Louis Walsh has just called me. I think he's just been fired from *The X Factor*.'

'You think he has?'

'Well, he's definitely going but he's making it sound as though it was his decision.'

'He's bound to isn't he? Was it?'

'Don't know. I know he's got a lot on with Boyzone coming back but at heart he loves that show. He always moans about it but he loves it really.'

'Blimey. Anything else?'

'Oh yeah, Kate's leaving.'

'Tell me something I don't know.'

'Louis has just got off the phone to her. He says she's distraught, absolutely inconsolable.'

Thursday 8 March

Remember where you heard it first ... ITV today confirmed what we'd known for six months. Kate Thornton is leaving *The X Factor*.

The press release comes through just before 4 p.m:

NEW FORMAT AND FACES FOR THE X FACTOR

The next series of the UK's biggest entertainment show, The X Factor, *is to see a number of changes to the format, which includes two new judges, a new presenter, a new category and the age limit lowered.*

After three years with the hugely successful show, Louis Walsh and Kate Thornton will be leaving. Simon Cowell and Sharon Osbourne will be joined by two new names to judge and mentor the pop hopefuls, taking the number on the judging panel to four. The show will also feature a new presenter.

Louis will continue to work with the show managing the acts off air. He said: 'After three incredible years, I have decided to leave The X Factor *to completely focus my energy on my day job as an artist manager. I will be having the busiest year of my career with Westlife, Shayne Ward and the re-launch of Boyzone. I am also looking forward to continuing my work with Simon and* The X Factor *team managing the stars from this year's series.'*

Kate Thornton said: 'Presenting The X Factor *these last three years has been fantastic and I truly believe I have taken the show as far as I can. I wish the new host every success; it will be an experience they will never forget. I'm looking forward to getting stuck in to some new programmes with ITV.'*

Louis is sticking to his 'I wanted to leave' line with us. Hannah spoke to him again this morning and he's so adamant that that's the reason, he almost believes it himself.

'Honestly, for me, I'm glad. I don't want to be on TV any more. I want to relax and enjoy myself.'

Louis also talked more about Kate – how Simon couldn't face calling her and instead asked the show's producer Richard Holloway to do it and how 'Kate really believed Simon when he told her that her job was safe. This was her baby, her show, and now she is going to have to watch someone else do it.'

Thursday 29 March

Dermot O'Leary was today announced as the new presenter of *The X Factor*. He'd turned it down once, but Simon Cowell is a very persuasive man and now he's said yes.

Tuesday 3 April

Today we ran an interview with Vernon Kay. It was conducted before Dermot was named *X Factor* host but after Kate was given the boot. Previously Vernon was very disparaging of all the press talk about Kate possibly being fired. He thought we were making it all up, basically, and called on other presenters not to put themselves up as potential replacements out of loyalty towards Kate. Now he knows that Kate has been let go – and that it wasn't just wild press-invented speculation – he's left with egg on his face. It's almost as if Vernon has just realised that the world is a crueller place than he ever expected.

'I feel for her. I really, really do. I think the way that it's come out and the way that it's made front-page news ... I can only put myself in her shoes and say that if I woke up one morning and got a phone call, then went to the newsagent's and saw that I'd lost my job, I would be absolutely devastated.'

Hannah then put it to him that he'd blamed the press for the speculation – but that we were right all along. (Is an apology too much to expect?)

'It pans out that what we were hearing was true and, like I said, if I put myself in her shoes and I heard that someone else was going to be the new host of *Family Fortunes* [the show that Kay currently presents on Saturday nights on ITV] and I was given a vote of confidence, then I found out it was true, I would be devastated.'

Vernon says he wasn't asked to present the show and would have said no if he had.

'It wouldn't fit in the diary with *Family Fortunes*. It's a great gig – one of the most popular shows in the country. You know, it's a personal choice.' Hmmm.

Wednesday 11 April

Oh, good God, that's the last thing she needs – Kate Moss is now wearing Pete Doherty's engagement ring and last night he introduced her onstage at London's Hackney Empire as 'my beautiful fiancée'.

We're *still* not doing anything about them in *Heat*. The team *still* think I've completely lost it.

Friday 13 April

I'm not superstitious but on days like this it's tempting. It's Friday the 13th and there's more bad news – early figures indicate our latest issue is going to end up selling no more than 450,000 copies, down 200,000 since our *Celebrity Big Brother* high. This time last year we were doing 550,000 a week. Maybe it *is* all over? Maybe Jade and the whole *Big Brother* thing has made people mistrust celebrities, hate them even? If so, where does that leave us?

Saturday 14 April

Oh, great. The *Guardian* have run an interview with Gordon Brown – just nine weeks away from his expected ascension to Prime Minister – on their front page as their main splash. The photo is him looking moodily out to sea in his constituency. The headline does nothing for *my* mood.

Brown: 'Britain has fallen out of love with celebrity'

The interview – on all manner of topics – has chosen to lead on the least weighty of the subjects covered. With commentators wondering whether Brown will throw a Blair-style Cool Britannia bash when Brown makes his way into Number 10, he gives the celebrity industry both barrels: 'I think we're moving from this period when, if you like, celebrity matters. It is a remarkable culture where people appear on television and are famous simply for the act of appearing on television.'

It's hard not to take it personally. My magazine has done more than anyone to usher in this whole 'famous for being famous' culture. I have a stake in it. You could even say my life, earnings and family wholly depend on it. And the next Prime Minister has just said it's all going to end. The last thing we need at the moment – with high sales hard to come by – is a situation where our readers are made to feel bad about being interested in celebrities. I just hope they're all reading some other newspaper today. Coincidentally, I'm due to meet him next week at a meet-and-greet with other editors at 11 Downing Street.

Great. Now he can tell me I'm finished in person.

KERRY

MORE BABY REVELATIONS

■ Bombshell: was she expecting twins?
■ Spotted smoking by *heat* reader only two weeks ago!

This week's hottest celebrity news

£1.65 *ie*£3.30 excl ROI: €2.90 Spain & Canary Islands 6 – 12 October 2007

www.heatworld.com

heat

'CHANELLE AND BILLI HAD SEX!'

THIS WEEK'S HOTTEST RUMOUR!

Making herself sick after meals
CHANTELLE

Bingeing on junk food, booze & drugs
BRITNEY

Downward spiral of diets & surgery
COURTNEY

GET SOME HELP!

ISSUE 444

TROUBLED STARS AT ROCK BOTTOM – CAN ANYONE SAVE THEM?

CHAPTER EIGHTEEN
It's all going wrong

April – November 2007

Thursday 19 April

5.30 p.m. What am I doing? Here I am, in my suit, *the* suit, standing by the office photocopier, photocopying pages from the *Guardian* and shoving them in my pocket. I have decided I'm on a mission: I'm going to go to Downing Street, I'm going to talk to our future PM and I'm going to confront him about this damn interview. I may even have a drink. I am OUT of control.

6.15 p.m. Arrive at Downing Street, go through the security process (suspicious-looking policeman followed by suspicious-looking policeman with an X-ray machine followed by suspicious-looking door-men – hmm, maybe they know I'm going to cause trouble?) and head upstairs. Bump into the lovely Merope Mills, editor of the *Guardian*'s *Weekend* magazine, and invite her to peer into my jacket pocket.

'I have the interview! Look!'

'What exactly are you planning to do with it?'

'I'm going to speak to him about it.'

'Riiight …'

I somehow manage to persuade her to join me at the entrance to the function room facing the stairs, the stairs Gordon Brown is about to walk up. I decide to have a glass of wine.

6.35 p.m. I finish the drink. Feel a bit funny.

6.45 p.m. There's some activity down at the bottom of the stairs and then an entourage moves up the stairs. At the centre is Gordon Brown. And we're ready for him. He walks through the door and Merope and I go straight up to him. I introduce myself.

'Mr Brown, I'm the editor of a celebrity magazine. Apparently we're on our way out.'

The colour drains from his face.

'No, I didn't say that.'

'You did!'

'I don't mean the kind of people you put in your magazine, obviously, I mean these people who are only famous for being on TV'.

'That's who his magazine covers every week!' chips in Merope, helpfully.

Three and a half million celebrity magazines were sold last week, I tell him – people like what we have to offer.

He looks mortified and tries to change the subject.

'Who was on the cover that week then?' he asks.

'Well, er, different people were on different covers ... erm, Victoria Beckham was on a couple of them,' I reply, wondering what the hell he's trying to get at.

'Right ... and how does Jordan sell for you?' asks Brown.

'Er, she sells all right.' (Jesus, I'm talking about Jordan with the man who's two months away from being our Prime Minister!)

He wants to get away. I'm not letting him.

'Would you put Victoria Beckham in that category of celebrities who are famous for doing nothing?' I ask.

'No,' he replies. 'She has her own fashion range. And she does a lot of work for charity ... listen, I'm sorry if I offended you.'

He then turns to talk to Merope who, after a few seconds of conversation, appears to be telling him that he looked 'hot' in his *Guardian* photo.

7 p.m. I decide to leave. In a typical politician way, Gordon Brown has completely contradicted what he said before. He's met someone who might be able to help him one day and he's being nice, whereas actually he thinks we shouldn't exist and that the people we write about are, basically, all idiots.

Friday 20 April

I emailed Merope this morning to compare notes on last night and to tell her that if I ever write my memoirs she'll be in them, mainly because she called Gordon Brown 'hot' to his face.

She replied straightaway. 'Wasn't it great? Incidentally, for the memoirs, I think I said "quite hot" and accidentally put the emphasis on "quite". I told my boyfriend and he was appalled! "Who calls the next Prime Minister 'quite hot'?" he kept saying all night.'

In other news: received a letter today 'From the office of *Who's Who*' telling me that I'm going to be in the next edition. Eh, Gordon, hear that?

Monday 23 April

Today we hear that Jordan's husband Peter Andre was taken into hospital on Saturday, discharged and readmitted on Sunday. It seems quite serious – so serious, in fact, that he had to be carried into the ambulance that took him there the second time – but no one's sure what it is that's wrong with him.

Friday 27 April

Got a press release from Can Associates, the management team for Jordan and Peter Andre.

> *Friday 27 April 2007*
> *Following recent tests on Peter Andre at the East Surrey Hospital, it is believed that Peter is suffering from suspected meningitis.*
> *Peter was admitted last weekend, and at this time we do not have an expected date of discharge. We would ask all the press to respect Peter and Katie's privacy, and to not contact or visit the hospital, and also to allow Katie to continue as normal, and support Peter and the family during this worrying time.*

It's going to be difficult for them to have any kind of privacy. Peter and Jordan don't keep anything private – every thought, revelation or photo opportunity is sold to a magazine or a TV channel in the shape of a fly-on-the-wall TV show. There is no privacy in these people's lives. Everything is sold. The hospital is going to be under siege.

Tuesday 1 May

So much for Jordan's privacy. She's quoted in today's *OK* magazine saying how Peter doesn't even know she's there and that he spends most of his days sleeping or drifting in and out of sleep.

She's managed to find the time to do an interview and photo

session with son Harvey too. 'He's doing brilliantly,' she says. 'On this shoot he was so good we actually had fun. It was just at the end when he wanted his egg sandwich he got a bit grouchy.'

Thursday 3 May

Another press release from Can Associates.

> *Thursday 3 May 2007*
> *Peter Andre has been discharged from East Surrey Hospital this morning.*
> *He now needs to be left alone with his family to recover and we ask that all the press respect Peter and Katie's privacy at this time.*
> *Please do not contact the hospital; any enquiries should be made to Can Associates.*

Friday 4 May

After seven and a half years of tireless service, today was Louise Matthews' last day as my boss. She will be missed. Her deputy Sophie Wybrew-Bond – fresh from huge success looking after *Closer* on a day-to-day basis – now has the thankless task of trying to manage me and keep momentum going at a very difficult time. The celebrity world post-Jade has many difficulties but it's good to know there's someone as good as Sophie going through them with me.

Tuesday 15 May

Twelve days after leaving hospital, Peter Andre has give an exclusive interview to *OK* magazine where he reveals at times he didn't know what day it was and that it was like being in a nightmare.

Amazing stuff.

Now, I know all about magazine deadlines. Most of *OK* will have gone to press last Thursday (10 May), seven days after he was released from hospital. Which means they will have had to do the interview with him at the beginning of last week, just four or five days after leaving hospital. Incredible. The things people will do to get their private exclusive into a magazine.

Friday 18 May

Amy Winehouse married her boyfriend Blake Fielder-Civil this morning at The Shore Club hotel, South Beach, Miami. The couple have been on and off for nearly three years but recently things have got serious. Both are clearly troubled, with a history of drug problems – we're not going to be able to escape hearing about this couple, the papers are just going to love it.

Tuesday 22 May

My birthday. And the launch day of our website, heatworld.com. Julian's done a great job. It's funny, full of character and people are going to love it. Whereas most websites have some kind of 'bing' noise to alert the visitor that a new story has just gone on to the site, Julian decided that was boring and we needed something more 'us'.

We've decided that Bronagh – whose loud, shrill catchphrases have become a feature of the *Heat* office – will record our alerts. Which is why this morning, when visiting the site for the first time, heatworlders will have been regaled by Bronagh shouting the words 'Don't Lie!' or 'Shut Up!' in a booming Cockney accent.

Tuesday 29 May

Jordan's son Harvey is back in hospital after a mirror toppled on him and smashed, cutting him badly. He's had six deep stitches under the skin and a few smaller ones on the surface. 'This year has been a nightmare so far,' says Jordan. 'We'd barely got over Pete and now this. It was an accident but goodness knows what people think.'

Wednesday 30 May

Big Brother kicked off this evening. The show is under a hell of a lot of pressure this summer after what happened at the beginning of the year. Although different in style to *Celebrity Big Brother*, the programme – in all its forms – has been tarnished by the Jade Goody controversy. Tonight's show seems subdued in comparison with others but there's two people in the initial all-female intake who seem very feisty characters. Charley is a mouthy, confrontational south-east London girl who will, I'm pretty sure, be trouble, while Chanelle is a Victoria Beckham obsessive who dresses like her, has her hair styled like her and (most annoyingly of all) performs a ridiculous Posh Spice-style pout and poses just like her as she makes her way into the house this evening. She looks ludicrous. Victoria will be thoroughly amused by her.

Not only is this summer's series make-or-break for the show, it's also crucial to us. Last year, with all the Pete and Nikki drama (and Grace too) we got some huge sales.

This year we need some more big numbers. Summer used to be known as the silly season for newspapers and magazines, but for us May–September is our busiest time. And that's all down to *Big Brother*. Readers can't get enough of the show and particularly the exclusive interviews up for grabs as each leave – so much so that the canny contestants now know not to give away too much at their post-eviction press conference because it could jeopardise their buy-ups. Thank God the show still exists and people still watch it. Without it, we're in big trouble.

Friday 1 June

They're being quite clever this year, the *Big Brother* lot. So far the house has been all-female but now they're gradually adding in blokes, one man at a time. Neat idea. The first bloke is a perfect choice – blond, handsome, a bit sweet and sensitive. Just right. Except for one thing – he's actually semi-famous, being an ex-member of a boy band called Northern Line. He gets a good reaction in the house but has caused consternation with one member of my team.

Jordan Paramor worked at *Smash Hits* with me but stayed for a couple of years after I left. She got to know all the boy bands – one of them in particular, it seems. I get a text from her five minutes after Ziggy makes his entrance into the house.

'Oh dear,' reads her text, 'I've snogged him.'

Tuesday 5 June

Got a text from Gaby this morning while I'm in a very dull financial meeting. It's exciting news: 'Danny can quack!'

Clearly I need to be spending a bit more time at home.

Thursday 7 June

I've been asked by Emap to sit on their weekly executive meeting. Feel very flattered. Editors don't usually get asked on to this kind of forum.

It's big-league stuff – the exec oversees all Emap's London-based magazines. Today my concentration was broken by a text from Boyd telling me that this morning one of the current crop of *Big Brother* contestants, a girl called Emily, has been thrown out for using racist language.

There's been so much apprehension about the new series after what happened in January that this, as I was sitting there in the meeting, felt like the end of the show. In fact, I went into utter panic mode when I should have been concentrating on the meeting: surely this was it? Surely the show, hanging by a thread anyway, is now going to be put out of its misery?

At 11.30 I headed out of the meeting, back to the office and straight over to Boyd's desk.

'Well, that's that then!'

He seems bemused.

'Huh?'

'That's that for *Big Brother*.'

'It's fine. They dealt with it quickly, she's gone already.'

'But after all the *Celebrity Big Brother* stuff! Are you sure?'

'The problem there was how Channel 4 dealt with it all. They just didn't do anything about it quickly enough then. Here they have.'

He's right, of course. But it bemuses me. How many lives does this show have? And how good is it for us as a magazine to be so dependent on one show, a show that could come crashing to the ground at any moment?

Wednesday 20 June

Hannah has spoken to Louis Walsh again today – and he's just told her that he's been offered his *X Factor* job back.

Thursday 21 June

He wasn't lying, Louis definitely is back. He's just given an interview to Radio 1 and he's jubilant. 'I got sacked and I threw all the toys out of the pram,' he said. 'But when they started having auditions, Simon and Sharon were texting me to tell me they missed me. Then I was asked to be part of Simon's appearance on *This Is Your Life*, and he said, "I wish you were back on the show again."'

Louis is replacing his own replacement Brian Friedman, who has now been shunted to some backstage role.

Wednesday 27 June

Tomorrow in London, the Spice Girls will give a press conference to announce the worst-kept secret of the year – they're getting back together for a world tour. And I have decided that there's only one man for an assignment like this: Mr Daniel Fulvio.

It's important, I believe, to be able to put certain things behind you. To get over them, to move on. So what if Dan got into a bit of a ruckus with Kate Thornton? Stuff like that goes on all the time. So what if Dan did gatecrash Cheryl and Ashley's wedding and then find out it wasn't Cheryl and Ashley's wedding at all? It could have happened to anyone.

Anyway, going along to a press conference to ask a question: what's the worst that can happen?

We met up at the end of the day to go through Dan's list of questions, compiled with the help of the rest of the team.

'I was going to ask them what the last argument they had was?'

'Yep, good, not sure whether they'll answer it, but go ahead.'

'Then I was going to ask them if they're sure they want Victoria to sing her solo stuff because I'm worried everyone might walk out.'

'That's funny! Brilliant. Love that one.'

'Then there's one asking what sort of things they'll be wearing onstage.'

'Bit boring that one, you've got better ones.'

'Erm, then there's one asking whether, because they're that bit older and mums now, they think they're going to be too out of shape for all those energetic dance routines now.'

'That's good too'.

We have arranged to reconvene tomorrow morning and think of a couple more. May be pointless – there'll be hundreds of people there, from all over the world; we may not even get a chance to ask anything.

Thursday 28 June

Dan was heading off to the Spice Girls at 10.30 so we didn't have long.

'Right, Dan. You've got the address, we don't want you ending up in the wrong press conference.'

'Ha ha, yes it's fine, I know where I'm going.'

'Thinking about it some more I reckon you've got one shot, if you're lucky. One question at the very most. We've got to go with the best one.'

'Okay, which one do you reckon?'

'Let's do the one about them being out of shape. It's a bit mean but it's good. Call me when you're out of there.'

'Will do.'

I really don't know why I'm excited about the Spice Girls coming back. I didn't like them very much in the first place, really couldn't see what all the fuss was about. But this reunion just feels *very* showbiz, very us. Our readers – average age 25 or 26 – were 15 when they were at their peak so this is a big deal for them. But also, if Dan does his job and gets on well with them we could, I think, become friends with them again. That might help us be a bit less dependent on *Big Brother*.

At just after 1 p.m., the phone rings. It's Dan.

'Mark, it's Dan! I asked the question!'

'That's great news …'

'Yes, and they all shouted at me then …'

He starts cackling at this point.

'… then, Mel B comes offstage, tries to take my shirt off and grabs my arse!'

'You are joking!'

'No! It was brilliant!'

He comes back to the office and I listen to the tape that Dan made of the press conference. He fast forwards to his question and presses play. Loads of it is just whooping and laughter and I can even make out a scuffle between photographers, but I can also hear clearly what is said in the exchange.

'Dan from *Heat* magazine in the UK. Obviously a lot of you are mums and mums-to-be. Are any of you worried that you might be a teensy-weensy bit too unfit to do the routines?'

There is a very noticeable gasp from the audience at this point before Richard E. Grant, who's hosting the press conference, asks the band whether they want to answer the question.

'No,' shouts Posh.

Then you can hear Mel B's broad West Yorkshire accent.

'Get him fired … you don't look very fit yourself, may I add!'

Posh again: 'And you're in the dark! In the light you may be even worse.'

Geri joins in now …

'Take your shirt off!'

Then all five of them start chanting 'Off! Off! Off!'

Dan's laughing away as the tape plays.

'Ooh, ooh, this is the bit where Mel B leaps off the stage and heads for me!'

I can just about make out Dan's voice as he says the words, 'But I haven't waxed my back for ages!'

There's a muffled noise for a few seconds.

'What the hell is happening here?'

'They're pushing me forward to the area in front of the stage. Mel B is tugging at the sides of my shirt and trying to pull it over my head. It's only because I've got my tie on really tight that she's not managed it. Then she grabbed my arse.'

The excitement is just too much. I am a proud, proud editor.

'This is *Heat* magazine's finest moment!' I declare to anyone listening. 'One of our reporters has just been sexually assaulted by a Spice Girl!'

Friday 29 June

Dan's molestation at the hands of Mel B is all over the papers this morning.

'They even threatened to STRIP one reporter who questioned whether they were still fit enough to do their old dance routines,' reported the *Sun*.

Even *The Times* were there:

'The reporter from *Heat* magazine asks if, "as the girls are now mothers", they're "fit enough to dance. Mel B wades into the audience, trying to pull his shirt off, and accuses him of having a "fat back".'

At just after 1 p.m. I get sent another press release from Can Associates.

PRESS RELEASE
Peter Andre and Katie Price are happy to announce the birth of their first daughter.

The baby was born at 8.49 a.m. on 29 June 2007 and weighed 6lb and 13 ounces.

Both Peter and Katie are absolutely over the moon with the new addition to their family and delighted to have a sister for Harvey and Junior – it is a dream come true!

Both Katie and the baby are healthy and happy and will be spending the next few days resting in hospital.

However, we respectfully ask the press to allow them time and space over the coming weeks to get to know their new baby and introduce her to Harvey and Junior.

Again – the privacy line. Incredible. In reality, of course, they will be spending the time getting to know their new baby, introducing her to Harvey and Junior and working out the best backdrops for their highly lucrative first baby pictures.

Wednesday 4 July
Lunch with Simon Cowell today. Never dull. We went to his favourite Italian restaurant just off the King's Road and sat outside because Simon wanted to smoke (favoured brand: Kool, cigarette fact fans!). He always sits outside, probably at exactly the same table. Only today he was in for a shock …

'Mr Cowell, we're sorry but you can't smoke here.'

'But we're outside!'

'Yes, but under an awning. So technically we're inside.'

'You are joking! Are you being serious?'

Now the waiter knows what it must be like to audition for him …

Simon is in a good mood, if a little tetchy about the four-day-old national smoking ban.

He was at the Diana concert at Wembley Stadium at the weekend and was forced to leave the venue and smoke in the car. He was livid – and this little incident hasn't made him any happier.

He's full of excitement about the new series of *The X Factor* – and thinks it could be even bigger than before. Louis has been back on the audition panel for a couple of weeks and he's happy things are back to normal at last.

'I knew after an hour of auditions that it wasn't working out with

Brian. An hour. I snuck out of the auditions, texted Louis and said, "Pack your bags and get up here now." He didn't think I was being serious so ignored me. Now I realise he just wanted us to send him some more texts so he felt more wanted!'

With his main course finished he decided he'd gone without his beloved nicotine for long enough and went outside the front of the restaurant for some speed-smoking (two Kools in eight minutes!), and made it back to the table just in time – it started pouring. Then the rain got even heavier.

I had no jacket and no umbrella so was grateful that he offered me a lift.

This, I decided as I was transported back to my office in a powder blue Rolls-Royce, is the life, a feeling of complete happiness only slightly spoilt by my rummage through the magazines in the pocket at the back of the driver's seat: *Top Gear* (fair enough), *Country Life* (for the property section I'd imagine) and ... *Closer*. Yes, no *Heat*. But, with the rain bucketing it down outside, I realised it was neither the time nor the place to mention it. Another day, maybe ...

Thursday 5 July
Well, thank the Lord for that. Kate Moss and Pete Doherty have now split up 'for good' according to reports. Pictures have emerged of a removal van taking away his stuff – guitars, paintings and even a piano.

Friday 13 July
I love this job!

A letter arrived today from Portakabin Limited ('Quality this time, next time, every time'). It's addressed to Lucie Cave but this is clearly a matter for an editor ...

> *Dear Ms Cave,*
>
> *In an article in* Heat *on 7 July entitled 'Spotted!' the following was stated:*
>
> *'Rhys Ifans announcing to everyone that he was "going for a shit" before entering the Portaloos...'*
>
> *I am writing to point out that 'Portaloo' is a registered trademark, which may only be used to describe buildings manufactured by this company.*

In order to protect our rights to the exclusive use of the mark, we must take active steps to discourage its use as a generic term, and would ask that the attention of your staff be drawn to this letter and they be asked to use the designation 'Portaloo' only in reference to the toilet units of this company.

It is clearly not practicable for you to check whether all reports you receive mentioning 'Portaloo' are in fact referring to genuine Portaloo toilet units. In view of this, may I ask that, in any future cases of this kind, you use the term 'portable toilets' or similar, there can then be no possibility of error.

I do assure you that this is of considerable importance to us and would, therefore, be most grateful for your cooperation in this matter.

Yours sincerely,

Dick Ellershaw

Trademarks Officer

In the hours between receiving this and leaving the office at 5 p.m., this letter has gained cult status in the office mainly for quoting the 'going for a shit' line. And, like any other items of cult status in the *Heat* office it has been sellotaped to the door alongside the pictures of the dwarves, the man with his face covered in thick hair and, for some reason, Dr Fox in the middle of an ice-skating rink.

Tuesday 17 July

Drama. Amy Winehouse is due to play at the Eden Project in Cornwall this evening after two weeks of cancelled gigs, but by the sound of things she might not make it onstage this evening either. The Eden Project is a vast environmental complex with areas replicating tropical rainforests and Californian orchards, and this week it's staging a series of concerts. Sue Hawken, Emap's ex-Managing Director and the person who gave me the editor's job on that fateful day at the end of 1999, is married to one of the guys involved in the venture so we've been getting regular updates from her. Amy's clearly in a bad way with talk of drug problems and other issues but this afternoon she had another problem: no shoes.

Now, I don't know how bad a state you have to be in to lose your shoes but that's what Amy Winehouse did at some point today. So the call went out for some new ballet pumps – size 6 – and various parties went to the local shops and drew a blank. Two hours till show time and Amy has no shoes. No shoes – no show. And it's at this point that Sue stepped in. Her 13-year-old daughter Ellie has a pair of battered pink ballet shoes in Amy's size and is prepared to lend them to her. So, tonight, most of the Hawken family will head off to the Amy Winehouse concert knowing that they saved the day. She may be troubled, she may be drugged up to her eyeballs, but tonight she at least has shoes.

Wednesday 18 July

So, Amy Winehouse played at the Eden Project in Cornwall last night and it didn't go to plan. She spent much of the set in tears, forgot lyrics, hit herself on the head with her microphone before finally storming offstage during her final song, a cover of the Zutons' 'Valerie'. The shoes, though, behaved themselves impeccably.

Tuesday 31 July

Three weeks after she was born, Peter and Jordan announce their baby daughter has a name. And they announce this, naturally, through the pages of *OK* magazine, having held it back for the week when the baby pictures appear.

Friday 3 August

The feud between *Heat* and *OK* has just taken a major turn for the worse.

Tomorrow one of Boyd Hilton's best friends, a TV producer called Dan Baldwin, is getting married to the TV presenter Holly Willoughby. He was invited months ago. Today Boyd has been uninvited.

Someone at the magazine went through the list of guests yesterday, spotted Boyd's name, recognised it from *Heat* magazine and told the now not-very-happy couple that their friend couldn't come to their big day.

That's correct – a bloke who works for a magazine company can tell a man and a woman who are about to get married that their friend can't come to their wedding.

What then hell did he think Boyd was going to do? Bring his own camera and tripod, push the official photographer out of the way and start taking his own photographs?

Dan Baldwin is livid and has told the magazine that Boyd *will* be coming. *OK* are still saying no – Boyd's barred unless he's prepared to sign a contract that, according to the groom's lawyer, will state that he is not allowed to discuss the wedding with anyone, especially not anyone Boyd knows in a work capacity. If he signs it and goes against that, says the lawyer, Boyd could well be sued. Boyd said no, he won't sign a contract. He's now not going to his friend's wedding.

He's angry and Dan, who has spent much of the day before his wedding – the day before his wedding! – trying to sort things out all because someone felt threatened by a journalist going along to his mate's big day, is also angry.

It's flattering they're that threatened by us. *OK* is this huge magazine empire – way bigger than *Heat* will ever be – that throws millions at celebrities for their weddings and the like. The fact that they're concerned enough by us and our TV editor to ban him from one of their weddings is truly something. We've really got to them, to the point where they're playing dirty.

Saturday 4 August

Dan and Holly's wedding took place today without Boyd.

Elsewhere in the world, Eddie Murphy has finally admitted he's the father of Mel B's baby. About bloody time too.

Tuesday 7 August

The Kate Thornton drama is still rumbling on, but now Kate – who hasn't given any interviews since being fired – isn't involved. I don't know enough about Dermot O'Leary and Vernon Kay to know if there's any history between the two of them, but there's something going on we don't know about because the two of them are having a go at each other through the pages of our magazine. Which is fine by us.

Back in April Vernon gave us an interview where he said that despite it being the biggest show in Britain, he'd turn down the presenter role on *The X Factor* if he was offered it. In today's issue, Dermot has a go back.

'There are probably only two people in the country who would turn down that job. Everyone else who says they'd turn it down, they're lying. They've said it to you. It's the biggest show in the country. Unless you're Jonathan Ross or Ant and Dec ... if you say you'd turn it down, you're full of shit.'

That's told Vernon.

Wednesday 8 August

Amy Winehouse has overdosed after bingeing on coke, ketamine, Jack Daniels and various pills. Talk is she's on her way to the Priory.

But that's nothing to the drama we've had today. Victoria Beckham wannabe Chanelle has walked out of *Big Brother* and today we did a shoot with her. She is a nightmare: she doesn't want to wear any of the clothes Bronagh has got in for her, goes into constant sulks and is driving the *Heat* team to distraction. I asked Al Dunne to keep me up to date as the shoot went on.

At 3.15 p.m. I got a text from her. It wasn't great news.

'Jesus Christ, She's crying now! Pics look amazing but she hates them. Fortunately I'm not interested in her opinion, she is a complete idiot.'

Thursday 23 August

Amy Winehouse and her husband Blake had a huge fight at the Sanderson Hotel last night. Huge and bloody. Guests reportedly heard the pair screaming at each other and, at one point, they even chased each other along the hotel's corridors, bleeding. Amy ran outside on three different occasions during the night, much to the happiness of the waiting paparazzi photographers. (Amy Winehouse's recent behaviour has completely changed the life of a pap photographer – whereas before they could knock off at three when the clubs turn out their guests, Winehouse's nocturnal behaviour means they're still working – and still getting dramatic pictures – at five or six in the morning.

The pictures are everywhere. Particularly noticeable are the battered and now bloodstained ballet shoes – all the articles mention them. A quick call confirms my suspicion – the shoes are the very same ones 'lent' to Winehouse just hours before the Eden Project gig. Now they're blood-drenched, unreturnable but part of celebrity history.

I look at these photos and despair. This is a severely damaged young woman who no one appears to be able to help. Yet, somehow, we have to cover this story.

My heart isn't in it. The pictures are awful. I don't believe any of our readers really want to see them. The celebrity world they love is the fun one, not this. We've discarded endless shots – the bloody ones, the ones where she's obviously been self-harming and we're left with not much else. A depressing story, a depressing day.

Saturday 1 September

Big Brother 8 finished last night with a victory for Brian, a childlike gentle giant. Of most interest to us, though, are Ziggy and Chanelle. The two hooked up in the house, he then dumped her, she walked out and last week *Big Brother* organised a brief reconciliation for the two of them. In what was a dull series the machinations of this couple are of considerable interest to our readers. Unfortunately, the pair have different agents so it's an organisational nightmare. I'm at a wedding today but keep dipping out of the reception to speak to Chanelle's agent, a guy called Dave Read who worked with Jordan in her pre-Peter Andre days as her agent and now has a roster of models, ex-*BB* contestants and notorious playboy Calum Best. Read is fine for us to do a joint shoot and is being great to deal with. One down, one to go. Only problem is, I can't speak to Ziggy's agent until tomorrow. The other problem? It's my old friend Darryn Lyons.

Sunday 2 September

What a day.

Big Brother got relatively poor ratings this year but according to our recent sales, and the emails we've been getting, our readers are still interested enough in it to want to read the magazine when it's on the cover. So Chanelle and Ziggy is the cover we want. But nothing – no amount of sales – is worth what I had to go through today.

Lyons called at midday. He was angry. Good start.

'Mark, I hear from Dave Read that you've already done the deal for this shoot.'

I wandered outside into the garden. I don't really want to be raising my voice in front of the family.

'Not true. He's told me Chanelle is up for it but that's all.'

'And have you discussed money?'

'Yes.'

'How much are you paying her?'

'I can't say.'

'You're going to have to say because however much you're paying her Ziggy is getting more.'

This is getting ridiculous already. As well he knows, anyone who does a joint shoot will get equal billing and the same money.

'Call me when you can tell me how much she is getting paid and how much my boy is getting paid.'

Love the 'my boy' bit.

He puts the phone down.

Half an hour later I call him back and tell him how much we'd be prepared to pay Ziggy.

'And how much will she get?'

'The same.'

'Mark – let me tell you something. You are very misguided to treat my client in the same way that you're treating Dave Read's client. You have no idea where my boy is going. If we do this deal I will need your support with everything he does in the future.'

At last we're getting somewhere. My support is utterly meaningless because Ziggy won't do *anything* in the future. He'll get his old job back being the security guy on the door at a West End club if he's lucky. This bit is easy.

'Darryn, Ziggy has *Heat*'s complete support. We will support all his future TV projects.'

'Oh no! Not TV.'

'Right. What then?'

'Mark, we're going to take this all the way.'

'Right.'

'We're taking Ziggy all the way to …'

I clamp the phone tightly to my ear. This will be good.

'… HOLLYWOOD.'

Silence.

'Hollywood?'

Lyons sounds very perturbed by my less-than-enthusiastic reaction.

'Yeah, Hollywood. What's so weird about that?'

'Oh nothing. Darryn, rest assured we'll support Ziggy as he breaks Hollywood.'

'Good man, you've got a deal. We'll sort out the details tomorrow.'

The phone line goes dead.

Thursday 6 September

Just before he becomes the biggest film star in the world, Ziggy (and Chanelle) stopped off at *Heat*'s cover shoot this afternoon. It's a tough one for two good reasons.

1. Last time we did a Chanelle shoot she was a nightmare.
2. We're trying to get them both to go topless and re-enact various classic Calvin Klein poses.

As usual I ask the team to keep me in touch.

At 2.46 p.m. Jordan Paramor sends me a text.

'She's going topless! Yay!'

At 2.48 p.m. she sends me another.

'I don't mean yay because I want to have a look.'

Message understood Jordan.

Well, we got there in the end.

Friday 21 September

This morning I interviewed Chris Moyles for our '*Heat* Interview' slot – the '*Heat* Interview' is the part of the magazine where we ask lots of tough questions over four pages. This is the first time since our huge falling out that we've had a chance to talk about the nose-picking incident of four years ago. It'll be fine. How annoyed can someone be about a set of photos after four years?

Still rather angry it seems.

You got very upset once when *Heat* printed a picture of you picking your nose – what was the problem?

I wasn't picking my nose.

That was the only problem?

That was the problem. It said I was picking my nose and I don't pick my nose. That annoyed me. And it was a libellous article.

It was libellous? In what way?

Because it was a lie!

That doesn't make something libellous!

Okay, it was defamatory. It was one of those big words. I was doing this, look ... (Rubs his index finger up the outside of his left nostril.)

But you ...

(Interrupting) Look, look, look! (Does the same thing again.)

But you having a problem with this ...

(Interrupting) Look, look!

All right! I get the message!

Am I picking my nose?

No.

No. See!

But you see ...

You have to admit that now.

Do you want a public apology?

No, that will do me.

The weird thing is, you pitch yourself as a man of the people, but that makes you sound a bit diva-ish ...

Well, no, it's not that. It's just ... who really wants to be on two pages of a magazine with their finger like that? (Does it again.)

Come on, let's be friends.

We are friends! Jesus Christ, you're so sensitive! Just relax!

I think we're friends again.

Monday 1 October

Britney Spears has been charged over a hit-and-run incident and for driving without a valid licence. This reckless behaviour concerns the Californian authorities so much that they have handed temporary custody of two-year-old Sean Preston and one-year-old Jayden James to their father, Kevin Federline.

Tuesday 2 October

A very timely cover for us this week.

The stories about Amy Winehouse and Britney Spears are so high profile that we need to address them in detail. Last week we commissioned a piece that looked at stars' problems and what they were doing (if anything) to solve them.

We go into Amy's plight in detail inside – but for the cover we go with pictures of Britney, Courtney Love and Chantelle Houghton, one-time *Celebrity Big Brother* contestant.

To our readers this will be a startling, very different cover.

BRITNEY: Bingeing on junk food, booze & drugs
CHANTELLE: Making herself sick after meals
COURTNEY: Downward spiral of diets & surgery
GET SOME HELP!
TROUBLED STARS AT ROCK BOTTOM –
CAN ANYONE SAVE THEM?

I don't like the cover. Nothing wrong with the design or the coverlines: it's just a grim subject.

Tuesday 16 October

As dramatic as our 'Get Some Help' cover was it's done little to help our figures. Sales have been down for a while – up to 10 per cent lower than a year ago in fact. We need to do something about it. And, as that old magazine maxim goes, if sales are down, give away a free gift.

We're going to give away stickers. It's been a pet idea of mine for two years. The readers love anything nostalgic – and stickers are a real reminder of their teen magazine-reading habits. Today we put an email out for ideas. Headlined 'At last! We're doing stickers!' I elicit ideas for slogans, logos, pictures that we should do. I get hundreds of replies and I put together a list. There's 'I'm not on drugs, it's my bipolar medicine' (a reference to Kerry Katona's constant drugs denial), a picture of Jordan's son Harvey with the words 'Harvey wants to eat me' (a reference to the interviews Jordan gives the press about her son's ravenous food intake) and, my favourite, 'Posh, will you f**king smile?' complete with typical Victoria Beckham stony-faced grimace. Then there's a topless picture of David Beckham, cute cats and rabbits, Borat and the Take That logo.

Wednesday 17 October

This week we're aiming to put our seven-year-long feud with Kelly Brook to bed. For good. I've just seen the proof of an interview Kay Ribeiro did with her that's in next week's issue and we've gone completely over the top in our apologising.

Brook is currently a huge hit on *Strictly Come Dancing* and we've decided to read out a poem to her that we've been working on for a few days.

It's a work of utter genius.

There was once a young girl called Kelly,
when Heat *was a new magazine.*
The girl could be seen on the telly
and the mag was occasionally mean.
They said she couldn't present,
which wasn't entirely true.
So it's fair she came to resent,
everything else that we do.
So let's get it out of the way quickly:
We know we commited a sin.
And when you're performing on Strictly,
We totally hope that you win!

When we finished writing it I decided she'd either love it, or think we're taking the piss and fall out with her all over again. Luckily, she loves it.

Thursday 18 October

Finally – after 11½ months – *Heat* seem to be forgiven by Sharon Osbourne over the hair thing. She invites us down to *Parkinson* to spend the evening with her. She's on superb form today: indiscreet, jocular, full of beans. Reminds me how much we love her, how our job would be so much easier if every famous person was like her. She is quite happy to sound off about everything. She loves Parky (and he adores her) but he *hates* her beloved dogs – because, in her words, they 'piss in front of his dressing-room door'. She also loves the goody bags she gets whenever she's on his show (everyone else's are 'crap' apparently, but she gets Mont Blanc pens and travel clocks from him). She gives Piers Morgan a Hitler moustache when she finds a photo of him in the Green Room then complains about how Orlando Bloom – another recent guest – won't stop bothering her asking for a date and that she had to change her number to avoid him. She also tells us she's had botox that very morning (you can still see the bruises). So weird that she'd be happy about admitting all of this but just a year earlier be annoyed when we talked about her hair. They're all mad, of course.

Friday 19 October

Tonight I was a guest on *Strictly Come Dancing: It Takes Two*, the sister show to the ridiculously successful Saturday night extravaganza. A few hours before heading to the studio I discover Kelly Brook will be the other guest. We've never met but I'm sure she'll be completely fine. After all we've just apologised and she liked the apology. She even – and we liked this quote so much we made it the headline – said the words '*Heat* magazine, you're forgiven.'

This could be quite a special moment: I imagine that we will chat, laugh and eventually part amidst hugs, kisses and plans for drinks at SoHo House (New York, of course).

Seeing her in the corridor I seize my opportunity.

'Kelly! Hi, I'm Mark, the editor of *Heat* magazine.'

'Right.'

Not a great start.

'Listen, I know Kay passed on our apologies the other week and I wanted you to know that it was sincere and that we are sorry about what happened.'

'I should hope you are. But frankly this is seven years too late.'

And off she went.

I quickly look around to see if anyone saw that. Coast is clear. Phew. There are some things, I realise, that you can never truly apologise for.

Friday 2 November

Today was the day the stickers went off to the printers.

I'm out of the office when the final selection leave but I'm not too concerned as I've okayed them all weeks ago.

The stickers are due to leave for the printers at midday and Jo calls me about a problem that's arisen just before noon.

'Some of the team have a real problem with the Harvey one. They say people will take offence and we shouldn't do it.'

'Jo, no one will take offence. Everyone knows Jordan is always on the cover of magazines with Harvey and she's always joking about the amount he eats. She goes on about it endlessly.'

'Okay. Al says it will be a nightmare to take it out anyway. She'd have to redesign the whole lot.'

'Jo, we're leaving it in. It'll be fine.'

Posh and Geri's bitch fight!

CELEBS WITHOUT MAKE-UP 10-PAGE SPECIAL!

This week's hottest celebrity news

£1.65 (€3.70 excl ROI, €2.90 Spain & Canary Islands) 1 – 7 December 2007

www.heatworld.com

heat

ISSUE 452

JORDAN SAGGY BOOBS

50 STICKERS FREE INSIDE!

XTINA PREGNANT & BLOATED

LINDSAY CHUNKY THIGHS

Stars who hate their bodies

POSH WILL YOU SMILE?

I'm going to London to buy heat magazine!

Hiro's my hero

CRABS

I STINK

Mum OF THE

SURFER OF THE 2008

Stick them anywhere you fancy!

CHAPTER NINETEEN
A stupid mistake

November – December 2007

Wednesday 14 November

Tonight we had a spy in the front row at the first date of Amy Winehouse's tour and it's grim stuff. Winehouse has been entertaining tabloid readers with her disintegrating life for a few months now, but the reporter has a shocking story to tell. The singer was in a complete state – over the course of an hour and a half the front row was spat at and sworn at. Charming.

Thursday 22 November

Back in the bunker this week. Every year we (Creative Director Al Dunne and myself) have taken time away from the magazine to redesign bits and that's what we're doing this week and next. We find it far easier to do this outside of the office so have relocated to Mappin House (the grungier cousin of our very corporate usual home, Endeavour House) and a small room at the end of the *Mojo* office. It's great to be back among the music magazines even if the weird stuff they play on the office stereo is a little outside my music tastes (Girls Aloud at the moment). I've always got on well with *Mojo*'s editor Phil Alexander: passionate, full of ideas and brilliant at pulling off memorable exclusive cover features. Today I bumped into him in a crowded lift and he told me about the next one they've got planned: Amy Winehouse has blown out huge chunks of her tours so far this year but they've had a journalist on the road with her for some of the bits she did do and they've managed to get an interview with her. Another well-deserved feather in the cap for Phil and, I'd wager, a big seller.

Friday 23 November

More Amy Winehouse drama – it never rains, it pours. Amy's husband Blake is still behind bars this evening and will stay there until well into the New Year. He's been charged with conspiracy to pervert the course of justice for allegedly trying to bribe a pub landlord called James King not to give evidence against him (Blake was accused of assaulting King last summer). This clearly is the best thing for Amy but, naturally, she doesn't see it like that. She was in court this morning as Blake's bail was refused and there was a slight altercation with photographers outside.

Monday 26 November

The new issue is back from the printers. There's still major disquiet about the Harvey sticker in parts of the office and, seeing it there, attached to the middle of the magazine, in my mind too, now. We should have taken it out. It feels all wrong.

At the end of the day I talked to Clare Hepworth, my PA, and the teams's Editorial Assistant. 'There's a chance we may get a couple of calls tomorrow about the Harvey sticker.'

She gave me a classic look, one that says 'have you only just realised that now?'

'Yes, I think you will,' she says.

'So, if you can put them through to the TV room that would be great.'

'Okay, will do.'

The TV Room. The room of doom.

Tuesday 27 November

I spent most of the morning speaking to an ad agency.

The presentation, although essentially a way of getting more business out of them, is also a chance for us to shout about how different *Heat* is to other magazines, how we push things that little bit further. I used the stickers as an example of that.

Back at the office there was an email from Peter Robinson. When I was at *Smash Hits* Peter was the magazine's number one fan – he'd phone me occasionally (mainly to discuss his favourite band, the KLF) and eventually got to write for the magazine. A few years ago he launched his own website about the pop music he loves called Popjustice. He also shares an office with the guy behind Holy Moly, so is party to much of the media and celebrity gossip of the day.

> *Hello Mark,*
>> *Hope you're well.*
>> *Erm … Wasn't sure whether to get in touch re this but I'm on a sort of industry messageboard thing where they've gone mental about the Harvey sticker and are on the verge of going to town –* Times, Guardian, *BBC, one of them's an author whose son is disabled …*
>> *Not sure what feedback you've already had on it but thought I'd try and give you a bit of a heads up that there might be a media shitstorm on the horizon.*
>> *Peter*

Shit.

Unbeknownst to me, *The Times'* Caitlin Moran – a long-time *Heat* subscriber – had been writing about the sticker already this morning on *The Times'* website on her regular parenting blog. In fact, she appears to have peeled the sticker off from the sheet they were attached to, stuck it to a surface in her home, taken a picture of it with her mobile phone and put it on her site.

The headline for her piece is direct: '*Heat* magazine sticker taunts Jordan's disabled kid.'

I look at it again. 'Taunts'? There was no 'taunting' going on. What is she talking about?

Every couple of months Jordan poses with her son, for money, on the cover of magazines. In many of them, often unprompted, she'll talk about his eating habits. She'll joke about them, often, and seems unconcerned about doing so. Our sticker is a reference to those comments – our readers live in a world where they read these interviews, see these comments and no one takes offence.

Until today. Of course, what has happened now is that these stickers have put us outside of that world – the world where we all read the interviews and see Harvey on the magazine covers and get the reference. In the cold light of day this sticker does not wash. It offends people. Big time.

In her editorial Moran is shocked. And Caitlin Moran is not some-one to give in to the simplistic 'I'm shocked by everything' journo approach. In fact I'd guess that very little shocks Caitlin Moran. Today, though, she is.

'Has anyone seen *Heat* magazine today? They're giving away free stickers, one of which is of Harvey Price – Jordan's kid – with "Harvey wants to eat me!" written across it. That's Harvey Price, the four-year-old autistic child with septo-optic dysplasmia and a hormonal growth disorder.'

Moran herself has come under fire recently from her own readers after writing a post asking why Madonna's daughter Lourdes didn't pluck her eyebrows when she really should. This, though, she states, quite rightly, is a whole different thing.

'Obviously after my Madonna's-daughter's-eyebrow thing I realise I'm not probably the most squeaky clean commentator on this issue, but my God. A sticker of a disabled child's face with "Harvey's going to eat you!" written across it? I know *Heat* has long since stopped doing anything except barracking C-list celebrities into body dysmorphia, but even for *Heat*, this is pretty outrageous.'

There's lots of comments below her piece. Although several question Jordan's policy of posing with and talking about Harvey on the cover of magazines, most are shocked and angry.

'Quite apart from its offensiveness, I don't see the point of it. What are they trying to say with this sticker? Is there some joke I'm not getting? I've always felt huge distaste for the way in which Jordan parades her disabled child in celebrity magazines. But this is beyond.'

'On what PLANET could this EVER have been considered a good idea?! Even if (and I struggle to see what …) there's some "awareness raising" good-deed-type mentality (I'm thinking of the "look, it's got everybody talking about disability") behind this, it's still a pretty misguided way to go about it.'

'Really distasteful. definitely calls for a protest, I think.'

At just before one o'clock I went out for lunch with my friend Kath Viner who works at the *Guardian*, thinking it would be nice to have a diversion, to be able to talk about something else other than this.

On the way I left a message with Stuart Higgins. Stuart is in charge of placing our articles and pictures in newspapers in exchange for a hefty plug and, as a former editor of the *Sun*, he is also very useful to me when I need advice in a crisis. (Proof of just how good Stuart can be in a situation like this is the work he did with Kate Moss to improve her image after the *Daily Mirror*'s 'Cocaine Kate' cover.)

Lunch with Kath is ruined by texts and phone calls.

One from Sarah Ewing telling me that the story had just gone on Holy Moly, as I expected it would, and then a phone call from Jo Carnegie to say that *Five Live* and the *Mirror* had been on the phone (we later looked into both of these and discovered that, oddly, the *Mirror* call was a hoax).

'Is everything all right?' asked Kath after the third interruption.

'Fine, fine. The usual stuff.'

I really didn't want to discuss this now.

At two I finished lunch with Kath and decided to walk back to the office rather than get a cab. I wanted to try and think this through.

I called Stuart Higgins again. This time, and despite him being on a conference with another of his clients, he was able to take the call.

From the off, he was direct, to-the-point and just what I needed to hear.

'You'll need to write an apology to Jordan and Peter.'

'Right. Of course.'

'And then make sure you have something you can send out to any media outlets that ask for it.'

'Can you read through them after I've written them? I know the sort of thing I'd like to say but it's going to be helpful for you to see it too.'

Back in the office I shut myself away in the meeting room. Within an hour there's two letters ready to go out – one to the press and one to Peter and Jordan themselves.

First there's the letter to all the press outlets:

Statement from editor of Heat *magazine, Mark Frith:*

Katie Price, her husband Peter Andre and her family are great friends of Heat *magazine and we have had an excellent working relationship over the years.*

We had no intention of offending Katie, Peter or their friends or family in our latest edition and we apologise for any distress caused on this occasion.

I am writing a private letter to them to personally apologise and I regret any distress caused to any of our loyal readers.

Then the one to Jordan:

Dear Katie and Peter,

As you are now undoubtedly aware we have published a sticker in our latest edition showing a photograph of Harvey saying 'Harvey Wants To Eat Me'.

In hindsight this has been an error of judgement on our part and I would like to personally apologise to both of you for any offence or distress caused to you.

I would like to think that we have had a very successful and valuable working relationship over the years, which has been of mutual benefit and I am both grateful and appreciative of the support you have shown Heat.

Again, I would like you to accept my profound and personal apologies for this error and please feel free to call me at your earliest convenience to discuss further any published apology you would wish us to run in our next edition.

Yours sincerely,

Mark Frith

While Stuart is giving the letters the final once-over I took the opportunity to catch up on the Holy Moly story. They are saying I was out of the country when the stickers were decided upon (not true) but that I should carry the can for this (absolutely, as any editor should).

The letters come back okayed by Stuart and we send them out by 4 p.m.

Half an hour later I'm calling Jordan's management from the TV room – my new home. Claire Blake is Jordan's manager and, PR-wise, her contact with the media. I know Blake from her former life as a pop music PR and manager but we weren't particularly close and anyway she's hardly going to show any warmth to me today.

'Claire – I just want to make sure you got the letter we sent you in the office. I wanted to apologise personally for the sticker – it was an error of judgement and we're very sorry.'

'I'll pass that on. What I want to know is who thought this was a good idea? Who came up with it?'

'Claire, I can't go into that. All I'll say is that as I'm the editor, I'm responsible for it going in there and I'm the one who is taking the blame.'

'Jordan was just bemused by it, utterly bemused.'

We have agreed to speak again tomorrow where we'll discuss exactly how we'll apologise in the next issue.

Wednesday 28 November

Rotten night's sleep. But I wake up to a calmer world: none of the tabloid newspapers are reporting the sticker story (either out of loyalty to us or because they're just not interested) and neither are any of the news channels. Could this already be old news?

Just after midday an email pops up from Stuart Higgins: 'It's all quiet on this front.'

But this quieter period at least gave me some time to get on with what I should have been doing – editing a magazine.

Just after lunch Lucie forwards me an email from one of Claire Blake's team, a woman called Carli Davies. Carli works in Claire's office answering the phone and playing an active part in organising Jordan's interviews and press coverage. She knows about most things going on with Jordan. This is the email I least expected to get.

> *To: Lucie Cave*
> *Cc: Jo Carnegie*
> *Subject: Katie Price*
> *Hi Lucie*
> > *Hope you are well!*
> > *I just wanted to see if you were doing a Christmas gift guide or a similar piece in any issues out Dec? It would be great to feature some of Katie's products – we have her new calendar, her haircare electricals range and lingerie. Let me know your thoughts.*
> > *Best Wishes*
> > ***Carli x***

How odd. They're not that pissed off with us then. Sure, they're just after some free plugs but usually in these situations all communication closes down, except for legal letters. The drawbridge comes down, you are *persona non grata*.

But this is friendly, with a kiss at the end from the woman who will surely have been taking all the calls at their end about the stickers. But the email is written as though nothing has happened. Or rather, nothing has happened that would get in the way of their selling machine.

I told Lucie not to bother replying, assuming – fairly, we conclude – that they'd sent it to us by mistake.

Then, just 15 minutes later, a story appears on *Brand Republic* – the online site for industry magazine *Campaign* – that proves this morning really was the calm before the storm. They're reporting that the Press Complaints Commision has already received 30 complaints about the sticker. Thirty is a lot in 24 hours – the number is bound to be increasing all the time.

Here we go again.

Sarah Ewing – who has just seen the story – calls again, in major panic mode this time.

'Have you spoken to Jordan's management today? We need to avoid a PCC complaint from them. Stay close to them and make sure they're as happy as they can possibly be.

At 3.30 I phone Claire Blake again. She still wants to know who came up with the sticker slogan and I repeat that it's my responsibility. She mentions that people have been urging her to complain to the PCC but gives me the impression she won't. She is also keen to discuss the magazine version of the apology and how we'll do it. I tell her that it's completely up to her.

'Claire, you can do this how you want. Either you can have an apology from us or we can print a couple of the letters coming in to the office on the letters page, to show the strength of feeling, and our reply can be us expressing our regret about the sticker. It's completely up to you.'

'Okay. Thank you.'

'Do you want to think about it and call me back in an hour or so?'

She seems distracted and keen to get me off the phone.

'Yes. I'll do that. I've got your number.'

At just before 4 p.m., I call Sarah Ewing again in a triumphant mood.

'Great news. They're not going to the PCC and we're talking about how we do the apology. We've got a good dialogue going and she's calling me back later. She's fine, Sarah, really.'

Oh, what a naive fool I am.

At 4.30 a story appears on the *Media Guardian* website that Jordan is in the process of complaining to the Press Complaints Commision. A PCC spokesperson is quoted in the piece as saying, 'We have received an indication of a formal complaint from representatives of Katie Price and Peter Andre.'

Twenty minutes later a letter arrives by fax from Jordan's lawyers. They're suing us.

The letter is pretty full-on – they require an apology on our website by midday tomorrow and promise to write back to us to discuss what we need to print in the magazine above and beyond that. We were going to do all of this anyway, that's what the conversations with Claire Blake were all leading up to, but clearly they have decided that either we weren't doing it quickly enough or just that they couldn't be bothered dealing with us on the phone and had better things to do (fair enough, can't really blame them).

Within minutes the story that Jordan is suing has gone everywhere.

Thursday 29 November

There are hourly stories on the Radio 1 news this morning about Jordan's complaint. Her move has helped crystallise the story so that it has an angle; it's now more than just a media story.

On my way in, I decided that today, in the *Heat* office, we are going to have an 'iPod day' and I sent an email to the team inviting them to plug their iPods into the stereo and to play anything they want to. What I didn't tell them is that this is my way of avoiding us having to listen to the Harvey story on Radio 1 every hour. This disaster is already so high profile that the last thing we need is it being broadcast at loud volume (we have the volume on our office stereo up VERY, VERY HIGH).

As it's press day I have much to take my mind off things. Approximately 40 pages that need passing for a start. I appreciate the diversion but wonder sometimes if the team think I'm putting some kind of brave face on things as I wander round the office, as chirpy as always, distributing passed pages and looking at photos, headlines and lists for the next issue. The truth is, I'm not. But being able to throw myself into press day genuinely does make me happy, especially as it means that at the moment, when I'm working on the magazine, I'm not dealing with lawyers or media journalists or PCC complaints or apologies. It's a genuine, much-needed relief.

Although we're not listening, it's obvious that Radio 1 are becoming even more obsessed by the story as the day goes on. I know this by the number of emails and phone calls I get from them. Then, thrillingly, one of their reporters turns up in our reception six floors down from where I work. This I've never had before. Despite all the feathers we've ruffled, all the people we've upset, I've never had a journalist turn up to try and get to speak to me. It's all very very weird. Security send her on her way.

Other than that, life goes on in as normal a way as possible. We had a Dermot O'Leary shoot this afternoon, which goes off without a hitch – although I don't think we'll be using the shot of Dermot, happily posing for our cameras wearing the Harvey sticker. He's astonished by the fuss and pummels Boyd for information about it.

His reaction isn't unusual: other journalists are either fascinated or bemused by the drama, often both.

A friend of our Creative Director Al, who works at the *Observer* sends her an email relaying the story of how she tried to put the sticker on the *Observer* fridge 'but the boss caught me and stopped me. Instead I've put it on my Smythson diary.'

I get calls and texts from all sorts of people, many of whom think we're stupid for what we did (they're right) but keen to express sympathy and the hope that I'm all right.

David Davies, former editor of *Heat*, now Emap bigwig, rings me to commiserate, see how I am and share stories of his mistakes when he was an editor (very kind of him, but none of his cock-ups were quite in the same league as this). Ally Oliver, our Art Director's sister-in-law currently working at *Closer*, also sends me a very sweet email telling me that she is thinking of me. That's all in a period of just two or three hours. The messages are constant and much needed.

Then, at half five, an email from my number one fan: Janice Turner, ex of *Press Gazette* now of *The Times*. No one has written more positive editorial about me and about *Heat*.

Janice, it's fair to say, is my number one fan no more.

Hi Mark,

I'm going to be writing about the stickers in my Times *column tomorrow (for Saturday) and would really like to have a chat about what happened and why. Off the record is fine, for background.*

Anyway if you feel like putting your side, please give me a call. I've long been a fan of Heat, *as you know, and have written in praise many times, but there does seem to be a change in the tone of celebrity magazines of late, I would be very interested to hear your take on this.*

All the best

Janice

Her number is at the bottom of the email but I don't call it. What will be, will be I decide. Roll on Saturday. But first I need to get through Friday.

Friday 30 November

The apology is approved and will go into next Tuesday's magazine. The website apology is already on *heatworld* and has been the number one story for the last two days (page impressions on the website are booming because of this story; all week we've had bigger numbers than ever before either from people wanting to read the apology, leave a comment or just see us squirm).

Stuart Higgins, the man who kept me sane at the beginning of the week, came in to see me this morning. Every Friday he and his team plough through the dummy version of the magazine in the hope of finding PR-able photographs and interviews. He's only been looking at it for five minutes before he comes rushing up to me.

'Has this printed yet?'

'They're about to start now.'

'You've got to stop it being printed.'

'What? Why?'

He holds up a page of our 'Week In Pictures' section, a page we put through on Monday before any of the Jordan fuss erupted.

It's a shot of Jordan wearing a tight-fitting dress. Just weeks away from a planned breast-reduction operation, her chest looks huge. The headline?

**JORDAN – IT'S TIME TO GET
THOSE BABIES REDUCED**

'Mark, you have to change this.'

'Really?'

'Really. At the moment if you do anything that makes you look insensitive, anything that makes it look as though you are in some way alluding to what you did or laughing about it, you're in big trouble.'

I stare at the page. It was a page designed in more innocent times, where 'babies' was a euphemism for breasts. Life was so much simpler back then. Not any more.

I speak to the production team.

'To change this at this late stage will cost £20,000.'

'Fine. Do it.'

It's not fine, of course, it's ridiculous. Sophie agrees. But I tell her we have to do this. More expense. It's a good job I've made this company millions and millions of pounds over the last eight years. If this was anyone else making this mistake, someone at a magazine that doesn't make quite as much as mine does, they could well be out on their ear for this. And if this goes in I could still be.

We have ten minutes to change the page. We consider ditching it altogether but that will take too long, so we just change the headline.

**JORDAN – IT'S TIME TO GET
THOSE BABIES REDUCED**

becomes

**JORDAN – IS IT TIME TO GET
THE PUPPIES REDUCED?**

Now, what next?

Another email, sent to Kellie Turner in our Marketing Department from the Deputy Editor of *Disability Now*.

> *Kellie*
>
> *As agreed just now, we are looking for a quote from Emap about the* Heat *stickers. We are aware that Heat has already apologised for the Harvey 'joke', but having just seen them, there is another potentially offensive sticker: 'I'm not on drugs, it's my bipolar medicine.'*
>
> *Granted, it doesn't poke fun at a particular disabled person, but it surely runs the risk of offending a lot of people with mental health problems and exposing them to ridicule and bullying. You might also bear in mind a new MIND survey which found that more than 70 per cent of people with mental health distress had been victimised in the last two years.*
>
> *I'd be grateful if you could let me have a response from the magazine on why the magazine thinks it was appropriate to include these two stickers.*
>
> *Many thanks.*
>
> *Best wishes,*
>
> **John Pring**

Sarah Ewing offers to speak to him and gives him a quote he's happy with.

Then, for me, a much-needed lunchtime walk to help clear my head. I've no idea what the afternoon will hold – this thing seems to be building and building.

The afternoon begins quietly. Stuart Higgins calls me to check that the Jordan headline has been changed and to mention that Radio 1 are sniffing around us again.

A reporter called Frances Cronin from *Newsbeat* has sent him an email that he's about to forward.

'It's coming over to you now.'

I read it straightaway while Stuart is still on the line.

Hi there

I'm writing from Radio 1 Newsbeat regarding Heat magazine. We have heard that this week's issue of the magazine is having to be reprinted without the stickers, can you confirm if this is correct?

Many thanks

Frances

'How odd. It's not true.'

'Okay, I'll let her know.'

Just 15 minutes later he gets another email from her that he forwards to me.

Apologies I had the wrong end of the stick there – it was actually that Jordan has asked for changes to a caption of herself in next week's issue of Heat. They referred to her breasts that are going to be reduced in an op as 'babies' but she asked for it to be changed to 'puppies'.

Can you confirm this?

Many thanks

Frances

In all my time at *Heat* we've not had a single leak. We kept the revelations about Gareth Gates quiet until the day we came on sale. No one knew we'd nicked someone else's Robbie Williams interview until that fateful day the issue came out. We've kept all sorts of revelations, exclusive shoots and scandal under wraps before. Now though, as my whole world falls apart, the thing I thought I could rely on more than any other – the confidentiality of the team involved in getting this magazine on to the news-stands of Britain – has evaporated. We have a mole. But I neither have the time nor the energy to seek them out.

Sometimes I hate this job.

I call Stuart.

'Can you get back to them and say that Jordan hasn't asked for any changes to be made in next week's issue. We're working together on an apology that will be in the magazine but that's it.'

Saturday 1 December

Today's *Times* has Janice Turner's column in it.

It dissects how magazines portray celebrities (and their children), how the way we pay attention to their lives, physique and relationships dehumanises them and dehumanises us, too. She also portrays an (entirely inaccurate) scenario where the entire *Heat* office – cackling manically – conspired to mock Jordan's disabled son. She explains to the *Times* reader, using her 'credibility' as an ex-magazine editor, that the sticker will have been decided upon in a meeting (not true), that at least ten people (she actually quotes the number) in the office will have been party to it happening (not true).

All nonsense, but after the week I've just had, pretty par for the course.

What most surprises me, though, is the headline. It's a goodie.

THE LOWEST POINT IN BRITISH JOURNALISM

In 1989, *The Times'* sister newspaper the *Sun* ran a front page headlined THE TRUTH. The article was about the Hillsborough football disaster and alleged, among other things, that Liverpool fans had picked the pockets of victims as they lay dying on the pitch, urinated on police officers who were trying to help the injured and even assaulted a police officer who was trying to give the kiss of life to one of the victims. The *Sun* had to admit that none of the allegations were true and apologise in the paper – yet they have, even now, never really been forgiven by the people of Liverpool. In fact there are large sections of the city where newsagents refuse to stock it 18 years later. Three years ago the paper's Managing Editor Graham Dudman said that this coverage of the Hillsborough disaster was 'a terrible mistake. It was a terrible, insensitive, horrible article, with a dreadful headline.'

Yet our sticker was, according to the headline on Turner's piece, worse than that.

A big mistake? Undoubtedly.

A misjudgement on my part? Guilty as charged.

The lowest point in British journalism? I don't think so.

Still, the pressure on me is mounting. Although the support for me inside the company has been total, outside the magazine world people are calling for my scalp.

Radio 5 Live's Stephen Nolan hosted a phone-in discussion on his show this evening all about the sticker. I know it's going to be tough on me when he trails it before the news.

'It's been called the lowest point in British journalism. The magazine editor has apologised – but should he still be in a job?'

First up was Piers Hernu, ex-editor of lads' mag *Front* and a contributing editor to *FHM*. He's meant to be on defending me but keeps changing his mind.

'This is a major error of judgement. It's tasteless, it's crass, it's insensitive. But he shouldn't lose his job and he shouldn't resign. In the very competitive magazine world there is a lot of pressure from above to push the boundaries and be controversial.'

Nolan comes back at him.

'Why are you being sympathetic? Why shouldn't he go because of this?'

'I don't think there was any malice in this. Jordan has put Harvey in the public eye. This has backfired on her. If no one knew about Harvey, if he hadn't been on this fly-on-the-wall documentary Mark Frith wouldn't have seen him as fair game.'

And so on. People call for me to be fired, others for a boycott. Just another day in the life of the editor of *Heat* magazine.

Monday 3 December

Today, for some reason, feels like the toughest so far. I guess it's because the weekend offered no respite from the negative press so I haven't had a chance to recharge my batteries. So far I've been able to put a brave face on things. I really don't feel like it today.

We're entering into the final days of production on our Christmas double issue, the most important issue of the year.

As usual the celebs send in cards to us or, if they need a little bit of persuasion, we send one to them which they sign and get back to us.

Today we sent a courier – with a card – to Alesha Dixon, currently competing in *Strictly Come Dancing*.

By mid-afternoon there's still no card. I get Lucie on the case. After half an hour of investigation she drags me into the TV room.

'She refused to sign it.'

'Really? Wow. Because of the Harvey thing?'

Lucie shrugged. This is a whole new situation that I hadn't dared contemplate. What if people don't want to deal with us because of this? What then?

Some better news at the end of the day. Because of our heartfelt (and very public) apology, Jordan's side have withdrawn their PCC complaint.

This sticker was a stupid mistake. A stupid, stupid, stupid mistake. Much of what is being written about Harveygate assumes that what we did was malicious in some way. Not true. But a lot of what was said about us assumed that, and just went on from there. The *Heat* team aren't malicious. But they – and our readers – *do* live in a world where Jordan sells access to her son for cash and where she talks about his huge food intake in a jokey manner. These are our reference points, like them or not.

What we are probably guilty of, and this has to change, is the feeling that we can say whatever we want about whoever we want. The whole 'here's what celebrities are really like' thing was meant to lead to a democratisation of fame: 'They're just like you and me.' Increasingly, however, it has led to some of us (and by that I mean some of my own team, including me) going too far – when you see celebrities as your playthings (as we have for several years, successfully) how much do you play with them?

I have to make 100 different decisions every week. I got this one badly wrong. Whether the magazine is allowed to move on from it, as though nothing has happened, remains to be seen.

CHAPTER TWENTY
Enough
is enough
December 2007 – February 2008

Tuesday 4 December

Counting down the days now until the end of the year.

For the first time ever, this job is HARD WORK. But this morning brings a cheery bit of respite – shockingly, I have a good bit of press.

The *Daily Telegraph* has gone big on the new edition of *Who's Who*. There's a couple of hundred new additions to the book, out this week, and the *Daily Telegraph* have put us all together and formed a theory that we're all part of some group that are shaking up the old guard. Their headline is bold and quite exciting:

Meet The New Establishment

There's Kate Moss, Stella McCartney, TV producer and writer Armando Iannucci, hot new Radio 1 DJ Nihal Arthanayake, fledgling *Newsnight* presenter Emily Maitlis … and me.

The writer Nigel Reynolds seems particularly surprised about the inclusion of Nihal and myself in the list: 'times really do seem to be a changin'' before reminding me that my entry lists my recreations as 'clumsiness, finding things to read in other people's recycling bins and Dostoevsky (not really!)'. It seemed funny at the time. I was going to put '*stealing* things from other people's recycling bins' until Gaby pointed out that such a thing was probably illegal and, anyway, I don't actually steal them, just read them then put them back. I know that's odd, trust me I do.

I didn't realise quite how many people read the *Daily Telegraph* until today – get a lot of congratulations emails and my parents are both properly made-up that I'm in *Who's Who*.

Tuesday 11 December

Email pops up from Sarah Ewing this afternoon. Bound to be bad news I decide.

> From: Sarah Ewing
> To: Mark Frith
> Subject: Mojo?
> Importance: High
> Mark,
> This guy has heard from a good source that you are off to edit MOJO?!
> Sx

Sarah has attached a message to call her from a guy called Ben at the *Media Guardian*. When she did the guy was adamant that I, Britain's number one Girls Aloud fan, am off to edit a magazine that's the spiritual home of Pink Floyd and Led Zeppelin. Utter nonsense but, in terms of press profile, just the kind of story I need out there at the moment after Harveygate.

Sarah dug around a bit more and has traced the *Guardian*'s call to a media website called Madame Arcati that two hours earlier had posted a story that was beginning to attract a few comments.

The story was brief but direct. And utterly wrong.

Mark Frith on the move?
Heat's Mark Frith to edit *Mojo*? Surely not?

As well as being nonsense the story is unfair on Phil – he's an exceptional editor and the last thing he needs is some story undermining his leadership.

Throughout the day the story has gathered pace – other people have called Sarah about it and the guy from the *Guardian* is still claiming it's true (we have patiently explained to him that his 'good source' is Madame Arcati but he's adamant it's true and says that we're lying). I have told the *Heat* team there's no truth in it at all, Phil has done the same with his team. Presumably the story will die overnight.

Wednesday 12 December

The story isn't dead. I *am* off to edit *Mojo*, apparently.

Madame Arcati posts further 'breaking news' this morning.

The story has yet to be confirmed – but my understanding is that Frith wanted to edit *Mojo* and Emap is keen to keep him happy, given his great track record.

It all sounds rather exciting. Here I am desperately trying to think of ideas for our New Year issues (it's not easy putting out a celebrity news-based magazine when there's no celebrity news) when the outside world thinks I'm in high-powered contract negotiations *and* planning a 24-page Joy Division retrospective at the same time.

This means we have to issue yet more denials. Phil and I have talked about this and have come to the conclusion that the conversation in the lift about Amy Winehouse (and maybe the fact that at the end of last month I was redesigning *Heat* in a room near the *Mojo* office) kicked off the rumours. Truly bizarre. But after the nightmare of the past few weeks it's nice to know that *someone* thinks I'm in demand. Even if they are – on this occasion – a complete fantasist.

The alarming thing about this – and Harveygate too – is that I and the team are now the story. We must embrace this and get used to it – it's a side effect of our success. It doesn't get in the way of what we do but it always seems odd. However, we wanted to be THE magazine of the decade and we are – so we need to deal with it, simple as.

Tuesday 1 January 2008

Enjoyed a relaxing (as much as you can relax with a two-year-old) Christmas and New Year. Enjoyed doing nothing. Whether I've recharged my batteries enough remains to be seen.

Friday 4 January

It's our first week back and already the New Year has begun to turn sour.

I got into the office at 9 a.m. this morning to be confronted by two of the darkest, most depressing celebrity stories we've ever been forced to cover.

Firstly, Britney Spears. Over the past few months, *Heat* has covered – with growing horror – the problems in Britney's life. Last night, though, the story moved on to another level and it's uncomfortable stuff.

At 7 p.m. LA time, Spears had been due to return her kids to her ex, Kevin Federline, who has temporary primary custody rights at the moment. However, when Federline's bodyguard arrived at the appointed hour Spears wouldn't hand over the kids. Within an hour Federline's lawyer, Mark Kaplan, had arrived with court papers making it clear that Federline's team were in the right. Shortly afterwards the cops turned up.

This was Britney's cue to barricade herself and her kids in the house. After a two and a half hour stand-off, she finally handed them over just before 11 p.m. Then, half an hour later, the news channels captured one of the most shocking celebrity moments any of us has ever seen: Britney Spears, the biggest pop star of the last decade, was stretchered out of her own home strapped into leg restraints.

As the drama happened during the night UK-time, the first I saw of it was on that morning's *GMTV*. It was startling stuff, a shock to the system for anyone watching this, often light-hearted, breakfast show.

But then an even bigger shock was about to come minutes after I arrived in the office. *Sky News* flashed up the news that kids' TV presenter Mark Speight had been arrested and was being questioned about the murder of his girlfriend, Natasha Collins, who had been found dead in the bath of the flat they shared.

Nine a.m. is usually a quiet time in the office. Not today. The web team were running around, trying to juggle two huge, developing stories.

And I'm sitting at my desk, staring at the screen thinking to myself: what the hell happened to the fun world of celebrity? Where did it go? And when, exactly, did it go?

Did it go with Kate and Pete's dark, dysfunctional relationship and very public drug-taking? Did it go with Amy Winehouse (and her husband) engaging in brutal physical fights in hotel rooms and her spilling blood on a child's ballet shoes?

Did it go with Britney last night?

I fell in love with this world because it was about what made people tick, how they got on (or don't get on), the constant fascination I have in how people relate to other people. Now the way they are relating is in a pretty brutal way.

Last year, I finished on a major low but came back to work on

Wednesday reinvigorated, excited and ready for a new year of celebrity fun. But already, 48 hours later, we're swamped by a sea of death, mental illness, possible child neglect (although one of the web rumours about the Britney stand-off – that one of the children was harmed in the process – was soon discovered to be untrue) and utter utter human desperation.

The rest of the team seem to be able to deal with it all just fine. To me, it's faintly depressing.

I want out.

Saturday 5 January

Perhaps I was a bit over the top last night. Maybe I just had a bad day. I simply got two depressing stories on one day. That's a real rarity. Well, that's what I told Gaby over breakfast.

But this morning I got sent the figures for yesterday's web traffic. It was huge. The interest in Britney and Mark Speight (after police enquiries, now no longer a murder suspect) has sent us to a record high. This prompted me to log on to the site and look through some of the stories we posted yesterday and some of the comments that appear afterwards.

Some of our readers are clearly as disturbed by events as me.

Two of the comments after the Mark Speight story particularly strike me:

One, from someone called EdinPinkPrincess, shows how shocking yesterday will have been for people.

'Oh my word! It isn't half kicking off today isn't it? What on earth is going to happen next?'

Then, a reply from another poster. I love its simplicity and directness.

'It's at times like these that you want to throw a party to thank your lucky stars that you're not a celebrity.'

Other posters soon agree with her.

We're constantly told that people of these posters' age only want to be celebrities. It's all they live for. They don't want to be scientists or teachers or doctors, we're told: they want to be on the telly, have their picture taken by the paparazzi and get handbags for free. If that ever was the case, I suspect that now it is a trend that's on the wane.

Seriously, who on God's earth would want to be a celebrity?

Wednesday 9 January

After last year's *Celebrity Big Brother* nightmare, Channel 4 have been forced to drop this year's show. However, so they don't seem to be losing faith in the whole concept and (I suspect) because there's a whole load of advertising money they can't afford to turn down, they've reinvented *Celebrity Big Brother* as *Big Brother: Celebrity Hijack*, where a group of young 'high achievers' go into the BB house and have their lives directed by a series of celebrity *Big Brothers* who are in charge of their destiny.

It's an interesting idea, but a week in, its numbers are low (not helped by a switch from Channel 4 to digital sister channel E4) and the critical verdict is generally poor.

Sensing a widespread lethargy in the *Big Brother* brand and particularly this series, the head of E4 (and *Big Brother*'s Commisioning Editor) Angela Jain has asked to meet up with me and *Heat*'s TV Editor, Boyd.

Boyd, bless him, really likes *Celebrity Hijack* and was hooked by the first show, where the hijacker was his friend Matt Lucas. But he also thinks this version of the show has reinvented the *Big Brother* brand in a neat way, likes a lot of the contestants (all successful in their chosen career, there's less wannabes among this bunch) and is watching every night.

I'm not. And I'm also not putting anything about it in the magazine either, which is what is really concerning E4.

The three of us – plus *Big Brother* PR chief Loretta De Souza – met at Covent Garden Hotel, just opposite Heat Towers. The conversation moved swiftly on to *Heat*'s coverage, or lack of it, of *Big Brother: Celebrity Hijack*. Angela, understandably, wants to know why.

'Angela, it's just not a big-enough show. Putting it on E4 immediately means you're only reaching a percentage of the people you were reaching before – it's now a far smaller show.'

'But you will cover it in time.'

'On the website, yes. Not in the magazine.'

'Really?'

'Really. Just as you've moved it from your big channel to your smaller one, we've moved it from the magazine to the website. It feels right.'

This isn't going the way she wanted it to, I suspect. As she and Loretta head off, Angela's last words to me are, 'I hope you want to put something in the magazine later in the run!'

Heat deserting *Big Brother* is probably one of Channel 4's biggest fears. We're not at that point yet but we're closer to it than they ever thought possible.

Tuesday 15 January

Last night, all Britney Spears' visitation rights to her kids were taken away from her.

Britney failed to turn up in court to hear the reasons Federline and his legal team were putting forward explaining why they thought the father should have sole custody and Britney should have no access. She spent the day smoking outside her Beverly Hills mansion, praying in church and driving aimlessly around LA (this last activity has become a regular occupation for Britney).

As everyone will be covering this story in their issues next week we have gone for a coverline that will really get us noticed against all the others. It's extreme, though, and there's a lot of people in the office (including Sophie) who are nervous about it. We're running part of an interview with Dr Lillian Glass, a prominent US psychologist. 'She doesn't have the motivation to work or live because she's alienated everybody. In my opinion she is a candidate for suicide if not treated immediately'. Our coverline is Britney 'could be dead in six months'. It's over the top but everything to do with this escalating story is.

Monday 21 January

Ah, tussling with celebrities, can there be anything more fun? Today we're in the process of falling out with John Barrowman of *Doctor Who* and *Torchwood* fame. Our readers like him so we've requested an interview. It's in his interests to do it too – he's got a new autobiography out, is one of the panellists on *I'd Do Anything*, BBC1's search for the stars of the forthcoming West End revival of *Oliver* and *Torchwood* is back on telly.

This morning we met to discuss how we'd like him to look in the accompanying picture – our photos are the main things that get us PR so they're important. The more noticeable the better. So we think it will be funny for him to play against his boy-you'd-want-to-take-home-to-your-mother(-if-he-wasn't-gay) image by dressing him as Rambo. The idea amuses us. Kay suggests it to his PR. The PR says no.

'Fair enough,' I say, 'his prerogative. What did the PR's email say?'

Kay reads it out to me.

'It says "I'm sorry to say that John and his agent aren't keen on the Rambo idea. The BBC won't be happy with him sending up his tough guy image ..."'

'He doesn't have a tough guy image! He's John Barrowman! And like the BBC care about that!'

We reconvene the original visual meeting attendees – me, Lucie, Kay, Al and Russ.

We're keeping pretty upbeat.

'How about,' says Lucie, 'Tom Cruise in *Cocktail*! He looks so much like him.'

'Good idea,' I say. 'That could be great. The papers will love that.'

Kay calls them. They say they'll think about it. Half an hour later ...

'They've said no.'

'What? Why have they said no?'

She reads out the message.

'"We feel that this image will make John look like a poor man's Tom Cruise. He is not a poor man's Tom Cruise. He is a rich man's John Barrowman."'

That's it, I'm resigning. This is not Madonna, this is John bloody Barrowman!

'What shall I say?'

'Tell them to sod off.'

'We can't,' chips in Lucie, 'we've no one else for that week.'

'Don't tell them to sod off. Lets have another meeting, then.'

Tuesday 22 January

Spent the evening at home catching up on bits of work and listening to the Tottenham/Arsenal match on Radio 5 live. In the closing stages there's a news-flash: Heath Ledger has been found dead in New York. I think back to that website comment in response to the Mark Speight story: 'What on earth is going to happen next?'

I bet that person never imagined anything like this.

No one really knows what happened, although sleeping tablets were found near his bed. I'd be astonished if it was suicide – he had so much to live for, including a truly adorable daughter who he doted on completely.

Wednesday 23 January

Hundreds of emails have come in paying tribute to Heath Ledger. It's a battle trying to edit them down to a page. The news team have a great piece on it and Film Editor Charles has filed a brilliant article about his movie achievements (with some fantastic, iconic pictures from his films researched by über-fan Steph Seelan).

More Barrowman nonsense this afternoon: he will be a bartender but he can't look too much like the Tom Cruise character in *Cocktail*. Also he needs his own make-up person there, apparently, who not only costs more than the make-up people we use but needs transporting down from Wales and possibly putting up in a hotel. We're broke, we can't afford that, we tell them. They'll have to use one of our regular make-up artists.

Thursday 24 January

TMZ, the hot American celebrity website, today put an alarming alert on to their site:

> **TMZ IS LIVE AT FRANK E. CAMPBELL FUNERAL CHAPEL**
> **We are streaming today from the New York funeral chapel where Heath Ledger was brought yesterday, and where, we've learned, a viewing will take place sometime today.**

Truly stomach-churning stuff. Is this what it has come to?

Some essential light relief this afternoon, courtesy of John Barrowman. An email from his agent explains why he needs his usual make-up artist.

'John has to have Claire – she uses a specific type of make-up (air brushing) which is a fairly new and unique type of make-up, and Claire is an expert in that field. John won't do it without Claire – sorry.'

'Air brushing'. I love it.

Thursday 31 January

Britney Spears was sectioned last night.

Yet again we're putting together an article about this troubled woman with the usual line-up of photos: a disturbed-looking Britney, some police cars, an array of hangers-on.

Tuesday 5 February

Our – and other magazines and newspapers – coverage of Britney's breakdown is receiving a lot of complaints. The letter we receive today is typical:

> *Dear* Heat,
>   *Has it occurred to you that it is because of publications like yours that Britney Spears is in such a state? The paparazzi that hound her continually do so in order to get paid by tabloid magazines like* Heat. *Maybe if you stopped paying these people they might leave her alone and you wouldn't need to dedicate a whole issue to her well-being!! Well done you guys!!*

There's no easy solution to this – the magazine or newspaper that stops featuring pictures of Britney is the one that will lose sales to rivals that do. But at the same time it's impossible to gauge how much the attentions of the paparazzi are affecting her well-being. I wince when I see pictures of her being surrounded by photographers but I do not believe, in all honesty, that her state of mind is how it is because of them.

However, something needs to change and the initiatives being discussed in California this week – especially ideas about setting a buffer zone of privacy, so that photographers can't get within a certain distance of the celebrity they're taking a shot of – sound wise to me.

Monday 11 February

Every week for the past couple of months we've been getting in some dreadful sets of Amy Winehouse pictures.

Amy looking distressed at four in the morning wandering the streets of Camden. Amy with self-inflicted cuts on her upper arm.

I've put a ban on us running any of them, for several reasons. She's in a troubled state and the paparazzi presence around her isn't helping. The pictures are just unpleasant to look at. People want to be entertained by their celebrity magazines, not dread turning the page fearful of what they might find.

The main reason, though, is this: our readers want to be able to identify, in some way, with the people they see in their magazines or on their TV. When a celebrity is in the middle of the Australian jungle, in tears because they're missing their kids, the viewer will watch it and think 'How would I deal with it if *I* was stuck there, away from my kids?' Celebrity culture – and reality TV in particular – has given us all something to compare ourselves to. Would we wear that dress to a premiere? Those shoes? If we were Suzanne Shaw, would we have gone anywhere near Darren Day, never mind have a child with him? Would we kiss someone else, in a house that's being filmed by 40 different cameras, live on TV?

We can't even begin to identify with Amy or Britney because the majority of us will never fight with our partner until we both bleed profusely or communicate with the outside world by cutting ourselves ALL THE TIME or driving around the town we live in with our child on our laps. A big, thick barrier has been put up between our readers and these celebrities – they can't even begin to understand them and what they're going through.

Recently, I've found myself pining for the days of Helen and Paul and, my God, even Hear'say. The days when, in the words of Ian Birch who, along with Louise Matthews, understood this more than anyone else, we had become the new generation *Smash Hits*. Fun, daft (my favourite word), and *life-affirming*.

This isn't life-affirming, 'Troubled Britney and Tragic Amy', it's just horrible. I never wanted to edit the *National Enquirer*. I don't like the dark stuff. Other people are fine with it, not me.

This isn't fun any more. I want to leave. I've arranged to meet up with the bosses here early next week. I think I know what I'm going to say but need the weekend to be completely sure.

In the meantime I've got a magazine to finish.

This morning I turned down today's glut of grim, gruesome paparazzi pictures to go big on a happy event.

Last night Amy Winehouse won five Grammy Awards. She didn't get a visa in time so couldn't travel to the ceremony. Instead she performed at the Riverside Studios in Hammersmith, London and collected her awards by satellite link. For an evening we were able to forget her problems, pretend she was on the mend and revel in the warm glow that awards ceremonies bring, a warm glow that can mask all kinds of ills.

This was a happy moment for Amy and a diversion for the family, friends, management and record company that have to share her problems on an hourly basis.

It was joyous. You could watch it – as I did on *GMTV* this morning – with tears in your eyes and believe that she really was getting better. Her mum Janis, lost in the moment, gave a tearful interview to *Sky News*. 'She will see a therapist and she will be getting help because she wants [it]. Amy's coming back – she's on the road back.'

She's not, of course. She's still very troubled, pining for her imprisoned husband Blake (and she can't even begin to get better, begin to put drugs behind her until she's away from him).

But last night we could forget all that and pretend.

We've gone big on her victory, possibly too big. It will be part of our cover and we've given it a few pages inside, saying it was the 'TV moment of the year'. We've run Amy's brilliant speech in full, report that she stayed away from the booze at the after-show party and have ended with her mum's hopeful words. A positive, feel-good piece about a train-wreck of a celebrity.

Am I in denial now? Trying to pretend that everything is all right with this world, that it's all happy news? That damaged drug addicts will get better because they won some awards? That Britney will get her kids back and live happy ever after?

Tuesday 12 February
The guy behind Holy Moly has given an interview to the *Media Guardian*'s website today, telling them that he has instigated a ban on his site running paparazzi photos where the subject has been pursued by bike or car.

Now, I've been on Holy Moly before and they don't run paparazzi photographs – as you and I know them – anywhere. The pictures of celebrities they run are usually head shots at promotional events, the kind of thing where you can just about make out a film poster or drinks logo in the background. They can't afford exclusive sets of photos anyway. Whatever, it's a good ruse and the *Media Guardian* have fallen for it hook, line and sinker so good for him.

Monday 18 February

Tomorrow I meet with Sophie and Marcus to hand in my notice: it's scheduled for mid-afternoon. After thinking it through over the weekend I've decided I'm definitely going to go through with it.

Tuesday 19 February

Today I handed in my notice. I really am leaving.

It went as well as could be expected. First I met up with Sophie who was supportive and not that surprised. Then I met up with Marcus – a man who has a lot on his plate, being responsible, as he is, for more than a dozen magazines – who will have the burden of finding another editor so was pre-occupied with that and the other side-issues involved with someone leaving.

Both asked me why and I gave them the same reasons.

I've been on this 'project' for ten years as of last Christmas – a good run for anyone.

I didn't feel I could take sales any higher than they currently were but as I'd taken them from 60,000 to over 500,000 already, I had no real concerns on that front and was quite happy to quit while ahead. (Both of them reminded me what an incredible achievement that was as I said it and I blushed at that point, as you would.)

I then told them both my main reason. As much as I love the celebrity world it had, for me, become terribly dark over the last few months. I – and I was only speaking for myself here – was fed up of seeing pictures of tormented famous people. The stars I had come to know and love had either moved on or were becoming increasingly distressed. I didn't have the energy for the next season's crop. Time to let someone else have a go.

They asked me what on earth I am going to do next? That's a very good question.

Is Blake about to dump Amy?

This week's hottest celebrity news

£1.65 (€3.30 excl ROI) (€2.90 Spain & Canary Islands) 17 – 23 May 2008

www.heatworld.com

heat.

POSH
WEIRD NEW
MAKEOVER

MEL B!

CURVY
GIRLS
HIT THE
BEACH!

COLEEN!

CORRR-DEN!

EXCLUSIVE!
James
Corden
RECREATES CLASSIC PHOTOS

Epilogue
February – May 2008

Thursday 28 February

My departure was announced this afternoon. The team were shocked – I was there before any of them and I often think magazine people see editors as part of the furniture. They think they'll always be there.

Marcus said a few words, told everyone that Julian would be in charge until he'd found a new editor, then I spoke for a couple of minutes.

'It's really important for me to enjoy these last few weeks – really enjoy them. I'll never forgive myself if I don't have fun. We need to make the magazine look as good as possible, but I really want to enjoy the rest of my time here.'

I leave on Friday 9 May.

Monday 3 March

Well, the celebrity world doesn't seem to be calming down at all. Today we received pictures, taken on Saturday, of Paris Hilton in an LA café being 'blessed' by a monk. Yes, a bloke with huge long beard, hair down to his stomach and wearing orange robes was holding the palm of his hand against Paris Hilton's forehead while LA's finest paps – not, I note, keeping a buffer-style distance between them and her – took their photo. At one point, apparently, he even persuaded her to give a diamond necklace she was wearing away to a complete stranger. She went through with it, willingly. Utterly bizarre – what the hell is she playing at now?

Thursday 6 March

Oh. Okay. The Paris Hilton thing was a wind-up. Ashton Kutcher – aka Mr Demi Moore – is producing a new TV series called *Pop Fiction*, a show that attempts to fool the media. It worked. The guru is an actor called Maxie Santillan Jnr and he was pretty convincing (although looking at the photos again this afternoon after hearing the news I was embarrassed that I didn't notice the decidedly un-gurulike mobile phone that he was clutching in his hand).

This programme will use 20 celebrities in total to fool the media. It seems to me that the show is fuelled by the programme-makers' anger at the things magazines like us do. They want to trip us up. We've been running things for way too long, they think. Kutcher's business partner, Jason Goldberg, went on record this afternoon to explain why they were doing the show.

'We live in a culture that's driven by media and obsessed with celebrity, to the point where they don't have private lives anymore. Two people going out to eat turns into, "They're engaged." It's a feeding frenzy. It's dangerous and it's irresponsible in some cases. We're having fun, but we want to say to people, "Can you really believe everything you read and see?"'

Celebrities have seen themselves as the hunted for a while – now they want to be the hunters again. We're going to have to be on our guard.

Tuesday 15 April

Late yesterday the French parliament adopted a bill that now makes it illegal for anyone – and this includes fashion magazines – to promote extreme thinness or dangerous weight loss.

Although the law seems to have been brought in to put a stop to the growing number of pro-anorexic websites judges could – if they felt it was necessary – prosecute a magazine where a photo shows a model or even a celebrity whose weight loss has detrimentally affected their health.

French magazine editors or even their fashion editors could be fined up to (the French equivalent of) £25,000 and could even be imprisoned.

The idea of editors and fashion editors being imprisoned is extreme but it's a very effective deterrent. For the French equivalent of our big fashion glossies life will never be the same.

Sunday 27 April

As I told the team when my resignation was announced I really want to enjoy my last few weeks. I've got just two weeks left and today was a real highlight. Today, Lucie Cave became a *Gladiator* for just a few hours. The show is back on TV, on Sky One, in a couple of weeks and Lucie filmed her role at the vast Shepperton Studios.

Usually when journalists take part in a TV show it's just for a photo opportunity. They wear the clothes or hold the prop, have the picture taken then go home for the evening. Not with us, not with this. Lucie really *did* become a Gladiator today. At about 6 p.m. she phones me in a state of breathless excitement – Richard Woolfe (the boss of Sky One) had introduced her onstage as the show's new Gladiator 'Cockroach' (small, but indestructible). She may never recover …

'So,' she's still pretty breathless, 'I ran out on to the stage, all the crowd are waving their foam hands and then I nearly tripped over the cables! It was amazing! We tried to think of what signature move a Cockroach would do but I didn't want to lie on my back kicking my feet in the air so I just walked to the front of the stage and did a "Grrrr" motion.'

I may be about to leave but I wouldn't have missed this opportunity for the world.

Friday 9 May

Today was my last day as editor of *Heat* magazine.

I got one hell of a send-off. Secretly the team have been filming various people giving me 'Good Luck' video messages over the last few weeks and put them all together on a DVD. Dermot was on there as well and even the presenters and team behind *Gladiators* (sadly, minus Cockroach).

I didn't want a big do, preferring a few drinks with the current team. However, as is often the way with these things, a few other faces from my past were invited along.

I'll miss them all – so much – but will I miss celebrity magazines?

Tuesday 13 May

The final issue of *Heat* with me as editor is on the news-stands today. It's also the first one I've ever paid money for. That hurt, I can tell you.

The magazine contains one final treat for me. Every week *Heat* lists its contributors, the team of people who put it together. This week everyone has been asked the question, 'What will you most miss about Mark?'

Oh dear. Might need to prepare myself for this, I decide. This is bound to be an emotional experience.

Or not.

At a time when on other magazines it is customary to pay a tearful tribute to a departing leader, a large number of my team have decided to do what *Heat* people do best: take the piss. The gags come thick and fast:

'His cuban stacked heels' (thank you, Jo Carnegie, oh faithful deputy).

'His disgusting impressions of Boyd Hilton' (courtesy of Ms Al Dunne – Boyd, that's so not true).

'His weekly motivational table-dance' (okay, that one is true. Well, as Dan Biddulph knows all too well it's important to educate the youngsters).

Then, my particular favourite from Rhiannon Cox in our ad department:

'Mark who?'

Couldn't have put it better myself.

Acknowledgements

I want to say a heartfelt thank you to the readers. Readers of celebrity magazines are a much-maligned bunch – but the ones I've met and the ones who wrote to me (and I read every single letter or email) are sussed, intelligent and just get it. Get that this whole thing is entertainment, get that it should never be the centre of your life, get that famous people have as many foibles and issues as they do (actually, probably a lot more).

Huge thanks go to my agent at William Morris, Eugenie Furniss. I've seen Eugenie's name appear a few times in the acknowledgements bit of books and now I've got to know her I can confirm that she's as great as everyone says. Eugenie, your encouragement, enthusiastic emails and attention to 'the project' has been incredible to me. I was never 100 per cent sure I had a book in me but you were. Thank you.

To Jake Lingwood, my editor at Ebury. You've always been patient, you've always been right (damn you) and my *X factor*-style journey from getting it all wrong to getting only most of it wrong has been fulfilling and enjoyable because of your guidance and positivity. Thanks also to Sarah, Di, Charlotte and the whole Ebury team. Thanks also to Gail Rebuck for her support.

To the team at the William Morris Agency, not just in London but also the teams in Beverly Hills, New York, Miami Beach, Shanghai and Nashville too. (Actually, I've had nothing to do with any of the other offices, I just wanted to show off a bit. Nashville, eh? Wow.) Particular thanks go to WMA-ers Rowan Lawton (the fastest-speaking woman this side of Miami Beach) and Sophie Laurimore (without whom none of this would have happened). Thank you too to Piers (for the inspiration) and Simon (for the quote).

Thanks to James, Bryony, Emma, Lesley and the team at Taylor Herring who have done an incredible job at making this book a huge hit. Unless it isn't and you're all reading this in a shop with absolutely no intention of buying it, in which case they've done a terrible job.

To Louise Matthews and Ian Birch – always inspiring, always supportive. I owe all of this to the two of you. Didn't we have the best time? To the bosses who gave me the confidence to edit magazines for a living: Mike Soutar, David Bostock, Sue Hawken, Baz, Marcus Rich, Mark Ellen, Paul Keenan and Sophie Wybrew-Bond.

To David Hepworth, my magazine hero ... and I'll stop right there cos I know you hate that sort of thing. To David Davies for persuading 'them' to keep the magazine going at a crucial point.

To all the *Heat* staff, past and present. You made all of this such fun. I miss you all. Special thanks to Julian Linley, Dan Fulvio, Dan Wakeford, Boyd Hilton and Hannah Fernando for help with the moments where my memory failed me. Thanks also to Steph Seelan and Clare Hepworth.

To the columnists and opinion-makers who wrote about *Heat* when others had written us off or no one knew we existed: Emily Bell, Janine Gibson, Janice Turner, Kathryn Flett, Barbara Ellen, India Knight, Philip Hensher, Leigh Holmwood, Grace Dent and, of course, Dame Julie Burchill (surely it's only a matter of time?) for being *Heat*'s most vocal supporter.

To Mum and Dad – you're the best. To Caroline and Sally – you're pretty good too.

To Leila and Jonathan – thank you for the office space. This book probably wouldn't have been possible without you. James, thank you too.

To Danny, who likes the Venga Boys even more than I do. And that's saying something.

And to Gaby. For your love, support and for never asking the question: 'Why the hell are you leaving that nicely paid job, you complete idiot?' I love you.